The Serpentine Butterfly

Celestra Forever After

Book 3

ADDISON MOORE

Edited by Paige Maroney Smith
Cover and Interior Design: Gaffey Media

Copyright © 2016 by Addison Moore

http://addisonmoorewrites.blogspot.com/
This novel is a work of fiction. Any resemblance to peoples either living or deceased is purely coincidental. Names, places, and characters are figments of the author's imagination. The author holds all rights to this work. It is illegal to reproduce this novel without written expressed consent from the author herself.

All Rights Reserved

Books by Addison Moore

Romance

Burning Through Gravity (Burning Through Gravity 1)
A Thousand Starry Nights (Burning Through Gravity 2)
Fire in an Amber Sky (Burning Through Gravity 3)

Beautiful Oblivion (Beautiful Oblivion 1)
Beautiful Illusions (Beautiful Oblivion 2)
Beautiful Elixir (Beautiful Oblivion 3)

The Solitude of Passion

Someone to Love (Someone to Love 1)
Someone Like You (Someone to Love 2)
Someone For Me (Someone to Love 3)

3:AM Kisses (3:AM Kisses 1)
Winter Kisses (3:AM Kisses 2)
Sugar Kisses (3:AM Kisses 3)
Whiskey Kisses (3:AM Kisses 4)
Rock Candy Kisses (3:AM Kisses 5)
Velvet Kisses (3:AM Kisses 6)
Wild Kisses (3:AM Kisses 7)
Country Kisses (3:AM Kisses 8) Coming Soon

Celestra Forever After (Celestra Forever After 1)
The Dragon and the Rose (Celestra Forever After 2)
The Serpentine Butterfly (Celestra Forever After 3)
Crown of Ashes (Celestra Forever After 4) Coming Soon!

Perfect Love (A Celestra Novella)

Young Adult Romance

Melt With You (A Totally '80s Romance 1)
Tainted Love (A Totally '80s Romance 2)
Hold Me Now (A Totally '80s Romance 3)

Ethereal (Celestra Series Book 1)
Tremble (Celestra Series Book 2)
Burn (Celestra Series Book 3)
Wicked (Celestra Series Book 4)
Vex (Celestra Series Book 5)
Expel (Celestra Series Book 6)
Toxic Part One (Celestra Series Book 7)
Toxic Part Two (Celestra Series Book 8)
Elysian (Celestra Series Book 9)

Ephemeral (The Countenance Trilogy 1)
Evanescent (The Countenance Trilogy 2)
Entropy (The Countenance Trilogy 3)

Ethereal Knights (Celestra Knights)

Season of the Witch (A Celestra Companion)

For we do not wrestle against flesh and blood, but against principalities, against powers, against the rulers of the darkness of this age, against spiritual hosts of wickedness in the heavenly places.

—Ephesians 6:12 (*NKJV*)

Prologue

Skyla

Long ago in Eden, the serpent ushered in the fall. The serpent—a devious foe who clothes himself in light— is sharp and handsome, so cunningly clever you can hardly resist his magnificent charm. His sole desire is to consume, devour all that is good in one swift bite. The serpent longs to herald a new era, a season of agony, a season of sorrow. The serpent is my lover. The serpent owns my heart. He is my most nearest, dearest enemy.

Time was an opiate we were consumed to inhale right down to our bones. We evaded death, begged for mercy, but it dug its necrotic talons into our mortal flesh and took what it wanted. Now, forever gone are those years of yearning, where the dry forests of our hearts burned like tinder. Gone are those heated sentimental days. The war of our youth had evaporated before our eyes. And now, a new war wages, a beautiful war. Perhaps it was an esoteric war all along.

Change. It comes to everyone with the passage of ages and stages, the details as irrelevant as dust or smoke, the curling of a fire that snaps and roars until finally it is blown out in the night like death. It is an ironic constant embedded in our lives from the cradle to the grave. It is inevitable, necessary, and inescapable at best. One thing is for certain in this fearful journey—change will come in abundance. After all, destiny is most interested in its revisions, its daily mutations of what we thought we knew.

Change has infiltrated my world, struck me down, brought me to my knees once again. Destiny arrived with first her scourge, then her blessing. She bestowed on me a crown of beauty for ashes, the oil of joy instead of mourning, a garment of praise in exchange for a spirit of debilitating despair.

Destiny is molding me, scolding me, loving me all at once. A transformation is taking place—a heart-wrenching, agonizing metamorphosis.

In nature, it is the butterfly that perhaps undergoes the greatest transformation. And so it was in my life, my mother's planting of her egg, the feasting off my father's love, the transition to a life without him—one on foreign soil which brought me the knowledge of who I am, who I have been all along. Then, finally, the painful stretching, the expanding, the unfolding of my very being as I struggle to break free from the vellum sheath of restriction I've lived in for so long.

Change has come, wielding all of its power, all of its threats, its knife-sharp convictions—its cowardice skirting around the corners.

The enemy is removing his mask, standing at the foot of his throne, readying to come to power, readying to embrace his rightful place from time immemorial—his long sought-after most precious dominion.

I am here, and I am ready. No longer am I a little girl, cloistered and naïve. A new season of my life is emerging. I will burst through the chrysalis of my existence, and unfurl the glory and the majesty of my beautiful, beautiful wings.

Change has come into my life—and I am anticipating all that it will bring.

I am ready.

Long ago in Eden, the serpent ushered in the fall—but destiny offered up a way out of it.

Redemption is coming.

It is already on its way.

1

The Jackal of All Trades

Skyla

Fate wove her fingers through the tapestry of our lives and skewed the design just enough to make me hate it. The sky blackens. The clouds boil. Paragon twists and writhes, her branches arch with the violent wind, even the dusty crags are groaning. A pang of numbness spreads throughout my body like a disease, like a betrayal, like death. Waves crash over the thick cap of hair lying silently on the rocks below as Gage stares vacantly up at the heavens—up at me for every grievance and disappointment I have ever caused him. After all, it was me who drove him to the cliff's edge. It must have been. I was his lousy wife, his lousy bedmate, his lousy leader who never really understood who he was at the core—who knew nothing of the battle waging in his heart that drove him to the brink of oblivion, then ungraciously tipped him over the edge.

Howling screams shrill from my lungs as a pair of strong arms wraps themselves around me.

"Get to him *now!*" Logan roars to Marshall.

The ocean swells over my beloved's body as his arms ebb toward the shore. There's a knot in my throat, a building dread that spells out the impossible. I refuse to believe it. My husband, the beautiful, beautiful man that God himself destined for me could never leave this planet. I couldn't bear it. I wouldn't.

"I love you," I push the words out in a whisper as Marshall somehow appears down below by his side and pulls Gage out of the water. He glances up at the cliff that Logan is determined to keep me from leaping from as if he were affirming the worst news possible. A crowd has gathered at the base as the howl of an ambulance pierces my incessant sobbing.

"Let's go." Logan does his best to pry me from the ledge, but that horrible scream eviscerates from my throat on a loop. My hands extend below, begging for Gage to latch on as if that is ever a possibility. It can't end like this. I won't let it.

The roars, the howls—frightening shrieks expel from my throat as Logan whisks us into his truck. We follow the flashing lights of the ambulance all the way to the hospital, and I jump out just as the EMTs open the back.

"Sorry, ma'am, you'll have to wait out here." A young man with arms the size of logs tries to curb me from the scene.

"That's my husband." The words grunt out of me, as I break through the stronghold, easy as wet paper, my hands shaking his ragged limbs. "*Gage!*" My voice vibrates through the tiny interior, but my precious husband doesn't move. His eyes lie open, staring to the ceiling, his limbs rubbery and cold, motionless. I touch my lips to his and pump in a lungful of air. "Come on, baby," I pant over him as I push in breath after breath.

Voices murmur from behind; hands fish for my body as they try to pull me away. Logan tries to reason with the men in charge, tries to reason with me.

"Why isn't anybody helping him?" I choke the words out through tears. Gage continues to ignore me with his marble pale skin, his lips blue as the sea that took him from me. "Please." My body convulses over his, washing him with the tears of my desperation. "Don't leave me!" My voice curdles in a childlike manner. "Gage!" I touch my lips to his cold flesh and writhe in agony over death's cruel victory. "I can't let you go." Tears burn down my cheeks in hot fiery tracks. He's so beautiful, with his hair slicked, black as midnight, his eyes still glowing the way only his can.

My fingers grip over his shoulders, dig in, nail to bone, and in a fit of aching frustration, in a fit of fury, I shake the shit out of him.

"Wake the hell up!" My voice alone has the power to rouse the dead, but Gage isn't budging.

Strong arms manage to pluck me off his body. My fingernails rip his iced flesh one last time before I'm suctioned back into the light of day, back into a world without my lover.

They never take Gage out of the ambulance.

They drive him straight to the morgue instead.

Lights. So many lights hit me at once. I'm disoriented, dizzy, floating as Logan leads me down the corridor of the Paragon mortuary, owned by none other than Gage's father—the one who raised him.

"Barron!" I give him a violent shake as he rises to greet us. "They're bringing him. Do something."

"What's this about?" A bell rings in the back, and he nods. "Just a moment. Looks as if I've got a customer." He gives a slight wink, stalking off before Logan and I dare tell him the horrible truth. Our legs carry us to the back. The walls revolve around us as if we're in a dream, and we find ourselves next to Barron once again where a garage door rolls up in the rear of the room he unceremoniously refers to as "the kitchen." It's the area where the body prep takes place, and today the body will belong to—

"*Barron*"—Logan says it loud and stern, causing his older brother, uncle, whichever they feel like referring to themselves at the moment to lurch—"it's Gage. You're going to find Gage on the other end of that wall."

The door recedes like a scroll, like a story that had reached its completion and would be no more in this earthen realm. I run out into the open just as they're wheeling him in, a white sheet resting over his form, thin as gossamer.

"Don't do that!" I whip the sheet off with a marked aggression. "He can't breathe!" The men gurgle out the brunt of their dismay with me, but I can't make sense of the English language anymore. I can't make sense of the endless howling escaping from my throat. I can't make sense of this version of my husband who refuses to look at me, who refuses to wrap his loving arms around my body. I can't bear this inhuman pain.

"If Gage has died, then I want to die, too," I pant over his sculpted face, his eyes still looking through me into the invisible face of God. "You hear that, *Mother*?" I scream so loud my skull begs to shatter from the effort.

Time passes. Gage is laid out in the stainless tub in the middle of Barron's chop shop. Emma runs in with her hands flailing, her hair escaping her signature bun as she literally unspools before us. And in a moment of solidarity like never before, the two of us weep over him like a pair of injured doves. This is madness, a special brand of hell I never want a piece of. Death is a bastard that doesn't mind knifing your heart out and feeding it to you for dessert. I know this intimately from losing Logan—from the tragic time of my father. But Gage—something about this feels far more grievous, nefarious in every sense of the word.

Logan yells into his phone. People show up; warm bodies fill the space around us as I sit holding Gage's hand on one side, as does Emma on the other. Liam, Giselle, Ellis, Ezrina, Nev, and Marshall all seem to explode into the room at once.

"Marshall." I grip the lapel of his jacket and pull him down to me, hard. I stand on my tiptoes and land my nose to his, my heavy panting landing directly over his mouth. "Do something," I grit the words through my teeth with a tremor in my voice, a threat lying just beneath that. "Wake him the fuck up—and don't you dare tell me a thing about language. Make this better. I swear to you, I will do whatever the hell you wish. Please"—my eyes close with desperation—"just please."

Marshall turns his cheek to me, and from a side-glance he bears a striking resemblance to Logan. "I'm sorry, Ms. Messenger. I'm afraid your beloved's predicament is out of my jurisdiction."

"Predicament?" I whisper, trying to decode his words.

I leap to Ezrina and grip her shoulders, pressing in, bruising her Chloe-inspired flesh, and not even the idea of it brings me an ounce of pleasure. Instead, I resist the urge to shake her like a rag doll. Chloe. She's all I see now when I stare at Ezrina. I know that evil has long since vacated the premises, but that black halo Chloe wore like a badge of wicked courage, the venom she bore—they're still floating around on the surface.

"Ezrina." I close my eyes a moment, reducing my voice to a whisper. "You must—you absolutely *must* heal Gage."

"Skyla," she hums my name, sweet and low, like a honey-drenched lullaby. "You do realize he's not ill, child. I can no more heal him than I can wake him. I'm sorry, Skyla. He's gone."

"No." It pumps from me with a dull whimper.

A pair of warm arms pulls me in. Logan wraps himself around me, tight and safe, like the very wings of God.

"We need to fix this." I twist, burying my face in the warmth of his chest. "We need to make him better. We need to find a way, and we need to fix this shit." I repeat the words on a loop until a sharp gasp comes from Emma. "What is it?" I dash over and take up Gage's hand once again, but Emma isn't focused on her beautiful baby boy. Not an eye is on my precious husband. They're all transfixed on the doorway. I spin slowly on my heels, my stomach clenching because I already know. I can feel the heated evil, the heart of darkness thickening the air with his monstrosity. They say death owns the night we know as life, but today it feels as if this wicked Fem owns us all.

Demetri. There he is, in all his tall, dark Fem glory, his black cape dusting off his shoulders like elongated feathers. He shares the same midnight hair, the same high cheekbones as his son, and for the first time ever, I see the family resemblance between my gorgeous husband and the demon haunting the door.

Demetri doesn't say a word. He simply nods and bows his head in an earnest show of disrespect.

Demetri Edinger is wicked incarnate, the very devil whom Chloe employed to kill my father. In a cosmic, arabesque twist, Gage Oliver's father killed mine before we ever met.

There's an irony in there somewhere I don't care to ever dissect.

I bring my husband's cold fingers to my lips before returning his hand gently to his chest. My body slides off the stool as my feet slowly propel me toward the shadowed devil at the door.

"Skyla, no," Logan pleads, but I don't bother to listen. We both know where this desperate train is headed, and it's already left the hellish station.

Demetri's eyes connect with mine, a cesspool of radiated darkness. He holds a desperately grieved expression, one that rivals my own, and for a moment, I let myself believe that it's genuine. For the first time in the history of our passing, I believe Demetri Edinger is exhibiting a human emotion, and that emotion just so happens to be desolate pain sponsored by death.

I fall prostrate before him, clasping my hands over his ankles before touching my lips to the leather—kissing the shoes of the devil himself—hell, I would kiss his heels, lick his bare soles to bring back Gage.

"I beg of you, in the name of all that is good, all that is holy, all that is right, bring my husband back to me. Do this, and I will forever be in your debt."

"Ms. Messenger," Marshall barks from behind. "I bid you to stand, right this moment."

"*Demetri.*" His name whispers from my lips over and over like an ancient chant, a holy hymn, like a demonic incantation that's already come to fruition, but unlike all of the times I've hissed his name before, this time the inflection falls in his favor. This time Demetri can right all of the wrongs he has pressed upon me and prove to be my savior. "Bring your son back. The only son you love, the only son who can and will bring you the glory you so achingly yearn for." There. I'm offering the keys to the kingdom, the keys to his cherished dominion. This act, right here, is damnation for my people on a silver platter, and I want it. I demand it. I need Gage back, no matter how high the cost. Life is priceless, and for me that means there is no ceiling, no demand too high, or unreasonable—not in this black hour of my deepest grief. There is no man on Earth who can bring Gage back to me. My own mother in heaven isn't answering my plea for mercy—nor would she. Perhaps this monster, whom I've long touted as my enemy, this storm cloud of a presence in my life can finally bring some respite. "Give me Gage. Bring him back to me."

His hands float down to mine as he helps me to my feet. Demetri doesn't meet my gaze. Instead, he strides toward the center of the room where my heart is splayed out inside a steel casket awaiting the grisly detailing of last rites that only a mortician can provide. I rush to my husband's side and feather his hair back with my fingertips. Emma still dutifully holds his hand, quietly sobbing into the stillness of her child.

"Come, my son," Demetri calls to Gage as if he could hear him.

Instinctually, I lean in and offer one last kiss to those precious lips I hunger for.

"I love you," I whisper as we part.

A brilliant white light envelops the room. It swallows the color, steals the definition from the borders of the objects, the people, as the brightness expands from the nexus of that steel tub, and in a flash both Demetri and Gage dissipate to nothing. The light, the evil, the dead, all have vanished. Gage is gone, and for the first time since I laid eyes on him at the bottom of that cliff, my chest swells with a sense of relief.

"Holy shit." Ellis staggers forward. "*Fuck*. You've done it now, Messenger."

I smack him on the arm. "It's Oliver." *Mrs. Gage Oliver*, I remind myself. And that's what I intend to be until kingdom come, so my mother and her destination station hippy-dippy friends can suck it.

My gaze snaps back to Marshall. "Take me to the Elysian Fields, Ahava, wherever the heck my mother is holed up—hell, take me to the throne room. I need to speak to someone about this right now. Better yet, take me to the Transport. Is he there? Can you take me to see Gage?" A renewed hope fills me as startlingly honest as the one that filled me a moment ago when Demetri disappeared with his body.

Marshall taps his finger over his lips, his brows redefining themselves as if he were thinking this through.

"I said *now!*" My voice rattles off the stainless counters and hollow walls as if it were my intention to wake the dead, and, in this case, it might be too late.

"Skyla"—Logan wraps an arm around my waist, his voice warm and moist over my neck—"I'm going with you."

The sky lets out a horrible growl as darkness covers the dismal afternoon, and it looks more like evening outside the opened mouth of the room. Rain sets in, hard and fast, as if someone flipped a switch.

"Neither of you shall go anywhere." Marshall pulls out his driving gloves as the rain hacks down like axes over the island. "At least not with me. I assure you, Ms. Messenger, you are in good hands with The Pretty One." He nods from me to Logan; a solemn expression takes over his features. "I am so very sorry for your loss."

"The hell you are." The words speed out of me before I can properly assess them. I've pissed Marshall off once before and swore I wouldn't touch those flames again, but now I'm the one who's pissed, and for Gage I'd dance in a bonfire. I am.

"Emma, Barron"—he turns to the Olivers without paying any further attention to me—"please accept my condolences. Your son was a good man. I'm sure the memory of him will live on in ways you could never imagine." He glances to me without meeting my eyes. "I'll be around if you need me."

Emma gives a stiff nod before turning to me. Her eyes round out in two blood-red spheres. Her nostrils flare with anger.

"Where in the hell did you send my son?" Her tone is curt, her eyes narrowed to hateful slits. Gage isn't gone five minutes, and the gloves come off—not surprising. It's no secret that Emma has never been a fan of my marriage, a fan of me in general. Although, she didn't seem to mind me too much when I was with Logan. Emma, just like my own mother, has been Team Logan right from the beginning, each for their own nefarious reasons.

I step in close until we're just about nose-to-nose, not an ounce of pity running through me for this woman. "Your son is with the man whom you thought best to father him."

Marshall glances back before exiting and pauses.

"*Skyla*." Nevermore steps in and gently tugs at my elbow.

"No." I yank out of his grasp without ever taking my eyes off hers. "*You* tell us where that wicked bastard might take your son. You're the one who knew him intimately, not me."

"Skyla." Ezrina clicks her tongue. "The devil has ears. There's no use in name calling once you ask a favor."

Emma seethes at me. Her orange-stained lips pull erratic at the sides of her mouth as if she were holding back a river of damning words.

"Go ahead and say it." I dare her—I want her to.

Her body flexes in a brief moment of retaliation as if I had pricked a pin in her uptight, self-righteous anger.

"At the end of the day, Skyla"—a thin smile flirts with her lips—"this will all pencil out to be your fault. You and I both know it, don't we?"

"Emma!" Barron objects, pulling his wife out of the room as if breaking up a fistfight. Her words were far more effective than a slap.

"*Mom!*" Giselle cries as she scuttles out right along with them. Giselle who looks eerily like her brother in female skin—Kragger genes aside. I'm glad she followed them out. I don't think I could take more than a glance in her direction.

"Let me get you out of here." Logan clasps my hand and pulls me toward the back exit, the very same hole in the wall they rolled Gage through on a gurney. "Where do you want to go?" He swipes an umbrella off the ground as we head into the rain-soaked Paragon afternoon.

"I want to go home."

Logan drives me to the Landon house as my tears rival the flood streaming from the sky. I tell my mother I'm not feeling well as I charge upstairs and vomit convulsively into the toilet for an hour straight.

Logan stays with me the rest of the day and well into the evening. He asks to spend the night, but I tell him to go. I lie and assure him that I'm okay.

The truth is, the only man I want to spend the night with is the one I can't—I desperately want to spend the night in the arms of my loving husband, Gage.

Logan

The clouds twist and turn, laboring to deliver their trauma over Paragon. Any more anguish, any more grief, and I'll crawl into the hell Demetri has Gage holed up in and put an end to this nightmare myself. If Gage is truly dead, if his time—although spurned by his own hand—had finally come, I have a backup plan that just might work out for my nephew, regardless if he wants it or not. I plan on shoving life down his throat, then wringing his neck for even thinking of taking his existence off the shelf in the first place.

What in the fuck has gotten into him? As much as the evidence points to suicide, there's no way in hell Gage would pitch his soul into eternal darkness. That's what life without Skyla would be. I should know. My own death has led me to the answer.

Damn. I head down the steps just outside of the Landon house and hear voices coming from the street. An expensive SUV sits blocking the driveway as three shadowed figures hold a lively discussion at a furtive pace. I jog on over to check it out. Skyla's stepfather, Tad, comes into view, then Chloe and—my stomach drops. It's Wes. I know it's Wesley Edinger, or whatever the hell his last name is, but it's his startling likeness to Gage that knifes me—a twin to my nephew, the deepest cut in the most mortal wound.

"What's going on?" I nod into their tightknit circle.

"I'll see you both later." Tad waves them off with an exasperated hand. "I'm sure once Althorpe gets wind of this, they won't be happy. A bonus is a bonus!"

"I'll double your bonus," Wesley offers with a forced smile. "No need to involve Althorpe when it isn't necessary. I'll notify payroll. You'll have your check in the morning."

"You better believe it, Greg. I've worked my ass off for that good-for-nothing company for years. It's about damn time Tad Landon gets his due." He storms up the steep driveway, up the rickety wooden stairs, and into the log cabin with the slam of the door.

"You'll get your due, all right, old man." Wes needles the doorway with a glare that spells out broken neck more than it does paycheck.

"So, did you hear the news?" I turn to Chloe and her wicked brand of beauty. Her whiskey eyes shine like cut glass in the dim light, and her high-cut cheekbones, her oversized bow-shaped lips are all marketable as beauty, but, to tell the truth, I've always thought there was something reptilian in nature about her. Chloe, who has both obsessed and professed her love for Gage over the years, looks oddly composed tonight as if she hasn't shed a single tear, not vomited once in the toilet, unlike Skyla. I've never seen anyone so sick with grief. No, it's safe to say they haven't heard—in the least, not Chloe.

She and Wes exchange a brief, yet secretive glance.

"What news?" Wes nods as if he were taking over the conversation, as if I needed to get through him to speak with Chloe. I'm not sure I like his protective, chest puffed out, this-is-my-girl attitude when it comes to the demon to my right, but then again, they are breeding. Maybe it's his kid he's really trying to protect.

"Gage is dead." I look directly into Chloe's soulless eyes as I say it. I want to twist the knife a little. It's her constant, furtive effort to derail Skyla that has caused this. Emma was wrong. At the end of the day, this wouldn't pencil out to be Skyla's fault. It would be Chloe's fault in ink, in stone every single time. She and Demetri, her demonic supervising spirit, have collectively killed both Gage and me. After all, it was Chloe who sliced my head off during the Faction War. She's the reason I'm standing here on borrowed time in a Treble that was drummed up just for me. I'm nothing more than a visitor on this planet, a sojourner on some grim, pointless mission.

"What's this about?" She looks from me to Wes. Her face twists in knots, because deep down, Chloe knows I wouldn't shit around about something like this. "I knew something happened." She swats Wesley on the arm. "You tried to tell me that everything was fine! But I knew. I *knew*." The veins in her forehead bulge as her rage directs at Gage's lookalike.

I remember when I was young, this go around, life felt so free and ridiculously long, as if it had the power to stretch into a golden eternity. Death's sting was for others, something I would never have to taste. I was a foolish youth who believed that deep down in his misshapen heart he was immortal. But life doesn't work that way. I'm non-living proof, and unfortunately now, so is Gage.

Wes lets out an exasperated sigh as the wind picks up; a light peppering of rain sizzles against my flesh. "What happened?"

"He fell off Devil's Peak." I shoot Chloe a quick look. A long while ago, after Skyla killed Chloe, the Counts took her body. Once they were through with her, they buried her in a shallow grave at the base of the nefarious locale. I'm sure Chloe finds the irony somehow bittersweet. Her burial plot is the exact marker of his demise.

"He *fell* off Devil's Peak?" Chloe's entire person goes rigid. "Gage wouldn't kill himself—not the Gage Oliver I know. Somebody must have pushed him."

Pushed him. Something in me wants to cling to Chloe's theory. The rain starts in as I stagger toward my truck. "Nobody pushed him. He left a note."

The night sours. The bourbon-colored sky pisses down its wrath, erasing any memory of the fact it's springtime. If it was a few years back, Gage and I would be suiting up, getting our asses kicked on the field by the coach as we ran that extra mile we knew we couldn't. I miss those golden West Paragon High days—Gage and I front and center, leading the team to victory after victory. Then, Skyla showed up like a rainbow after a storm, the promise of brighter tomorrows buried in her smile, and cheered us from the sidelines. But we weren't a unified front around Skyla. Gage and I entered into a war long before the factions ever did.

My phone goes off in a series of consecutive texts, and I check it. None of the messages are from Skyla, so I ignore them for now.

I do another drive-by of the bowling alley, the house on White Horse, the cemetery, the Landon house in some OCD figure eight loop—two times, maybe six. I know where I really belong, behind the gates at the Paragon Estates with Emma and Barron, with Liam and Giselle while we bury ourselves in grief. But Gage is out there somewhere, with *Demetri* of all fucking people. Where the hell did he take him? The Transfer? Tenebrous? Heaven, hell? It all seems like one in the same these days.

A thought comes to me. Candace. She likes me. For whatever reason, I've found favor in her eyes. Thank God Skyla is unable to gain access to her mother tonight. It would have ended in disaster. She's too hopped up on rage. And as much favor as I've found in her mother's eyes, Gage has left that much of a bitter taste in her mouth. Skyla vying for Gage through marked aggression would not have gone over well in the heavenlies, at least not with the original Ms. Messenger around. But maybe I can talk to her. Reason with her—in the least, discover where Demetri is holing up his body. The body. I grimace at the thought of my nephew—hell, my brother, relegated to nothing more than a corpse, an empty human vessel.

I pull over and shoot Dudley a text. **We need to talk. I'm headed over.** Marshall Dudley has been my supervising spirit for a few unsettling years now, and it's about damn time I start tapping into a few favors. I scroll through the rest of the messages that are vexing my phone. Ellis wanting to know if he can do anything. Liam letting me know Barron and Emma have gone to bed. Giselle wishing I would save the day and bring Gage back before the sun went down. They were all sent hours ago. I'm sure Giselle is disappointed to see that I'm nobody's savior, just a dead man walking, driving as it were.

Our family is staggering, right along with the heartbreak of our friends. Just trying to imagine a life, a single moment without Gage, is hollow and cruel, and I don't want any part of that horrific reality. I do love Skyla, but if having her married to Gage is the only way I can keep that blue-eyed ball of trouble around, I'm all for a lasting union between the two of them. My stomach clenches as if it objects my valiant effort.

"Fuck you," I say out loud before killing the engine and making a run for Dudley's overgrown estate. The door is unlocked, so I let myself in.

"I'm here," I growl as I enter. It's warm inside, toasty in fact. A swell of voices warbles from above, and I try to distinguish for a moment if he has a woman up there, or judging by the giggling sounds of it, a couple of them.

"Here you are." Dudley jogs down the stairs, still dressed to impress the ovarian crowd with his tailored Italian suit, his sleek silver tie that wags from side to side like a metallic tongue. I've never seen him in anything but a suit. At the most, his jacket comes off. Who knows, maybe he'll lose his welcome-to-Earth pass if he dresses down for the occasion. Candace and her cohorts are all a bit formal and uptight. "What is it you need? I have visitors that have spanned continents and generations, time continuums as it were. They're quite entertained by modern advances. It's exhausting me to no end. One of them attempted to stick a fork in a socket." He gives a bored grimace as he leads the way to the living room. Dudley doesn't bother to take a seat, just crosses his arms and continues to glare in my general direction, his impatience growing like bread mold.

"Gage is dead." I sit hard on the unforgiveable sofa cushions. It's as if he had this crap crafted and imported from the Stone Age. Probably did.

"So it would seem. My condolences. I suppose you came to see if I happen to have a magic wand handy, or a spirit sword that works in the reverse. I'm afraid to inform you I can no more reanimate Jock Strap than I could yours truly. And, as I am not his indentured servant, my supervising capabilities are relegated to you and you alone. I have no jurisdiction in death's department. I am no more able to resurrect Skyla's formerly betrothed than I am—"

"Stop!" I bark over at him. "Enough already, I get it." I jump to my feet and pull him in tight by the collar. "You piece of shit. You couldn't care less that Gage has bit the big one. You couldn't care less that he was *murdered*, and now Skyla is forced to believe that he took his own life." I give him a stiff rattle. "You couldn't care less, because all you really care about is your damn self," I spit the words in his face like a storm.

Dudley lifts me off the floor with his fists balled up in my shirt so tight. His knuckles sit just beneath my neck, cutting off my breathing.

"You don't get to call me whatever piece of filth your dirty mouth desires," he seethes. His eyes boil, each its own shade of fire. "You do not get to slander *this* celestial being." His voice sears over my ears with excruciating heat, blistering my eardrums, if that were at all possible. "You want the truth? The truth, Mr. Oliver, is that I don't have time for your little tirade. I'm not so interested in whether or not Jock Strap is swimming through cosmic dust up there or down below, because right this minute I have a very real problem brewing like a witch's stew right up those stairs. And if I don't tend to it soon, both you and I will be very, very sorry."

My lungs struggle to take in the slightest gasp of air.

"Can't breathe," is all I can manage as I struggle to kick the living shit out of him.

"Say it loud and bold just the way you did when you dared to compare my existence to excrement."

My entire body writhes as I try to employ my Celestra strength to buck him off. But not a muscle can prosper against his Holy Jackass Highness.

"I heard that." He flings me into the fireplace, and I bounce right back, rolling the flames out on my flannel.

"Shit." I gasp for air, just lying there, staring at the ceiling for a moment, my body smoldering from the flames. "You win." I wave him off. "Do what you have to do. I'll take care of Gage."

Take care of Gage. I want to laugh and cry at the thought. Destiny has already taken care of Gage.

Dudley stills a moment before sighing toward me. "Ask what you came for. I've no doubt I'm already apprised of the favor."

"Then take me there. I want to witness Gage's darkest hour. I need to see for myself what happened." My eyes stay trained on the beams that run in dark, thick, lines over the ceiling. I'm too exhausted, too beat down to look at those boiling cauldrons he calls eyes. Don't want to.

"I'm afraid that's not possible."

"It's possible because I said it's possible. Take me now. Devil's Peak. Rewind time as far back as his arrival. I want to see it all."

"It's not possible because I've already attempted the effort. There's a binding spirit in play. We have no ability to penetrate that slice of time. If that is all, please do excuse me. I have a fire that needs to be doused in my bedchamber."

Shit. "Douse away."

I wait until his footsteps scuttle back up the stairs before hauling my ass off the floor and getting out of Dodge.

Binding spirit? I smell a dirty rat bastard Fem at the other end of this time continuum.

Unless, of course, Gage planted it there himself.

And if nothing else, this has been a day full of unless...

Skyla.

I think of her all the lonely way to White Horse. I stare up at the monolithic home I built for the two of us—as much as a gift for her as it was a reassurance to myself that I would be back—that one day in a future not that far away we really would have it all. Skyla and I should have it all. At least that was my belief once upon a time.

I get out and jog up through the rain before letting myself in. Technically, I won't be alone tonight since Nevermore—*Heathcliff*—whatever it is he's referring to himself these days, and Ezrina are taking up residency here. They're actually underground somewhere in the vast labyrinth of this new and improved lab I constructed under Ezrina's watchful eye. I wanted to give her the edge she'd need once she came to work for Celestra full-time, and now she has it. The lab spans far beyond the reaches of this property, so in a sense Nev and Ezrina have an entire village to call their own.

The house itself is sparsely furnished. I've purchased a small table for the dining room, a couch, and a nice oversized high-definition television for those game days when I don't want to bother Emma by way of cursing at my team. Although, the truth is, I've spent far more time at Dudley's than I'd like to admit. It's not easy being a displaced soul. I'd stay here full-time, but I was hopeful that Gage and Skyla would take up residency here rather than holing up in her bedroom at the Landon house. I don't know how Gage can stand to live with her batshit stepfather. Tad can make any rational person consider jumping off a cliff.

I pause on my way up the stairs. I didn't mean that. Gage would never...There's no way in hell he would ever leave Skyla and take a flying leap off Devil's Peak. He couldn't. He wouldn't.

That note comes back to me. I dig in my pocket and fish it out.

Skyla,
Farther down the road I see you,
a heart that measures in time with mine.
We breathe the air of a world forgiven.
Spin on this planet, once thought divine.
I'll stand beside you until I am driven,
into the light so brilliant—into the light sublime.
And if that moment has finally come, my wish for you is this;
love without abandon knowing we'll hold each other again in eternity.
My heart breaks writing this.
I pray you never find it.

All of my love, forever,

Gage

It knocks the breath out of me each time I see it. Still don't get it. I sink it back into my pocket as I head upstairs and make a beeline for the master bedroom. I might have had a bed delivered, a dusty end table, and a lamp, but none of it was intended for me. Emma gave me some discarded sheets and blankets, a nice fluffy comforter with blue bonnets stamped all over it, and thus was born an opulent version of a thirteen-year-old girl's bedroom, with frilly curtains she dug up to finish off the windows. But I don't mind. I've only spent a handful of nights here—and, again, I had Skyla and Gage in mind when I piecemealed this stuff together.

I fall onto the mattress and close my eyes, the world around me growing dark as my heart. This was to be their bed. The exact place Gage would have happily made love to my wife, Skyla. Where Skyla would have called out his name like she did mine during our brief three-day union—a marriage and honeymoon all rolled into one. That's what Skyla and I had—a shooting star of a covenant that lasted seventy-two blissful hours. Those heated nights come back to me in jags. Her limbs intertwined with mine, the two of us naked, sheathed in night sweat that we pulled from one another with passion. We were exploratory you could say without sounding crass. All tongues and teeth, all fingers and hair and mouths, connecting as husband and wife all through the night, through the throes of a magnificent sunrise, through the bliss-filled afternoons and the heady anxious evenings. We were a miracle together, a revelation to the universe, that yes, there was still some magic, something better that two people could bring to the holy table. We were lovers for three brief days and nights, a hopeless whisper in the grand scheme of time.

But Gage and Skyla have been married for months. He had what I could only dream of, and, now that he's gone, ironically, I only want one thing—him back, him with Skyla. If she's the key to his existence, then I'll reheat those three passion-filled days in my heart until my Treble expires and I have to turn in this borrowed coat of flesh. Those memories will have to be enough. Deep down, I know it will never be even close, but Gage is at stake. And, in truth, I could still love Skyla as much as I would if we were still together, and I do. The difference being, my dick is now a very sad and depressed member of my body. There's no one else for me. There could never be another Skyla. My heart and all of my despondent members will always belong to her.

An hour drifts by, two, then three. An unsettled knock comes from the door, and I startle enough to open my eyes.

"Who's there?" My voice rumbles out, hollow in this oversized bedroom.

"It's me." The sound of a sweet female rings from behind the door, and my mind reels with the possibilities of who *me* might be. Brielle, Michelle, Lexy, Emma, Giselle, Ezrina—Chloe herself are all possibilities.

My eyes adjust to the moon-drenched room and find a girl in a white nightgown, airy and light with ruffles around her knees. Her hair is sprayed in full curls surrounding her delicate features like a lion's mane.

"Skyla?"

Her eyes are stained red, her lips swollen twice their size as she scuttles to the bed and climbs under the covers with me.

"Hope you don't mind, but I'm freezing." Her teeth chatter as if attesting to the fact.

My hand runs through her damp hair, the moonlight exposing the water beading over her curls like a thousand tiny stars. Skyla is her own universe, my sun. Her iced feet swim up my jeans, and I pull her in.

"You're barefoot. How did you get here?"

She hesitates a moment, trying to choke the words out. "I drove. I just ran out of the house. I wanted to go there, but I couldn't."

"Devil's Peak?" My eyes close at the thought of Skyla driving there alone in the middle of the night. I should never have left her. I should have waved off the idea she would be fine for the night, left with her mother and her family under that nutty roof. The only real person to lean on in the vicinity would have been Brielle. Skyla needed me, and I failed her.

"Skyla." I bury my face in her wild hair and take in her soft, sweet perfume, lilacs and vanilla. It's a wholesome scent, one that I've memorized, one that I've desperately claimed as mine, and I hate myself for even thinking it.

"Can I stay?" She scoots back until the steely wash of moonlight bleaches out her features. "I promise, I'll leave before the sun comes up. I just couldn't stop thinking about him. I couldn't stop the tears." Her eyes spill their deluge as if to prove a point, and I draw her near to me, crushing her chest to mine as we sniff our pain into one another's necks.

"Yes. Of course, you can stay. I want you to."

"Thank you." Her cool fingers brush over my face. Her pure vellum eyes lock onto mine, and it's as if a spell has been cast. I can't look away. Skyla always has that effect on me. "I need you, Logan," she says it so low that for a moment I wonder if I manufactured the words from thin air. "Like no other time in my life, I need you. Hold me tight, and don't let go."

I nod like an obedient schoolboy. Here it is—our pain merging into one lonely highway. I don't think I could have survived this night without her. Skyla and I leash ourselves around one another, tight as a vine. Her chest moves in rhythm to my own. Her ragged breathing warms my shoulder, but it's her smooth thighs, her iced feet that my hands keep gravitating toward. I tell myself it's an effort to warm her, bring her to room temperature so she can finally get some rest, forget this misery we're sunk in if for a night—but the aftereffect of being so close, of touching her bare flesh has my body enlivening to uncalled for heights of arousal. I haven't held Skyla this close, with this much determination, since all those nights long ago we spent in one another's arms. Her tears track down her face and burn through my shirt. She presses her agony into my neck, my shoulder, twisting and writhing as her body bucks beneath mine, her misery so physical I long to quell it.

Something soft—far softer than tears—presses against my lips, and my eyes squeeze tight with a new level of pain.

Teeth graze over my Adam's apple, and I realize where we are—where we're about to go.

"Skyla," I whisper. "No." As much as she needs me, needs my body to comfort her, it wouldn't be right. Tomorrow, in the light of the scathing day, she'll regret this far more than I ever could.

Her iced hands slip up my T-shirt and warm themselves against my skin. Her lips rake one long track up my jaw, meandering in a heated stream over my cheek until her soft mouth covers mine. A sigh expels from her, just one, as if she's finally found the solace she so desperately needed.

"Skyla," I moan right into her throat, but it does nothing to stall her efforts. Her hands claw at my clothes. Her tongue mingles with mine—a few sorrowful swipes before increasing in its fervency. "Skyla, no." I give one more anemic protest before she dips her hand into my jeans, into my boxers.

My clothes come off at record pace. Skyla bathes me with her tears, her mouth, as we make love for the entire agonizing stretch of night, our bodies begging to find comfort while buried deep in one another. This is our honeymoon revisited in a horrible and horrific manner. A bitter night washed in bitter sins that neither of us will care to remember.

This was a terrible, terrible thing we had done. Are still doing.

We are killing Gage all over again.

2

Beauty For Ashes

Skyla

The sun brightens our world through the vellum fog. I'm not sure I slept a wink last night. My eyes desperately tried to seal themselves shut with a reprieve then snapped to attention as soon as I realized it wasn't Gage next to me. I swam through a nightmare, only to have the harsh reality coursing through my veins like a current.

A pair of arms floats near my hips as a soft moan comes from the other side of the bed.

"Morning," I say, rolling over to look at my blonde friend with her wild mane that rivals my own. I couldn't bring myself to say *good* morning. There's nothing good about it.

"What time is it?" Laken wipes the sleep from her eyes.

"It's seven thirty. Do you have class?" I'm so disoriented, I have no clue what day it is. It feels as if weeks have drifted by—years of agony, all without Gage. What day follows the worst day of your life? These were all deep thoughts I wasn't ready for, nor would I ever be.

"No." She gives a wary smile that dissipates into sadness. "School is over, Skyla. We don't go back until fall." She swipes the hair from my face and hitches it behind my ear. As soon as Logan left, Laken appeared as if on cue. I tried telling her I didn't need anyone to stay with me, but Laken insisted. Deep down, I'm glad. If Logan had stayed, who knows what disaster that might have led to? If my sweltering overly sexual dreams were any indication, nothing good and nothing needed.

All the waking night I was incensed, outraged over the audacity of Gage leaving me, as ridiculous as it sounds. For a brief and shallow moment, I considered his death nothing short of treason and demanded revenge. If Laken hadn't shown up, God knows I would have wandered out into the storm and tracked Logan down for comfort. If those dreams I had last night offered an inkling of where things would have led...No, for certain, Laken was the best solution.

"I'm sorry." I grip my temples a moment and squeeze my eyes shut. "My mind is all muddied up. I just can't wrap my head around any of this." Tears sting my eyes again, and before I know it, I'm blubbering into my damp pillow.

"I know." She cradles me like a child, smoothing my hair with her fingers. "I'm going to stay with you. We're going to talk to Demetri. We need to get to the bottom of this mystery. We need to know where he's taken Gage—and what he could be doing with him."

"He wouldn't hurt him. He couldn't—he's...he's dead." Those last few words warble from my throat.

A hard thump unsettles my window. We look up to find Nevermore, correction Holden, pecking at the glass. Dear God, he's so annoying. I used to love that bird when it was filled with sweet, knowledgeable Nevermore, but now that Holden has taken over the poor winged creature, he feels more of a burden than a gift. He gives a few more thunderous taps.

"Ignore him..." I trail the words into my pillow.

"He might have information." Laken springs up and opens the window enough to let him in. The ripe scent of earth, the woodsy scent of the forest just south of here filters inside, and I take in a lungful. I've always loved fresh morning air, but for some reason, the scent of damp Paragon soil combined with the evergreens reminds me of the cemetery, the day I buried my father, the day we eulogized Logan—all rolled into one grievous event. And now it's a sharp reminder of Gage and that immovable stare that's haunted me for the last several hours. I'm usually the biggest fan of Gage Oliver's cobalt blue eyes. Nothing makes me feel more alive, sexier, more wanted than that anticipatory gaze he settles over me night after night, but, yesterday, his eyes were hollow, staring up into the nothingness of the sky, unseeing, unmoving, a testament to his horrible demise.

Holden twitches and flaps his wings, shuddering like a dog while spraying the early morning dew over everything in a five-foot vicinity.

I swab my lips over my pillow before sitting up. "What do you want?"

He lets out a series of blood-curdling caws, and both Laken and I cover our ears.

"Okay, enough." I reach over and tender his feathers with my hand until they're settled once again against his back. With my Celestra powers, I can hear Holden telepathically, but only if we're touching. "Speak your peace. My head is snowy, and all I want to do is sleep." Actually, it's *weep*, but I thought I'd spare Laken my new reality. Tears will be my bread, sorrow, my only comfort. It's a strange world that grief plunges you into. There's no world I want a part of without Gage Oliver in it. My heart shreds at the thought.

Nev summoned me. He said you'd need my services. What's up, Messenger? Tell me what you want me to do. You know I'm here for you. I want to prove myself.

"Why?" I'm suspicious—far from trusting when it comes to Holden Kragger—any Kragger for that matter. Holden once took residency in Logan's body and tried to aggressively have his way with me. I still haven't quite forgiven him for that malfeasance, not to mention he took possession of Ethan for a time. Holden has spread his disease in far too many people, but now he's fully committed—in an imprisoned sort of way—to being my personal on-call feathered friend, willing and ready for duty. Which is mostly a joke since the only thing he's capable of is suppressing Chloe's presence. He literally makes her barf on command. That alone is why I'll be keeping Holden around forever. The very idea of Chloe retching should make me smile but doesn't. Nothing makes me smile anymore.

I'm going to prove myself to you and your mother, too. She'll get me out of bird jail once and for

all, you'll see. I'm reformed, Skyla. I'm not the asshole I used to be.

I'm only slightly amused. "I'm afraid I don't have any tasks for you. Why don't you go out and enjoy the day? Find a tree to squat in and shit on Tad, or whatever it is you do to get your feathered rocks off. I have other things on my mind right now."

Like?

"Skyla"—Laken touches her hand over Nev's old feathers until he turns toward her—"Holden, something terrible happened to Gage yesterday. Skyla found his body at the bottom of Devil's Peak. We don't know all the details, but Demetri took him out of the morgue. We need to know where they went. Can you find them?"

Holden lets out a riotous squawk. ***Shit. Sorry, Messenger. Look, I know you probably don't even believe me, but I am sorry. I know how much death sucks. I hated losing my sister. It changed my entire family. My mother took off, my father turned into a monster, and, well, you saw what happened to my brother and me. I'm going to do this for you. I'm going to track down Demetri, and I'm going to find out what the hell he's done with Gage.***

Holden hops to the window and squeezes his way right back out.

"He says he's going to find Demetri—to find Gage," I whisper as we watch Holden spread his coal black wings into the pale, soft, cruel world outside my window.

"What else can we do?" Laken gives my hand a quick tug.

I like the way her urgency rivals my own. At this point, it far outweighs my own. I seem to be locked in a daze, a haze, an unsettling fog of my own. It's as if the island has wrapped itself around my head, and I can't see the world through the dark and twisted forest, the ever-present mist. This is worse than Tenebrous. This is worse than hell.

"Who do you think can help us?" She bounces over the mattress, her determination reaching its pinnacle. "What about

Professor Dudley? He's a Sector, right? He can pull a few strings."

I moan into the idea. "I don't think so. Marshall made it clear yesterday he was stepping back from the situation. He's about as useful as my mother at this point. Neither of them cares if Gage makes a living, breathing reprisal." It's true. My mother is out for Logan, and Marshall is out for himself.

"Knock, knock!" my mother—other *earthly* mother—chimes from the hall. "I've got breakfast for my two favorite lovebirds! *Gage*, I made chocolate chip pancakes just for you! They even have those Mickey Mouse ears you love!"

She claps with glee all the way down the stairs.

Laken's jaw goes slack in that is-this-what-you-have-to-put-up-with kind of way. "Sounds pretty special." Her face drenches in sorrow as she says it. "I'm sure he would have loved them."

I nod through tears. He would have. My mother loves Gage almost as much as I do. She's made it a point to find out all his favorite meals and proceeded to dish them up on a rotational basis. Nobody seems to notice the nightly resurrection of all Gage's greatest digestive hits, but I did, so did Gage. We both appreciate my mother's effort to make him feel like family. He is family. Was.

Laken steps into my closet, rummaging for fresh clothes. My fingers extend toward Gage's cell phone just out of reach. He left it here. Gage never took off anywhere without his phone—and yet, yesterday he did, which only manages to paint an even more ominous picture. I'm too lazy to reach for it, but my hand stretches to touch it as if it were a manifestation of Gage himself that I was struggling to graze, and the phone gives a violent jerk. I startle for a moment. What the hell? I get up on my elbow and try again with outstretched fingers, demanding the phone to dance a little jig, and in a moment of incredulous defiance against gravity and just about every law of physics, it slowly drags across the nightstand like a snail until it's compressed in my hand. My mouth falls open at the miracle. In a fit of unbelievable reality, I'm cradling an object I neither made the effort to retrieve nor deserve to be holding at present.

A ragged sigh comes from me as I marvel over this. I must be learning a whole new power. Figures. My mother always did have lousy timing. I let the phone slip out of my hand as Laken tosses me a sweatshirt.

I don't say a word about the cellular miracle. Instead, I let Laken help pull me together just enough, hair in a ponytail, a fresh pair of sweats, my face scrubbed clean from a long night of mascara-stained tears before we head downstairs. My stomach is clawing for food, an oddity since I've never been able to eat through my grief before. I suppose there is a first time for everything, but I'd like to think it's because I know for a fact Gage Oliver is coming back to me.

Demetri owes me that much.

"Morning!" my mother sings as she spins toward us, a spatula in one hand and baby Misty in the other, aka Mystery-No-More since I now know who her baby daddy is. Daddy is interchangeable with Demon at this point because it just so happens to be that infamous Fem who fathered her. One day I'll find out that Demetri spawned half of this island. He's probably been spraying his seed freely for generations upon generations. It wouldn't surprise me one bit if Chloe were his demon spawn as well. Evil begets evil. Although, neither Misty nor Gage is evil. *Was* evil. *Are*. Oh hell. My head starts to pound as if on cue. My stomach is still demanding I pay it attention, but I'm too despondent to make any nutritional decisions at the moment. How the hell am I to eat while Gage is out there hurting, or worse, not feeling a single thing?

"Oh." Mom's expression falls flat as she spies Laken in place of my handsome husband. Gage has the ability to make my mother's morning with simply a smile just like he does mine.

Misty lifts Mom's shirt, picks up her slouched boob, and suctions the nipple into her mouth. Really? When a kid can clear a three-step process like that, aren't they a little old for momma milk?

"Laken dropped by last night and crashed." A drunken haze of grief encapsulates my words, makes them sound as if I just shouted from the bottom of a well.

"Oh, that's fine!" Mom does a little tap dance. "I keep meaning to convert Drake's old bedroom into a full-blown nursery for Baby Beau. You know—decorate it with those cute wall decals, lots of boys' stuff, and sports memorabilia. Gage can help with that. But if I knew you were having a guest, I would have put fresh sheets on the bed."

Baby Beau waddles in and tugs on my mother's shirt until she puts down Misty and hoists him up. His mouth lands right where Misty's was a moment before, and I catch Laken openly wincing at the sight. It's true. It's an odd one. Beau Geste is a bona fide toddler now. A part of me is sorry for Laken for having to witness the madness that makes the Landon house go round. I'd run her out of here, but my entire body is stuck in this grieving molasses. Nothing is real. This is all a dream—a living nightmare that has swallowed me whole. It has to be.

Laken shakes her head nervously. "No, really. You never have to go out of your way for me."

Mom and Laken carry on an entire conversation, but my mind chops up the words, mixes them, and throws them into the air until they all sound like gibberish.

"Ugh!" Mia shuffles in from behind with her robe cinched tight, her hair in full electric socket mode. "Get a life, Mom. That kid is like turning twelve next week, and he's not even yours. Stop stealing kids, and pay attention to the ones you have."

"Mia." I meant to scold her, but it came out a faint whisper. Honestly, I don't have time for any Landon family piss-poor dynamics. My husband is somewhere out there, and I want him back. If my mother won't make arrangements to breathe new life into him, if Ezrina can't, then it looks as if Demetri really is my only strangled hope. I cringe at the thought.

I give Laken's arm a weak tug. This entire morning feels like an illusion, as if at any moment the family room will melt away, and I'll be standing in Ahava, and I wish it would. I'm in desperate need to speak with the wicked witch of the nethersphere—my birth mother.

"Anyone want an omelet?" Mom gives the eggs in the pan a quick stir, and the yolks bleed orange in slow, oozing circles. Their tendrils coil like fingers, and my stomach clenches at the sight. She plucks out the garlic salt, and the kitchen explodes with the stench of the stinking white rose.

A hard groan comes from me, guttural and deep. "Can't breathe." I pull Laken along to the foyer as a hard wave of nausea rips through me. Laken swings open the front door, and a body pops up as Tad stands between the fresh Paragon air and me.

I moan in lieu of a word and forcibly push him out of my way. In a boxy staggering move, I stumble out onto the porch, inhaling vats of sweet, island fog as the nausea begins to subside. A cold sweat breaks out all over my body as if I've just escaped a fire.

"You okay?" Laken whispers, pulling me away from a screaming Tad, something about his shoe.

"Yes. I just—I don't know what came over me. I took one look at those eggs, and—that smell." I gag at the memory before taking in another few lungfuls of air. "But I'm better." Only a partial lie, I think.

"Are you now?" Tad hops over on one boot, his other foot simply in his sock, showing off a hole where his big pale toe leers out at the world. "And no regard for my bad back— have you? I don't see anyone asking *me* if *I'm* okay!" His face reddens in a quick burst, and I wonder if we should be on alert for stroke symptoms soon. His dark hair is peppered with just as much silver these days, and his gut is starting to spill over his belt. If he keeps up his love for all things carbohydrate, he'll morph into the Pillsbury Doughboy by Christmas. "And tell Greg I never got that check he promised! I've got mouths to feed, you know—and his grouper-like lips happen to be the biggest of them all."

"What check?" I give a side-glance to Laken. I very much doubt Tad has a clue about anything that's happened to *Gage*. On most occasions, all Tad is good for is your run-of-the-mill chaos and confusion, but now that Gage is missing and horrifyingly enough no longer with us in other respects, I'm curious as to what he might know—or in the least, thinks he knows.

"He'll understand what I'm talking about. It's official Althorpe business, that's what. I was paid a king's ransom to escort those two suits from the mainland. And I did my duty." His arms flail as he rages. Each day, Tad becomes more and more a caricature of himself, a scary thought since he was just a rough outline with a bad sense of humor the day my mother brought him home from the shelter. One day, I fully expect to come downstairs and find he's made the full transformation to an animated character. That sounds about right in this lunatic life of mine. Soon, we'll all morph into a cartoon, and along someone will come and turn the channel—my mother most likely. I scowl at the sky.

My phone buzzes, and I fish it out of my purse, like trying to save a drowning child.

"Gage?" I spit into the phone without glancing at the screen to see who it is. My stomach growls out a roar as if demanding to speak with him itself.

"I'm sorry, love," a familiar voice warms the other line with a formal tone. "It's just me, Nevermore."

"Oh—yes." I shake my head as if coming to and whisper to Laken, "It's Nev."

Tad opens his mouth as if ramping up his tirade, and I turn my back to him. His voice goes off like a bomb as he wanders deeper into the house. It looks as if my mother will have to bear the brunt of his shoeless adventure.

"What's going on? Did you find Gage?" My voice twists when I say his name, and that painful stone settles in my throat again.

"No. In fact, Rina and I drove by Demetri's." He gives an audible swallow. "I would suggest you spare yourself the misfortune." He pauses a moment too long. "The house is gone, Skyla."

"Shit," I hiss. "It figures the first thing Demetri does is take off." I squeeze my eyes shut and spin in a silent circle. "I might stop by anyhow and prowl around. If anything, I can scream my head off in there, demanding to speak with my mother. God knows Marshall is no help—"

"Skyla." His voice firms into my ear. "You may *not* go to Demetri's home."

I pull the phone back and scowl at Nev as if he were in front of me. I get it. Nevermore has always had this paternal vibe going with me. He has my best interests at heart. He wants to keep me safe. And a Fem hovel is the very last place I'd theoretically be safe in. But I'm still wearing the protective hedge around my neck.

My hand reaches up to confirm this and comes up bare. Oh shit. I completely forgot that Chloe hacked the chain off, and I've yet to replace it. Nevertheless, I'm feeling ballsy.

"I'm going. You can't stop me. Love you. Thank you for thinking of me. Tell Ezrina I said the same. I'll catch up with you later. If I don't find you at Marshall's, I'll track you down at the lab." I hang up before he can protest. I nod toward the Mustang and pull the keys from my pocket. "Let's hit Demetri's."

"Done"—Laken plucks the keys from my hand—"but you're not in any shape to drive. I got this."

Laken and I head down toward West Paragon High, but the lights are all out along the intersection, so we take the coastal route that hugs the hips of the island, offering us a quick drive-by of the bowling alley. My stomach is so racked up with hunger, my arm presses tight against it in a weak attempt to satisfy the craving.

A marked sadness builds in me. The bowling alley is where I first laid eyes on Gage—in that very facility. That day rushes by like a blur. Gage was all dimples and butterfly blue eyes. I was star-struck by him even then—by both him and Logan. I take a hard sniffling breath and shift in my seat, only to see the gift Logan gave me for my birthday a few years back.

"There's the house that Logan built for us." The words come out hoarse, but Laken nods while inspecting it. "White Horse." I point to the two-story gem that shines like lightning against the water. "Right on the sand—last beachfront lot available. Logan borrowed from the bowling alley to make it happen." It wasn't the best move financially, but it warmed me to the bones, humbled me beyond recognition that Logan would rearrange his world to gift me, us, something so wonderful. Has Laken been to White Horse? My mind swirls as I try to piece together the last few dizzying years, and I come up blank.

"I've been to the lab with Coop," she assures as if answering the question I never asked. "It's a beautiful house. In fact, it looks as if he's here. Should we stop by?" Sure enough, Logan's truck is tucked high up in the driveway.

"No, please don't. Logan will be the first to protest the thought of me heading to Demetri's, especially if I plan on letting myself in—if I plan on digging through the bowels of that haunted hotel until I come up with where he hid my heart. Logan would want to do this for me, but it's something I need to do for myself. Besides, I'm positive Gage"—*his body*, I want to say but don't—"is safe with Demetri. I'm sort of hoping..."

"I know." Laken brushes her hand over mine a moment.

We drive the long gray tongue of Paragon road to the Estates, and I make up some excuse about visiting Ellis to the guard before he lets us through. God forbid I lie about visiting Emma, and she gets wind of it. I suppose I could have said Marshall, but much like Logan, he would frown upon my decision to break and enter, smash a mirror or two for bad luck, because God knows I don't have enough of that.

"I should go in alone." It occurs to me Laken will want to keep her record clean. It wouldn't surprise me if Demetri decides to throw the book at me.

"No can do. Not without me, Skyla. Not on your Celestra life." She gets that devilish look in her eye, and for a moment, it feels as if we're something more than friends, more than would-be felons—and I do believe that Demetri could pull a felony from me—it feels as if Laken and I are sisters. Strangely enough, I feel a stronger bond with Laken than I do with Mia or Melissa. Of course, I hardly know Misty yet, but I'm hoping to be close with her one day, too. Mia and I have never really clicked, especially since we've moved to Paragon, but I'm ready to fight for that, too. And Melissa, well, that relationship still remains to be fleshed out. She's been nothing but a ball of anger these last few years.

"You're too quiet. What's on your brain?" She frowns as if the idea of having anything on my brain is not a good idea.

It's Gage. Everything else is an afterthought, but I go with it. "My sisters. I'd like to bond with them. I think we've drifted." Not necessarily true. True. True.

"Funny you should say that. I'm feeling the same way. I mean, Lacey and Marky have each other, but I'd love to bond along with them. Especially now since Marky will be my sister-in-law." She bites back a smile. Cooper popped the question last New Year's Eve, and I couldn't be happier for them.

"Let that smile loose." I give her a soft nudge. "Gage and I are both happy for you." My voice breaks just as we round the corner to the final stretch of road leading to Demetri's hideous house. It's an exact replica of the haunted mansion in the Transfer, which I'm not entirely sure is actually haunted more than it is filled with the vaporous Transfer dwellers—a dapper crowd of ghosts from another century entirely. The Transfer is a strange, dark, twisted world the Countenance created. Figures. Give the Counts an entire dimensional plane, and they putz it up with bad décor and ghouls who have long since departed. I'll have to ask Ezrina to tell me the full story on that polluted playhouse one day—especially now that I'm the overseer of the factions. Done are the days when I don't know shit, when I'm kept in the dark for my dumb-blonde benefit. I think it's time to start wielding my lady balls a little more liberally.

I give a hard glare to the sky. Sorry, Mother. There's a new sheriff in this celestial town, one who isn't afraid to call you out on your bullshit. Killing Gage—allowing him to die, it's beyond bullshit, and my mother knows it. Why else would she avoid me in my hour of need? Other than the fact there's not a motherly bone in her celestial body.

"It's gone." Laken slams on the brakes abruptly and backs the Mustang up to the easement leading to an overgrown hill.

"What's gone?" I pant, staring out the window at a ratty looking embankment covered with weeds—not a trace of an opulent stoned paved driveway in the vicinity. "We must have taken a wrong turn."

"I'm sorry. Of course, you're right." She spins the car around, and we drive from the corner right back to this ominous stretch of vacant land. "Oh my shit," she whispers, coming to a rolling stop as her head leans deep toward the windshield.

"What's going on?" My heart thumps in and out of rhythm as if in the throes of its final moments. "Where the hell did it go?" I stare up at the blank, weed-riddled hillside as if it held the answer.

"It's just gone." Laken jumps out, and I do the same.

A sports car comes barreling down the street, and Marshall, Nev, and Ezrina all file out.

Ezrina's face contorts a moment as she ogles the barren site, bemused. "Gone!"

"Yes, in fact it is," Nevermore confirms.

"Where is it?" I demand, stalking up the lot with its enormous bald spot where the house once set its architecturally decrepit footprint. "Where the *fuck* did it go, Marshall?" My voice shrills to the heavens, piercing the monochrome membrane that Paragon is locked in.

His brows rise with the expletive, but he doesn't bother with an admonishment.

"Tell me!" I stagger toward him in a fury. "Where is the damn house?" My eyes bug out as I examine the three of them.

"Skyla!" Laken calls from the top of the hill, and we charge our way up to meet her. "Look at that." Her hand swings over the expanse of what was once the backyard. A dark impression lies embedded into the soil, expanding enormously in girth and width. "If you turn around and follow the pattern, it almost looks like a—"

"Butterfly." I spin slowly, examining the freshly singed soil. "He's mocking me." The knife of grief stabs right through my heart once again. "Give Demetri your most prized possession, and this is what you get," I admonish myself.

"Skyla." Marshall steps in, lifting his chin to inspect the carnage. "I wouldn't be overly concerned about this. Demetri has simply stepped out for some air. He'll be back. I can assure it."

"Stepped out?" My voice rises from my throat, incredulous. "For some freaking *air*? He didn't simply make a beer run to the gas station. He didn't just grab his wallet and walk out the door. He took the entire fucking house!"

"Enough," Marshall barks so loud a trio of crows darts out of an evergreen. "I'll see to it that he's located at once. In the meantime, I bid you one thing." His eyes glower into mine, sparking and snapping like red licking flames. "You do not see your mother without me. Do you understand the gravity of this, Skyla?" There's an earnestness, a curtness I'm not used to coming from his voice. Marshall has been adamant before but never like this.

"Why?" I'm suddenly suspicious of my saintly Sector pulling rank. As much as Marshall is a down-to-the-letter alpha male, he has yet to insist I do as he says. Well, okay, there was this one time—and, oh yes, one other. Okay, maybe a third, but that's beside the damn point. He should know by now that if he plays the you'll-do-as-I-say-card I'll most certainly do the opposite.

He gives the slight hint of a nod as if I were right. "Because I said so." His lips curve up one side. "You will do as I say, Ms. Messenger." He tips his imaginary hat in my direction before striding down to his sports car and speeding the hell out of here.

"I suppose we'll need a lift," Nevermore muses.

Laken steps in close and whispers, "Where do you think he went?"

"I don't know." My feet travel over the surface of this haunted soil, numb, afraid to move in the event the ground swallows me whole. I wish it would. "The Sectors, the Fems—maybe they're all packing up their houses and closing up their little shops of horror. Maybe their silly little Paragon project is finally over."

A dull chortle rises from Ezrina. "Dear child, don't you know? We've yet to leave the gate."

I glance to Nev for a translation. Ezrina is the queen of brevity.

"She's right." Nev nods as if affirming her theory. "This little Paragon project, as you call it, hasn't truly begun. Ezrina and I have been mapping out Nephilim history. We pulled thousands of prophecies from the Viden people. From what we can surmount, everything up until this point has been one long preface of what's to come."

"Correct." Ezrina steps forward, her eyes lift in the distance toward Devil's Peak, toward the exact spot where Gage took his last God-given breath. "This story has yet to begin." She turns her head to the north as if waiting for the wind to whisper a secret directly into her ear. "We truly haven't even left the gate."

Laken and I shudder simultaneously.

They're wrong. They have to be. There has been a war, several hundred deaths—*Logan's* death—a victory for Celestra, the closing of those wicked tunnels, the heavenlies rearranged with myself named as the overseer of the factions and all their crappy decisions. It sounds more like the end of a story than a beginning. But Gage is missing. Gage is dead. My heavenly mother, who has the power to change these horrible truths, is suspiciously quiet.

The wind picks up violently around us, and we draw our collective attention to the white caps in the ocean, thrashing like the arms of a thousand dying men.

Yes, Gage is missing. My Gage. My life is missing. I glare at the heavenly expanse. Perhaps it's time to have more than a chat with my mother. Perhaps it's time to cut the celestial apron strings, take the reins, and write my own damn story—*rewrite* it, redraft this entire nightmare until there are much more palatable circumstances. I think I will.

"You're right." I sniff into the wind. "This story hasn't even gotten off the ground yet. Come on, let's go." I take off for the Mustang still idling in the street.

"Where to?" Laken catches up, breathless. "The bowling alley? The cemetery?"

"No." I walk around to the driver's side. It's about time I take the wheel in both this reality and the ethereal plane. "I was thinking more like the Burger Shack first. I could really go for a cheeseburger. Or ten. Then, once I settle this ravenous appetite of mine, I'm going to find Gage."

Damn straight I will.

Logan

The Paragon Bowling Alley isn't merely my anemic claim to fame. It isn't simply an inheritance from my dead parents. It's become the fabric of who I am, so each time I toy with the idea of selling it, I wonder if it's me I'm really trying to get rid of.

Lightning flickers through the windows like ghostly fingers attempting to snatch my soul right out of the room. The entire structure quakes as thunder growls its way through the cavernous, mostly deserted establishment.

Ellis bounds through the entry and heads on over, his clothes lightly freckled with rain. The storm is just ratcheting up. It's due to wreak havoc through the weekend. Then, just in time for Monday, it should be fogged-over sunshine and rainbows. The Weather Channel is what happens to you once you're old and dead. It's happened to me, although last night Skyla made me feel anything but like a corpse.

Those erotic hours speed through my mind on a loop. Her legs roped around me, her naked chest pressed against mine. Her heated cries, her tear-stained face. The thought of our braided bodies sears me right down to the bone with a level of ecstasy I wish I never knew. I can't believe I let it get that far, but we needed each other. We needed to push through the grief together, and unfortunately, we chose the most inappropriate route. I'm not sure what possessed us. I know for a fact I'm going to see Gage again, whether it's on Paragon or eternity, and he'll want to deck me for it. The truth is, as much I've needed Skyla, craved her body, to drink her mouth down like priceless wine, I feel like shit. The idea that I've taken advantage of her ricochets in my mind, but a stubborn part of me refuses to own it. I refuse to own it on many levels, but, deep down, I know it must be true. I am lower than the shit on the bottom of Demetri Edinger's shoe. I'm a greedy pig of a man for what I've done to Skyla—to *Gage*.

"*Hey*." Ellis slaps me five and pulls me into a partial hug. "I'm sorry, dude. Any word?"

"Nope."

"G is pretty torn up."

G is his nickname for Giselle who still goes by Emerson Kragger to the free world. Giselle died as a toddler, but Skyla's mother was kind enough to resurrect her and gift her Emerson's body. Giselle doesn't seem to mind. She especially doesn't seem to mind the Kragger credit limit, sports cars, or casita that Big Daddy K has offered up to her on a very real silver platter. She has everything she could ask for out of life—and then she has Ellis.

Ellis Harrison isn't such a bad guy, mostly. He's a little loose around the edges, mellow, one might say, but that's strictly a result of his lifetime reefer addiction. Ellis grew up across the street from Gage and me. I know his ins and outs. I know he's a Count who stands against the Barricade, even though his father is a very prominent member of the Countenance who stands *with* the Barricade—hell, he is the very definition of the Barricade. I know Ellis's heart, and it's a good one. So if my niece feels he's the love of her life, then so be it.

"I need to stop by and talk to Emma and Barron. I went home last night for the first time in a long while." I nod across the street toward White Horse, the scene of the fornicating crime.

Ellis ticks his head back a notch. "Dude, you left Skyla? What the hell? Gage would have your balls. You know he'd want you taking care of her."

"I know." My hands ride up a moment as if surrendering. "I was with her at the house until late—she wanted to sleep. She told me it was okay to go. Trust me, I wouldn't have left if she didn't insist. Plus, she was sick—vomiting. In fact, I'm about to put a call in to her now—just wanted to give her a chance to sleep in." Okay, so that's mostly true—hell, it's all true. I'm simply leaving out the fact that once she felt better, she drove over to White Horse, and we went off in my bed like a grenade. Skyla begged me not to talk about it. And I get it. The things that are done in darkness, in the thick of the night—a night coated with grief—are better off left in a murky world that never felt real in the first place. For some reason, bringing it up, repeating the effort in broad daylight would make it a reality. Last night was a fantasy wrapped in a fog for both of us, a surreal error that I won't let happen again.

"You should go to her." Ellis leans against the counter, pushing in at me with his patriotic red, white, and blue stoned eyes. He's all American that way when he's baked, and he's usually baked. "Dude, I got this." He nods for me to get lost. "Liam isn't even coming in today. Why the hell are you playing superhero? Go be with your family. Skyla is your family."

Skyla is my family. The words sink down to the deepest part of my soul. Who knew Ellis would hand-feed me the best truths?

"You're right." Two words that have a hard time choking from my throat whenever Harrison is around.

When I backed out of the driveway this morning, I had fully intended on heading to Barron's. I know my brother and his wife need just as much comfort as I do. But as soon as those iron gates that divide the Paragon Estates from the rest of the world came up on me, I flipped a U-turn and landed in the parking lot of the bowling alley instead. I'm too plagued with guilt to face them. I'm afraid as soon as I step through their front door, both Barron and Emma will know what I've done to Skyla, what I've inadvertently done to Gage. I'm not sure I could ever face them without feeling weighted down with this tonnage of guilt. It's adhered to me as the hours bleed by, melted over my flesh like a scarlet letter—*S* for Skyla.

"Call her." Ellis strums his impatient fingers over the counter. "Right now. And then get the hell out. I can handle this place with my eyes closed."

That's what I'm afraid of.

"Will do," I say. Not sure when Ellis started making sense, but it's nice to know someone hasn't lost their ever-loving shit after what happened yesterday. We need someone— anyone, to stay grounded, someone still moored to the port before we all drift away in a fog of grief and take each other down. Gage was the life vest that kept us afloat for so long, and with him gone, we'll all drown in this misery. I love Gage more than I could ever admit or even hope to express. And what happened between Skyla and me last night sickens me—makes my stomach churn. If Gage didn't hate me before, he should now.

No sooner do I dig out my phone than Skyla walks through the door with Laken Stewart by her side. It's like a breath of fresh air. Every cell in my body stands at attention whenever Skyla is around, always has. In fact, something about the way the light shines down on her reminds me of that first day she strolled right through the very same doors all those years ago with Brielle. I thought—here she is, my beautiful girl. I knew, just *knew* she was meant for me. Gage shared a vision with me that morning that I would meet my soul mate, and then later that afternoon, she was right there in the flesh. Once I laid eyes on Skyla, I claimed her. I did. I claimed Skyla like some grunting caveman, full of hormones and dumb lust because all of my good judgments were put on ice. That's what Skyla does to me. She scrambles my good senses. That's exactly how I justify what happened last night. My judgment was more than slightly derailed. Her pain was palpable. I tasted her boiling grief in every kiss.

"Come here." I wrap my arms around her tight. Her tiny body melts into mine just like it did a few hours ago, only this time with a few more layers of clothing between us.

Skyla sniffs into my neck. Her chest bucks wild before pulling away.

"We went to Demetri's." Her eyes fill with tears and rage simultaneously. "The house is gone."

"What house?" Ellis heads over. "Did they demo the old Edinger place?"

"No—there's just a plot of land." Skyla explains how they drove over and found nothing but dirt where Demetri's shit shack once stood, the burnout of a butterfly in its wake. "What do you make of it?"

Crap. I try not to show my panic. "What did Dudley say?"

Laken gently pulls Skyla over by the shoulders. "He said Demetri would be back. I believe him. Demetri loves

Gage—he loves both of his sons." Her eyes flit to the floor a moment. Laken has a sordid history with Wesley.

Skyla gives a long, disgusted blink. "I'm not sure Demetri knows what love is. His version is a bit more psychotic, but he is attentive. I'll give him that."

"Indeed." Holy shit. I try to digest what this might mean. "Why don't we head over to Barron's, and we can try to process all this?" For sure, I'll need to speak with Candace today. The only way I have access to the Elysian Fields is through my very unhandy dandy supervising spirit. Dudley and I will have to do a road trip whether he likes it or not.

"That sounds like a good plan." Laken wipes a tear from Skyla's cheek. "You need to be around family. And you should probably tell your mother about Gage, too."

Skyla shakes her head. "I don't want to worry her or anyone at the Landon house. Besides, he's coming back to me. That's the only reason I gave that devil my most prized possession."

"Yeah, well"—Laken averts her eyes a moment—"Coop has practice until four, then we're headed to the Transfer. That devil happens to have another prized possession, and if anyone knows how to get in touch with Demetri, it's Wes."

"I'll go with you," Skyla says the words so fast it sounds as if she's panting.

"*We'll* go with you," I correct.

"Fine." Laken offers Skyla a firm embrace. "Meet us at Devil's Peak at four-thirty. I have to take off for a bit. I can walk to the ferry from here." She points over to me as she heads toward the door. "Bring a fast car!"

"Will do." My truck hasn't busted through that granite wall in a while, hasn't needed to. The only thing I really need to bring is a fast Sector.

A group of teenagers strides in, laughing, chatting it up as if the world still carried on like normal, and it is. I hate that the world doesn't bat a lash at death. Gage is gone—missing at best. The world should quake at the thought of my nephew, my brother forgoing a single breath on this planet.

Ellis holds his hands up as he strides toward the register. "I'd shake the shit out of Wes myself, but I'll be closing this place down for you. Don't worry about a thing, Oliver. You do what you need to do." He hits the registers before backtracking a few steps. "Almost forgot. Barricade's got a big meeting in a few nights. Some big shit is about to go down. They want to prep the masses." He turns around and is swallowed up in a cloud of giggling preteen girls.

"The Counts are prepping the masses?" Skyla's chest rises and falls as she considers the idea. "If the Counts—the Steel Barricade—is about anything, it's about keeping the masses in the dark."

"Power and darkness. That about sums it up."

Gage was powerful, and now he's gone. Skyla and I are the ones left in darkness.

I pull her in just enough to create a bubble for the two of us.

"How are you holding up?"

"I'm great." She shakes her head as if contradicting herself. "Now that I'm with you I don't feel quite so lost. Do you think we'll find Demetri?"

"I know we will."

"How do you know?" Her pink lips knot up as she holds back tears.

"Because after we leave the Transfer, I'm going to speak with your mother."

A dull smile comes and goes on her lips. "We're going to speak with my mother."

"Can I stop you?"

"No."

"I didn't think so." I lean my head over hers as we head for the exit. "Let's get out of here."

Skyla and I head straight over to the Paragon Estates. The rain has let up, and the sky is still set with a thick layer of steel-colored clouds. I bypass Barron's home and head for

Demetri's, only because I have to see this travesty for myself, and sure as hell there's nothing but a gaping hole, as the Paragon hillside where the Fem's house once sat offers a toothless smile.

"What the hell is he thinking? What's the logic behind this?" I muse out loud.

"It's to prove a point. He's powerful. He can and will get what he wants. And when he does, he is free to do whatever the hell he pleases. I don't know what I was thinking serving Gage up to him like an offering." Skyla buries her face in her shoulder as if ashamed by her actions.

"Hey"—I take up her hand—"you were desperate with grief, we all were—still *are*. If Demetri brings back Gage—and I'm hoping he will without any fucked-up strings—it was for the best."

We drive over to Barron's, and I help Skyla out of the truck. Giselle is inside, curled up in a ball on the sofa with Emma wrapped around her, the two of them raw from endless tears.

I offer my brother a strong hug. "How are you doing?"

"Considering the circumstances"—Barron pushes his glasses up the bridge of his nose—"I'm devastated. Come sit with us." He pulls Skyla into a long hug and whispers something into her ear, eliciting a nod from her.

Emma and I exchange an embrace, and I sit on the other side of Giselle, far from Skyla. I don't want Barron or Emma to think I'm stepping in and taking their son's place with his wife. Last night wafts through my mind like a rancid piece of meat, and I wave it away.

Skyla and Emma exchange an awkward embrace before they both land hard on the couch.

"Logan and I are going to do everything we can to find him," Skyla assures both Emma and Barron. I know she feels responsible for the sudden disappearance of her husband, but the fact of the matter is that he's dead—*was* dead in the least. I'm sure everyone here understands that she was just doing her best at the moment. In all honesty, Demetri is Gage Oliver's only blessed hope. You know you're in deep shit when the only hope of rescue comes from the king of the wicked.

"Doing everything you can?" Emma's voice rises with a mock amusement.

Okay, perhaps not everyone here understands that Skyla was simply trying to make things better. I'm pretty sure I was next in line to beg Demetri to breathe life back into his son. And as much as I hate to admit it, Skyla is right. Emma is not in her fan club. I'm not in Lizbeth's fan club, but I'm positive that I don't mind as much as Skyla does in this case.

Emma gives a dry laugh, and Giselle slowly sits up straight as if readying to bolt. "I don't think we'd be sitting here wondering where my son's corpse is if you didn't hand him off to a madman yesterday."

Shit.

Skyla's mouth opens and then closes abruptly. Wise move. Less is more in a situation like this. Emma is blind with grief. She has no clue what she's saying.

"You know"—Skyla shakes her head, incredulous—"I don't believe any of us would be sitting here if you didn't sleep with that madman in the first place."

"Skyla! That was a very low blow!" Giselle gives a sharp clap. Her face is lit up with glee as if she's enjoying the start to this verbal sparing match. Giselle doesn't quite have a grasp on appropriate social etiquette. I'm pleading the fifth on whether Skyla or Emma does.

"It is a low blow." Emma pulls a tight smile. "But I'd expect nothing less from the snake that sold my son to the devil."

"*Emma!*" Both Barron and I bark at the same time.

"Enough." Barron swipes off his glasses and massages his eyes for a moment. "Tensions are high. Let's not resort to name-calling. Skyla, please, accept my apology on behalf of my wife."

"Don't you dare apologize for me." Emma's voice shakes as she says the words.

Giselle leans toward me, hard. "What's happening?" She's gone from gleefully amused to confused as hell. "Aren't we all worried for my brother?"

"I'll answer that!" Emma cracks through the silence with her voice like a whip. "My son is missing, my son is *dead,* and it's all because of this cheerleading barracuda."

Skyla rises to her feet, her mouth wide open as she gags on a million fresh comebacks all aimed at her mother-in-law.

"Gage is my husband." Her breathing becomes erratic, and I head over to steady her. "He loves me, and I love him."

Emma jumps to her feet and gets nose-to-nose with her daughter-in-law. "You tricked him into an ambush marriage! Gage would never have agreed to such a foolish arrangement if you didn't somehow finagle your way into it. As soon as Logan died, you pinned yourself to my son's side. You're one of those weak girls who always needs a man around."

Skyla sucks in a lungful of air. "Says the one who slept with a *Fem* behind her boyfriend's back!" Her body shakes so hard, I wrap myself around her arms in the event she decides to make this physical. "My husband loves me. I forgive your erratic behavior, Emma, because I understand that you are grieving. But if Gage were here, he would march me the hell away from this living room because he would *never* want you to speak to me this way."

Emma's eyes boil with rage. I've never seen her lose her sanity quite like this. "Logan, why don't you march Little Miss *Oliver* out of here because I'm about to speak to her again that way."

A thick silence clogs up the room.

"That's right," Emma seethes. "I not only blame you for my son's death, but for the quality of his life just prior to his unfortunate demise. You're the worst thing that has ever happened to that boy, Skyla!" She lurches forward, and Barron jumps up to hold her back.

Holy shit. Never would I have dreamed that it would be Emma looking for a fistfight.

Skyla bucks like a wild bull in an effort to escape my grasp, but I hustle her to the door, employing my Celestra powers to ensure we get there.

"Take that back!" Skyla screams. "Gage would have your head for that!"

"Once Gage is cremated, he won't have a head because of you! Isn't that right, Logan?" Emma screams from the living room. "None of Skyla's suitors survive with their heads intact! You love people to death, Skyla! And then you arrange to have their heads removed!"

Crap. I may have lost my head in the war, but it was Chloe who sliced it off at the finish line. It's not a memory I care to relive, but Skyla had nothing to do with my decapitation.

"You *witch*!" Skyla wriggles out of my grasp and bullets back to the living room. "How dare you!" The veins in her neck bulge with fury. "And how dare you even suggest we burn Gage up as if he were trash. That body, those bones, my precious, *precious* husband is *mine*!" She digs her finger into her chest. "You do not have a say in anything that happens to him ever again."

"I wish he never met you." Emma's eyes all but close with grief. "I wish he met a nice girl, a sweet cherry of a girl who would have treated him better than you ever could. Oh, I know, Skyla. He was your everything, and so was Logan, and that math professor of yours is your everything, too! Who knows how many other special men mean so very much to you? My son deserved someone whose whole heart was devoted to him, and as soon as I got wind of your perverse behavior, I knew it wouldn't be you."

Skyla's face cinches back as if she were slapped.

"Gage Oliver is my world. He has my whole heart, Emma, and if you never believe that, I'm okay with it because Gage knows it."

She stalks out of the room, and I pause for a moment. Skyla's words burn a hole right through me.

Of course, I know that Skyla loves Gage.

It just makes what I let happen last night that much more tragic.

A crown of storm clouds circles just above Barron's home as we head back out. Skyla speeds for my truck, and I block her before she can jump into the passenger's side.

"That was pretty brutal." I gently touch her cheek with my thumb. Skyla's skin has always felt like silk to me—something too soft to ever be true like water. "Emma's not herself today."

"Bullshit." She frowns back at the house a moment. "She's exactly herself today. Those were her real feelings, Logan. That woman has hated me ever since Gage even hinted that he might want me as his own. I used to think Emma wouldn't approve of Gage being with anyone—that no one was good enough for her baby, but then, along came Kresley. She sort of destroyed that theory singlehandedly."

Kresley Fisher is Emma's old classmate's daughter. Back in high school, Kresley was obsessed with Wes, Gage's long lost half-brother. I wish he were still lost. I know for a fact the hardest part of today will be seeing Wesley Edinger's face. It just so happens to be identical to my nephew's.

"Forget about Kresley. Forget about Emma," I encourage, pulling her close. Skyla rests her head onto my chest, her body rising and falling with her deep sighs. She looks up and lays that baby blue gaze over mine, and the two of us sit there despondent beyond measure, just breathing God.

"I'm so sorry," I whisper into her hair—too much of a coward to ever look her in the eye and say it because I could never really lie to Skyla's face.

"Don't be. We're going to find him."

"I'm sorry about last night." It needs to be said. I am sorry. I'm sorry for everything. Emma was wrong; everything that's happened can be directly traced to me. I started a war the day I thought it was a good idea to globe trot killing Counts. I enraged Chloe a long time ago, and that's why she killed me. I was dead, and so Skyla married Gage.

I pause a moment because I know deep down Gage was never a conciliatory prize to Skyla, and that's the deepest knife. It's only fair—after all, I was the deepest knife to Gage.

"Logan." A heavy sigh expels from her as she cradles my face in her hands. "Don't apologize. That's what I wanted. It's what I needed. I hope you understand." Her arms thrust around me as I bury my face in her beautiful hair. My breath warms her neck, her beautiful face, those lips I swallowed down all night long, and a seizure of guilt hooks me in the gut. Skyla doesn't want me to feel bad. Last night is what she needed. It still guts me to think that way, but I get it. Grief brings out strange things in people, even stranger needs, and I happen to feed into one of them.

I take Skyla to the Burger Shack, and we hit the drive-thru before heading out toward Devil's Peak, to the nexus of all this misery. It's almost time to meet up with Laken and Coop. God knows I'm not summoning Marshall until the very last moment.

"What's on your mind?" she asks between bites. When Skyla ordered three cheeseburgers, I was sure she meant the two additional ones were for Laken and Coop, but she's proven me wrong by wolfing them down, one right after the other. It's a rather impressive feat I've only seen Harrison accomplish, and that was after a fresh high. It's true. Grief affects us all in different ways.

"I'm just admiring you." I flex a dull smile, and it comes and goes. "You're a rock, you know that?"

"Are you kidding?" She flashes a glance to the sky. "I'm a mess. I can't wait for the Transfer part of the day to be over, because that supervising spirit of yours is going to land us straight into the presence of my mother," she seethes those last few words out. I know Skyla doesn't get along with Candace. Not that I can blame her. She's not exactly the coddling type. Skyla is pretty much left to her own devices.

"You're all about getting things done," I say without thinking. She's fighting for her dead husband. Of course, she's going to get shit done.

"That's right." She crumples the wrapper to the last burger and tosses the bag to her feet. "I'm kicking ass and taking names." She nods behind me. "Here they are. Call Marshall, and let's get this party started. I've got a husband to find."

Laken and Coop wait by the cliff while I text Dudley. No sooner do Skyla and I get out of the truck than our pet Sector appears with a nefarious grin on his face.

"Shall we jump to the Kingdom of Darkness?" he asks politely as if inviting us to afternoon tea. "A mass suicide of sorts?"

"Marshall!" Skyla's voice shrills out, curling up to the clouds. "That is in very poor taste."

He narrows his gaze in on hers. "You don't think—" He tilts his head, further, silently examining.

"*You* don't think!" I shout in his face. "We're not jumping." I hold my hands out, and we form a circle. "Why don't you lead us in prayer, Dudley?"

"Dear Heavenly Father"—Dudley starts, and both Laken and Coop bow their heads—"we are gathered here today to bid you to reconsider this erroneous Treble your maidservant Candace has granted the dolt known as Logan Oliver. He is a petulant ass who believes all the world should bow to his every whim."

Skyla and I exchange glances. She rattles his hand, but the bowed-head, closed-eyed talking yak proceeds with his rumblings.

"Though I might dream of snuffing out the flame of his questionable existence myself, I do implore a higher wisdom to prevail in such matters. May he go the way of all the Earth so as to ease my burden in these few short years I've chosen to dwell among humans and Nephilim alike. By the power of your holy name, and in the blood, and in the spirit, we all say." His voice echoes out those last few words, hollow and sharp, as if we were in a tunnel. "Amen."

A cloying darkness robes us, the earth quakes beneath our feet, as the ground fog lifts and suctions us right off the cliff side, right into another dimension entirely as our feet touch down gently onto the hard, cracked soil of the Transfer. This is the dark dimension the Counts were granted, by who and when I have no clue nor do I want to. It's morbidly creepy, fully equipped with seventeenth century Counts, all of them disembodied. Ezrina's old laboratory that spans for miles, formerly known as the chop shop, sits in the center of this demonic city. The original haunted mansion where Skyla was held during her entrapment lies just to the north. In truth, I've spent time there, too, and last but not by a long shot least, Wesley's overgrown, new and improved version of the haunted mansion, a replica of Demetri's home which itself is a cheap replica of the hellish hotel that sits impatiently in front of us.

"Ah, yes"—Dudley gives a bored, deluded look of practical delight—"here we are again. Where's the fire, Ms. Messenger?"

"This way." Skyla speeds to Wesley's house of horrors, and we jog along to keep up the pace.

"Wesley?" Skyla's voice fills the entry to the douchebag's playhouse. It's absolutely huge, and for a second, I make a game of guessing how many versions of White Horse can fit into this place. My guess is twelve, easy.

Skyla bustles her way into the grand room where a raging blaze fills the enormous fireplace, the size of a one-car garage. I'm betting Wesley has some serious compensation issues. Big ego, little—

"Skyla." Wes appears from the elongated corridor along with Chloe, his wingman *woman*. She's trapped in the Transfer, mostly, as per her punishment doled out by the Decision Council after the war. She's the reason I'm in this Treble. I wouldn't be surprised if she had something, anything, to do with the fact Gage ended up in eternity yesterday as well.

"I bet you had a long night." Chloe grabs on to Skyla's finger, her face filled with mock remorse. "Do tell, are you exhausted? I bet you can hardly walk."

"Shut up." Skyla extracts her hands and speeds toward Wes, crashing into his chest, her fingers strumming over his features as if she were reading Braille. "Oh God," she whispers, her knees buckle as Wes holds her up.

"I've got you," he says it low and husky, sounding eerily like Gage in the process, and for a second, I'm left wondering. "I know this is hard for you."

Dudley steps in and gently extracts Skyla from Wesley's wicked claws. He's an Edinger, his father's son through and through. Gage might have Demetri's DNA as well, but he is nothing like his father. He might have drifted a bit this last year, but we left things off on good terms. That final conversation we had where he asked me to take care of Skyla comes back. Those erotic images of last night's grief counseling session follow suit. I'm pretty sure Gage didn't mean for me to jump into bed with her night fucking one. I'm an ass of the highest order. I deserve all the curses Marshall can rain down on me. If the roles were reversed, and Gage did the same the night I died, I wouldn't be too impressed with his lack of self-control, perhaps not hers either, and this grieves me the most. I know for a fact they waited until their wedding night after I died. Gage didn't morph into an asshole upon my demise. Nope, the only asshole around here would be me.

"I need Gage." Skyla's voice is weak as she struggles to get close to Wesley. "Please, find your father. His house is gone. It's just disappeared off that God forsaken rock. Tell him to come back, to bring Gage with him. Or in the least show me where he buried the body. I can't bear this pain, Wes. I will give you all of my blood. All of my favor if you do this one thing."

"And we're leaving." I scoop Skyla out of Dudley's arms without asking permission and head out of the monstrous castle.

Coop follows and nods to me as I place Skyla back onto solid ground.

"Skyla"—Coop takes her by the hand—"why don't you show me the old lab? Ezrina mentioned something about checking the tanks next time I had the chance."

"Yeah, sure." She shudders as if waking from a dream. Skyla slips her hand over her stomach and closes her eyes a moment too long. "I might need to find a bush to puke in first. Those burgers aren't sitting too well with me." She offers a shy smile before they take off toward Ezrina's old lair.

I didn't think the burgers were that great of an idea, at least not in that quantity. Once Skyla and Coop drown in darkness, I head back inside, and Chloe cuts me off before I can head into the grand room. I know for a fact that Laken is probably sweet-talking Wes into giving her as much information as possible. A few months back, he manipulated her into kissing him in an effort to shut down the tunnels. It weighed heavy on her to end that carnal madness ever since her own sister and mother were trapped down there with Counts sucking off their necks as if they were water coolers. Coop forgave Laken for kissing Wes. It's pretty easy to see that her heart is steadfast for Cooper Flanders, so much so that she's about to take his name and become his wife.

Chloe slaps me over the chest with both of her hands as if rebuffing a sexual advance.

"How haven't you found him yet?" Chloe is incensed as if I've purposely slacked in my search for Gage.

A flash of last night's lovemaking jolts through my mind again. Okay, that might qualify as slacking.

Her eyes glow bright as flames. Now that she's no longer on the planet proper, Chloe has garnered physical morphing capabilities. She's taken Ezrina's old form, and, in doing so, she's morphed right back to herself—a new and improved version with longer, darker, stronger hair, more demanding eyes, her face far more cutting and beautiful than that of her earthly countenance, although that too was stunning. I thought I could love Chloe once. I slept with her in high school. It was stupid. Her heart was set on Gage even then.

"How haven't *you* found him?" I turn the question around. Skyla might have come to lure information out of Wes, but my intentions were set on Chloe all along and her obsessive Gage-shaped heart. "Where is he, Chloe? You are a master of his whereabouts. Gage might be dead, but he still needs to be with his family."

"I don't care about his family." Her eyes flash like mirrors in the sun. Chloe steps in and brings her finger to my cheek, running it down my neck throbbingly slow. "Maybe just you—a little." She smirks. "Besides, Gage can't be dead. I need him. I need him to see my precious baby." She cradles her still flat stomach. Chloe is with child. I don't know the specifics, and I'm not gunning for them either. The kid belongs to Wes. I'm guessing that's hard for Laken. Speaking of which, I try to brush by Chloe, and she blocks me off at the pass.

"I can find him for you—I swear I can." Her voice strings out the words with urgency.

"But?" I slip my hands into my back pockets and wait for it. I can't quite pinpoint the last time Chloe asked a favor of me, but I'm guessing it wasn't good then, and it isn't good now.

"But I might need your help."

"Shit." I motion for her to move it along.

"I'm having these cravings." Her neck bends back. Her eyes roll into her head like some devilish doll. "I need at least six Burger Shack double doubles, extra cheese, extra pickles. And throw in a Neapolitan shake. Oh hell, make it two. I fucking hate sharing with Wes."

"Are you serious?"

"Deadly."

"Would you like some fries with that?" There's no reason for heavy sarcasm when Chloe makes it so simple.

"Hell yes! Make it two large chili fries. I might as well go for the gold."

"I was being facetious, Chloe. You've got Wes for that. He has both a license to thrive and drive on Paragon. There's no reason he can't make those burger runs for you."

I manage to step past her, and this time she pulls me back by the sleeve.

"Are you kidding? He's a real-life burger miser. All he wants me to eat are carrots and celery. Do I look like a deer to you? I'm a carnivore! I need red-blooded meat to survive, not to mention to feed his wicked spawn."

My lips cinch tight in the event an easy dig decides to plume out.

"So, I make the food run, and you'll find Gage?"

She gives a furtive nod like that of a compliant child. Who knew hostage negotiations for Gage would heavily hinge on the

Burger Shack menu? They should change their slogan. *The Burger Shack, rich in cholesterol and negotiating power!*

"All right. Deal." I make my way past her into the grand room to find Wes and Laken whispering near the fireplace. Dudley is busying himself with staring at the rolling blue stone in the center of the room. It's a fountain of some sort, a globe made of granite bobbing in a pool of water. The globe itself stands about four feet tall, and there's a slight moat around the entire unit while the sphere spins in a continual cool wash.

"What do you see?"

"I see nothing. This is a portal of darkness. I wouldn't expect it to open to me, a creature of light. Have you said your peace? I've business to tend to in another century."

"Let me talk to Wes, and we'll head out. Skyla and Coop are in the lab, checking out the tanks. Why don't you round them up, and we'll take off?"

"Very well." He heads for the exit.

"Dudley." He pauses and turns—his constant annoyance with me perpetually visible. "Fair warning, you'll have to put off any light drives you have planned for the evening. We're heading to Ahava to visit Candace."

His chest expands as he sets his sights on an invisible horizon. "Absolutely no good will come of this."

"I didn't think so." I head over to Wes and step between him and the flame of his heart, Laken.

"Logan," Wes says with a marked disdain while still holding Laken's gaze. "I want to be clear about something."

It's an unnerving thing to have someone speak to you, with that aggressive tone no less, without having them look at you.

He sighs deeply, still staring her down as if this directly involved her. And, knowing Wes, it does. Wesley is as obsessed with Laken as Chloe is with Gage. Oddly, with him looking like Gage, and Chloe morphing into Laken in her spare time, it only sponsors a peculiar brand of hell for the two of them.

"What is it you need to be clear about?" I try not to sound exasperated.

"I'm as deeply saddened as anyone regarding my brother. But in no way am I responsible for the tragedy that befell Gage. I can't get in touch with my father. I've tried. When I do, I'll make sure he touches base with Skyla. It's the least I can do."

"Sounds good." I nod Laken over toward the door. No use in negotiating with the devil. It's bad enough I've already promised Chloe a side of charred beef.

"And Logan—" Wes bows his head slightly. His green eyes are the only distinguishing factor between him and Gage. It's eerie, unnerving, and for a second, I entertain the thought that he's somehow absorbed him. "I really am sorry."

Before I can say anything, he steps in, those lucent eyes painfully piercing through mine.

Wes gives the impression of a wicked grin. "And I'm sorry for what's about to become of the rest of you."

Laken lifts her head toward him. "Just out of curiosity, Wes, what could we have ever done to have avoided any of this?" She's pissed, curious, but pissed. "If we had all joined the Barricade from the beginning, would that have really been enough?"

Wes stares into the fire a few seconds too long. "No, I suppose it wouldn't." He turns toward her fully, his thumb brushing over her cheek. "Because I still wouldn't have you."

I usher Laken the hell out of there, and we meet up with Dudley, Skyla, and Coop outside.

"Where to now?" Coop takes Laken back into his arms and swipes a kiss over her cheek as if he just pulled her from a fire.

"You're headed home to Host, my friend." I look to Skyla, my beautiful girl whom I would melt the universe to cinders for. In that respect, I understand Wesley's pain, his roiling frustration. "We, however, are headed to Ahava."

Skyla takes my hand, her thumb rubbing a quick circle over my palm, and I'm not sure how to read it. "After you, my Elysian."

A dull smile rides over my lips as Dudley whisks us out of darkness and off through time and dimensions, through the material world and into the spiritual. My thoughts shield themselves from her in the event I enter into a play-by-play of those heated hours we shared. It's true. I am Skyla's Elysian—her guide in the spiritual realm, at least as far as the Counts are concerned. I was once her husband, and according to Candace, will be again, but last night I was her lover, and that's the title I'd take down heaven and Earth for. If Wesley feels even a fraction of that diehard angst I do toward Skyla, then Celestra, all of the Nephilim, and all of mankind are in a hell of a lot of trouble.

3

Fruit of the Rose

Skyla

My father once said that time is circular—a constant river that flows in and out of itself. People think it's linear, that one day progresses to the next, but it's merely an illusion, the sun rising, the sun setting, the moon cut and quartered for all to see—it's all a play on a single moment in time. We age, we move, we parcel out activities that feel as if we're marching on, but it's the same day, same God's breath repeated on a loop. People enter and exit this realm at all hours, every day, week, month, and year. The comings and the goings are endless. The bold entrances, the grand departures—those are the crowning moments, not the idolized sentiments we fill the interim with. It is a miracle you arrive on this planet. It is a miracle you exit—a dark miracle, but a miracle nonetheless. Gage is somewhere here or there, conscious either way—I'm hoping in flesh clothes, tucked warm and safe somewhere as the treasure he is to both Demetri and me. I knew if I couldn't protect him, the only other being that could was that demon I dread to call upon. Desperation makes you do strange things. And now, I'm about to embark on another one of those odd adventures.

Ahava forms around us. The tiered falls sparkle just past the expansive crystalline lake. My mother and her three cohorts that form the rest of the Decision Council sit firm above the water hoisted up in their glassy thrones. There is the long-haired, one-eyed delight, Rothello, who proclaimed the Faction War in my honor. I'll refrain from name calling at the moment since my thoughts are not entirely my own in this sphere. Then, there are the Marshall twins who flank her on either side—two alarmingly stunning Sectors much like the one holding my hand at the moment, although Marshall is in a class all by himself. He's perfection, sublime, with just the right touch of arrogance to make any girl swoon.

"I heard that, and I approve of your summation." He gives my hand a squeeze.

"I figured you would." I quickly untangle our fingers before turning to my Elysian. "Logan, use your *sensibilities*." Confession, I had to grapple with that last word. What I really want is for Logan to charm my mother senseless until she vomits up Gage like I did those cheeseburgers back in the Transfer. Funny thing is, no sooner did I puke onto the dry, cracked soil of that jackal haunt than an entire crop of red-tipped mushrooms sprouted. Coop thought they might mean something, so he tucked a few away in his pocket. The thought is disgusting enough to make me want to retch again.

"My sensibilities." He gives a crooked smile, and that longitudinal dimple I gifted him inverts. I cut Logan once with a bottle. It was after a fight, and I've regretted it ever since, but I'd be remiss if I didn't admit it only added to his good "sensibilities." My mother herself isn't impervious to Logan's appeal. I only wish she cared for Gage or even me a fraction as much.

The air tingles, the breeze moves in swiftly, and the sand swirls around our feet as my mother materializes at the shoreline in a sparkle-filled fog—her own rendition of Glinda the Good Witch of the South.

"I am not a witch." Her expression sours—correction, my expression. My mother is my exact representation. I'm a carbon copy minus a few millennium and superpowers removed. "And, you have all my powers, Skyla." She gives an impish grin. "Were you unaware of that?"

I hate that she can read my thoughts here. My brain cramps up just trying to erect a wall to keep her out.

"All your powers?" I'm stumped by the idea. "Let me guess. They're disabled?"

"Harsh verbiage." She turns and offers a coy smile to Logan, her chief pet.

"*Skyla*," she purrs as if reprimanding me. "What brings the three of you to Oz?" That smile of hers sours, and she's right back to being her curt self. It looks as if Logan's charming sensibilities only go so far.

Marshall lifts his chin. "We came to see if the wizard is a wizard who will serve."

"Very funny." I offer a light smack to his arm. "Gage is dead." I step toward my mother. My eyes lock onto her crystal orbs and don't let go. "And missing."

"Oh dear." Her brows hike an inch. "It appears you have quite the conundrum. And you need me to locate the body?"

"No. We need you to *resurrect* the body," I correct.

"Speak for yourself," Marshall adds with that same look of boredom he's worn throughout this entire ordeal.

I barrel on without acknowledging him. "Point the way, and I'll get Gage myself. Where's that rat-faced Fem hiding out?" I look over her shoulder as if I might actually see Demetri clogging up precious Ahava real estate. "Just make this better, and I will do whatever you please." Demetri is the only one who's taken me up on this offer so far. It's true. I would do anything to have Gage alive once again, including putting him right back in this mysterious predicament with his father. Demetri will prove to be a saint if I get Gage back, warm and breathing.

"Let me see." She retreats within herself for a moment, her expression sober, the look in her eye distant and foggy. "Skyla. This simply isn't my jurisdiction. Sector Marshall, you're more than equipped to handle the situation from here. Make yourself useful, would you? I must get going. The yearlings are running."

"Is it that time of year again?" Marshall bounces on his feet, delighted by this nonsensical turn of events. "I do miss the pomp and circumstance surrounding opening day."

"It really is a treasure." My mother offers him a wink, and it more than weirds me out.

A slow boiling rage enlivens me. "Look, I'm really glad you'll get to feast your winking eyes on a bunch of baby horses running amuck, but your daughter's husband just passed away—as in major life-altering crisis marked by horrendous torrents of *grief*. How about an *I'm so sorry, Skyla! Oh my goodness, I'll go pluck him from eternity so you can say a proper goodbye!* Or *Let me make this better, baby girl, by breathing life back into his body right this fucking minute.* But, no! You have yearling races to get to!" My voice hits a crescendo just as Logan secures his arm around my waist. "And here I thought Marshall was being rather cold-hearted about the entire event."

"Ms. Messenger!" he crows, but I don't bother acknowledging him.

My mother and I lock eyes. It's like staring down my own reflection, and then a thought occurs to me. There's something cold and disconnected in her gaze and...

"Oh my God," I whisper. "Are you even on my side?"

"What side?" She shakes her head incredulously as if the concept were the most ridiculous thing in the heavens.

"Celestra's side, the good side, the side not affiliated with the Steel Barricade, i.e., Wesley Edinger's ploy for power."

"Is Wesley at it again?" Her cheek pulls back just enough to get a rise out of me.

"Oh, wow, you're not even hiding it. You are mocking me! You know damn well Gage is no longer on the planet. You were the same way during the Faction War, and now you're being just as elusive and coy as ever. What was the purpose of having me? What is the purpose of having this relationship?"

Something in her darkens. "I never sought you out, Skyla."

And there it is. The Celestial slap in the face.

I take in a sharp breath. Those words were mean, cruel as a kick in the teeth.

"That's right," I whisper. "You didn't care to. You dumped me into Lizbeth Landon's arms and took off for greener celestial pastures. Are you going to help me get Gage or not?" I'm sick of beating around the ethereal bush.

"No. And to set the record straight, I did not dump you in Lizbeth Landon's arms. I had the Fems and the Counts set my feet to flames until I succumbed. Something only Logan would fully understand." Her nostrils flare at me. "Gage Oliver is not of my concern at the moment, nor do I see that changing in the foreseeable future." She glances to Logan.

A hard groan crawls right out of my throat. "I get it. You're waiting it out until Logan has a turn at bat, and then you'll be all over my business. Is that right? You'll tune in when The Skyla Show takes a dramatic Oliver plot twist."

"I am vested in Logan, yes." Her lips turn down at the tips when she says it. My mother turns to him fully; any look of pleasure is wiped from her face. In fact, she's downright glaring at him. "I know what you have done," she says the words slow and staggered as if he were responsible for the greatest offense.

Whatever Logan has "done," she's not too pleased with it. For whatever the reason, she's lost that sparkle in her eyes while ogling the Golden Oliver.

She continues, "What I am not vested in is this conversation. Skyla, I am deeply sorry that your heart is broken. That is a very real hurt that no one can cradle but you. As for altering destinies, I'm simply not in the mood, nor do I find it necessary." She examines me up and down with a scrutinizing stare. "Please take care of your health. Get plenty of rest, and for goodness' sake, drink a glass of water once in a while, will you?"

I'm stunned. Is she really pausing our tit-for-tat mother-daughter spat to give me a rudimentary health lecture?

"Drink plenty of water?" I say, incredulous. "I am drinking buckets of tears! I love Gage. Gage is my husband. You have the power to make him appear to me, and you are all but denying me that right."

"I'm not all but denying that right—I am flat-out denying it. I don't wish to see him in Ahava. I don't need him in my presence, Skyla. Gage is with his father—both of which are Fems, in the event you have forgotten. I'm very slow to entertain Fems for anybody. Don't take offense." Her lips pinch. "With the exception of..." Her eyes ride down the length of my body. "Let's just say there are exceptions to every rule. There are some Fems I will welcome with open arms. And that day has not yet arrived."

Anger shoots through my veins in short bursts of rage. Gage. My beautiful husband is out there somewhere. He needs me. Dear God, I need him. And my own mother, this wicked, *wicked* witch is denying me the help I so desperately need to find him.

She turns to leave, and I violently yank her back by the arm. "I hope you are in desperate need someday." My chest heaves as I spit the words out. "I hope you know the pain of such ripe grief that you would do anything to have your heart set right again. I hope the power is out of your hands to restore the situation, and I hope you are ripped with anguish when the one who can rectify it refuses to make things right. I curse you with this. I curse you at this moment so that you begin to feel that deep-welled anguish right this very minute."

"Skyla!" Rage mixed with terror transforms her features.

"Remember this day because I am parting ways with you, Mother."

A hard groan comes from behind, and I can't tell if it's Marshall or Logan—both perhaps.

"You are parting ways with *me*?" Her mouth opens. Anger percolates fresh in her eyes. "I bore you. I nursed you at my bosom." She beats her chest just once. "I died a horrific death for *you*, Skyla."

"And you've resented me ever since!"

Marshall takes up my hand and pulls me back. "Time to leave, Ms. Messenger. Come, I shall aid you in finding Jock Strap once and for all."

"Parting ways with me." She shakes her head in disbelief. A sharp cracking sound emits, filling the air with its harsh snap. "Oh, Skyla." She holds her hands out in front of her as her fingertips turn a cool glacial blue. Before long, the icy color spreads up her arms and throughout her body, turning her into nothing more than a glacial sculpture.

"What's happening?" I've never seen my mother in such a strange capacity.

"It's the curse," Marshall whispers. "Don't feel too bad. This was inevitable on some level."

"I didn't really curse you." I reach out to touch my mother in her brilliant blue state, and she retracts. "I don't even know *how* to put a curse on anyone."

"*Skyla*." Her features melt with grief. "I can't bear this pain. Why must it be this way?" She staggers toward the lake, her feet striding over the water as if it were solid ground. "I could have focused on the situation much better without all this anguish." The words howl from her in agony. Candace Messenger weeps bitter tears all the way back to her glassy throne, and not even her cohorts from the big DC can comfort her.

"What the hell just happened, Marshall?"

"Those bitter tears are for you as well."

"Over Gage?"

"No, dear." He draws me near as we ready to leave Ahava. "Over something far more dear to her heart."

We begin to dissipate, and I grab ahold of Logan's hand. "What did you do?" I whisper to him, but Logan doesn't answer.

Paragon forms around us with the night wrapped around her like a robe. The island moans and creaks as a harsh south wind whistles throughout the evergreens. It's been a long, grueling day and still no Gage.

"I'm ready for bed," I say, pulling Logan in for a hug, and his body goes rigid beneath me. "You mind taking me home?"

"I'll do the honors." Marshall lands an arm over my shoulders, and that deep, electrifying, warm buzz his body emits takes over my senses.

In a blink, we're standing in his living room sans Logan.

"I meant the Landon house."

"This is your home, Skyla. That's simply your temporary abode."

"Okay, well, can you get me to Gage tonight? Because if not, I'd really like to cuddle with my pillow over at my temporary abode. My bones hurt. I've never been so tired. Grief will do that to you." I'm familiar.

"Yes, well, I'll track down Demetri while you catch up on some shut-eye. I have a feeling I'll do better on my own. I'll leave you a message if I make headway."

The lights dim. The faint sound of music permeates the air. Marshall pulls me in by the fingertips, and before I know it, we're slow dancing.

"You do realize I'm in deep mourning." I lay my head against his chest, so very, very tired, and let his rhythmic swaying lull me to sleep.

"I would very much appreciate one last dance."

"Before?"

"Before our lives change, Skyla."

My eyelids fly open. "What's going to change, Marshall?"

"The landscape of your world."

"*Oh*. I suppose it already has."

"No, not quite yet."

"Why do I get the feeling you're not talking about Gage?"

"Why would I ruin a perfectly good moment by bringing up Jock Strap?"

"Thought so." I pull back and study his ruggedly handsome features. "Wait a minute. You keep calling him Jock Strap...You're still full throttle rude to him as if he were—"

His brows rise, confirming my theory.

A swell of relief hits me as wide and tall as Devil's Peak. "You don't think he's dead, do you?"

"Get some rest, Skyla. You heard your mother, plenty of sleep, plenty of water."

"Right." I bite down on my lip so hard I taste blood. "Gage is *alive*." I want to cry, to *laugh*. "And all either you or my mother can think about is my lack of sleep, my hydration habits."

Marshall drops a lone kiss to my forehead, and when he pulls back, I find myself standing in the Landon foyer.

"Good night, Ms. Messenger." He evaporates slowly into a vapor.

"Text me if you hear anything," I whisper.

"Text who?" my mother calls from behind, and I jump.

"Oh, nothing. I was just talking out loud—my head is sort of on overload these days," I say, trotting up the first few steps. "Hey, Mom?"

"Yeah?" She backtracks with her arms cradling a laundry basket.

"You're sort of like a doctor...I mean, you're up on a lot of medical things." Okay, so I'm buttering her up, but in a way, I'm right. My mother is very health conscious. I suppose it couldn't hurt to have her solve my heavenly mother's cryptic riddle that even seemed to spook Marshall on some level. "A friend of mine mentioned her *doctor* told her to get lots of rest and drink plenty of water. What do you think could be wrong with her?"

Her forehead wrinkles. "Gee, Skyla, that could be just about anything. Sorry. It's just too broad to narrow anything down. Has she been feeling anything else that you're aware of?"

"Oh, yes, she can hardly hold anything down. Just puking, tired, and crying all the time."

A sharp laugh comes from her throat. "That's easy, Skyla. I'd bet a million bucks your friend is expecting."

"Expecting what?" I give a few innocent blinks.

"A baby. Your friend has all the classic signs. It's safe to say your friend is pregnant."

"What?" The ground beneath my feet gives way. My entire body goes numb with shock.

"Oh, and Skyla?" She steps back into my view. "I wouldn't go ruining the surprise for her. You never forget where you were when you found out you're carrying new life inside you. It's really a magical moment." She bites down a smile with that faraway look in her eye as if she's revisiting each and every occasion herself. "Would you mind dropping this off at the foot of my door?" She hands me the laundry basket and disappears down the hall.

Oh my God, a *baby*?

I stare down at Tad's yellowed socks, his permanently stained underwear, and absorb right into my cellular level the moment I am never going to forget.
Could I be? Am I?
Pregnant?

Logan

The storm clears out in time to allow the night fog to seep in, slowly crawling over the island, finger walking at a glacial pace over Paragon's every curve, licking every private place in between.

Something about seeing Wes and Chloe tonight felt familiar. I can't quite put my finger on it, but seeing Wes with his Gage face and those large Gage eyes, I don't give a damn if they're not the correct hue. It was tough. I know that weighed heavy on Skyla, so much so that she vomited in the bushes no less than twenty feet from that house of horrors. I can't imagine what it would be like having someone else with Skyla's face running around after the unthinkable happened to her. Candace bounces through my mind, quick and slippery like a rubber ball. That horrible visit clings to my palate, about as pleasant as sucking on rust and ashes. Her clear-cut eyes narrowed in on mine, and she pointed, *pointed* at me when she said those cryptic words. *I know what you have done.*

She knows. And I know, too. I've made Skyla mine in the carnal sense.

After a short meal with Emma and Barron, I decide to head back to White Horse. I'm not sure what my reasoning is. Liam and Ellis invited me to stay up and watch a movie with them—a wartime shoot 'em up classic that the normal me would have loved. I try to tell myself that it wouldn't be right without Gage. After all, he's still out there. Skyla is still a mess. I don't really have the right to enjoy myself, but I know what's really triggering my antisocial behavior, and it has very little to do with grief.

I warm my bones in a nice hot shower that lasts for what feels like weeks. Skyla didn't say much about last night, and I'm glad. She's going through a shitstorm, and that visit with her mother didn't exactly help. What the hell is it with Candace anyway? She's a cold fish when it comes to her own daughter, and yet, when we're alone, it's as if she's visiting with royalty. Maybe that's what I need to do, speak with her alone. I'm pretty sure Skyla didn't mean what she said about cutting off ties with her. As much as Skyla doesn't want to admit it, we *need* Candace. We need her for...I grapple for a single concept of why we might need her and come up with nothing. I'm not sure why we need Candace Messenger, but hell, I'm pretty sure we do.

"Knock, knock!" a female voice floats through the thick, steaming vapors, and my stomach clenches.

I swipe my hand over the glass door to find Skyla's blurred image, quickly disrobing on the other side.

"Don't say a word," she whispers, opening the door and slipping in beside me. Her bare skin brushes over mine, her perfect tits graze my chest, and my hard-on springs up out of nowhere. "I guess you don't really mind, do you?" Her fingers collapse over me as she takes my length in her hand.

"Shit," I hiss the word out, closing my eyes as if she's causing me just as much pain as she is pleasure. It's only psychologically true. "Skyla." I take a step back into the heated spray, and she stays close to me. Her hair fills with vaporous beads floating around her face like a thousand sparkling stars. "We shouldn't be doing this."

Her features pull heavy. Her lower lip quivers, and I want to kiss it, to hold her and to let her know everything will be okay when I know it won't, not like this.

"I'm so sorry. I don't know what's gotten into me." She touches the handle and cracks the door just enough to let in a cool breeze.

"No, come here." I pull her back to me, greedy, afraid she'll sober up and leave for good. I guess I'm not the white knight I've always painted myself to be, more like the bruised, downtrodden anti-hero. I'm just another asshole willing to comfort my best friend's widow—for all practical purposes, brother's widow with my own body. There are moral codes and laws about this in the heavenly books, and if there aren't, there should be because it feels wrong. It feels insanely horrible to think that Gage's death is the catalyst we're using to fall into bed together. Skyla and I have always had a strong sexual bond. After all, our relationship was initially built on lust. Trust came much later, and what happened with that was mostly my fault.

But in truth, we are most certainly grieving, afraid for Gage, afraid to live in a world without him. Alone we're weak, but together, we're strong enough to hold up a suspension bridge.

"We don't have to say anything." Her cool finger glides over my lips. Her beautiful eyes sear over mine. "If we don't say anything, none of this is real. This is just some twisted fantasy, a waking dream that neither you nor I can control. But I need you, Logan. I need your touch, your body pressed against mine." Her bare hip presses over mine, and I start to lose it. "You were my husband once. You are my greatest comforter—my best friend. I don't want you to feel guilty. I just want you to feel me." Her lips fall to my chest in a single soft kiss, and she stays that way for a long while, warming me with her hot tears.

I pull her chin up gently until she's looking at me with those watery eyes, her lips raw and swollen. It hurts me to see her in so much pain. It hurts me to be in so much pain. I can't stand what life has dealt us—what it took from us. But I would give it all away if we could have Gage back. I would be just fine with Gage and Skyla being a couple forever as long as I could have them both on Paragon with me. Or at least this version of me, the one with his hard-on pressed to her stomach believes so.

"You know I have always loved you," I whisper as the steam rises between us, judging us for our sins. "I would do anything for you, Skyla."

"Prove it." Her lips crash to mine as she offers a spirited kiss, an aching kiss mixed with tears, and I join her right there, my own tears mingling with hers. Our tongues fall into rhythm with one another as our bodies start in on a slow dance. I selfishly love the way her familiar curves press against me, the way my fingers feel when they're knotted up in her hair.

Skyla takes my hand and moves it down over her hips, lower still until I'm at that sweet spot between her legs, so soft, so *fucking* soft. A dull groan comes from me as I pick her up and lay her gently against the warm stone wall, the water washing away our tears, our sins, as my body penetrates her. Her mouth opens, her head arches back as she struggles to catch her breath. I can't help but watch. Skyla is a testament to her own beauty. She is the nexus of all things beautiful in this life and the next, at least to me. I know she was to Gage.

I plunge in, thrust after thrust lost in ecstasy with the girl I've loved since as far back as my dreams. Skyla is my girl, my wife, my everything. Always has been, always will be. She slips down, pushing me away abruptly, and my heart seizes, my eyes widen into hers as she drops to her knees and swallows me deep into her mouth, loving me that way, pulling me down her throat to unimaginable lengths, taking me in like that over and over.

"*Shit.*" My head falls back. My fingers tangle in her hair as the water melts her curly tendrils to her skin. Skyla and I are lost in lust. There's no turning back from this.

Skyla had me roped and tied from the beginning. I couldn't refuse her. I wouldn't want to.

Candace comes back to me with the bite of judgment falling from her like a hammer. *I know what you have done.*

But I was already found guilty before she ever made the charge.

The harshest judge of my immoral character just so happens to be me.

The first few awful days drift by. Then a full awful week. Then two. Skyla has become increasingly withdrawn. I try to get her out of the house, but she's anchored to her bed—says she's not feeling well. I know for a fact she told her mother that Gage is working on a secret project on Host. That he'll be back soon. That part, right there, tore me to shreds. She's hopeful Dudley will come up with a lead, but he's proven useless per usual. I've even tried to infiltrate Gage's dreams but keep coming up with nothing but static. Not that I've been having all that much sleep. Skyla comes to White Horse each and every night. She refuses to stay, and I get it. This is our dark secret, kept under the covers, literally. Something dirty for the night that we never discuss during waking hours. It's odd. The Skyla of the night is playful, rejuvenated, and carefree much like she was when she first came to the island. She offers me consolation by way of her tongue, her wandering hands, the open-mouthed giggles she pours right down my throat. The Skyla of the day is still very much morose—lost in grief, bags under her eyes, her stomach soured, life passing her by like a nightmare she can't wake up from.

Around noon, I head over to the Landon house, pry her out of bed, and drive her down to the Gas Lab for a quick bite. Nev and Ezrina have managed to turn what most of the island referred to as the "Gas Bag" into something just short of a five-star restaurant right here on Paragon. And they wisely cater to everyone, the gluten-free, vegan, pescatarian, you name it, anyone and everyone can find something to eat at this culinary café. Too bad about the unfortunate name—although, Ethan has all but stepped out of the picture. This might have been his brainchild, but as soon as he discovered there was actual work involved, he left on his lunch break one day and never returned.

Inside it's light and bright. The once plain walls are painted a cheery yellow, and vases filled with flowers sit on every table. A few men stand near the bar, yanking tubes from the floor. A dolly filled with oxygen tanks is wheeled out in front of us.

"What's going on?" Skyla asks as we find a table. The thick scent of coffee is the first thing that lights up our senses.

"Looks like the oxygen bar is no more." The oxygen bar was a very poor idea to begin with. Trying to digest your food while watching patrons inserting and removing plastic tubes from their noses did nothing for the atmosphere—let alone the appetites.

"Good riddance." Skyla falls hard in her seat, and I help scoot her in. Her hair is disheveled, her mascara slightly smeared, but she's still as beautiful as ever. I thought maybe today would be a good time to talk about what's going on between us. As much as my body would beg to differ, it doesn't feel right. I'm all for helping Skyla feel better, but I think I've jumped the bounds of good behavior. I'm not here to screw things up between her and Gage. And I very much still believe he's out there.

"Afternoon. The usual?" Nevermore comes up with two cups of coffee and sets them down. Nev and Ezrina bought a roaster, as in they roast their own beans. I'm not sure there's a better scent in the universe, with the exclusion of Skyla. Skyla is roses, lilacs, vanilla, and cinnamon, her own blend of perfect spices.

"If it's not too much trouble, do you think I can have decaf?" Skyla glides the coffee toward him, and he happily picks it up.

"Not a problem." Nev nods to me. "The couple in the back has aroused Rina's suspicions." He takes off, leaving me to crane my neck at a tall stalky man and a redheaded woman who looks as if she's been sucking on a lemon. Probably tourists. Paragon gets her fair share. The island is lovely. You can't blame the rest of the world for admiring her sheer scope and beauty.

"What do you feel like eating? Donuts? Omelets? I hear the saltimbocca melts in your mouth."

"I'm not hungry." She folds a napkin into the shape of a butterfly and drops it onto the table. The disappointment, the hollowness in her eyes has taken up residence.

"I talked to your mom—Lizbeth." I reach over and interlace our fingers, and her eyes widen as if this were treason. "She says you're hardly eating." I'm not too worried because I know for a fact her energy levels are up in the evening.

"You talked to my mom?" It comes out peeved.

"She says she's worried about you and Gage."

"I let her know he's away at Host. School stuff. She's not a fan of his absence." She arches her brows at me. "The Decision Council may have thought it was a good time for him to die, but I'm not buying it." Nev drops off her coffee on his way to another table, and she perks right up. "There's a faction meeting in a few weeks. I'll be appointing a new officer for the education division. It's something new I've been thinking about."

"You've been banned, Skyla. They're taking you to court. They think your leadership is deceptive because of your—"

"Union with a Fem." She openly smirks at me. "Yes, I know. I was there. The threat of court, evisceration, decapitation, blah, blah, blah. I don't really give a shit. You'll be the temporary overseer until I can clear my name."

"Says who?"

"Says me." Determination is written all over her features. "I'm still running this celestial circus whether or not my mother likes it."

"It's not your mother who kicked you out of the hot seat. It was almost a unanimous decision. Besides, they won't accept me. I'm in a Treble. And some still view me as a traitor toward Celestra. They'll think I'm with the Barricade because of my ties to Gage—to you."

She glances down, staring at her coffee through that thicket of lashes. Skyla has always had the most beautiful eyes, but those lashes...She made a point to run them over my abs last night. It was the best feeling, a surreal sensation. Everything about those heated, stolen nights has been surreal.

"Then I'll have Dr. Booth take the role. People like him. He's an established part of the Nephilim community. He'll be your mouthpiece."

"Why not cut the middle man and have him be your mouthpiece?"

She shakes her head, her lips still set in that perennial frown. "I'm not myself lately. My head is all over the place. I just can't right now. I need you to carry me through this, Logan." She leans in hard. "Help Celestra. Help the Nephilim for me. I'll try my best to spring back into step." Her eyes close as she tries to digest the thought. "Right now, all I can think about is getting Gage back. I think I might have to put my tail between my legs and grovel to my mother—although, traditionally, that gets me nowhere. There has to be something that will work."

Coop and Laken waltz in, literally spinning and laughing, their lips finding one another as if they were on their first date. It's nice to see them so in love, so very public about it. I wonder if Skyla and I will ever get to that point again. I'm pretty sure I don't deserve to be that happy ever again after what I've done.

"Look who's here," Laken says it in a sweet, humble voice as she wraps her arms around Skyla. Laken has been nothing but a rock for her. Bree, too, but Bree and Drake have been a little wrapped up in the multiple business ventures they're branching off into. There was a rip-roaring discussion between those two going on at the Landon house when I arrived, but my primary purpose was Skyla, and what Skyla wanted was to find the nearest exit and fast, so here we are.

"How are you two holding up?" Coop motions to a couple of chairs, and I nod.

"We're doing the best we can." I wrap my arm around Skyla as if I'm sending some subliminal message to Coop—look at us! We are together. And I am a piping hot piece of shit. "We're there for each other. I couldn't do this without her." A part of me wants to hurl. Gage would be sickened by the way we're *there for each other*. It's no wonder Skyla is physically ill. She knows what we're doing is damning.

"Did you get over that bad flu?" Coop examines Skyla with a renewed scrutiny, like he's speaking in code.

"Not quite."

Skyla has had the flu ever since Gage—since he disappeared. I think the thought of having Gage out of her life simply makes Skyla sick to her stomach. I know it does me.

She wrinkles her nose. "Did you ever give Ezrina those mushrooms to examine?" I know for a fact it was Coop's idea to do so.

"Did." Ezrina and Nev come and fill in our circle. She glares at Skyla a moment. Ezrina wears Chloe's body like it were some designer suit, although given the fact Ezrina and Chloe have opposite sensibilities about fashion, hair, and makeup, you can hardly tell Ezrina's face once belonged to Chloe Bishop. "However, we shall not discuss that at the moment. That is a personal matter for later." She tears her gaze from Skyla. "Did Heathcliff inform you of the interlopers?"

"What interlopers?" Coop glances around until he lands on them. "Huh?" He takes in the rather pedestrian scene.

I lean in toward Ezrina and Nev. "What makes you so suspect of them?"

"They stiff you on a tip?" Skyla's cheek glides up one side at a feeble attempt at humor. It's strange. At night, Skyla sheds her smile as easy as she does her clothes. And while the sun is still up, she's drugged with grief. Not that I think any of her heartache is an act. It's just odd.

"They asked questions." Nevermore shifts in closer. "Unfriendly questions."

"Like?" Laken seems perturbed. You can tell she isn't in the mood to turn this into a guessing game.

"Like have we seen anything out of the ordinary?" Nev nods as if we should read between the lines.

Laken smirks. "They do realize they're on Paragon?"

Coop strains to get a better look at them. "I'm going to head to the restroom and snap a few candid shots."

"*Cooper.*" Ezrina tries to stop him, but he's already walking away, pretending to text, snapping up a storm.

"Don't worry. He's smart, Ezrina." Laken twirls her engagement ring absentmindedly. "He won't get caught."

"I'm not worried about him getting caught. I'm worried about the entire lot of us getting caught and carted away like cattle."

"Don't you see?" Nevermore leans in. "The Barricade has the planet in a fury over these mass 'UFO' sightings, strange lights appearing over large cities, these strange happenings regarding the release of the tunnel victims. Mark my words. Mass hysteria is brewing."

"Are you sure there's not mass hysteria brewing in here?" I ask. "I don't mean to burst your paranoid bubble, but Paragon isn't exactly on anyone's radar. Unless...shit"—my mind zeros in on one horrific theory—"unless someone threw a dart at the island and said have at it."

"*Wesley,*" Skyla and Laken say in unison.

Sometimes, a theory can materialize into an undeniable fact without so much as a swing of the pendulum. If those hardboiled humans sitting in the corner were appointed here by Wes, that pretty much takes them off your average tourist list. Wes wouldn't just bring in anyone—he'd haul in the ball-cracking cavalry.

"He's sheltering the DNA of every person in the Barricade." Nev looks pissed. That look on his face in a nutshell is how I remember Pierce Kragger—Pierce being the original owner of the body Nev has been granted. Pierce was one serious son-of-a-bitch, and I mean that quite literally. In this case, the bitch is Arson Kragger, whom I'm sure is in on this little deal if there is one. "What's left to do but expose the rest of us?"

"He's right." Laken looks to Skyla.

"We need to stop this madness before Wes lands us in government-issued holding pens." Skyla takes in a long, ragged breath. "I think it's time I start compartmentalizing my pain and get back to helping the Nephilim. There's a faction meeting coming up. I've appointed Logan to act in my place." She shakes her head as if she got it wrong. "Actually Dr. Booth. Would you pass it on? He'll be Logan's mouthpiece since they'd never allow Logan to hold the position as a Celestra traitor." She looks to me. "A title I plan on having stripped as soon as I'm back in power, and I will be."

Something in Skyla enlivens as if somehow she's already compartmentalized her pain and shifted it straight to anger. Anger toward the Barricade is always productive. If there could be an acceptable outcome to her grief, that would be it. Kicking ass and taking names is a good lane to switch to—those were her words the very next day Gage disappeared, and now, it looks as if she's ready to implement them.

Coop comes back, and he and Laken head out. He's determined to start the research party.

Ezrina and Nev matriculate back to their bourgeoning customers.

"Looks like it's just you and me." I scoot in close and pick up her hands from across the table.

"I do love it that way." She gives an anemic smile, her eyes wary with thinly veiled agony, and my heart breaks seeing her like this.

"I have a feeling we'll get some answers soon."

"You do?" She perks up. "Why? Did Marshall say something?"

"No, not at all. It's just a feeling, I can't explain it." I put up a wall around my thoughts. Skyla is in so much misery—I doubt she can focus enough to read my mind. And truth be told, the real reason I can feel Gage coming back to us is because I'm ashamed to admit on a sick level I've enjoyed having Skyla all to myself. As much as I love Gage, I didn't realize until these last few weeks that my body has craved hers so much more than I could have imagined. I've loved having her in my bed, naked in my arms, hearing her sweet whimpers as we make love. It's been a warped dream come true—one I'm not sure I want to be roused from. And, understandably, I hate myself for it.

"I hope you're right." The bags under her eyes swell, and her cheeks glow florescent pink. "I can't bear to think that was all we'll ever see of him until eternity. It's as if Demetri is holding both his body and soul hostage. I should never have trusted him with my heart's treasure." She bats her lashes, wet with tears. Her eyes steady over mine, serious as death. "I want you to know, Logan, that the things you've done for me, the way you've been here for me are all beyond the call of duty. I hope you don't feel like I'm taking advantage of you." Her chest expands with her next lungful.

"No, God, no. I feel like I owe you an apology. *Skyla...*" I close my eyes and bow my head a moment. I bear into her beautiful eyes lined with crimson tracks. "We can talk about it. It's okay."

Her mouth falls open. She cocks her head as if she's unsure.

"Logan. You know me so well—or perhaps you've read my thoughts." She pulls her fingers from mine. "I swear, my head is all over the place these days. Half the time I don't know what I'm thinking. I mean, I'm not even sure yet. I want to talk about it, but I'm sorry. I'm just not ready. This is *big*. It's life-changing. Once those words are spoken"—she closes her eyes as she goes rigid—"it will all become real. And, are you going to be okay with this? Am *I*?" She shakes her head. "This is so huge,

Logan. Please don't say anything. I'm going to need you every step of the way." Her lips tremble as she gathers her purse and rises.

We head out into the dull day, the sun breaking out from the clouds just enough to make the rain-slicked sidewalks shine like a dime.

I take Skyla home and head over to White Horse. Long after the sun goes down I wait for her, and she comes.

"Logan Oliver." She wraps her arms around me, her hands floating up my shirt. "I hope you don't mind. I just couldn't sleep. You're the only one that can help me get through this. You're the only thing I want and need."

We fall into bed, into each other, her mouth over mine, my body heavy over hers. Skyla and I make easy love, we fuck hard, we outright drown in our passion.

I can't believe how much I've grown to love her.

I can't believe how much I've grown to hate myself.

4

The Ultimate Reception, the Ultimate Deception

Skyla

Long ago, when we lived in Los Angeles, when my father was still alive—still happily married to my mother—there was just Mia and I. Our little family drew great pleasure in the simple things. We loved the ocean. The beaches in L.A. are a stark contrast to Paragon's cold, dismal, pewter water—nothing but a storm thatch. Back home, the water was so blue, so glassy it matched the unblemished turquoise sky. I miss the sand and surf, our shoulders pinching from a fresh sunburn—my mother chasing me with a hat and sunscreen. I miss lying on my belly on the warm sand, rinsing my hair with salt water in hopes to tame my curls. I miss the endless supply of brighter days, the palm trees swaying in the nonexistent breeze, the vanilla sand, the tangerine sun, the sky hanging heavy with cobalt. I miss it all, but most of all I miss my family—Messenger family proper, Mom, Dad, Mia and me. We were a nice, neat square, an even number perfect for rides at Disneyland, which we often partook in. The right number to take a vacation without breaking the bank, having to rent a bus, or having an odd man out seated alone or with a stranger. We fit in my father's cozy sedan just right—the same sedan he lost his life in. We were perfect in this imperfect jagged-edged world. We knew nothing of Paragon. We knew very little about who we really were. Sometimes in life, some things are better kept a mystery.

I examine myself sideways in the full-length mirror attached to my closet door and try to distinguish if I'm completely out of shape, if I'm simply distending my stomach for the sake of buying into my mother's theory, or God forbid, my stomach is growing because there is the seedling of a teeny tiny Gage growing in there. I don't have the balls to verify this.

I give a side-eye to the pregnancy test I swiped from my mother's bathroom and stashed inside my desk. She has a stockpile of little white sticks just waiting for urine to rain down on them, so I doubt she'll notice that one happened to wander away from the herd.

I want to take the test. I'm determined to take the test. All of my agony—my *misery* funnels in on that single desk drawer. I want that test in my hand so bad I can feel it, and with that thought, my desk begins to rattle. The drawer glides open in a jarring manner.

"Holy shit," I hiss. This is just like the incident with Gage's phone. "Did I really just do that?" I head over, opening and shutting the tiny compartment as if testing its durability. It seems to be working like normal. I close it tight.

"Open," I say it like some silly command, but it remains staunchly shut. Then I do the unthinkable. I imagine how bad I want that test, how I crave to memorize the wording on the box like a prayer, and the drawer slowly jerks open. The box jumps back and forth like a dying fish until it's halfway out of its confinement.

"Oh my God," I whisper, staring in disbelief. Something has happened. Something *is* happening. My eyes narrow in on the potentially life-altering box with a newfound fear. I don't really want to take that test. I suddenly both resent and hate that tiny purple box, and the drawer slams shut with a crisp, loud slap.

I swallow hard. This is a sign. I should not take that test. I should not be anywhere *near* that test. Besides, I can't be pregnant. Am I pregnant? Crap. There is nothing in me that wants to confirm this on a scientific level.

Sure, I am very, *very* late with my period, but I've researched the subject enough to know that heavy grieving can mess with your body in all kinds of crappy ways. Sleep deprivation can knock off your cycle, too. And God knows I haven't been getting any shut-eye. There is nothing worse than swimming over the sheets and finding the spot next to you cold and barren. For a brief moment, every morning when I first wake up, I forget all of this heartache and reach over to greet Gage with a good morning embrace. But I come up empty-handed. My bed is now nothing but sterile and lonely as hell. It's a cruel hoax that the morning plays on you. Although, for one delusionary moment, having Gage in my life is still a happy reality. I'll take an illusion to a harsh reality any day.

"Skyla?" Melissa's voice calls from the other side of my bedroom door before she bangs over it as if the house were on fire. Melissa is a Landon add-on—one of the many stepsiblings Mia and I earned in the Landon-Messenger merger that took place shortly after my father passed away. "That math teacher of yours is here, and he looks horny as hell! Can you please give him a hand job or something so he'll go the heck away and leave us alone? He's creepy. I'm sure he's here because he wants you to alleviate some of that sexual tension for him. You know, do it *old* school."

I roll my eyes. By the time I open the door, Melissa is long gone. That haunted drawer runs through my mind, and I decide to try something a little more exciting than opening furniture. I close my eyes, the way Gage used to before teleporting us, and imagine myself already at the base of the stairs.

My body shifts and warbles, my limbs feel airy and light, and the smell of my stuffy bedroom is soon replaced with the robust aroma of bacon. My lids flutter open and take in the foyer.

"Oh my God." I take a deep breath while glancing up at the stairwell that my feet never touched. I did it. In a strange way, it's as if I'm becoming Gage. God, maybe Gage has possessed me? Or, maybe when he died he bequeathed me his powers? That last theory floats right back out of my mind, and I try not to study it too in-depth. I'm not going there. Gage is not dead. Besides, I have Marshall to deal with—a horny version of him no less. On second thought, is there any other version?

I head into the family room to find Melissa and Mia feuding over the remote. Drake and Bree shovel cereal into their mouths with a fierce amount of focus, probably training for some carbohydrate inhaling competition that they will medal in, of course, and garner themselves many more millions. It's not that I'm unhappy about their success; it's just that I'm more than slightly baffled by it. Suffice it to say, Bree and Drake are winning at life while Gage and I are struggling to keep it.

"Ms. Messenger." Marshall steps into view, and a breath hitches in my throat. He's dressed to the nines, his features cut and comely. I've always known Marshall to be handsome as hell, but there is something about him this morning that shines with a radiant light. My hormones kick into high gear, and suddenly, I'm overcome with the urge to take Melissa up on her sexual alleviating suggestion of the naughty Sector.

I close my eyes with a tight squeeze.

Must not lust after Marshall. Must not lust after Marshall.

I don't know what in the hell has gotten into me lately, but my sex drive has been uncontainable. Of course, I've been nothing but celibate post Gage's disappearance, but I've had the most inappropriate dreams about Logan. Usually it's Marshall who clutters up my carnal nocturnal desires, but ever since Gage disappeared, strangely enough it's been all Logan, all the time. If that's my mother's cruel way of saying "next," she is a much bigger bitch than I ever thought she could be.

"It's Mrs. *Oliver*," Mom corrects him with wink. "Gage is on Host working on a very intense research project."

"Oh?" Marshall looks mildly amused. "And what pray tell is he researching?"

"Unexplained disappearances," I offer, glaring at my favorite Sector for egging my mother on.

Tad ruffles the newspaper in his hands. Newspaper? Really? Where exactly does he get his copy? All of the paperboys on Paragon rolled themselves in that good-for-nothing fish wrapper and died off at the turn of the century.

"Unexplained disappearances?" Tad chokes in his seat, and for a moment, I'm hopeful. "Get Gregory on the phone right now!" he demands.

"It's *Gage*," I say half-heartedly because I know for a fact it won't matter. Tad's brain is impervious to correction.

I glance to Marshall. There is nothing in me that can tolerate Tad's drama this morning.

"If he thinks he can go around spouting off Althorpe's top secrets, he's got another thing coming! Why, I'll call the top brass myself and rat that human garbage disposal out. He'll have both our necks in a noose if he doesn't clam up!"

A part of me wants to brush Tad off. But another part of me, the I'm-so-fucking-concerned-about-my-husband's-whereabouts part of me demands I press on.

Althorpe has top secrets? Such as what?

I've suspected for a while that Althorpe is simply the Counts thinly veiled attempt at running a legitimate business—in other words, a front for wickedness. I've always wondered what in the hell they were doing with Tad. *He* knows secrets? It doesn't make sense. The Counts are too cuttingly smart to spill the big beans to someone so low on the evil totem pole. No offense to Tad, but he's more of a lackey than a trusted advisor.

Unless—a horrible scenario sifts through my mind—I can practically feel my eyes spinning like pinwheels. Unless they have people like Tad do their dirty work so that the top brass keeps their noses clean. The thought alone sends a sharp roll of nausea through me. Not that actual part about Tad being used, but the dirty noses part. I've never been a fan of nostrils. Having two, dark, hairy orifices dead center on your face seems like more of a design flaw. I'm betting my mother had a say in that little holey misnomer.

Marshall steps in toward Tad. "And what position is it that you hold at the esteemed corporation?"

Misty crawls up to Marshall and uses his pant leg to get herself to a standing position. It's hard to believe Misty is already trying to walk. Mom scuttles forward and snatches up the baby just as she's about to take a giant bite out of Marshall's shin. The faint smile she inspired glides right off my face as I remember exactly who her father is. Hey? Maybe I should take off with Misty. Once Demetri learns I'm holding his precious daughter hostage, he'll give me back my husband.

I'm quick to shake the ridiculous thought away since we're all sort of "hostage" in the Landon house.

Mom waves a hand at Marshall. "Tad is a male escort at Althorpe. All of the bigwigs request him by name. I've never seen a group of men so gaga over another man."

"*Eww!*" Melissa and Mia scream in tandem from the couch.

"That's so fucking sick!" Melissa adds the expletive because she's classy with a K like that these days.

Bree and Drake hack a laugh right through their cereal-loaded mouths, and I'm on alert in the event a marshmallow charm blows out through their nose.

"Language!" Marshall and my mother say at the same time before glancing at one another in awe.

"I'm a *VIP* escort, Lizbeth." Tad dips his chin with disdain at my mother's word choice. "In fact, I'm a very important person myself." He refocuses his asinine attention to Marshall. "I have an expense account *and* a travel schedule that take me to the mainland at least twice a month. And as of late, I've been granted a personal assistant. Tad Landon is moving up in this world"—he beats his chest like a gorilla—"and there's not a damn thing the universe can do to stop it."

I groan inwardly, waiting for a lightning bolt to strike. That type of talk is usually an invitation for misfortune. Although, realistically, is it even possible for him to move down in this world? I think not. Misty and her not-so-lucky DNA bounce through my mind. I suppose if he were jilted by my mother that would be quite the demotion—and by demotion, I mean my mother's. Just the thought of her with Demetri is sacrilegious. Who the hell hooks up with their dead husband's murderer? My mother. That's who.

"Personal assistant?" Marshall appears amused.

Wait—why is he here, and why is he egging Tad on in a conversation?

I'm waiting for you to put the pieces together, Ms. Messenger.

Marshall is the only one who I can hear telepathically without touching. He had lost the power for a time, but it was restored as a gift my mother granted him after the war. After the war. God, I sound old. Antebellum, anti-Faction War. Anti-Gage. Anti-knife-in-the-gut. Speaking of gut, my hand rises protectively over my belly without putting too much thought into it.

Focus, Ms. Messenger.

"Oh, right." I shake myself out of my stupor. Nothing about the state of my belly has been confirmed, and a part of me likes it that way. I don't mind living in the dark. It's all darkness without Gage. "Tad? Who is your assistant?"

"The one and only, Isis Edinger." He dazes off with a faraway, slightly perverse gleam in his eye. "No one gets it done quite like she can."

Good God. And when exactly do I start accusing both him and my mother of having their own affairs? Should I even care at this point?

"Isis, of course." I shrug at Marshall, and then it hits me. Isis might be a better point of contact for that demon than Misty. "Isis!" My eyes brighten, and both Tad and my mother stare at me curiously. "Well, she's great. I'm really excited for you." I offer him a simple smile before frowning at my mother. Isis is "great" if you like big, blonde, breasty women who have a propensity to be scantily clad at all times and usually barefoot. She's forever molesting Tad for all to see. I don't know how my mother can stand it.

"Marshall, I have those papers you came for." I give a slight nod, insinuating he should play along—although, let's be real, Marshall is always two steps ahead of the game. "Why don't you come with me?"

Bree waves her hand spastically at me, her cheeks chipmunked out with her morning confection. "Wait! I didn't get to tell you! Drake and I are starting a nail polish line!"

"We'll catch up in a bit!" I call out.

I lead Marshall down the hall and hear both Mia and Melissa gasp as we take the turn for the stairwell.

"God, she really is taking him upstairs!" Mia giggles.

Melissa growls, "I bet they're going to do it."

I shoot Marshall a sharp look because I don't want to hear a single quip about us doing *it*.

"They are not. That's totally cheating!" Mia is quick to defend me. Funny how once her proposal takes a turn toward reality, she's not so quick to surmise a sexual student-teacher relationship. "Skyla would never cheat on Gage."

"It's not cheating if they both masturbate."

"Melissa!" My mother's reprimanding tone is the last thing we hear as I entomb Marshall inside my bedroom—the very room I shared with Gage all too briefly.

"Shall we touch genitals?" he says it bored, examining the scene as if he were a CSI investigator.

"Never say genitals to me again. Or God forbid the *M* word. Melissa is growing up to be quite the little pig."

"My, my, testy, are we?"

"I can't help it. I've been such a terrible bitch lately. All I want to do is scream at people and then hack off their heads for good measure. It used to be that Chloe was the only one I loathed, and now, I want to swing a sickle in a crowd of innocent bystanders for looking at me crooked. I don't know what the heck has gotten into me. And Isis—*really*? You and I both know we don't need her. That was just a ploy to get in my bedroom." Oh, wait—that part was sort of my idea.

"Where is it?" He gives an indiscriminate glance around.

Figures. I pour my heart out, my *bitchy* little heart, and he promptly ignores me.

"What, Marshall?" I sigh, lying back on the bed. "Where is what?"

"The chess set I gave you."

"I don't know. I probably misplaced it like I misplaced my husband." I sit up on my elbows. "Actually, I do know where it is. I put it in a box and hid it in my closet. No offense, but I found it a little creepy."

His left brow arches so high into his forehead I'm afraid it's about to levitate right off his face.

"Skyla, it has properties." His affect flattens. "And it was a gift. I crafted that for you myself."

"And I appreciate it very much." A tiny smile cinches on my lips. "Properties, huh? I don't suppose you'll tell me what those are. You and my mother—I swear—you're all about the guessing games."

"Did you ever cradle the pieces in your hand?"

"Chloe the *Bishop*? No thank you. Although, come to think of it, I might find snapping her neck a bit therapeutic. By the way, she's due for a punishment from you. She stole Ezrina's bed warmer, remember?"

"I'm well aware. And I will dole out the punishment when I feel the time is right. Back to the pieces—they were amulets, Skyla." His gaze lifts to the ceiling, exasperated. "I crafted them myself from dream stone."

"Dream stone?"

"From Ahava. I gathered them from the River of Life myself."

"Ahava?" My heart pinches. Just the thought of Marshall plucking stones from the river, weighing their heft in the hollow of his hand, lovingly selecting each one warms me. Ahava is a part of paradise, and just the thought of having a piece of Gage and Logan's true home makes my heart swell. I swallow hard at the thought. Both Gage and Logan are gone. I can hardly believe it. I refuse to.

I clear my throat. "I'll dig it out of the closet later today. Gage and I have so much stuff crammed in there I can hardly get to my clothes." My hand drifts to just below my stomach again like some automatic response, and Marshall eyes it. I'm quick to replace my hand to my side. "I don't know why I did that." Before another excuse can fly from my lips, he lifts his chin in defiance.

"I do."

"You d-d-do?" I stutter that last word out until it sounds almost comical. "You *know*." Crap. We just took a big step toward this being a reality. "I guess I should confirm it—

nothing a little science won't reveal." I pluck the magic wand from my desk, i.e., the stick I will take a piss on to reveal my future destiny like some urine-soaked crystal ball—and fondle it in my hand a moment. This doesn't really feel like some twentieth century innovation that was a giant leap for procreating man, rather a step back into the dark days, something just this side of witchcraft. My entire body goes numb just looking at it. "I can't believe I'm going to do this." I wave it at him. "A plus sign means I'm having a baby. A minus means I'm losing my sanity." I take a few bold steps until I cross the threshold into the bathroom, and Marshall enters on my heels. "Excuse me? This is sort of a private affair."

"I can hold the stick if you like."

How he managed to say that without an ounce of lewdness, I will never know.

"I'm good." I give him a gentle shove back into the room and lock the door behind him.

The thing with urinating is, I'm good at it. I can literally almost always pee on command. It might very well be one of my ubiquitous superpowers (endowed by my vindictive mother, no doubt).

I do the deed, then promptly wash my hands with boiling water because I may have just sprinkled while I tinkled. I snatch the stick back up, head to my room, and nestle against Marshall as we stare at it as if it were about to do something truly miraculous like tell us where the hell Gage is.

"Wait." I tuck it behind my back as a newfound panic grips me. "Maybe I should call Logan. He should probably be here for this."

"Skyla." Marshall is clearly not impressed with this suggestion. "We're having a moment."

"We're having a moment?" I look to him, puzzled. "Oh! We're having a moment." I melt into the sweetness of it all. "Thank you," I whisper. "Thank you so much for being here—right at this moment. I couldn't have done this without you."

"You will never be alone, Skyla." Those boiling cauldrons he calls eyes enliven an earthy shade of red. "I will always be here in the wings waiting, on center stage, alongside you—in your bed while you fondle your genitals." He gives the ghostly impression of a Cheshire cat's grin.

"Stop." I swat him with the stick, forgetting all about its importance for a second. I pull it forward and hold it between us as the tiny window washes a faded blue. Slowly, tragically slowly, one line appears—negative. It begins to brighten, and a swell of relief the size of the entire ocean rinses through me. A weight has been lifted off my shoulders as heavy as a thousand newborns. "It's—" Just as I'm about to declare my emancipation, another line appears, quick and strong as if mocking me, creating a perfect plus sign right before our eyes. I take a breath and hold it, numb with shock, my mind completely blank.

"Congratulations, Ms. Messenger. I do believe this is the very first test you've passed in my presence."

My head tips back, and I let out a harrowing cry. Marshall pulls me into his arms and holds me like that for a very long time.

Outside, the world turns to soot as the orb that illuminates our planet is shrouded with storm clouds. Darkness had already set over my life. To have Gage's child without him here to experience it is a cruelty beyond measure.

I glare up at the sky, toward the Decision Council, toward the mother who bore me.

Life is not a cruel bitch.

My mother is.

Marshall takes me for a late afternoon drive. Logan has called a thousand times—left impatient messages that I haven't bothered to check. He's texted sweetly, just wanting to make sure I'm fine—letting me know that the Olivers have invited both him and me to dinner. I'm sure it's innocent enough, but in my twisted mind I think this is Emma's way of cementing Logan and me as a couple. It's her final good riddance to me— as Gage's wife, anyway. After all, according to her, I was the disease that ravaged her son—that took him away from her long before death ever did.

"Where are we going?" I ask lazily as Paragon sweeps by in a blue-gray blur. The evening fog is rolling in, thick and heavy, stripping the evergreens of their color. I can't get my mind off how my life has changed so dramatically, twice, in a little over a month. Soon enough, it will become obvious to all what Gage left behind in this world, but, for now, this child, this tiny piece of my beloved husband, is safely, secretly growing in my belly.

"There was a reason I came for you." Marshall's expression sours as we drive past West Paragon High. That oversized painting of Cerberus looms like a dark omen over his shoulder—Cerberus with his large glowing eyes—all six of them—bearing his teeth with the promise to eviscerate with each of his ugly heads. Whoever thought it was a great idea to make a three-headed hellhound the school's mascot must have had a touch of Count in them. The Countenance as a whole are a nefarious bunch. Although, I hate painting the entire Count population with such a broad brush, considering most of my family, most of my friends, *Logan*, all are a part of that branch of Nephilim.

Speaking of Logan, Marshall takes a turn, and we catch a glimpse of the bowling alley sitting lonely on the left side of the street with the *O* in the neon sign blown out. I'll have to tell Logan about that, although I'm sure he's already aware. He's been working very hard to resurrect that dying corpse for as long as I can remember.

"This is a two-part journey, Ms. Messenger." Marshall pulls in across from the bowling alley into White Horse, the house that Logan built for me. Logan's truck is parked in the driveway, and just the sight of it makes me pinch with grief.

I'll tell Logan next. He'll be hurt that Marshall was the first to know. I'm sure Logan will be filled with just as much pain as I am at the thought of Gage never seeing his child.

Those faraway thoughts creep into my brain—the ones that have tried to surface ever since Gage died. Logan and I together was a prophecy my mother gave me, but I didn't really need a prophet to expend that notion to me. Logan and I were in love before I ever fell hard for Gage. These thoughts all seem so cruel in nature, so barbaric toward the genuine love, lust, affection, toward everything I felt and still very much feel for Gage. I've always stood by the maxim that I would rather be married to Gage forever than have him leave Logan and me alone on this planet. Logan and I had three blissful days. Our mouths, our limbs, exploring, tearing one another to pieces, then lovingly putting ourselves back together as one. We are still very connected. He still feels like my husband, and, I know it sounds dubious, but Gage does, too. It's a twisted world to live in when you accidentally give your heart to two people. I glance to Marshall. Three. But it's Gage I'm married to, and, God willing, will be for a very long time. The one thing death fails to do, at least in the beginning, is to take away the feeling that the other person might still walk through that door, still warm your bed at night. I wasn't able to disconnect from the notion with Logan, and, now, I can't seem to do it with Gage. That's death's cruelest trick of all. It leaves you with the illusion that the one you lost is still very much a part of you when all you're really left with are the memories.

"Two-part adventure?" I hop out, and Marshall comes around and takes up my hand. He leads us to a quiet thicket of pines that butt right up to the shoreline. The thing I love best about White Horse is that it sits on a pale sandy beach. It's funny how Gage and I love Rockaway—that's our special place with its onyx shores, and, here, Logan has chosen the white sands of Silent Cove. Gage drives a black truck, Logan a white one. Gage is a Fem, Logan—Celestra, mostly.

"Anyway"—I startle back to life and twist into Marshall and all his physical brilliance—"you are sweet to me and perhaps too gorgeous for me to ever be safely around. You do know that my hormones are already on overdrive. Please do me a favor and promise you won't take advantage of me like that." My lips quiver. "I'm weak, Marshall, and my body will want things that Gage isn't here to offer. If I can give him one more gift, it's to be chaste while his child is inside me."

He gives a long blink. "You've foiled my plan so soon," he says it dry, teasing. "I suppose The Pretty One will be the next to hear those heartfelt words stream from your ruby lips." Marshall rubs his finger along the seam of my mouth, and those erotic dreams I've had of him, over the months I've been married to Gage, come back in one encapsulated sound bite.

A sharp, pulsating stream of ecstasy rips through that sweet spot between my thighs, and I lean into Marshall's chest to steady myself a moment.

"Wow, you are really not good at taking direction," I pant through the powerful pleasure he's just elicited in me.

"It's your own physiological response to me, but do let your imbalanced hormones know that I'm flattered. Nevertheless, I've not brought you here to make your body hum with delight." He pulls my chin up with his finger and steadies his dark crimson irises over mine. Marshall's eyes pop with intensity against the dismal sky. "I've brought you here to—"

"Skyla!" a husky, comfortably familiar voice calls from our left, and we turn to find Logan jogging his way over. In an instant, he snatches me from Marshall's arms and embraces me hard with his own. "I've been trying to reach you. It worries me when you don't pick up. I was just about to head to the Landon house." His warm breath pulsates over my lips. Logan, with his dark blonde hair, those liquid amber eyes that have never been able to hide his unending ache for me. He's so stunningly handsome I want to cry. "You up for dinner?" He sheds a brief smile. "I think Emma is ready to bury the hatchet."

"In my skull?" I quip without meaning to. But the truth is, I can't face Emma and Barron now, not knowing what I do.

"What do you know?" Logan's brows dip into a sharp V, and my stomach pinches. He can hear me. Of course, he can— his hand is touching my bare arm, so I pull away. For whatever reason, I'm always forgetting that Logan has access to my brain.

Marshall pulls me back a moment. "Never mind what she knows. What's important at this hour is what I know." **Don't tell him about the child just yet.** He nods to me. "I'm taking you both somewhere. Come, we must leave now."

"Are you okay?" Logan whispers as Marshall treads ahead.

"I'm fine." I shake my head as if refuting my own theory. "Really I am."

Marshall heads to his car, and Logan and I follow. He drives us to the Paragon Estates, and we watch as we pass the Olivers' home and Ellis's house with his big monster truck out front. We pass Marshall's own elaborate estate and then Nicholas Haver's property. There is only one other home out this far, surrounded by a vast lonely thicket of woods and gray dusty skies—Demetri's. My stomach boils as we head in that direction. Paragon sheds its dull pencil-gray coat for a carefree, ethereal blue. Even though this eerie glowing mist generally represents wickedness, I've come to love it in theory. It's beautiful. The color itself breathes new life into me. If only it can breathe new life into—

I take in a sharp breath. There it is. Demetri's haunted hovel is back like a phoenix rising from the ashes.

Demetri Edinger's home sits high on the ridge in all of its wicked, arrogant glory as if it dares us to accuse it of ever leaving in the first place.

Logan and I jump out of the car before it comes to a complete stop.

A dark winged creature caws from the sky as Holden flaps down onto my shoulder rather dramatically, and I reach up to touch his feathers.

I led him here, Skyla. I was the one who alerted Dudley as soon as the house reappeared.

"Good job," I pant, never taking my eyes off the over-constructed hall of horrors. "You will be rewarded." I jerk him away as he takes flight. My heart hammers over my chest so hard I expect it to be the very next thing that takes flight. "This is the second leg of the adventure," I say it breathless, my eyes never leaving what is now officially the most beautiful mansion I have ever laid eyes on.

"Let's go find Gage." Logan takes up my hand, and we race up the marble steps to the palace of what has always represented darkness, and now here, today, it represents light.

My heart beats wildly as we come upon the overgrown double doors shrouded in dark mahogany, the leaded glass ensconced in wrought iron.

A tiny smile comes to my lips for the very first time in so long as I pant into a future with so much hope.

"Let's go find Gage."

Gage

There have been times in my life that I have wished to be anywhere but in my body. Most of those concern my discomfort of Skyla being with Logan, but this last one has to do with the unimaginable pain I've gone through these last few weeks.

My spine was not severed. That is the good news. The shit news is that my back endured enough impact to require copious and stringent amounts of physical therapy from here to eternity.

I'm human. It's finally happened, although not at all in the way I had envisioned. When I finally convinced Candace that I was committed to shed my Nephilim heritage and become mortal through and through, she was quick to fill me in on the fact this was a no-go. I'm still a Fem. I've simply been stripped of my powers. Good enough for now. Although, in all heartbreaking honesty, I regretted the words as soon as they sailed from my lips. Sure, I was an asshole at the height of my power. Sure, I had turned into a megalomaniac who believed he was invincible and able to rule the universe. In effect, I had fully morphed into my half-brother, Wesley.

I give a quick grimace as I readjust my position on the leather recliner. One of the assistants Demetri hired, and he has hired an entire infantry of them, helped get me settled in the media room. I'm pretty sure a decent amount of time has drifted by since the accident, and I'm also pretty damn sure there's a very good reason why Logan and Skyla haven't swung by. I'm not angry about that, or in the least concerned this means they don't care. I know that my father, and, yes, I have claimed Demetri as such, much to his delight, has bound this madhouse of his somehow in an effort to keep them at bay. In truth, I don't think I would have healed quite so well, quite so quickly on the outside. It's safe to say supernatural forces have been busily at work, in addition to the ground troops he's enlisted to mend me.

I remember the sky twisting above, the sound of my voice as I called out for my wife, my pregnant, beautiful wife, and then a giant errant wave breaking my fall, soft as concrete. Nevertheless, I'm apprised of what's been going on in Paragon for the duration of my absence, namely in Logan's bedroom. Fucker.

I'm not really all that pissed at Logan. More or less from what I could see, and Demetri made sure I could see every last bit, he was trying to ward her off—at least in the beginning. And I get that Skyla has needs. I just wish she didn't have them so soon after I vacated the premises. I'm not upset with anybody, just extremely annoyed that I put everyone in this position to begin with. Although, I'm not sure what's to become of Skyla and me. I'm not so sure we can get past this. Does she even want me anymore? Has she ever? If Demetri has done one thing efficiently, aside from my healing, he's cast a shadow of doubt over my marriage, wide as a dragon's wings.

A rustle emits from the entry. The lights go on in the theater room, and I fully expect to find two assistants filing in to help me back to my room. I can almost make it on my own now. I just a need a cane to get by. I'm almost healed, but not quite. Aside from physical therapy, Demetri has flown in the best of the best in just about every related field of medicine. I've downed concoction after concoction just hoping to restore my body to a useable state. I need to get back to Skyla, if she'll have me—to our baby.

"Son."

Glancing back, I startle a bit to see Demetri coming this way.

I grab ahold of my cane, an electric blue metal rod that's light yet sturdy, and I'm betting not of this planet, and struggle to rise.

"No need for that." He glides over until he's square in front of me and bows his head as a show of respect. It's strange. Having Demetri Edinger bow in my presence makes me feel anything but human. "You have visitors."

"Skyla?" I'm ready to bolt at first mention. I'm sure I have enough adrenaline in me to circle this palace twice looking for her.

"I'm bringing them to you."

Them? Logan is with her.

I glance up at the overgrown screen where I saw the damning evidence for myself.

"Not in here." I wouldn't put it past dear old Dad to produce a sound bite of all their most carnal moments—the white-hot horror of it all played out in surround sound. I don't want them to know that *I* know. How juvenile is that? Furthermore, I don't want them to see what I saw. They lived it. That should be enough. "And not in the Fem trophy room, or the throne room (He does indeed have one, and, yes, I have my very own gilded seat). Have them wait in the living room. I'll make my way down."

"They're well past the living room. She has your uncle in tow, as well as Sector Marshall. It's quite a rude crew the way they've ambled inside without knocking, shouting and screaming your name as if I were holding you prisoner. Might I suggest the terrace?"

Prisoner. I'd scoff in his face, but I'm not in the mood.

"Yes." I struggle to balance myself and limp the hell out of here as fast as I can. "You might."

The terrace is located one flight up and overlooks the west side of Paragon with an unobstructed ocean view. It's where I've spent most of my days recuperating. I like the fresh air. I like knowing that Skyla can see the same blue water, the same dismal sky. The thought brought an ounce of pleasure to me. Just that, an ounce. Without her beside me, it could never be full measure.

Demetri walks me to the baluster railing before heading to the door. I take in a lungful of fresh Paragon fog and observe the sky above lamp-lit by the papery moon. There's a certainty about the airy mist, the sound of the evergreens rustling in the breeze. Something feels far more familiar about Paragon on this day than it has these last few, and I can't put my finger on it.

"Do me a favor and divert the Sector," I say without looking back. "I'd like to be alone with Skyla and Logan." I doubt that Dudley, nor anyone else, is in on their nighttime comfort sessions. Not that I plan on lambasting them. Hell, I don't even plan on bringing it up. But that gloating Sector is the last person I want to see. I need this first visit to be pure, perfect, as I try to explain my way out of the paper bag I've crawled into.

No sooner does Demetri disappear than I see two shadowed figures bulleting toward me. Skyla and Logan race out into the night and crash into my broken body. Their arms compress around me so tight, I can't breathe—don't want to. I want this moment to last forever with the three of us locked in this holy huddle. Logan isn't merely my uncle—he's something more than a brother. We are a single coin, each one side. And Skyla. My lips find her beautiful face, and I douse her with kisses.

"I've missed you." I pull her in closer still and bury my lips in her ear. "My God, I have missed you, Skyla Oliver, in the very worst way."

A trill of laughter bubbles from her as she pulls back, her face tear-slicked, as are Logan's and mine.

"What the hell happened?" Logan steps back and examines me. His eyes trace over my cane with a morbid curiosity.

"You look fantastic." Skyla tilts her head as she inspects me herself. "Gage? Are you alive?"

"Yes." I pull her in by the hips, letting my cane drop to the floor. "God, yes. I'm here. I had an accident. It's a long story."

"We have all night," Logan says it sober before I can add another word. His features harden as if I owed them an explanation, as if I'm the one who's done something morally incomprehensible in the meantime.

"We do have all night." I rub my thumb along Skyla's cheek like a promise. "I'm coming home. No one can stop me."

Skyla cups my face with both hands. Her eyes penetrate mine with that drunken look she wears just before we make love, and I can tell she's making promises that she very much intends to keep beneath the sheets. I can't wait. Her chest swells with her next breath. Her smile expands as wide as the sea as she steps into Logan and offers him an exuberant hug as well, and my ego drops off its high horse.

"Gage, where were you?" Her breath plumes out white as feathers, her arm still linked over Logan's shoulder in a congratulatory manner. "This was the first place we looked. Well, the house was gone, but you know that."

I glance back to the gaping open doors that lead to the terrace. The house was gone?

"Demetri didn't mention you came."

"Are you kidding?" Skyla is incensed by this. "We came by every day for weeks. I had—"

Weeks? I cut her off without meaning to, "How long was I gone?"

"Six weeks, four days." Logan gives my arm a quick tap. "But we're damn glad to have you back."

"Six weeks?" I hiss below my breath as I glare at the monstrosity behind them. "He didn't let you in for six weeks?" I can't believe I find this shocking, but I do. First of all, I thought it was days, four solid, one week at the most. And second of all, Demetri seemed to be helpful, on my side, assuring me that Skyla would be here any moment. Not that I could have done anything to change that fact. I was pretty much out of it in the beginning.

Skyla shakes her head, confused. "He didn't let us in because there was no house to be let into. No sooner did he take your body from the morgue than he took the entire house and up and disappeared."

A red rage brews in me. "He took the *house*? Wait, why was I in the morgue?"

Skyla and Logan exchange glances. It's clear information, *vital* information, might I add, was withheld from me.

"Never mind it for now." Skyla's hand touches over her stomach, and my heart lurches. Does she know? If it's been six weeks, she must. "I'll tell you all about it once we get you home. I don't want to spend one extra moment here than necessary."

I look to Logan, who is suddenly very quiet, very wary of the situation.

"Six and a half weeks is a long time. Did anything happen while I was gone that I should know about?" I don't know why I brought it up. It's not exactly a conversation I'd want to continue on the drive back to the Landon house. It will certainly rile things up between Skyla and me.

"Nothing." Skyla's eyes widen, and she shrugs as if she means it.

Logan remains stiff and quiet as a statue—put him in the yard and watch the birds crap all over him. He's not talking. I get it. I wouldn't expect him to pony up that kind of salacious news, but Skyla seems to have forgotten all about it. Her joy is genuine. Her teeth illuminate the night with her smile.

"Actually." She looks to Logan. "There is something big I have to tell you." Her chest pulsates like a heartbeat all its own as she struggles to catch her breath. "I can't believe this is how it's going to happen, but Marshall knows, and I think I'd rather tell you both at the same time."

The slight curve of a smile struggles to break free, but I resist. I want to savor this moment. Candace has already told me that Skyla is having my child. It was all I could think about these last few days—weeks. She and that precious life inside her have been my motivation to get better, to get home.

"Give me your hands." She motions to both Logan and me. "I want to get us out of here. This is the last place I want to remember when we think back on this moment."

"I can't transport us." Teleportation is the one gift I'll miss.

Skyla wets her lips as she considers this. "I can."

Both Logan and I exchange a glance of suspicion.

"Take my hands," she coaxes again, and we're quick to comply. I bend over and grab my cane in the event we don't come back, and I'm hoping we won't. "I'm going to take you someplace special. And after our little trip, none of us will ever be the same again."

My muscles tense as every cell in my body rearranges itself from the flight over.

I open my eyes, slow, dreamlike, my back still aching, my legs weak from standing so long. I recognize this bluff, the sound of the roaring ocean down below, the feel of the pressing dark clouds as they meet up with this dismal horizon. The world spins for a moment as that dreaded day comes back to me. I steady myself on my cane to keep from reprising that fateful fall to the rocks below.

"Devil's Peak?" Logan asks for both of us.

"Yes." Skyla walks over to the edge and peers down. Her shoulders press back, her chin up as if she's just defeated the enemy.

I glance around at the vicinity. A group of stoners sits in the dirt field adjacent to the parking lot, and a group of girls not too far from that sits in the flat bed of a truck. It's all so normal. Six weeks I was gone, and life simply went on without a stoner hiccup. I'm not sure why this pains me. I'm back. I pull Skyla in and get lost for a moment in that beautiful mass of curls that surrounds her, those ruby lips that wait for me.

"I want to make this place special—take back the power it has over us." She takes a step toward the safety rail. "I never want to look at Devil's Peak again and be covered with grief. I want this to be the place where I tell you both the most incredible news of my life."

My heart sings as I glance to Logan. I'm glad he's here to share our news. A very small yet vindictive part of me wants him to know that Skyla and I did this. We knitted this beautiful being into existence—that despite what happened between the two of them, our love burns bright.

"Okay." Her hand floats back to her belly. "I thought I might be, but I wasn't sure." She bites down on her lip, hardly able to contain her joy. "Logan, Gage..."

Her eyes remained focused on mine even when she said his name, and I'm only slightly ashamed at how much satisfaction that gives me.

"Skyla, what it is?" Logan focuses on the fact her hand is pressed to her stomach. "Are you feeling sick again?"

"No—well, maybe just a tiny bit, but with Gage back, I can handle whatever my body wants to give me." She nods into me, her eyes brimming with excitement. "Even a baby."

"*Skyla*." I pull her in and crush her body to mine. The waves taunt me just past her shoulder with their familiar chorus, but I choose to ignore them. I choose to focus on this one blessed moment, and all feels right with the universe.

"A baby?" Logan is stunned. His face bleaches out, his lips pursed as he tries to decipher exactly what she means.

She gives a furtive nod, and he lunges at her. His arms replace mine as he greedily pulls her to him and spins her in a celebratory circle.

His laughter lights up the vicinity as he pours kisses over her face before backing away, his demeanor softening once he realizes I'm still here. Figures.

"Skyla." His fingertips graze her waist as if it was holy ground, and it is. Logan's features melt with grief. "Gage, I'm so sorry." He shakes his head as if he's somehow responsible— wait. "It was really hard with you gone. You don't know the level of agony we went through. It was never our intention."

"What was never our intention?" Skyla tries to step in front of him, tries to hook his gaze, but he doesn't waver.

"It's okay, Skyla." Logan's nostrils flare, his eyes gloss with moisture.

I can see the intense level of grief in him, and a part of me wants to put him out of his misery. I know damn well that baby is mine. Candace told me so herself right before she pushed me off this very cliff.

"Skyla and I never intended to fall into bed together. This baby wasn't brought into being over the glee of your passing," he pleads his case with watery eyes. "We needed one another. I'm so sorry that it led to that, but I'm hoping you can forgive me. It wasn't my intention to take advantage of her."

Skyla smacks him over the arm. "What the hell are you talking about? Are you trying to steal my thunder? I'm pregnant! I'm having Gage's *baby*—" Her mouth falls open as she puts the pieces together. "Why would you think I'm having your child, Logan?" Her head cocks to the side as she weighs his intentions.

"Skyla." He ticks back a notch. "It's okay. Our secret is out. It's best we not play any mind games." He looks to me in earnest. "Forgive us for sleeping together, Gage. Please, just forgive us."

"Oh no, you don't." Skyla wags her finger, first at him, then at me. "You don't forgive me." Her voice is low and husky.

Skyla is incredulous that Logan would out them this way, and, quite frankly, I don't get it. Logan is right. It's best we lay everything out onto the table right now. No mind games.

"I am having *your* baby, Gage." The whites of her eyes glow like hot coals. She looks to Logan and seethes, "I don't know what you're up to, but you are acting a hell of a lot like Chloe Bishop than you ever are yourself."

Logan steps in to settle her, then freezes midflight. His eyes bug out like eggs.

"You don't think?" I stop myself from finishing the thought. A rush of relief fills me. "Skyla? You didn't sleep with Logan, did you?"

"No." She shakes her head, baffled. "He didn't even stay the night. Laken was with me almost every night for a week. I swear, I haven't touched him—not in that way." Her demeanor changes on a dime from defensive to stunned. A deep guttural groan escapes her. "*Chloe.*"

Skyla and I look to Logan, his face somber as shit, his eyes focused just past us at some unknowable horizon where he is undoubtedly wrapping his hands around Bishop's neck.

"Demetri showed me the whole thing." I swallow hard. "In the viewing room. I saw you with her, and I thought it was Skyla. She was uncanny." I threw that last part in on behalf of Logan's defense. Not sure why.

"It wasn't me. I swear on all that is holy." Skyla's speech is pressured, desperate for both of us to believe her. "Oh, that fucking *bitch!*" Her voice twists like a tornado into the sky, piercing the thin layer of hope that divides this plane and the ethereal. Skyla lunges at Logan, knotting up his shirt with her hands with a vengeance. "You slept with Chloe?" She offers up a violent shake until he tosses his hands in the air in surrender. "How could you do that?" she rages. "What on God's Earth would possess you to think she was me? She's nothing but an evil chameleon! When did this happen?"

Logan twists his lips, and that hard divot Skyla dug into his cheek years ago depresses.

He winces. "It was a reoccurring event."

Skyla snaps her head back and lets out an arduous roar.

"*Enough.*" I try to pull them apart, but Skyla is too hopped up on rage to let go.

"How could you?" Her voice breaks for just a moment before her pissed-off resolve rises again. "She will *never* be me! How dare you not know the difference! Chloe Bishop is a *cunt* who is about to have her head handed to her on a paper plate. I don't care how many kids that beast has brewing in her belly. That witch is mine." Skyla takes off like a bullet toward an opening in the fence before leaping off the side of Devil's Peak like an angel who forgot her wings. Her hands lift over her head, and her wedding ring catches the light, giving me a wink as she falls through the earth, right through to the Transfer.

"Go get her," I riot in Logan's face.

"You're coming with me."

"I'm human. The last fall almost killed me."

"You're not human." He wraps his arms around me and launches us both off the side of the cliff. "You only wish you were."

Logan

There is something about the act of falling that has the power to lull me to sleep. It's hypnotic, an adrenaline rush with the ability to soothe me on many levels. My life can be broken down into a series of falls, not at all hypnotic or soothing. There was the initial fall, the burn I sustained over most of my body from the Counts that sought to incinerate my parents alive. Then, there was the second fall through time where I came back, only to be raised by my brother, Barron, as his nephew. Next comes the infamous fall in which I traded my allegiance from Celestra to the Countenance all in the name of aiding the girl I love, leading to my death, of course, the day Chloe saw fit to sever my head from my body and make it bow to my own feet. Then, perhaps the lesser fall in which I accepted the Treble handed to me by Candace that allows me to exist among the living. And, last, but not least, and, in all honesty, probably far from last is the great immoral dive I took into Chloe Bishop's body. I had been there once or twice before on a strictly voluntary basis, but this deception she's managed to pull off only makes me want to shake her violently until her own head pops right off its base. It would be poetry in motion. I have never wanted to hurt another human being, a woman no less, in the way I want to hurt Chloe. This ordeal is over for her, but for the rest of my existence, I'll have to live with the memory of how I loved her as if she were Skyla. For me, in those few brief moments, she was.

The Transfer forms around us, dark as a cave. A dank blue fog is settled over the landscape that we usually don't experience here.

Gage and I hit the ground running. Skyla beat us to the punch, and now we're afraid she's literally punching Chloe's brains out. Not that I would usually mind, but now that Skyla is with child—*Gage's* child, which I'm sure he will never let me forget—I don't want a hair on her head harmed. I'm relieved it's his child. And I'm damn relieved he's back.

The doors to Wesley's not-so humble home are sealed shut, and Gage slams his shoulder into one as he struggles to break in.

"Let me." I pull him back and kick down the door with all the Celestra rage I can muster. Gage winces as he holds his arm. He limps by my side with his cane as we head inside as the sounds of screaming and yelling fill the great room.

We rush over and find the veins in Skyla's neck bulging as she screams at Chloe, who is wisely hiding behind Wes for protection. I hope Skyla drives a stake through her temple. Hell, I might suggest it, hand her the stake just to ensure it happens.

"Out of my way!" she roars at Wes just as he does a double take in our direction.

"Gage?" He heads over and pulls his brother into a quick embrace. It's eerie how much they look alike. It's as if somehow Demetri harnessed the power to extract Gage's reflection from a mirror.

Skyla doesn't miss a beat. She leaps onto Chloe, wrapping her hands around her throat until they both knock over like bowling pins with Skyla on top.

"You bitch! How dare you! How *dare* you!" Skyla throttles Chloe, bouncing her head over the limestone until her eyes rattle into her skull.

Wesley jumps to break them apart, and I secure the beast tight, channeling all my reserves to keep him immovable as stone.

"What the hell is going on?" His voice thunders through the room, but Skyla continues, unabated. Chloe claws at Skyla's arms, her skin enlivening in streaks of crimson as Chloe's nails bite into her flesh. "She's having a baby! Get the hell off her. That's my kid in there, Skyla!" It's his spawn Wesley wants to protect—Chloe not so much, and now I feel bad that Skyla is using Chloe as a battering ram.

The room shakes; the fire explodes in shades of blue and crimson. Chloe's body bucks in death throes just as Wesley breaks free from my hold.

Wes wraps himself around Skyla, his hands hardly able to remove her grip. Chloe gasps, crawling away, clinging to her neck just as Gage throws himself over Wes, and Skyla makes her escape.

Skyla flies across the room, slamming her body hard against Chloe, sending Bishop into the fire with a lurch.

"Oh shit." I'm not sure if I'm amused or truly worried for Chloe, more to the point, her child.

"Skyla!" Wes pauses from his wrestling match with his younger, injured brother, and both Gage and he rise to their feet.

Skyla whips Chloe around the living room. Chloe's back is still ablaze, her hair in flames.

"You don't fuck with me." Skyla thrashes Chloe's body against the rug over and over until she puts out the fire herself. "And you don't ever fuck with Logan again."

"Wesley," Chloe gurgles out his name, her hand falling limp toward him. "Help me. The baby. She's killing our baby."

Skyla's mouth rounds out in horror as if she's just come to and realizes it's not just Chloe in that body anymore.

Wes plucks Chloe off the floor and holds her stiff in his arms.

"What the hell did you do now?" he growls at her. "Skyla, what happened?"

I head over to Skyla and wipe the tears from her face. Her anger has her so worked up I doubt she realizes she shed them.

"Let's get out of here." My stomach turns just looking at Chloe. "I feel the sudden need for a shower."

"Oh, Logan"—Skyla looks up with the underpinnings of her rage still very much intact—"there is not enough holy water on the planet to wash that scourge off you."

Gage hobbles over, and I land Skyla safe in her husband's arms. "Why don't you get her home? I'll hang out here for a while." I turn to glare at Chloe for a moment, and she lifts her chin in defiance.

"Logan." Skyla struggles to reach for me as Gage helps her to the door. "Don't you let her off the hook. This is a crime subject to a higher court. I will take her to the Justice Alliance. I want her morphing abilities revoked! And I want her ass nailed to a chair in this Count coven!" She shifts her anger toward Chloe. "You will pay for this. I will not forget what you've done."

Chloe lets out an insolent laugh. "What are you going to do? Rat me out to Mommy Dearest? Newsflash, Messenger, I'm not afraid of your big, bad momma."

Skyla breaks away from Gage's stronghold and takes a few bold steps forward.

"You don't need to fear my mother, Chloe." Her jaw tightens as she bares her teeth in a show of aggression. "You need to fear me."

I nod to Gage, and he wraps his arm around Skyla's waist, ushering her right out the door. The house falls silent for a moment as I glare over at the woman I buried my body in for the last six weeks.

"Why?" The word curdles from my throat like a razor.

Chloe takes in a deep breath, struggling free from Wesley's hold.

"Yes, Chloe?" he barks, sharp and loud. "*Why* are you fucking another man with my baby tucked in your belly?" His jaw pops, his dark brows narrow, thick like worms. It's hard for me to look away when he emulates Gage so completely.

"Look at you, so self-righteous." She smirks, tossing her singed hair at him. It's a well-known fact that Wesley had Chloe morph into Laken's likeness for him on more than one occasion. I guess that good time is a one-way street as far as he's concerned.

"I was lonely." She rubs at her arms, and soot falls from her like necrotic snow. "I had a craving for an Oliver." She scowls at me. "Besides, the baby is fine."

"You had a craving for an Oliver?" I'm stymied that she'd even consider me. "It's Gage you're obsessed with. You're living—sleeping—with his twin, you dumbfuck!"

Chloe's mouth drops open. She gasps and clutches at her neck as if I struck her, and I might have with my words. It's as close as I'll let myself get to the real thing. And for the most part, it was satisfying.

"Don't you speak to me that way," she seethes. "And here I thought we were friends." That last word elongates like the hissing of a snake.

"Friends?" A hot glowing rage boils through my veins. "Friends don't sleep with one another under false pretenses." I pick up a heavily carved, heavily dated, irreplaceable looking end table and smash it against the jagged stone wall. "Friends don't decapitate friends, Chloe." I stomp over and pant my anger, my hatred down over her face. "That's what *enemies* do."

Chloe shrinks, her features crumbling with manufactured fear. "Oh, come on, Logan. Don't get so worked up." She bows her head a moment, her eyes still set to seduce. "I really think we can have a good thing going. I can be Skyla for you anytime you like."

"What the hell?" Wesley rages, pulling her away from me. "You will not be Skyla. You will not screw other guys while our child is growing in your womb. Get that sick filth out of your head. I am here to fill your every desire. *Me!*" The veins in his neck jump like cables. You would think Wesley really does care about Chloe on some level based on this visceral response. "And mark this"—he leans in hard over her—"you will never wear this face in bed with me again. Because right now, I can't stand the sight of you." He bullets out of the room without so much as a goodbye.

So maybe he doesn't care about her so much.

"You essentially have Gage, Chloe." My voice softens as I wave to the gaping doors Wes just flew out of. "Why mess with me other than to hurt Skyla?"

Chloe takes in a breath. She removes her coat and lets the crusted, singed garment fall to the floor as it cracks in two.

"I do have *Gage*." She mimics me by flailing her hand in that direction. "But he's not my Gage. He's Wesley Edinger. He loves Laken. Correction, he *worships* that nitwit. He makes love to me like I'm Chloe even if I look like the woman who has his balls in a vise grip." She plops herself onto the dark velvet sofa, and a plume of dust rises like a nuclear cloud. "I have long suspected I was missing out on something. I thought about it, the way Gage—the *real* Gage makes love to Skyla." Her eyes look past reality, straight into Gage and Skyla's marriage bed. "I thought there must be this unbelievable passion they share." Tears come to her eyes, and I don't want to see them. Everything in me screams *get the hell out*, but my feet are nailed to the floor. "I wondered who would ever make love to me with that much passion. Gage was dead. My hormones were raging, and I needed to have it. Without Gage in this world"— she glances toward the ceiling— "*that* world—I figured why am I always so damn nice?"

My chest bucks with a laugh, but I won't give it. If Chloe is faking nice because Gage is on the planet, good God, that boy can never die.

She rises to her feet and struts over, a lone tear still on display for all to see. "I thought why not go and get some of that good loving?" Her finger curves under my jaw as she slowly steps past me. "Who could love me so ferociously? And then, of course, I was sickened by the thought of you comforting Skyla with your incredibly ripped, hot body. So I beat her to the punch." Her finger freezes on my lips. "And you know what?" Chloe smolders into me. Her eyes glaze over, and for the first time I see a shred of what I had seen all those nights—that electrified lust brewing in her. "You were fan-fucking-tastic." Her tongue does a quick revolution over her lips. "You and I were explosive. The way you made love to me was insanity. The way you moved, the things you did with your body—that delicious tongue." Her eyes widen. Her breathing is clipped. "Logan, I knew you loved Skyla, but I had no idea the level of intensity. It only makes me hate her more." She takes a breath and blinks away the tears adhering to her lashes. "We were on fire. You can't deny that. Make love to me again, Logan. I will be her for you every day of the week."

I shake my head. My entire body sags with anger, with pity. "None of that was for you, Chloe. It was all for her. In my heart, where it truly counts, I was making love to Skyla."

Chloe arches her head back and lets out a mighty roar. "When will you stop hating me?"

I think about this, consider if it's even a possibility.

"I don't hate you, Chloe. It's too much energy for me at this point. I simply pity you."

And with that, I get the hell out of the Transfer.

With a long, lonely night ahead of me, I cruise down to Dudley's and sit in the driveway. White Horse has become a wound—a place where my body betrayed Skyla instead of comforting her.

Skyla.

I close my eyes and let the burn penetrate my body. For one, small, selfish moment, I believed we had found our way back. I even believed that I would trade that shining miracle to have Gage back on this planet, and now that I do, my entire world seems to have unraveled. It's easy to wish for something altruistic when you think you'll never get it. But when it does come to pass, it doesn't feel quite as good as you thought.

I take a breath and jump out of my truck, letting the thick Paragon fog encapsulate me in its icy embrace. Skyla and Gage will be parents soon. Skyla has new life forming in her body—life that Gage himself placed there. And I'll be damned if it's not a beautiful, beautiful thing. I'm happy for them. Happy for Gage, especially since he almost missed this miracle. His child deserves to have him in his life. So does Skyla—so do I. And no matter how much it hurts to gift Skyla back to him, I'm glad he's here to have her.

It's a slow walk to Dudley's door. It's unlocked, so I let myself in. The television is on in the living room obnoxiously loud, an action scene with lots of guns and the sound of a roaring engine. I'm betting either Liam or Ellis is at the helm of this dick-flick. I head over and confirm my theory. In fact, they're both here, right along with the Sector himself.

"You left me." He frowns before shifting his attention back to the screen.

"Gage is back," I say mostly to Liam and Ellis, who both give a raucous shout just as a giant explosion takes over the screen.

"They should have seen that coming," Dudley chimes in, and I'm a bit surprised to see him in the testosterone trenches with the two stooges. He snaps off the television, and the room grows dim. "What is it you want?"

"I'm just here." I plop on the couch. "Hanging with my boys."

"Go hang with your other boy." Dudley flips the TV back on just as Ellis tries to swipe the remote. "I'm sure an Oliver reunion is called for this evening."

"He's right." Liam smacks my leg. "Emma's got a hell of a surprise headed in her direction. Dudley told me the good news. So, what happened?"

"We don't know. By the sound of it, he's not aware of much." I scowl at Dudley. "And I did not leave you. We had someplace to be. Skyla had some news she wanted to share." My expression sours as I glare into the fire. I'm still happy for them—just pissed at myself in the interim.

"So you know." Dudley lifts his chin. Skyla mentioned he was aware of her big news before she shared it.

"Yes, I know." I glance to Liam and Ellis, who have disbanded to raid the refrigerator. "I thought it was mine." I'm not sure what's sponsoring this late-night confession. I don't exactly consider Dudley to be anything more than my supervising spirit, certainly not a friend. "I thought I was comforting Skyla—turns out, it was Chloe."

"What?" Ellis squawks as he heads back into the room with a near beer in hand. "You fucked Bishop?" He belts out a laugh. "She's not that great." His affect changes on a dime. Chloe obliterated Ellis's heart and ego in a one-two punch back in high school. Ellis has always carried a very real torch for the Queen of Mean, and I've wondered if his self-medicating began on the coattails of that heartbreak. Chloe has never inspired anything good in anyone.

"Don't go spreading rumors. And believe me, Giselle is the last person who needs to know." I shoot a hard look to my brother. "Or God forbid Michelle."

"What doesn't Michelle need to know?" a female voice chimes from the stairwell as Michelle herself glides on down.

"Shit." I grind my palm into my eye. Michelle Miller is Liam's current house pet. She's smitten with him, perhaps far more than she ever was with Dudley or me. Liam hasn't quite settled on the fact if he's committed to keeping her around, but for now she doesn't seem to mind warming his bed.

"Don't worry, Logan," she chirps. "I heard the whole thing, and my lips are sealed. I think it's totally romantic that you were with Chloe because you desperately wanted to be with Skyla and couldn't. So, what's Skyla trying to keep classified? Is she secretly harboring boy parts? Come on, I won't tell." She falls into the seat next to me, her finger tracing out my jawline just the way Chloe did earlier. What's with that anyway? Is that some maneuver they developed in the time of the bitch squad? I've actually never called them that. It was Skyla's nickname for a few of the girls who happened to be in cheer with her. In truth, all of the girls on campus called them that. The bitch squad, which consisted of Michelle, Chloe, Emily Morgan, and Lexy Bakova, were infamous cheerleaders—basically, mean girls personified. High school feels like a million years ago, and here it was simply just one.

"Skyla doesn't have anything she'd like to share with any of you. That was my point. And as for Gage—I guess I'll head over to Barron's in a bit. I'd hate to ruin the surprise, so I think I'll drop by later."

"We'll do the same." Liam offers up a knuckle bump.

Dudley gives a huff of a laugh, his dark nefarious humor bubbling to surface for no apparent reason. He heads toward the piano in the rear of the cavernous room, and I follow.

"What the hell is so funny?"

"You thought you were sleeping with Skyla. You didn't know the difference. I'm sure Ms. Messenger was completely impressed with your lack of intuition." Dudley pulls that haunted speculum forward and runs his hand over the border.

The mirror itself was a gift to Dudley that acts as a portal. It mostly leads to haunted planes. It was a twisted revenge gift, seeing that Dudley gifted Demetri with a mirror resembling this one. Only *that* mirror, the Realm of Possibilities, was just that, a realm in which you can conjure your deepest fantasies and have them projected to reality once you step inside. It didn't go over too well once Demetri realized his least favorite Sector offered him a world in which he could make believe the Fems were in charge. Demetri wants that control, and he wants it in this world. But the only way he can ever achieve dominion is through—

"Shit." I give Dudley a shove to the arm, and his gaze drifts to the place I tapped him as if I just lit his mother on fire. "Skyla's child will give Demetri—"

"Dominion, yes." He glowers at his reflection as if it were Demetri himself. "I am more than aware."

"Crap. So this is pretty big." As happy as an occasion this child's birth will be, it will also be a blow for the Nephilim, particularly Celestra. "There's a horrible irony in there."

"Isn't there always a horrible irony when Candace is involved?" He pulls a handkerchief from his pocket and begins meticulously wiping down the mirror.

"What are you doing? What's this housekeeping bug that's suddenly crawled up your pants? You have traveling plans, don't you?"

"This I do." He shakes out his handkerchief in my face and settles it back into his pocket. "I've places to go and"—he gives a brief grimace—"unfortunate people to see." Dudley offers me a hard look of disdain. "I've business to tend to that involves yours truly."

"What do you mean it involves me? Does this involve Skyla?"

He glances to the mirror with an eerie look. "I'm not certain."

"You and I both know everything involves Skyla. She's been her mother's pawn long before she was ever born."

"Young Oliver"—he expels a deep sigh—"I'm beginning to think we all were." A lavender fog pours from the speculum as the glass liquefies like mercury. He steps into the looking glass without so much as a goodbye, and I'm half-tempted to follow. "Open your palm," his disembodied voice commands, and I do it. A flash of lightning streams from the mirror straight into my hand, and I stumble back from the sudden burst of energy.

"What was that for?"

"That, young Oliver, is a new game we're going to play. Memorize it. Demand the current to come to you, and it will. It's time you learn new powers—sharpen them like a spear. You will need them, sooner than you think."

And just like that, he and his rumbling voice vanish.

"Logan!" Michelle calls from the living room, and I head over. "You've got a lady caller."

Great. Probably one of Dudley's mid-century whores. More than a few have taken a liking to me. I give a smug half-smile for no particular reason. I suppose my ego needed the boost.

"Tell her I'm—" Just before the lie can speed out of my mouth, I notice a familiar body clogging up the space before me. Turns out, the lady caller is none other than Lexy Bakova. Her hair is a bit shorter, a dark copper mold that cradles her jawline perfectly. She's pretty in a cutthroat kind of way, but still not for me. "What's up, Lex?"

She speeds over and wraps her arms around me hard as if it were me who had just come back from the other side. Little does she know—no fanfare needed—I'm just plain dead.

"It's terrible, Logan. You won't believe all the BS I just went through. Wesley has really lost his shit."

I pull back, peeling her off me while glancing to Ellis and Liam who look equally stumped.

"What are you talking about? What's Wes done now?"

"You don't know?" Her large brown eyes press into mine. "Wesley's started a small army of super Nephs. He's training in superpowers that have never been available before to our people." She rolls her eyes at Michelle a moment. "Do you mind?" Miller leaves for the kitchen without even blinking. Michelle is the only one in the room without a drop of Nephilim blood in her. "I'm on his dream team, Logan."

"What's he training you for?"

"For the end. It's almost here. It's going to be game over for the rest of you. Only the Barricade survives. This is the big one, and there's not a soul in heaven or down below who can save us—not even your precious little Skyla."

That baby brewing in her belly blinks through my mind.

The enemy has us bound, surrounded.

We need a hero. A savior.

Just who is that going to be?

Maybe—just maybe—it could be me.

5

Dominion Rising

Skyla

The enemy lurks in the darkest places, sometimes in the open as an angel of light, and, sometimes, the enemy manages to plant themselves in the most unassuming place of all, right in the nexus of your being.

Gage rubs my belly with his hand, skin on skin, the look of heartache and love all folded into one. Here he is, with his hair a little longer, dark scruff taking over his cheeks. His eyes glow, very much alive and sexy like my own personal jack-o-lantern.

We've been standing outside of the Landon house for the better part of an hour—our eyes remain locked on one another. We're unable to move, unable to look away. Gage and I are beyond words, content with the silence for now. We pour our love into one another through this deep, meaningful gaze. Gage bows down and lands his soft lips to mine, his tongue finds its home in my mouth, and we get lost in our magical kisses. We surrender what feels like hours to this very task.

Gage pulls back, his eyes glittering with tears. "I'm so happy, Skyla." He peppers my face with his precious lips. "Words aren't enough to convey this."

"I am, too. I really am, Gage." I cross my wrists behind his neck, pulling him closer. Gage wanted to come here first and shower before we head to his parents' house. I've told him how worried they are—leaving out the screaming match I had with Emma. I suppose that's in the past. "I know what you're probably thinking." I glance down at my stomach and press my lips together so hard it's painful.

"Dominion." His jaw tightens as he gives a tiny nod.

"I'm not afraid," I whisper. "This is our child. Our love is greater than any wickedness in all creation. Our child won't have an evil bone in its body. The Good Book says train a child up in the way he should go—and we will train this child to love our people."

"Yes." He presses a hard kiss to my cheek. His stubble rubs me raw, and I love it. There are so many things I've missed about Gage—and his rough stubble, his greedy kisses were at the top of the carnal list.

"This child has the power to change things." I swallow hard, my hand covering his as he warms my stomach. "This is Celestra—Caelestis, united with a Fem." My gut pinches. It's the first time I've said it out loud. "Instead of giving into Demetri's wicked scheme of gaining dominion, this child will be a symbol that unites all of the Nephilim races—and maybe then even the Sectors and the Fems can finally move forward as one." I frown at the theory. "I suppose there's no Sector in the mix, but nevertheless, I refuse to let this pan out the way Demetri wishes."

"He still gets dominion." Gage blows out a hard breath that plumes to life, white as smoke. "But you're right. There's no reason our child can't channel the factions—the Fems away from their power-hungry ways, and bond us all as a united front." He touches his finger to my nose with a veil of sadness lingering in his eyes. "That is a mighty big task for a tiny little baby. I say we let 'em be for a while."

"I second that." I nod toward the house. "Let's make this quick so we can get to your parents' house. I'm dying to get you into bed." I close my eyes a moment and cringe. "I'm so sorry that you thought I did those things with Logan—that you saw my likeness doing them. It was wicked of Chloe, but it was wicked of Demetri as well."

"They never give up, do they?"

We head inside, and my mother drops a load of laundry in one hand and Misty loosens in her grip in the other.

"Gage Oliver?" Her voice rings out like a bullhorn. "Is that really you?" She lunges at him. I narrowly escape having my head hacked off by her forearm and manage to swipe Misty to safety in the process. My hand glides over Misty's bare arms in the event the baby Fem-slash-Count has anything she might like to reveal. She's already babbling away a storm, and I assume in a few short weeks she'll be speaking well enough for all to understand. But if there's anything at all going on in that tiny little brain of hers, I would love to be apprised. It's too young for normal *human* children to start spouting off, but she is her father's daughter. Who knows what kind of maleficent thoughts might be circulating around in there?

There's your brother—and your uncle, I suppose. Aren't you glad to see him? I take her hand and point over to where my mother is molesting the hell out of my husband. In truth, that's the kind of homecoming I can't wait to give him, with the exception that far more fondling will take place in far more intimate places.

Misty yanks her hand free and turns her attention to my shirt. She plucks and plucks—looking for a spare boob, I'm sure. My mother will probably nurse her until she's thirteen. She keeps threatening to stop and then remembers *last one out!*

"No, no," I softly reprimand, but Misty lands her sharp fingernails over my bare stomach. Her entire face lights up as if I were Santa or a giant purple dinosaur or whatever it is that gets almost one-year-olds overly excited these days.

My mind fills with her baby gibberish. Her feet dance and kick as she coos and giggles with the best of them. Her hand warms over my belly, oven hot, and Misty shoots her gaze to mine and gasps as though she just had a stark realization.

"Would you look at that?" Mom plays with Misty's hand. "I've never seen her so excited! It looks like Misty-Pie is glad Gage is home, too."

"What the hell is all that racket?" Tad comes staggering down the stairs in an unfortunate pair of flesh-toned pants—his knees picketing in opposing directions with every step he takes. Oh, wait—oh my shit! Those aren't flesh-colored pants—that's actual flesh he's exposing. In fact, he's in nothing but his boxers, black knee-high socks and—good God—is that a garter belt? What the hell? I don't even want to know.

"Gage is back!" my mother cries. "Girls!" Her high-pitched wail startles the baby, and now they're both screaming. "Gage is *back*, everyone!"

Mia and Melissa run down as if this were a fire drill.

"Oh, it's just you," Melissa snarks before making an abrupt U-turn, and Mia gives her the finger on the way down.

"Nice to see they're getting along." He forces a smile to come and go.

"Never mind that," Tad barks, like spitting out nails. "Where's the dough Althorpe promised? I knew I shouldn't have left the goods in your hands. You failed to deliver!"

Gage shoots me a questioning look, and I give a little shrug.

"It's been a long day for him," I say, handing a wailing Misty back to my star-struck mother. "He just came by to change before we head over to the Olivers.'"

I give Gage a pat toward the stairs, and he gives a noticeable limp on the way up. He steadies himself on his cane, and it breaks my heart to see it. "I'll be right up!" I call after him.

"I can give his boss a message if you like." I blink into Tad, trying to look unassuming, but all I really want is to shake the crap out of Taddy Dearest for treating Gage like dirt on his first night back. Who at Althorpe thought it was a good idea to put Tad Landon in charge of anything? A couple of morons. Arson and Morley, that's who. I cringe as I recall them offering him a promotion. So that's how the Counts plan on keeping their noses clean—relying on dolts to do their dirty work.

"Tell 'em I brought those two hoity-toity government officials to Paragon myself, and your idiot of a husband took all the credit. And poof! There went my ribeye dinner! There was another bonus involved if I took them to the Paragon Palms Hotel, too, and I blew it because Greg here promised he had the whole thing handled. It's no coincidence that Jock Strap of yours and my cash bonus both disappeared around the same time. I bet he went to Vegas on my dime! And now he's ready to limp around the lap of Landon until he can figure out how to steal my next paycheck!"

I want to laugh at the thought of Tad calling Gage by his Marshall-inspired nickname, but I also want to smack him for making fun of Gage's new limp.

"Tad!" Mom yanks him toward the kitchen by his ear.

Good riddance.

Hold on—government officials? A mean shudder runs through me. What the hell is he babbling about? Why would Althorpe drag government officials to Paragon? Wait... Tad's "Greg" just might be Wes! No wonder it feels as if we're in another dimension when he's spouting off things regarding paychecks and *hand-offs* of government officials. Crap. Wes has gone too far. I'd make it a note to talk to Wes when I get a chance, but I'm afraid I already know what the government is here to inspect.

Those "Interlopers," as Nev dubbed them, run through my mind. Nev and Ezrina thought there was something strange about those two. I'm betting the Interlopers and Tad's guests are one in the same. Thank God the Nephilim are impossible to detect, despite our genetic markers. Wes has his work cut out for himself if he wants to screw us—or at least I hope he has his work cut out for himself.

"Guess what?" Mia blocks my path, as I'm about to head upstairs. She's exactly my height. Same face, same body—for now.

"What's up?"

She sizzles a pendant across her chain and taunts me with the tiny silver ring, hardly big enough to fit Misty.

"I have a new boyfriend."

"Rev gave you that?" I'm not impressed. Revelyn is Dr. Booth's son. He's a student at Host, and as much as I dislike their ginormous age difference, Rev seems to be a decent guy.

"What? *No.*" Her face contorts in horror. "It's from Gabe. I stole Gabriel Armistead right from underneath that little slut's nose."

"Oh my God." I glance up the stairs, hoping Melissa is nowhere near this toxic conversation. Mia and Melissa have been warring over Gabriel Armistead for years now. "Are you nuts? First of all, *she* stole him from *you*. He's disgusting. You can both do better. And what happened to Rev?" Mia and Rev were sharing a dog named Bullet and everything.

"Relax. We're still co-parenting D-O-G." That's right. The dog has two names, two homes, the best of both worlds, blah, blah, blah. Still, anything is an improvement from an Armistead. His sister, Carson, is a certified asshole. I can't stand her high-pitched squeaky voice—or was that her annoying friend Carly? My mind is so fogged up these days that my entire high school experience is strung out like one long nightmare. Nevertheless if they both hadn't abandoned me in the woods ever so long ago, Ezrina wouldn't have hacked my arm off. I wince. It was actually per Marshall's orders—the Ezrina hacking part, not the Carson run-in. Why haven't I made Marshall pay for that yet? Turns out, he's not big on stealing, and I did snag a few treasures from him once—against my better judgment. A thought comes to me. Chloe stole that antique bed warmer from Ezrina right in front of Marshall's face, and he promised she would pay for that. I hope he chops her head off. Oh, what poetic justice that would be. Wes could raise their spawn. I can't believe they teamed up and are actually going to pollute this world with their seed. I wouldn't be surprised at all if she gave birth to a giant cockroach.

"Hello?" Mia waves a hand over my face before glaring at me with her discontent. "Figures. It's like I'm invisible to you. Nobody cares about me around here. I hate it. As soon as I turn eighteen, I'm out of here."

"I'm sorry! I'm just—my head is everywhere these days. I just zoned out for a second. So, you're seeing Gabe? Is this really what your heart wants, or is this some sort of revenge-based relationship?"

She gives an indifferent shrug. "A little of both."

At least she's honest. "How long does this need to last? I mean, is it worth ruining things with Rev over?"

I cannot believe I'm advocating that leather jacket bad boy to my sweet little sister. A few months ago, I was threatening him with stat rape charges if he even had a wet dream regarding my sister, and now I've all but put on my old West Paragon cheer uniform and spelled out his name while doing high kicks.

"Oh, Rev is cool with it." She waves it off. "He totally doesn't mind. Plus, I want him to sow his wild oats while he can. Once we're official, there's only going to be me rocking his bed, if you know what I mean."

"No, I don't know what you mean. You're a kid. The only bed you should be rocking is your own while jumping on it. Get your head out of the gutter and cut both of those clowns loose. You need a good boy. Someone who will love you and only you with every fiber of his being."

Her eyes flit to the ceiling as she considers this. "Maybe so, but it sure does feel good to know I'm the reason Melissa's eyes are red as apples—*poison* apples. That girl is a witch. She laughed in my face when I cried over Gabe, and I plan on doing the very same thing." She speeds up the stairs as I shout her name, but the door to her room slams with defiance before I can get another word in.

"This isn't over!"

Gage ambles down as quickly as he can with his cane supporting him every step of the way. His hair is freshly slicked back. He holds the scent of mint and subtle spiced cologne.

"What isn't over?" He pulls me into a tight embrace, his lips covering mine, moist and heated. God, he feels, smells, and tastes like heaven.

"Us." I close my eyes a moment and just soak in the feel of my husband in my arms. "We are not over by a long shot, Gage Oliver."

It occurs to me as Gage gives a firm knock over his parents' front door that Emma very much wishes we were over.

"*Hey.*" I pull his scruffy cheeks down toward me and bury a kiss into one of his dimples, my tongue dipping in deep for no other reason than I love the feel of that happy divot. "There's a preview for later."

"Love it." He dives in with a quick kiss of his own. "You want to mention anything about our big surprise?" His fingers graze over my stomach.

I shake my head. "Let tonight be about you. Plus, that gives us some time to get creative."

The door swings wide, and Barron stands there, stunned. Before we know it, Gage is mobbed by both of his parents as they huddle to him, raining their tears over their son for an eternal hour. There are happy tears, and then there are grievously happy tears, and these just so happen to fall in the second category. There is no greater separation than death and no greater relief than to hold your loved one in your arms once again after thinking you've lost them forever. A ripe sadness comes over me because that's not something true humans can experience. It's a gift that seems to come sparingly in Nephilim circles as well. I'm glad for the times I've seen my father. Seeing him in Ahava—here on Earth postmortem takes the edge off, but I still miss him. I still wish he were here on a day-to-day basis. And I'm eternally grateful for Logan's Treble. I grit my teeth because I'm sure Chloe is, too. Wench.

"Come." Emma pulls him into the living room, and Barron and I follow. "Skyla, call Giselle." She doesn't take her eyes off Gage.

I'm quick to oblige and shoot a text off to Liam and Ellis as well. I send a separate text to Logan.

At the Olivers'. Missing a very important Oliver. YOU. Come quick!

After what Chloe pulled, I plan on being extra careful around Logan. I'm sure he's torn up about what happened—what he thought for sure had happened. My face fills with heat at the things he thought he was doing to comfort me. I hope this doesn't widen the rift between Logan and Gage. Those dreams I had while Gage was away come back to me, and I blush ten times deeper. Crap. I find it awfully coincidental that

I had porn-grade dreams about Logan while he believed he was making love to me. I shake all thoughts of porn and Logan out of my head.

"My God, son! Please tell us everything," Barron implores.

"How are you alive?" Emma wails. "How is any of this possible? Is this a Treble? Are you visiting from the great beyond?" Her voice rails against the walls before boomeranging back to us in an echo, and I smirk over at her for not giving Gage the chance to get a word in edgewise. I can't believe Emma is getting under my skin for merely shedding some concern over her son. Honestly, it's as if I can't get ahold of my emotions when I'm around her.

"Slow down." Gage gives a dull laugh. "You sound a lot like Skyla."

Emma and I exchange glances. It's clear we both take umbrage to that.

"I didn't think I was gone for that long," he continues. "I hurt my back. Demetri flew in specialists from around the world."

More like he flew Gage to them. I bet that's why the house is gone. The ridiculous Fem was using it as a transportation unit. It's bad enough Wes is shaking up the world with his bogus moving lights in the sky attraction. We don't need Demetri trying to one-up him by freaking out the masses with his pop-up mansion.

"You were gone for six weeks, Gage." Emma shakes her head, disappointed in her son's ability to keep track of the calendar in light of his spectacular fall. "Your heart stopped."

Barron nods. "I examined you myself. I called it. However, Demetri has done the impossible. He's brought you back." He jumps up and pulls his medical bag from the hall closet. "I'll check your vitals." He proceeds to poke and prod, sticking his stethoscope under Gage's shirt, and I get my first mouthwatering glance at those hard as sheetrock muscles, and my panties drench in an instant. To say that my hormones are on overdrive is putting it mildly. Ever since this afternoon, my mind has been compiling a pornographic bucket list, and I plan on checking off every single item later tonight. It's safe to say Gage won't get a whole lot of sleeping done his first night back.

"Everything is as it should be." Barron shrugs into this wonderful news. "It might not hurt to ask how you came to have breath in your lungs once again. I'll be curious to know how the resurrection was performed."

"So will I." My thigh presses to his, and an erotic rush pulses over me, stronger than anything—stronger than death, and if this sexual appetite of mine keeps increasing, I'll soon harness the power to resurrect a few corpses myself. I've never felt so solidly aroused.

Giselle and Ellis burst into the room along with Liam and Logan holding up the rear. They all attack Gage while Logan takes a seat on the ottoman.

"*Dude.*" Ellis pulls Gage into a long, strong man-hug. I must admit, it warms my heart. They've been friends forever. We can trust Ellis with just about anything. "Heard about the kid! I can't believe it! You and—"

"Yeah—that kid," Logan booms from across the room. "He pointed out the fact Demetri's house was back on its evil perch."

Nice save.

I glare at Harrison. My God, you just can't trust Ellis with a damn thing, can you? And who the hell told Ellis in the first place?

My eyes bug out as I transfer my stare to Logan. Oh, never mind. I bet the entire topic came up because of that bitch, Chloe. A boiling anger courses through my veins. It's like I'm running hot and cold, one emotion to the next. I'm like a nuclear bomb just waiting to go off, and Chloe knows exactly how to light my fuse.

"Yeah"—Gage gives my hand a hard squeeze as everyone falls into a seat—"lucky he was there." ***That was close.***

"Wasn't it?" I whisper.

The joy drips from Emma's face. "Wasn't it what, Skyla?" I guess the fact I brought Gage over like a trophy is small potatoes while there's still fresh hate to be had. Face it, we are never going to get along.

"Just a private word I was sharing with my husband."

Emma squints at Gage before whispering something into Barron's ear, and now they're both eyeing my poor husband as if he were a thief who came to steal the silverware.

"What?" Gage doesn't have the patience, and, for one, I'm glad. I'm so over Emma and her head games. Maybe he'll give her the finger, and we can all go home.

I touch my hand to my lips. I can't believe I said that, even if it wasn't out loud.

Emma clears her throat and nods in my direction. "How can we be sure this is your husband?"

"I'm not Wes." Gage is the first to contest this theory.

Oh shit. What if Emma is onto something? I mean, we did see Wes tonight, but what's to stop Demetri from pulling more Gage doppelgangers out of his ass for the next thirty years? He's about as obsessed with Gage as Chloe is—as I am. My hormones purr once again, and I push the thought, the horrid theory, to the far reaches of my mind. Leave it to Emma to throw a wrench of doubt into my fuck-Gage-until-my-ears-bleed plan. As soon as I land him in that bed, I'll know for damn sure.

My eyes flit to Logan for a moment. Again, how could he not know? But then, I suppose three days wasn't enough to memorize my every nuance. Plus, I'm more than positive Chloe brought her dark vaginal magic to the table. I shudder just thinking about that Bermuda Triangle-shaped bear trap of hers.

"Look"—Gage takes a deep breath, his eyes hood with fatigue (but I can work with that because it looks like lust to me)—"I hurt my back in the fall. A wave came and softened the blow, so it wasn't as bad as it could have been. There was some spinal damage. Demetri had me injected with some stem cell treatment not approved yet in this country. And I knew Skyla and Logan would come as soon as they could."

Logan winces when Gage says that last part. Dirty, dirty, boy. My hormones rev up again, and those dreams replay in my mind as I force my eyes back to my husband.

"And we did." Logan furrows his brows as if thrown that the words actually came from his mouth, but we know what he meant. Mostly.

Liam looks to Logan with a serious look of discontent. "Should we let them in on what happened?"

"Oh God, no!" I straighten in my seat, gripping Gage hard by the shoulder. I don't care if it was Chloe who lured Logan into bed, Emma's hatred for me will proliferate if she finds out that Logan slept with me—in theory. Plus, *hello?* It's just a touch embarrassing for Logan. I'm stomping this topic out like an oven fire for both of our sakes.

"It's okay." Logan lifts a finger.

I'm hating the finger lift.

"Shouldn't you consult with me first?" I make large, concerned-as-hell eyes at him, and he holds back a smile. Not liking the withheld smile either.

"This concerns Lexy."

"Did you sleep with her, too?" My hand clamps over my mouth, and I can feel Gage's chest buck with a laugh.

"No, Skyla." He glances to Liam because I do believe it's Liam who's tapping both that well and Michelle's. Hey, I wonder if when it's Michelle's turn he says, *It's Miller time!*

"Lexy came over to Dudley's and told us about some recruitment project Wes is undertaking." Logan gives me a curt nod as if to say, *See? You can trust me.* "He selected a few willing members of the Barricade to form a special ops team, if you will." He shrugs as if not really. "She didn't say much, just that they're in the process of learning new powers."

Barron looks to Gage a moment. "Why would she volunteer this information? Do you think that brother of yours is trying to plant a mole?"

Emma's head twitches toward Gage as if her own son were the mole in question. Really, Emma? Oh, ye of little faith.

But *God*—what if he is? At this point, I'm just so thrilled to have him back I probably couldn't care less. My one-track mind is screaming *clothes off, Oliver!* Hell, I'm ready to bark out all sorts of physical demands, and I just pray his poor back can take it.

"What do you think, Logan?" Gage leans in. "Do you think Lex is setting you up? Or do you think she's heard how vulnerable you've been and is ready to offer up a little physical comfort?"

The room quiets down to a deafening silence.

Giselle raises her hand as if we were in school. "I think that's very nice of Lexy to offer Logan some physical comfort. Especially now that Gage is back, and Skyla can't physically comfort him anymore." She gives a few innocent blinks, and her mouth opens again.

Oh my fuck.

"I saw you behind the bowling alley." She bites down on a nervous giggle. "Ellis says people don't usually do those things outside, but I caught you!" she says it with the pointing-laughing enthusiasm of a three-year-old.

Emma tweaks her head like a bird. "What did you catch them doing?"

"We were going over numbers." Logan clears his throat. "End-of-the-month stuff. I really should hire an accountant."

"Me, too," Barron chimes, obviously trying to cover for our fictional coital misdeeds, and now I wish the ground would open, and I could fall through. Leave it to Chloe to humiliate me and ruin my reputation in one fell swoop. "Gage, if you need a supplemental income, I'm willing to bet you can earn the business of the bowling alley along with the mortuary. Just a thought. Isn't that right, dear?" He glances to Emma, but she's still too busy shooting her beams of destruction at me to notice. Not only am I the daughter-in-law she never wanted, but now I'm the female version of a philanderer as well.

"I'll think about it." Gage rises, and everyone in the room follows suit.

"You weren't talking about numbers," Giselle blurts out while looking at Logan. "She said you were checking her internal temperature with a *special* thermometer." She turns to me accusingly.

Oh God, I can't breathe.

Giselle widens her doe eyes at me. "Are you still hot-to-trot, Skyla?"

Emma lets out a roar and tosses up her arms. "Oh, for God's sake!"

Logan opens his mouth as if to rectify the situation and swats the idea down before it ever leaves his lips.

"Save it, Logan," I sigh, exasperated. "She already thinks the worst of me."

Gage says his goodbyes as we speed the hell out of the house. Logan calls after us just before we get into the truck.

"I'm sorry." He looks from me to Gage. "I swear, I would take it all back if I could. Forgive me." The hurt in his eyes is painful to witness. Logan meant those words with every cell in his body. I could feel the apology etching into my heart like fire over stone.

"We'll talk later," Gage says rather unimpressed as he helps me into the truck. "Get what info you can out of Lex. I'll talk to Wes. We need to shut this shit down. He's moving faster than I thought he would."

Gage gets into the truck, and we take off for the Landon house.

I watch as Logan grows smaller in the rearview mirror, and my heart breaks for him.

Damn Chloe. As soon as she spits that child out from between her legs, I'm going to go off on her ass with a spirit sword.

There has to be a way to kill the devil.

Gage growls out a tiny laugh and shakes his head as we leave the Paragon Estates.

It was as if he heard me.

And I wonder.

My world stopped the day my father died. It did. Time went on, I went on, but nothing was ever the same. Tad came into our lives, we moved to Paragon, all hell broke loose in this realm and the next, and I wish I could say *the end*, but I'm still here, moving through time without my father. The safe little girl that knew nothing of pain was forever erased the day we lost him.

Gage and I head straight upstairs. He tries to hide his noticeable limp, as if his cane was merely for show, but I see it. I'll be as mindful as I can of his injuries. Now that Gage is human—according to the father of lies—I'll have to see where his thresholds are. I'm so very thankful I haven't lost Gage. I'm not sure what's brought him back to us—hell, *he's* not sure what's brought him back to us, but I am sure about one thing, this is indeed my husband.

The rhythmic squeak of a mattress comes from the left just as we hit the top of the stairs, and Gage and I cast a suspicious glance at one another.

"What the—" Drake's room has been empty for a while, ever since he and Brielle moved into a trailer in the backyard. Drake and Bree are rolling in it. They have no need for cheap mattress sex in the Landon house anymore. I swing the door open, bracing for just about anything—even a chubby-cheeked toddler with a carpet full of blond hair.

"Baby Beau!" I say, relieved. It looks like Mom and Tad finally gave him an eviction notice from his casket-slash-bassinet. He'll be two in a few weeks, and he's absolutely huge.

He offers a toothy grin as he bounces up and down in a bona fide crib.

"I can't believe this is what we have to look forward to." In truth, it terrifies me. Babies can be very demanding. All they do for the livelong day is dangle from their mother's boobs and poop. Gah! My boobs!

"Kyla! Out!" he coos, trying to latch on to me so he can hitch a ride out of baby prison.

"Sorry, buddy. This is exactly where Mee-Maw wants you." I offer a kiss to his forehead before we step out of the room again.

"Think he'll go to sleep?" Gage winces as we leave him in the dark to his own devices.

"He's a Count. He'll probably think of ways to rule the world until he passes out."

We share a brief, quiet laugh on behalf of the Countenance, which isn't really fair since we're on the friends and family plan with that rotten faction. Speaking of which...

Gage and I step into my bedroom, *our* bedroom, and I push my dresser over the door, old school.

"I've got a faction meeting coming up, and I want you to come with."

"No." Gage closes his eyes as if the thought of attending physically pained him. "I'm not allowed, and from what I remember neither are you."

"Well, I'm going, and I'm hoping you will, too." I peel off his T-shirt in one quick motion, and he leaves his hands in the air as if daring me to inspect him.

The breath vacates my lungs at the sight of him.

"Holy, wow," I marvel at Gage's newly ripped body. Gage was muscular before, but this is definition beyond reason. "Being human suits you well."

"That's exactly what's happened." His features sag for a moment. "I needed to rely on my own strength—all of that Levatio power—the Fem in me is gone, sort of." He winces. "I'm only human in theory. Demetri doesn't have the authority to strip my DNA, and apparently neither does your mother." He pulls off my sweater, and a dirty grin blooms on his face.

"I'm just glad you're back." I work his jeans open and glide my hands into the back of his boxers. Gage Oliver is hot both physically and literally. I let my fingers smooth over his flesh, his tight as a rock ass, and then grin up at him. "Speaking of *back*, how careful do we have to be?"

He shakes his head. "Don't think about it. I'll be fine. It's really just my leg that needs to heal now. My back can take anything you dish out. Mostly."

I cock my head to the side and crimp a smile. "Guess what you don't have to dish out?"

"A one-liner to get you into bed?" His lids hood over so low, all I see are two blue slits.

"A condom. So, if that's your pick-up line, you're right." I poke him hard in the stomach, pulling him out of his sexed-up stupor. "And how the hell did this happen anyway?" There go my emotions again. It's like I'm ice skating, gliding a million miles an hour without a bit of control, from one end of the emotional sphere to the other.

His mouth opens with promise, then closes with defeat. "I'm sorry. It was something Ellis said." He walks me backward until I fall over the bed with him landing beside me.

I swat him over the chest. "You know the first rule of dealing with Ellis is never listen to anything Ellis says." I bury my face in his chest a moment before looking back up. "What did he say? I'll need this info while I'm beating him later. Harrison is not going to get away with knocking me up—inadvertently."

"It was a back-to-front issue." He winces, and those adorable dimples dig in, and I die at the sight of them. Dear God, have I ever missed this boy.

"Front-to-back? Is this a condom thing? Is there another way to put them on? Wow, have we been using them inside out the entire time? I'm totally confused."

"No, actually, it was the night we tried—I tried—something new. You were quick to evict me, and, well, I couldn't take the condom to the front so I flicked it off and went commando." More wincing.

"*Oh.* I do remember that." I gently knock my forehead to his. "I guess Ellis was technically right, but he forgot one crucial detail—put another condom on." I scratch his chest as the memory of that night swims through me. "You'd better fill Ellis in on that little detail, or your poor sister is going to be incubating a miniature Harrison before you know it."

"Ugh—no." His hands ride to cover his face. "Let's not talk about Giselle and Ellis. The visual—I can't."

"Apparently, he can. We both know they're doing it. You caught them firsthand, and I know for a fact Brielle has been mentoring her for months. And don't even say you're going to kill Bree because this is all that stoner's fault to begin with. He's the one that corrupted her—is still corrupting her. And how the fuck did Ellis manage to knock me up again?" I fall back and pull a pillow over my face.

"Whoa." Gage runs his finger up my belly. "I hate to sound like Dudley, but you might want to watch the language. And believe me—Ellis had nothing to do with landing that tiny being in your body." He bows his face to my belly and delivers a searing hot kiss to my flesh. "It was all me." He looks in my direction, his eyes tugging with sadness. "Skyla, I know this is life-changing, that perhaps you're upset, but the baby, it's already here." He rubs a finger over my stomach. "I think we should find joy in this moment. I'm glad to be back, for you and for the baby."

"Gage." I knot my fingers up in that slick, glossy mane of his. How I have missed every hair on his body. "I think you're right. My head is all over the place, but I get what you're saying. And I want to. I want to embrace this magic—this miracle—that we get to share together." It comes out uncertain.

"Have you been sick? Are you having cravings? I couldn't stop thinking about those things while I was in Demetri's hostage hospital." His mouth covers mine for a moment.

"I've been kind of sick, and, yes, I've been craving anything I can get my hands on. I'm sort of an equal opportunity foodie at this point." I bite down on my lip, hard, as all kinds of paranoid thoughts run through my mind.

"What's the doctor say?"

"I just took the test. I haven't seen a doctor."

"That means I haven't missed an appointment yet." Gage is relishing this, and it warms my heart to see it. "We'll find a doctor together."

"Perfect. And we'll have to devise the perfect way to tell our parents. We should probably sew Ellis's mouth shut in the meantime."

"Agree and agree. And we'll have to figure out where we'll live."

I glance around my tiny room. "I guess the butterfly room isn't exactly the best place to have a nursery, but, hey, it's all we can afford right now. Babies aren't cheap."

That smile he's been wearing all night deflates. "I'll figure something out. Something that doesn't involve Demetri." He gently pushes my hair back. "I promise, I'm going to take care of you, Skyla."

"I'm not a hamster." I give him a playful tickle. "We'll do this together."

"I like the sound of that."

"How about less talking, more fucking?"

"Language." He gives a deep-dimpled smile, and my insides melt.

"You do sound like Dudley." I gurgle out a dark laugh. "And, actually, I have had one strong craving that I, nor anyone else, wasn't able to fulfill."

"Anything. Name it, and I'll have it here by midnight."

"You between my legs."

He raises a brow, amused. "Which part of me?"

"This part." My hand reaches down and caresses the blooming hardness in his boxers. "And this part." I trace out his perfect, full lips. Gage's lips are the envy of the world. His hair, those sea glass eyes—every part of him is the envy of the universe.

"That's funny. Those were the exact parts I planned on latching on to you with first."

"Really?" I tease. "Well, you just made this part and this part extremely jealous." I point to the girls, each in turn.

He leans over and offers a simple kiss to each of them over my bra.

"My efforts are being hampered." Gage reaches back and unhooks it, tossing the fragile lace across the room like a missile.

"We forgot to turn off the light." I glance up and try to will it off, but it simply dims and comes back full strength, mocking me.

"Leave it. Everything is better with the lights on."

I suck in a quick breath. "Gage! You're going to see all my bits and pieces." I make a face. "I'm going to jiggle."

"Looking forward to it."

"I'm going to die of embarrassment."

"You're going to love it. Besides, you're beautiful. I want to watch you." His eyes melt to mine, drunk off the idea of seeing me exposed.

"That means I get to watch you." I ride a finger up his rock solid chest, skin over steel. "But I'm still going to die of embarrassment."

"I'm going to worship you with my body." He takes a gentle bite of my lower lip and pulls out slowly. The thought of Gage Oliver in all of his unearthly sexual perfection worshiping me with those rock-hard abs makes me heady in a whole new way. "And you keep breathing—no dying of embarrassment allowed."

"Sounds good." My voice squeaks when I say it.

His hand slips between my thighs, riding slowly home to where it belongs, where I need him to be, and his finger plunges deep inside me, inciting a dizzying rush that sends me into a high like I have never known.

"God, I love you," I pant as we struggle to evict the rest of our clothes.

Gage and I put those carpeted, soundproof walls to the test as we start in on a wrestling match fueled by passion. His kisses drip with honey as I drink down the maddening wine of our love straight from his mouth. Gage moans into this kiss as if he's waited a lifetime to place his lips over mine. It feels as if an entire eternity has passed in these last six weeks. My limbs secure over his body, my legs riding up over his back. I take the length of him into my hands—marvel at how hard, how outrageously long he is as I navigate him home, deep inside me. This right here, this moment with Gage, with his love filling me in every possible way is what it feels as I was born to do.

I find it perfectly romantic that he was wondering how I felt with the baby, what I was craving while he was incarcerated in that light-driving, light-traveling nuthouse. Then it occurs to me—how did Gage know to wonder about those things when I didn't get a chance to tell him that I was pregnant until today?

And now it's me who's left to wonder.

Morning comes with a violent roll of nausea as I groan my way to the bathroom. Gage finds me naked and retching into the toilet—worst nightmare affirmed. I suppose he was right. I had nothing to be embarrassed about last night. It's this morning that would bring me ripe humiliation. Afterward, I gargle with that blue poison Gage likes to use religiously and moan my way right back to bed.

"Here." He sweetly hands me a bottle of water he found in the less-than-hygienic stockpile I've amassed in the crevasses of the bed. I wasn't exactly keeping our room tidy while he was away. It wasn't my top concern. "Is it bad?"

Gage is so achingly handsome I once believed that just looking at his beautiful eyes alone had the power to heal any ailment—now, not so much.

"No. It's—" Another hard roll of nausea treks through me, and this time I simply groan my way through it. I've already given that damn toilet everything I've got. "It's bad." My voice shakes as I say it. I pull him in until his arms wrap around me. I've never needed Gage like I do now.

"As soon as you're able, we'll head to the doctor's office. In fact, I'll look up a few right now." He reaches for my laptop. "Only the best will do," he says it with an uptick to his voice, because unlike me, Gage is blissfully excited about this baby. Not that I'm not blissfully excited—I am—it's just hard to convey while my intestines are so diligently struggling to swim up my throat.

"My insurance is Alta Pacific, so just those providers." My voice is graveled and weak. I sound as if I've spent the last twenty years smoking a thousand cigarettes.

"We should look into our own insurance. We're married now, so it's probably the best time to break from our parents' policies." He slides the laptop back onto the nightstand. "I'll talk to my dad about it this afternoon. We'll get something quick."

"No." I twist into him, shivering from my naked jaunt to the loo. Gage tucks the covers around my back as he pulls me into the warmth of his body. "I want us to tell everyone at the same time. We'll do it soon, I promise."

"I won't tell him about the baby, just the need for healthcare." His dimples dig in, and I plunge my finger in one, grinning as best I can through the ick rolling around inside me. "Tell me," he whispers, landing his warm hand on my belly. Here we are, just the three of us, lost in a circle of love. "How do you want to do this? We could throw a party?"

"That might arouse suspicion. We don't throw parties. We generally avoid them."

"True."

"Misty and Beau are having a together birthday party in two weeks. She's turning one, and he's turning two. Maybe after they open their gifts, we could do the big reveal."

He winces. "It's their special day. Brielle and your mother already have to share the spotlight. Do you think they'll mind?"

"I didn't think of it that way. Any other events coming up that we can latch on to?"

"Laken and Coop are getting married."

I shake my head. "A solid no. Now *that's* a special day. The only other thing I can think of is Logan's birthday, and that's a *hell* no to that one."

"I double that." He touches his finger to my nose, and his chest drums with the idea of a laugh. "Now that's a totally acceptable expletive."

"That's funny, because the biggest, baddest expletive of them all is your father." I make a face. "It's true. Having Demetri's name roll off my tongue has always stung both my heart and my ears."

"If I could change everything, I would." His features morph with agony, and now I'm sorry I mentioned it at all.

"That's because you're a prince." Actually, he's a king—Demetri's spawn and pawn. An idea begins to percolate. "Hey, I know. We should have Demetri throw some ridiculous party—that beginning-of-summer bash of his—I'd happily announce the fact we're having a child in his home."

Gage touches his palm to my forehead as if he's reading a fever. "You're delirious."

"No, I'm serious. Think about it. You and I will declare a victory for Celestra, for the Nephilim people right in the heart of wickedness. It's bold. It's daring. It's *courageous*. It screams we've got bigger balls than you can ever hope to have. Most importantly, it says F.U. to the chief Fem and Fems in general—no offense." I shrink a little in his arms. "It might just be an insane idea, but I think it works."

His lips twist as he considers this. Gage glides his warm, thick hand over my shoulder, dripping down my torso before landing on my hip and giving a gentle squeeze.

"I think you're right. It might just be an insane idea, but I think it works." He gives a light tap over my hip. "Plus, he pays for the food."

I hold my hand up as he meets me with a high five. "Plus, he pays for the food."

I plan on having Demetri pay for a lot of things, and none of them have to do with a monetary exchange.

Once Gage and I shower and dress, we finally manage to head downstairs. Rain trembles over the windows, thunder shudders through the walls, and somehow this unexpected storm soothes me. Something about it feels familiar, like home, as if with Gage back everything has fallen into place, even the horrible weather.

The thick scent of bacon—the utterly disgusting underlayer of garlic-riddled eggs comes from the kitchen, and it takes everything in me to march in that general direction. My sisters are both at school since West Paragon doesn't get out for another few weeks. Out in the back, I spot Drake and Brielle making their way toward the house, running through the rain with their hands over their heads as if that was enough to shield them from the downpour.

My mother holds Misty while whirling around the kitchen, and Beau holds on to her legs, screaming with glee as if he were on a thrill ride. He giggles incessantly while pecking at Misty's toes with his toy dinosaur.

"I going to eat yo' feet!" he shouts over and over. It's nice to see his language skills are developing. Note to self: buy Misty steel-toed boots for her birthday.

"I'm making a list for Cost Club!" Mom trills in a melodic manner. What's with the operatic revival this morning? "If you need anything, just let me know!"

"Will do!" Bree shouts from the back door, and Tad snarls at both her and Drake as they shake off like a couple of shaggy dogs.

"I need lots of shit." Ethan walks into the room with a serious case of bedhead, his sweats so loose they threaten to fall off. I'm pretty sure nothing could make me yak faster than getting a surprise glimpse of Landon bits and pieces. "Get some of those protein shakes. I'm bulking up. Getting me some muscle on this skeleton." He flexes his bicep, and both Gage and I exchange glances. "Hey—come look at this, dude." He calls Gage over with a wave, and reluctantly he limps over.

Oh gosh. I watch as Gage struggles to get across the room, and my heart weighs heavy with guilt. He wasn't that bad when we came home, was he? I was so excited to see him I might have overlooked a limp or two. It's pretty evident our all night rodeo has taken its toll. Note to self: go easy on your man. A dull ache of a laugh rattles through my chest. Like that will ever happen. I can't get enough of the man candy that is Gage Oliver. He's lucky he can move at all after the aerial acrobatics that went on last night. I'll admit, I might have been a bit more forceful than usual. I couldn't believe he was real, on top of me, below me, beside me, over, under, lusting, thrusting. I couldn't believe it was his very own warm flesh I was touching, sucking—*swallowing*—loving all night long. A part of me still wonders if I'll wake up from this beautiful dream.

Ethan proceeds to show off his nonexistent six-pack while extracting some workout tips from the master—aka my husband. Speaking of masters, I head over to Mom and take Misty from her.

"I have a question." I wrinkle my nose at the glibbery egg white she's swirling with the spatula. "A friend of mine is having a baby, and, well, she's sort of new to Paragon—is there any doctor in particular you'd suggest she use? Perhaps even stay away from?" God, I bet there are all kinds of freaks out there. I've only had a doctor examine that area once in my life, and thankfully, it was a female. I don't even know what I'd do if I had a man staring down at my lady garden, poking around in there no less with ice cold metal objects. God, this is going to be a nightmare either way.

"Oh gosh, yes!" Her eyes light up, and she gives a wild nod as if not only was I wise to ask this very question, but there is no one better to answer it than her—which I totally agree with.

"Great! Who is it?"

"You first." She switches off the stove and takes Misty back, lifting her shirt and pushing the poor kid's head toward a free hanging boob. Her nipple looks as if it's a bruise that's simply trying to slide right off.

God, are they supposed to hang that low? *Can* they hang that low? I've seen my mother's boobs before, but I haven't *seen* seen them. I'm not into inspecting my mother's privates on a regular basis, but right now I'm sort of interested in postbaby anatomy.

"I know what you're thinking." She waves me off, and I follow her to the couch where Emily and Bree gawk over a knitting project Em has been working on for a while now. It vaguely resembles a cactus, green and oddly fat and long. I thought it was a doggie sweater for Sprinkles, but it turns out it's a warmer for Ethan's man parts. I shake my head at the idea once again. I can't even look at it or the nausea comes back full force.

"What am I thinking?" I whisper, hoping to God that Bree and Em don't latch on to this conversation.

Mom gesticulates. "You're thinking, oh, look at my crazy mother still nursing Misty—trying to hold on to her youth!"

Wow, she's spot on! Only I wasn't actually thinking that at the moment. Besides, I'm not sure if she's talking about her youth or my sister's, but truthfully both apply.

"Anyway, on to the gossip!" She jumps a little in her seat when she says it, mashing Misty's face into her flesh unnaturally. "Which one of your friends is knocked up?"

Gage shoots me a look, and I cringe. Geez, I'm pretty sure me blurting out the truth with less than half of our families present isn't going to please him, so I do the right thing—lie.

"You don't know her." I avert my eyes, because for one, Bree and Em are now totally glued to our conversation. Just crap.

"You said she was new to Paragon." Mom gives me a playful shove with her Misty-free hand. "I bet you it's that Laken girl. Isn't it? I really do like her."

"Oh Em Gee!" Brielle says it with a touch of gossip-giddy malice. "Did little Miss Perfect go and accidentally knock herself up? Ha!" She belts out a howl. It's safe to say Bree isn't Laken's biggest fan. "So, now what? She has you doing her dirty work for her? I thought she was oh-so-smart going to Host and everything. *Look at me—I'm a university girl! Living in a university world!*" Bree makes Laken sound like a ridiculous airhead. "*And Skyla Laurel Messenger is my best friend!*" She shoves her finger down her throat and retches.

"Oh, stop. She is *not* knocked up." I know Paragon. It's best to squash these rumors right over their vicious beastly bellies before they ever get started.

Em looks at me with a meticulous level of intrigue. Crap, I bet she's getting one of those freaky premonitions. Emily is a Viden, a people that have drifted down in lineage from Rothello of the Soullennium, one of the big four of the Decision Council right along with my mother. Apparently, he had an earthly indiscretion and spawned an entire line of soothsaying, hippy artist types such as Em. Rothello sold his children and their children's children, like the great father he is, to another demented father—Demetri. Gage was recently crowned their king. It's twisted.

My mother lifts a finger in my direction. "Well, if it was Laken, I was going to give you all my best tips. But I won't do that for just anyone. Tell your friend to visit that free clinic down on Center Street or see her general practitioner. I'm sure she'll make out just fine. People have babies every single day, Skyla. She'll figure it out."

Every single day? Not me. Figure it out? Again, so not me. Free clinic on Center Street—aka STD Central? Ha! So not me.

I give an anxious glance to Gage who's busy entertaining Ethan's fantasy regarding a future on the weight training circuit. Extorting this info from my mother is becoming quite the challenge without telling her the truth. I want all of my mother's so-called best-kept secrets, and I want them right fucking now. I can feel myself getting a little testy. Who knows when Demetri will get around to hosting his stupid summer shindig? My baby needs a doctor asap. *Aw!* I just called it *my baby*. My hand floats to my stomach as I give a dreamy smile, and Bree's eyes enlarge.

"You're right!" I shout to Bree as if she just guessed the answer on a quiz show. "Laken is *totally* knocked up." I cover my mouth for a moment, shocked as hell at what just flew from my lips. "Coop is the dad, of course." Honestly, what good would one lie be without the other? Laken is completely going to freak out, and then, of course, I'll have to confide in her, seeing she is my "bestie." I give a Bree a dirty look for pushing me to the fabricated brink.

Mom rattles on and on about doctors and hospitals, something called a doula, and midwives. I glance back at Gage and note he's holding his phone particularly low, and I see the red light at the tip. He's wisely recording all of this. There's no way I'd ever be able to keep track.

Tad calls her from the hall, and she hops up like a trained circus poodle. My mother would literally jump through fiery hoops for him, and considering they sleep in the same bed, she technically has.

"So, Laken and Coop, huh?" Emily considers this as she plucks baby Ember from under her shirt. Gah! I didn't even realize she was harboring a fugitive in there. I can't believe this is going to be my life in just under a year, doctors and doulas, and pulling babies (singular, of course, no reason to jinx myself at this point) from under my shirt—from between my legs no less.

"Yes, *Laken*," I say, weak. I happened to be in the room when baby Ember was born, and it was a bloody nightmare in the most tragically literal sense. "Are you thinking about more kids?" I look to Em as if somehow her words might have the power to quell my fear of all things maternal. If Em would willingly go through that bloodbath again, then it couldn't be so bad. Right?

"Are you fucking kidding me?"

I jump at the expletive. Emily is sort of Ezrina-esque in her use of the English language. Brevity is king, and, well, expletives don't happen all that often unless, of course, they are abso-fucking-lutely necessary. That can only mean one thing—this is very, very bad.

She helps Ember steady herself on her cute, chunky legs, her arms gripping on to the coffee table for dear life. Ember is Drake's lovechild. Em and Drake had a brief thing while he and Bree were on a break, and, well, the rest is DNA history. Ethan gladly took Em under his wing and under his body once Drake rejected her. I really feel bad for Em. Bedding two Landons in one lifetime is asking a bit much of anyone.

"I'd rather have someone chop off both of my arms and beat me with them then go through that horrific pain again." Em retches. "I'd rather have every single one of my teeth plucked out, and then have a lemon squeezed into my mouth before I ever even think of procreating. I'd rather have a snake crawl up my—"

"Oh, for God's sake, we get it!" I shout, and the room quiets unnaturally.

It takes a few good seconds for Ethan, Drake, and Gage to resume their brilliant conversation on roid rage, and for Tad and my mother to start up their buzzing argument in the hall.

"Bitch, feed me," Ethan croaks, and Em snarls in response.

"I'd leave him if he weren't so damn cute." She gets up and heads to the kitchen.

Bree glides in and grabs me hard by the arm, her eyes pressing into mine as if she were about to demand a ransom.

"You're not fooling me, Oliver." She gives a hard wink when she says it. "I'm your best friend, and I know when you are full of shit, and you are brimming to your eyelids in horse manure. You got knocked up by Dudley while Gage was away, didn't you?"

"What? No!" It's going to be a breeze lying to Brielle because she's so far off base it's ludicrous. "What on earth would make you connect those crazy dots?" And on the bright side, I have no problem lying to Bree. For one, she's the town gossip if ever there was one, and two, she spent the first few years of our friendship under Chloe's control. Our entire relationship is sort of built on a foundation of lies, but I mean that in a good way because at the end of the day she really is my bestie—Laken, too, but I'll never admit that to Bree.

"I heard him talking to someone in the barn. He said now that he's a father there's a newfound responsibility he feels. Something about *Skyla*."

I gasp and try to think of a million different scenarios that could have sponsored that conversation, but come up empty. Marshall doesn't think I'm having his baby, does he? I mean, all those dreams I've been having have been rather racy in nature and most of them recently involved Logan. Regardless, I'm pretty sure sperm don't thrive well in a theoretic environment. Although, this is Marshall we're talking about...Marshall is probably loaded with miracle sperm that can transcend time and dimension and apparently physical vaginas. I shake the thought loose.

God, no, that can't be happening.

"I'll talk to Marshall." Like stat. "But rest assured, this isn't his baby." I slap my hand over my face, and now it's my eyes that are bugging out.

Shit, shit, shit!

"*Aw!*" she mewls in one, loud, dragged-out form of affection. "Congratulations!" she whisper-shouts and dives over me with a hug. "Your secret is safe with me! I promise." She pulls back, and her mouth contorts. Her features crumble as if she's putting the pieces to a very unfortunate puzzle together. "Wait a minute. You and Laken planned this, didn't you? You're having *together* babies. She really is your new bestie." She swats me across the arm, because apparently Bree has no problem hitting a pregnant woman. Chloe and that brawl we had flushes through my mind, and I flush it right back out. "What's the matter, Skyla? You didn't think to ask me to get knocked up so that we could have babies close in age, too? I can just see it now—you and Laken will be doing everything together for the next eighteen years. I bet you these babies are just a means to exclude me further in your life. Well, three can play at that game!" She spikes up and drags Drake toward the back door as if the house were on fire. "Come on"—she bellows—"we've got work to do back home."

"What the hell?" Drake gives a weak attempt at breaking free from her stronghold. "Did we forget something in the tin can?"

"Yes! A brand new baby!"

"Wait!" I call after them. "None of that was true!" Mostly.

Shit. I get up and walk over to Gage, totally exhausted from the bizarre exchange.

Em looks over at us, bored. Her lids hang heavy. A dribble of milk spills down her chin as she shovels in cereal.

"You guys headed to Silent Cove tonight?" she grouses through her next bite.

"What's tonight?" Gage rumbles, and my body adheres to his, just craving his soothing rhythm.

"If it doesn't rain, Logan is hosting a mattress burning."

"A what?" Why does this sound particularly satanic?

"Logan says he needs to torch his mattress and invited everyone down for a party."

"Mattress burning." I nod to Gage. Of course, it sounds satanic. Chloe is involved. "He couldn't keep us away if he tried. In fact, I'll bring the gasoline and matches."

"Cool," she says it unmoved. "I'll bring my notebook. I'm feeling moved to do some drawing."

"Very cool." Ethan scruffs her hair up until it blossoms like a chia pet. "That's what I like about you, babe. You're smart and shit. Draw a picture of us sitting on a stack of hundred dollar bills, would you?"

"It doesn't work like that."

They banter back and forth as I spin into Gage. Emily's visions haven't exactly been that great for me in the past. In fact, they've been sort of scary in a this-is-your-freaky-ass-future kind of way.

Before I can open my mouth to say something to the father of my child, Marshall flits through my mind for no reason.

Mom and Tad barrel into the room.

"Cripes almighty! It's a job, Lizbeth, not a death sentence!" Tad locks his elbows and balls his fists, looking every bit the cartoon version of himself.

"Well, I don't like you gone so often!" she wails back. "You're *my* man—not that blonde, big boobied hussy's!"

I giggle a little because Mom just said "boobied." Her life sort of revolves around the "girls" so it shouldn't come as a surprise to me that she's developed an entire vocabulary for them. And besides, I'm completely on her side. I can't stand Tad's so-called assistant, Isis, Demetri's demented "big boobied" niece. She's a blow-up doll, inflated with nothing but wickedness. Come to think of it, I'm betting a blow-up doll was the prototype Demetri used when creating that vapid vixen.

"What do you want me to do?" he bellows. "*Quit?* Who's going to feed all these mouths, Lizbeth? I've got to keep on trucking."

"Not when trucking means spending the night on the mainland with a blonde, big boobied hussy! It's your choice, Tad Landon! But don't forget. I'm packing, too!" Her blouse flies open, and she flashes him for a lightning quick moment—thankfully with her back turned to the crowded room.

Gah! Perhaps she should have chosen another weapon from her arsenal. My mother's boobs shouldn't be enlisted as lures to keep Tad Landon at home. They've been through enough already.

The room quiets down to nothing as we all wait with bated breath.

I glance to Gage, and in a moment, he's by my side, holding me, his hand warming our growing child.

Why in the hell would my mother give Tad such a harsh ultimatum? Tad has been with Althorpe for as long as we've known him. He has no marketable skills. He's completely useless in this jobless economy. It's almost as if my mother is setting herself up for splitsville.

I suck in a sharp breath.

"Don't answer that!" I jump over to Tad, waving my hand in his face. "Mom has been under a lot of pressure lately." I glare over at her briefly with a look that says *I'm on to you, saggy boobs and all*. "I'm sure given a little time, the two of you could come up with an amicable solution."

"I meant every word," Mom growls from over my shoulder.

Sheesh! I need to stop this Demetri bound train before we accidentally add another Fem to the family—well, other than the one my body is currently engineering.

"How about a compromise?" I give a little hop while looking to Gage for help.

"Yes." Gage steps in. "Tad, why don't you bring your work home? Lots of people work from home. I'm sure if you ask your boss, he'll happily let you spend a few extra hours here rather than the office."

Who the hell gave Tad an office?

"I don't have an office, *Greg*," he barks out the wrong moniker as if it were laden with acid.

Thought so.

Tad staggers toward Gage. "And I still don't have payment for those wise guys I handed off to you at the landing a few months back. You, my gimpy friend, are the reason I have been denied a T-bone dinner!"

"That's a great idea!" I clap like a trained seal. "Invite them to dinner. You know, as an apology for handing them off to the wrong person. Gage and I will buy the food and make a wonderful meal. In fact, invite your boss right along with them." Wait, why would that be a good idea?

"Arson Kragger will not be a guest in this house. As far as I'm concerned, he's just as much a dinner thief as this person standing right in front of me," he rages at Gage. "But"—he walks in a brisk circle—"I like the idea of having the loons I dragged to the island for a night on the Landon town. Maybe if I accidentally leak the fact my idiot boss never made good on his promise, they'll put in a good word for me." He points hard at Gage. "You are going to be a man and grill those steaks to perfection." He pulls his pants up by the belt loops. "Get dressed, Lizbeth. All this talk about steak has made me hungry. We're headed to Cost Club."

"I'll grab my pocketbook!" Mom sings with glee. She's become a Cost Club addict, even going as far as eschewing her couponing ways to pony up for a gallon of mayo.

"No pocketbook needed," he says as they take off out of the room. "If we leave now, we'll make it just in time for the sample fare."

Gage looks to me with a measure of concern. "Who are these people that are coming to dinner, Skyla?"

"I don't know who they are or if they're people, but I'm for damn sure going to find out."

Late in the evening, the moon hangs low over Silent Cove, casting its pale shadow over the water like a splendid, dancing ghost.

A small crowd has already amassed by the shore as lawn chairs are strewn about. At least half a dozen bonfires illuminate the night as people roast hot dogs and marshmallows while their mouths are filled with laughter.

Gage and I come upon Logan, and I don't hesitate to wrap my arms around him. I know he's still hurting, and my heart aches for him to the point of bleeding.

"You throw a party and don't invite your two best friends?" I pull back and give his arm a playful squeeze. "I hope you don't mind, but we've decided to crash."

"Crash away." He gives Gage a light sock to the arm. "You know how it goes. You invite a couple of people—one of them being Brielle—and, before you know it, it's a class reunion."

Gage wraps his arms around me, his hand warming my belly, and Logan's gaze drifts to it momentarily. His affect falls. The joy he held in his eyes a moment ago dissipates to sadness. "I got Dudley in the house." He shakes his head, hitching his thumb toward the back patio. "He and Ezrina are up to no good. Let me get them out here. I'm sure they'll be glad to see you." He jogs back toward White Horse.

"Why do I feel as if we've just been avoided," I say, twisting into Gage.

"Normally I'd disagree, but since he'd rather spend time with Dudley, I'm afraid you're right."

"I still can't believe you're back." The words swim from me dreamily as the fog begins to infiltrate the vicinity as if it were an invited guest. The entire island glows a little brighter with Gage back on Paragon soil.

A sharp howl of a laugh expels from down the beach, and we see the bitch squad with its original fear leader, Chloe.

"This is going to be a long night," I sigh just as I spot Bree heading over to Laken. "Oh shit," I whisper. "Why don't you go in and talk to Logan? I've got a fire of my own to put out."

"Come here." Gage gently pulls my lips to his and offers a kiss that warms me right through the layer of fog sealing over us. "I will be right back."

As Gage heads in, I speed over to Bree. God, I pray I'm not too late.

"Well, look who's here." Laken crosses her arms, the look on her face amused and slightly affronted.

I'm too late.

Laken is beautiful, with her long golden-washed hair, her pale eyes that glow in the night. She and Cooper are the quintessential perfect couple, and I, for one, cannot wait to see them tie the knot in a few weeks. Plus, she might need all the reinforcements, front and center, to make that happen. I can't see her demonic ex, Wesley, going down without a dirty fight.

"I miss anything?" I glare at Bree a moment. Brielle is beautiful, too, with her strawberry-blonde hair, her perennial crooked grin. She's forever up to no good, which is one of the reasons I adore the living hell out of her.

"You didn't miss a thing," Laken is quick to reply. "But *I* did— apparently, my entire first trimester."

"Crap," I say it lower than a whisper.

"The rumors are true, by the way." She offers an exaggerative shrug. "I just hope poor Coop doesn't get wind of it before I can properly surprise him." And now it's her glaring at Bree. "Do you think you can keep your pie hole shut for about five minutes?" She pokes Bree hard in the chest, and I half expect some hair pulling action to quickly ensue. Laken looks back to me. "You might say this news had startled me as well when I first heard it this afternoon." Her eyes harden over mine. Apparently, Bree's good news traveled faster than I thought. "At first, I was very upset, but then I had an epiphany in the shower."

"Eww." Bree glances down at Laken's crotch for no good reason.

"An epiphany is not a bodily function," she says it curt to Bree before turning to me. "I was thinking of Skyla. Why would my best friend...in the whole world"—she drags the words out in an apparent effort to crawl under Brielle's skin, and judging by the jacked-up look on Bree's face, mission accomplished— "make up such a terrible lie about me? I mean, an unplanned pregnancy? Unless, of course, it was simply a cover-up for her own unplanned pregnancy." Her brows rise as she awaits confirmation.

"Wow, she's good," Bree muses. "She totally just busted you." Bree makes a face. "But I'm still onto your little pregnancy pact. I bet Chloe's been in on it since the beginning, too. It's not fair, Skyla. All my best friends are having babies, and nobody thought to clue me in on this little sperm-fest? Well, screw you!" She looks to Laken when she says that last part. I don't really think Bree would have the balls to say something like that to my face. "And screw you, Skyla Messenger! I thought we were better friends."

"Oh, look!" I say, giving Bree a gentle shove toward the bitch squad. "Another expectant mother is here—Chloe! Rumor has it she knows the baby's gender, and she's just about to tattle."

Brielle gives an excited squeal. "I'm going to find out if I'm going to be an uncle or an aunt!" She takes off running, spraying sand at the two of us, but Laken doesn't flinch.

"Really, Skyla? A fake pregnancy?" She shakes her head. "What's the story? Spill it fast. I need to find Cooper before he busts out the cigars. And does Chloe really know what she's having?" She cranes her neck in the witch's general direction, and I block her. Laken might be a little more emotionally vested than necessary in Chloe's child since it's technically Wesley's baby, too. There's no denying Wesley broke her heart in a roundabout way. They had something special, and he ruined it like he ruins everything. Damn Count—*Fem*.

My eyes snag on Gage having a conversation with what looks like himself. Great. Wes is here, too.

"No—I don't know or care if Chloe knows what she's having. Probably a cloven hooved child with horns and a tail." It comes out small and weak, exactly how I feel for spreading such a nasty rumor about Laken to begin with. "I'm sorry about the rumor." I latch on to her as I beg for forgiveness. "I'm so sorry. I swear—my hands were tied. It's me who's having the baby. And my mother was in the room, and I wanted to surprise everyone, and she was holding a very good doctor's name hostage and—"

"Skyla?" She gives my arms a squeeze, her eyes wide and white as flames. "Oh my God! *Skyla*! Congratulations!" She pulls me in tight with her body hard over mine, and I can feel the genuine joy exuding from her. As much as I love Bree, and I do, I know that with Laken all I'll get is support—not some strange inkling that I might be trying to start some baby cult behind her back.

"I'll help you get through this." She pulls back, her eyes glistening with tears. "I want to help you with the factions as well. Let me be there for you. Don't shut me out."

I nod through tears. Laken feels like so much more than a friend—more than a sister.

"Thank you. And I won't shut you out."

"Hey, ladies." Coop is winded, his eyes large with surprise, and it's safe to say he's just a moment away from "busting out the cigars" as Laken put it. Wes jogs up alongside him, and I cringe. Usually in this dim setting, with the Paragon's papery breath swirling thick between us, I would mistake him for Gage, but the way his eyes are glued to Laken— that perennial look of lust mixed with the eternal agony on his face, there isn't a doubt that it's Wesley. Wes and Laken were each other's first loves. She chose the light, and he chose the darkness. They both swore it was true love. I guess even true love has its boundaries.

"Coop." Laken shakes her head, and before another word can fly from her mouth, Wes steps in.

"Laken, is it true?" He's panting, his eyes wild with concern. It's going to kill Wes when this becomes a reality one day. "Are you having Cooper's baby?"

You can feel the weight of his grief. His voice is heavy with sadness. If he's anything like his father, and he is, he'll pine over Laken for the rest of his days. I've seen Demetri pine firsthand for my mother, only my mother rewarded the demon by bearing him a child—Misty. I'm still so unhinged about that I've yet to speak with her about it.

"Wes!" Laken is incredulous. "Is this any of your business?" She softens into him as she wraps her arms around Coop. "I'm marrying this man. I'm taking his name. He will be my family, already is. Cooper and I want at least five children." Coop doesn't flinch when she says it, so it must be true. "If it happened in a few months, it wouldn't really make a difference." She pulls Coop's chin toward her and plants one on him.

Crap. Even I feel sorry for the douche standing here wearing Gage's drop-dead gorgeous face, albeit with a very wounded expression.

"Wow, babe. This is truly a blessing." Coop is brimming. Not sure if he has a clue either way, but he's always been a good sport.

Laken's eyes glint back to her ex. "Say your peace or leave, Wes." There's something different about Laken, about the way she's treating Wesley. Usually, she's a little more careful, a little more cordial, and I wonder if the real reason she's riding the coattails of this pregnancy hearsay is to give him a taste of his own in-the-family-way medicine. As much as she loves Coop with her whole heart, it still knifed her to hear Wes was procreating with Chloe.

Wes lets out a heated breath, a paper dragon with nothing but steam shooting from his nostrils. He's impotent compared to Gage's brilliance in just about every single way.

"I know you love Coop." He offers an anemic smile at his adversary. "And, please believe me when I say this. If it's not me that you're with, I'd rather it be Cooper. We were friends once. I'd like to get there again one day."

Tears come so fast I can't control them.

"But." Coop is unmoved by Wesley's soliloquy, and I let out a little laugh.

"But"—Wesley's chest expands with his next breath, his heavy stare returning to Laken—"you're going to wake up one day and realize that you made a very big mistake. Know this— my arms, my life, my bed will always be open to you."

Arrogant much? And to think he almost had all of my sympathy. Teaches me to mourn for a devil. I blame my hormones. I'm completely off balance, crying one moment, laughing the next.

"Really?" Laken hauls off and slaps him—a nice, loud crackle of a whack—and the crowd around us grows quiet for a few moments before the party atmosphere picks right up again. Laken has the biggest lady balls I have ever seen. I'm taking notes.

"Don't insult me," Laken seethes. "Even if you were to renounce the Countenance, your Fem lineage, we are *through*. Do not offer me your bed in front of my soon-to-be husband ever again. It's offensive to him, and it's offensive to me. The only way Coop and I will ever befriend you is if you step down from the wicked throne you've planted yourself on—help us save the Nephilim, not destroy them. That slap was a wake-up call, Wes. Deep down, I would like to believe you're the same boy I used to know—you're just lost."

"It's true." Coop relaxes with Laken in his arms. "I think you're lost, too, Wes. You're dazzled by all the power. You can't see the forest for the trees. One day *you'll* wake up and realize you made a very big mistake. And when you do, Laken and I will both be here for you, as friends. I miss you, man. Come back from this nightmare. It doesn't have to be this way. This doesn't have to be your legacy."

Wesley swallows hard. His eyes narrow to slits as he soaks in their words.

"I will never renounce who I am." His jaw pops. "I can no sooner remove myself from the Barricade, from my lineage, than I can my body. This is the fabric of my being. I am a Count born of a Fem." He takes a step toward Coop and sticks his finger just shy of Coop's chest. "I will have no mercy on the Nephilim that have removed themselves from my charge. Those outside the Barricade will fight to get in as soon as they realize what they're up against. My ranks will grow, and I predict *you*, my old friend, will be among them." He looks to Laken. "And you will be mine. The prophets have spoken, Laken. I have no doubts about this." He stalks off into the night, his form slowly evaporating until he's faded into the fog like a bad dream.

"Wow, I feel like I should apologize for him." I shudder. "You know—since he looks like Gage and all."

Laken and Coop are still staring at that black hole Wesley left in his wake.

"I think I'll let you guys work things out," I say, backing away. "Oh, and, Laken, do as you wish with that whole rumor thing." Who knew she'd get so darn creative with it?

I take off toward the party and run smack into Marshall and Ezrina having a heated conversation.

"What's this?" I'm almost amused. I don't remember the last time I've heard either of them raise their voices.

"Nothing," Ezrina hisses, her eyes still fixed hard on Marshall's. "I'm off to find Heathcliff." She pulls Marshall in tight by his dress shirt. "Do *not* visit me again. And you most certainly do not visit Clara. Not all of us want the demons from the past parading around Paragon." Ezrina stalks off quickly as the fog swallows her down.

"What was that about?"

"Believe me, Ms. Messenger, you will be the last to know." He speeds toward the street with blatant disregard for my curiosity. Doesn't he know he just added fuel to the curious fire?

"I will find out, you know!" I call after him.

He revs his engine and takes off with the squeal of his tires as they embed themselves into the pavement.

Huh. Wesley is in a rage. Marshall and Ezrina are in a rage. Let me take a wild guess how this night is going to end...

I find Gage down by the water's edge, his arms welcoming me, warming me—most definitely not in a rage.

A giant mattress sits in the middle of the sand with dry brush strewn over it.

Coop helps water it down with gasoline while Logan strikes a match and holds it in the air.

"I want to thank you all for showing up tonight. To old friends, to new friends, and to those I've yet to meet—I cherish you all. Sometimes, it isn't enough to move on from a deep regret; sometimes, you need to watch it burn." He tosses the match, and the bed erupts in an inferno. The deafening roar of the fire shouts Logan's grievance into the night.

Chloe stands just a few feet from Gage with her hand to her throat as the flames dance wild in her eyes. In this shadowed light, I see the outline of her distended belly. Chloe is actually showing, and for some reason, this stuns me. Thank God she was knocked up long before she bedded Logan, or I would have nightmares about this for the rest of my life—plus, a child to look at as a constant reminder of their twisted season together. My heart aches for a moment. I wonder if that's what my baby will be for Logan—a constant reminder.

Gage holds me tight as the bitch squad comes alongside us.

"So, what's up with the bed burning?" Em bleats it out without affect like only Em can.

Lex cuts me the side-eye. "Rumor has it he was bedding some skank because her husband was MIA."

A growl works its way up my throat.

"It's not worth it," Gage whispers.

"Yeah, well"—Chloe blows out a breath as a plume of smoke streams from her nostrils—"I bet his touch was electric. I bet his tongue felt like a fire all on its own while he ran up and down her body, licking every last nook and cranny—drinking her down in all the right places, making her do things for him that require an incredible amount of flexibility. That boy can—"

Logan takes the lighter fuel from Coop and feeds the hungry flames as they rise ever higher, growling over her incessant need to relive her fantasy.

I step in close to Chloe, my eyes never leaving the mesmerizing blaze. "Do you know what people burn, Chloe? Trash. Nobody burns a treasure. It's the garbage they wish to be rid of that they take a match to. But to throw a party? To add fuel to the fire as though the flames can never be enough? This is a special brand of filth he's purging himself of. Logan is purifying his life, deleting you from the hardware of his mind and heart. You are the dross, and this is the refiner's fire. One day you are going to burn, Chloe. And I pray both Logan and I will be there to see it."

Her chest thumps with a silent laugh. "How does it feel to always be left out of the equation, Gage?" Her eyes zero in on mine. "That's okay, Skyla. The Barricade is moving so swiftly, so efficiently, both you and Logan—along with all of your useless minions will soon be eradicated." Her dark eyes shift back to Gage. "And that will leave you to me."

"Never." Gage doesn't hesitate with the answer.

"Soon. I know this, Gage. With this child inside me, I have powers that I never knew existed. I have the gift of knowing. And I know things about you and about me. Suffice it to say I am sleeping a lot better these days. In fact, one can say I am downright happy." A horrific cackle escapes her as she walks toward the fire. Her feet touch down at the base of the blaze, but Chloe doesn't slow down.

"Bishop!" Em calls after her as she edges toward the flames. She tries to snatch her back, but I hook on to Em's sweater and put an end to that good time.

Suicide by fire? I can only wish. Chloe's baby bounces through my mind. And now it's me leaping for her. I'll admit, I felt like shit for beating her senseless, knowing that she's with child, but once I learned she was slithering beneath Logan's sheets, I couldn't help myself.

"Chloe, wait!" I call after her just as she leaps into the flames.

The crowd lights up with a scream, then laughter as soon as we realize Chloe isn't dancing in the fire. To the others it looks like nothing more than a clever party trick. The blaze seemingly swallowed her whole, and she's simply gone.

Chloe has new powers now that she's with child.

I touch my hand to my belly and glare at the flames, willing them to the sky, and a horrific rush ignites before us as the fire rises as tall as a tower, into a violent twisting tornado, leaving the entire population of the party running for higher ground.

Chloe has powers she never knew existed—and so do I.

Gage

Viden Council meets at midnight. Get to the Transfer a few minutes prior to talk shop. We'll head out together.

I stare at Wesley's text a few moments too long, trying to digest it. It's early—that strange time of dawn when the light of the moon and the sun are equal in strength. I'm glad to say it wasn't Wesley's early morning wake-up text that roused me out of my dreams—more like nightmares. Every night it's been the same one, me falling to my supposed death from Devil's Peak. It's as if my mind is reaching, as if there is some message in there that my brain is stubbornly holding on to but refuses to release. It's as if it's protecting me, taunting me, *both*. But no, it's not Wes who pulled me out of my nocturnal state—it's the woman I love, whose wet kisses currently stream up and down my neck. Her tiny body has crawled on top of mine, and she's working me with her soft form, her smooth thighs riding over my sides.

"Someone is very hungry for breakfast," I tease. Skyla has her first doctor's appointment later this afternoon, and I'm more than a little excited. I'm dying for any news about the baby—to hear its beating heart. I'm like a kid on Christmas, and Skyla is giving me the greatest gift.

Her chest rattles with a laugh. "I'll take my Gage sunny side up." She lands a wet kiss to my ear. "Upside down." Her lips rake over my stubbled cheek. "Sideways." Skyla drags her tongue along my jawline. "Backwards." Her teeth graze the ridge of my chin. "Oh, wait." She slaps her hands over my chest and sits up. Her bare bottom misses being impaled by less than an inch. "Going back door is exactly how we got into this mess." She rains her hair over me and lands a biting kiss over my lips. "You do realize it's as much Brielle's fault as it is Ellis's. All that *you two are so vanilla* crap." She slaps my chest harder this time and barks out a short-lived laugh. "And we fell for it! Hook, line, and penis!" Skyla rolls her head back and closes her eyes. "I'm sorry." She grinds her hips into me. "I've just been all over the place lately. One second I'm up, the next I'm down. I'm laughing, I'm crying, I'm jumping into a fire after Chloe—actually, and thankfully, I'm not that insane."

"You did try to stop her. Even I thought that was erratic."

"You're the one with the heart, Gage. I'm shocked you didn't try to pluck her out. Besides, I did it for Wes Junior. Chloe is a python who should never have been allowed to breed. She's horrid. She's vile. She is absolutely sickening." Her chest expands with her next breath. "I think she actually got off on that whole bed burning thing." Her eyes widen the size of baseballs. "I just had an epiphany."

"We need a code word."

"We need a code word." She holds up her hand, and I offer a high five. "Great minds!"

"How about forever? That's how long I'm going to love you." I slip my hand high up on her thigh.

"Love it." She gives a light bounce over my hips. "But knowing that monster, she'll crack it. How about Celestra blue? I'm a Celestra, and your eyes are too beautiful. God, I hope our baby has your eyes, and your dimples, and your full, gorgeous lips." Her cool fingertips float over my face.

"Celestra blue—sounds good to me. How about we tack on forever to the end of that?"

"Love it." Skyla leans in, her tits falling over my chest, heavier, fuller than usual, and I smile into our kiss. My hands float up to her stomach, and I can feel her abdomen just slightly raised. Skyla has always had a flat, concaved, in fact, stomach. Soon, her body will change. Our baby will grow, and before we know it, we'll hold that beautiful being in our arms.

She pulls back, her eyes slightly glossed as she gets that high look right before we get down to business.

"That was beautiful, Gage." She places her hand over mine as we both hover over the spot where our child incubates, nestled deep inside Skyla, nestled safe in our love. For a brief moment, I forgot that Skyla has the capability to read my thoughts when we touch. As if it were a knee-jerk reaction, that wall of static goes up without any real effort on my part. I've kept Skyla at bay for so long that it's become a natural defense, and we both share a small laugh.

"Sorry. I can't help it." I seem to have less control over it now that I've been demoted to human. "Wes wants to talk about the Videns later today. I'm just being honest." I hold up my hands a moment as if testifying. "I'm going to do it. I want to tell them to shove the Videns up their asses for all I care. I'm done. I'm out." I swallow hard. "And I need to talk to Demetri, first about the party, and second, I want to thank him for that damn cane. I'm not sure what it's infused with, but it takes away the ache. Sometimes, the pain is so unbearable I'd gladly defer to a Fem walking stick than suffer." I wince. "Don't shoot me."

"I'm not shooting you." She glides off, and her hand drifts down to my happy-to-see-you command center. Skyla glides her hand up and down my cock, a lazy smile budding on her lips. "I'm most certainly not going to add to any of your pain."

"Are you kidding? You weigh less than a bag of chips." I twist around until I'm straddling her. "There is no way in hell I'm not taking advantage of the next few condom-free months. I'm not missing this." I enter her a little rougher than necessary, greedy as hell, watching as she bites down hard over her lip, her head bows back with pleasure. "And neither are you."

Skyla and I start in with the pulling, tugging, a wrestling match of a love-making session that says *I love you, I've missed you, I'm going to punish you with my body for all of the misery you've given me*—her words to me last night. We make love far longer than any human should be able to withstand, so in that respect, I'm thankful my genetics are still strong. I bury my face in her newly plump chest, bury my lips down in that intimate part of her that seems perennially wet and waiting for me. Her fingernails hook into my shoulders as she hits her climax, and I wait for the eviction before my mouth leaves that sweet spot. My body spears into hers, easy because there's an occupant in there now that I don't want to rattle. Her body is still as tight as the very first time. I come long and deep, my entire body shaking with a heightened sense of nirvana. Skyla has always felt like family, like my wife long before we were ever married, but now with our baby knitting inside her womb, we've moved on to some extraordinary plane, our bond that much deeper than my heart could have imagined.

My lids flutter open. My body is still buried in hers, my chest crushing her just enough. I love the feeling of her beating against mine once we're through, one violent knock after another like a tennis ball hitting a wall over and over.

The room is significantly darker, the air tinged blue, and then I see we're no longer in bed at all—we're in the butterfly room.

"Shit." I pull up on my elbows and take a good look around to make sure I'm not hallucinating.

"Now it's my turn to say sorry." She shrinks a little, and I fall out of her. "I was thinking about how much I missed you holding me here. How I missed being with you in this room. I know your back can't take it. Anyway"—she gives the room a circular glance—"but now here we are."

"You did this?" My heart drums hard as if some tribal ritual were about to get underway, in which we all die a horrible death by way of teleportation. I'm probably not far off base. "Skyla, you think—"

"The baby." She nods. "I have powers, Gage. I'm able to do things that I never imagined. This is something more than Levatio, Gage. Our baby—" her voice crumbles as her lips press tight.

"Shh." I hold her to me, rocking her steady.

Skyla is amassing powers. She's taken on the skills of our unborn child, who is smaller than a thumbnail.

And now I have something new to ask. Yet another in a long string of questions for that demented father of mine.

And not for a minute do I believe he will give me the truth.

"Let's go out for breakfast. My treat. I've got some spare change burning a hole in my pocket." I try to coax Skyla out the door as soon as we hit the bottom of the stairs, but instead of answering, she leans against the railing and expels a deep horrific groan.

"Can't." She heaves, her eyes squinting in pain. "Please don't mention food to me again."

"It's morning sickness, isn't it?" A very twisted part of me is excited about this on some level. Although, I wish it was me who was riddled with the urge to vomit and not Skyla—never Skyla.

"Yeah. It kind of hit me upstairs while we were—" She wiggles her fingers. "I think it's more like motion sickness." She bites her lip and mouths the word *sorry*.

"Let's get you some water."

We head to the kitchen. The heavy scent of breakfast that usually permeates this place has all but dissipated. Skyla and I lounged in bed until almost noon. Her prenatal appointment isn't for another hour and a half, and I'm secretly counting down the minutes.

Tad and Lizbeth are at the table arguing over a pile of mail. I help Skyla take a seat next to Emily as I get her a water bottle from the fridge.

"We need a racket!" Tad shouts, fisting the bills in his hands and shaking them. "If this keeps up, we're going to miss a mortgage payment, and I can't miss a single payment, Lizbeth. They take your damn house after three!"

"Would you hush?" She tries desperately to coax him to a whisper just as Ethan sits down at the bar.

"Just fucking sue someone," he grunts over his cereal. "Get yourselves down to the grocery store and turn aisle five into a slip and slide. You'll be rolling in dough all the way home."

I give Skyla a wary look as I hand her a drink.

"Do *not* turn aisle five into a freaking slip and slide!" she shouts before guzzling half the bottle. "Oh, wow, that's better," she whispers, her eyes closed as she sighs with relief.

Tad grunts, "They don't pay out like they used to. These national chains have insurance up the wazoo. In the good old days, if you took a tumble like that, they'd take you to the back room and shove a fistful of cash in your hand and tell you to never show your smarmy face again." He gives a wistful smile as if relieving a memory, and I'm sure he is. "Papa Landon hit all the local markets back in the day. He was a man you could really look up to."

"Maybe we should go," Skyla whispers. "I wouldn't want Celestra Blue to pick up on any nasty habits." She bites down on a smile as if relishing our secret.

My brows dip. I sort of like the fact she just referred to our child as Celestra Blue. It looks as if Skyla and I will need more code words than the FBI these days. I love it. Love her.

"You can't go anywhere." Em grips the edge of the sofa. Her breathing becomes erratic as if she's about to be sick herself. "I have a message. I need paper. Somebody get me some fucking paper!" she belts it out, and Ethan springs into action.

I glance over at Tad and Lizbeth, but they're too absorbed in their financial misery to care about any roving expletives.

Ethan comes back with a Post-it note and a crayon.

"What the hell is this, you fucktard?" Her head snaps back as she lets out a riotous groan. Em jumps up and runs to the back patio. Skyla and I try to rush out after her, my hip nearly falling out of its socket in the process, but Em zips back in with two handfuls of something dark and lumpy.

"What the hell?" Ethan plucks one out of her grasp. "Is this fucking charcoal?"

Em doesn't answer, just goes about her business like a woman possessed. She glides the china hutch down to the other end of the room with her hip until a bare white canvas of a wall appears behind it.

"What in tarnation is she doing?" Tad calls out, but nobody moves, and nobody says a thing, because face it, this is Em. Nobody truly knows what the hell she's doing.

She starts in with both hands, drawing, sketching over the white blank surface, and everyone in the room gasps at the defacement taking place.

Skyla gives me a nervous look before edging toward Em and her frenetic movements. "You really don't have to do this."

"Darn right, you don't!" Tad leaps over, causing Ethan to hold him back as if he were restraining him from a fistfight. "Let go, son." He struggles to break free. "You're holding back the wrong person, you moron! What the hell is going on around here?"

"Emily doesn't like the color of the walls." Skyla looks to me for help.

"Yeah—she's thinking about getting into decorating." Shit. "She really wants Ethan's support." I shrug over at Ethan. He and Drake are pretty close in both age and features, but Ethan is a little more aloof if that's at all possible.

"That's right," Ethan grumbles as if pissed that he's forced to play along. "She thought it might need a fresh coat of paint."

The veins bulge in the side of Tad's neck. "Well, it sure as hell needs it now!"

"Okay, honey, that's enough!" Lizbeth calls out to Em while gathering the children off the floor as if snatching them from a mad woman.

"Here." I take Beau Geste from her. "Hey—what's up, little guy?" I whisper as we watch Em with awe and trepidation.

Drake and Bree walk in, and they both let out a riotous caw.

"What the fuck?" Drake shouts, partial amusement in his tone. "Dude, she is batshit."

Em spears them with a look. "I need lipstick, stat!"

"I'm on it!" Brielle cries, digging through her purse while Skyla bolts to the bathroom down the hall. Both offer up a bright red tube at the very same time, and Emily swiftly snatches them away, continuing her hostile makeover of the Landon living room. The wall darkens with an entire body of movement. Squiggles, lines, shapes of people, of things emerge. An entire forest of ideas takes over the wall from floor to ceiling.

Holy shit. I don't think I've ever witnessed an event quite like this. The walls fill with color, black intermarried with blood red. Emily's body zips back and forth so fast, I swear, she's becoming a blur, the diagram itself still too crude to decipher.

"So—um—what color do you think we should paint it?" Lizbeth asks while keeping her gaze morbidly dialed into Em's psychotic drawing.

"I'm thinking padded walls will work best." Tad frees himself from Ethan's grip and storms out of the room. "Call me when the nightmare is over!"

The slam of the front door signifies his departure, and Skyla shudders as if she's the next to bolt out the door.

"There." Em staggers back, her face dripping with sweat, her hair perfectly round like a pompom. "It's yours, Messenger." She takes Ember from Lizbeth without an apology.

"I think you do good work." Skyla's mother seems only vaguely irritated. "*Say*—do you think you can hit a few walls in my bedroom? Tad hasn't painted since we bought the house, and it's the most God awful shade of green."

"Sure. How about a PB and J sammy, and I'll get it done for you this afternoon?"

"One PB and J sammy coming up!" Lizbeth sings her way to the kitchen. "And I'll cut the crusts off, too!"

"What the hell is this?" Skyla and I take a step back, and then it appears at once like some bad optical illusion painting—a foreground background mindfuck that you stare at until it comes into focus, and we both react to it at the same time.

"Oh my God." Skyla buries her head in my chest.

Staining the wall before us is a hideous beast, a snake of some sort with wings that sits under a deep well of dark clouds with its talons perched over the globe of the Earth.

"It's a three-headed serpent," I whisper. And behind it are enormous wings with detailed images in each and every feather where a million other pictures emerge.

"It's a dragon with three heads," Brielle says it plain. "The first head is breathing fire." She traces just shy of it with her finger. "The second head is asleep." She pretends to pat it. "Aw, sleep tight, you little bugger! And the third one looks as if it's screaming bloody murder."

"It looks like it's in agony." Skyla pulls out her phone and begins a paparazzi-worthy snapping session. "Em, what is this?"

"I couldn't care less," Drake announces, plucking Ethan to the side. "Dude, I've got an opening in the company. A real shitload of money to be made, you in?"

My stomach pinches. I wouldn't have minded if Drake asked me to join him in making "a shitload of money." Right about now, both Skyla and I could use a serious infusion to our bank account. I believe our account total is running in the negatives.

"Is this my future?" Skyla asks breathlessly while trying to make sense of the disaster-piece.

"Yup," Em says matter-of-factly. "I'm not an interpreter or anything, but I think it's pretty obvious."

Skyla's eyes enlarge with rage. Right now it looks as if the only thing stopping her from clocking Em is that baby she's holding.

"What's obvious, Em? I'm a fucking blonde. Spill!"

Skyla did mention she's been moody—a testament to the fact her hormones are all over the place.

"Okay, geez, I might be wrong, but I kept getting a family vibe. Like maybe these are the kids you'll have one day with Gage." She shrugs as if it were no big deal, as if they were looking at the menu at the bowling alley trying to decide between hot dogs or pizza.

"My kids?" Skyla takes a wobbly step forward. "Three kids." Her chest huffs with a dull laugh, and I wrap my arms around her. "We're going to have three kids, Gage," she whispers, burying a quick kiss of relief on my neck. "That means I'm going to have you with me for a very long time."

"Yes, you will." I want to add *I promise*, but I know better.

My eyes drift back to that demonic image, our frightening family portrait that has brought my sweet wife to tears. Our three-headed child who looks as if it belongs right up there with

Cerberus, the fire-breathing dragon, the sleeping serpent, the anguished one. They sit on the world as if it is their own dominion, and knowing my father, it most certainly is.

"Look at the wings!" Bree marvels.

The charcoal veining bleeds out, spanning the girth of those enormous, powerful wings turning them a—

"Celestra blue." Skyla swallows hard. "They're butterfly wings."

"A serpentine butterfly." My gut sinks. Skyla and I have created a new breed of species.

Great. Just great.

"They're going to be beautiful." She buries her head in my chest, and tears soak my T-shirt.

"Yes." I kiss the top of her head. "They will be."

"Three kids," Skyla marvels as we drive out to the West Side Medical Building adjacent to Paragon's only hospital. It's almost go time at the doctor's office, and my heart is racing at the prospect of it. This appointment makes it real, *official*. Truth is, I'm dying to get inside. "This is the type of knowledge we can use to our advantage." Her eyes grow big and wild. I've seen this look before—she's determined. "We'll space them out. We won't have the last one for a good long while. That way—" She sinks in her seat, pulling her flannel over her lips. Her eyes close as she gives a soft moan.

"Is it bad?" I park under the shade of an oak that's lifting concrete with its roots and roll down the windows. I know what Skyla was going to say before her nausea cut in. That way we can keep me around for years to come by putting off our final child. It's very sweet that she's fixated on holding off my expiration date. I've always known that my time would be cut short on this planet. I guess you could say I've come to terms with the idea a while ago, but now that Skyla is my wife, that the baby is on the way, I want to do anything I can to keep my exit from sneaking up on me. I want to stay. It's simple math. I want to be where Skyla and the baby are.

Skyla groans twice as hard, writhing from side to side as I unhitch her seatbelt.

"Here." I hand her a water bottle, and she pushes it away.

"I can't do this, Gage. I don't know how I'm going to walk into that building. Do you think it's safe to teleport us?"

"Sorry." I give a brief glance around. "Too many witnesses."

She lets out another hard groan.

"Let me carry you." I open the door, and an anguished cry comes from her.

"*No*—I'll pull it together. Just give me a minute."

It takes twenty minutes to get to the elevator—that's with us stopping under every tree just praying the nausea lets up a bit.

"I can't believe anyone would voluntarily do this to themselves on a repeated basis," she whimpers into my shoulder as we finally make our way into the office.

"I think once the baby comes, they forget all about the pain. At least that's what I hear."

"It sounds like a bunch of BS." We share a simple laugh before filling out a mountain of paperwork. Skyla leans against me in the waiting room, eyeing the distended bellies of each of the dozens of women around us. Most are young with their tight-fitted shirts and yoga pants, their contouring dresses proudly displaying their baby bumps. Others are middle-aged, the Lizbeth sect, happy to have a baby in their body at their mature stage in life. I know Lizbeth had to go to medical extremes to have her latest child, Misty. And, apparently when those didn't work, Skyla is certain she went to alarming extremes by calling on my father to save the day. It's one of the topics of conversation I plan on bringing up to him the next time we meet. That and the party, along with about six million questions all pertaining to the fact I was dead and now I'm alive. Yes, you can say that the questions are piling up for my demonic father. Never was I looking forward to speaking with him more.

"Skyla Oliver?" the nurse calls out, and we follow her to a back room where Skyla is asked to pee in a cup, then disrobe and put on a paper gown. I sit patiently by her side as we wait for the doctor to come in.

She pokes her feet into the stirrups and lies back, spread eagle, biting her lip at me. It looks degrading, uncomfortable, and I can't believe in this day and age that is the position all women assume when waiting for an exam.

"I take it you're feeling better."

"Only enough to flirt with you." She wrinkles her nose. "I'm really nervous about this. Rumor has it this doctor is drop-dead gorgeous—and by rumor, I mean Bree." Skyla looks as if she's about to be sick, literally this time.

"What?" I pull a couple of paper towels out of the dispenser and hand them to her in the event this isn't a drill.

"You heard me." She sits up on her elbows as the gown splits open in the front, and I can see her beautiful tits peeking out at me.

"Well, I'll try not to flirt with her." I give a quick wink.

"Excuse me?" She gives a light smack to my arm. Her mouth fills with laughter, and something in me loosens. I needed to see her smile, hear her beautiful laugh. This is all too serious. She's been way too sick. I need us to feel in control again, even if it's over something as ridiculous as a laugh.

"She is a *he*, Gage. And *he* is rumored to be divine." She shrugs a little and mouths the word *sorry*.

A dude? "Oh shit."

"Yes, oh shit. And he's going to stick his head and his hand in my—"

The door swings open, and, swear to God, I feel like I might pass out and simultaneously punch the guy who's about to walk into the room. My blood pressure spikes, and I'm blind with rage. For a split second, I think Skyla might be messing with me, trying to get me worked up, and meanwhile in will walk a beautiful woman or a sickly, hairy man sporting a bad spray tan.

But he's not a gorgeous woman or a sickly orange man.

"Skyla Oliver?" Shit. "Hello!" In walks an over-cheery, white teeth gleaming, fake bake, roid rage muscles bulging from his dress shirt, stethoscope swinging questionable MD. He can't be serious. "Nice to meet you both. I'm Dr. Baxter!"

He extends his hand to me first, his teeth moving in one solid marble clump. Plastic is the best way to describe him—from his sunburnt smile to his over-dyed hair. I can see the gray roots coming in at the temples. He's not fooling anyone.

Where the hell did they dig up this guy? The Hollywood extras discard pile?

"Skyla, how are you feeling?" He sits down, eye level with her parted knees, and now I'm sorry she ever put her legs in those stirrups.

"Not so good. I've been really sick."

"I'll have Janice give you a list of natural remedies. I like to see if we can settle things the homeopathic way before delving into anything too serious. The baby's best interest always comes first."

A nurse walks in and quietly hands him a tray. He sits back and gloves up like he's about to perform surgery. His chair glides between Skyla's feet, and he scoots in so close her gown sheaths half of his face.

Shit. I think I'd rather be anywhere but here right about now—not entirely true for obvious reasons, but a serious thought nonetheless.

Skyla reaches over and takes my hand, and I stand up next to her.

There's a gleam in his eyes as he hand selects from a tray of torturous looking instruments that look like they belong to Ezrina.

"This might feel uncomfortable." He chooses a metal speculum from the tray and pulls it down toward her body, past the curtain her paper gown is inadvertently creating. "I'm going to enter you now." Just fuck. "This might feel cold." My stomach clenches. Every muscle in my body demands I rip his head off. Only I can't see his head because he buried it between my wife's fucking legs. "I'm opening you now."

I'm going to open his skull in about five seconds!

"*Ouch.*" Skyla flinches and gives me a tight squeeze.

"Careful down there." I try to sound light, but it comes out like a threat.

He doesn't take his eyes off the area he's spent his entire medical education specializing in. It makes me sick that my wife's vagina is on full display for this pervert.

"I'm pulling out now." He holds up the metal speculum for me to view, a shallow grin blooming on his sick-as-fuck face. Okay, so I'm getting a little heated, but I don't appreciate another dude touching my wife, and the fact I'm witness to it isn't helping. I don't care how many scholastic degrees this guy has after his name. I don't want his filthy hands on my wife—or *in* her. "Okay, Skyla." He gives her thigh a quick rub while looking deep into her eyes, and my body starts to shake. "Now I'm going to put my hand inside you." He spreads his fingers wide in the air for show.

Shitfuckshitfuck.

Sure enough, his entire damn arm disappears under her gown, leaving Skyla wincing and squirming. I glance to the nurse who looks away uncomfortably, but Dr. Baxter's lids hood over. His eyes oscillate as if he were at the height of pleasure, and I want to decapitate the son of a bitch.

Shit. I'm about to throw this dude out the fucking window. Shove *my* arm down *his* ass. He is not getting away with this crap. I'm calling the authorities and turning his ass in. He's a fucking pervert. This is just a cover to feel up hot girls.

"Now"—he rises from beneath her gown, his eyes glossy as if he were suddenly stoned—"I'm going to insert my finger into your rectum."

"Oh my *God*," I huff under my breath. My entire body goes rigid.

His torso disappears under her gown. Where the fuck is his body?

"There we go." His voice sounds far away and hollow like he's speaking from the inside of a vagina bowl.

Is this guy serious? Is this the sodomy that goes on in places like this, or is this dude getting off by way of hand fucking my wife?

"Relax, Gage," Skyla whispers, her face still slightly strained. "I can hear you," she practically mouths the words.

"Right." Crap.

The not-so good doctor emerges, red-faced, gasping for air as if he were momentarily submerged.

"Beautiful," he purrs. "Everything is *perfect*."

Steam—I've got fucking steam coming from my ears.

"Now for the fun part!" He flicks off his gloves and replaces them with a clean set. "Janice, dim the lights. It's time to set the mood." He waggles his brows, and I'm about to lose my ever-loving shit. If that crude molestation is his cold-call, I'd hate to see his warm-up.

He hums a little ditty.

Great. Now he gets romantic.

The room darkens to pitch-black, and he turns a computer monitor toward us.

"We're going to see and listen to the baby."

"Oh my God!" Skyla shrieks, and for a second, I'm about to play defense because I'm half-afraid he's penetrating my wife again. "I can't believe this! Am I going to get one of those cute black and white pictures to take home, too? My mom has dozens of them plastered all over the fridge."

"Anything your pretty little heart desires." His teeth glow in the dark as he says it. But all I heard was *Anything your pretty little pussy desires!*

Knew it. He's fucking flirting with her.

Skyla gives my hand a yank that suggests I behave.

He gives a pleasurable growl. I'm betting he cut the lights so he could toss off to the memory of dipping into my wife. And I can't see shit to quantify this.

"What's going on down there?" Again trying to sound light, again failing miserably.

"I need to make sure I see everything as clear as possible," he assures.

Shit. I bet he's recording all of this on his phone. Skyla's privates will go viral by midnight.

"*Gage,*" Skyla sings my name, and, surprisingly, sounds just like her mother in the process. "*Gage!*" she hisses it out so fast, both the demented doctor and his silent sidekick bless her.
I apologize. You do not sound like your mother.
Dr. Dick gives a deep moan. If I see him shake off to completion, he'll soon be Dr. Dickless.
"I'm afraid I'm going to have to use the internal wand." He feigns a look of disappointment.
Why do I get the feeling this guy is going to pull the "internal wand" from his boxers?
"I prefer a transvaginal view at this early stage of the game," he continues. If he dons a pair of goggles and says he's going in, I'll pummel him. "Although, according to the chart, your last period was March eighth. You'll soon be exiting your first trimester. We do encourage women to come in as soon as they think they might be expecting." He turns to his nurse while adjusting his belt. "I'll be needing a condom for the internal."
Knew it. "Wait one fucking minute!" I bark.
The whites of every eye in the room glint in my direction as the pervert breaks out into a slow laugh.
"Oh my. You first-time fathers are a barrel full of monkeys, aren't you?" He tears open the condom and rolls it onto a long, plastic—for lack of a better word, *wand*. "This is all different to you. I can't blame you one bit in the least. Everything is so new the first time around." He shakes the wand in my direction with a cajoling laugh. "Behave this way again, and I'll make sure security finds you."
His vague threat runs right past my ears. The truth is, I'm still stuck on the word *father*. I'm going to be a father—somebody's father, and eventually, one day, three somebodies' father. My entire body goes numb with shock, and half of what this life-size Ken doll says, while probing my wife's vagina with the condom on a stick, goes right over my head. The monitor lights up, and the room fills with rhythmic static.
"Hear that?" He holds up a finger, and I try hard not to smack it before he sticks it into one of Skyla's orifices in the name of Western medicine. "It sounds like a baseball bat

cutting through the air on a loop. *That* is your baby's heartbeat. Although—" He sticks his face close to the screen, his hand maneuvering the wand he's probing her with, twisting his wrist like it was some video game controller.

"*What is it?*" Skyla and I say in unison, and she gives my hand another squeeze.

"What?" Skyla cries as if she's in anguish, and if the fact half of his arm is missing were any indication, I'd say this space invader has finally caused some bodily harm.

"It seems"—he leans in further until the front of his bouffant hairdo touches the screen—"do multiples run in your family, Skyla?"

"Multiples?"

What the hell is he talking about? Swear to God, if he's hinting at orgasms—

"Twins." He gives a Cheshire cat's grin.

"*What?*" Skyla and I belt it out together again like some macabre choir.

"Actually"—he looks to the screen slightly confused—"in your case, triplets."

"Oh God." Skyla thumps back onto the table, and I lose my grip on her as the room starts to sway.

He's fucking with us. I've pissed him off, and now he's fucking with us.

"Now"—he pulls out the glistening wand and points as if it were some extension of his hand—"They're fraternal—meaning they each have their own sack and won't be identical, but I have to ask. Did you come to this naturally? Although, not entirely unheard of, triplets are still a rarity."

"Oh, believe you me"—Skyla hikes back up on her elbows with a glazed look in her eyes that I haven't seen before, some strange combination of elation and anger—"there is not one natural thing about the way I conceived." She mutters Demetri's name under her breath along with Ellis's, and she might have thrown Chloe's and Wes's in there for good measure.

"It was completely natural," I assure. Supernatural.

"Nevertheless"—he points to the darkened screen with its charcoal images flashing in and out of focus—"here is baby number one."

"*Oh my God*," Skyla and I say it together. This time it's in awe, nothing short of a God-breathed miracle we're experiencing.

"It has a perfect little head." She sniffles. I kneel in until my cheek is close to Skyla's as we stare at the screen in wonder. The tiny being on the screen has a perfect human form, tiny limbs, a slightly larger head and belly.

"Is it sucking its thumb?" I ask.

The doctor nods into the screen. "I'd say yes."

I'm done. I've melted, fallen into a puddle of love, and I never want to get up.

"We did that," I whisper to her. Skyla and I have created a perfect little being—dear God Almighty—three of them.

"Baby number two." He moves to another small sac, and the image of yet another perfect child emerges. "And last, but not least, baby number three."

"They're so beautiful." Tears stream down both Skyla's face and mine. Here we are, our eyes feasted upon our children—*children*—for the very first time. Tiny glowing beings with perfectly formed everything, moving lethargically as we watch from this technological vantage point.

"It looks like you have a due date of December thirteenth," he announces victoriously as if he just discovered the answer to some difficult to solve crossword puzzle.

Skyla sucks in a breath and holds it.

"What's wrong?" I gently turn her chin toward me, and then I see it in her eyes. Logan. December thirteenth. Of course, this year that day would have been their second wedding anniversary. "We don't need to tell him. We can change it a day or so."

"No." She fans her fingers through the air as if it were useless trying to fight it. "We'll tell him. No more lies."

No more lies, just another dagger through his heart. I hate that Logan and I take turns killing each other by loving Skyla.

Dr. Baxter and the nurse leave the room, and I help Skyla with her clothes, but in no way have we come back down to Earth.

"Parents." I pull Skyla in, my lips searing over hers. "We're going to be parents."

"We already are." Her lips quiver, the tears flow like an open faucet. "Times three." Her voice breaks when she says it.

Three. Emily's prediction wasn't some far-off future event she was trying to decipher. It was for today, this season of our lives. Skyla and I would have all of our kids in one shot.

Her cool fingers wipe a tear from my own eye that I didn't even realize I shed.

"I'm going to make sure you're here with me for a very long time, Gage. Three kids." She shakes her head. "I'll never survive without you."

Three kids. For the first time, I feel completely against the idea of my early demise. I want to live to that promised ripe old age I once predicted for Skyla and Logan—Logan, who is factually dead but here in a Treble. A hollow, sad laugh tries to buck through me. Dear God, I do not want a Treble. No offense to the forces that be that provided it to Logan, but I want life blood pumping through my veins—a real beating heart. I want to be a part of the blueprint, not a ghost in the flesh. I'm not feeling so generous toward Logan anymore. Skyla and I aren't just dating, aren't simply husband and wife, a family of two. We've upgraded to five in the blink of an eye, and I want to make sure that number stays right where it is.

"I'll be here for you and the kids, Skyla, until you're old and gray." I can feel the impossibility begging to jump from my throat so I give in. "I promise."

Now to make that happen.

Skyla and I hit the Burger Shack on the way home, then I settle her in bed before heading out on a few errands, all of which concern my own biological father.

Demetri's haunted estate sits crooked on a hillside not six miles from where I grew up. It doesn't surprise me. My brother and I have been his pet projects for some time, although who knows how many siblings I might have running around this planet.

I don't bother to knock, just let myself in.

"Yo, Pops!" I shout sarcastically. Not that it matters. Any attempt at humor is lost on the demonic coot. The scent of something familiar baking in the oven catches me off guard, and this alarms me for two reasons—one, I've only ever smelled this vanilla cinnamon goodness from the Landon home. And two, I seriously doubt Demetri is swapping recipes with Lizbeth.

"Son!" Demetri materializes from the stairwell, his body coming into full form as he touches down in the foyer. "You've come for a visit."

"Not quite."

A pair of heels click-clack in this direction, and the sound of a baby fussing lights up the room.

Lizbeth bursts in from the direction of the kitchen with little Misty squirming in her arms.

"Oh." She takes a step back as we examine one another with a vague look of shock, although nothing, and I mean nothing, can shock me more than I've already been shocked today. I've met a lifetime quota of surprises in the span of thirty seconds this afternoon. "You're here." Her affect falls flat at the sight of me. Not something I'm used to with my mother-in-law. "Is Skyla here, too?" She glances nervously past my shoulder.

"No. She's not feeling well. She's resting back at the house."

Lizbeth Landon is dressed to the nines with a skirt that sits uncomfortably too high above her knee, black kitten heels, and a skin-tight sweater. What the heck? Is she trying to seduce him?

Demetri takes Misty into his arms. "There, there." He rocks her back and forth, and she immediately settles down.

"Dada!" she coos as she plucks at his chin.

"Oh!" Lizbeth's face lights up neon red like the butt of a cigarette. "Goodness! Well, she just calls every man that these days." She waves a hand in my direction.

I've held Misty dozens of times. I'd venture to say more times than Tad himself, and she's never once called me that—or him for that matter. My gut boils because it just confirms Skyla's theory.

"I was just baking some cookies." Lizbeth's face fills with color.

Why do I suddenly feel like I'm intruding?

Little Misty gives a giggle and a wave in my direction, and my stomach sours. Crap. Lizbeth Landon is a cheat, and that baby is tangible proof of her infidelity. I knew this. Skyla told me herself, but something about seeing them in action, or at least as close as I ever want to get, makes me want to vomit on my shoes.

"What can I do for you? Is everything okay?" Demetri's eyes press hard into mine. He knows about Skyla's condition. Hell, we talked about it.

"Yeah. Skyla and I were just wondering what weekend you were thinking of throwing that kickoff to summer shindig you've been known to host."

"A party! Yes!" Lizbeth jumps an inch in her heels and almost eats it on the slick marble floor. "Why, we were just about to schedule that. I'm his official party planning hostess, you know." She nods in heavy anticipation of my agreement so I give a stiff nod back.

"Week after next." He's studying me, smiling with those dangerous, cunning eyes that only know evil. "Lizbeth will fill you in on the details."

"Sounds good." I head for the door.

"Wesley is expecting you tonight for dinner."

I turn back, sickened by the sight of the three of them playing the part of happy little nuclear family.

"And what will he be serving?" Bullshit, I assume.

"You'll see once you get there. I assure you, Gage, it is a feast fit for a king."

I bet.

But that's one meal I don't crave anymore.

Late in the night, as the clock ticks to midnight, I stare at my phone, at the anxious texts Wes keeps sending, but I'm determined to fall back to sleep with Skyla in my arms. Skyla, who is host to our three children. Skyla, who I promised that I would live to a ripe old age for. My heart breaks just being next to her, knowing I'm impotent to add a single moment to my life.

My phone buzzes in my hand.

Brother. Finally, Wesley has mastered brevity.

Perhaps, just perhaps...

I swing slowly out of bed and head for the restroom. Skyla will know I am gone. She always knows when I leave. And this time I won't hide anything from her.

I text him back. **Need your help getting down there.**

And just like that, the room disappears.

Logan

For an entire week, I've successfully avoided both Skyla and Gage, burying myself in making the world a better place, one bowling alley at a time, mine to be exact. I'm not actually avoiding Skyla and Gage, but by the looks of it, they're avoiding me. In truth, I kind of like the story in reverse. My ego tends to bruise a little easy these days.

"Knock, knock."

I glance up to find Gage himself standing at the office door, slumped over, a somewhat bashful smile on his face.

"Speak of the devil." Shit. Did I just say that out loud? "I'd say come in, but there's only room for one." I get up and pull him into a hug. I want to hug Gage. I want to feel his solid form next to mine, because the entire time I thought he was dead, this is what I craved. "Congratulations, man. I never did get to say it to you the way I wanted. You're going to make a damn good dad."

"Yeah, well, the jury is still out on that one. I'll give it one hell of a go, that's for sure. You'll be a great uncle. I already know that firsthand. You got a minute?"

"For you? Always." *Uncle.* My heart warms at the idea. It's not a title I had considered. For whatever reason, I imagined the baby coming into the world and me blinking right out. That still might be the best-case scenario.

We head into the bowling alley proper and find a seat toward the back, the exact table we sat at that first summer Skyla walked through the door with Brielle. It feels like eons ago that fate brought her to Paragon. I remember the instant I fell in love with her, and now Gage has put a ring on her finger and a baby deep inside her.

"How is she?" I ask as we take a seat. I don't have it in me to beat around the bush.

"She's pretty sick, but all is well on the baby front. Skyla cries at the drop of a hat. There's this rage that rears its head about three times a day. It's pretty wild. There are some tiny details about the pregnancy"—he cuts his hand through the air—"but Skyla probably wants to share those with you. She's spending lots of time up in the butterfly room—says it calms her."

"That's good. I'm glad she's doing okay. I'd like to see her." I'm dying to see her. Hell, I'm already a corpse waiting in line to catch a glimpse, hold her, tell her how proud I am of her for hanging on, how happy I am that she has Gage back.

Lexy breezes by with a friendly wave. She and Ellis are on staff today along with Liam. A skeletal crew is working the kitchen.

"Lex, huh?" His brows hike an inch.

"She's been as faithful as a Golden Retriever. She even volunteered to furnish White Horse, on my dime, of course. She says it's a gift to me, no strings. She wants to be an interior designer, and I volunteered to be her first victim."

"White Horse?"

I know what he's thinking. First, I fucked Chloe in the bedroom that I built for Skyla—although, technically, I did fuck Chloe thoroughly all throughout that massive house, the mattress burning was simply symbolic—and now I've employed Lexy to decorate the place. White Horse is ironically barren of Skyla in every capacity.

"I thought it could use a woman's touch." I'm not feeling up to explaining myself further. What the hell? "She's leaking me info on your brother's new endeavor. The Barricade's dream team. Her words, not mine."

"Nice. I've been to see him myself. Each night, all week. Skyla hasn't called me on it, but I'm guessing she knows. She's too sick to bring it up, or I might have done it myself."

"What did you glean?" A week? He's right back to pulling his old bullshit, and my blood boils for Skyla.

"I'm in discussions with him and the Videns. Demetri wants this to be my decision—should I go back and how much authority I wish to assume. I'm still sucked dry, no powers to speak of in any respect." He holds his hands up. "I flip the switch, and nothing happens." His dimples go off. "Just the way I wanted." He gives a wry smile as if he's changed his mind.

"Only it's not." I know the feeling.

"Only it's not." He nods in sober agreement. "I want to get together with you and Dudley and talk this over."

"Dudley?" He couldn't have thrown me more if he had said Tad.

"Yes. He's a part of Skyla's future, and so are you. I need to make the best decision, the only decision." He leans in, pleading for me to get on board. "I'm playing with fire, Logan. If I fall in, we all get burned."

"First rational thing I've heard coming from your lips in months." I grind my teeth at the thought of us consulting Dudley about anything, but it makes sense. "Okay. Sounds good. I'm good with Dudley."

"Thanks, man." Gage gives a quick grimace. "And I want to ask you one more thing."

"As long as it doesn't involve Dudley, I'm all ears."

"No, it involves the bowling alley. I just took my dad up on his offer to take over the accounting for the morgue. If your offer stills stands, I'm looking to fill the position."

A tiny relief of a laugh comes from me. "It looks like I'm staring at my new accountant." I lean over and give him a pat on the shoulder. "I like the sound of that. I'll shoot you an email tonight. I'll send enough raw numerical sewage that both you and your laptop will be sick for a week."

"It's on."

Down at the last lane, Drake bowls a strike.

I nod to him, and Gage catches a quick glimpse from over his shoulder.

"He's been here nearly every single day, bowling game after game all by his lonesome. Not that I mind. His money is as green as anyone else's—greener, in fact."

Gage shakes his head, a smile dying on his lips. "Drake. Can you believe he and Brielle are the great success story of West Paragon High? I'd say our entire class, but most likely all of West Paragon history."

"No kidding." We both offer a disparaging look in his direction, and he jogs on over.

"We need to think of an idea—something to pump some serious green into both of our bank accounts."

Gage nods just as Drake takes a seat, sweat dripping from his temples. He's the only one I've yet to see actually break a sweat while bowling. That probably means he's doing it right, and the rest of us are just slackers, a metaphor for life in general.

"What's up, Olivers?" He kicks off his shoes, and the stench of vinegar lights up around us. Looks like I'll be putting those puppies in the discard pile.

"Just talking about what a success you are." I offer a thin smile. Drake is okay. He's just Drake. "What's your secret?"

"Dude, it's my girl. She's the fucking brains of the organization."

Ellis comes by and slips Drake a soda.

"Thanks, bud." He salutes us before gulping it down. "You should get your bitches to work. They're good at that shit. That's what God put 'em on this Earth to do, right? Take care of our sorry asses while we bowl the day away."

"Giselle's a genius." Ellis cuts Gage a side-glance. "It's too bad her family treats her like a three-year-old. She could really flourish if you guys weren't holding her back."

"What?" Gage recoils as if Ellis just decked him. "Nobody's holding her back. And you're right. She's a smart kid."

"There you go again." Ellis lifts his hands as if the evidence were before us. "She's trying to get her GED, and her parents are getting in her way. You should really talk some sense into them."

"Her *GED*?" Gage and I exchange glances. I have no clue about this, and apparently neither does Gage.

"I thought she liked high school?" I'm stumped by the revelation myself. "She'll be a senior next year."

"She hates it." Ellis slaps his hand on the table, and the sound drums through our ears. "She hates the cheer squad, and she can't effing stand Dudley's class. She's over it. She's ready to start the rest of her life." He pulls a small plastic bag from his shirt pocket filled with questionably legal vegetation.

"Would you put that away?" I smack it out of his hand. "I don't give a shit if the state of Washington made it legal. It's still illegal in my bowling alley."

"Got it, boss." He buries it back inside his pocket. "I was just about to call my supplier. I'm running low."

Drake perks up. "Who's your supplier?"

"Some idiot named Rev. He's over on Host, but grows the shit at his dad's house."

"Dr. Booth?" Gage seems both irate and irritated by the idea. "His son is an idiot. He's been messing around with Mia, and the dude is like twenty."

"That's sick," Drake says without any real emotion behind it while plucking the dime bag out of Ellis's shirt pocket once again. "How much?"

"Ten bucks. I like to buy in bulk, if you know what I mean."

"In bulk, huh?" Drake's eyes spin with marijuana-laced dollar signs. "Tell your supplier you won't be needing him anymore." He flicks the bag as he rises from the table. "I just found myself a new business venture. See that, boys?" He throws a few odd wannabe gang symbols with his hands, and I try not to laugh. "I didn't need my bitch to think of my next move. I'm going to be raking in the green *with* the green." He lets out a mean whoop before his eyes snag at something at the entry.

We look over to find Tad with a tall block of a man and redheaded woman, the "Interlopers" as Nev affectionately referred to them.

"Shit." I knock Gage in the side until he turns his attention to the door.

"What's up?" Ellis turns around. "Lucy and Ricky?" He shakes his head. "I've had about enough of their shit." He gets up, and I pull him right back down by the sleeve.

"What are you talking about?"

"They've been coming around here and there—sniffing for shit. They keep asking questions. Probably DEA."

"Did you say anything?"

"Hell no." It's hard to irritate Ellis, but by the looks of things, Lucy and Ricky have very much achieved this. "I know a narc when I see one. Every time they ask me some weird question trying to 'break the ice,' I simply shrug and find myself something to do."

"And here's the owner!" Tad squawks as the three of them make their way over.

Gage and I stand and meet them along with Drake.

"Logan Oliver." I shake the dude's hand first, firm and strong, and I hold on a little longer than necessary hoping to hear some incriminating thought, but there's zero going on up there.

"Nylan Moser," he offers a little too voluntarily, and it makes me wonder if he made it up on the spot. I don't know what these two are up to, but I'm betting telling the truth isn't too high up on the list.

I shake the redhead's hand. "Gillian Killion."

My eyes widen as I glance to Gage. *Do not laugh, dude. I know you want to because I do, too.*

"Nice to meet you both. This is Gage, my nephew, and Drake, Tad's son."

"This boy is my pride and joy." Tad puts Drake in a chokehold and offers up a noogie. "Out of all the ankle biters I've produced, I'm proud to admit this one is my favorite!"

"Cool it, Pops." Drake shoves him off. "You don't mess with the hair." He nods over at the two of them. "You check out my shop?"

"First place I took 'em!" Tad beams. And he should beam. Drake's business, Made in Paragon, is booming both on and off the island. Bree tells me that Internet sales are outpacing in-store purchases by triple. If this keeps up, they'll both land on the Forbes list. Somehow I believe this to be true.

"What can I do for you?" I smile bleakly at the two of them. Mostly I just want to put us all out of our misery.

Tad puffs out his chest like the proud silly peacock he is. "These, here, are inspectors from Althorpe. They've come to scout Paragon for a new site. The big guns are thinking of planting a building somewhere downtown. Imagine that. Althorpe changing the skyline of Paragon Island."

I'm sure they're here to change something, and now that I know Althorpe is involved, I'm guessing it's a shift of Nephilim power.

"Do you have any identification?" I went there. It's purely routine. Show me an Althorpe badge, a union card, anything that doesn't scream Uncle Sam, and I'll be good to go.

They glance at one another without any form of affect, not a hint of humor, or the warm feeling you might get after having someone welcome you to their business establishment. Nope. These two are cold fish without a pulse. Something is definitely amiss.

"No need to card them"—Tad flashes his palm in my face—"I'm buying the booze. Make it cold and frosty. Two tall ones?" He mock shoots them, and yet, they don't raise so much as an eyebrow.

"No thank you." Moser tips his head. His features iron out, smooth as the moment he walked in. "We should be going."

"Where are we headed?" Tad plucks out his keys, already edging toward the door.

"We'll be leaving alone."

"Wait—" Gage nods to Tad as if speaking in code. "Aren't we having them over for dinner?"

A growl comes from him. Tad snarls at Gage as if he were a rabid animal trying to protect its prey. "Always trying to one-up me, aren't you?" He hikes his pants to his chest. "I was thinking"—he steps toward the two of them, and they simultaneously take a step back—"you really haven't experienced Paragon until you've had a good home-cooked meal."

"No thank you." The woman with the rhyming name doesn't waste any time in shutting Tad down. "What's the quickest way to West Paragon High from here?"

"Six blocks, then take a hard left," Drake offers. "There's a giant mural of a dog with three heads painted on the side of the gym. Can't miss it. My wife's a cheerleader there." He heads back to his lane to pick up his shoes, and the two inspectors stare at him, baffled. Brielle is a cheer instructor. I'm sure that little detail would have made things sound a little less perverse.

"What are you doing at West?" Gage isn't buying the fact they're scouting for a building, and neither am I.

"There's a teacher we've heard is particularly helpful with the lay of the land. Althorpe recommended we look into him. A Mr. Marshall Dudley."

Crap.

"We're having him for dinner!" Tad shouts while spinning his finger through the air like a lasso. "We're serving him up! I mean, he's serving us up! For cripes' sake—he'll be a guest!"

They glance at one another and give an indiscriminate shrug.

"When will this be?" Gill Kill seems suddenly interested in chowing down on some Landon cuisine. Little does she know it might actually kill her.

"Friday night. Six thirty. Come hungry." Tad flicks his belt loops as if they were suspenders.

"Very well." Her features squint with disdain. "I'm allergic to shellfish, tree nuts, dairy, eggs, and wheat."

The tall brooding one leans in. "I'm a vegan, but I make exceptions for grass-fed, non-antibiotic organic Kobe."

They both offer a polite nod before heading back out under the cover of a grim Paragon sky.

Shit. I pull out my phone and send a text to Dudley. **Althorpe inspectors want to speak with you. They have no sense of humor. Do not entertain them. They will not find you witty or charming.**

He shoots back. **I speak to whom I wish when I wish with the amount of wit and charm I deem necessary. As you were.**

Figures. It will be Dudley's ego that leads them to the celestial prize.

Tad takes off and challenges Drake to a quick game while Gage and I stare at the empty door.

"What do you think?"

"I don't need to think. I know—Wesley sent them. It can only mean one thing—they will somehow further the Barricade's efforts."

"I'll run their names, see what I come up with. I'll put Dudley to the task as well."

Lexy comes up out of breath. "Are they gone?"

"You know them?"

"Sort of, not really." She flicks her short copper hair. "But I've been bumping into them wherever I go out. It's creepy. I swear, it's like they're following me. They're making it impossible for me to grow my new powers." She smacks Gage across the arm. "Tell that brother of yours we need more time in the Transfer. It's not safe up here." She gives a mean shiver before tending to a swelling crowd at the cash register.

"Wes has his dream team growing out their powers, practicing right here on Paragon for all to see." I shake my head at Gage.

He looks out the gaping front doors. "And he's got inspectors checking out Paragon. Conflicting interests?"

"Sounds like the perfect setup."

Paragon shakes and rattles as a thunderstorm roars its way over the island. Paragon spreads her wings, opens herself to all of the fury that the sky has to offer, drinking down its juices like a love tonic. Some might say the weather has ruined what was shaping up to be a rather nice summer, but it's the rain that reminds us of who we are. It tells us not to get too excited about a few balmy afternoons. It's the rain, the reprimand of the thunder, the flashes of lightning that surge overhead like a giant haunted chandelier that keep us all in check and remind us exactly where we are.

Dudley's home is brimming with life as Gage and I head inside. Michelle and Liam paw each other on the sofa while Ellis and Giselle sit uncomfortably close to one another—*on* one another. I'm shocked Gage hasn't ripped off Ellis's stoned balls yet. Lexy tries very hard to mimic the actions of both Michelle and Giselle, but I've kept a good arm's length from her. And absolutely no one is paying attention to the movie, a sci-fi flick about a dinosaur eating its way through Manhattan.

"How's Nat?" I take a swig of my drink. Natalie Coleman went to high school with us, and I haven't seen her in months, but in truth, I'm simply trying to throw out some platonic vibes in Lexy's direction, and what better way than to bring up a mutual friend.

"Dead as a doornail," she sighs dreamily while leaning into me, her chin resting comfortably on my arm.

"What?" Gage and I say at the same time.

"She's fine." She flicks her wrist. "She's dating some soon-to-be senior on Host. She's pre-med. Who knew? Nat is the smart one." She averts her eyes to the ceiling. "Just kidding, I'm the smart one because I'm sitting here with you." She walks her fingers down my chest, and I catch them before she gets to the boys.

"Whoa. So tell us more about this field trip you're taking to the Transfer," I whisper as not to break Michelle from her lust-driven trance. My brother is lapping up the love, and, quite frankly, I'm about five minutes out from telling them to get a room.

Lexy blows out a breath. "It's called the Immunity League." She shrugs. "Um"—she cuts a quick glance over her shoulder—"I'm not really supposed to talk about this, but, well, you're in it." She flicks a finger at Gage. He's in it? My stomach bottoms out, but I pretend it's old news. "And, well, you're like my boyfriend." Lex bites down on her lip and tugs at my T-shirt as she reels me in.

A clap of thunder comes from the back of the room, near that dusty haunted piano of Dudley's, and I look to find the Sector himself materializing in a plume of white smoke.

Thankfully, Michelle is too busy burying her tongue down my brother's throat to notice. Come to think of it, Michelle doesn't notice too much else when my brother is around. Who knows, maybe this will pan out to be the real deal?

"Would you excuse us?" I gently place Lexy's wandering arm back to her side as Gage and I motion Dudley into the dining room. Gage mentioned he wanted to talk about his future tonight—with Dudley present.

We sit round table style with each of us at opposing ends, Dudley glaring at the two of us like we ate the last piece of pie.

"What?" he barks it out unordinarily perturbed.

I'll bite. "What has your panties in a bunch, sweetheart?"

Dudley gives a low-lying growl, his eyes changing colors in every hue of red like a bubbling kaleidoscope.

"Dare you speak to me that way? I'll have your tongue on a spit should you choose to negate the respect I deserve."

"*Huh*," I muse. "It seems each time you crawl out of that haunted mirror you're a bit more ornery than the last. What's going on? You finally fuck your way through every whorehouse this side of the seventeenth century?" I meet the disdain in his eyes with a minutia of intrigue. "Let me say it for you— *Language, Mr. Oliver.*" I do my best Dudley impression, and yet, not even Gage seems amused.

Dudley steadies his hands onto the lip of the table. His jaw flexes tight as if I've gone too far. "You know not to whom you speak."

"Oh, I think I know." Somewhere during this bizarre exchange, I've crossed the line from mocking to outright antagonizing.

"All right." Gage raps his knuckles over the table. "Save this shit for later. I need the two of you to help me make a decision, and quick. I've got a wife in bed waiting for me."

Both Dudley and I give a disconcerting growl in his direction.

"She's sick." He glares at us with those glowing eyes. "I need to get going." He motions with his hand as if speeding things along. "Look, Demetri is after me to shit or get off the paranormal pot. He wants a commitment. He gets that I'm not power-hungry. Apparently, all the megalomaniac genes went to Wesley. He just wants me in on the fun. He wants me to participate as an active member along with Wes. Apparently, Demetri is all about family."

"Who knew?" I muse without an ounce of feeling. I've got news for Gage. Demetri is all about Demetri.

"Lizbeth and that kid of hers—Misty." He looks to Dudley. "She's Demetri's in the event either of you didn't realize."

"Skyla mentioned it a few months back." I wince at the thought. "It's still hard to believe."

"Believe?" Dudley seems incensed. "What's there to believe? Lizbeth Landon would no more trollop behind her husband's back than leave the buffoon. This is a child of maniacal manipulation. I assure you I stand by the virtue of my future mother-in-law." He gives the curve of a careless grin to my nephew, and Gage turns a few shades of purple. As soon as he uttered the words *future mother-in-law*, Gage's jaw began to clench.

"Okay, before you two kill each other. Why do you need us to make this decision?"

"Yes, Jock Strap"—Dudley groans—"why are you depleting both my time and oxygen?"

Gage looks from Dudley to me, his expression serious as stone. "I'm thinking about staying."

A loud pop emits from the chandelier overhead as a light bulb blows out, then another and another loud as a firecracker display, as the room quickly dims to nothing.

In the corner, the form of a woman appears, slowly at first, one molecule at a time, hair wild and frizzy as a haystack, the outline of a sweatshirt with the word *Host* printed across the front, sweats, then finally Skyla's exhausted face, bags under her red eyes as if she hasn't slept in days. She looks more like the Ezrina of old than any version of Skyla I have ever known, and just seeing her warms my heart. I did love Skyla through her Ezrina phase way back when while she was actually in possession of Ezrina's body and vice versa. Skyla has my entire heart, no matter what form she's in.

"Are you okay?" Gage hops up, not at all alarmed by the fact she just materialized before us like a ghost.

"What the hell is going on?" I'm by her side before anyone can protest.

Skyla staggers forward and falls into a seat. "You tell *me* what the hell is going on." Her eyes are bloodied and full of rage. Her face offers not a hint of any friendly demeanor. Skyla is pissed, and I have a feeling we're all going to hear about it.

Gage swallows hard, examining her like this. It's as if Skyla has gone feral, and Gage hadn't bothered to notify us.

"I'm not feral Logan, for fuck's sake." She flicks my hand off her arm. "I've got morning sickness—all freaking day." She glares hard at Dudley. "You aren't picking up your phone, or answering your texts, and every time I try to materialize in front of you, I'm deflected!" Her voice rails to the ceiling with those final words. Good. Maybe it's just Dudley she's pissed at. "I have a very short shit list these days, and you are quickly rising to the top, buddy, but before a single excuse bubbles from your lips, I want to know what this little powwow is about. Why the hell wasn't I invited?" She glares at us all in turn.

Now it's me swallowing hard, as I take a breath just before taking one for the team. "Lexy shared a little more about her new project with us. It's a group of elite Counts—they're developing new powers outside of their realm. It's called the Immunity League. He's having them train right here on Paragon. We're afraid they'll arouse suspicion."

"Immunity League," Skyla tests it out on her lips. "They're going to frame us. They're not going to kill us. They're going to tie us to a stake and let the government burn us alive. The news is filled with supernatural occurrences all over the world—twenty-four hours a supernatural day. All they need is a few volunteers to set things in motion, and the rest of us are as good as in holding cells."

"It is a possibility." I take up her hand without asking.

"It's happening," she assures. "Why are you here, Gage?" She snaps at her husband. "Is Lexy's Immunity League that much of a concern to you?"

Skyla's tone is harsh and curt. What's this? A lover's spat we're witnessing?

She plucks her hand from mine, still waiting for his answer.

"It appears Jock Strap is in need of council," Dudley offers like the rat he is. I'm fine with it. If Dudley didn't say something, I would have. I'm through with keeping things from her. It's already cost me my life. The next time it might just cost hers.

Gage sinks deeper into his seat, his hands both collapsed over her fingers. "Skyla—Demetri wants me back. He wants me as the Videns' leader. He wants me as Wesley's equal, although we all know that will never happen because our morals happen to be running in opposite directions—and he wants me to claim heir to my Fem heritage. I need to give him definitiveness. I wanted Dudley and Logan to help me figure out what was best for you and me."

Shit. Someone should really work with Gage on how to speak with a woman—namely his wife. He was doing pretty good right up until that last sentence.

"You need *them* to figure out what's best for you and me?" Her face deepens a peculiar shade of plum. Her lips purse as her eyes roll back into her head a moment. "So, let me get this straight"—words you never want to hear from your sweetheart—"you called *Dudley* and Logan here for this very important life-changing, destiny-wielding, eternal ramifications decision, and yet, it never occurred to you to include your own wife?"

There it is. A big old pile of crap just fell over Gage, and I'm afraid ain't nobody able to dig that boy out.

"I'd better get going." I try to rise, and Skyla pushes me into the seat next to her.

"Nobody goes anywhere."

"I'm sorry," Gage pleads. It's a good start, but the race is over. Skyla is already pissed into next week.

"There's a faction meeting coming up. You won't be going, Gage. Logan, I expect you to take over like I asked. I'll talk to Dr. Booth and fill him in. And for the love of God, do me a favor and make sure there isn't a chicken in the vicinity. Deorsum is always bringing food. It's not a damn potluck. The smell of chicken—the *thought* of chicken makes me gag."

"Done." No chicken. Does that mean Gage can't bunk up with her tonight? I withhold a private smile.

"Look"—he tries to turn over the engine again—"I wanted to include you. I was *going* to include you, but you've been too sick to move, let alone sit up. I wanted to hear what these two thought, and then run it all by you tonight."

"Is that before or after you sneak off to be with your *real* family?" She smears it with such venom it almost hurts to watch.

Gage inches back. His features pinch with grief. "You are my real family."

"Save it," she snipes. "I'm the one you're keeping things from, not Demetri or Wes."

Gage slams his hands down over the table so hard the thunderous clatter stills the entire oversized house. "I did *not* want to stress you out!" he roars. Crap. I cut my hand in the air for him to knock this shit off, because for one—he's stressing her out. "I want to keep you and our babies safe, Skyla."

Babies?

"I love you." His voice softens. His eyes water as if there were an ocean in each one. "I would do anything for you. That's why I went to see your mother that day and begged her to make me human. That's why I came back to Paragon—to live as your husband—your human husband. She's the one that told me you were expecting. She's also the one who tossed me to Devil's Peak—or I should say just shy of it—that's when..."

"Blasphemy!" Marshall doesn't waste any time in calling Gage on his bullshit, only I for one don't think he's shitting us. "Candace Messenger is a lot of things, but a murderer? Of her daughter's husband no less?" Even Dudley seems incensed by the notion.

"Oh, come off it." Skyla scoffs openly at her spirit husband, and a dull smile rides on my face. "You and I both know she's capable."

"Perhaps she's willing, but according to ancient bylaws, she is very much forbidden from harming your spouse. It's not yet Jock Strap's time, and thus she would be culpable for attempted murder. His story has more holes in it than a yard of

French lace. Speaking of which—" He checks his phone and gets up from the table. "I've a meeting to tend to," he grouses at me as if I were at the nexus of this unchaste exchange.

"You're not off the hook!" she calls after him as he disintegrates while walking through the wall.

"Neither are you, Skyla." His voice warbles as if in a tunnel.

"What's that supposed to mean?" she asks quietly, mostly to herself, and suddenly, she's the most subdued she's been all evening.

"What do you want me to do, Skyla?" Gage asks, a little more amicable himself.

"Do you have to answer him tonight?" Her voice is even, and dare I say, tender. It's as if just like that they've gone from volcanic to loving in a single bound. Not surprising, everything seems a little calmer with Dudley out of the room.

"I have time."

"Good, we'll need it. I'll talk to Dudley, but I already know my answer. Tell me what your thoughts are, and I'll tell you mine." Skyla gives a cold look to both Gage and me.

It feels like a trap—a trap only her husband should fall into, but technically, we both fit the bill, Gage more so than myself at the moment.

Gage nods. "I think I should stay. I'll still be here for you, for Celestra, minus the power trip I had the last time I joined in on the fun. I can help you from the inside. They're going to try to derail our people with or without me there."

He has a valid point, although I very much hate the thought of Gage getting knotted up in the barbed wire of the Barricade once again.

She cups the side of his face, and, for a minute there, I thought she was going for a slap.

"And you, Logan?" she asks without bothering to turn her head in my direction. "What do you think Gage should do?"

"Easy," I say. "I've known from the beginning. Stay." I look right at him with a genuine earnestness in my heart. "Glean what you can, and bring it all back. Demetri and Wes already know you're going to report to Skyla. Either they're going to feed you a load of bullshit or they genuinely don't give a rat's ass. And I tend to believe it's the latter."

"Why is that?" Skyla twists in my direction. Her swollen lips are so beautiful it's all I can do not to lean in and steal a kiss.

"Because they think they're infallible. They think they are gods—that nothing Gage knows and tells you will ever come back to bite them in the ass." I can feel the sad truth bubbling from me, and selfishly I'm slow to give it. "And—they simply want Gage. He's one of them, the missing link in Demetri's eyes. Your baby has given him the thing he coveted most, dominion. Demetri has already won the prize, and Gage is the ultimate bonus. Demetri and Wes are both greedy to a fault. Neither has a friend in the world, and in Gage they have a friend and family. Who wouldn't want Gage on their side?"

Skyla gives a hard sniff before a flood of tears trickles down her face, her skin blotching with large, pomegranate stains.

"Come here." I pull her in, hug her hard, dig my face in her unruly hair, and I don't really give a shit if anyone is watching, not even Gage. I needed to do this. God, we haven't even talked in private in so very long. The things I need to properly apologize for, ask her about, are piling higher than my mental ceiling has the capacity to handle.

"I'd better get going." Gage pulls out his phone and starts texting. "I'll be home late, Skyla. I'll tell Demetri I'm not sure. Once you square things away with Dudley, with your own heart, let me know, and I'll make it official. I'm just hanging out on the sidelines as less than an observer for the time being."

He leans in and kisses her on the cheek before glancing over at me.

"Why don't you talk to Logan and fill him in on a few things?" He slaps me a slow five before heading out the door.

"What's going on, Skyla?" The fact Gage is intent she talk to me alone is alarming enough. "Is it bad? Did something happen to the baby?"

She shakes her head. "Can we go somewhere?"

"Half of West is in the living room. It's raining sickles outside. The bowling alley is hosting the youth group from church tonight. I can't think of anywhere."

"How about the butterfly room at White Horse?" Her gaze dips a moment. "Did you and Chloe?" She offers a slow nod, and I close my eyes in response. "I don't care." She sniffs the air hard. "I'm sick of her stealing everything that's mine. I'm taking it back." She holds out her hand. "To the new butterfly room built with your love for me."

I take her hand, and the room disappears in a swirl of iridescent blue. "To the butterfly room."

The butterfly room at White Horse is more or less an exact representation of the one at the Landon house with the exception of its size. This one can easily swallow Skyla's entire bedroom, let alone the original room above her closet at least twice over.

I casually take in a deep breath, looking for the slightest incriminating evidence as if the room still might hold the scent of Chloe and me fucking. I cringe at the thought while detangling my hand from hers.

"That's not necessary." She pulls me down until we're seated on the floor, the light of the cobalt wings fluttering around us. "There will be many seasons of our lives that we will not be able to hold one another—this isn't one of them." She wraps my arms around her, twisting to look up at me.

"This reminds me of that day back in the old butterfly room when you asked what we had to do to be together, and I said—"

"Take down the Counts," she finishes.

"We're still taking them down." I swallow, waiting for some inevitable news, something so horrific that Skyla is willing to whitewash my oversight with Chloe.

"No. Chloe is responsible, not you."

"In my heart, I was making love to you, Skyla." Tears burn as I struggle to keep my gaze on hers. "I was loving you, only you."

"I know. And had I needed that, I know it would have been special." She shakes her head. "There was something strange happening at that time—I was having these dreams of you and me. We were—" She motions with her hand.

"Together?"

She nods. "While Gage was away. I'm forever having these sexed-up dreams—they usually star Marshall, but for those six weeks..." She looks up at me, her eyes shining like stars. "They were so real, Logan." She nods. "We were in every single room in this house. Right here in this room." She looks to the sheath of cobalt fluttering wings. "You had me up against that wall. The butterflies flew all around us. You spun me in a circle and said—"

"I will love you through this." Tears come to my eyes, but I don't let them fall. Someway, somehow, I was indeed making love to Skyla.

She shakes her head, her steely gaze never leaving mine. "I don't know what this means. I'm sorry. I didn't want to upset you."

"No. I'm the one who needs to apologize until I'm blue in the face—no pun intended." Counts are spiritually blue. That is, after all, how Dudley exposed me as such.

"I wish I knew about the baby sooner." Her hand floats down to her belly. "I didn't know until that day, Logan, or I would have confided in you as soon as I found out." She readjusts herself until her beautiful face is close to mine, her features serious as stone. "Gage and I are having—"

"Twins?" My gut wrenches with both pleasure and pain. Of course, that's why Gage said babies.

Skyla shrinks in my arms as she holds up three fingers.

"What?"

"I know." She covers her face with her hands. "It's freakish, but it's true." Her body turns until we're facing one another fully. "And there's one more thing you should know,

Logan." Her chest hiccups as she struggles to hold back tears. "My due date is December thirteenth."

"December thirteenth? That sounds so far and yet so close. God, three," I say through a huff of a laugh. Then it hits me. Skyla is having her children with Gage on our wedding anniversary. "Yes—the thirteenth." My eyes close involuntarily. Even I know that babies rarely arrive on their due date, but the irony is symbolic for everything we have ever been—that we are. "Skyla, this is a blessing. I couldn't think of a better day for something so wonderful to happen in your life—in all of our lives."

Skyla lets me hold her, and I rock her slowly in my arms for hours. And for hours, I ponder just what kind of message the universe is trying to send me.

Skyla reaches up and offers a simple pat to my cheek. "I'm heading home." She rises, and I join her, wobbling on my feet a moment. "We *are* going to take down the Counts, Logan—the Barricade to be exact. I want you to talk to Ellis for me—Brody Bishop, too. We're going to start our own version of the Immunity League."

"What for?"

"We need to stop this insanity before it stops us. Who knows—" Skyla's body, her clothes take on a transparent state— "we might even get back into the killing game."

The killing game.

What's gotten into Skyla?

Three Fems, that's what.

6

Enter the Dragon

Skyla

In this new world of sleeping and moaning, I'm lost in a delirious fit of physical aversion. Anything and everything makes me squeamish, and my only hope lies in a seizure-like regurgitation of food I hardly can stand to get down to begin with. I have many dreams in this—what I have dubbed the Retching Season. I dream in blues, in purples, in fog, and in rain. I dream of Marshall, stubbornly only of him. He is my anchor in this madness. And though he refuses to come to me in the waking hours, his presence is never absent in my sleep. These dreams are littered with his naked, rock-hard body pressed to mine. His hungry tongue-lashing over my quivering flesh, his strong arms pining me down with the promise of a harder lashing, a good thrusting from his body to mine. Marshall has me in ways that are inhuman, indescribable with the mere English vocabulary. He takes me to heights that are neither organic, nor in my nature. I beg him for more every hour. I can only deduce this means I need him so desperately. Just one touch from his sizzling flesh, and I'm sure—positive that my nausea will flee, and I'll receive the respite my weary soul aches for.

Gage comes in well after three in the morning and drops a kiss to my temple. My lids flutter to greet him. He's holding something in his hands, a brown square that reeks of recycled dead raccoons.

"That smell." I push it away from me. "I can't take it."

"This box? I have my father's papers in it. Just some accounting stuff I need to go through."

"Ugh, I can't stand the smell of boxes."

"Are you sure?" He pulls it in and takes a sniff. "I don't think boxes smell."

I shoot him a look that contests his theory, and he slides the inspiring parchment to the other end of the room.

"You're feeling pretty bad, huh?"

A hard moan shrills from me. After nearly vomiting on poor Logan, I barely had the energy to transport myself home.

"Skyla." Gage flicks off his shoes and glides in bed next to me, pulling me in until we're face-to-face. The moonlight kisses his features, kisses his tar-colored hair until it glows an eerie shade of blue. "Do you remember how sick I would get if I teleported too much? I don't want to make anything worse for you. I just want you to be safe—for the babies to be safe."

I give a furtive nod. "I'll never do it again, I swear." My teeth chatter as a chill spirals through me. "*Gage*"—I touch my forehead to his—"I beg of you. Call Marshall. Tell him that I'm dying. And when he arrives, tie him to the bloody bed—to my body."

Gage lets out a moan of his own. "I won't go that far, but"—he fishes his phone out and shoots Marshall a text—"but consider the call done."

"Thank you." Everything in me exhales. "God, I hope he shows. What did you say?"

He gives a depleted smile before flashing his phone at me.

"Get your ass over here, ASAP. Oh, Gage—Marshall doesn't take well to orders. We need to ply his ego." I take his phone and type into it, showing off my work of genius to my gorgeous husband.

"*I'm having a serious craving for a Sector. Know of any, big boy? Skyla!*" Gage ticks back incredulously, but a laugh is buried deep in his chest. "And this is coming from my phone."

"Sorry. I can't help it. I'm not above begging or lying."

"I don't approve. But if you are having a craving..." His dimples go off as he hits *Send*.

"You're the only man I crave, Gage Oliver." I pull him in tight, trying to quell the nausea, but nothing seems to work. This is ceaseless, endless agony.

The room illuminates in a spray of stars before muting to a soft glow in the shape of—

"Marshall!" I gasp. It takes all of my strength to push Gage in his direction. "Quick, catch him!"

"Lay a hand on me and taste eternity, Jock Strap." Marshall offers his devilish grin, his eyes speaking to mine the way they have in my dreams. But I didn't summons Marshall here for sex, or even anything remotely inappropriate.

Marshall bends over and smooths my hair back with his hand, and I feel it.

A delicious moan escapes me. "There it is," I hum. This wonderful buzzing vibration is the exact thing I've needed all these weeks. "How could you avoid me?" I latch on to his collar and bring his body close to mine. "Quick! Touch me everywhere."

"As you wish." Marshall lies over me, the bulk of his weight distributed on his elbows as that electric strumming pulses through my veins, my bones and all signs of nausea, the horrific sick feeling I've had for weeks, up and dissipates.

"Oh God, that's better." I can breathe for once without the urge to hurl.

"Skyla." I glance over to find Gage sitting in the chair behind his desk, the look of distinct irritation on his face. When Tad and Mom redecorated this bedroom for us, they were kind enough to gift us both a desk. Unfortunately, we'll most likely have to do away with them and put in an entire row of cribs, or open air caskets if Brielle has anything to do with it. That was her alternative choice of bedding for baby Beau.

"Gage, I can't help you right now. I can hardly help myself with Marshall on top of me." My entire body bubbles with relief. My blood flows effervescently through my veins, and I feel physically better than I have for as long as I can remember. "Marshall has gifted me a new lease on life." One I never plan on giving up. I mouth the word *sorry* over at my disgruntled husband. "You understand, right?"

He folds his arms across his chest. His dimples depress right along with his mood.

Marshall takes up both of my hands and gives a gentle squeeze into my palm.

"Oh, Marshall!" I moan at the top of my lungs as a wave of luxurious healing pulsates through me.

"Don't be alarmed, Jock Strap, just a little acupressure. I know the right places to inject myself into a woman's body to ensure she's filled with pleasure."

Crap. Marshall also knows the right buttons to push to ensure a husband is filled with fury.

"This is fucked," Gage says mostly under his breath, so I let it go for the moment.

"Just need one more hit," I stutter. It's a complete lie. I need Marshall chained to my body. Hell, let's face it, to my very *naked* body for the next few months just to survive the outright hostility my stomach is demonstrating. I've never felt so horrible. Scratch that. I never knew I could feel so completely wretched on a daily basis. I don't know how humans do this without a Sector to lie over them and pulsate waves of orgasmic relief throughout their growing bodies. There's no way on Earth women ever get this sick while expecting, or the human race would have long since died out. I bet I'm allergic to my own children. There simply is no other explanation.

Marshall flexes his muscles, pressing into me while maneuvering his face near mine before landing cheek-to-cheek.

That volatile pleasure excels into the stratosphere, and I roar with an intense pang of deliverance from the ongoing trauma that this pregnancy has inflicted.

"Yes, right there! Oh my God!" I bleat. "Don't stop!"

"That's it. Get the hell off my wife." Gage plucks Marshall off and sends him sailing into the wall, well, through it, and Marshall dissipates into a blast of nuclear precision.

"I won't stay where I'm not respected." His voice is hollow and distant. "It's easy to see how having that Fem by your side—in you—is making you ill. If I'm not away on business, I'll be at your beck and call."

"Away on business?" I call after him, but all traces of his glowing cellular structure have up and disappeared. "I am his business." I cover my face with a pillow before sliding it off. "I'm so sorry, Gage." I pull him over me as all of Marshall's good vibrations peter away to nothing.

"I'm sorry. I should be able to check my emotions. I just want you feeling better. What I don't want is Dudley copping a feel."

"Oh, he wouldn't dare. Oddly enough, he has the upmost respect for the marriage covenant." I land a tender kiss to his lips. "And that's exactly what I have with you."

"What's that chess set doing on your desk again?" He nods over at the haunted game board.

"Marshall said they were amulets, that they had power. I've been tinkering with them, trying to figure out his riddle. Next time he's around, we need to shake a few answers out of him."

"I'll do the shaking."

I pinch his sides, and he bucks. "Sounds like a plan."

"Do you mind if I bring you comfort the only way I know how?"

A naughty smile tugs on my lips, but I won't give it. "I beg of you."

Gage starts in with methodical kisses, his tongue twisting over mine achingly slow, so careful and tender my insides melt with yearning. Gage knows how to stir the passion, bring it to a roiling boil before devouring me in the best way possible. Gage makes love to me with his whole body. His mouth loving me over every limb, over the most tender part of me—and that's where he lingers, his hair touching over my belly like a kiss of its own. His tongue devours me, swift and greedy, licking me in long, broad strokes. His fingers bury themselves inside me over and over, ratcheting me up from every angle. Gage brings me to a heightened state of pleasure that far exceeds anything that Marshall is capable of doing in or out of those perverse dreams. It's bliss like this with Gage, touching the stratosphere, riding on the tail of a star. Gage and I are our own galaxy, the children buried deep in my belly, each their own secret solar system.

We are inextricably related.
We are our own blessed dominion.

Happily, Gage and I rouse at the lazy hour of three in the afternoon. We trek downstairs, only to be met with a disgruntled Tad, glasses on, clinging to his laptop with a sunny-colored legal pad next to him and an arsenal of wadded-up papers. Whatever literary adventure he's embarked on, it's not going well. The china hutch is placed right back where it belongs with the hideous charcoal and lipstick wall art peering at the room from behind.

"Whatcha' doin'?" I practically have a skip in my step. Marshall's feel-good vibes haven't quite worn off enough to open the floodgates to Barfland again. I'm feeling more like my normal self and less like a human incubator with a faulty stomach. And the memories of those kisses Gage imparted last night, the ones he buried between my thighs to be exact, still vibrate warm in that intimate part of me.

"Planning for those damn guests you suggested I invite. They're both on some kind of hippy-dippy diets."

Gage leans in and whispers, "The Interlopers."

It's hysterical that the silly nickname is sticking, but in truth, that is what they are.

"I think we'd best have a variety, and that way they can pick and choose what they want." My mother's disembodied voice drifts from the family room, and I do a quick scan, still unable to locate her. My mother has always been part ventriloquist, but she's not this good. "In fact, we'll just have a buffet!"

"Buffet?" Tad squawks. "I suppose you'll want actual food at this buff-it and stuff-it. You have any idea how we're going to pay for this shindig?"

"More importantly, where are you?" I crane my neck to find her on the floor in front of the television with her legs awkwardly spread eagle in front of her, Mia and Melissa are each at the helm of her feet, gripping at her ankles as if they were about to turn her into a wishbone.

"Should I ask?" Really that was just me talking out loud. I totally know I should not be asking.

"She wants to do the splits," Melissa grouses as she twists my mother's ankle abnormally to the left, and Mom's face wrenches in pain.

"God, you're going to dislocate her hips! Or God forbid shatter them." It's a well-known medical fact that elderly people die within a year of fracturing their hips, not that my mother is elderly, but still, with three children underfoot I'll need her around for a very long time.

"No, I'm fine." Mom is quick to wave me off. "The girls are just helping me out. This is all for Tad." She whispers that last half, and my nausea makes a momentary comeback.

"I see." I glance to Gage with that hold-me look on my face, and he wraps his arms around me tight. I love how he knows me so well.

"Speaking of the splits." Mia pounces on my mother's shin so hard I half expect to hear a bone snap. "Coach Bishop has gotten herself knocked up, and she wanted me to ask if you'd be willing to assist the cheer squad."

"Ha!" I belt out the laugh before I can fully even process the madness. "Chloe wants me to assist? I bet she'd love to bark orders at me once again. It'd be just like the old days." And sadly, I sort of miss those—minus the Chloe part.

"Chloe is pregnant, too?" Mom's entire affect dissipates to something shy of envy. "Wow, first Laken and now Chloe." She shakes her head at both Gage and me. "No offense to those girls, but I'm really proud of you two for waiting before getting into trouble like that. Can you imagine?"

Trouble?

"Oh, right." I give a nervous laugh as Gage increases his grip on me. "I totally cannot imagine my life with children in it right now." True as God. "But I'm sure it'll all work out for the young mothers-to-be." Myself included.

"You keep those rubber baby stoppers on hand, young man!" Tad scolds from the table, and both Mia and Melissa groan in unison. "The last thing we need is another mouth to feed."

"Or three," I whisper as the room starts to spin.

"Come on, Lizbeth"—he motions for her to stand—"we don't have all day. There are fine highfalutin establishments to visit, falls to be had, lawyers to be called. I've got one right here that says *Call before you fall!* And he offers a comprehensive plan of action guaranteed to earn us millions! *Millions!* Can you believe that? Tad Landon, a millionaire! We're going to be rich, Lizbeth!"

Call before you fall? Just crap.

"You will not do this." I try to block my mother's path, but a light bulb goes off in her head, and she's already on to her next thought. When my mother gets an idea, you can see her eyes spinning as if she's hit a jackpot—usually an empty one.

"Demetri's summer soirée!" she shouts as if she just won the lottery.

"God, yes!" And just like that, I've hopped onto Tad's genius plan. "You can bilk him for *billions* actually." The truth is, all she would have to do is ask, and Demetri would print the money in his living room to gift her.

"Not that, Skyla. He's hosting an event next Saturday. We'll simply move our party to the following day. That's how we'll get the food for our get-together."

Tad growls at the mention of the nefarious demon. "I like Skyla's idea better."

"Don't be ridiculous. I'm the party planner for his big bash. I'll simply order twice the amount of food we'll need and take the leftovers home for our own party the next day. He's forever encouraging me to take whatever I need."

Like sperm.

A small wave of nausea pulses through me. Why would she think it's okay to host an event with someone else's sperm? Gah! I mean leftovers. Namely her lover's leftovers. My stomach churns again.

"God"—I whisper to Gage—"we're all going to get food poisoning from the macaroni salad." Another dull wave washes over me, and I clamp my hand over my stomach. I've never been a fan of the mayonnaised-glibbery noodles. "We need to leave."

"I'm taking Skyla out for a bite." Gage ushers toward the hall.

"Wait!" Mia calls out. "What will I tell Coach Bishop?"

I think on this for a moment. "Tell her to find a permanent replacement." She doesn't belong at West. She doesn't belong on Paragon. My goal is to make that happen one day. I don't need my mother to do it, but I just might need the added boost to my powers that these precious little beings floating in my tummy offer.

I have a feeling Chloe's eviction is going to be Femtacular.

Of all the places on the island to eat, I choose the Gas Lab. For one, the food is pretty damn great now that Ethan has all but been voted out of the kitchen. And two, Nev refuses to take my money—which in and of itself is an irony since my mother used my meager inheritance from my father to get this gas bag up and running. Not that it's a gas bag anymore. It's a bona fide treat.

"What will it be?" Nevermore, who for whatever reason I still find very hard to call Heathcliff, waits patiently. But I'm too distracted to peruse the menu properly because Logan and Marshall are off in the corner with Brielle of all people. I'm not sure if I should find this combination of company charming or alarming—perhaps a little of both.

"Surprise me!" I give a manufactured grin. "No garlic or chicken, though."

"And hold the box." Gage tweaks his brows at me.

We wait until Nev disappears before breaking out our we-have-a-secret goofy grins. I suppose half of our friends already know, but still—three babies!

"We should be terrified," I whisper, pulling his hand over to me and giggling into it.

"We shouldn't be terrified. Those kids should be terrified because they're going to have us as parents." His dimples wink at me. "You'll be a great mother—already are."

"You'll be a great father—already are." My voice grows somber as a dull ache fills my chest. "Tell Demetri whatever it is he wants to hear—you know, just to make sure you see your grandchildren one day. I don't care about the destination game my mother plays."

A cool breeze whistles past my bare ankles as Coop and Laken walk in.

"Coop dawg." Gage slaps him five, and I pull a seat out for Laken as they join us.

"How are you feeling?" Her eyes glitter with joy for me, and I feel that much closer to her.

"Usually not so great, but I'm hanging tough right now." I shrug a little at Gage because we both know whose magic touch we can thank for getting me out of bed.

"She had a slimy Sector roll all over her." Gage is still not impressed with the less than kosher methods of reducing my nausea. "But I was there and supervised the entire fiasco." He shakes his head at Coop. "Dude, I don't know what's worse—watching Dudley getting physical with my wife or watching that nutcase of a doctor sodomizing her. When the time comes, do yourselves a favor and either get a female doctor, or a male equivalent of a goat."

Coop barks out a laugh. Coop is a dark blond, same cut features and cunning good looks as Logan. Coop could easily pass for an Oliver in that respect. He's part Celestra and Noster, so he was able to help in the Faction War. I couldn't think of anyone better for Laken—especially not Wes.

"How's the wedding coming along?" I'm convinced that I'm just as excited for them as they are.

"Great." Coop gives a slow nod.

"Not so great." Laken cocks her head at him as if daring him to tell the truth. "Our venue had a roof leak, and now we not only have to make last-minute changes, but we need to contact everyone on the guest list and somehow reroute the entire event."

"We'll send a text," Coop offers. "It's a small wedding."

"A text?" Laken looks as if she doesn't know if she should laugh or cry.

"I think it would be fine." I pat her on the hand. "In fact, it screams modern bride. Just make sure you add hashtag wedding."

She rolls her eyes. "And hashtag disaster, hashtag screwed. Anyway, that's what we're doing today, scouting for a new venue."

"You can have it outside," a familiar voice chimes from behind as Logan flashes his killer smile before pulling up a chair. "You can have it at White Horse—on the beach."

"Really?" Laken's eyes sparkle with instant tears. It looks like we're both wearing our emotions out in the open—a vest of feathered armor.

"I don't mean to be a killjoy"—Coop leans in—"but what if it rains? I've been on the island for a couple of years, and I can count on one hand how many times I've seen the sun—and at that it was just an impression."

It's true. Paragon loves to play in the rain, have her every orifice washed and licked by the dismal skies. It's their crooked love affair I'll have to thank when my children one day ask me to describe the solar unit the rest of the planet bathes in—otherwise known as the sun.

"I might be able to take care of that." I glance out the window at the dull day and stare pensively at the western sky. A dark shroud moves over the already moody canopy above, and lightning sizzles outside the window. "Oops. Looks like rain." The words tremble out of me. I haven't tried messing with the weather until now, but I remember Gage having that capability. "I'll get it right."

"Be careful," Gage warns. "That was the one trick your mother did not care for."

"*Skyla*," Laken says it breathless. "My God." She pats her chest a moment as if she's shelving her thoughts. "Yes, White Horse it is, as long as I can coordinate with my weather girl." She says that last part sarcastically. "I think I'll have tents on hand just in case."

Bree saunters over, a pissed pout on her lips. Brielle is the queen of wearing her emotions on her sleeve.

"Well, look what we have here!" Her voice is high and peppered with an accusatory tone. "Two knocked-up besties and their husbands." She looks to Logan. "Don't worry, hon. That covers you, too." She makes a face at me.

I'm about to say something to set her straight until I spot Marshall having a spirited chat with Nev and Ezrina, and a part of me wonders what that's about.

Nev comes by and drops off an omelet the size of my head, brimming with veggies and cheese. It's perfect, and surprisingly, I feel as if I can devour this monstrosity in one sitting.

He leans toward Gage and Logan. "Would you gentlemen mind stepping over to the counter? There's something I'd like to discuss with you."

"Does this concern the Barricade?" I'm just about to get up myself.

"No." Nevermore shoots a quick glance behind him. "It has to do with a certain young man's bachelor party."

"You don't have to do that." Coop raises his hands to rebuff the idea.

"Actually, it's not me." Nev nods toward the so-called Slimy Sector whom I feel as though I owe my new lease on life to. "Sir Dudley would like to do the honors."

"Oh no," I protest. "If this involves some seventeenth century whorehouse, he can just shelve the idea."

"I'll keep them in line." Nev zips away with Logan and Gage, and Coop is quick to follow.

"I think you had them at whorehouse." Bree nods, satisfied with the idea.

"Doubtful." I scowl over at them all huddled with glee. "So, what's new with you?"

"I did a little shopping!" Bree sings, à la my mother. Me thinks Bree is hanging out a little too much at Landon Central. "Just a little something for you." She tosses a small wad of white fabric at my face, and I tug and pull at it before gasping at the sight.

"Bree!" Now it's me singing, although a much whinier, amused version. "This is adorable." It's the tiniest cotton onesie in the world with the words *Made in Paragon* scrawled across the front with a Sharpie.

Laken moans with delight and takes it from me to inspect.

"So stinking tiny and cute!"

"I love it. Thank you, Bree."

"Don't thank me yet. It's part of a gift set." She smacks me in the face with another, much larger wad of fabric, and I pause before untangling this one. "Is that a thing? Is throwing gifts in people's faces the in thing to do now?" I'm not sure if I'm being bitchy, or if I'm asking a genuine question. God knows I feel out of the loop after spending the last few weeks holed up in the butterfly room.

I pull a much larger T-shirt open in front of me and laugh. "Made in Paragon!" I chirp. There's an arrow pointing down to the bottom of the shirt where my belly would be. "It's perfect."

"Are you kidding?" Bree snaps it back and inspects it. "It's solid gold. I just thought of this idea last night. Drake and I just finished having the most delicious food sex, and you were the first thing that popped into my head."

God.

Laken titters enough for both of us, only I don't find it all that funny.

"What?" Bree squawks at her. "She's my BFF. She's always on my mind. It's just something true BFFs do." Bree tosses her head side-to-side while staring at the ceiling. "So I was like, *wow, that was amazing mind-blowing sex*. I bet that's the exact kind of sex Skyla and Gage had when they made that cute little bugger floating around in her belly. Of course, you guys probably didn't have a ketchup fight that led to a hotdog fight, then finished it off with some relish in hard to reach places."

"Oh, gross." Laken taps her hand over her chest like she might be sick.

"Skyla and the G-Man are pretty vanilla." She wrinkles her nose, and for a second, I contemplate smacking that look right off her face. It was that exact ridiculous comment that landed Gage and me into an anal sex aborting position, which sponsored the *G-Man* to remember another one of our asinine friend's cryptic words—I'm looking at you, Ellis—and thus filling my body with three floating—angels. Furthermore, I'd never refer to my babies as something slimy that drips from your nose. I glare at Bree for a moment for even insinuating they were.

"Ketchup?" Laken nods as if looking for clarity. "Wow, you really do know how to party. You're right, *Bree*"—she lays the sarcasm a little heavy when she says her nickname—"that is the very opposite of vanilla."

"Oh, honey"—Brielle flicks her wrist—"you don't know the half of it. I should write a how-to book." Her eyes round out like a pair of shiny new half dollars. "I should totally write a book! Think of all the tips and tricks I have to share! I can call it something like *Power Positions*. Wait—I should totally work the name Paragon in there somewhere. *Paragon Power Positions!*" She's pretty much speaking to herself at this point, staring off at some invisible horizon, laden with wealth building ideas, I'm sure. It seems neither she nor Drake can do no wrong when it comes to business ventures—sexual as they may be. "I mean, the Made in Paragon line is pretty much set in stone. We have fifteen national retailers and boutiques purchasing from us. We don't even make that shit by hand anymore." She leans in aggressively. "But I totally made yours. By the way, thank you for that thunder bolt. As of today, Made in Paragon has officially expanded into maternity wear and infants. I just got off the phone with my marketing team back in L.A."

She has a marketing team back in L.A.? Wow, I never thought I'd say this, but I envy Brielle Landon, nee Johnson, in a very big way. She's really made something of herself—sans the whole hotdog condiment nightmare she's wrapped up in between the very stained sheets.

"I bet the book will be a best-seller," Laken says it dry as if coming to terms with Bree's stubborn success herself.

Brielle waves it off. "I'll have to shelve it for now. Get it? *Shelve* it?" She fans her turquoise fingernails at the two of us. "I'm too busy working on my new line of Paragon Polish—

Spellbound. I've got nuChloe to help out." She jerks her polished thumb behind the counter. "This shit never chips."

I glace over at Ezrina helping with the customers. "I'll take a bottle." Not that I can afford one. But if Ezrina had anything to do with the chemical makeup of that product, you can bet that both gel nails and acrylics will never see this coming.

"Me, too," Laken muses while fondling Bree's fingers. "So, is that what you do all day? Think of great ideas?" Again, she looks far more pensive than necessary. Laken is still not on board with Brielle in general.

"That's right. Someone's gotta make this world a better place. Right now, I've got two hundred bottles to name. Do you know how hard it is to name a bottle of nail polish? It's like I've got to channel freaking Einstein just to get through this nightmare."

"It can't be that hard." Laken blinks a smile. "Nail polishes have all kinds of crazy, fun names like Pale Moon, Red Christmas Ribbon, and Sugar Cookie."

"Oh!" Bree jumps in her seat, making a quick note of Laken's ideas on her phone.

"Plus, you could put a Paragon spin on it," I add. "Like for the black sand beach—Rockaway Noir. And for a dark blood red, you can call it Devil's Peak. Pale blue can be Rolling Mist."

Brielle taps onto her phone so fast it nearly skips from her hands. "Keep 'em coming."

"How about Chloe's Breath for a putrid shade of yellow?" Hey! I'm really getting into this.

"Charming," a voice chirps from behind, and I turn to find the she-devil herself. "I've got one, Bree. How about for the most beautiful shade of Celestra blue, you call it Making Love to Logan?" Her finger strums over my cheek as she heads toward the back.

Celestra blue? So much for a code word.

"Anyway, I have news." I pull a tiny piece of paper from my purse and carefully present it to both Brielle and Laken. "It's from my ultrasound."

"Is this the baby?" Brielle leans in and coos at the picture as if they were already here.

"That's wonderful!" Laken's forehead wrinkles. "I'm not really good at reading these. Where exactly is the baby?"

"Well, *duh*." Bree takes great delight in being the knowledgeable one in all things maternity. "Here's the head, here's the tail, and that's the trunk." Maybe not so knowledgeable.

"Um, no tail." My face heats because for whatever reason this feels like impossible news to share. "That's baby number one. That's baby number two. And that's baby number three." My heart races as if I've just finished the Ironman. I watch their expressions as they dissipate from delighted to significantly concerned. It's alarming to see them agreeing on anything, even if it is on an emotional level.

"Skyla!" Brielle lifts both hands in the air as if I just took first place in the Mommy Marathon.

"Skyla?" Laken looks as if I just swallowed a live goldfish—three of them to be exact.

There's the wide divide I know and love—sort of.

"I know." I bring my hands to my ears. "It's so odd, and yet"—I shrug—"I'm strangely okay with having these three tiny beings come into my life, that I can neither afford to clothe nor feed at the moment."

"Come here." Laken pulls me into a tight embrace, and spontaneously I sob over her shoulder. Damn hormones. But mostly, I'm just scared as all hell.

"Group hug!" Brielle dives in over me, and for the first time in a long while, I feel the weight of their love, literally.

"Having a threesome?" Chloe gargles as she makes herself at home. "In public no less?" She clucks her tongue like the poultry I wish she'd morph into. "Nice little picture of baby? Oh, wow—it looks like I should I say *babies*. My, Skyla, aren't you ambitious? Having the entire junior department at once. I always did think you tried too hard." She twists her lips, amused.

Bree nods. "If one of them is a girl, you should totally give her your ship name."

Laken and I stare at her as if this should start making sense in just a few seconds.

"You know, your couple's name—Skyla and Gage—*Sage*."

"Oh, right." I consider it a moment. But in my mind, they're all girls.

Chloe leans in closer to inspect the slim piece of paper, and I snap it off the table, burying it back inside my purse.

"No worries." Chloe drums her nails over the Formica, and the sound is almost as annoying as her presence. "Your secret is safe with me." She leans in, and instantly, I know she's coming in for the kill. "You have a habit of spilling your own secrets, Skyla. You know that little weather phenomenon you caused about an hour ago? It only rained over the Gas Lab. Some very important people have taken note. In fact, here's a heads-up for you; some very important people are taking a lot of fucking notes. Keep up the good work, Messenger. You'll have the Nephilim locked up in no time."

She rises from her seat just as Logan, Gage, and Coop come back.

"Ta-ta for now." Chloe runs her finger over my husband's lips, and he flinches from her reach. "See you in my dreams." She hums as she heads out the door.

"Chloe says there are people watching us." My heart thumps because she's right about that whole spilling my own secrets thing.

"We know." Logan is telling me something with his eyes. It's not a very good thing when he does this. "The Interlopers"—he says in air quotes—"came by the other day with Tad and introduced themselves. We had Marshall run their names. Turns out, Agent Moser and Agent Killion don't work for Althorpe at all."

My body pulsates and quivers. Already I know this is going to be a crap piece of news.

"Who do they work for?" The words tremble out of me like a flock of frightened birds.

Gage closes his eyes a moment. "They work for the government."

And there it is.

The end as we know it has come to the island.

A small tremor runs through the establishment as if Paragon herself were quivering.

Gage

Night falls, and Skyla and I opt to hang out at Dudley's. Scratch that. Skyla strongly suggests we remain fastidiously planted at Dudley's. I have a feeling I know where this night is headed. The other alternative was dinner at my parents', and truthfully, I've been avoiding them a bit. I'm afraid I might blurt out the fact that Skyla and I are having a baby, three of them to be exact. I don't care for keeping things from them, and this is something huge that my entire heart is dying to share with the world. I don't know how I'll make it all the way to Demetri's party.

"Marshall?" Skyla calls as she bursts through the doors first. Her voice rises with that nausea-inspired twang. I'll admit, it wrenches my balls just a little that I'm not the man that can bring Skyla comfort when she needs it most. And it's in hours like these that I seriously have myself reconsidering my newly human-issued status. All of the genetics of a Fem, none of the fun. Brilliant. And that's exactly what I'm not.

"What's up?" Logan comes over and gives me five, pulling me in for a hug. "Dudley's outside."

Skyla bolts toward the back without hesitation, and I grimace.

"She's not feeling so hot."

"Sorry about that. Everyone's healthy, so I guess that's all that matters."

"There is one person I wouldn't exactly call healthy." Here it goes. I've been avoiding this conversation, but it's bound to happen.

"What's wrong? Is it your back? I talked to Brody, and he says he'll work on you for free."

Turns out, Brody Bishop is a newly minted physical therapist who is more than willing to work on my broken body.

"Cool. I know where to find him." He's been shacking up with Brookelynn next door. Although walking up the mile long staircase to the Johnson house will be therapy enough. "But, no, it's not me. It's you, dude."

"I'm not healthy?" He raises his brows as if questioning my sanity.

"I know—I get it. You're dead. But it's what I did to your body, the earthly one." I gave it to Wes who reduced it to mincemeat and bones. And for now, as far as I know, the remains are in a fridge down in Ezrina's new lab. "I'm so pissed at myself. You don't know the half of it."

"It's okay." His face fills with color a moment. "I know you're beating yourself up over it. I know it's the reason you did what you did at Devil's Peak. Don't worry about me."

"What did I do at Devil's Peak?"

He doesn't say anything, and it's easy enough to fill in the blank.

The room explodes with laughter as both Ellis and Giselle titter at whatever it is they're watching.

"Shit." I pull Logan toward the back door. "I told you. It was that fucking psychotic mother of hers." The night sky ignites in a fit of lightning so thick and wide the room glows bright as noon.

Giselle lets out a viral scream at the sight, and Michelle Miller runs down the stairs, partially dressed.

I pull Logan outside. There's not a lot of drama I've got room for tonight.

"I know that's your story." He pulls loose from my grip. "But you left that fucking cryptic poem. It's hard to believe you intended on coming back." He needles those dark eyes into mine until I feel the sting.

"I wouldn't hurt myself. I wouldn't do that to Skyla, to our children, our family." I steady into him with my sharp gaze. Of all the people on the planet, I would think Logan would know me well enough. "Forget it. I was just about to say that I'm going to talk to Demetri about restoring you. I'd bring it up to Candace, but she's not having it with me."

"Don't worry about my body. I don't need it. You need yours. Keep your nose clean, and stick around for a good long while for those three kids that will be here soon. You're going to be a dad, Gage." A smile pumps from his lips. "Can you believe it?"

I want to meet him right there with his joy, but the truth about his body rises up in the back of my throat like bile.

"The reason I gave Wes and Demetri your body was so that I could live to a ripe old age." I swallow hard with the admission. "I tried to steal your life, Logan. I'm so sorry. I can't live with the guilt. I don't want something that was never meant for me in the first place."

His jaw pops in light of the revelation.

"I was a selfish bastard, and it ate me up inside until I made my way to Candace that night. I thought I was hot shit when Demetri crowned me King of the Videns. That I was just coming into my own as the Prince of Darkness at all those underworld roundtables with Wes and the Barricade. I thought I could straddle both sides of the fence—and I was wrong. But here I am, thinking about doing it all over again. What the hell is wrong with me?"

"This time you're going in with both eyes open." He clamps his hand down over my shoulder. "You can do this, Gage. With my support, with Skyla's, you've got this in the bag. But now you're not just protecting the Nephilim people; you're protecting your own children as well. You've already toyed with the power, and it took a shit on you. And now you go in as the spy you were born to be and take them down from the inside. You're our only hope, Gage. Nobody else has the kind of access they're offering you." He slaps my back. "Now, what are you waiting for?"

Skyla and Dudley come upon us, and I groan inwardly. "Permission."

I glare at the smug Sector a moment. God only knows what the hell he just did to my wife.

Dudley sneers at the two of us. "It appears you seek reentrance to your father's lair. Why is this even a thought I was forced to entertain? Wickedness begets wickedness—"

Skyla smacks him over the arm. "Behave."

Dudley's shoulders sag a moment. "Do as you wish, young Oliver. Do remember this—your wife and child rely on you to be honest, upstanding, and a noble head of the family. Dive into evil at your own peril."

"I'm not diving into evil. I'm done. I'll talk to Demetri tonight. If he wants me to take down the Nephilim right along with him, he's in for a rude awakening."

Dudley closes his eyes as if he's run out of patience "He'll know you're there to keep watch. What is the purpose of this farce?"

Deep down I know, but I'm not too eager to pour it out. But as much as I'd like to keep the lid on it, I've seen where that's taken me.

"It's my family."

Both Skyla and Logan take a breath and hold it.

"Breathe." I kiss her over the cheek. "You are the only family that I am concerned with. What I mean is, it's a part of who I am—I can't deny it. I'm genuine in wanting to understand how his demented genes have navigated themselves into my body. And if I'm not evil, if I have a heart and compassion for the Nephilim people, of which our children—his grandchildren belong to—maybe I can get him to lighten up."

"The mercy plea." Logan nods as if he doesn't like it, but he gets it. "Be careful."

"And no secrets." Skyla doesn't look sold on the idea, but, like Logan, she seems to get it.

"Who are these children you speak of?" He looks to Skyla for explanation.

"This tells the story." She pulls the sonogram out of her purse. "These are my children, Marshall. All three of them."

"Good heavens," he sighs into the grainy black and white slick piece of paper.

"And this"—Skyla pulls out her phone and shows them both that haunted wall mural Emily outlined in the Landon dining room—"is perhaps another picture of my children."

"Dear Skyla." Dudley's voice dips, dejected as if it were the worst possible news.

"I know." Now it's my turn to sigh. "It's not their best side."

Logan taps on the screen. "Why is the one in the middle asleep?"

Skyla shrugs. "I'm more concerned with the fact the one to the left is breathing fire."

Then, there's the third with a silent scream locked in its throat. It's frightening. Unnerving. Everything about that mural makes my hair stand on end.

"What's everyone looking at?" Giselle pops up in our midst with Ellis in tow. My eyes automatically fall to their conjoined hands. It seems every time I see Giselle these days she's connected to Ellis in some way. I still haven't had a chance to talk to her about her wanting to drop out of school early.

"Nothing at all." Skyla plops her phone back into her purse. "What's new with you two? Enjoying your summer?"

"What summer?" Giselle motions to the barn where the rain drums over the steel roof.

"Well, it's going to be summer." Skyla bites over her lip in an effort to hide her blooming grin. "Next Saturday at Demetri's. He's having his annual summer bash. Be sure to invite your parents."

"Okay." She shrugs. "But I'm not sure they'll go. My dad isn't exactly Demetri's biggest fan."

"Crap," Skyla whispers while looking up at me. "We might have overlooked that tiny little detail."

"They'll be there," I assure. I know this for a fact because my parents love me enough to support me in just about anything I do. If I tell them I'll need them at that party, they'll be there. They won't mind being at Demetri's one bit.

Skyla gives my hand a squeeze, a sure sign she heard my inner dialogue, loud and clear.

She hikes up on her tiptoes and whispers into my ear, "Let's hope your father feels the same way."

He had better. There's a lot more riding on this than a life-changing announcement. There is a genocide in the making, and I plan on saving my people the only way I can, from the inside of the enemy's chambers.

†††

Late in the night, technically early in the morning, I kiss Skyla on the cheek and head downstairs out into the damp two a.m. air and meet up with Wes who waits for me at the bottom of the driveway.

"Brother." It comes from him dry and sarcastic as the fog plumes from his mouth like a smoke bomb. He clasps his hand over my shoulder, and the ground shifts. Our bodies dematerialize into thin vellum sheets until the Transfer forms around us.

"Demetri is waiting inside." He leads the way into his haunted house. It's dark save for the enormous fireplace that mirrors shards of light over the cavernous room. Chloe and the devil himself stand by the flames, and for a second, I consider tackling them, knocking them both into the mouth of the hungry blaze, at least him. Chloe, after all, is with child.

"Son."

I grimace. I'm not as into pronouns as Wes and Demetri seem to be.

"What have you decided?" Demetri's smile spreads wide as if he already knows, but then again, he always has that shit-eating grin on his demented face.

"Yes, Gage." Chloe steps in and tugs at my collar, breathlessly, the lust boiling over in her eyes as if she's ready to knock me onto the nearest bed. "Tell me who you choose. Me or Skyla?" Her hands spread wide over my chest before I can stop her. "Say my name."

"Control her," I growl to Wes, and he has her subdued and by his side without so much as a glance. Figures. Wes has become the Chloe-whisperer. "I'm here." I look to my brother, then the man who is technically my father. "I'm going to be straight with you both. I'm not taking down Celestra—not the Nephilim, not anybody who doesn't agree with your philosophy in life. I'm here of my own volition—I've come to terms with the fact you're the blood of my blood, that my DNA lives in you both. I'm here because we're family, and I'd like to see if this can lead to a positive place. I'm not here as a spy. I'm here as a brother—as a son." It looks as if the pronoun disease is catching after all.

Chloe squawks before offering a round of applause. "They're going to eat your wife's people for breakfast. You do remember your wife? The scrawny, soon-to-be enormously bloated whiny little witch who killed me and snatched you away in her talons like a rat in a field? I love that you have so little regard for her." Chloe's dark eyes enliven with a fire all their own.

"I have regard for my wife." I cut the words sharp as a knife. "I'm in love with Skyla. I'm willing to die for Skyla and for our children. I want to be clear about that. I'm rejecting the Barricade."

Demetri lands his heavy paw on my shoulder. "You have made the right decision."

I frown into the idea. How is rejecting the Barricade the right decision in his eyes?

"It is good for you to know me"—he continues—"to know your brother. There is much we will accomplish. We have never needed your blessing to carry on with the Barricade, but the price is yours to pay for choosing to turn away from the purpose."

Purpose. I almost want to laugh. Most people would have said "cause," but Demetri actually believes mass annihilation is his purpose—same with my dolt of a brother. Only the scary thing is that Wes is not at all stupid. He's brilliant. It's a shame he's squandering his genius trying to fill a void on the dark side.

"I realize this," I whisper. There was a vague threat Wesley relayed to me on behalf of Demetri a few months back, but I push it out of my mind for now.

Wes nods to our father. "And what about the Videns?"

"They need your leadership, Gage." Demetri's eyes dance with the flames. He's saying something subtle that I'm not quite grasping.

"Are they truly mine? How can they be if they've sided with the Barricade?" That was Wesley's great victory, getting the Videns to sell their souls to the Steel Barricade. "I was just a puppet with the Videns. I don't want that anymore. I want full authority. None of this partial bullshit, or they can go and find themselves another leader."

"Done." Demetri opens his palms like a dicey magician. Wes taps him on the arm as if trying to draw him out of a trance. "What do you mean, *done*?"

"We don't need them." Demetri doesn't take his smiling eyes off me. "We don't need him." He steps in and takes up my hand, his flesh uncomfortably thick and coarse, scaly to be exact. "I don't need you, Gage. I *want* you. You have gifted me my most richest treasure, and I will never forget what you have done for me."

My heart pounds erratically until it's drumming in my throat, my ears. Maybe, just maybe, he'll soften to me, to my causes, to my wife, and to my children. I'm starting to feel this was the right decision. Getting to know my father and brother will not be the curse it was just months before. This time it just might be a blessing.

Demetri nods as if he heard, and I don't doubt he did.

"We have a council meeting in Tenebrous." Demetri's smile broadens. "Let's say good night to the young lady and be on our way."

Chloe flings herself onto me, her hands racing over my chest, my neck. "I only think of you, Gage. When Logan was deep inside me, it was you my heart was with."

Wes tries to pluck her off, but she's sticking like a spider to its web.

"Yours is the only face I see." Her fingers dab over my features as her growing belly touches over my hip. It's as if she's gone mad, but then, this is Chloe. Mad is her natural state of being. "I will do anything to be with you. We don't have to tell Skyla." Her speech is pressured as I pull her away. "We don't have to tell a mortal soul."

Demetri calls something out in a language I can't decipher, and the room melts as Tenebrous forms around us. Not a sign of crazed Chloe in sight.

"Sorry, dude. She's all sexed up. She can't get enough these days." Wes slaps me on the back as the soot and the rot of the tunnels light up my senses. An electric blue flog colors this otherwise monochromatic world, but the stone of sacrifice sits off in the distance, illuminated with a twinge of red. I've never seen it that way—bleeding into the parched earth below, and I'm curious. A small mob is gathered around it, and from this distance, they sound like a beehive.

"Chloe is horny as hell," he continues. "She has me nailing her to every corner of that overgrown house. I'm probably the only one who's not too sorry that Logan took a 'shift,' if you know what I mean. And, before you go there, I had no idea what the dirty wench was up to. Chloe is her own—"

"Monster," I say, staring at the stone in the distance as a nest of lightning begins to form over it like a crown.

"I bet Skyla is all over you, too. It's the only benefit of this entire incubation period. I'll tell you the truth, though—I can't wait to lay my eyes on my child for the very first time. I didn't think I'd feel this way, and yet, I can't stop romanticizing the idea of being a father." His features crumble. "And I'd be lying if I didn't tell you that it's killing me that Laken is having Coop's kid."

"What? No, she's not having a baby. Skyla just used her as a cover."

"Really?" His eyes widen with hope. His entire person pulsates with relief. "Shit!" He rakes his fingers through his hair. "Thank you, thank you for letting me know. You didn't have to do that. You could have watched me wallow in my misery, but I'm damn glad you didn't."

"I meant what I said back there. I'm in this for family—you in particular. You're lost, Wes. You need a ray of hope, a ray of light. I want to be the voice of reason, and I'm hoping you'll be open to what I have to say."

"Gage." He closes his eyes a moment as if the only thing he's lost in is regret. "If Laken couldn't sway me, what makes you so sure you can?"

He takes off toward the commotion happening around the stone, and I follow.

Six men stand around it in a military-like formation with their legs set in defiance, their hands behind their backs, hand over wrist.

"What's going on?" I nod to Demetri as he wields a silver sword through the air until it glows a beautiful shade of blue—Celestra blue and I try to hide the smile.

"A sacrifice is to be made." His laughing eyes glint at Wesley. "Tell your brother your wonderful plan."

Wes takes a deep breath, his eyes darting across at the men standing at attention, faces down, their gazes set on that glowing red stone.

"It's time to let the world know what the Nephilim are capable of. I put out a call for a very small number of volunteers—your wife's people—tapped them on the shoulder, no big announcement, and here they are. They simply do their thing, call attention to the danger that is the Nephilim—only we're not painting them as angels. People love angels. The simpler humans worship them. We're painting them as something far more nefarious—something unknown—something out of this world."

"Aliens and shit," I grumble, unimpressed. "So, what has you switching sides?" I call out to the motley crew. A few of them look vaguely familiar as if perhaps they were island grown.

"*Dude.*" Wes smacks me on the arm, but Demetri holds up a hand as if to allow my outburst.

I am curious, though. "So, what is it?" I call out again, and not one of them speaks up.

A tall man covered in tats with scruffy hair and a beard long enough to house a bird's nest points his finger at me as if conducting an orchestra.

"I know you. You're married to that what's-her-name, the one that's overseeing the factions. Yeah, she hasn't done shit." His eyes glow a menacing shade of green. "That's what put me in this position to begin with. Somebody has to defend my family. It might as well be me."

"What are you talking about? How is this defending your family?"

"Is he shitting us?" a lanky dude with a backward mullet pipes up.

"He's as clueless as his wife!" tat boy pipes up again, and the entire lot of them breaks out in mockery of Skyla.

"Shit." I stalk over with a vengeance, and a white-hot pain shoots up my leg, all the way through my spine until it decimates my skull. "*Fuck.*"

"Careful." Demetri pulls me back and secures my cane beneath me. He wrenches it, and it illuminates the same color as that spirit sword in his hand. "Proper posture, proper care." He gives a sly wink.

The cane radiates a soft hum throughout my body, and instantly, I feel relief. It feels like heaven, and I never want to let go. Crap. This must be how Skyla feels when Dudley is around. No wonder she's begging for his touch. This can cure anything.

"What the hell is going on?" I nod over at the hairy bunch of traitors gathered around the stone.

Wes takes a breath. "In exchange for their earthly sacrifice, the Barricade will protect their families. Though they chose not to side with us when it was time, they see the value in becoming our associates." Wes steps forward. "No harm may come to your wives"—he projects his voice so loud it booms across the acrid expanse—"or your children, or your children's children. This is a generational covenant with your hearts and the Barricade. All who agree shall say amen!"

Wes says *ah*-men as oppose to *a*-men the way my family does it, the way Skyla and I do, and even this little nonsensical detail irritates me about my new brother.

Wesley leads them into the traditional Count chant usually hummed out and botched up at New Moon ceremonies.

"*I am an immortal. Flesh and bones and such as these are not tethered to my soul.*

In this world and outside its bounds, I stand shoulder to shoulder with my brothers.

This pledge is delivered from my heart. With one another and with God,

We shall conquer and hold down our enemies until they rest beneath us like a footstool.

In accordance to the hierarchy, so shall it be for one, so shall it be for all."

Their voices unite into a thunderous appeal as one by one Wesley taps them over their bowed head with the spirit sword. It glows electric blue in this dark, bitter night that reeks of rust and pools of dehydrated Celestra blood.

Here we are again, the Counts—the *Fems*—taking down the other factions any way they know how. This is personal. They want to wipe Celestra off the map, first and foremost. Things are looking pretty shitty right about now for the other side.

"Lie on the stone and seal your fate!" Wesley's voice vibrates through the still of this dead night.

Bodies fall like flies as they lie prone on this marred granite that has seen and tasted the blood of their Nephilim brothers and sisters—and here they are, trying to do right by their families while voluntarily killing their extended branches.

That nest of lightning above crackles and hums to life. It spins furiously with its lavender illuminations, its spectacular show of strength and light. A single bolt touches down over the stone with knife-like precision and ignites the granite the exact shade of blue as the sword in my brother's hand, as my brother. Wesley is a shadow as his bones glow through his flesh like an x-ray.

"Tonight you have pledged your loyalty to the Barricade!" Wesley's voice booms with insolent pride.

Adrenaline courses through my veins. Blood pumps through me in a surge. I can't do this. I can't watch as these men sacrifice themselves as pawns of the enemy.

"This is bullshit!" I jump onto the stone. My body jolts with the power of a million watts of electricity. My limbs go rigid. My jaw wires shut. The world glows with the brilliance of the noonday sun before blinking to darkness, and everything around me takes on the obscurity of a negative. "Get up!" The words grit through my teeth. "You don't have to do this. We can find a way." Thunder roars through the sky. It quakes through my bones as a gravitational force pulls me to my knees.

Wesley holds the sword to the sky, and the lightning licks it clean.

"Who here is for the Barricade say I!"

A uniform cry breaks out as they all seal their fate.

"Traitors!" I howl above the swell of nature rising around us, the riotous rumble convulsing the stone, shaking us to our very souls.

Wesley points the spirit sword in my direction, his eyes filled with venom and fury. A lone bolt of lightning glowing in blues and purples, dazzling in its parade of horror, streamlines its way from the tip of his blade to me, and I reach my hand up to greet it.

My flesh, my every cell that I'm comprised of ignites with vigor. My body rises to the sky, up to the crackling nest of lightning with its dizzying ring of fire, as black wings spread wide from my back, my body traded for the scales of a serpent drenched in soot.

I look down to find I am no longer who I thought I was.

If every disappointment, every failure I have ever experienced were rolled into one, it wouldn't come close to expressing the horror that this moment brings.

My back arches unnaturally. My elongated neck twists and writhes. I growl out my aggression as an immeasurably long stream of fire pours from my mouth. My howls lick through the air in flames.

Here I am, home at last.

The dragon.

Logan

Sometimes, life tosses one hell of a surprise your way that you never in your wildest dreams saw coming. Gage is back—a great surprise, better than great. Skyla is with child—*children*—an amazing surprise, better than amazing.

Sometimes, life tosses one hell of a surprise your way that you never saw coming, and right now, that is Skyla here with me at White Horse. She's not afraid to visit, to take back what's hers after Chloe so viciously tried to burn the spirit of this home down with her wickedness. I watch as Skyla sleeps on the couch of the newly decorated home I built for her while marveling at her tiny body—at the three beautiful angels she has buried deep inside her. Surprised doesn't begin to describe how I felt when I found out about the babies, how I still feel—stunned feels more accurate. It's been like living in a state of shock, a waking dream, some kind of a strange illusion that Demetri is asking us all to partake in. Skyla still looks in every way like her old self, her pre-pregnancy self. It's easy for me to believe that none of this is real. But the truth is, Gage and Skyla will be parents. I will be an uncle. Things have changed. Skyla and Gage have cemented their family by combining their DNA and knitting three beautiful beings that will bear both their attributes. I'm curious about them. I already love them as much as I love their parents.

"What's the big sigh for?" Lexy attempts to whisper from across the room. She came by right after Skyla nodded off. I had originally brought Skyla by to see the big decorating reveal, and Lex happened to pull up an hour later with some finishing touches for the upstairs. I had taken Skyla out to the Burger Shack and watched her wolf down three cheeseburgers—one for each child—before heading here, where she proceeded to pass out on the sofa.

"Just counting my blessings." Three new ones to be exact.

Skyla lets out a sharp cry. Her body twitches and writhes, and her eyes oscillate from underneath her lids.

"Skyla?" I say it low as I swoop in beside her.

"*No,*" she cries as her entire body startles with a jolt. Her lids spring open like roller shades as her eyes bolt from side-to-side taking in the scene. "Where am I?" she pants in a panic.

"White Horse." I brush back the hair from her damp face. "With me. You're safe, I promise."

"Oh—good." Her breathing grows erratic as she struggles to sit up. "Lexy?" She gives a few hard blinks.

"The one and only." Lex pauses a moment to snarl. "Just spit-shining my latest, greatest project." She has a photographer dropping by this afternoon. Since this was her first big project, she asked if it could be included in her portfolio. "I'm going to be a well sought-after interior decorator one day. If you and Gage ever get a place, give me a call. After all, we're practically family. We should all go out sometime. You know, double date. You and Gage, and me and my man." She points a svelte, long finger in my direction. Shit. Lex has always reminded me a little of someone who was stretched like taffy—a little too long in the limbs, in the fingers, but she's a stunner, just not the one for me. Liam maybe. He seems to take a sexual swing at her every now and again, much to Michelle's chagrin.

"Your man?" Skyla belts out a short-lived laugh—an angry warning shot of a chortle that has me both amused and alarmed. Gage mentioned Skyla has been moody. And it's no secret that she's not a member of the Lexy Bakova Fan Club.

"That's right." Lexy comes over and sits herself square over my knee. I try gently to evict her, but she burrows in. Crap.

A high-pitched combination of a laugh and a cry gets caught in Skyla's throat, and now I'm afraid Lex might be moved to injure both her and the babies, so I lower my knee, rolling her off like a dump truck.

"Let's get one thing straight, Lex." Skyla struggles to keep her voice even-keeled. Her demeanor is calm, but her nostrils flare, telling a different story. "He is not, now, nor will he ever be your anything. So scoot your little tramp stamp, copper-haired bob right on out of here."

"Oh, please, Messenger." Lex slaps at her bottom like she's shaking sand off from a long day at the beach. "You only wish you have that kind of say. You're nothing but an old married woman who has no more control over who Logan fucks than what he eats for breakfast!"

"Whore!" Skyla doesn't miss a beat.

"Whoa!" I hold my hands out in an effort to keep things from escalating. "If we're going to do this, we need to try to get along."

"Do what?" Skyla's eyes enlarge with equal parts horror and rage. "Oh my God, are you seeing Lex?" Her voice grows soft, incredulous, and I brace myself in the event she decides to shove a foot in my face.

"No, no. I'm not seeing Lex. We're just—"

"Would you look at that?" Lexy jumps, her entire person revolted. "You've got him afraid to tell you that he's ready to move on. Look, Messenger—have you ever heard that expression 'If you love someone set them free'?"

Skyla ticks her head back in annoyance. "And how the hell does that have anything to do with you touching my husband?"

"Ha!" Lex points at Skyla with the laugh still buried in her throat, and suddenly, it feels as if we've all been transported back to third grade. "You can't take it, can you? Logan and I are tired of waiting for your permission." We are? "This is getting hard, Skyla. We're not waiting for your twisted blessing anymore. And, yes, I will call him my man whenever the mood strikes." She folds her arms in defiance, and I wonder how in the hell I wandered into this alternate reality.

Skyla cuts me a hard look, and I give the slightest shake of the head. My hand glides over her bare ankle, well out of Lexy's range of vision.

We need her. I nod into Skyla.

She looks to Lex, and her demeanor sours. "Lex"—she closes her eyes as if girding herself for the impossible—"please report to us when you get marching orders from Wes. I want to see all the party tricks, all the special effects he's pumping you full of. I want to know what our people are up against."

"Your people," Lex corrects. "I've sided with the Barricade. I'm only doing this for my *man*." She overannunciates the last word, and Skyla gives a heavy sigh as if resigning to this on some level.

"Fine." Skyla's jaw redefines itself. "Show us what you've got. We need this, Lex. A lot is riding on the information you give us."

"What about Gage?"

Skyla glances to me for the briefest of moments, her face filled with grief. "You might have more insight—at least unadulterated insight. Gage sees what Demetri wants him to see."

"This might be true." Hell, I know it is.

"Anyway, I'd better get going." Skyla swings her legs off the sofa. "Gage is probably home by now."

Gage has been auditing the books at the morgue for the last few days. He briefly mentioned there was something he wanted to discuss regarding his Transfer jaunts.

The doorbell rings, and Lexy answers it, leading a photographer in with a cheery smile.

Skyla heads for the exit, and I follow her out.

"Demetri's party is this weekend." She winces. "We're making our big announcement. Please come."

"Of course. I wouldn't miss it."

Her hand floats over her stomach. "We're not telling anyone we're having three. I mean, how insane does that even sound? As of right now, we're just going to surprise everyone on D-day. Unless, of course, Chloe spills. Which wouldn't surprise me at all." Her face fills with grief for a moment. "I still can't believe my due date is our anniversary." She frowns. "Sorry how that worked out."

"Don't apologize. It makes the day that much more special."

I walk her down to the Mustang and open the door as she gets inside.

"Hey, Skyla?" I drop to one knee as if I'm about to propose. All I really want is to look up at her in the natural light that Paragon is willing to give. Skyla deserves to be venerated. "I'm here for you. I'm here for the Nephilim, for Celestra—but really I'm here for you."

Her hand warms over mine as she gives it a tight squeeze. "I know." She leans in and offers a chaste kiss to my cheek. "I'll see you at the faction meeting." She gives a knowing nod. "I talked to Dr. Booth. He's willing to help us out if anyone gives you trouble."

"They're going to give you trouble. You're not allowed to be there."

She laughs as she shuts the door and rolls down the window.

"Come here." She pulls me in by the curl of her finger. "I love you, Logan Oliver. We're still going to kick some Count ass."

A groan draws from deep inside me. "We might have to kick the government's ass as well."

"Then that's what we'll do." She winks as she takes off into a bloom of powder white fog.

Famous last words.

I head inside and spend the next hour reluctantly posing for pictures of my new home with Lexy Bakova right by my side.

This is not going to end well—not much does on Paragon.

The faction meeting is old school tonight. Gage isn't welcome now that Demetri outed him as his son, and, well, technically, I'm both dead and under thirty, both valid reasons as to why I shouldn't be here. A long time ago, the factions made an edict about the age which one should attend these sensitive gatherings, and they came up with the ripe old age of thirty. Although, now that I'm barreling toward that third decade of life, it doesn't feel so ripe or old anymore. But Skyla has obliterated most old rules, or at least she's about to in a very big way.

Nicholas Haver likes to play host to this event, and so far nobody has contested the idea, so if we're going old school, it's always at Big Nick's.

"Logan Oliver," a deep voice rumbles from behind. It's Nev and Ezrina.

"What's up?" I slap him some skin, and he shakes the sting off my hand. I pull Ezrina in for a hug. "You guys slumming? You know you're not allowed."

"We're well past thirty." Ezrina smirks. "Besides, Skyla mentioned she was working on abolishing that bylaw."

Nev leans in with a touch of pride in his eyes. "You may not realize this, but it was Rina who sponsored the law in the first place."

"Stop." She flattens her hand over her forehead. "It was a trying time. Everything just went to hell in a hand basket."

Nev leans in again. "She coined that phrase as well."

The crowd heads in, and I linger out in the yard a moment while various familiar faces stride by. Nicholas Haver's converted barn-slash-poolhouse is cavernous, but I'm still able to peer in and see that Skyla is nowhere inside. Skyla is like a flower that brightens the vicinity with her presence—pink and beautiful, holding the fragrance of sugar and cinnamon, night jasmine and aloe all rolled into one. Without her, I'm living in a sepia world that stinks of sweaty gym socks and sneakers that have landed in dog crap. Speaking of which, Skyla once stepped in dog crap right here in the Havers' backyard, and I chuckle at the ridiculous memory.

"Glad to see you smiling." Her voice hums in my ear, and I turn to find her with Ellis by her side while Giselle distracts herself with the Havers' German Shepherd.

"He's a lot friendlier these days," Skyla muses at the pooch. "So"—she takes in a breath and gives a brief smile—"I told Ellis about our meeting at your place later. You know, to discuss the landscaping." She gives a sly wink.

"Right." I nod. "I hear Brody is handy with a pair of shears. I'll make sure he's there as well."

Her face sours as she doubles over a bit.

"Are you okay? Is it the babies?" Shit, I didn't even bother whispering that last bit.

"I'm fine. It's just morning sickness, which apparently doesn't really give a flying F what time of day it is. Marshall makes it better, but he's been hard to find lately. Is there something going on with him that I should know about?"

"Not that I know of, but he has been kind of MIA as of late. Maybe he's having a hard time with this." I glance to her oversized shirt, and my heart drops. For some reason, I envisioned Skyla going through all nine months with three kids growing in her belly while still thin enough to fit in her cheer uniform. Skyla's bodily transformation will be beautiful. I'm sure of it. In fact, I think it should be commemorated in photographs.

The thunderous clanging of a gavel echoes from inside, and Skyla doesn't hesitate pulling me toward the front.

Her hand firms over mine. *Logan, I don't want to alarm you, but my powers are growing. I have a very special gift that I'm going to utilize tonight.*

A smile pushes from me. The thought of Skyla's powers growing brings me relief on some level. As if she'll need them to keep up with Gage, regardless of the fact he's been reduced to human. His lineage alone gives him a dangerous edge. The proximity he keeps to his father each night highlights the fact.

Should I have the fire department on standby? I tease.

"You're not funny." She swats me. "*No.* I can project my thoughts to you," she whispers. "I tested it out on Laken this morning. It's most likely a temporary gift, so we might as well take advantage of it."

Temporary due to the fact once the babies arrive, Skyla's new powers might be evicted from her right along with her children.

"Skyla"—my voice drips with sadness—"I know you're frustrated that you're no longer in charge. You went through a lot to get there in the first place, but why don't you simply relay your thoughts to Dr. Booth? You don't need me as a middleman."

"I do need you." She tugs me in by the shirt, and something in her eyes testifies to her words. "I need your presence. Only you could ever be a true extension of my power, not Dr. Booth. Do this for me."

"Anything for you."

Nicholas Haver sounds the gavel once more. "In light of the current situation, Dr. Eugene Booth will assume the overseer's position as well as council leader. If you can all please join me in making him feel welcome."

A slow, unenthusiastic response breaks out as Dr. Booth makes his way to the front.

Skyla leans in. "The good news is, he says he'll be your mouthpiece."

Dr. Booth nods me over, and I jump to my feet as we make our way to the elongated table that lines the front of this late-night revival.

"Thank you." The applause builds, and Dr. Booth raises his hands in the air like a seasoned politician. "I'd like to let you all know that I have nothing but the best intentions and will fight tooth and nail to keep our people safe."

Nicholas hands him an itinerary of local bullshit that eats through a solid half hour.

Skyla nods to me. *Tell him to inform everyone he'll be the acting overseer at the Council of the Superiors meeting later this summer. If anyone has concerns or questions, they should state them now. Then, tell him the Barricade will not prosper, and that we're doing everything we can to make sure our members are safe.*

I lean in and relay the message to Dr. Booth, who politely waits until a rousing discussion on civic planning yawns to completion regarding little to nothing to do with the faction's impending doom.

Dr. Booth relays the message with a sense of authority and believability that puts the already tense crowd at ease—mostly.

A small rumble comes from the side as a short, boxy woman stands to her feet. "My uncle is in the Barricade. He says that soon we'll all wish we had joined—something about *markers*? Is this true? Are we marked for the slaughter?"

"No, no." Dr. Booth is quick to assure as he glances to me for reference.

Tell him the Barricade is all bark and no bite. They're about as harmful as an old dog with no teeth.

I jot it down and slip it over it Dr. B who glances at it before relaying the message as smoothly as if he thought of it himself.

The room breaks out into a soft roll of laughter.

Tell him that the Barricade is going to hang for what it's trying to do.

I shake my head ever so slightly. This right here is most likely why Skyla needed me as a go-between. Deep down, she knew she needed a filter.

Her eyes narrow in on mine, sharp as pins. *Do it.*

I shake my head again. It's too violent. Just about every single person in here has a relative or friend in the Barricade. Telling them we're going to kill their loved ones puts us on par with the Barricade themselves.

"No," I say to her, and her lips part in horror as if I've just stepped on a puppy's neck.

Skyla glares at Dr. Booth as if she's trying to will his head to explode.

"What?" He glances toward Skyla, confused, his hands grabbing at his temples.

Shit. It looks like my job as her mouthpiece was short-lived. She does only need the one.

"I see," Dr. Booth says under his breath, and someone from the back shouts that they can't hear a damn thing.

"He's cracking up!" another cries.

"I assure you I'm fine." He pushes out a forced grin. "I also want to assure you all that the factions are safe. The Barricade is a weak vessel with unwilling participants. We are in no danger. Oh my God, I think I'm going to be sick." He looks over at Skyla, confused, and the room breaks out into a rumble.

Nicholas Haver hammers his gavel in an attempt to bring the room to attention once more. "Silence." He leans toward the good doctor. "Do you need a glass of water?"

"No." He shoots Skyla a death stare. "I'm fine." He clears his throat. "One last word to the local factions—if anyone has information they feel might be vital as far as the Barricade is concerned, please do bring it to the board's attention. Consider it a duty to your fellow brothers and sisters. All eyes and ears are needed. I charge each one of you to do your part. We will take those rat bastards down by the balls before they hurt a hair on our heads." He takes the gavel from Nick and crashes it to the table, concluding the meeting the way it began.

Bodies swim through the oversized barn as Skyla makes her way over.

"You did great!" She beams at him. "Sorry about the puking commentary."

"Yes, well, some might say I caught on a tad too late. Second verse same as the first? We'll do this again at the Council of the Superiors." He stands and nods to both of us. "Good night."

"We'll see you tomorrow at the party!" She gives a cheery wave before her affect dissolves, and she turns toward me. "You, on the other hand, didn't do so great." Her face turns ashen as she steadies herself over the table.

"Let's get you out of here." I usher us out the door, and she pulls me to the side of the facility. We head opposite the crowd and sink into the cool, oxygen-rich fog that Skyla swims through as if treading water, her moans becoming more audible with every step we take.

"Logan." She gives an anguished cry before hurling into the bushes. The warm splatter hits over my jeans, and I cringe.

"What the fuck!" Ellis and Giselle pop out of the wiry bush, half-dressed, each with their own joint pinched between their fingers.

"Are you kidding me?" I slap the shit out of Ellis's chest because I can't quite reach him and still hold on to Skyla. She drops to the ground and lies on the grass, and Giselle follows her cue.

"Give me that." I take the smoldering joint from her hand while she busily adjusts her clothes.

"Please don't tell." Her dimples dig in just the way they do on Gage, and for a second, I consider keeping her slightly illegal secret. That is, until she breaks out into an uncontrollable giggle fit and rolls on top of Skyla.

"Harrison!" I bark into his face.

"Dude." He drops his joint and grinds it out with his heel. "No worries. This was cheap shit. Nothing but oregano, I swear."

I pull him in by his disheveled shirt. "I don't want to do this, but I have to." My knuckles connect with his jaw, and Ellis falls right back into the bush that vomited him out.

Speaking of vomit, I help both Skyla and Giselle to their feet, one moaning, the other laughing uncontrollably.

This is going to be a long ride home, and ironically, it's moments like these when I'm able to help those I love that I'm glad I stayed.

Perhaps coming back, perhaps this Caelestis-issued Treble, was worth all of the heartache.

Who am I kidding? There isn't any heartache when I'm near Skyla. As long as we're together—even if it's as friends, as family, is all that ever matters to me.

Skyla leans in, relaxing her arm over my shoulder as she lets out a retching moan. A wall of vomit splashes onto my lap, hot, reeking of soured milk with the discards of just about every meal Skyla has ever eaten.

I guess there are some Fems in the universe, perhaps in the pit of Skyla's belly that don't particularly care for me being near her.

We drive to Barron's, and I hose off while Emma rips into Giselle about the evils of drug abuse. It turns out I didn't have to say a word. They could smell it on her.

Skyla and I take a seat on the lawn with the hose running over our laps like a fountain. Every now and again she rinses her face off and drinks from the stream, her head falling to my shoulder with a sigh of relief.

I pull her in close and wrap my arm around her waist. "I'd do anything if I could make you feel better."

"I wish that damn Sector would say the same thing."

"That's funny. He's usually the first to volunteer."

"Yeah, well, he's got other things on his mind these days. I'm so sorry I threw up on you. Can you ever forgive me?" Her eyes pull down with sorrow, her face still as green as it was earlier.

"There's nothing to forgive." I plant a kiss on the top of her head.

What the hell could Marshall care about more than Skyla? Nothing, that's what. Therefore, whatever it is that has him distracted must be directly related to her.

Sounds like I have a Sector to track down.

My phone buzzes, and I pluck it out. It's a text from Gage.

How did the meeting go? Everything all right? Can't get in touch with Skyla.

On our way home. I text back.

I hold Skyla like that for just a little while longer.

An eternity wouldn't be enough.

Soon, she'll have three little beings to care for. She has Gage. I'm pretty sure my nights of holding Skyla are numbered.

7

The Big News

Skyla

My dreams, my emotions, every up and down is far more vivid these days. It's as if my life before was simply an impression of what it could be. If housing these three precious angels has brought me anything, it's clarity in acres, colors in hues I hadn't known existed, feelings in ranges that run from exuberant to lethal. And the sex. Oh. My. God. You would think I had never been touched before. Making love to Gage is pure insanity—and sadly, that includes the subconscious salacious night moves I'm having with a certain dirty Sector in those X-rated midnight romps I can't seem to shut off. And yet, it doesn't discount the amazing, real-life sex I'm experiencing with my stunning, tall, dark and hopelessly handsome husband. I've never been so thrilled to be alive. And yet, I've never wanted to kill another human being more in my life. First Lexy. When I spotted the newest issue of *Paragon People* on the sofa, I about gagged on my own vomit. She and Logan made the cover with the headline, *Check Out the Exciting Renovations to the Happy Couple's New Home!*

Next up on my homicidal to-do list is Wesley, of course. My fingers crave to wrap around his neck about as bad as I'm dying for a burger fix. That about sums up my life and its rainbow of emotions. I want more of this God-breathed time on the planet with Gage by my side, and I want Wesley and his Barricade dreams dashed and smashed until the only thing he's capable of taking over is a cemetery plot. I'm sure his brother can arrange to have that done for free.

I give a black smile over at Wes and Chloe who are cozying up to a table lined with miniature palm trees, festooned with shrimp and pineapple stabbed into their trunks.

It's the day of Demetri's big summer bash, and, low and behold, the sun too has chosen to show its shining face for the big event. It's so hot I'm melting in my long navy maxi dress. My stomach is already starting to bulge to the point I can no longer consider crop tops as an option. But I'm loving my new curves, my fuller breasts and lips—both of which Gage finds quite delicious.

I pan the crowd for my dark prince, but my eyes snag on Bishop again. Chloe looks ridiculous in her ultra short, ultra tight bandage dress. Her tummy is hardly noticeable, but I'm sure her shape-shifting maniacal self had something to do with that. Even if I had the capability to morph myself to perfection, I'm pretty sure I wouldn't risk my children's wellbeing just to alter my waistline.

"Why are you smiling at Wes?" Gage whispers from behind as he wraps his arms around me.

"Sorry. He's making me sick, actually. Both he and the witch he's with. Let's go find Bree."

Demetri's backyard, if you can call it that, is filled with just about every inhabitant on the island, plus all of the scholastic dwellers on Host, and perhaps most of the mainland as well. It's wall-to-wall bodies—correction, bathing suits, teeny, teeny bikinis that make me blush and simultaneously want to cover my husband's eyes—and I can't seem to find Bree or anyone else that I remotely know.

"Where did all these people come from? And why are they so underdressed?"

"Word got out that the food was pretty great last year. Free food plus a heated pool is a rare treat for the people of Paragon. Your mom knows how to throw a mean party."

"Yeah, well, your dad knows how to foot the bill." Gah! I can't believe I just referred to Demetri as Gage's father! "I'm so sorry. I swear, I think of Barron as your dad, well, because he is. Quick, find a match so I can disinfect my tongue of that lunacy."

A deep rumble comes from his chest. "It's okay. I've actually come to terms with it. I'm a part of him. I can't deny it."

"Can't deny what?" a female voice comes from behind, and we spin to find Emma and Barron himself.

"That we're glad to see you." Gage pulls his parents in for a hug, and I stand off to the side, uneasy, and give a slight wave. As much as I hate to admit it, Emma and I have more than a strained relationship.

"Did Skyla fill you in all that nonsense with your sister?"

"What nonsense?" He looks to me, and I shrug. A vague memory of Giselle riding home from the faction meeting with Logan and me struggles to break free.

She smirks at me as if to say *figures*. "That Harrison boy forced her into doing drugs. She came home reeking of marijuana, and now she's upset with me because I've forbidden her to go anywhere near him."

Barron nods. "I told her that would never work. You can't keep two people apart who demand to be together."

"Wait"—a slow fury builds in Gage—"Ellis and G were smoking pot?" He shakes his head, pissed to hell. "He's going to wish he never heard of the stuff when I find him. I'm going to kill him."

"Murder is a felony." I'm quick to remind. Knowing how pissed Gage is, a homicide might truly be on the table. "And Ellis didn't mean any harm."

"You would defend him," Emma says under her breath, her eyes rolling toward the newly manufactured sunshine.

"What's that supposed to mean?" I'm just looking for a fight today, and don't think I won't hesitate to launch her to the bottom of the pool. I've already imagined pinning Chloe down in the deep end, twice since we've arrived, but, hey, if Emma wants to go first...

Barron steps between us. "It means we're all family, and we love one another. I'm sure Skyla had a very good reason for not telling Gage."

"Oh, well"—I give his hand a squeeze, but his eyes are demanding rapport—"you might say I was a little distracted. I wasn't feeling too well that night."

Emma makes a face. She's calling bullshit, and that pisses me off ten times more than before. I can't wait to make our big announcement. I bet she'll feel like crap for thinking so little of me. I'm the vessel of her future grandchildren. She'll practically be required to like me at least a little for the next six months—emphasis on *little*.

"Never mind that." Barron turns his attention to Gage. "How is the accounting business going?"

"So far so good. Both you and Logan are in the black. And I think as soon as this next quarter is over, the bowling alley is actually going to turn a nice profit. It'll just take some minor tweaking."

"That's great to hear." Barron chuckles. "You do realize that for the morgue to do well we'd have to lose half the residents on the island!" Both he and Gage share a laugh over the thought of mass casualties while Emma takes the moment to openly glare at me.

God, it's as if she'd like to populate the cemetery right now—starting with me.

"Tell them the news, Emma." Barron takes his glasses off and wipes them down, still recovering from his graveside guffaw.

"Oh!" She pats her chest, her eyes wide as if she were momentarily sidetracked from giving some goodness of her own. "The Walshes are moving!" She practically jumps on Gage while jiggling his shoulder.

"Watch it, woman." I pluck her off with very little remorse. "He's still injured, you know."

"Sorry." She dusts him off as if he were a knick-knack. "Anyway, we've been having an awful rash of gophers, and so I called next door to see if they were experiencing them, too, and they mentioned they'd be moving this fall!" She screws her lips up in a tight little bow. "If you and Skyla are looking into a place of your own, I bet you can get quite the discount on the Walsh's place."

"Where is this house?" I'm suddenly interested in holding down a conversation with Emma Oliver. That hasn't happened since, well, a very long time, if ever.

"Right next door!" She beams as if this were a great idea.

Next door? As in next door to Emma and Barron? As in can I borrow a cup of sugar, and can you throw in a little of your bullshit on the side because my day hasn't gotten off to a rotten enough start? Uh, huh. No way, no how. Not happening.

"The Walshes have lived next door for years," Gage elaborates. "Sort of a reclusive bunch. If you're facing the house, they're on the right."

"Oh?" I rack my brain, trying to remember ever seeing a house there. "I thought that was a forest." Dear God. A house next door to the Olivers'? And that would make us—next-door *neighbors*? Is she insane? I've never been so thrilled to be poor.

"Well, we're just this side of broke." I toss my hands in the air—because let's face it—for once this is cause for celebration. "But if we could swing it, I'm sure we'd be right on board. Who would pass up the chance to live behind the gates? And so close to family? When the kids arrive, we'd have built-in babysitters and right next door." Crap!

"What?" Emma gives a few steady blinks.

"You know in the future." Gage gives my hand a slight tug. "I'm sure we'll have a rowdy bunch—ten or twelve."

"We'd make terrible neighbors," I add. I'm sure three screaming babies in the middle of the night will make them rethink their plan—plus, still broke.

"Well, if you change your mind"—Barron shrugs—"it may not be that far off the mark financially. Rumor has it the place is a mess. They won't get much more than dirt value. Emma and I were thinking of investing ourselves—or helping out the two of you. Keep it in the back of your mind."

"That's very generous of you. We will." In the very back of our minds it will stay. "Oh, look!" I point over to my mother and give a wild wave, motioning both her and Tad over. Heck, I'd flag Demetri himself down to join our unholy huddle just to get me out of this insane conversation.

Mom traipses over in her one-piece that qualifies as a prom dress in comparison to what the harlots from Host have donned. She click-clacks in this direction in her kitten heels with her auburn hair coifed to perfection, and I can't help wondering who she's all dolled up for—her husband or her lover. Tad trails behind with white tracks of sunscreen swathed over his nose and cheeks that give off a tribal effect while he swills a tropical drink in one hand. Tad, plus alcohol, equals an entertaining disaster in the making.

The Olivers exchange niceties with Mom and Tad, and everything seems cordial for about thirty seconds.

"We were just trying to convince Skyla and Gage to purchase the home right next door to us." Emma beams as if this is still a real thing.

"Ha!" Tad balks, and for once, I feel like balking right along with him. "What are you two smoking? They can't pay a mortgage. Heck, they can't pay a grocery bill!" His head twitches back a moment. "Come to think of it, my grocery bill will go down significantly once they pitch a tent in your neighborhood." He looks to Gage. "Figure out how to pay a mortgage, would you?"

"Crap," Gage murmurs because suddenly our familial conversations have gone from bad to worse. I know it's bruising his ego—not being able to provide a place for the two of us has driven him to the brink of insanity—that and living with Tad.

"We're willing to take a second on the house to help them," Emma announces rather piously.

"Are we headed down this road again?" It's Mom's turn to balk. "The last time the Olivers suggested they team up and purchase us real estate, it didn't go so well."

"Heavens no." Emma pretends to fan herself from the heat, but most likely it's because she can feel a Landon-style throw-down about to take place. "But your lack of participation isn't going to stop Barron and me from providing our only son with a gift. They'll be celebrating their one-year anniversary soon. I'd like to see them in a place of their own."

"Our lack of participation?" Mom is still on first base. "Let me frame this for you, *Emma*." Mom says her name staggering slow, and both Gage and I exchange a brief glance. He looks pensively worried, but I'm amused beyond reason. "Tad and I are not lacking in team spirit as far as supporting Skyla and Gage with moving on to the next phase of their lives. In fact, we support them so much we have opened up our home to them for as long as they would like to stay."

"Says who?" Tad puts his drink to his mouth just as Mom ribs him and causes his liquor to slosh.

Emma chortles Mom's diatribe away. "I'm afraid you've misunderstood me. Of course, Barron and I realize that you and Tad aren't well-to-do."

Mom sucks in a lungful of air. "Is that some sort of code for poor? Excuse me, but Tad and I have more than one child we need to provide for, and they all need to eat."

"Speaking of eats." Tad burps. "Would you look at this spread? This is enough to feed us for weeks."

Again, grateful for Tad and his stomach for stealing the spotlight.

Although Mom has it partially right. Technically, the Olivers have more than one child—the second being Giselle—but Giselle can buy us each our own home behind the gates and still have room on her credit card to outfit them all with designer furniture thanks to Big Daddy K.

"Don't just stand there"—Mom bumps Tad with her shoulder—"they think we're poor!"

More like destitute.

"We're not poor." Tad shakes a fist in the air, his demeanor suddenly serious as shit. "I happen to have a prominent position at Althorpe, and my wife here is in training with the hospital to become Paragon's resident nipple twister."

Good God. Kill me.

"Lactation consultant," Mom is swift to clarify. "But nonetheless, it's a voluntary position for now. It'll take several months and courses before I can get certified. The female breasts are a very complex system."

Emma's face goes white, and this pleases me on a small mammary level. *Take that!* I want to say, but—well, *nipple twisting for the win* just doesn't have the right ring to it.

Demetri's ugly mug pops up, and I swell with relief. If anyone can derail this crazy next-door neighbor nipple twisting train, it's the frightening Fem himself.

"Lizbeth, you've outdone yourself." He pulls her in to offer a brazen kiss to her cheek, but Mom flinches just enough to land his lips square over hers. And we've just gone off the rails.

They both laugh it off, with Demetri nodding to Tad and Mom giggling herself into a Demetri-gasm while patting her lips as if they were her new favorite pets.

"So, where's that beautiful child of yours?" Demetri looks to Tad as he asks the mocking question. "The beautiful Mystery Landon."

Gag me. Never mind I'm sick to my stomach at the thought of the two of them flaunting their affair. It's sickening. An anger-fueled adrenaline spikes through me at the thought.

"Why are you so interested in Mystery?" My jaw is set tight as I seethe out the words. I should just walk away, but a part of me wants this non-chaste coital confrontation to go down right this very minute.

"Misty is with Emily, my soon-to-be daughter-in-law." Mom is quick to silence my line of questioning. "Emily is allergic to sunlight come to find out. Truthfully, I think she just appreciates her lily-white skin."

Tad scoffs. "Allergic to sunshine? I'll give you allergic to sunshine! The only thing the entire lot of those teenagers shacking up under our roof is allergic to is gainful employment! When are *her* parents going to offer to buy her a brand new home?" He turns to Emma while sloshing the Mai Tai in his hand. "How about you buy up an entire city block, hot shot? The way the kids today multiply like rabbits you'll need to gobble up the entire west side of the island!" He swills his drink in Barron's direction. "The death business must be pretty brisk these days, eh? You two making routine trips to all the nursing homes in the area—dropping off a little homemade spice cake, eh? A little arsenic in the mix, eh?"

Did Tad just accuse the Olivers of mass murder? And why is he suddenly Canadian? And why am I secretly cheering on Drunk Tad?

Barron and Emma make up an entire slew of unintelligible excuses before scooting along.

"I have an announcement to make in just a few moments!" Demetri calls after them. "Make sure to stay a few extra minutes if you can."

Tad spills his drink in Demetri's direction. "Whatcha got going? Cakewalk? A raffle?"

"Yes." Demetri is clearly bored and tired of Drunk Tad. One day Tad is going to eat an arsenic spice cake, and I will damn well know who served it. "A raffle." He looks to Gage, dismayed. "The winner takes all—the highest prize in the land is his to have."

"How long does this prize last?" My heart thumps as the words drum out of me. Demetri might just be the key to keeping Gage around until I'm dead as a doornail. There's no way in heck I'm letting my husband get away with impregnating me with three little Fems (cute and special as they may be) and then cashing in on his one-way ticket to paradise. "Wouldn't it be great if that prize were made to last for decades to come? About seven more would be nice. Seven is a nice round number." Technically, it's not, but the only math genius here is Gage, and I'm pretty sure he'd agree with me.

Demetri winces before transferring his attention to his son. "The prize has already been doled out. It was won on the bed of a promise. All that's left is accepting this generous offering."

Gage takes a breath that expands his chest wide as a city. "Sometimes, an offering isn't the gift you hope it to be. Too many strings make it unacceptable. It's more blackmail than it ever is a gift."

"Let's go, Lizbeth. I'm running on empty." Tad tries to drag off my mother, but she's standing staunch with her boy toy.

"You go ahead. I'm pretty interested in this raffle."

"Me, too," I whisper.

Isis struts her blonde self by with a jiggle and wiggle, and honest to God, I'm praying a bikini is buried somewhere in the folds of all that overexposed flesh. Tad doesn't waste a second running toward her like some cartoon roadrunner.

"I guess you two have your Mystery, and Tad has his triple D Greek goddess."

"Skyla!" Mom barks. "What has gotten into you?"

My mouth opens to snark out some smart-ass comeback (which, oddly, each time something truthful, yet more than slightly disrespectful, flies from my lips, I find it eases my nausea a bit—a cure I'm willing to explore since Marshall has decided to up and pull a disappearing act), but I'm waylaid with an obnoxious sight from across the pool. Lexy Bakova stands, all greased and buttered a delicious golden brown with her body draped over Logan like a wet towel. He's carefully removing her hands, trying to wiggle from her grasp, but she's relentless in her pursuit of him.

"What the hell?"

"Skyla, no," Gage moans with that I-know-this-is-inevitable tone in his voice.

Bree and Drake, along with Chloe and Wes, have formed a circle around them, talking and laughing as if they were a part of some obnoxious couple's clique.

"I'm going to drown them all in the pool." I glide over the water so fast my feet touch back on dry land before I register what I've done in full public view. All six pairs of eyes expand in my direction, agog at my sudden presence as Logan backs up from Lex with his hands in the air.

"You." I poke a finger into Lexy's hard as steel stomach and snarl at how tone, fit, perky, and pretty she is this afternoon. "Who do you think you are dripping over him like honey?"

Lex gets right in my face, baring her fangs at me as if to say it's on. "Who do *you* think you are hovering over him like some helicopter ex-girlfriend?"

Gage runs up, out of breath, cane in hand, as he tries to pluck me away, but I resist.

"I *think* I don't like how you're shoving yourself down everybody's throat," I snipe at the copper-headed queen of mean.

"I think *you're* trying to shove yourself down your ex-boyfriend's throat. Maybe all those rumors about the two of you having an affair have a ring of truth to them." Her eyes glint with a wickedness I had only ever seen in Chloe before.

"Are you kidding me? I would *never* be unfaithful to my husband!"

"Save it, Messenger. I watched you for years at West, shoving your tongue down both their throats because you couldn't decide between them." She glances over my shoulder. "Where's Dudley? Rumor has it you lost your virginity to him just to get a passing grade in his class. Are you that bad with numbers, Messenger, that the only thing you could figure out was two spread legs plus one math teacher's penis equals—"

My hand connects with her face so fast I recoil in horror. My heart beats like a jackrabbit on fire, and my head pounds, because for one, I'm not physically able to finish what I just started. Out of the entire bitch squad, I think Lexy is the last one I could take on a *fit* day minus three babies in my belly. Lucky for me, Gage will never let this get that far.

Before I know it, Lexy is over me, and we're plunging into the deep end of Demetri's never-ending swimming pool.

My fingers claw at her neck as I struggle to break free and swim to the surface.

I'm having a baby! I plead with her, my mind using all of its reserves to pound that thought into her ridiculous Deorsum brain.

I don't give a flying shit! Her eyes are wild as she swims us deeper away from the waterline, and my lungs begin to ache for a breath.

Bodies dive into the vicinity like dark missiles born with a dusting of bubbles. A familiar pair of limbs rips me free from her terror hold. A mouth covers mine and lends me a much-needed breath before we rise to the surface, and I gasp and struggle to fill my lungs with precious, fresh Paragon air.

I turn to find Gage popping up beside me, about six feet away, and he swims over. But the arms of this mystery man who lent me a breath when I needed it most are still secured around my body. I twist myself free as I struggle to turn around. It's him.

"*Marshall.*" I pull him in for a brief hug, whispering a breathless *thank you* into his ear before Gage helps pull me out of the water.

"Attention, everyone!" Demetri's voice booms over the expanse like a loud speaker. That auditory oddity alone should warrant concern among the humans among us. Forget Wes and his nefarious plans. It's going to be Demetri's idiocy that gets us all killed. "I have a wonderful announcement to make, and I would bid you a moment of your time to share in this wonderful news with me."

A crowd amasses toward the back terrace where Demetri stands with Chloe and Wes faithfully by his side.

Laken and Coop greet Gage and me with dry towels and a slew of questions about my wellbeing, but I can't take my eyes off the strange sight before me.

"What's he doing?" I take the towel Laken hands me without looking.

Demetri holds up a glass of champagne. "Today I want to share with you the blessed news that my son and his wife are expecting their very first child!"

The crowd breaks out into cheers.

"Shouldn't we be up there?" I ask Gage while pressing my back into the warmth of his chest.

"I don't think this is our announcement."

"To the new Mr. and Mrs. Edinger." Demetri raises his glass even higher. "May your child bring you as much delight as you've both given the world."

"Dear God, he's just cursed that poor thing." I almost want to look away as Wes grabs Chloe and kisses her like he means it.

A hard groan comes from Laken as she turns around abruptly.

"You want to go?" Coop asks sweetly.

"No. I'm here to hang out with friends and eat all the free snow crab I can cram into my body and my purse. Besides, this is old news."

"Dude!" Brielle runs over with a turkey leg in hand. "Chloe is freaking married!"

"I guess that's the real news." I shake my head at Laken like *what gives?*

My mother races over to Chloe, and before I know it, she's feeling her up, probably twisting her nipples for good measure. Apparently, nipple twisting is my mother's love language. I hope it hurts. I hope Chloe's tits fall off, and she begs to die of embarrassment. Knowing Bishop, she's getting off on having her nipples pinched in public.

"He's trying to one-up me." Laken averts her eyes, and I catch a glint of moisture in them. "I'm getting married, so he has to get married. Plus, he still thinks I'm knocked up."

I happen to know that's not true anymore. Gage put a pin in that happy little delusionary balloon, and Wes is happier than ever.

"It's killing him," Coop adds. "By the way, I had Ezrina check those mushrooms."

"Mushrooms?" My stomach turns.

"You vomited in the Transfer, and they blossomed on sight."

"That's right." Coop was fascinated by my talented stomach regurgitations.

"Turns out, they're laced with an unidentifiable metal."

"What?" Gage leans over my back a little too heavy, but I don't say anything.

"She says there's no known substance like it on Earth. It has no likeness to any mineral, any chemical she could compare it to."

"Maybe it has a compound unique to the Transfer," Gage offers, because for one, he's brilliant. As much as I like to be unique, I hate the idea of being extraterrestrial in a world that's hungry for just that.

"It's not." Coop flexes a dry smile and looks surprisingly like Logan in the process. "I asked. She knows the Transfer better than she knows herself. She says it's all you, Skyla."

"Perfect. I'll talk to her about my magical metallic mushrooms when I get a chance." God, what if they're worth millions? I can see the headlines now—*Couple Hits Forbes Upon Profit Yielded from Vomit.*

I wish.

The stench of cheap cologne fills the vicinity as Demetri's face pops up. "Are you ready to make your announcement?"

"*No!*" Gage and I say in unison, and with just the same amount of pissed-off inflection. I love it when we're a unified front.

"What was that about?" Gage is openly disgruntled with the frenemy.

"It was about fulfilling a request. Wes and Chloe thought it best their news be shared first. It's only fair. Their child arrives sooner than yours. If all goes well." He looks to me when he says that last part.

"What's with the not-so vague threat?" My hand flies to my stomach and lands over Gage's fingers, already securing a stronghold over our children.

"No threat. Birthing can be a complicated, messy process. Things don't always go the way we assume they will." His face clouds over with grief. "You mustn't toss yourself about like that anymore. A moment of carelessness can lead to eternal consequences. It may have already." He bows and leaves with those cryptic words.

Laken, Coop, Gage, and I get out of Dodge. Logan's truck is missing from where it was parked when we arrived, so already I feel better that Long Legs Bakova won't be able to drown him with her perky little breasts. But a part of me feels guilty. Why am I so against Lexy being with Logan? I am married after all. I know I should be fine with it in theory, but, the truth is, I'll never be fine with anyone trying to claim Logan as their own. I'm sickened by how egotistical that is. I'd love to chalk it up to hormones, but I know better.

The four of us hit Rockaway and enjoy the flickering light of a bonfire, and when the winds blow it out, I reignite it with a flick of my fingers.

An eerie feeling comes over me, a startle of electrocution as my head snaps toward the forest.

Someone or something is watching us. Watching me. Watching all of Paragon. I can feel them. I know they're right here with us.

Wesley's decision to involve the government has escalated this conflict into a new warfront. Nothing sets a rage in me like Wesley and his piss-poor decisions. This time people will have to be contained, be killed. This time I won't need my mother's help. This time I'm not involving all of the remaining factions.

Logan and I are going to take these bastards down the way we set out to do in the first place.

Ourselves.

The best part of being married to Gage Oliver is having the privilege to bed Gage Oliver on a nightly basis. Lex and her scrunched-up angry face come back to haunt me. I know that she—and the rest of the world—don't realize what Logan, Gage, and I went through, that from an outsider's point of view, I'm nothing but a whoring monster who teased two boys all through high school and still claims them both for myself, but our story is much more complicated than that. Yes, I loved two boys, and, yes, I still do. Logan was my husband, and now he is dead. Gage is my husband, and even though my mother turned the hourglass over on his life a long time ago, I still want to do everything in my power to keep him here with me. I'm not looking to kick him to the grave anytime soon. I'm no devil. Ironically, half the time I don't feel like an angel either—perhaps something in between. Logan and Gage are the great loves of my life. There is no denying it. Lexy can never understand that. Half the time I can't wrap my head around it either. Marshall comes to mind as that heated breath he gave me in Demetri's pool comes back. Marshall is always saving me. I can't deny him the right to my heart. He already has it.

I peer out my bedroom window as Gage talks to Wes on the phone about not going to some Viden event tonight. It's sweet the way he insists on me falling asleep in his arms, but tonight, he simply wants an uninterrupted night with his wife, and I'll be the last to stop him, considering I'm the lucky wife in question.

I roll open my bedroom window as Paragon gleams while the ground clouds roll across her woodlands in batches. A sharp bite of fog-fresh air penetrates my nostrils. I love the cool, wet, alive scent of the midnight mist as it swirls deep in my lungs like an opiate.

The cawing of a bird comes from the western sky as Holden spreads his wings wide over the night while gliding his talons first in this direction. A white bird, with the same girth and width, glides up next to him. For a second, I think maybe Emerson escaped her wrought iron cage in Mia's room. She does complain that she doesn't see enough of her brother. Who would have thought that I would one day become the keeper of the Kraggers? But it's not Emerson for sure, not an owl by a long shot. It's a stark white raven, a perfect match to Holden in every capacity.

Just as I'm about to inquire of his ghostly buddy, I spot a note in his beak and take it from him.

Skyla,

Report to the Justice Alliance for a briefing of the charges against you. Please arrive within the week. I've granted you administrative access for the time being.

Mother

"What?" I spin to find Gage already reading the note over my shoulder.

"Shit." He takes the fragile parchment from me, and it ignites into flames, curling to cinder before we have a chance to read it again. Gage drops it before it singes his fingers and stomps it out with his shoe. "Fuck," he mumbles as it stains the wood floor.

"Well, there's that. Life just keeps on truckin'. It seems every time I feel the slightest bit relaxed, the world bends, and I have to find my center of gravity all over again." I turn to Holden. "We're having triplets."

He twitches until I put my hand over his back.

Triplets? Congratulations!

"He's happy for us," I say, unenthused. "So, who's the hot blonde?" I'm tempted to pat the pretty white bird on the head but hold back in the event I don't like his answer.

Serena Taylor. Mid-century—Deorsum. She once partook in an unholy pact with the Fems—they took her to court, and the Justice Alliance sentenced her to featherdom.

"God." I relay the message to Gage. "That's exactly what I'm being called to court for."

"Don't worry," Gage hums into my ear. "Things have changed. You're Candace's daughter. You didn't create an unholy pact with me—"

"I married you. It doesn't get any holier—or, depending on how you look at it, unholier."

"I was going to say, you didn't create an unholy pact with me—the Fem—*knowingly*."

The white bird squawks, and I place my hand over her delicate wing, my other over Gage so he can hear as well. I can feel the barrier—the fact he is all but human is simply another hurdle for my newfound powers. I glare hard into my husband's beautiful eyes, the color of Caribbean waters, until an unexplainable awareness lets me know I've penetrated his thoughts. Gage nods, letting me know he can hear me.

He's right. Serena trembles as her feathers disperse. *I went in knowing full well I was crawling into bed with wickedness. His name was Axel Thicket, and he was every girl's dream. Only in my case, he ended up more of a nightmare. He asked for my hand in marriage, and my father said no, so we ran off and lived in the woods, ate berries and tree bark, caught fish in the lake when we could. The winter was harsh, and we nearly died, so we had no other choice but to* *go home. Father was angry that I had been defiled and took poor Axel to the Justice Alliance.*

"Wait," I interrupt. "If Axel went to the Justice Alliance, why were you punished?"

The Justice Alliance decided I was truly to blame. They reasoned Axel was only doing his wicked deeds by pulling me in. I was the one who should have known better.

"Ugh!" I can feel my blood pressure spike. "I'm so sick of this bullshit! The Justice Alliance has no right to tell someone who to fall in love with. Who are they to say you can't marry a Fem? I'm married to a Fem, and I'm damn proud of it." Oh, for fuck's sake, where did that come from?

Gage rumbles with a quiet laugh. His dimples dig in and stay that way.

That's not all, she continues. *Axel indeed wanted to please his father, and, of course, I went along with whatever my new husband decided. He was a half-breed, Genesis Josiah. His father was the Fem in question. His mother was Noster. In order to please his father, he was told he had to capture Celestra and imprison them in the dungeons. It was a new concept at the time. I hear you've closed them down. Congratulations.*

"So, you were sentenced for kidnapping, and possibly murder?" My hand slips from her back. I knew I should hesitate before falling for her cuteness. "Well, it's nice to meet you. So glad you've survived the hunter's bow." I start winding up the window, and Holden lets out an ear-piercing cry, so very loud, I'm convinced I've hacked his wings off. "What?" I land over him in a near panic.

Thank you for accepting her. She's my new lady, and it means a lot that you were nice to her.

I'm not too sure how nice I was. I offer a peaceable smile to Holden's main squeeze. "You're welcome. If you two need anything, you know where to find me. Please stay close tomorrow. We're having a party, and the place is due for a Bishop haunting. I need all the help I can to keep her at bay."

Especially since my biggest craving to date is to claw her eyes out.

They both give a twitching nod and fly off into the forest. Serena's feathers glow like fireflies.

"At least they have each other," I say as I lean into Gage.

"I still don't like the idea of the Justice Alliance having the power to turn a person into an animal. It's barbaric."

"I think the alternative is to be extinguished from existence."

"Which sucks."

"It does suck"—my lips twitch at the thought—"but at least they're not alligators, snakes, or kitchen mice."

"The Justice Alliance would probably turn me into a donkey." His dimples dig in once again, and I'm completely his.

"Yes, but you would be my very own ass." I suck in my bottom lip.

"For now, I just want a bite out of your ass." His mouth finds its way down my neck.

"Let's go somewhere," I moan as he buries a kiss behind my ear. "I'll teleport us. Rockaway? Our little love shack built for two?"

He shakes his head. "How about the butterfly room? I'm starting to miss that place."

I blink us up faster than we've ever teleported anywhere before.

"Skyla." Gage furrows his brows as if he's worried for me. His hand finds a home over my belly.

"We're fine." I lift a finger, and the brightness of the trembling wings that surround us goes up, easy as a light switch. In a burst, they unleash from the walls, alive and beautiful, whirling through the tiny space like a blue tornado. I touch my fingers to their wings as they flutter around the room in a flurry, around us, between us, above and below us. It's a frenzy of electric Celestra blue, so beautiful I wish I could share it with the world.

"Well done." His grin widens, and I take my time burying a kiss into each of his dimples.

"We are far from done." I snuggle up in his arms and give a wicked grin. "Make love to me, Gage."

"Yes, my queen," he whispers, the clothes already sailing from his body.

Gage covers my bare flesh with his wild, hot kisses. He drops to his knees and runs his searing tongue over my belly, kissing me, kissing the temporary home of his children, loving them, loving me. Gage takes his time licking over every last inch of my body until he's bathed me with the hot of his mouth. His limbs slowly entwine with mine. His rock-hard muscles tense as he cages me in beneath him. It feels safe like this with Gage. With all of these new powers, the old ones combined, I'd like nothing more than to freeze this moment, trapping both of us in time. Gage has my heart now and forever more. There is simply no greater truth than this. I would do anything to encapsulate this feeling, my love for Gage frozen forever in a teardrop. I need to know he'll always be safe by my side. I need to know that there is no chance that I'll ever lose him to death. It's too much for me to bear.

Gage and I writhe, we wrestle, we reignite every passion we have ever felt for one another during these stolen hours in a room filled with electric blue dancing butterflies. We make achingly sweet love. We fuck like our lives depend on it. This isn't your average coupling before bedtime. This is the knowing, the sensing that a big change is on the horizon, and, in our shared fright, we unite the only way we know, the best way we can think of. Making love to Gage is a pleasure, a treasure. This is the only pure truth I know.

I love Gage Oliver.

Yes, I do.

Sunday, just minutes prior to the Landon bash in which my mother smiles and serves potato salad that sat in the hot sun for over eight hours yesterday, Ethan and Drake sit at the edge of their seats watching the news as if it was Hollywood's latest, greatest release—a horror flick to be exact.

"Would you fucking look at this?" Drake squeals with excitement while patting his head like a monkey.

Gage humors them by plopping down on the couch, but Bree and I stand staunchly in the corner, crossing our arms in rebellion.

The talking heads go on and on about UFO sightings, strange lights under the ocean near Southern California, and Baja, Mexico. An entire rash of lakes in Russia have turned blood red overnight. But the most disconcerting is a beast that washed up on shore in Spain. It's pale and sickly looking, a cross between a giant fish and a dog.

"It's fake!" Melissa chirps as she and Mia bop into the room.

"It's badly photoshopped," Mia adds. "We could do better than that with an app on my phone." She and Melissa share a fist bump.

"It's nice to see you two getting along," I say, following them to the kitchen. "You guys iron everything out?"

"I'll say they did." Bree winks at the girls, and my stomach does a revolution. Who knew winking had the power to make me physically ill?

Mia nods while plucking a wrapper off a Popsicle. "Brielle was the one who came up with the brilliant plan."

Second roll of nausea. Brielle and brilliance don't often go hand in hand. Oh, wait...

"What's the brilliant plan? I'm dying here." God, what if she's endowed them with the Midas touch, and now everyone else in this family will be millionaires? Of course, Gage and I will still be paupers holed up in my old bedroom with our growing little brood. For a second, I picture the entire lot of us begging at the front door with dirty knit caps and fingerless gloves while Tad tries to chase us away with a broom.

"We gave up boys for the summer." Mia offers a lip-stained smile.

"That *is* brilliant!" I high-five Bree just as a stream of guests floods the backyard. Tad has a big sign that sends the masses straight to the rear of the property, lest they trample through the house and steal his valuables—his words not mine. "Looks like it's showtime."

The back of the Landon micro-mini estate is meticulously festooned for this leftover extravaganza. Mom and Tad went all out with the twinkle lights, even though the sun is theoretically still hiding behind the clouds. Rows and rows of tables covered with crisp white linens and ladder-back chairs dot the landscape all the way to the forest's edge. Even Drake and Brielle's mobile home is trimmed with lights as if it were Christmas Eve.

To the left, an enormous spread of Demetri's leftovers, still displayed in those giant plastic clamshells he had them in, sit just waiting to put a pox on the evening. Someone should put the emergency room on high alert. A catastrophic triage will be taking place in less than a few hours. Just the sight of Demetri's glistening discards makes me want to vomit until my eyes fall out.

Gage comes over, and we inspect the scene together.

"We can't go anywhere near the buffet," I push the words out, trying to hold back the urge to puke. "That slippery Sector had better show. And not to be disrespectful, but would you mind throwing him my way as soon as he does?"

"Consider it done."

Gage and I spot Demetri and Mom yakking it up while passing Misty between them like a hot out-of-wedlock potato.

"Not going there," I whisper. Instead, we migrate toward Logan, Coop, and Laken—three people I would gladly spend the next few hours with.

"Don't eat the food," I offer the gentle warning before giving them each a quick hug. "My mother thinks it's fine, but my better judgment begs to differ."

"So"—I turn to Laken while the boys talk Host football—"someone has a wedding coming right up!" I sing. I wanted to discuss it at length yesterday, but I was too drained after Lexy's failed drowning attempt.

Bree pops her head over my shoulder. "I smell a bachelorette party!" Her voice shrills over the crowd, and half the guests turn to inspect us. It's odd that Bree would want in on the action, considering she and Laken hardly qualify as friends, but, seeing that there is a party (with potentially naughty implications), this doesn't surprise me one plastic penis bit. "So, what are we planning?"

"We?" Laken raises a brow.

"Yes. The three musketeers." Bree hops with enthusiasm when she says it. "I mean, I know you guys are knocked up at the same time and all, but there's no reason to exclude me from the real fun. Besides, with the Landon I'm sleeping with, I'll catch up in no time. Drake isn't known for firing blanks."

"*Geez.*" I land my hands over her shoulders and give a sturdy shake. "Do not get yourself knocked up, Bree. You already have a beautiful, beautiful, child." My voice dips to its most pathetic register as I start to cry. "I'm sorry." I attempt to sniff back tears. "I'm just so emotional lately."

"It's okay. So am I." Laken pulls me in. "Of course, not for the same reasons. So, where is this bachelorette thingy going to take place?" She presses in with a sweet smile trying to make me feel better.

"Skyla's obviously too sick—and perhaps out of her mind to properly plan out the event." Bree sweeps the hair from my face, and the cool Paragon mist swoops in and kisses my forehead. "I'll handle all the dirty details. Friday night before the wedding, you bitches are mine."

"Not the night before my wedding," Laken protests.

"Fine, we'll do it earlier that week." Bree shrugs it off as she skips her way past us. "Get those fake IDs ready, girls!" She lets out a riotous howl.

"I don't drink," Laken says just under her breath.

"Under the circumstances, neither do I." A couple at the edge of the woods catches my attention—a tall, boxy Frankenstein lookalike and his redheaded villainous girlfriend. "The Interlopers!"

Logan and Gage turn to me before following my gaze.

"I've seen them everywhere." Coop looks unimpressed with our government-issued spies. "They even spent a few hours on Host the other day."

"Great," I hiss. My mother cackles so loud the hair stands up on the back of my neck. I glance over and spot her still glued to the hip with the demented demon, the exact one who spawned the child bouncing between them. "Hey, what if we hand-feed them Demetri?"

"He's got an umbrella around his DNA." Gage frowns, his arms finding a home around my waist. "So does Wes."

"What's new with the Barricade?" Coop widens his stance, his arms cross over his chest in the same way Logan is positioned, and they look like twins—twins that happen to be a little skeptical of Gage at the moment. It's probably just the way the light is hitting their eyes, but they do look rather pissed.

Gage sighs, his chest rises and falls against my back. "They've been accepting faction sacrifices all week. About ten a night, so far I've counted sixty men."

"What?" I spin into him. "Why didn't you tell me this?" My adrenaline spikes. My skin grows so hot with rage it feels as if it's about to melt off the bone. "Why would you keep this from me?"

"I'm not keeping anything from you," he says it sweetly, measured. His eyes bear into mine as if to assert this is the truth. "I wanted to tell all of you at the same time, and I didn't want anything to upset you—like it clearly has. Besides, it's given me a little time to do some homework. I was able to track down the identities of all those participating thus far."

"Where's the list?" Logan isn't nearly as ticked as I am that Gage waited over a week to fill us in on this tidbit, but I suppose his argument is valid. Plus, now, apparently there's a list.

"Dudley has it."

"Dudley?" Coop and Logan say in unison.

"Popular, aren't I?" Marshall appears from out of the shadows, his crimson eyes glowing like cauldrons. "Ms. Messenger." He extends his hand to me, and I take ahold of it. Gage doesn't release me, and I don't fight him. Marshall's feel-good sensations strum from his limb to mine, radiating all throughout my body like a poem inscribed on a diamond—sheer perfection, sheer delight.

"*Yes*," I moan with a little too much pleasure, and Laken shakes her head just enough to let me know it's so not cool. "I mean, of course. Tell us about the list."

"They're your people, Skyla." Gage warms my neck with his words. "It's mutiny at its best. The Barricade has convinced them this will offer immunity to their families, their children, and their children's children. People are signing on by the droves."

"What's the sacrifice?" Laken's eyes round out with a mixture of horror and heartbreak.

Gage leans in. "They pull a few circus stunts, convince the world 'they' are out there and dangerous. Call attention to themselves for all the wrong reasons."

"That's it?" I'm shocked Wes has made it so easy. "Drake and Ethan do that for free on a daily basis."

Gage drops his gaze to the ground a moment. "This is sort of a death-do-you-part commitment. They're married to the cause. If the government catches them, they play along. They do all their show-pony tricks until the rest of us—*you*"—he grimaces—"are walking around with targets on your backs."

"You can't see our targets," Coop points out.

"Not until there's a mandatory blood test—or something far simpler, a swab of the lining of your cheek." Gage takes in a breath. "Some sort of DNA purging will take place until the Nephilim, those outside of the Barricade have been contained."

My heart wallops in my chest like a dying carp. "We need Ezrina."

"She and Heathcliff have been informed." Marshall gives my hand a squeeze, and my body settles down.

You do look stunning tonight, Ms. Messenger. He raises his brows, his smile transforming into something just this side of lewd.

Down, boy. No flirting.

"Skyla!" Mom sings from across the way with Emma and Barron by her side.

"We'd better get over there." I lean hard into Gage as we step away from our small group, my fingers lingering onto Marshall's until the distance breaks us apart. We head over toward Brielle and Drake's love shack to where our families have converged for yet another awkward exchange.

"Look who's here!" Mom's eyebrows dig into her forehead unnaturally, and I take Misty from her while giving a little wave to Emma and Barron.

***Sky*—la.**

I glance down at the tiny half-breed Fem in my arms and startle.

Misty! Oh my God. Oh my God. Oh my God! ***Can you hear me?***

"La-la!" She smacks my chest over and over again, enthused. Her cute little dimples press in, and my stomach clenches. She looks so much like Gage—her half-brother-slash-uncle. The need to vomit ratchets up again. Stupid Demetri.

"Aw!" Mom coos. "I think she's trying to say *Skyla*."

"She is a smart one." I stare into her beautiful dark blue eyes. ***What's going on, Misty? Is there something you'd like to say to me?*** Perhaps a plea to help get her as far away from Demetri as possible? A request like that would make her extremely bright.

She pinches my nose as if expecting it to honk. ***Skyla.*** A cute gurgle of a laugh escapes her.

Hmm. Turns out, she's a one-hit wonder for now. I smile down at her while rubbing my nose over hers.

"Dada." Her tiny little fingers point to the side, straight to the demon *Dada* himself. Geez. I glare at Demetri from across the yard. It would figure. His ego could never deny her the pleasure of calling him Daddy. I'm sure as a cover he'll request that all the Landon children do so. Fat chance, buddy. I glance to Gage and frown because he happens to belong to the Dada in question.

The backyard is teeming with bodies, and it feels as if twice as many people are here than were at Demetri's oversized pool party. *God*, forget about the Olivers committing mass murder with poisoned spiced cake—with the tepid temptations Mom is offering tonight, she'll revive the morgue's economy by midnight.

Barron nudges Emma, and she scowls a moment before forcing a smile in my direction. "You look just lovely tonight, Skyla."

What's this? A faux compliment for yours truly? Wow. I wonder if Gage put her up to this. But then again, it was Barron practically beating her into submission.

I twist my lips. "Why thank you, Emma. You look quite nice yourself." No lie. Emma is always put together with her hair in an oppressively tight bun, which happens to be dyed an unfortunate shade circus clown orange this week. Her outfit is always a fitted business casual as if she's about to negotiate contract terms for that preschool she runs right here in Paragon's backyard. She's the school dictator, director, whichever.

Emma bends her wrist in my direction. "You should both come by tomorrow night for dinner. I've got haggis on the menu and—"

My body convulses on cue, and I slap a hand over my retching mouth to keep the projectile vomit in check. Haggis is sheep heart, liver, and lungs all cooked in a debatably delicious pudding inside the poor creature's very own stomach. Nothing says yum quite like vital organs.

"Ha!" Emma balks. "See that?" Now she's the one nudging Barron. "She's *mocking* me. I've never met anyone so abruptly rude. Honestly"—she hisses toward Gage—"it's like you've married a child."

Mom and I exchange smackgobbed looks.

"Emma!" Barron cries. "How do you ever plan on getting along with your daughter-in-law with your own juvenile behavior on display?"

"Someone just got called out," I pant while fanning myself, trying my damnedest not to pass out. Lord knows Emma will take it personally.

Gage gives an aggressive huff. "Listen, before this goes any further, I have an announcement I want to make."

Tad meanders into our caustic circle and smacks Gage in the arm, and it's then I note that the terrible two are with him. Crap. Agent Killion has her auburn hair fashioned into tentacles, and Agent Moser looks as if his head elongated just for the occasion. I swear, in the mother of all ironies, I bet we'll find out *they* are the true aliens.

"Hold off on the gas, Greg, would you?" He cozies up next to Mom. "Jilly—Ny the Science Guy, this is my wife, Lizbeth Landon. She's responsible for all this delicious food and the spectacular entertainment."

God, I'm pretty sure pegging Mom for this meal will prove to be regretful in about twenty-four hours. And what spectacular entertainment? I do a quick sweep of the vicinity to make sure Drake and Bree aren't procreating in full view of the masses.

Mom bats his compliment away, as she should. For one, he's just pinned an island wide homicide on her. I bet Tad has plans to cash out of Casa de Landon once that happens and take off with the Titty Temptress, aka, Isis the Idiot.

Agent Killion reluctantly takes my mother's hand and shakes it. "I assure you we don't go by Jilly, or Ny the Science Guy." She shoots Tad a lethal look. "It's Killion and Moser. We prefer surnames only."

"Personable, aren't they?" I whisper to Gage, and Killion's head turns eerily in a clean snap toward me. There's something disturbing about her eyes, something reptilian that I can't quite put my finger on. Misty whines in my arms, and I turn her head away from the mean snake-like lady. "It's nice to meet you," I say, bouncing Misty over my growing stomach. "I'm Skyla. This is my husband, Gage."

"Have we met before?" Her forehead wrinkles into three solid lines as she inspects Gage. Come to think of it, the two of them are looking more cartoon-like by the second.

"I believe you're thinking of my brother, Wesley. We resemble one another quite a bit."

Gage just handed them their first paranormal morsel, not that they'll pick up on it.

Emma juts her neck out like a turkey. "So, what brings the two of you to Paragon?"

"*Research*," they chime in unison, dry and monotone, as if they've spent their whole lives spewing that singular excuse.

Barron's thick brows lift in the exact same manner that Gage's do, and I marvel at how much alike they are for not being genetically related. "What type of research?"

"Plant life," the girl bot says without an ounce of inflection.

"We work for Althorpe," the male drone offers. "Biotech department. We're looking to lay roots to a new department here."

Tad gives an awkward fist pump to Ny that narrowly misses Emma's face, and I frown. What the hell is wrong with me? I would never want Tad to haul off and coldcock Emma—well, maybe just the once, accidentally, of course. "It's all about cleaner living!" Tad shouts his cheer loud and proud for all to hear. "Nothing says green like Althorpe. We're leading the world in reduced fossils emissions by powering the future with smarter people."

Wow. I'm really embarrassed for Tad. He sounds like some walking pamphlet that got stepped on by a shit-covered shoe and now nothing makes sense, it just sort of stinks.

Killion and Moser look down on him in both the traditional and literal way.

"If you'll excuse us, we have an announcement to make," Gage says, pushing his smile to each of their faces.

"What? Right now?" I give his arm a slight tug. I'm not so sure our baby news should mix with the exact people who are looking to lock our children up in cages. Just the thought makes me see red, and now I'd love nothing more than to kick some government-issued ass.

Misty yelps as if she agrees.

"Yes, right now." He settles a sweet kiss to the top of my head before dipping his mouth to my ear. "We want the night to seem as normal as possible—family oriented," he whispers. "They're looking for a Count coven, a faction meeting, and that's the last thing they're going to find."

"Agree." I look to my mother and beam. "Is there a way to get everyone's attention?"

"Tad"—she nods while taking back Misty—"do your thing."

"Listen up!" He claps up a storm, and no one pays him any mind. "I said listen up!" he barks, giving an affirmative nod of authority to Agent One and Agent Two, but still not a cricket has stopped chirping. "Anyone lose a fifty-dollar bill?"

The entire island shuts the hell up and turns around.

Well played, Tad Landon. Well played.

"Gets 'em every single time," Tad honks with pride.

Demetri edges his way over. Rat. He smells a baby announcement coming, and speaking of smells, what is that rank odor? I glance around and spot Bree coming in close with a platter full of detestable looking meats and gah! *Tentacles*! An entire bed of squid lies strewn about with their tiny little legs frozen midair. Glibbery, glistening, pink, purple, and gray, with miniature suction cups dotting their extremities.

Holy shit. I openly retch for all to see, and unfortunately, hear. Bree's eyes meet up with mine, and she bolts like a deer with a double-barreled shotgun staring down her face. My stomach squeezes tight just as Gage raises his arm to the crowd.

"If I could hold your attention for just a moment," he starts before looking to me lovingly, and my eyes swell with instant tears. "I think everyone here knows that just under a year ago I was fortunate enough to marry my best friend, the love of my life, Skyla Messenger."

The crowd breaks out into a soft sigh, and, one by one, I recognize faces from West. It's like a high school reunion right here in our backyard, each one of them with an overflowing poisonous plate in hand. Lovely. My mother will slaughter the entire graduating class, sans Logan, of course, whom Chloe managed to slaughter first because she's a moron. Speaking of the witch, she and Wes slink over for front row seats, and I openly scowl at the two of them. Figures. Come for the free food and entertainment. Fifty fake bucks says she's about to usurp our announcement.

"I want to take this moment to tell the world how very lucky I am, and how madly in love I am with this woman." My husband's voice catches on his words while the crowd gives another round of coos.

Chloe coughs as if she's about to be sick.

"It is with great excitement"—he continues—"and a touch of fear of the unknown that Skyla and I would like to announce that we're excepting a baby later this year."

A slight gasp emits before the crowd breaks out into deafening cheers, and congratulations are shouted from the four corners of the Earth.

Mom and Tad drop their jaws to the floor while the Olivers look as pale as ghosts.

"Skyla?" Mom nods as if needing further proof.

"It's true." I give a little shrug before she pounces over me.

"Oh, my baby girl is going to have a baby! I'm so proud of you!" she squeals straight into my ear and extinguishes the hearing on my right side. "I can't believe this!" She pulls back, still bracing me at the shoulders, her face filled with tears of joy. "Is this for real? I can't bear it, Skyla. Are we really having a baby?"

I note the pronoun shift that just took place and smile. In every way, I want my mother involved.

"Yes." I pull Gage in close. "We're having a baby."

"Well, congratulations." Tad spits it out with a sarcastic enthusiasm generally reserved for buffoons and idiots. "Let's get one thing straight. There's no more room at the Landon Inn. Get back on that orange donkey of yours and keep on keeping on." He hitches his thumb toward the Mustang. "We're knee-deep in rugrats as it is. We've caught our limit."

"Oh, stop." Mom smacks him.

"Was this planned?" Emma snaps as if demanding an explanation. "I thought you were on birth control!" she snips at me as if this entire mess were my fault. She so wishes.

Before I can open my mouth to say a word, Mom scoffs her off with a wave.

"Two can play the contraception game." She makes a face that's indicative of her newfound disdain for Emma. "And—two *have* to play the conception game. I say we call it a tie and forget about the name calling."

Boom! Mom just seriously laid it all down. And the rush of relief she just inspired has actually lessened my nausea.

"Congratulations, you two." Barron pulls me into a hug first before bringing Gage in on the action. His enthusiasm is so genuine, so beautiful and light, that I want to bask in it all night. "I just know you'll make fantastic parents."

"Yes—congratulations." Emma looks just as sick as I feel. "I suppose I wasn't expecting this so soon. You'll finish college, Gage, don't you worry. Skyla and this baby won't get in the way." She offers up a hard embrace to her son as if he's about to go off to war. Thermonuclear war. Little does she know he's already gone to war—a war with my vagina—in which he carpet-bombed my uterus with his amazingly speedy and ultra determined semen.

Three babies! I feel like shouting in her face. We're having *three!*

I bet it would kill both her and Tad if we told them the truth. Now there's a twofer I might be interested in.

Emily and Ethan come up and offer their congratulations.

"*Dude.*" Ethan slaps Gage some skin. "Welcome to the club. You're going to be fucking broke forever." I think it's great the way he's stepped up and become a true father to Ember. Not that Drake isn't being a true father to her—it's just that, well, he's Drake.

Em looks straight at me with that dead look in her eyes. "We have a lot to talk about."

God. I'm not too sure I want advice on anything that concerns the living, especially not the three living beings swimming around in my belly. Hey, I've practically become a human aquarium! I perk up at the thought until a vision of those tentacles comes back, and a wave of serious nausea pulses through me again.

Where is Dudley?

"You'll go natural," Mom insists as she pulls me in by the hand.

"It's going to hurt like a motherfucker," Em bleats without an ounce of emotion.

Crap.

"I probably won't be going natural," I mumble, because for one, I'm not really ready to have this conversation just yet. It's just a fact. I'm not trying to start a war of the vaginas with my mother.

"Brielle went natural, and so will you," she says through her teeth like a bad ventriloquist.

"Brielle's a freak of nature. Besides, she gave birth in a parking lot with the aid of my boyfriend who was a junior at the time." I grind my teeth. This is all Brielle's fault to begin with—tricking me with all that no-vanilla bullshit. I bet it was all a ploy to get me to join that baby-making cult she founded with my mother.

Speaking of Bree—she and Drake come over, and soon we're landlocked by our old senior class. Everyone seems excited and thrilled for us, well, everyone but Emma, of course.

She gives a wobbly smile as she and Barron successfully excavate us from the crowd. "I've got a sudden headache."

Barron offers another brief hug. "Come for dinner one night, and we'll open a bottle of our finest apple cider." He offers me a wink before his features sag, depleted of the smile he held just a moment before. "I suppose there are faction ramifications."

Gage gives a slow nod. "This offers Demetri—"

"Dominion," a deep voice strums from behind as the beast himself lands in our midst. "But let's not allow that technicality overshadow this joyous occasion. This child is so much more than its lineage. This child is a unique being created from the love of these two amazing young people." Demetri bows to me slightly. "Don't you ever let its DNA define it. This child, like everyone else, will get one shot on this spinning blue rock, and I imagine it will be magnificent. I'm truly elated for the two of you. A love like yours deserves a rich legacy to see it through time."

Gage and I seize, unsure of how to respond to this unusual act of kindness.

"Thank you." The words stutter from me. I'm suddenly gripped with grief over the fact my own father isn't here to experience this moment, and to make it worse, I just thanked the man who killed him. Sometimes, I can be a real moron.

"When will it arrive?" Emma shudders as if we've summoned a demon.

"December thirteenth." A shiver runs through me as I say the date of my anniversary with Logan out loud. "At least that's when I'm due."

"What?" Mom shrieks her way over. "Skyla, that means you're fifteen weeks!"

Dear God, the woman is a genius when it comes to prenatal mathematics.

"I've missed your entire first trimester!" she cries, her face crumbling, because for one, my mother is genuinely sorry about this unlike ungrateful Emma who is still looking to pin this whole conception deception on me.

"Don't feel bad," I offer. "I sort of did, too."

Mia and Melissa make their way over, and I happily use my sisters in an effort to excuse both Gage and me from Emma's allergic reaction to my children.

"Did you see that?" I whisper. "She wasn't even happy for us!"

Gage glances back a moment. "It's too new. She's freaked out. I can tell."

"She's been freaked out ever since we said I do. It's a sad day when we tell her we're gifting her a grandbaby, and Demetri out nices her by a mile."

"She'll be better by morning." He lovingly smooths the hair off my face. "She's going to spoil you from here on out with dinner and dessert. Just you wait and see."

"If haggis is number one on her menu, then she's already spoiled something—my appetite."

My sisters come upon us, and Melissa is the first to offer up a high five to both of us.

"Hey, skank. Congrats." Melissa offers an awkward hug, and Mia pulls her back abruptly.

"You can't call my sister a skank. You're the skank. Don't think I didn't see you with Rev."

"What's the matter?" Melissa bites over her cherry-colored lips. They're both wearing matching micro-miniskirts and pancake white powder and red lips. It's an eerie look. And not a good one. "I thought you wanted your freedom before the two of you get tied down. Isn't that what you said? Now is the time to *sow* your wild oats."

"No wild oat sowing," I interject, patting my stomach. "This is a direct result of sowing wild oats." Not really in the traditional sense, but if it weren't for Brielle's non-vanilla sex competition and Ellis's newfound hygiene practices when it comes to anal sex, we wouldn't be in this predicament right now.

Mia gets right in her face. "You suck, Melissa! You're only interested in Rev because I'm with Gabriel, and you know it pisses me off!"

"You're just with Gabriel because you know it pisses *me* off." Melissa pulls back like she's about to slug her, and Gage breaks it up.

"*Enough*," he barks. "No throwing punches. There's not a guy on the planet worth this."

Go, Gage. And what happened to giving up guys for the summer? Their pledge didn't last one full day. I'm beginning to think both of my sisters have a serious addiction to testosterone. I give Gage a quick squeeze—me included.

Mom comes over and drags them both off to the house like the toddlers they're acting like.

"This is just sick. What kind of person dates someone just to make someone else jealous? Mia should just pick one. She can't have two boyfriends."

"Oh, come on, Messenger." I turn to find Chloe and her glowing teeth, sparkling like shards in this dim light. "You practically invented that game. It looks like the skanky little sister didn't roll far from the rotten family tree."

Bree comes up with Natalie Coleman, Michelle Miller, and Lexy—who instantly infuses me with both rage and DEFCON 1 level nausea.

"Congratulations, Messenger." Lexy is the first to offer up her approval. "Logan and I will be sure to send a gift when the time is right."

Gage takes up my hand. ***Ignore her.***

"That won't be necessary." I scowl just as Logan, Coop, and Laken make their way over.

"Sure, it will." Lex is quick to wrap herself around his body like a python. "Uncle Logan and Auntie Lexy are going to spoil little Baby Oliver with all of the gifts and attention we can afford."

Logan peels her off with a gentle smile.

"You see that, Lex?" I snip. "He's peeling you off like an old coat. Logan is too much of a gentleman to toss you into the deep end." Plus, no pool.

"Wow," Chloe bleats. "Even with another man's baby in your belly, you insist on peeing a circle around your favorite Oliver. How does that make you feel, Gage?"

I glare at the sky for that stupid bird. If Holden wants to prove himself, he's doing a lousy job. My blood turns to lava as my general frustration with the night begins to hit a boiling point.

"I'll show you how it makes him feel." I step up and offer a crisp slap to Bishop's bitchy little face, and the crowd around us gasps.

I glance around in horror. Usually, I just dream about whacking her, about hitting her so hard her teeth fly into the back of her throat, and she chokes to death on those chunky calcified rocks, but, for whatever reason, I couldn't control myself. Oh my God. I stare down at my hand, still stinging from the effort. It's as if I have no filter and no control over my emotions anymore. I've become a danger to myself and society at large. The next thing you know, I'll be mowing the bitch squad down with the Mustang.

"Skyla!" Bree is quick to comfort her. "She's with child."

"So is she." Laken comes to my defense. "And all that bratty little witch ever does is antagonize her." Laken's rage against Chloe is mostly personal, but I love the show of camaraderie.

Wes shows up and nods to Gage as if to ask what's going on, but it's not him I'm worried about. It's the two that have followed him over. Lingering near the back of Bree and Drake's trailer are Killion and Moser, looking ever so interested in our adolescent exchange.

Chloe gets up in my face, her eyes glossy with hatred, and it's all I can do to keep from strangling her just to satisfy the craving.

"You little bitch." She smooths her hand over the side of her face, swollen with the imprint of my hand. I used every Celestra-Fem-based ounce of strength in me to whack her into tomorrow. "You're going to pay for that."

The urge to finish the job bounces through me. The downright hand-trembling intense desire to claw her face to shreds jolts through me, and I roll my head back and cry, "*Holden!*"

She huffs a laugh, and I taste her breath as she leans into me, hard. Wes comes over and tries to pull her away as Gage secures his arm around me.

Chloe spits in my face. "There will be an hour, Messenger, that you will beg for my help, but I will be the last to give it!"

"Oh, tell me something new," I hiss as I wipe the filth off my eye. A dark shadow of a bird circles overhead, and behind him a glowing white flame, Serena. Holden and his fair-feathered beauty make the rounds, lower and lower with each revolution as Chloe begins to sputter and cough.

"Come on." Wes tries to pull her into the woods. "We'd better go. This isn't good for the baby." But Chloe digs her spiked heels into the soil as her eyes start to glow an eerie shade of Satan, and, swear on my life, I'm seeing the inkling of horns sprouting from her head.

"I'm not done!" She gags on the words as Holden flies ever so much closer, his lady friend soaring over him in concert, and it's a mesmerizing sight.

I spot Killion pulling out her phone and recording the strange phenomenon. Scratch that. There isn't one paranormal thing about a couple of birds looking to scavenge off a piece of stale bread.

"Go back to hell, you little witch!" The words heave from me. "And do us both a favor, and stay there this time!"

Holden comes in low until he lands soft over my shoulder, and Chloe lets out a harrowing cry.

"I hate you, Skyla Messenger! I *hate* you!" A thunderous roar emits from her as she explodes in a flash of fire and ashes.

"Holy shit!" someone cries from deep in the crowd. "Did you see that?"

Crap. Leave it to Chloe to inadvertently start the apocalypse.

I glance over to the government dream scheme and find their faces set agog.

"They saw," I hum the words without moving my lips.

"They don't know she's really gone." Logan forms a huddle with Coop and Laken, motioning for us to join in. "Walk to the woods."

We walk toward the wall of evergreens as Nat tries to calm a hysterical Michelle Miller.

Where is Liam and his magical dick when you need him most?

We hit the periphery of the property until I'm unable to see ether Killjoy or Poser anymore.

"Coast is clear," I whisper.

Wes calls to Gage from a good distance away and excuses himself before heading over. I can't help but frown at their newfound solidarity. Or at least it seems as if they're enjoying a harmonious relationship these days.

I pull Logan to the side. "Thanks to Chloe, we've just fed those government minions exactly what they wanted—paranormal proof that Bishop is an idiot."

He pumps a dry smile, and that horizontal divot I gave him inverts. "I'm more worried about the people Wes recruited to work against the Barricade."

"Yes, I know. We have to get to those people, Logan," I pant. For a brief moment, I entertain the thought of letting Laken and Coop in on our plan, but then Holden does a fly by with his blonde bombshell, and I cringe at the thought of putting anyone else in danger. The Justice Alliance will not hesitate to turn the whole lot of us into a flock of angry birds should they find out what we're up to.

Gage heads back in this direction.

"We're shutting this shit down," I say to Logan, low as a whisper. "Wes might have the Immunity League, but we have a league of our own. The Don't-Fuck-with-my-People League." I give a curt nod. "Wes is about to fight dirty, and so are we."

"Yes, we are." Logan steadies his gaze over mine. That smile of his has long since dissipated. "Is there a reason we're not letting them in on this?" He ticks his head toward Laken and Coop.

"I don't want the Justice Alliance to turn us all into a bunch of glorified homing pigeons."

He winces. "Got it. But they won't. I'm dead, they can't charge me with jack, and you're untouchable. You and I both know that."

Laken and Coop come over.

"What's going on?" Coop asks with his chin tucked in the same manner as Logan's, and, for a moment, I think I'm seeing double.

"Nothing." I straighten as Gage joins us, and I pull him in. "We'd better head back to the party."

I don't say a word to Gage about what Logan and I talked about. I'm not sure why I don't feel too guilty about this.

Perhaps it's because he waited a week to tell me about the traitors. Maybe I'll wait a week before I tell him about the fact I'll be hunting those exact deserters down myself.

I smile up at my beautiful husband.

Fair is fair.

Gage

There is a lethargy, a calm like no other that comes from telling the truth. Skyla and I lay in bed for the better half of the next day. Lizbeth spent the majority of the afternoon at Demetri's, cleaning up from the party he had two days ago so it was beautifully restful with Skyla in my arms—me taking care of her, bringing her food when she could stomach to look at it. Come Tuesday, Dad asks me to run by Cost Club and pick up a few things for Mom who insists on cooking us a big meal.

"You sure you're up for this? Logan mentioned he needed to make a food run for the bowling alley, so if you want to stay here and rest, I'm more than okay with it."

"No way, no how. You can't stop me." She pulls on a pair of long leather boots over her jeans. It's pouring caskets outside. Those two days of sunshine were completely manufactured, and if Chloe's sudden disappearance from the party the other night didn't tip off Thing One and Thing Two, then the miraculous weather event for sure did the trick. "Besides, I want to look into a few things myself like, you know, baby stuff. Three babies are going to need a ton of supplies. We may as well take a peek and see what we're up against."

"Sounds good." I wrap my arms around her before we head downstairs. "I just want to let you know that I really think we're going to be okay. Accounting agrees with me. I can't believe my dad and Logan were shelling out the big bucks to some pricey firm on the mainland. Not only am I saving them some serious cash, but we're finally making it. I swear, I think I found my calling. All I do is put the game on in the background and sit and crunch numbers. It's a cakewalk."

"Really?" Skyla's eyes shine like river stones. "That's great. How about writing? You're not giving up on that, are you?"

"To quote you—no way, no how. You can't stop me." I lean in and take a bite out of her bottom lip as we make our way into the family room. It's true. I've been hacking away at the novel I'm working on whenever I get the chance. I'm hoping that one day I'll make something out of it. I take another bite of her lip before moving to her ear.

"Get a room," Melissa snips. Crap. I'm sort of hoping both of my new sisters-in-law will outgrow their snippy stage. Or in the least, Skyla and I will outgrow, outrun, or simply get out of this house and avoid the tension altogether.

"We just *left* our room." Skyla gives a placid smile. "You wouldn't believe the mayhem that went on in there." She gives me a quick wink, and my dick starts to tick.

Skyla has always had the ability to get me going with just a wink and a smile.

"You're sick!" Melissa tosses a pillow at her.

"Watch it!" Mia shouts, too late to intercept the throw. "She's having a baby!"

"She's not having it now."

Lizbeth scurries out of the kitchen and cups Skyla's cheeks with her palms. "I still can't believe my baby girl is having a baby! How are you feeling? Are your breasts sore? Have they exploded in size? Are they killing you yet? Do you need a bigger bra? Are you leaking?"

"*Mom.*" Skyla gently removes herself from her mother's clutches while Mia and Melissa pretend to retch. "There are people around."

"What people? The girls don't care. Are you talking about Gage? Oh, hon, I'm sure long before you ever got to this stage he's quite familiar with what's happening in your brassiere. Besides, I'm sure he wants you to feel your best, too. That's why I'm taking you shopping to invest in a good nursing bra. And I'm going to give you a few tips. It's never too early to roughen up your nipples, you know. Most young mothers don't think to do that, and then they're shocked that breastfeeding hurts so much in the beginning. Nipple treatment is an integral part of—"

"*Crap.* Excuse me." Skyla groans under her breath as she rushes to the coffee pot.

"Oh no, you don't, missy!" Lizbeth cuts her off at the pass. "Your caffeinated days are over."

"That's okay." I pull Skyla back before she commits an all out assault over her inability to caffeinate herself properly. "I'm taking her to breakfast. We're headed to Cost Club after. You need anything?"

"Well, look at this." Tad pops into the room. "Mr. Hot Shot offering to pick up the grocery tab."

Shit.

Lizbeth holds up a hand as if to stave off his lunacy—not that it were possible. Tad Landon's lunacy is an unstoppable force. "Actually, I was headed that way myself. Why don't we go together? Demetri asked me to pick up a few things for him." She cuts a glance to her questionable better half. "It's for an event he's hosting this fall."

Buying food now for an event that's not scheduled for months? Sounds about right. If I can say one thing about Demetri, it's that he likes to plan ahead—twenty years in my case.

Skyla grunts, "Serving up a little listeria with his lunchmeat? What event is he hosting so I'll know to steer clear?"

"It's a wedding and no lunch meat for you either, young lady. Do you have Dr. Cara Vale's new book? *What Happens When You're Expecting: A Step-by-Step Guide Through the Most Important Nine Months of Your Child's Life*?"

"Nope. Haven't read it."

"Oh, I'll have to pick up another copy. I just gifted one to Chloe. It even has a pullout calendar we can put right here on the fridge, and that way the whole family can track your uterine changes right along with you!"

"Gross." Melissa plucks the coffee pot right in front of Skyla. "Can't wait to read all about your separating pelvic bones."

"You're so smart!" Lizbeth pats her on the head. "But that won't happen for another few months."

Mia gives a disgruntled moan. "Well, actually, I can't wait to learn what size the baby is in your stomach right now. Can I feel it?" She lands her hand over Skyla's belly. "Oh, wow. You're already huge!"

"I'm not huge." Skyla's face blushes ten shades.

Lizbeth pulls back Skyla's T-shirt, revealing a rather round budding belly.

Where did that come from?

"I know." She looks up. "It's like I woke up this morning, and my stomach sort of arrived in big-bellied style. It's just weird. I can't even button my jeans without this silly rubber band trick that Brielle used to do." She wiggles the button on her jeans, and sure enough, it's suspended by a rubber band.

"Skyla"—Lizbeth runs her hand over her daughter's swollen belly—"you need a whole new wardrobe."

"Your mom is right. We need to get you some clothes." Knowing Skyla, she'll refuse the offer, but it doesn't change the fact this is happening.

"Don't even worry about it. I can wear sweats. I love sweats. This is the perfect excuse to live in them."

"What am I thinking?" Lizbeth squeals so loud both Misty and Beau toddle in to see what's the matter. "I have an entire box of maternity clothes I can gift you."

"Again, I can wear sweats." Skyla turns toward me and winces at the thought of donning her mother's maternity discards.

Little Misty lifts her mother's shirt and ducks inside.

"Looks like someone wants a snack." Tad is clearly irritated at the sight, then again when isn't he irritated?

"I'm trying to break her," Lizbeth whispers as if keeping the news from the baby.

"Mommy!" Beau tugs at her shirt. "I thirsty, too! Beau wants snack!" Misty kicks him in the head, and the wailing ensues.

"I'm sorry, Tad, but I've got to get to the store with Gage and Skyla." She plucks Misty from her top and tries to hand her off, but Tad makes a break for the door himself.

"Sorry, Tits, I gotta see some people about some things."

I warm Skyla's bare arm with my hand. ***Did he just call her Tits?***

Skyla makes a face. *I'm pretty sure it was Toots. Or at least that's what I'm choosing to believe. Sometimes, you need a delusion just to get by.*

"What people about what things?" Lizbeth's own irritation grows.

"I've got a meeting at Althorpe!" And with that, we hear the slam of the door.

"I'll watch Beau," Mia offers.

"Great!" Lizbeth tosses a few things into her oversized diaper bag, and Skyla watches with careful attention as if taking notes. She looks worried, afraid, as Lizbeth mules up with her bag and the car seat, so I offer to take both from her. "We'll take the minivan, if that's okay. Gage, can you drive if you don't mind?" Lizbeth has a way of singing every single sentence. She really does live in a bubble of joy, despite being married to Tad.

"I don't mind one bit."

We head out to Cost Club with Skyla sitting up front next to me and Lizbeth chatting all the way there about bloody cracked nipples, stretch marks, and the extreme importance of orgasms.

I offered to stop off at the Pancake House, but Skyla cut the air with her hand, her shirt firmly planted over her mouth letting me know that was a no-go.

"Not many people know this fact"—Lizbeth continues as we each get our separate carts—"but a female orgasm is very beneficial with helping to implant the baby." She waves me off. "Sorry, Gage, but, let's face it, you win at that game every time. This is Skyla's time to shine."

"Kill me," Skyla whispers just under her breath.

"Anyway, you're well past the implanting phase. The next trimester is going to be a breeze." She straps Misty in a blanket-like contraption that swaddles the entire front of the cart into a baby fun zone before taking off. "Text me when you're ready!" And with that, she takes off inside.

Skyla latches on to my arm. "Wait, don't we need her to get in?"

"Not anymore." I pull out the credit card my dad gifted me. "It's an expense account for the morgue, and I'm on it." In truth, I think this was my father's way of lending us a helping hand. He said it was okay for personal use in case of an emergency, or my mother's grocery requests, which this happens to be.

Skyla turns and catches her reflection in the oversized window to the tire department. "Ha!" A laugh bottlenecks in her throat. "Would you look at that? It looks as if I have two baby bumps—one in the front and one in the back! I look ridiculous." She gives her bottom a quick shake and giggles. "I love that funhouse mirror effect." She glances over at my reflection, and the smile glides right off her face. "Um—I was sort of expecting to find you short and stalky, or in the least have your features stretched like taffy, but they're not. You look suspiciously like yourself." She walks me back and forth, still inspecting our reflections, and the horror grows on her face.

"Oh my shit." She buries her face in my chest, and I'm quick to offer a consolatory pat on the back. "My ass is growing in girth and width!"

"It's not that bad," I whisper.

"Wrong words," she buzzes against my chest.

"You look perfect."

"That's better." She looks up with her face blotched with heat. "Although really it's not."

"You're cute as hell." I give her a pat on the ass, and she giggles with delight, back to her usual self.

We head inside, and Skyla tugs and points us toward an aisle infiltrated with baby formula, oversized boxes of diapers, plastic cups in a rainbow of colors, and mystery boxes filled with medicinal looking things. The entire vicinity smells nice, baby fresh, and for some reason, everything about this aisle is beginning to scare me.

"God"—she gives my arm a squeeze—"this is so exciting." That last word rings to the ceiling. "Wait, $39.99 for a box of diapers? That sounds a little pricey, don't you think?"

"I don't know." My stomach lurches like maybe it's agreeing with her. "It is a pretty big box—192 diapers."

"How many do you think they'll need? I think when Misty was born my mother was changing her a million times a day. I'll just ask, and that way we can do a little math and be in the know." She sends a quick text to her mom and instantly gets a reply. "Eight to twelve times?" Her voice pitches like she might be sick. "Somebody get me a bed and a burger."

We stare at the pallet full of diapers a good long while.

I grunt into the tower of boxes, "Let's say it's ten diapers a day—a nice round number. That means one box will last about nineteen days."

"For one baby, Gage." Tears roll down her cheeks before I can stop them. "We'll need about five or six boxes each and every month. What's the math?" She looks up at me in haste.

I swallow hard, almost afraid to tell her. "Let's try not to think about that right now." I push the cart quickly past the diapers, the wipes, the formula, all of which I'm secretly adding up, and I'm pretty sure my own nausea is rivaling hers right about now. "Why don't we hurry up and get the food for my mom, and I'll buy you a hot dog?"

"Sounds like a plan." She leans her head on my shoulder and sighs. Her phone bleats, and she holds it up. It's a text from Lizbeth. **Don't you worry about a thing. You are going to be a great mom!**

Skyla bucks as she buries her face in my chest a moment. "I can't believe this. I'm actually going to be someone's mom." Her watery eyes fill with a touch of joy, and for a moment, my beautiful wife looks as if she's won the lottery, and she has. We both have.

I pull her in and hold her like that for a very long while as her tears warm over my chest. The urge to weep right along with her hits, and I fight it. Everything is changing. Soon, Skyla and I will have three very tiny beings crowding the space between us. We will never be alone. I'm betting we'll wonder how we ever survived without them. I'm betting we'll never want to be alone, again—mostly.

"*Gage,*" Skyla moans as we make our way past the guard shack at the Paragon Estates. Mom sent an entire spasm of texts letting me know she was home, and I could drop the food off so she can get right to the meal she's set out to create. I believe the word she used to describe it was *complicated*.

Lizbeth just speeds on with her nonstop speech about some wedding Demetri is hosting this fall. "You won't believe the guest list. Oh, I'm sure the two of you will be invited." She peppers it with a schoolgirl giggle.

"Skyla"—I reach over and pick up her hand, limp as paper—"are you okay?"

"I can't," she moans, and instantly, I know her stomach is about to empty its contents. I tried to talk her out of that third hot dog—then when she had the berry and chocolate vanilla shake, I suspected we might have to pull over. I speed to my parents' driveway and help her to the porch while Lizbeth frees Misty from her car seat.

Mom swings the door open wide with a smile. "Well, hello, you two! I have to say I'm really warming to the idea of having a grandchild!" Her voice is all sunshine and roses, but Skyla is to busy clawing at the wall, moaning incessantly, and I know—

Skyla pukes a steady river into my mother's prized bed of impatiens, their violet blooms suddenly covered with three regurgitated all beef hot dogs and one berry chocolate shake.

"I'll hose that off," I assure her as Skyla retches to completion. "Let's get you inside."

"Inside?" Mom panics. "Are you sure the fresh air won't do her better?" she asks, trailing us into the living room. "I can bring a water dish out for you."

"She's not a dog." I help Skyla lie down on my mother's pristine white sofa, and I really don't give a shit if it's a mistake. I just want my wife to feel better.

"Here, honey." Lizbeth plucks a water bottle from her purse, and Skyla knocks half of it back. Her red-glazed eyes drift to mine. "Marshall." Her entire body writhes as she says it, so I don't hesitate pulling out my phone and sending him a text.

At my parents'. Get the hell over here. Skyla is really sick. She needs you.

I stare at that last line for a second. I hate that last line, especially that it's true.

The doorbells rings, and I hear my mother welcoming the wily Sector himself. That was quick.

"He's here," I whisper, bringing her hand to my face and meeting it with a kiss.

"Thank you." The words croak from her.

"No funny stuff." I give a stupid wink, but I mean it. *Please do not let him dry hump you in my parents' house in front of my eyes* I want to say, but let out a dull chuckle instead.

"Gage." Her brows furrow as she gives my hand a squeeze.

Shit. She heard.

Sorry.

"It's okay."

Dudley slaps me over the shoulder and evicts me from my spot.

"Good afternoon, Ms. Messenger. I hear you're not feeling well. Pity." He takes up her hand, and she gives an audible sigh.

There's that. Marshall can do for her what I can't. I head over to the foyer where Mom and Lizbeth are sounding off about something.

"*Gage*." Lizbeth pulls me in. "I'll be right back. I'm heading to Demetri's to drop off these supplies. Barron was kind enough of take your mother's groceries from the minivan. Tell Skyla, morning sickness can happen around the clock!" She spins to leave, then backtracks, "Oh, if you have ginger ale and crackers, that would be excellent. She needs to keep hydrated. It's so important for the baby. Amniotic fluid replenishes itself several times a day!" she sings as she heads back to the car with the baby in tow.

Lizbeth is a ball of knowledge of all things prenatal. And somehow, Skyla and I ambled right into her territory.

"She's like a walking Wikipedia page," I whisper, and my mother laughs a little too loud. "I mean that in a good way." I give my mother a stern look. "And be nice to Skyla. She's carrying your grandchild." It was hard not to say children. I'm not very good at keeping secrets from my parents, but, the sad truth is, it feels as if my marriage to Skyla has done nothing but drive a wedge between us.

"Did you have a chance to talk to your sister?" Mom's face fills with worry as she changes the subject on a dime. "Her education is of the utmost importance. She can't be serious about this quitting school business. That's not an Oliver thing to do. Even Logan is taking courses at Host through the adult program, and he's dead!"

"Pursuing academics beyond the grave—he always was an overachiever." No joke. That's why I've always looked up to Logan, still do.

I wince at what I'm about to say next. "Giselle isn't exactly just an Oliver." I hate to remind her of my sister's Kragger roots, but I'm afraid they're starting to show a bit—or at least influence. If I remember correctly, Emerson spent her last days as a Goth rebel who couldn't care less about her scholastic standing.

"Oh dear." Now it's Mom who looks as if she's about to be sick.

Skyla lets out a chipper laugh from the next room, and I head over without giving it a second thought.

"You feeling better?"

"God, yes." She leans on Dudley as he helps her to her feet. "Let's get out of here so I can go home and shower." She looks to my mother. "I promise, we won't be late for dinner. But if you don't mind, could you set the table for one more?" Her eyes flit to Dudley.

"Of course—I'd be glad to. Mr. Dudley is a welcome guest in our home anytime." She gives a high-pitched giggle, reminiscent of the one Lizbeth gives in his presence, and now it's me who's nauseated at the effect this douche of a Sector seems to have on all the women in my life. He glares at me a moment as if he heard.

"Is everything better?" Dad ambles inside from putting away the groceries.

"*Much*. Thank you." Skyla fans herself a moment.

"Barron"—my mother turns to him—"why don't we take the kids next door? The Walshes have already moved most of their belongings, and they've told me to feel free to bring them by anytime."

Skyla shudders as if the potential of moving next door had the power to bring back her nausea.

"We really can't afford it." I pull her in, away from Dudley, and she happily melts against my chest.

"Not to worry." Mom ushers us all out the door. "It certainly costs nothing to look. At least this way you'll know what you could be missing!" Now it's her voice singing through the air. Slowly, my mother and Lizbeth Landon are morphing into one person. I'm not sure if I should be horrified or grateful.

The Paragon fog skirts the street just as Logan's truck pulls in, narrowly missing Dudley by inches. I give a brief wave as he jumps out.

"Try harder next time." I offer up a knuckle bump.

"What's going on?" He pulls Skyla into a brief hug. "Everything okay?"

"It's fine. Emma just wants to show us the house next door." Her eyes enlarge, expressing her disdain in code.

"Ah." His head tips back. "Well, let's do it. It can't hurt to look." He nods her over as we walk toward the Walsh's home as a mob.

Ellis and Giselle jog over from across the street.

"What's up?" Ellis stinks like ass, looks like he hasn't showered in days, and then it hits me—he looks like he's just got laid.

"You keeping things chaste?" I say it low as my parents lead the pack toward the Walsh residence.

"Always and forever, dude. You checking out the old haunted house?"

"Haunted, huh?" Skyla folds her hand in mine. "And it's a firm *no* on the purchase. Come on, let's check this place out so we can head home, and I can throw myself in the shower." She leans in and whispers, "If you're good, I'll throw you in, too."

"I heard that." Giselle makes a face.

I can't help but frown at my baby sister. "And I heard some things about you and West. What's going on?" I pull Giselle in. Her hair smells like weed, and I want to clobber Harrison for ever getting to know my sweet sister, let alone corrupting her.

"I don't want to talk about it." She steps on ahead with Ellis just as Lizbeth pulls up with Demetri.

"Crap," I whisper. "Let's make this real quick."

It's hard to tell where the woods next to my parents' home end and the Walsh residence begins. It's wild, wooly, and dark. Nothing but a tangle of dead roots swinging over the dilapidated rooftop, the gray house stands two stories, heavily shadowed from the already dim light Paragon has to offer.

"Shit," I hiss upon first sight. It's fair to say I haven't actually seen the house in years, if ever. It's been shrouded in a cover of evergreens for as long as my memory serves. I certainly don't recall this parched, scraggly looking—for lack of a better word, haunted house with a few of the windows missing.

The wind howls through the vicinity, and the house offers a belated moan as if welcoming us, or telling us to stay the fuck away. It's a toss up, but I'm starting to find credence in Ellis's haunted house version of this reality. The fog brumes through the porch, and it looks as if the house is giving us a toothless grin with its crooked front door, its dilapidated balconies on the upper level. This place reeks architectural hazard far more than it ever does cozy new home, but to fulfill my mother's latest desire, I'm willing to do a quick run-through—let's hope nothing decides to give us a chase.

"Wow," Skyla marvels. "It's like there's a dark cloud over it—and, well—just it."

We head up the badly cracked tar driveway right after Dudley and Logan. All of the homes behind the gates had tar-covered driveways once upon a time, but one by one they ripped them out and installed stone driveways, stamp concrete, or interlocking bricks, anything but this pocked-up mess. But not the Walshes. They were steadfast in maintaining the home's original architecture, and apparently aesthetics. I can predict the crap we're about to see inside, and I certainly don't need the gift of knowing to figure that out.

"It's a bit of a fixer-upper," Mom chirps as she gives a brisk knock to the door, and a plume of dust radiates from her effort. "They're not home," she announces, pushing and kicking at the entry until the door simply falls off its hinges.

Good God. Did she just use her Deorsum strength to break and enter? My mother is chock full of surprises these days. One thing is for sure—she's gunning hard for this house.

"I'll admit, it needs a bit of a spit shine!" she announces a bit cheerier than necessary.

"A spit shine?" Skyla quips just low enough for me to hear. "Try a bonfire."

"What's everyone looking at?" Lizbeth and Demetri barrel up with their lovechild tucked between them.

"Oh, it's just a fixer." Skyla shakes her head at her mother. "The neighbors have moved out. They'll be putting the house on the market soon."

"This is perfect for the two of you!" Demetri beams.

I catch Dad scoffing at the demon, and don't know whether to laugh or to get ready to break up a fistfight.

"You can see it's quite spacious!" Mom shouts with joy, proudly accepting her role as tour guide to this neglected estate. "We should spread out. Divide and conquer. I'll open the back so you can see what a large yard you'll have. A great place to put up a swing set, and, perhaps, one day put in a swimming pool!"

"She's campaigning hard," Skyla sighs, taking it all in. "But there's no pool," she whispers. "My nonexistent swimming regime is already in peril."

We take the full tour. The dusty living room opens to a spacious kitchen with its stuck-in-the-sixties cabinetry and appliances. The refrigerator is a small, boxy Norge, and Logan seems most amused by this.

"The kitchen will need a few upgrades." Logan taps the counter, and a plume of dust rises to the ceiling like a poltergeist.

"Are you kidding?" Ellis barks out a laugh as he opens the decrepit fridge. "Skyla doesn't cook—she can hardly make a sammich."

"I can make popcorn." She gives a sly wink before hopping up on her tiptoes to offer a kiss.

Upstairs there are four bedrooms, each one a moderate size. It's not as large as my parents' home, but it's a palace compared to the eight-by-ten cell we share at the Landon Incarceration Facility.

"You've got the right number of bedrooms." Logan gives the wall a hard knock, and something collapses in the next room.

Skyla gasps. "We'd better get out of here before the roof falls in and kills us, then we won't need any rooms." She's quick to lead the way downstairs.

Logan pulls me back. "I take it she's not into this."

"Nope. We're just humoring the folks. It sure would be nice to get our own place, though."

"Life at the Landon house isn't all it's cracked up to be, huh?"

"Oh, it's all that it's cracked up to be. That's the problem."

We head downstairs and find Skyla in the backyard musing at an entire section of downed and dying trees. There's an Amazonian appeal, a jungle book look that I'm not too sure I can get used to. Just past a plethora of average evergreens stands a beast of a tree, a cross between an oak and a Jurassic-looking eucalyptus with a trunk the size of a double-car garage. Thick cable-like tendrils drip from its branches as if ten trees had melded together to form this one enormous botanical monstrosity.

"Why, this place is practically sacred." Lizbeth squeals with joy as she takes in the long, phallic extensions that drip to the ground. "And this is where we'll plant the placenta! Feed the tree, Skyla. Feed the tree!"

There's a moment of silence that none of us quite know what to do with.

"It's just begging for a tree house!" Dad shouts. And it saddens me a bit to see him get his hopes up.

Logan nudges me and nods over to the center of the yard. Skyla and I head over to find a dark circle burned into the soil with something that resembles the letter A running through it.

"Looks supernatural." Skyla runs her shoe through the soot.

Dudley looks back at the house while the rest of the party meanders back inside. Both my mother and Lizbeth are buzzing with excitement. You would think we just toured a model home.

Skyla steps next to Dudley and shakes her head at the monstrosity. "Do me a favor, and make sure this never happens."

"The architecture doesn't please you?" he muses.

"It's the neighbors. Neighbor to be exact," she tries to a whisper, but Logan and I are just a few feet away.

"Sorry, dude." He taps his shoulder to mine.

"I know how she feels." I grind my heel into the ash, marking the soil. "What do you think this burnout in the soil means?"

"Hell if I know." He gives a brief wave to Skyla before taking off.

Demetri comes my way, and we take a few steps into the mangled woods. "Are you interested in the place?"

"No," I flatline. No use in sugarcoating anything to Demetri. In that sense, he does feel like family, and, ironically, I know that I'll have to sugarcoat my feelings about this monstrosity to my parents. "What do you want?"

"Testy, are we? I take it your wife's state of displeasure is more than unsettling for you. I'm sorry she's been ill. I'm sure she'll feel better soon. It seems the Sector is able to quell her. Would you like the capability? Vibratronics is an easy gift for me to impart. Even a near-human is capable of such a second rate magician's trick."

"Vibratronics? Sounds robotic. Like something you might install on your hard drive. A cheap app they give away for free." I think about it for a second. "Yeah, maybe." Hell, it's necessary as far as I see it.

"Then, along with it, allow me to offer you another gift—sort of a package deal."

"What's that?" I'm only half-interested. In truth, I miss my powers. I miss the ever-living shit out of them, and I'm just a hair away from begging him to restore me to my fake Levatio standing. That's always who I'll see myself as—who I'll be deep down inside. Gage Oliver the Levatio. Such humble beginnings. I wish I could have stayed that way.

"Let me anoint you and Skyla in holy matrimony. If it's one thing I've wanted all your life to give you, it's a proper wedding. You already have the prize, Gage. Let me honor it in some small way."

"A wedding?" I tick my head back. "I don't think so. Skyla and I are sort of past that phase and on to the next."

"Nothing fancy then—a word or two in your honor. It'll be in the Transfer. Just a few minutes of your time."

"And when will I get my good vibrations? Skyla needs them now." I scowl over to where Dudley stands with Skyla and Logan.

Demetri claps his hand over my shoulder. "As soon as Skyla agrees to the anointing ceremony, we'll make arrangements. And once the ceremony is complete, the gift is yours through spontaneous commission. The sooner the better, don't you say?"

"I do." I nod as he takes off into the woods and explodes in a plume of boiling black fog.

I glance to where Dudley holds Skyla's hand.

It's time to convince her of a little vow exchange in the Transfer.

What could it hurt?

Demetri is right. I already have the prize.

Logan

Dinner at Barron and Emma's is usually something I look forward to, but, tonight, in the midst of Skyla's desperate need to cling to Marshall and moan, it's a bit less appetizing all the way around.

"Have you thought of names?" Emma waves a fork full of food at Skyla as if taunting her, and Skyla's poor face turns green as the lettuce wilting on her plate. She hasn't touched a bite of her meal.

"We haven't really," Gage answers for her.

Emma's pet, Kresley, is here, mopping up Gage's side of the table where he sloshed his water, offering him bread and butter as if she were his personal bed nurse. From an outsider's perspective, you wouldn't think Gage and Skyla were a couple at all. You would assume it were Gage and Kresley.

"I think you should consider Barron if it's a boy." Emma gives a sly wink to my brother. "Of course, unless you were thinking of Gage Junior. I'm all for that as well."

Liam holds a finger up while he swallows. "Liam is a fantastic name, but works well as a middle name, too."

Skyla tilts her head to the side, the color returning to her face just enough. "I sort of thought I might be having a girl. I don't really know boys." Her face deepens a dark shade of cherry. "I mean, I didn't grow up with a brother. Not that I would be intimately familiar with his body—um"—she looks to me for help. "Anyway, I think it would be fun to dress a girl." She closes her eyes in defeat.

"Boy's names for girls is all the rage." Kresley nods into Skyla as if they were old friends. "I'm actually named after my father's middle name. I didn't quite appreciate it, though, until I met Wes," she sighs, gazing dreamily into some unknown horizon. "Wesley and Kresley. It has such a nice ring to it."

"You should go find him and tell him." Skyla doesn't miss a beat. "Maybe you can cut his steak and wipe his face down with a napkin like you practiced on my husband tonight."

"Oh, for goodness' sake." Emma tosses down her utensil. "Can't you girls ever get along?"

"Only when she stops lusting after my man." Skyla picks up her knife and fingers the blade.

"Well"—Gage pushes his plate back—"I have a meeting to get to for the Videns. I'm planning on talking to the local chapter, getting to know a few of them a little better. I want to know how they really feel about the Barricade, about us."

"I'd like an update on the dolomites." Skyla taps her hand over Marshall's as she says it and shudders as if soaking in the hit. I get that he makes her feel better, and Skyla is the last person I want to feel bad, but the sight has taken my appetite and shot it down like a clay pigeon.

Gage glances at his phone. "Wes is outside. I'd better get going."

He and Skyla hug it out while Kresley runs and snatches her purse. "Thank you for dinner!" She offers Emma a quick embrace at the door.

Skyla gawks at the sight. "Where do you think you're going?"

"I figure Wes can give me a ride." She narrows her eyes at Skyla. "And I can wipe his chin, feed him my lips like you suggested."

"At least you have your sights on the right Edinger this time," Skyla whispers it low as not to offend Barron in the next room.

"You know, Skyla"—Kresley takes a step in, and I do the same in the event a catfight breaks out—"if you weren't with Gage, or whoever the hell it is you'd die to be without"—her hand pans both Marshall and me—"you'd understand the pain, the anguish I feel with Wes. Just know that you're lucky to have the man you want most in your arms, in your bed. Some people don't truly appreciate what they have until it's taken away from them forever. I know I didn't." She waves her off before stepping outside and joining Emma and Gage.

"Ignore her." I pull Skyla in by the shoulders for a moment.

"No, I get what she's saying." Her lips press white. "But she's wrong. I do know what it's like to love someone and lose them." She pulls me in briefly. "I'm glad you're still in my life, Logan."

We step outside and wave goodbye to Gage as he and Kresley take off in Wesley's SUV.

"What should we do with the rest of the night?" I ask as the fog dances between our bodies, mocking us like a restless spirit. It's saying *here she is, you can't have her. You didn't plant that baby, those babies inside her beautiful body.* My eyes keep straying to her rounded belly. Out of nowhere, Skyla wears her tribute to her love for Gage like a badge whether she's ready or not.

"Get Ellis," she whispers. "We're going to Marshall's." We met up with both Brody and Ellis a few nights ago just to feel them out. I think tonight we cement our new standing with them.

Dudley finishes saying good night as he tips his invisible hat at the two of us.

"We'll be there in just a few minutes!" Skyla waves after him.

"You can't keep your hands off me, can you, Ms. Messenger?" He's more than happy to tease. Asshole.

"Don't you know it! I expect a full body massage before I go home!"

"*Skyla.*" I give a disapproving grunt.

"I can't help it. I'm just about dead with all this morning sickness. It's beyond terrible, Logan. In fact, I've thought of hiring out his services. We'll make millions if Brielle doesn't get to it first."

Emma and Barron poke their heads out the door. "We're off to bed, Logan!" Emma shouts.

"*Good night!*" Skyla and I chime in unison as she slams the door shut.

"See that? As soon as Gage leaves, I'm invisible. That woman hates me. I'm just an incubator for her grandchildren at this point. A machine she can feed her sheep guts to, and I pop children out in return. A haggis eating Pez dispenser." She wrinkles her nose at the idea. "Let's get to Marshall's. I'm ready to hack the Steel Barricade to pieces. Did you see all that bullshit on TV regarding the so-called otherworldly visitors? Drake and Ethan are talking about selling anti-terrestrial repellent. Soon, the entire world will be outfitted with little tinfoil hats no thanks to Wes and his impotent bid for earthly dominion."

"Earthly dominion." I think on this a sec. "You may be onto something." I nod across the street to the Harrison's house. "Let's walk to Dudley's. It's a nice night."

"Okay, but I might need to take a puking break or two."

"I'll carry you if I have to."

She leans her head over my shoulder as we cross the street. "I feel like you're always carrying me."

It warms me to hear that. "Thank you." I sneak a kiss to the top of her head as we reach the Harrison's oversized, overly ornate front doors.

Skyla rings the bell, and it tolls for a solid five minutes, loud enough for everyone on the planet to hear.

The door on the left swings open, revealing a glazed over Ellis and a disgruntled looking Giselle.

"I thought you were home with a stomachache?" Skyla pulls her in.

"I lied." She gives a dry smile, acting more like her predecessor, Emerson Kragger, by the minute.

"Why would you do that? We just had a nice family dinner." Now it's Skyla fabricating a story. "Liam was there without any of his annoying girlfriends."

"Liam's annoying girlfriends weren't the reason I wasn't there. It's that old witch." She scowls at the house.

"*Giselle.* That's your mother!" Skyla seems incensed by this, but I happen to know Skyla has felt close to the same on occasion.

"I don't care. She's not the boss of me."

It takes a lot to hold back a laugh. "I hate to break it to you, but she sort of is. Look, we're headed to Dudley's, and we need to borrow Ellis for a few minutes. You need a ride home?"

"No, I have my car." She nods to the glossy black Range Rover in the driveway. "Daddy's having fluffy pink seats put in for me next week. I can hardly wait."

I'm not quite sure how to respond to this. For one, by *Daddy*, she means Arson Kragger, and two, fluffy pink seats.

Ellis and Giselle share an uncomfortably long smooch good night that looks as if Ellis is snaking out her insides. We wait until Giselle drives off before heading over to Dudley's.

"Just the three of us." Ellis gets between Skyla and me, slinging his arms over our shoulders. "The three musketeers are back together again."

Skyla hitches her breath. "We've never been the three musketeers, Ellis."

"Yeah, but I like the sound of it."

"Me, too." She pulls him in.

We push through the fog, bathing in the cool mist as we make our way down the middle of the street. There's something pure about this moment, something reminiscent of softer days.

"Here's to a prosperous future," Ellis declares for no real reason.

"What do you think the future holds for you?" Skyla tucks her head toward his.

"I've got some serious ideas, dude. Designer LSD—we're talking llama lickers, peanut butter poppers, and tragic magic," he pants the words out, serious as can be. "Those obnoxious feds sniffing around? All we have to do is slip them roofie coladas, dismember them, and I'll use their remains to fertilize my reefer farm."

Skyla and I still a moment as we stand in silent judgment of our once favorite stoner.

"What?" he pipes up, irritated. "They're organic."

We hit Dudley's, and Marshall is already at the table along with Brody Bishop.

"The dream team unites. The Retribution League," Skyla muses while studying the brooding Bishop. "Are you up for playing nice?"

Brody's chest bucks with the idea of a laugh. "I didn't join this endeavor to play nice. I'm here to help you shut this shit down. And, in the event you've forgotten, I'm taking it up the ass for you." He nods to her stomach as if whatever he's sacrificing is in honor of the fact she's with child. "I'm giving the Counts their monthly blood draw in your place."

"Brody." Skyla closes her eyes for a moment. "Thank you. I had hoped there were other reasons they weren't claiming my neck. I owe you more than I can ever repay."

"I don't need repayment. I believe in doing what's right." He offers a short-lived smile. "Now, what's the game plan? I'm ready to get dirty."

The blood draw—another reason for me to hate the Counts. The tunnels might be closed, but they weren't about to give up control entirely. There are reserves to be met. I much rather they're met by a Bishop than by an Oliver—Skyla Oliver.

"Good." Skyla nods to Dudley. "You have the list?"

"Yes, my love." Dudley sits straight, shoulders back, chest puffed with pride at the fact Skyla has confided in him. I'd be lying if I didn't say I was resentful. He passes out a sheet of paper to each of us, and suddenly, it feels like I'm in fourth period all over again. Damn, who knew I could miss West so much?

"What's this?" I scan over it, and then it hits me. "These are the guys, huh?" Shit. Names for miles of the lunatics that are willing to out the Nephilim in order to save their necks.

Brody shakes his head while pouring over it. "The sad thing is, these people actually believe that the Barricade is capable of protecting their families."

"Can't they?" Skyla cocks her head to the side. "I'm sure Wes provided some sort of demonic covenant."

"And I'm sure he didn't," Dudley is quick to add. "There is no protective hedge strong enough to shield thousands of people from a large and powerful entity such as the U.S. government, or any government for that matter. What Wesley has done is offered a compact. Nothing more dynamic than that."

"He lied to them," Skyla says it breathless as if the wind were just knocked out of her.

"Not necessarily." Marshall claps his hand over hers, inspiring Skyla to take in a quivering lungful of air. "It's simply a matter of semantics—*and* the fact they were gullible enough to believe him."

Ellis folds his hands together. "So, what's going to happen?"

"I get it. I know what's going to happen." I close my eyes because I sincerely hope I *don't* get it—that I don't know what's about to unfold. My mind just so happened to flit to the worst-case scenario. "Wes is giving our own people the rope they need to hang themselves. We get enough defectors out there, and they won't have to do any of the dirty work themselves. The Barricade keeps its nose clean. We die a slow suicide."

"Wow," Skyla muses, obviously pissed. "Wes really is an evil mastermind."

"So, what now?" Brody folds his paper into the shape of an airplane. I can see Chloe there in his face, and it's unnerving if I look at him too long.

Skyla runs her finger down the page as if she were silently numbering them. "Now we figure out where we're going to store the bastards after we capture them."

"Capture?" Marshall isn't the least amused. "Detainment for the greater good of one or more factions is a non-punishable offense. Capturing and taking prisoners during a time of peace among factions is something the Justice Alliance loves to reward by turning the perpetrators into overgrown fowl and haggard factory workers for the enemy. There is a razor thin line between the two, Ms. Messenger. I suggest you tread lightly."

"Ezrina and Nev—so the punishment is old school." I nod. "It looks like we're about to detain a hell of a lot of people for the greater good of the Nephilim."

Brody nods. "And, once people realize it's not a means to an end like they thought, they'll think twice before performing circus tricks for humans. I like what we're doing here." He looks from Skyla to me. "I'm asking Brooke to marry me. I want kids—a big family. I don't want to think about my children being taken away and shoved in a cell while some freak in a lab conducts experiments on them. This is a good thing, Skyla." He stands to go. "My lips are sealed. Let me know when you need me to start hunting the bastards down."

"We need it now." Skyla looks to Dudley. "We'll keep them here."

Dudley's lips twitch as if he's amused. His eyes hood low as if he's taking a moment to seduce her. "I'm afraid I'm denying your request."

"It wasn't a request," Skyla huffs. "It's an order."

"I'm denying that as well."

"No, Marshall. We need to stick these assholes somewhere, anywhere. And this is the only place large enough that won't evoke suspicion."

"Language," he says it stern as hell and stills Skyla in her seat.

"This is my house," she snipes, pulling the spirit wife card. I like her moxie.

"My house for now," he growls back, and it looks as if we're witness to a lovers' quarrel, if the lovers were two powerful celestial beings who could turn this place into matchsticks in less than thirty seconds.

"How about the Haunted Speculum?" I offer. "It's a shit storm of destitution in there. A vast desert of nothingness. A haunt for jackals. A perfect holding cell for the traitors."

Dudley presses his thumb to his lips as he stares off in that direction.

"It'll have to be temporary," he decides. "There's no way to corral them once they're inside. Of course, there's no escape either. The true definition of detainment dictates a confined space—not an entire realm where they are welcome to roam freely. According to rules and regulations, a temporary residence may be in use for up to sixty days until proper confinement is provided."

"That means we start now." Skyla glances back at the list. "We'll each take ten."

"Heavens no. I can't partake in the fun." Marshall pushes out a silent laugh. "I'm simply here as The Pretty One's supervising spirit. I've no jurisdiction to participate in the detainment process. I'm a Sector. These are not my people."

I nod to Brody. "You take the first fifteen men on the list. Ellis, you take the next fifteen. I'll pick up the rest."

Skyla clasps her hand over my wrist as if to stop me. "We will pick up the rest."

"Sounds good." Brody taps Dudley over the shoulder with his paper jet. "I'll text you as soon as I catch one."

"Very well." Dudley stands and heads for the exit himself. "The speculum does love to entertain. This should be interesting. I have an appointment. I'll keep my phone on hand."

"Marshall, where do you keep going off to?" Skyla jumps up in frustration, but he's already halfway to the haunted mirror in question.

"Seventeenth century."

"What are you doing there? Does this have something to do with that Chloe look-alike skank?"

His expression sours as he looks over his shoulder at me. "I don't believe so. And if I'm fortunate, my business back in the Mother Country will have no ramifications in the present whatsoever." With that, he steps into the smoky fog of the looking glass and disappears out of sight.

"I'm out of here." Ellis wags his list at us. "Don't worry. I won't let anyone see this. I'm keeping this on the DL, dawg." He knuckle bumps Skyla and me. "Get it? *Dawg*? As in West? Man, I miss that shit."

"Me, too." I give a mournful grin. Maybe more of us are feeling the same. Maybe it's time to start plotting a get-together that doesn't end in one of us going up in flames.

Skyla rushes to him and pulls him in by the T-shirt with an aggressive jolt. "Ellis, you so much as breathe a word of any of this, you will force my hand to kill you. Do you understand?" She grits the words through her teeth. I've never seen her look so frighteningly serious. "And, if for whatever reason, you do decide to leak this—for *any* reason I deem necessary, I will kill Giselle first."

The room fills with a thick silence.

Ellis holds his hands up like it were a stick-up and lets loose a nervous laugh. "You're not a killer, Skyla."

She leans into him close until their noses are almost touching. "Let's be honest. I'm probably going to kill us all."

Ellis takes off, swearing up and down that he's not saying shit.

"You're a badass, Messenger!" he shouts as he heads out the door. "I'm glad I'm on your side!"

The door shuts, and the overgrown house is quiet as a church mouse.

"I'm glad I'm on your side, too," I whisper, leaning against the wall, just taking her in this way. Skyla is gorgeous on an average day, but, now, with new life budding inside her, she literally glows ethereal. She is a true testament to the beauty of an expectant woman. I should commission a painting of her in this delicate state as a gift to her and Gage. I think I will.

"What's that smile for?" She frowns as she says it.

"I was just thinking I need to commission a painting of you. You're too beautiful, Skyla. I want you to always remember what you looked like while with child—children." I wince.

"Are you kidding?" She backs up as if I offered to feed her a rat. "No way. I'm huge. I've already gained like twenty pounds. Yesterday, I fit into my jeans just barely, and today, I'm not even at the rubber band phase anymore. Nice try, but it ain't happening."

"You need to. At least let me hire a photographer to do some monthly shots from here on out. Trust me, you'll thank me later."

"I'll think about it. But nothing nude. Just something tasteful."

"Nothing nude." My eyes glide down her body, then up again like a reflex.

"Wipe that smile off your face, Oliver."

"I can't. You're one of the only people on the planet that I can't stop smiling around. I smile in my sleep when I think about you."

"Oh?" She raises a brow. "And these dreams, are they chaste?"

"That's one thing I don't have to tell you."

She bites down on a smile of her own, her hands balling up into fists at her hips. "Do I need to kick your ass?"

"You think you're up for it?" I can't help but mock her a little. "By the way, I love it when you talk dirty."

"You stop it, Logan Oliver." She needles into my chest with her finger. "Because I will so do it! I have enough rage in me to kick ten Celestra's behinds all the way to Tenebrous."

"You're damn cute. You know that?" I give the impression of a dirty grin. "You keep this up—I might be forced to kiss you."

Her eyes widen, completely not amused at my quasi-pass, and come to think of it, neither am I.

"You kiss me, and I might be forced to slap you."

My lips twitch. "I might like that just as much." It's the sad truth.

Our eyes lock for a moment, hers with curiosity and mine with a morbid undying love that wishes she were still completely mine. I knew I should have done it long ago—the descaling of Skyla from my heart—but it's an impossibility that will never happen. No matter whom she's with, deep down in my soul, she'll always belong to me.

We walk back to Barron's, and I pick up my truck and drive her home. Skyla invites me up to the butterfly room and shows me her new trick of making them dance in concert to music. Skyla is gaining power, and she's angry as hell. A dangerous combination if you ask me.

She falls asleep on a pile of pillows while telling me about a shopping trip to Cost Club with Gage, something about enough diapers to line the planet with.

But all I can think about is what a lucky bastard Gage Oliver is. What I wouldn't give to be in his shoes. One thing I wouldn't give up is Gage himself. If it were anyone else, I would have killed him by now.

Skyla might like to think she's a killer, but deep down, I've always known that the true killer around here is me.

If those traitors don't comply with detention, they'll find out the consequences the hard way.

Death will come, and I will bring it.

8

On a Butterfly's Wing and a Prayer

Skyla

Dinner at the Oliver house seems almost repetitious, as if we're on a loop with Emma's misadventures in cooking. Don't get me wrong. Emma is a fantastic chef, but her exploits of innards and non-vital organs have left my palate begging for mercy.

Gage and I make our way into the living room where Logan pats a spot on the sofa next to him, so I head over, and Gage lands on the other side of me. It feels nice like this, ensconced with my two favorite angels. Safe.

"Come here, princess." Logan starts in on a penetrating massage over my shoulders, and I twist into him and moan. "You look like you need a little TLC."

TLC? I give a nervous smile to Gage as I try not to moan with pleasure at the deep, careful prods of Logan's thick, strong fingers. Damn, that boy knows how to work his hands.

"What do you mean TLC?" Gage isn't too amused at what this might imply.

"You know what I mean." Logan leans in and drops a kiss over the back of my neck, and I gasp. But, no thanks to his demanding, highly skilled digital maneuvers, my back insists I hold still and keep my ever-loving mouth shut. Besides, Gage didn't seem to notice that innocent peck. He's too busy doing a similar maneuver to my knee, and, before I know it, my shoes are off, and Gage is offering up a brisk, thankfully tickle-free, massage to my poor tired feet.

"Look at her"—Logan gives my shoulders a tweak—"she's rode hard and put away wet. You need to take better care of the old girl if we're going to get some mileage out of her."

What the hell? Before I can gawk at him properly, Gage unhooks his belt and begins unbuttoning, *unzipping* his jeans.

"You're right." Gage smolders at me with heavy lids, that lustful look in his eyes that gets right before we get to business. "What she really needs is a slow, thorough body massage with my mouth." Gage dives in with a tongue-twisting kiss that manages to scoot me straight onto Logan's lap. Soon, that back massage Logan is offering up turns into something more as his hands ride up my blouse, his mouth falls over the back of my neck, biting my earlobe and the beginnings of a terribly large orgasm trembles through my body. I've never felt so intensely, deliciously loved before. So many groping hands. Their hot mouths moving over my flesh, biting, licking all at once. Before I know it, my clothes have been stripped from me, and Logan's cock is pressed against my lower back as Gage thrusts into me from the front. Someone is kneading my breasts, biting down over my neck. Our collective lust snowballs, hurdling toward a magnificent climax as inevitable as an avalanche. Logan grabs me and twists my body into his before plunging into me so deep I feel the pinch at the base of my neck.

"He can't have you forever, Skyla." His amber eyes burn into mine as he penetrates me deeper like a punishment.

"Fuck you!" Gage pummels his face so close to mine I'm afraid for both our teeth.

Emma walks into the room wearing a wedding dress while balancing a platter with a sheep's head on it. "Dinner is ready!"

And the three of us shout in unison, *"We don't want any!"*

I sit up in bed with a start, panting, pulling the covers off my sweat-drenched body as my bedroom slowly melts into view around me.

"Whoa." Gage lands a heavy arm over my lap, making a weak attempt to pull me in. "You have a bad dream?"

A dream. I close my eyes and arch my head back. God, I can still feel Logan deep inside me. This has got to stop.

"Yes, it was a very strange dream, actually. We were at your parents,' and your mother was making us dinner." I don't see the need to torment him with the details.

"Dinner, huh? Was it making you sick?" He pulls me over to him, those dimples of his darken in this early morning light, and my stomach pinches with lust for him, only him, my husband, just the way it should be.

"I guess you could say that." I land a sweet kiss to his lips before glancing over his shoulder just to confirm the fact there isn't a spare Oliver in the room with us. Not that Gage and I would ever consider a threesome—especially not with Logan, not with anyone. Not in my wildest dreams—well, technically, I guess that was my wildest dream. Sadly, I've had those threesome dreams before. This wasn't my first nocturnal rodeo with one too many horses to ride.

"It was one of those dreams again, wasn't it?" He pulls his cheek to the side. Gage is fully aware at what a nocturnal pervert I am—at least subconsciously. Although, oddly enough, he thinks Marshall is the one consistent star, and he usually is. Last night was simply an aftereffect of my secret meetings and late-night liaisons with the fair-haired Oliver to discuss some extracurricular faction business.

"It might have been." I'm slow to admit. "But on the upside, you were in it and offering up a nice massage." I'm too much of a wimp to admit to the nitty gritty truth, but I'm sure my throbbing thighs are filling in the blanks for him.

"Speaking of Dudley"—he grimaces at the thought—"I have a little surprise coming that might eliminate the need to have his intergalactic paws all over you."

"Really? You're going to chop him to pieces and have your mother fry him up in a pan? That's one way to get his feel good vibrations inside me," I growl as I take a playful bite from his bottom lip.

"Actually, *I* would be putting them inside you." He slaps my thigh with his amply large penis. "With this."

"You are a dirty, dirty boy, Oliver!" I think on this for a second. "But, God, if you could do that. I would lie flat on my back and let you bang the next few months away. And then we'd make lousy parents because I would never let you leave this bed."

"Sounds good to me." He tucks a kiss just under my ear. "In fact, I'll hold you to it. Demetri offered me the gift of 'vibratronics.'" His fingers encapsulate that last word in air quotes.

"Vibratronics?" I shake my head. First, it sounds like a cheesy sex toy, and second, I thought those good vibrations were something unique to my favorite Sector. A frown comes and goes without my permission. "What does he want in exchange?" I'm onto his bad daddy ways.

"A wedding—yours and mine. He wants us to exchange vows in front of him. Nothing fancy, just a few words."

"A few words?" Gage and I spend each day professing our love to one another. This would be like any other night before we make love—sans the making love part in front of the demented demon. Just the thought of those good sensations flowing through Gage, to me, *in* me! "Holy crap. Find him and tell him yes!"

"Really?" He pulls back in disbelief. "Are you sure? I didn't think you'd be so eager."

"I'm sure. Tell him yes. *Hell* yes—I'm sure he'll appreciate the nod to his homeland. Besides, this body has become a living nightmare. All I want to do is sleep, eat, and puke. It's sort of a nasty cycle I'm locked in, if you haven't noticed. Tell him we'll swing by around noon. Then we can hit the Burger Shack to celebrate, and no way am I letting you talk me out of the animal fries." My mouth waters just thinking of those golden delicious "potatoey" sticks floating in an orange sea of secret sauce, heaping with enough grilled onions to give me stink breath for years. Oh, wait...maybe that's why Gage is so against the animal fries.

"Okay. And, yes, to the fries. But we each get our own. I don't want to feel like I'm going to get my arm bit off just for reaching in."

"Oh, you think you're funny." I give his ribs a tickle, and he offers a deep massage to my hips in return. "Okay—that feels *good*." I close my eyes and sink into the mattress. "Just a little lower."

"A little lower?" He gives a dark laugh as his hands make their way to the inside of my thighs.

Looks like I'll be getting that massage I wanted after all.

Marshall calls about noon and asks if I'm free. For Marshall, I'd make myself free if I weren't. But, with Gage helping Logan out at the bowling alley for a few hours and me languishing in my prenatal misery, I decide to head over.

The lead-gray Paragon fog kisses my windshield all the way to Marshall's expansive estate where I find him lingering by the horses in the corral, hand-feeding them a bucket full of apples.

"Aren't we domestic?" I don't wait for his permission before snatching up his free hand and interlacing his fingers with mine. Those feel-good vibes wash over me like rain over a parched hillside, and I tilt my head back and enjoy the semi-orgasmic sensation. Oddly, it doesn't feel blatantly sexual. I've truly come to view Marshall as some sort of medic who helps to alleviate morning sickness in the most profound way. "I'll be needing your services during labor. There's no way I'm pushing out three human beings without you holding my hand." In the least.

"They're hardly human." He gives a quiet laugh while setting down the bucket. "And you'll need more than my hand, my love. Although, I'm not sure I'll be there."

"What?" I squawk so loud an entire flock of crows evicts themselves from the evergreens and races to the skies. "You'll be there," I assure.

"Jock Strap will be there. Modern medicine will be there—most importantly, you will be there. Every woman on the planet has given birth without my aid, Skyla. You'll soon join their ranks."

I suck in a breath at the audacity of the sneaky Sector before me.

"If you're not present for my birthing experience, I will personally hunt you down and hack off all four of your earthen limbs. Then I'll beat you with them for abandoning me in my time of need. I've done my research on the subject. Heck, I've watched *YouTube* extensively. This birthing experience will be a long, drawn-out lesson in agony. Not once did I see anything that might indicate otherwise."

Marshall gives me that dead stare for a solid ten seconds.

"Well, if *YouTube* has confirmed this." He smirks. "Modern conveniences have removed the element of surprise. In the old days, a woman wouldn't know what to expect on her wedding night. And if she thought that was a gruesome act, her surprise grew in acres upon the birth of her first child."

"They used to knock women out once upon a time in this great nation of ours." I frown as I pet a horse with a white star on its nose. "I wish they'd knock me out."

"Yes, well, when the time comes, summons me and we'll see what Jock Strap desires. I've sensed his discomfort with me on more than one occasion."

"Never mind what Jock Strap desires. *Jock Strap* is the one who put me in this predicament without my permission, so I think it's only fair I override his opinion just this once." I turn to him fully and pick up his other hand. *God*—this is euphoria. Marshall is sheer heavenly bliss. Why am I living at the Landon house again?

"Because you and Jock Strap are not welcome to fornicate on my property, Skyla."

"Oh, that's right." Drats. God knows I can't live without fornicating with Gage. Even if Gage is the one who put us in this pregnant pause of a predicament, I can't live without our wild bedtime romps, or early morning romps, or mid-afternoon—

"Yes, yes. I get the picture." His lids hood low with annoyance.

"So, what's the big secret?" I give his hand a little tug. "Is that why you've called me over? Gage and Logan say that you're forever stepping into the Haunted Speculum. Does this concern Marlena? And why can't you leave well enough alone in the seventeenth century?"

Marshall gives a lazy half-smile toward the corral. "No, I can't seem to leave that century alone, can I? And, yes, in a roundabout way it does involve that nefarious time in my life. You see, I might have"—he motions with his hand—"with a few women. And"—he motions with his hand again—"with others just prior to that. And it's been brought to my attention that a particular union had spawned a curious lineage."

"Marshall!" It's as if the world shakes around us, soft and subtle as a snow globe, only instead of snow and glitter floating to the ground, it's beautiful Sector DNA. "You're a daddy!" I gasp at the centuries' old implications. "Um—I guess, *were*. Sorry." It's a strange thing to congratulate someone on a child and apologize for its passing all in one breath. "But you have a family tree. I can hardly wait to trace it." It comes out sad and morose, because by now, who knows where his DNA has drifted.

"Yes, about that"—he gives a curious look toward the horizon—"you won't have to look far. In fact, you might say the branches are touching just a bit."

"What do you mean the branches are touching? Why does that sound incestuous? Did you have an affair with your sister? I mean, someone you didn't know you were related to?"

"I'm a created being, Skyla. I have no sister." He cuts me a quick, yet disturbed look. "And all of my doltish branches have since been spawned without my knowledge. Some of which are closer than you imagine."

"Oh my God! Marshall! You mean right here on Paragon?"

"Precisely so." He slouches, dejected at the thought. "It appears this knowledge has been held back from me for this specific time."

"Oh, wow. Who are they? Please, I'm dying here. If there are little tiny Studley Dudley's running around this island, I just have to know."

"In due time."

"Do I know them?"

His eyes flit to the barn as if avoiding my gaze.

"I *do* know them!"

"Nothing has been confirmed. And I shan't say a word until otherwise." He steps in and swings our hands between us. "Thank you."

"For what?" I shrug because I'm pretty much useless to someone as powerful as Marshall.

"Not true." He gives my hand a squeeze. "You listened. That was worth its weight in gold and just as powerful. I needed you, and you came."

"Don't forget to return the favor in a few short months." I give a slight wink. "But I'm glad I could be here for you." I pull his hand to my lips and give a simple kiss. "I'll always be here for you, Marshall."

He pulls me in and presses his mouth to the top of my head, and my body trembles with unspeakable ecstasy.

"I'd best go. I've a few more steps to complete with Ezrina before we confirm who the simpletons are." He takes off for the barn and melts into the ever-thickening fog.

"Word to the wise, don't call your offspring simpletons!" I shout after him, exploding with unspeakable joy.

Marshall has family right here on Paragon. Imagine that. Actually, I can imagine that. I am Marshall's family if you count the fact I'm his spirit wife.

I know this isn't easy for him, but I plan on being there for him every step of the DNA way.

And, if he's wise—I place my hand gently over my swollen belly—he'll return the favor right around December.

"Aw, fuck!" Beau Geste shouts as he struggles to retrieve something from beneath the couch.

The entire day has drifted by as Gage and I enter the family room where Drake and Ethan applaud Beau's potty-mouthed behavior.

"Ugh," I whisper to Gage. "I do believe Beau just used that word in the proper context." It was cute when he couldn't say *truck* quite the right way, but now that he's outright using it as a proper expletive, it's not so cute. Not really.

He winces. "That just exemplifies why we're going to have to watch our language once the babies come."

"I heard that." Drake gives us the stink eye. "You think your kid's going to be better than my kid? My kid's going to be a fucking millionaire. Ain't that right, you little piece of shit?" He pulls Beau in and cuddles with him until he's reduced the toddler to a puddle of giggles.

"Dude, you are fucking cute." Ethan moves Beau over a few inches with his foot. "But you're also in my way. Can't see the damn TV." Apparently, Drake does not have a lock on stupid.

"Charming," I say as Bree walks in wearing leather pants and a tube top, and a pair of ruby red heels that I'm positive I've borrowed from her before.

"What are you doing?" She scowls, inspecting me from head-to-toe.

"I swear, we don't think our kids will be better than yours. Beau is my favorite nephew." True story. Only nephew, but still very true.

"Who the hell cares about that?" Her eyes grow wild. "Why aren't you ready for our GNO?"

I stare at her blankly. "Do we have an appointment together at the gynecologist?" If so, it totally makes sense why she's decked out like she belongs on a street corner. Dr. Baxter is sort of a looker, or at least Bree might think so. Oh hell, he is.

"GNO, not *gyno*," a female voice gruffs from behind, and I'm stunned to see a decked out, belly out, Chloe Bishop patting Gage on the shoulder before making her way to the fridge.

Oh my shit.

"It's a girls' night out." Bree dances back and forth on her heels. "I'm throwing Laken a surprise bachelorette party tonight, only I sort of called and told her because I needed to know how much she weighed—anyway, that's for later. I guess you're the only one not in the know. The rest of the girls are in the limo, so let's get—shoo!" She gives me a loud slap over the ass in hopes to usher me along.

I do remember something about a bachelorette party being discussed a few weeks back, but I didn't think Bree would actually go through with it.

"Whoa." I'm still waylaid by the fact Bishop is in my home noshing on a piece of leftover cheesecake. "Why is the she-devil here?"

"Skyla!" Mom ambles from behind the stove. "Chloe is a guest." She turns to Chloe with a saccharin smile. "How are your nipples? Have you been toughening them up the way I taught you?"

Ha! That's what she gets for entering the Landon Loony Bin—a nipple interrogation.

"You, too, Skyla." She nods to Gage as if this somehow involves his participation. "Toughening her nipples can be a two-man job, you know." She gives a cheesy wink. "Oh, which reminds me"—she reverts her attention back to me—"you just make sure to do as many deep, strong Kegels as you can. I just went over this with Chloe."

"Kegels?" Do I really want to know?

"*Yes.* Oh goodness. How could I have let this slip by? They're very important for women of all ages and stages of life."

Why do I not like where this is headed?

"How do I put this?" Mom tips her head to the side and harrumphs. "They're like vagina push-ups. Yes! That's it!" She jumps a little with her vaginal epiphany. "They're exactly that! You just tighten your vaginal walls over and over and over again. It's an exquisite exercise that one can never get enough of! But they must be strong!"

Dear God. Sorry I asked.

"Strong?" Oh hell, I'm a glutton for punishment. "How can you tell?"

"That's easy." Mom glows. Clearly, all things areola and vaginal are right up her— "You just slip two fingers inside and test it out."

I'm quick to recoil at her words, and my perverted mother is quick to brush me off.

"Of course, not *here*," she sneers. "That's what showers are for."

God, I'm not too sure I want to hear about my mother's less than hygienic bathing practices.

"Of course, you can always get someone to help—you know, test the theory out for you." She wrinkles her nose at my husband as if the thought of his wandering hands makes her all warm and fuzzy inside.

Gah! The woman is like a predator.

Drake rises and plucks a beer from the fridge. "So— Perfect Parents—"

Great, we've obviously ticked him off without meaning to. Is this a bad time to tell him that Beau Geste sports the cutest little widow's peak on the planet? Both Drake and Melissa have what Mom has affectionately dubbed the "Landon Hairline," which has sort of a stereotypical vampire appeal. Mom has thanked God Almighty out loud on more than one occasion over the fact Misty doesn't have that hairy fish-hook sunk between her eyes. And why would she? Misty is clearly not a Landon.

Drake moves in. "Who's going to be the disciplinarian?"

"Neither," Gage rumbles as he wraps his arm around me. "Skyla and I are a unified front."

"My nipples are fine, Lizbeth," Chloe says it loud enough to penetrate our important discussion on discipline. Obviously, her parents didn't bother instating any behavior regulation in their home, or she wouldn't have so rudely interrupted. "Why they're pink and perky, just oh-so happy to be a part of my full, steadily growing ample soft breasts." She strides over with her dark hair eclipsing one side of her face, giving her a sultry appeal. "In fact, they're just aching to be touched," she whispers as she walks by Gage.

"I'll touch them," I offer. "With my fist."

Brielle clucks her tongue. "Oh, stop, you two. Skyla, get yourself into something girly. Tonight is going to be a blast."

"I don't have anything girly. All I fit in now are my husband's clothes—and I'm loving the manly side of fashion." It's true. I've been living in his T-shirts and old sweats. It's comfy as all hell, and I may never wear girly clothes again. Even though shopping for me is still high on Gage's to-do list, I'm stealthily avoiding the matter. There's no way I want to add to our financial stress by splurging on things I'll only wear for a few more months, and, not a shocker, maternity clothes do not come cheap.

"Don't be silly!" My mother ushers me all the way upstairs to her closet. "I have a few things I saved from my mommy-in-waiting days." She plucks out a navy tent with a huge white Peter Pan collar with a thin red stripe running through it. "Would you look at this? The pièce de résistance!" she sings in her best—read worse—French accent.

I take the archaic garment from her with caution. More like the pièce de I-must-resist-this.

"Oh, wow," is all I can manage.

"I know. You'll be the belle of the ball! Now you heard Brielle, *get!*"

Mom helps transform me from a cool chick in her husband's old football sweats to a mammoth, very pregnant, fashion-challenged teen. I inspect myself in the mirror and gasp.

"Look at me." My voice grows hoarse as I hold my hands out. I'm hideous. I'm the size of a battleship—a battleship with the fashion nonsense of someone stuck in the '80s. God, was this even in style back then?

Mom lands her hands on my shoulders—that look of frightening envy locked in her eyes. "It truly is timeless. I've thought of pairing it with a belt rather than letting it rot in my closet and wearing it out for a hot night on the town, but tonight, you're the lucky one." Mom wraps an arm around my shoulder. Tears glisten in her eyes. "You are the most beautiful creature in the world."

Gage steps in as a steady stream of tears falls from my eyes. Just as I was about to make a snide remark about her belting herself in this dress for a hot-to-trot date with her favorite Fem, she stopped me cold when she said I was beautiful. There's something special about hearing your mother say it. Damn hormones.

"Skyla." His dimples dig in, and his lips curve into that forever-warm smile he wears just for me. Gage wipes my tears away with the simple brush of his thumb. "You are simply gorgeous."

"And you are drunk off your love for me."

"Aw!" Mom melts. "Let me get my camera."

He pulls me in. "Go have fun."

"What are *you* going to do?" I'll be with Chloe, so already I know he'll be safe.

"I think Coop might be in need of some company tonight. Take the edge off the fact his wife-to-be is hanging out in some strip club geared for women."

"Please." I give a playful smack to his chest as my mother waves us to attention.

"Say baby makes three!" she chimes, snapping away a half dozen photographs as Gage places his hand over my stomach and lands a tender kiss on my lips.

Baby makes three? More like babies make five.

"Have a good time, Skyla!" she shouts as we make our way downstairs. "There won't be too many girls' nights out in the near future!"

I round my hand over my belly. Forget a girls' night out. Once the babies arrive, I don't think Gage and I will get a night out for the next two decades.

Sharing a limo with the bitch squad while dressed like a bloated sailor isn't something I thought I'd ever experience—correction, would never *want* to experience. Then there are Bree and Laken, not to mention Nat who wasn't in the original bitch squad but totally qualifies as an honorary member. Something tells me this entire night is going to be a mindfuck—pardon my French—I pat my bulging tummy.

"Hey, where are we?" Michelle squints hard, trying to understand our bleak surroundings. Paragon is basically one big powder puff of fog, so it's hard to determine at any given time where you're headed—never mind the fact if it's up or down.

"Near the water." Chloe presses her nose to the window like the good little bitch she is. "My sense of smell is practically bionic at this point. Being with child gives you powers you could never imagine. Isn't that right, Messenger?"

I don't bother answering because I'm no longer a Messenger. Ironic that I don't mind at all when Marshall invokes my maiden moniker.

"On to the next surprise!" Bree leads us out, and we quickly realize we're standing dockside at the harbor. Brielle shuttles us all on a boat before we get a chance to protest.

"Knew it." Lexy smirks while we all huddle down in the bowels of the ferry where it's nice and dry. Chloe and I sit side-by-side with our bellies protruding like twin missiles. "There are no adult clubs on this God forsaken island."

"Adult clubs?" I look to Laken because, dear God, I pray that's not where we're headed.

"Coop is not going to like this." She shakes her caramel-colored locks. Laken can easily be a cover model. She's going to make a beautiful bride. "I'm out. I'll find a coffee shop to sit in until you've had your fill of half-naked men flaunting their junk."

Chloe shifts while holding her belly. "They had better not be half-naked. If I'm expected to use my weekly allowance of hard to come by human currency, then I'd better have some very naked junk wagging in my face." She lets out a hard groan as if she's in labor. "Being knocked up sure makes you horny as all hell. Isn't that right, Messenger?"

Again not answering.

"You can't be *out*, Laken," Brielle growls. "This entire night is in your honor. It's your last GNO as a free woman."

I squish in closer to Laken and whisper, "Okay, so I thought of gyno again when she said GNO. I guess I'm a little vaginally preoccupied these days."

"Understandable since your vagina is currently occupied."

Gross—I think. Although, the thought of three miniature versions of Gage bobbing around in my tummy actually makes me smile. Not gross after all.

Miller bops in her seat as if she were on Liam's lap. "I'm with Bishop. I need me some dancing balls. Besides"—Michelle lifts a mini bottle of brown booze from her purse—"banana hammocks."

"What?" Nat snatches the bottle from her before she can take a sip and gives it a sniff. "This is eighty proof, guaranteed to produce some barf-in-your-purse action. I'm not carrying your ass back to Paragon." She tosses it into the waste bin beside her.

Michelle lowers her lids as if she were drugged. "Banana hammock, as in wienie bikini."

"Gah and *gah!*" I whisper. The visuals, they won't stop coming.

Laken sinks in her seat. "Ditto."

Chloe gives a dark smile. "Oh, come on, Lakey Pooh. Surely, you're not a prude. Or let me guess. You're saving the big banana hammock reveal for the wedding night." She smirks. "Doesn't Wesley wish? All that boy ever does is bitch and moan about Cider Plains—how he would change things if he could—how he would change you. Wesley could no more change his crooked destiny as dead Logan Oliver could. Isn't that right, Messenger?"

Not going there, no matter what she calls me—or calls Logan. Tonight is about celebrating Laken, not murdering Chloe—again.

She gives a museful moan. "Isn't it funny, Skyla, how both you and I ended up with men who could pass as twins? Knocked up before we could legally drink? And don't forget our living arrangements—you with the Looney Landons, and me in the Terrible Transfer—each in our own private living hell."

Now it's my turn to smirk. When you put it like that, Chloe and I are practically the same person—with the exception that I'm actually happy.

"I happen to be in heaven." An acrid heat expands throughout my body for speaking to the slithering serpent, bloated as she may be. I'm not too proud of myself for falling right into her ridiculous trap. It's Chloe who lives to try to get under my skin. Why should tonight be any different?

A blinding pain sears through my head as a wave of nausea pumps through me, and just as quick as it came it dissipates. That was close. All day I've felt as if I could pass out if I wanted, but I mostly blame that on the abnormally long love-making session Gage and I participated in this morning.

The ferry finally hits the dock, and we get out into town, take a lungful of fresh Seattle air, and start heading toward trouble.

The rest of the girls go on ahead as Chloe and I waddle at a much slower clip, holding up the rear. Laken stays by my side because she's loyal to a fault. She values our friendship so much that she's willing to risk mental torment by way of Bishop to help me out. She's a big believer in the leave-no-woman-behind campaign that only true besties participate in.

"Hey!" I pause a moment, taking in the odd new skyline of downtown Seattle. "When did they get another Space Needle?" I can't believe I haven't heard of this. This just goes to show that I'm pretty craptastic about keeping up with current affairs.

"What the fuck, Messenger?" Chloe presses her hand over her belly and blows a breath through her cheeks. "Stop hallucinating and pick up your pregnant pace. I'm losing sight of Em."

Laken leans in. "There's still just the one. Are you okay?" She places a cool hand over my forehead, and I hold it hostage there for a moment.

"I'm fine." I glance up at the twin spears piercing through the night and know that I am anything but okay. I have been feeling a little more woozy than usual today. I keep having this strange sensation of falling, and on top of that, it feels as if an extra pair of eyes is on me. Although, that last paranoid bit is totally justified as evidenced by Joy Killer and Nosy Mosey.

A darkness settles over me, a living fear as if an entire army of old school clown Fems were about to jump me from the bushes. I frown over at Bishop. I should have guessed no good would come of being around her.

Brielle leads us into what should be crowned as the *diciest dive bar of them all!* In the back, past a cheap black curtain that gives this place a your-creepy-uncle's-house appeal, we're led to the *All Male Review!*

"What exactly are we going to review?" Laken muses as we're seated at an enormous table that faces the stage with its long runway dotted with lights.

"Children's books," Lexy snarks. *"The Erotic Emperor Has No Clothes."*

"Yeah," Nat joins in. "I hear they have pop-up penises!"

The girls bust a gut as if it were the funniest thing they've heard. I start to laugh myself and feel a surge of warm liquid gush between my thighs. *Crap!* I just inadvertently pissed my pants. *Double Crap!* I press my lips tight and give a quick glance around as the spreading warmth grows down my thighs. Holy shnickies! I'm living my very worst nightmare—public urination! Just fuck. I'd head to the restroom to finish the job with a shred of decency, but, the truth is, I think I'm already done.

The music starts in, loud and unexpected, and I give several hard blinks as the room sways to the rhythm of the beat. The voices of hundreds of screaming women light up the place, deafening me from my own thoughts.

I try to say something to Laken, but my lips feel numb and tingly, and my head spins as if my brain just got on some psychotic merry-go-round.

An entire line of men files out onto the stage in various stages of undress. They pop the buttons off their shirts while pretending to struggle with their clothes. A few flash strip themselves of their Velcro pants before they even hit their marks. The bass picks up, and I can feel my body growing lighter with the ferocity of the rhythm. My chair feels as if it's falling right through the floor, and I clasp onto the table with both hands.

One of the men, the lead, with his bronzed chest, his Cheshire cat unstoppable grin strips his way in our direction, and ever so slowly reveals himself to be someone shockingly familiar.

"Marshall?" I gasp at the horror. Here we are, just one year out of high school, a majority of us mothers, or soon-to-be, and our math teacher is shaking his banana hammock just hoping we'll make it rain dollars. It's simply sickening.

Up next is an ebony-haired god with dimples you could sink your lips into.

"Hey!" I bark as I jump to my feet. "What the hell?" I shout, confused by the fact Gage just laughed in my face while revealing his amply endowed package with nothing more than a red silk sling to try to hide it. Behind him I spot Logan in a cowboy hat.

"Oh my...crap." The words *yee haw* ricochet through my head for no good reason. Cooper holds up the rear, and from this vantage point, Marshall, Logan, and Coop all look like the same person—triplets. My hand lands protectively over my stomach. I should probably get used to seeing things in triplicate.

Chloe jumps up next to me, cheering and whistling obnoxiously loud before leaning next to me hard. "Why the hell are we standing, Messenger? These guys look like they belong on a farm locked in a barn and saddled for a group of schoolgirls."

My head turns toward her, and the room expands in a visual echo.

I stagger back until I fall softly into my seat. The club breaks out into a riotous roar as Marshall snaps off his weenie bikini and starts swinging a flesh-colored lasso.

Gasps emanate from all around until finally giving way to an approving, quite enthusiastic, applause. Oh my God. That is no lasso he's wielding.

Nat leans in. "Check out the size of that cum gun!"

My stomach does a revolution at her crass analogy. Besides, it's more like a hose than a gun—any idiot can see that. Point in case, that's exactly why Emily was the valedictorian and not Nat.

Gage takes center stage and pulls off his man thong—and out flies one of those snakes in a can.

Another round of gasps.

Oh, wow. That sure is one nude looking snake—and it's meticulously attached to his body. My eyes can't seem to break away from the monstrosity.

"Is that what he's been stuffing into me each and every night?"

"Skyla!" Laken laughs, shocked at my admission.

"*God*, I'm so embarrassed. Could you please tell him to stop?" Everything in me wants to scream. "Would you please get the hell off the stage?" My voice booms through the facility as laughter and jeers circle around the room. "I can't believe you're doing this. Those are *my* body parts. That is *my* penis!"

A riot of laughter ensues once again as if I've offered the room the comic relief they've secretly been waiting for.

Brielle jumps onto the table and starts flashing her boobs, and Em jumps up after her as if she's about to wrestle her back down, but instead busts out her own boobs as well. Before too long, Lexy and Michelle are topless while Nat is busy getting all the dirt on her phone.

The room gives a heavy sway. Logan and Coop strip down, and soon enough, there is a sword fight of the flesh breaking out onstage.

"I can't take this!" I cry, covering my eyes.

"Skyla, what's the matter?" Laken pulls me in until my face is buried in her chest.

"How can you stand to see them this way? It's disgusting! This isn't funny. Everything about this is so very wrong. I don't know how you can stand to marry Coop after this. I'm going to hack off Gage's penis in his sleep tonight! And don't get me started on Marshall and Logan. Those perverts are no longer allowed to even look at me."

The chair and the table begin to melt, and I give a horrible groan. Dark shadowy figures fill the periphery of the room, and that horrible fear rides up my back in shivers.

"We have to leave." I hop up, and both Laken and Chloe shuttle me out of that den of depravity and down a narrow hall, landing us inside the safe haven of the restroom.

"We need to get Gage off that stage," I pant, my body breaking out into a sweat. I take my shoes off and land my bare feet onto the cool tile floor, and my entire body exhales.

Chloe grunts, "I don't know what shit you're on, Messenger, but your feet have the right idea." She takes off her shoes and does the same. The relief on her face is almost as palpable as mine.

"Skyla, look at me." Laken pulls me in. "Your pupils are dilated. Did you drink anything?"

"No." My mouth is dry as cotton.

"Gage isn't here." She leans in further, and her face flexes in concave. "Neither is Mr. Dudley, Logan, or Coop. Those were hillbilly geezers out on that stage tonight. There wasn't even a close resemblance."

Chloe heads for the sink and splashes water onto her face. "Again, I think your brain had the right idea." She waddles over with her newfound pregnancy gait, and something about her rounded belly catches my eye.

"Chloe," I whisper in awe as my hands cup the sides of her hard stomach. Beneath her clothes, beneath her skin, straight into her womb, I see the face of a beautiful, beautiful baby. In fact, its entire body is visible, with its bottom tucked toward me, knees up by its chin, and I can clearly see that Chloe is carrying a sweet baby girl. "My God—she is so perfect."

"Who's so perfect?" Laken tries to remove my hands from Chloe's belly, but I won't budge.

"The baby. There she is," I say dreamily, staring into Chloe's womb as if it had a window. "Dark hair, dimples—oh my God, yes, she does have them. She's sucking her thumb." I'm breathless at the sight of Chloe's little angel. I clasp on to my own stomach in hopes of more of the same, but there's nothing.

"Let me." Chloe lifts the tarp I'm wearing over my bulge.

"Hey—" Laken tries to stop her, but Chloe bats her away.

"I need to touch her skin." She lands her cool hands over the bourgeoning globe of my belly, and her mouth opens as she stares into my navel with wonder.

"What?" I touch my stomach, but I'm still denied the womb with a view.

Chloe's brows twitch like dying worms. "How many babies did you say you were carrying?"

"She's having triplets." Laken slaps Chloe's hands away and pulls down the king-sized sheet I'm trying to pass off as a dress. "Now, would you both cut it out? This is getting a little too freaky for me."

Chloe shakes her head with that same bored look on her face that she wears like a mask. "You'd better get to the doctor, Skyla."

"Why, is something wrong?" Before the words fully form in my mouth, one of the stall doors opens, and a large catlike creature, black thick fur, large yellow eyes the size of tennis balls comes out with its tail snapping around like a whip, and I lose it. I scream like a loon—thunder so riotously loud, the walls shake, and an entire slew of people rush inside, including a half dozen underdressed men.

Collectively, they stare at the beast as if it were your garden-variety grandma.

"Get it out! Kill it!" My throat rubs raw from the effort.

The beast stares me down a moment, giggles, washes its hands, and takes off back to Fem-riddled hell.

"What the heck?" I shout.

Laken is the first to usher me out the door and straight out of the haunted establishment. "What did you think was back there?"

"It was a classic Fem. I know what I saw. I've seen it before." I grip her for a moment. "They've been *following* me." My voice comes from my mouth in triplicate, rising to the sky in the shape of musical notes. "Did you see it?"

Her face grows increasingly somber. "No, Skyla. I didn't."

Chloe and the rest of the girls run out, most of them looking quite pissed, and they all start yelling at once—mostly at how I've dashed all of their banana hammock dreams.

"I'll take her home," Laken volunteers.

"I'm coming with you." Chloe waves her red-painted claws at the girls as we head back to the dock, and my mouth refuses to protest. If there is a Fem following me around, it can eat Chloe first, giving Laken and me a fighting chance.

We get on the boat, and I see them lining the seats along the underbelly of the ferry—tall, dark as soot creatures that closely resemble panthers with their long thrashing tails, their almond-shaped glowing citrine eyes.

"Oh my God," I whisper. "Do you see them?"

"No, Messenger. You're delusional." Chloe crosses her arms as if my delusional state offended her.

"I don't either," Laken whispers.

Chloe doesn't say another word. Here's her big chance to take a swipe at me, and she's squandering the moment.

"Something is wrong." The words spurt from my lips in a rainbow of colors.

Correction, something is very fucking wrong.

Gage

The bowling alley shakes with the rattle of thunder, sending such severe shock waves throughout the facility that I'm sure they register on the Richter scale.

"Dry storm." Logan nods toward the windows as if we could see it.

It's weird. Knowing that the wind, the thunder, and the lightning are all performing their duties, but the rain has somehow failed to show up. It's like having a wedding go on without the bride.

Bride. My lips twist as I hurdle that bowling ball down the lane and wait for it...so beautifully centered...almost...

"*Strike!*" I pull my fist toward my hip, high-fiving Coop as he readies to take his turn.

I glance up. Dudley is still in the corner, seated with a book in his hand. Who comes to a bowling alley to read a book? Conveniently, he's been stealing glances our way all night. Logan was a perfect gentleman and asked him to join us—which is odd in and of itself since Dudley helped spearhead the event. It's just a few guys—Logan, Ellis, Coop, Brody, and me. I thought about inviting Ethan and Drake, but I confess to having a bit of Landon fatigue.

Coop heads back, and I glance to find half the pins still vertical.

He takes a quick drink of his soda before sinking it back onto the table. It's been a soda and pizza kind of night, and not one of us seems to mind.

"Okay"—Ellis leans in—"so I've got another one."

Ellis has been doling out sex advice all night long. He's our very own Dr. Ruth. I only remember Dr. Ruth, because when I was little, my mother would have her on in the next room, and Logan and I would pretend to be busy while secretly listening to all the perverse advice.

Ellis motions us closer. "You know when you almost get her there, and you're like just fucking come already—"

Logan tosses a ball of wadded-up socks at him. "This is a family establishment. Speak in code, or forever hold your perverted peace."

I grunt at Harrison, "And if you value your balls, you had better not be speaking from experience with my sister." Just the thought of his stoned mitts manhandling Giselle makes my head spin.

"Not at all. She's actually pretty easy to plea—" He pauses a moment. "I'm actually referring to Bishop." He shakes his head with a wistful look in his eye. "She was a beast in bed. Didn't you think so?" He knocks his elbow into Logan, and it suddenly feels as if World War Three is about to break out.

"I've wiped my memory clean of the ordeal." He grimaces at the thought.

"Ordeal?" Now it's Brody growling at Logan.

"All right, let's change the subject," I offer.

Coop shrugs. "Spit the hot tip out, and we'll move on."

I know for a fact Coop and Laken are more than intimately familiar. Back when he was my roommate at Host, I caught them liberally exploring one another in more than one compromising position.

"You get your hand and—"

Dudley comes up just in time to spare my brain cells the effort of exploding.

"Evening," he says without a lot of conviction behind it. "Just stopping by to congratulate the groom-to-be." He flexes a dry smile at Coop. Not a lot of conviction behind that either. "I wish you and your lady love many years of happiness and prosperity." He snaps up a few cups off the table. "Why don't I remove some of this debris for you." He picks up a few empty paper plates as well before making a beeline for the trash. I watch as he tosses the plates, but leaves the establishment with the cups in hand.

"What was that about?" Brody leans in and takes a sip from his drink. He's lucky it survived Dudley's sudden need to tidy up the place.

Ellis slaps his hand over his knee as he jumps up to take his turn. "Just Dudley being effing Dudley." He takes off, and Brody gets up after him, queuing up to go next.

Logan raises his brows. "You notice anything strange about Dudley's little exercise in discretion?"

Coop smirks. "He wished me prosperity, then left me thirsty. What was that? Some kind of Sector curse?"

"He took my cup, too." Logan stares at the wall as if putting two and two together. Unfortunately for him, there's not enough arithmetic in the world to make sense of anything Dudley does.

My phone bleats. It's a group text to both Coop and me from Laken. **Where are you?**

Coop glances up. "I got this." **Bowling alley.** He shoots right back.

I'll bring her there. Give us five minutes. Don't leave.

"Bring who here?" I look to Coop as if he's got the answer. We have just enough time to worry and change back into our shoes before Laken and Chloe walk in with Skyla between them as if they were holding her up.

"What's wrong?" I rush over and help her take a seat.

"I'll get you some water." Logan disappears and comes back in a flash.

"Thank you." She gives a curt look to Laken. "I'm really fine. It was just a—" her mouth stays open as she searches for the words. "Oh hell, I don't know what it was."

"She was hallucinating," Chloe offers before jumping up and hugging her brother. "God, I miss you! Visit me sometime, would you?" She looks back to me. "Skyla thought you guys were up on stage stripping." Her dark brows wiggle with approval. "She's convinced you're able to slingshot your junk all the way across the room and lasso her in. Is that the kind of freaky shit that goes down between you two?" She wags her finger, and her brother brings her hand down.

"Skyla, look at me." I lift her by the chin until her gaze meets mine. "Your eyes—they're glazed and dilated."

"Everyone's eyes are slightly dilated. I'm fine, I promise. It was just some weird spiritual thing."

"I'm taking you to the hospital."

Logan stands and pulls on his jacket. "I'm going with you."

Skyla scoffs. "Well, you two will be there alone. I'm going home."

"She was seeing Fems." Laken is quick to point out. "Big, scary, shadowed Fems that look like oversized cats."

Shit. I've seen those back in our West Paragon days. "Maybe you're right. Maybe this is spiritual more than it is physical, but I want to have the babies checked out if you don't mind."

"I don't mind." She stands with an abrupt turnaround. "I happen to have a check-up in the morning, and I'll be glad to go then." She looks from me to Logan. "And there's not an angel or a devil on this planet that's going to get me there sooner."

"All right." I hold my hands up as Skyla and I say good night to everyone.

Chloe runs up with her belly almost the same size as Skyla's. It's strange seeing them side-by-side in general, but in this physically altered state, it's a mind-bender.

"Will I see you later?" There's something in her eyes that's pleading. It turns my stomach to see her so consciously desperate for my company. Why the heck can't she be happy with Wes? When will he ever be enough for her?

"Tell Wes I can't make it tonight. There's a feast with the Videns. Ask him to step in for me."

"Will do." She gives a quick wave of the fingers, and I can feel Skyla groaning beneath me. "Take care, Messenger." She glances to Skyla's stomach. "And I know you won't believe me, but I am sorry."

We get home, and I tuck Skyla into bed, massaging her back gently as she lies next to me. All night she cries and whispers feverishly in her sleep. I hear the words *Fems, fire, die, open Tenebrous, we must open Tenebrous*—and I'm too worried to catch a single wink.

Skyla should be relaxed, enjoying herself, soaking in this magical season without a care in the world, and by the sound of her nightmares, by the disturbing report Laken offered up, Skyla isn't relaxed, she isn't enjoying herself, and for darn sure she isn't soaking in this season. She's stressed to the max, and it's all the fault of my fucked-up lineage.

I just hope we get some good news from the doctor tomorrow.

If not, I don't know what I'll do.

Skyla thinks Fems are stalking her, and I have no doubt they are.

I pull her in tight and press a gentle kiss to the top of her head.

Skyla and the babies have to be okay.

I'll do anything to make it so.

At ten a.m. sharp, I have Skyla checked in and seated in the waiting room. It takes less than five minutes for them to call us back and another forty-five minutes until Dr. Baxter feels like doing us the honor of showing up.

Both his tanned skin and teeth glow unnaturally as he gloves up in an effort to get touchy-feely with my wife.

"How is everything? Have you felt the babies move yet?"

"Well, actually"—Skyla looks to me apprehensively—"I felt a little strange last night. And, no, I haven't felt the babies move yet."

"Not to worry." He takes a seat at the base of her makeshift bed and taps her thighs open until her feet are secured in the stirrups. As soon as she's spread eagle, he gives a shit-eating grin. Pervert. "So, tell me how you felt last night?" He pulls forth a long metal object, and it disappears beneath Skyla's paper gown. "This will be cold."

She winces. "Um, I don't know. I was seeing things that weren't really there. I was out with the girls. Someone probably slipped something into my drink."

"What were you drinking?" He glances up, alarmed, as if Skyla hasn't gotten the baby incubating basics down yet.

"Nothing actually. I'm not sure why I had such a weird night."

He pulls the metal speculum from her body and lays the glistening probe onto the table.

"Dim the lights," he instructs, motioning his assistant. "We'll get this party started with an ultrasound. Let's do a quick look-see. Typically, I use the Doppler, but, in the case of multiples, I prefer an ultrasound." He slathers her beautifully rounded stomach with blue gel and touches over it with a blunted instrument that looks like a wand. The room fills with the sound of a baseball bat swinging at about a hundred miles an hour. Then it dims until he settles over another part of her stomach, and it picks up again. On the screen, a white glowing orb shows up, then the faint distinction of an arm, a leg.

Everything in me wants to bawl with joy. Those arms, those legs were made by Skyla and me—with love. My heart warms just looking at the small fidgeting being nestled inside her.

"Let me see here." He continues to probe from side-to-side. "I'm afraid I have some news."

My stomach bottoms out. My heart wrenches, because as tiny as those little beings are, I don't want a thing to happen to them. I'm not sure I want to hear any "news."

"What's wrong?" Skyla's voice wavers as she gets up on her elbows.

"One of the babies has disappeared."

"*What?*" Skyla and I cry in disbelief.

"It's not uncommon," he reassures us. "It's phantom baby syndrome."

"What do you mean *phantom*?" Skyla says it breathy as if she's ready to pass out. "Where did it go?"

"It appears it was reabsorbed." He scans over a dark spot. "The sack is empty."

"Empty." Skyla falls back against the table, her fingers clasping hard over mine. "Like my heart."

The appointment wraps up, and I help Skyla get dressed. Dr. Baxter assured us bed rest wasn't needed. It was simply nature running its course, that the other two looked healthy and viable.

"This is terrible." She leans into me, her face slicked with tears.

"The Lord gives, and the Lord takes away." The words come from me slow, layered with grief. "Blessed be the name of the Lord."

Skyla settles her watery eyes over mine and gives the hint of a nod. "That's the most profound thing I've ever heard you say. You always know what to say."

It might be the most profound thing I've ever said, but when your family owns the only cemetery on the island, you tend to know what to say in times like these.

Skyla wraps her arms around me tight as her tears rain over my T-shirt.

With everything in me, I wish we didn't have to experience times like these.

Skyla and I hold one another in bed for the next several days, well into Saturday. It's the Fourth of July, the day of Laken and Coop's nuptials, so we dress to the nines and head down to Silent Cove just below White Horse.

"Looking good," I say as we come upon Coop. The wedding is literally on the white sandy beach below Logan's home. It's picturesque, dreamlike, and the most perfect venue for a wedding. Maybe when Demetri has Skyla and me renew our vows, we can do it here. Or Rockaway. For sure Rockaway. The Transfer pops back into my mind. That's right. The demented demon prefers darker, far more nefarious pastures.

"Thanks, man." Coop pulls both Skyla and me in for a hug. "The sun is up. The ocean is sparkling." He tweaks his brows at my beautiful wife. "To whom do we owe this amazing weather miracle?"

Skyla laughs, the first one in days, and it warms my heart to see her smile. "I may have exercised my abilities to make the dark clouds disappear. I mean, if I can't do it for my own life, I might as well do it for yours. Where's the bride?" She gives a quick glance around.

"In the house getting ready."

"Well, in that case, excuse me. I'm dying to see her. I just know she's going to make a stunning bride."

"That she is." Coop nods as Skyla makes a dash for the house.

"How did everything work out the other night? Laken said Skyla was pretty cryptic in her messages."

"We lost one of the babies."

"Shit." He pulls me in once again for a quick embrace. "Sorry, man. My heart is heavy for you."

"Destiny has a will. We'll see that child again one day." I know for a fact I will much sooner than Skyla. "But today is about you. Are you nervous?"

He takes in a full breath. His eyes cut to the house behind me. "Just enough. I want this with everything in me, Gage. There isn't another woman I want more than Laken."

"Why do I feel a but coming? You getting cold feet?"

"No. Wes contacted me yesterday. I was helping out at West, doing some coaching, and he just showed up on campus out of the blue. He actually tried to talk me out of it." He gives another nervous glance toward the house. "I know for a fact he's planning on trying to talk Laken out of it, and if I were a gambling man, I'd guess he'll choose that tender moment just before the wedding while her emotions are off the charts. No offense, but your brother can be a real asshole."

"No, I get it. Look, if it makes you feel better, I've got no problem making sure he doesn't show up." I start to pluck my phone out of my pocket, and he waves the idea off.

"He's already here. Chloe's milling around, showing off her belly. I know it makes Laken cringe, even if she won't admit it. Besides, it's best if Wes sees us making it official. Maybe that will drive the point home that she's never going back to him.

The Interlopers are here as well. I spotted them edging around the property."

"You don't have anything to worry about."

I spot Demetri speaking with Dudley and frown at the two of them.

"Look who's here." Logan pops up and catches Coop in a mock chokehold. He's wearing a suit that closely matches Coop's. Logan is in the wedding, so it only makes sense. "You want me to keep the truck idling for you?"

"I'm not running, dude." He gives Logan a playful shove off him.

For a second, Logan and Coop look like the exact same person, as close to twins or brothers as you can get, and my gut cinches. Twins. That's what Skyla and I have now. I'm grateful to God, but so saddened by our loss. Neither Skyla nor I knew we could grieve so deeply for a child we've never met.

"Is she okay?" Logan gives my arm a squeeze. We let him know, first thing, that we lost one of the babies. It was through a text, and I felt like an asshole, but at the same time, I didn't want to be around anyone but Skyla.

"She's okay."

He gives a slow, somber nod. "I'm sorry, man." Logan pulls me in and collapses his arms around me in a deep, strong hug, and it's all I can do to keep it together.

"Look, I got someone I need to talk to." I pull back and give several hard blinks, trying to keep it together. "Sorry." I don't wait for a response, just take off into the crowd and bump into Bishop of all people.

"Hey, gorgeous." She takes a sip from her fruity drink. "You mind putting me down on your dance card for later?" Her dark brows do the wave.

"Sorry. My dance card happens to be full for life." Not sorry. I try to make my way past her, and she blocks me with her ever-growing body.

"So, are you ready for fatherhood?" Her finger finds its way to my collar, and I take a full step back.

"As ready as you are for motherhood." Hell, I have no idea what kind of mother Chloe is going to make. A horrid one, I suspect.

"I'll never be ready for this thing." She makes a face at her stomach, and suddenly, I feel sorry for the kid she just referenced to as a *thing*.

"Yeah, well, Wes will love it."

"You should love it. It's your niece. I had suspected I was having a girl, but Skyla confirmed it."

"She did?" I'm skeptical. But I'm suddenly the tiniest bit interested in my niece. I may not like or appreciate Chloe in any way, but I do have a love for family, and whether or not I care to admit it, that baby is exactly that.

Chloe nods between sips. "The night she lost the baby. I'm sorry, by the way." She makes a face that looks something like grief. "I touched her belly, and I knew. Anyway, you got any names for the two that are sticking around?"

"Crap." I look past her in an effort to get away. "No names as of yet."

"I'm not dreaming up any keepers either, and all Wes can see, hear, or think about is Laken, Laken, Laken." She whines that last part out so loud that ten different people look in our direction.

"Well, I'm sure you'll come up with something." I spot Wes leaving the house. "Speak of the devil. If you'll excuse me, I'd like to have a word with my brother."

Chloe steps in, her fingernails dig into my arm. "Celestra has cockblocked him. Wes is pissed to high heaven. Whatever you have Skyla doing, it's working."

"What are you talking about?" I glance over my shoulder and spot Logan still chatting it up with Coop and wonder if Logan is the one I should be interrogating.

"You know, the pledges. They're disappearing faster than you can say *abracadabra*. Wes is seeing red, and all he talks about these days is revenge." She smirks. "I mean, what did he think would happen? He opens the door to all his secrets and expects you to keep it from the pinhead you're sleeping with? Although, I must give it to Messenger, she's really got him by the balls with this one. Where's she housing all these people? God knows if she doesn't play by the rules, the Justice Alliance will nail her ass to a feathered wall." She gives a dark giggle.

"Shit." I head over to Wes first. If Chloe assumes I know what the hell is going on, I'm sure he does as well. "What's up?" I give him a quick pat on the back. Placating. That's about my only weapon at this point.

"Just spoke with Laken." He blows out a breath, exasperated from the effort. He's all decked out in his Sunday finery. His Italian suit is cut just right, tailored just for him, no doubt. One might easily mistake him for the groom. I'm betting he hopes Laken will. "She's pissed." He shakes his head as if it were a revelation. "You know, I don't get it. We were and *are* the great loves of our lives. She and I—we were inseparable in Cider Plains. We've crossed every heartbreak together. We crossed death and made our way back to one another at Ephemeral. How can she do this to us?" He shakes his head in genuine disbelief.

"Wes." I press a hand against his chest to steady him. "You did this. You chose evil. No offense, but she doesn't want to dance with the devil."

His eyes harden over mine as he firmly removes my hand. "You are mistaken. I, my brother, much like you, am an angel, something greater than that even. I am of the Fem order of beings mingled with the blood of the Countenance—the blood of Laken's people. In that respect, we are one in the same."

"She doesn't want to see the Nephilim wiped from the planet. Is that a shared goal of yours, Wes?"

He touches his hand over his chin and holds back a laugh. "Do you think that's the end game for me? It's not. What's important is lifting the Fems back to their proper position above the Sectors. That's where we belong, and *we* are going to accomplish that." He jabs a finger from his chest to mine. "You and I with our seed, so don't go getting all high and mighty on me." He turns to leave, then spins back in my face with a vengeance. "And don't think because you ran off to tattle like a pussy that I don't have this in the bag. Demetri thinks it's ingenious to have you follow me like a shadow, had me sign a blood covenant that I wouldn't hold anything back from you, and this is the thanks we're both repaid." He strides past me, and I pull him back by his suit jacket.

"I can no more deny the Nephilim the help they need than Laken can. Why are you hell-bent on destroying your own people? Who the hell cares if the Fems are on top? It doesn't change who you are."

He shakes his head, incredulous that I'm not getting it. "It will change everything. You might have been born to breed, but I was born to *lead*. Chew on that and see how well it goes down. Demetri knew I wouldn't bow to the whim of any woman's heart when I know what's right for our people—the Fems. And that's why he created you. A softhearted poet who would be sympathetic to the enemy—marry the enemy. Because that's who you needed to fall in love with—a Celestra with Caelestis genes no less. Don't think for a minute that you are your own. You were bought for a price, and now he expects us both to perform. We're hardwired to be who we are, Gage. It's showtime, and I've no doubt you'll please the crowd." The music starts in, and bodies rush to their seats. "I just don't get why he's pitting us against each other." Wes takes off toward Chloe, and I take a seat down front closest to where Skyla will be standing.

A few of the bridesmaids walk down the aisle with friends of Coop's on their arms. I recognize the younger girls as Cooper and Laken's sisters. They look overjoyed, thrilled to be uniting their families in holy matrimony. A twinge of sadness spreads through me. Is this what I denied Skyla by eloping? Just looking around at the attention to detail, the beautiful flowers arching over the makeshift altar, Coop with his dapper, yet, casual suit, the family already weeping in the seats around me. If I could go back, I'd gladly gift this all to Skyla.

Up next, my beautiful bride comes down the aisle in a peach dress that hugs her luscious curves, her belly sways out in front and causes her to wobble slightly. She's arm in arm with Logan, and seeing them like this, so formal, shining and glowing, it makes it feel as if it's their wedding I'm attending.

"Don't they look like the perfect couple?" a female voice chirps in my ear, and I turn to find Chloe and Wes taking a seat beside me.

I don't answer. Instead, I turn my sole focus on my beautiful wife.

She's barefoot. Skyla had a hell of a time trying to get her feet into those heels, and with the sand, I didn't think it was safe. It looks as if she agreed. She blows a kiss my way as she passes me by, and I do the same.

Logan and Skyla take their respective spots at the top of the altar, and my heart drops down into my stomach. Yes, they do look like the perfect couple. A horrid grief rips through me because one day they'll be just that. I'm simply a road bump to their happily ever after. In the long stretch of Skyla's life, I'll simply be known as the Gage years. I would have given her twins, though. Those children will be my legacy. Tears come at the thought of leaving a wife and children behind. My chest bucks, and I struggle to fight it.

Logan turns to Skyla and takes up her hands, whispers something into her ear, and she gives a soft laugh.

The music shifts, and everyone turns to look at the bride. But my eyes snag on Logan's, and he drops Skyla's hands like a hot potato.

I offer a quick nod and smile to let him know it's all good. It takes all my effort to watch Laken as she makes her way bashfully down the aisle on the arm of a guy, who by the looks of it can pass as her brother. Yes, she is stunning. Skyla is right. Laken is a beautiful bride. But my heart transposes Skyla's face over hers, my face instead of Coop's. And sadly, the only face I can seem to juxtapose over Cooper's is Logan's. If and when I do die—if and when Skyla and Logan do get married, he had better gift her a damn big wedding. A thought comes to me. This very location will most likely be where they'll do the deed, and my heart breaks just thinking of it. It shatters in one magnificent explosion, nothing but fine dust left in the aftermath, because no matter how right that would be for them, it kills me on every level. Skyla is mine. It should only ever be the two of us together.

The ceremony goes off without a hitch. Once Laken and Coop exchange their vows, there's not a dry eye in the house, including mine. I can't help it. Laken and Coop belong together. There are some people whom you just know are meant to be, and those two are certainly meant to be. I glance to the side at Wes, his stoic expression, his jaw set tight in anger. I know this has to be a living hell for him, but it's good for him to see it, to bear witness to the fact he will never hold Laken in his arms again, at least not the way he demands.

Chloe leans in, her belly rubbing up against my arm. "That could have been us."

I don't even bother qualifying that with a statement. Chloe lives in her delusions as much as Wesley lives in his. Maybe Chloe needs to witness the wedding between Skyla and me when we renew our vows in front of Demetri.

Once the ceremony is through, Laken and Coop run down the aisle with pure unadulterated joy as bodies begin to mingle. The atmosphere immediately shifts to party mode. Skyla is busy speaking to Ellis and Giselle, so I take a moment to take care of business.

"You got a second?" I nod to Wes, and we step aside from the crowd. "I know that was tough for you, man. I'm sorry."

Wesley glances to the ground, doesn't say a word, and it breaks my heart. Wes is the exact effigy of myself, especially when he's locked in grief. It's painful to watch. Even more painful to know that one day that will be me. And I suppose in a way, it's Logan now.

"I love her," he says it low, about as audible as the wind. "That will never change."

"You're allowed to do that. No one can take that away from you."

"Someone just did." He takes off before I can stop him, and I catch up with him, blocking his path a moment.

"Are we on for tonight? There's a new moon." The Counts still hold their sacrificial round table. Now that it's on a voluntary basis, the numbers have dwindled considerably.

He stares off into the cold black water as the waves lap over the shore. "I'm thinking about taking the night off. The

Videns have questions. Come with answers. I'll be back later." He drifts away with the sea mist and eventually disappears into the woods that border the shoreline. Wes is in a tough place emotionally, and I almost feel sorry for him. Almost.

"Hey, you!" Giselle hops over with Ellis, Skyla, and Logan in tow. She rings my neck with the crook of her arm as laughter bubbles from her. That's one thing about my sister—no one will ever accuse her of being a killjoy. "Wasn't that wedding fabulous? Did you see her up there in that big white dress? I want a big white dress! As soon as Ellis and I can, we're going to get married. He's going to look handsome, and I'm going to sparkle."

"What?" I take a moment to glare at Harrison.

"Dude." He shakes his head as if half-heartily denying it. "We're talking years."

"But last night you said we could do a secret wedding like Gage and Skyla," Giselle whines. "Of course, we'll invite our families. It's not that secret, right, Ellie?"

"*Ellie*?" I growl out the moniker.

"That's right, G." He comes over and wraps his arm around her shoulder. "I can't blame you for being excited. You get all this to come home to." He waves a hand over his body.

"Please." I give Ellis a hard look. "She needs to stay in school, go to college, grad school, and then we'll talk." Maybe.

Giselle sucks in an audible breath, her face contorting in all kinds of shock. "You and Skyla didn't wait! In fact, Skyla had two husbands in one year!" she shouts loud enough to incite a small crowd to turn in our direction. "Skyla gets to have three babies all at once, too! When are you going to put three babies in my belly, Gage? Why are you letting her have all the fun? Sometimes, I think you love Skyla more than me!"

"Would you keep it down?" I pull her away from the crowd to a nearby evergreen as the rest of our small circle follows. "Do you even know where babies come from?"

She shifts uncomfortably, looking to Skyla for help. "Ellis says he'll put them in me with his magic wand."

"Shit." I look to Logan and shake my head at the lunacy we've let Harrison inflict on poor, innocent Giselle.

"Just kidding!" She laughs and hops, and it really doesn't do anything to solidify the fact she desperately wants to be an adult. "Ellie says he's going to put babies in my belly real soon. All he has to do is plow my field with his seed. Then I have to scream and scream and scream. And the more fun I have while he's seeding me, the better my chances of having more than one watermelon baby like Skyla." She turns to my wife. "Ellie says you screamed so loud that they had to put carpet on your bedroom walls to protect the ears of the rest of your family."

"Ellis!" Skyla whacks him in the arm before stepping toward my sister. "It might be a Tad Landon true. And what exactly is a *watermelon baby*?"

"Come on, Skyla." She rolls her eyes like a preteen. "Babies are born in watermelon pods. What do you think they eat for nine months straight? It's the most delicious food in the whole world, so I think they're really lucky."

I look to Harrison. "I'm going to kill you."

"No, no!" Skyla holds a hand out while herding Giselle back toward the party. "We're going to congratulate the bride and groom, and take a good look at that sparkly dress up close. You two feel free to have your way with *Ellie*." She smirks at him as they dissolve into the crowd.

"All right"—Harrison takes a full step back and holds up his hands—"just give me a running start." He turns around and books it the hell out of here.

"You think he went to the bowling alley?" I ask as he jets out of sight.

"If he's smart, he went to the mainland." Logan slaps his hand over my shoulder. "You okay?"

"Yeah. I'm just pissed at Ellis. What's new, right? I have a feeling I'm going to spend the next fifty years pissed at Ellis."

Logan belts out a laugh, and for a second, I catch myself in the absurdity of what I said. I get it, though. Logan is laughing because of the fact I see myself hating on Ellis for the next half a century, but the truth is, the real reason it's hilarious is because I won't be around long enough to do it.

"Whoa." He gives my arm a firm shake. "Come out of that black hole. You'll be here."

"How do you know?"

"I know because you traded the carcass of a certain Celestra for a wish at your last birthday. Isn't that how it worked? My dead body for length of years?"

I blink into him, more than slightly sucker-punched. Here, Logan remembered my wish, and I didn't. Of course, I may have mentioned it the night I tried to beg Candace to take me home. I had become a monster and didn't want to inflict any more of my ego on Skyla or the world.

Demetri stalks by in the distance like a shadow, edging his way toward the exit.

"Excuse me, dude. I've gotta dance with the devil before the night is through."

I sprint through the sand, up toward the house, and catch up with the demon.

"Hey, Daddy Dearest." I offer up a half-smile because I'm not too sure he gets the pop culture reference.

He turns, that dark line on his face curves up with the impression of a grin. "Do you wish for me to beat you with wire hangers?"

"Okay, you're a smart guy." I cross my arms over my chest in an effort to keep from decking him. "So, what's this blood covenant you had Wes partake in? What is the real story between my brother and me? You know we'll never be a unified front. Why have him expose his deep, dark secrets to me at the detriment to his cause?"

Demetri lifts his dark eyes and scans the crowd until he nods to my left, and I follow his gaze.

"Skyla." I let out a breath I didn't know I was holding. Skyla would have the power to calm me if I were tied to a stake with flames licking at my feet. "She's the reason for the blood covenant?" Makes sense in a demented Demetri sort of way.

"She's the reason. You'll thank me for it." He turns and heads into the woods and evaporates to nothing.

Skyla is the reason for the blood covenant.

Demetri is looking out for us, or at least our children. But knowing all of Wesley's best-laid plans only seems to benefit the Nephilim in the end—Skyla's people. Could this be his way of apologizing for killing her father? Demetri is gifting Skyla the keys to the kingdom through me. A kingdom in exchange for a dominion. I suppose that's fair in Demetri's eyes.

But something still does not add up.

Logan

"Come on"—I nod toward the crowd moving in rhythm to the music—"just one dance. It's not even a slow song." I've spent the last five minutes trying to herd Skyla toward the dance floor, but she keeps biting her lower lip apprehensively, eyeing the thick gyrating crowd as if it were a snake. Come to think of it, she was having hallucinations just a few nights ago. "Are you okay? Are you feeling strange again?"

"No." She gives an annoyed blink toward the two government agents who continue to skirt the periphery. For the most part, we've decided to ignore them. Coop said he didn't want to make a big deal out of it. "It was sort of a one-off. I'm just"—she rounds her hand over her growing belly—"I'm too big to dance. I'll look like a hippo having a seizure. I don't know where I end and the rest of the world begins."

Skyla is already pretty huge, but by no means is she a hippo. I love the fact that I'm here to witness the event firsthand, even if I am relegated to the sidelines. My insides pinch with heat as my gaze falls over her quickly changing body. Candace foretold that Skyla and I would one day have our own child, and right now, the thought makes my stomach turn because any day that zaps Gage out of reality is not a good day. Besides, those babies need him. Gage is going to make a great father—and great fathers should be the ones who live to a ripe old age.

"Do you know where you end and I begin?" I ask with my voice lowered, a smile playing on my lips, but I won't give it.

She cinches her mouth at the thought. "I give. Where? Keep it PG, Oliver."

"I don't know either, but I'm guessing we run a figure eight right in here." I tap my hand over my heart. "Is that PG enough for you?"

"Maybe." Her cheeks flush with color.

"And don't worry. It's appropriate. Dead husbands are allowed to venerate their wives for all eternity." A rush of sadness rips through me because I've happened to play the role of dead husband for quite some time now.

Skyla reaches up and brushes my cheek with her thumb as if wiping away tears. "I'm sorry it hurts, Logan. It hurts me, too."

The music switches gears and couples migrate into one another's arms.

I motion her close with the flick of my fingers. "Keep it PG, Oliver." I'm only partially teasing.

Her brows arch at the mention of her formal, very legal name, twice over.

Skyla extends her hands, and I take up her warm, soft fingers. It's only then I note the fact this is as close as her burgeoning stomach will allow.

"My how you've grown." I give a wry smile, and she gives one right back.

"Save it for your nieces or nephews as you watch them age. I hear childhood goes by in the blink of an eye."

We sway sullenly to the music, even though I happen to be enjoying the hell out of her, and I'm hoping she feels the same.

"Childhood may be fleeting, but rumor has it that it still takes eighteen years to pass the time." I give a quick wink. Her belly rubs up against my body, and something in me stirs to touch it. "May I?" My eyes fall to her beautiful bulge. Skyla is a stunning mother-to-be. Not even her enemies can deny her that.

Her hand rubs over the top. "By all means." She pulls me over, and I gently lay my open palm onto her surprisingly firm stomach.

"Wow." I'm breathless. And like some big dope, all I can say about the miracle taking place in Skyla's body, the miracle she and Gage put in there, is wow, over and over again.

"It is pretty wow." Her entire body beams with pride as she places her hand over mine.

How are we doing with the list? Her demeanor changes on a dime. **How many of them are captive?** Skyla is determined to shut down Wesley's dream team before it ever takes flight.

Twenty-two. Brody is a machine. He captured eleven. Ellis five.

And the other six? Her eyes widen as if she's offended before I can get the answer out.

Skyla, it was me. I give a little shrug in my own defense. *You do realize I'm in this with you. I want to nail those bastards to a wall as much as you do.*

If you're in this with me, then you'll take me the next time you decide to nail a bastard to the wall. She tilts her head in, her expression conveying her sarcasm far better than her voice ever could.

"Are you insane?" I don't bother filtering that one through telepathy. "I had to fight the last guy with my fists. He threw a chair at me, and not the kind that is conveniently made of balsa wood, but a genuine, heavy-as-all-shit clump of office metal." I touch my shoulder where the bastard nailed me. "I've got the battle wound to prove it."

"Logan." She gives my name in a severe whisper. "As the overseer of the factions, I forbid you to go without me."

"And as your Elysian, I refuse to listen. Your unborn children will thank me one day once they arrive without a dent in their skulls. These men are not going willingly into the haunted good night—otherwise known as the Speculum. Speaking of which—the clock is ticking— we need to find a replacement."

"You're right." She glares at me a moment. I hope to God it's hormones driving her to incite this kind of rage toward me.

"Skyla." I want to weep as I say her name. "You know I love you with all my heart, all my soul, every last fiber of my deceased and spiritual being. You are the love of my life, and I would do anything to protect you." *Already have. Still doing it.*

"I know you care."

"No." I'm emphatic this time. "My love for you is so strong, it dulls out the rest of the world in a blur. When you're not with me, all I do is count down the hours till Skyla. This love for you I feel is God-breathed—something spectacular and haunting. I love you, Skyla Oliver." What joy is left in me slips away as I remember which Oliver she's bound to at the moment. "I still love you, princess."

Skyla's stomach jumps beneath my hand as a foot bursts forth with a kick as if trying to evict me from the premises.

Both Skyla and I give an open-mouthed laugh of delight.

An explosion goes off overhead as the fireworks get underway.

"The babies—I think one of them just moved!" she squeals as spontaneous tears trickle down her cheeks. "Logan, they're both moving."

My fingers fan out, as I spread them wide and plant my other hand over her basketball of a stomach.

An aggressive assault takes place as if I were the last person on the planet they want touching their mother. Probably true.

Gage steps up, breathless. "Here you are." He glances down at the placement of my limbs, and for a second, I'm afraid he's going to remove them at the root. "What's going on?"

"They're kicking!" Skyla turns slightly toward him, and I lift my hands so Gage can experience it for himself.

"Already?" Gage is breathless at the idea of his children moving, kicking up a storm inside Skyla. Up until now, they had two-dimensional proof, the awkward flimsy papered picture that showed three round sacks with the grainy exposure that photographic technology has passed up by a mile.

"They're not moving anymore," he says, dejected.

"Maybe they're tired." Skyla softens into him, believing this theory herself.

Tired? Those kids were wide awake a second ago. In fact, if I had to guess, it felt as if I were about to be ousted.

Wait a minute...

I lay my hand over the side of her stomach, and a violent jolt comes my way.

"Oh shit!" Gage is speechless, something just this side of a miracle. "Logan, do that again." He taps the top of her belly, and I lay my hand down just as I was told.

Again, the baby, *babies*, give an aggressive thrust maneuver.

"Holy hell." I close my eyes just briefly. "I think they're trying to evict me." I've heard of people trying to poison our youth, and here I see that Demetri has wasted very little time. I'll be their least favorite person by default.

Gage puts his hand over mine and feels the thumping, the bumping, the very real get-the-heck-off-my-mother moves his kids are dispensing. Carefully, I move my hand, and Gage slips his beneath it. His grin widens the size of a football field.

"They're moving." His breathing picks up as he and Skyla lock eyes, and it feels special, romantic, and in no way like I should ever bear witness to it.

The fireworks go off in one last blaze of glory, the grand finale as Gage leans in for the kiss. Hell, I would have done the same. I can't help but feel emotional. Skyla and Gage just felt their children move for the very first time, and it all went down in a fit of fiery glory. If I didn't know better, I'd swear it was a sign, a prophecy for the spectacular life those two kids are going to live. They're very lucky to have such amazing parents. I walk backward a few paces as the crowd disperses. The music starts up again, and the party only seems to grow, not wither.

"Where you going?" Coop slaps his hand around my shoulder.

"Skyla!" Laken calls to her friend as she and Gage head over. "Thank you for all of your help. Your advice." She gives a knowing nod. "You really were a great friend today. And thank you for putting up with the Jens." She looks to me. "My sisters, both named Jen, but that's mostly the Counts' fault."

"It's quite a story, but one I'm glad I know." Skyla pulls her in. "You've been through so much." They hold tight for a moment. "I had a wonderful time. Everything was beautiful. I think you're both off to a great start."

A cool pair of arms swings around my waist as Lexy Bakova pops up from behind my shoulder. Her breath reeks of booze and cigarettes, a combo I don't care for either à la carte or together.

"Boo!" She breaks out into a fit of giggles. Michelle Miller is with her, looking a little ruffled—probably from something my goofy brother did to tick her off. "So"—she looks to Coop and Laken—"you two ready for some R and R in paradise?" I carefully slip her arms right back off me.

Skyla dips her knees a moment. "Yes! Where's the honeymoon? Somewhere tropical, I hope."

Coop and Laken exchange happy drugged glances that scream *let's get the hell out of here and into the nearest bed*.

Laken shrugs at Skyla. "I thought Logan told you. We're staying here for our honeymoon."

"Oh"—Skyla tries to wave it off as if it were no big deal—"Paragon is a great place to honeymoon. Gage and I didn't go far either. We just stayed on Host."

Just stayed on Host.

Gage glances my way, and an uncomfortable moment drifts between us.

Lex gives my side a pinch. "Logan here took Skyla to *Rome*." She swoons a little when she says it. "Where do you think we'll go, Logy-Poo? Venice? Milan? Ooh! I know! Tuscany! We should totally go to Tuscany. I hear they have amazing wine. And I'll let you take me to Paris for our first anniversary."

Skyla scoffs. "Wow, Bakova, you really are shit-faced. If I were you, Miller, I'd take her home while she can still stagger. She'll be one hefty carcass to lug when she passes out. Notice how I said when and not if."

There's the Skyla I know and love.

Lexy growls like a lioness about to take down her prey, but before she can pounce, Michelle holds her back.

"Who you calling hefty?" Lexy laughs a loud drunk chortle that sounds demented more than it does vindictive. "Honey, you give new meaning to the word *hefty*. The next time Logan needs to take out the trash, he might just call *you* to line his can." She snaps her fingers and swivels her head over her neck. Lining my can? It sounds sexual in nature, and I'm positive that's not the kill shot Lexy was gunning for.

"At least I'm not caught in some delusion about a honeymoon that will never take place! Maybe Miller here will take you to Tuscany, and you can both drink your body weight in wine. While you're at it, take Bishop with you and drown her in a vat of fermented grapes! And have someone ship me a bottle from that batch. Bishop Reserve sounds like it will be spectacular—after all, any year is a great year to lock Chloe in a bottle."

"You just don't give up, do you, Messenger?" Michelle gets in her face. "Lexy has been kind enough to distract Logan from the heartbreak you caused, and yet, all you can do is ridicule her, hoping to end their relationship. Don't you think Logan needs someone, too?" She gets in a little too close, and I pull her back. "You can't guilt him into being alone forever, Messenger!" she shouts as Lex plucks her away. "Chloe was right. All you ever think about is yourself!"

They drift onto the dance floor and start moving their bodies to the rhythm as if nothing at all just happened.

"Did I hear my name?" Chloe pops up like an apparition with Gage's no good brother dutifully by her side.

"Congratulations," Wes says to both Laken and Coop. He looks to Coop. "If it's not me, I'm glad it's you." He puts his hand out, and Coop eyes it a moment before shaking it. "Laken." He gives a partial bow. "I'm happy for you."

Chloe burps out a laugh. "No, you're not. You're cantankerously angry with her is what you are."

Wes glares at the mother of his child. I can't blame him. I'd glare at Chloe, too, if I had to be glued to the hip with her for any length of time.

"So, where is the honeymoon?" Chloe inches her head forward, feigning interest. "I heard you mention Paragon. Pitching a tent on Rockaway, I assume? It's a fan favorite of Gage and Skyla. They have a hut I'm sure they'll happily let you borrow," she sneers at Skyla as if that little grass love shack should have been hers to share with Gage.

"No, actually, we'll be living it up in style right here at White Horse." Laken bites down on her lip a moment as she looks to Skyla. "Logan was kind enough to gift it to us for two weeks, and we couldn't say no."

"White Horse?" Skyla nods, forcing a smile, but I can tell she didn't mean for it to come out as a question.

Wesley's chest pumps with a silent laugh. "Let me guess. You're still trying to exorcise Chloe from those walls." He shakes his head a moment. "Can't say I blame you. Exchanging bad love for good seems like the only way to make this place holy again."

"That's what I'm hoping."

Chloe's mouth falls open.

"Come on, Chloe." Wes gives her a nudge toward the front lawn. "It's time to head down to the bat cave for the night.

Skyla steps in, her lids hanging low with sorrow. "I see you're cleaning the house of all its mortal sorrows."

"If that's not enough, I'll bulldoze it and start all over," I offer. "Hell, I'll sell the land and find another lot to build you a palace on."

"Isn't that romantic, Gage?" Chloe coos as Wes tries to pry her into the crowd. "Doesn't it just appall you?"

"That's not what I meant." I cut Gage a quick look, but judging by the scowl on his face, he's not getting it.

"No." Skyla takes a step back before glowering at Chloe. "And it is romantic for Coop and Laken. They're the perfect couple to remove the scourge you've left on the place. Come on, Gage, we'd better get to bed ourselves." Her lips curve toward Chloe. "Isn't it romantic? Doesn't it just appall you that I'm the one that's with the man you truly desire? That he will never be yours, never love you?"

Chloe bares her teeth, her body inches ever so close to Skyla.

Coop nudges me from the side. "So, when do we step in?"

Chloe and Skyla begin growling and snapping at one another, whispering their I-hate-yous as efficiently as casting a spell. I've never seen Skyla lash out at so many people in so little time. It's safe to say she's wearing her hormones on her sleeve.

Laken lets out a nervous giggle. "God, it's like watching a pair of Weeble Wobbles go at it."

"Let's hope they don't fall down." They do look a bit comical for lack of a better word, with their distended bellies, their bodies locked in the epitome of a genteel motherhood while they war it out with their hearts.

The Interlopers come into view just as Chloe's hair jumps to the sky, projecting off her scalp as if it's trying to hang on for dear life.

"What the?" Laken leans in.

Skyla's hair does the same rendition of hairy scary, and it's odd seeing them both with their 'dos out to there like tumbleweeds, creating a perfect globe of tresses that stretches to the stars. Chloe's feet levitate off the ground as she pulls Skyla up with the command of her fingertips.

"Chloe, knock this shit off!" Wes barks, wrapping his arms around her legs before she floats off like a balloon, but it's too late. Killion and Moser are already taking notes, snapping pics on their phones as proof. Soon, Chloe and Skyla will be wanted for questioning, and I can't have Skyla incarcerated by the feds, not now, not ever, so I do the only thing I can.

I turn and spot Dudley, the perfect victim-slash-volunteer and hold a hand out to him just like he taught me that day in front of the Haunted Speculum. His eyes widen because he knows what's coming. He cocks his head, looking at Skyla, and then he gets it. He holds his hand out, and a bolt of lightning passes through him to me. An electrical current jets through my limbs, spearing me with an exquisite pain, sharp as a blade. My skin, my every last cell illuminates a demanding electric blue. Gasps fill the crowd. I hear Skyla scream my name as my body, my soul, they all drift back to paradise. Perhaps where I belong. Perhaps where I should remain for time immemorial.

Candace kicks me right back out on my shiny white ass, and I drift back to Dudley's where I spend the next few weeks while Coop and his new bride cleanse White Horse with the fire of their love. The dross of Chloe has been officially removed. I hope they used condoms. Or in the least held very sanitary love making practices. They spent two weeks exploring every inch of White Horse while exploring each other. I've hired a maid service to come out, twice now, to scrub it down from the rafters to the baseboards. As much I appreciate Coop, I don't care to have his bodily fluids spread far and wide over every square foot of my home.

"So, what's on the agenda tonight?" Michelle and Lexy have been impatient with my lack of desire to do anything with them.

"Nothing much. Skyla and Gage are taking me out to dinner."

"Out to dinner?" Lexy's mouth squares with rage. "It's your birthday. We should go old school and take a drive down to the Cape."

"I'm totally bummed you nixed our campout." Michelle glances to Liam. "Your brother used to throw himself the best birthday parties."

"Sounds pathetic." He offers me a beer, and I wave it off.

"It's only pathetic when you realize I didn't have a set of living parents to set one up for me." I give him a satisfied smile. "Besides, girls in bikinis all night long? It was a work of genius."

"There you go." He nods his beer toward me before downing it.

The doorbell rings, and Dudley stalks past us.

"Don't any of you bother to rise. I'll see who it is. After all, I live to serve you, feed you, offer you room and board, all free of charge, of course. There's nothing more satisfying than having those you hardly care for suckling off your energy and resources."

Liam grunts, "What the hell is he grumbling about?"

"Who knows, who cares?" I glance back to find a familiar good-looking couple chatting it up with my supervising spirit, so I hop to my feet as both Skyla and Gage wish me a happy birthday.

"It is now. Where to?"

Lex steps in, as her arms find their way around my waist. "We were all just headed to the Cape for old times' sake. You guys up for a little night surfing? Michelle and I will bring the real fun."

"And what's that?" Skyla isn't amused, but damn, is she ever beautiful. With each passing day, her lips grow fuller, her body illuminates like porcelain lit from within, and her eyes shine like a sea of blue topaz, wildly beautiful, exotic, expensive as hell. The price for Skyla has always been very high, but I'd pay with my life each and every day. She's worth it. Gage and I always swore we'd never war over a girl, but Skyla is worth that, too.

It takes less than a minute for everyone to agree that Lex and Michelle have had a stroke of genius, and before I know it, I'm seated next to Skyla as Gage drives us down to the Cape in what's turning out to be a long caravan. He tossed our surfboards and a couple of wet suits into the back, so we're set to go.

"What's up?" Gage glances over his shoulder at Ellis in his monster truck, the headlamps blinding him. "You've been pretty quiet as of late."

I have been pretty quiet as of late. I've been hunting down traitors like it's my new favorite hobby and have only managed to nab a couple more. Meanwhile, Wes has recruited a new batch by the dozens. Shutting down his little conspirator club is like trying to catch water through a sieve.

I take a breath, avoiding Skyla's pending gaze, her newly oversized boobs. I realize I'm not supposed to notice those things, that it borders on complete disrespect, but her skin glows like lit paper, and her tits have been rippling with every bump in the road, bursting through the top of her dress as if trying to find a way out of the contraption. It's getting harder to sit here by the minute.

"I've been laying low," I finally speak up as we take the turn past Pike's Reef, following Liam's taillights like a beacon. "You know, after the incident." The incident being the fact I morphed into an electrical wire in front of God and the government to distract the feds from Skyla. And now I have them sniffing around the bowling alley, the Gas Lab, the fucking morgue, asking questions about me because all of a sudden dead Logan Oliver is a person of electrical interest.

"Got it." Gage grimaces as Liam's truck hits the brakes a little hard, and his face glows red as a flame.

"So, what's new with you? The same could be said. You've been a little quiet yourself."

"Nothing new. Demetri and I are still doing the father-son tango. Meanwhile, back at the demented ranch, Wesley swears his dolomites are ready to spring into action."

"He has the ability to regenerate them?" Skyla jumps at the thought.

"Not quite, but he's ready to convince the world."

"And the Videns?" I ask simply out of curiosity. I'm not sure what role they play in anything other than the fact they seem to like Gage, a lot.

"They say they're sticking with the Barricade. I've talked to Coach Morgan, and he's determined to stay with a winner—the winner being Wes and his minions. He's holding sacrifice rites almost every other night now." He looks to me, cold and unfeeling, before shedding a frown. "You able to keep up with that shit list?"

I give a dry huff of a laugh. "So, you're up to date on that, huh?"

Skyla tenses. I know for a fact she's not the one who told him.

"I figure they're disappearing. It's a mighty big coincidence that I give you a list, and the people on it evaporate into thin air. So, where are you housing them? The basement at Dudley's? White Horse?"

Skyla gives a hard sigh. Her hand flattens over her belly. It's so huge it almost touches the dashboard. "The Haunted Speculum. Don't breathe a word."

"I won't," he assures.

We get to the Cape, and to my slightly amused surprise, there are bodies upon bodies here to greet me. A giant banner staked in the sand reads *Happy Birthda, Logan!*

Someone forgot the Y in *birthday*.

Giselle comes up and swings around me like a pole while gifting me a hug.

"Do you like the sign? I painted it myself!"

"Of course." I wince. "It's great." Only it won't strengthen her argument on why she should test out of high school early.

"Let's do this." Ellis high-fives me while running toward the waterline with his board in hand.

"I'll be right down." I head back to grab my wetsuit and stumble upon Gage with his mouth over Skyla's right tit, her dress downturned just enough to expose the girls.

They're glowing and white and huge as twin moons, and I force my feet to pivot the hell out of there.

"Fuck." I hear Gage grumble. "All's clear. Sorry, dude." He tosses me my board as if nothing happened, and Skyla is already gone.

We suit up and hit the water, but that image of his mouth where mine once was has stained my brain, and not in a good way. I should forget about it. I wish I could.

We hit the sapphire water, cold as fucking ice, and Gage and I surf our asses off. Even Dudley has gotten into the spirit and showed up unannounced with a board in hand. He's taking those waves like a master, riding them without wiping out once. All of the girls are riveted by his otherworldly moves, his undeniably impressive abs. Asshole.

Dudley outperforms us wave after wave. There's a nice swell out here that's pretty consistent. The set breaks about thirty yards out, each one topping out at about six feet. There's something nice about the carrying on of tradition—this one in particular. Even Liam is giving it a go. And who knows how long it's been since he's seen the water. Brody and Ellis whoop it up another fifty feet out. Both Gage and I are keeping an eye on Ellis in the event he's too stoned to make it back to shore.

We relax on our boards, just sitting out here in the warm bath of God's tears thinking about nothing and everything.

Dudley pops up with a roar and paddles up beside us. "Birthday, huh?" He falls back on his elbows, his chest expanding with his every next breath, and both Gage and I groan.

"Put it away." Gage splashes him in the face. "The girls aren't around. No need to impress."

"This is my natural state, Mr. Oliver. If I impress you, it's no fault of my own. What's with the puss? Afraid Skyla will abandon your brooding ways for someone as heaven sent as myself?"

"Skyla's not leaving Gage." I paddle up a few feet to get square between them.

"That's right. You keep trying to ensnare her, don't you?" Dudley huffs a silent laugh before closing his eyes as if he were sunbathing.

"I don't need to try. We had our shot. We were married. I died. The end." There's a little bite of the salty truth. What better way to commemorate the day I entered this planet than to douse it with the unfriendly facts of my death?

Gage clears his throat. "Don't act like you don't know there's a to-be-continued clause in there."

"There's not. I read the fine print." Not really, but both Skyla and I are determined to have him stay.

"Candace isn't keeping me around."

"No, but Demetri is willing. Have you talked to him about his promise yet? Or have you let my corpse rot for nothing?"

Not that it was doing much better in Ezrina's keeping solution, but it was a hell of a lot more comforting knowing I had a body lying around in the event I actually needed it one day—like a pair of sturdy running shoes you keep on the side just in case.

"Not yet."

"What the hell are you waiting for?" My voice echoes over the rippling waters.

Dudley gives my board a swift shove. "Perhaps he's waiting for you to die properly. You're the epitome of a man who can't seem to do anything right—death included."

"Ouch," Gage says it for me.

"Oh, I'm quite sorry," Dudley muses, shaking out his hair like the giant dog he is. "Did I hurt your feelings? You half-breeds seem to be full of those hard-to-control foibles. Go on now and weep." He gives my board another kick. "It's your party. You can cry if you want to."

"What the hell has gotten into you?" I paddle back to get a good look at the demented Sector. "You're my supervising spirit. That means you get a free ride on *my* dead coattails, and, as a bonus, you get to do my bidding."

"Free ride on your what?" He looks perplexed.

"It means—"

"I know what it means." He glowers at me a moment.

Dudley may have only one person on the planet he's zeroed his interests in on, but I've surmised that he was blown down from the heavens as much for me as he was Skyla.

"Never mind." The swells die out, and we head for shore. My swimming trunks are wet and crisp, and I'm starting to chaff—never a good thing.

Fire pits dot the shoreline with bodies gathered around them huddling for warmth. I find the blaze illuminating Skyla's beautiful face and know I'm at the right one. She's seated next to Laken and Bree. It's nice to see Skyla surrounding herself with good people. I want that for her. I want everything for her.

Ellis backs his truck up to the party and sets up a few stage lights in the back and a working microphone that screeches into the night like nails on a chalkboard.

"What's this? Entertainment?" I take a seat on the sand, amused, just as Lexy falls to my side.

"I'll say there's going to be entertainment," Skyla growls audibly at Lex, and I'd be lying if I didn't feel like that was gift enough.

Gage heads over and pulls Skyla onto his lap. It looks uncomfortable—for both of them.

Coop and Brody hop into the back of Ellis's truck with him.

Coop grabs the mic and taps it until it expels ear-piercing feedback, assuring the entire Western Hemisphere it is indeed on.

"Logan"—he says my name so loud it pops through the air like a firework—"I think everyone here wants to wish you a very happy birthday."

"Unbirthday!" a female voice shouts, and we turn to find Chloe meandering over. She offers a friendly wave of the middle finger as she lands in our circle.

I suppose she's the one responsible for the unbirthday party, considering she is the one who killed me—but, because I intend on having a good birthday, I ignore her.

Coop continues, "Dude, I don't do this for very many people. In fact, I haven't done this for anyone other than a few of my old classmates back at Ephemeral, so consider yourself a lucky bastard, or unlucky. You decide which."

A warm beat pumps from the speakers, thumping its rhythm over this distal tip of the island. The wind picks up, and the palm trees bend their ears our way as if Paragon herself were ready to hear Coop belt out a tune. The night is lit up with a party atmosphere as Coop grabs the mic hard, his head rocking out to the music, and just about every girl here screams her head off for him. Both Brody and Ellis turn around with a mic in hand and—holy—I think I'm about to be treated to an epic treat.

They start in on a familiar song—with Ellis and Brody as the backup singers and Coop taking the lead. It takes me a second to realize the lyrics belong to a popular rap song, only Coop is belting it out slow and dramatic, adding a comical, ironic spin. He's dead serious as he sings his way into every girl's heart with Laken howling and cheering the loudest.

I laugh my ass off as Ellis and Brody growl out the chorus. I'll admit, they do harmonize nicely. Coop sings the song softly, letting the expletives rip as uncomfortably and smooth as can be. It's fucking hilarious, and as the song nears completion, I'm bummed I didn't get a chance to record it.

Every single one of us gets up on our feet, wild with applause, as Coop jumps down, followed by his two-man crew. Ellis's speakers continue to whip out a playlist from his phone as bodies move and groove way too close to the fire if you ask me, but that about sums up my life, so why not?

"Dude." I give Coop a slap on the shoulder. "Well fucking done!" I nod over to Brody. "Not bad, Bishop. Who knew you had a set of pipes?"

"That's my brother!" Chloe swoops over to him, and they drift into the gyrating crowd.

Dudley comes up with his perennial bored expression, his I'm-better-than-you-and-I-fucking-know-it demeanor. "Nice show." He glares at Coop as if he's about to drum up a citizen's arrest. "You're quite talented." He nods solemnly as if digesting this bit of non-information. He clears his throat and swallows hard. "I'm proud of you." He gives Coop a slight bow before turning toward me. "You, however, not so much. But do keep trying. I'm sure there's something redeemable you can impress me with yet." He takes off in a plume of darkness, the visual equivalent of a black hole, and it would figure that Marshall alone could manufacture one.

"Wait!" I shout after him. "Why would I care to impress you?" But it's too late. He's long gone.

Skyla and Gage come over, and she wraps her arms around me from the side, her belly distending over mine. "Happy birthday, sweet prince," she whispers as she offers a brush of her lips to my neck. Skyla seems to have lost the ability to get up on her tiptoes, but I appreciate the effort. "We have a gift for you."

"No. I can't take anything from you guys." Skyla and Gage are broke with a capital everything. "I'd feel bad if you spent a single dollar."

"We knew you'd say that." Gage gives me a light sock to my arm. "So we didn't technically purchase anything—not something that you didn't once already own anyway."

"Okay." I'm almost afraid to ask.

Skyla frowns a moment before a tiny smile bleeds through. "We're gifting you back the Mustang." Her chest bucks as if she's about to bawl. "That is, after I have the babies if you don't mind. It'll be a million years until it's practical again. But I'm going to miss her, so, if it's no trouble, I'd still like a ride once in a while."

"Deal." My heart breaks a little. I gifted that to Skyla for her seventeenth birthday. I wanted her to keep it forever, but I get it. With the babies and the cost of insurance, it just doesn't make sense. "She'll still be yours. I'll just hold her for you indefinitely."

"Thanks, man." Gage pulls me into a hug. "You're my favorite brother." He gives a wry smile. Gage used to say that when we were growing up, and I'd shoot back *you don't have a brother,* only now he does, and it means a lot to me.

Laken and Coop pop up again. "We're taking off." Coop shakes my hand and pulls me in. "So, when are you going to fill me in on this secret shit you've got going on with Brody and Ellis?" He pulls back, the slight look of hurt ripe on his face.

"Dude, you trust Brody Bishop over me?" He shakes his head. "Let's talk sometime." He and Laken say their goodbyes to everyone, both looking equally stunned and pissed.

Laken leans into Skyla. "Are you in on this?"

Skyla doesn't say a word as Laken and Coop leave shaking their heads.

"Nice work." Chloe starts in on a slow clap. "Divide and conquer is usually the enemy's job, Logan. Sometimes, you just make it too easy."

Something bright flickers from the sky, and a few of the girls in the crowd scream as every person on the sand cranes their neck skyward.

"*Shit*," Gage seethes.

"Looky here!" Chloe sings. "It looks as if Wesley's gift showed up after all."

Four glowing orbs, fat and round as Volkswagen Beetles, settle just above the Cape, purple and green in nature, all of them hovering, floating, unidentifiable flying objects.

"*God*, this is going to make the news!" Brielle shouts.

Gage steps in until his shoulder touches mine. "This is going to set the entire world on edge."

"It's a beautiful sight, isn't it?" Chloe hums as she strides down the shoreline, her long, dark tendrils flowing behind her like vipers. "I insisted on having green in there somewhere since it is your favorite color," Chloe coos as the rest of the party snaps pictures to every social media outlet on the Internet. Chloe slithers her way between Gage and me, snapping away selfies of the three of us, the unnatural northern lights dotting over each of our heads like some demonic halo. "The end of your people is nigh, indeed. Happy birthday, Logan."

9

Blood Roses and Broken Promises

Skyla

The lights above the Cape remain a newsworthy event taking place on the distal tip of the island for the next few months. And now the feds, our United States government, heck, the governments of multiple nations have sent scientists to explain away this phenomenon.

Come September, Gage is back at Host full-time, and I'm left brooding at home, trapped alone with my mother and her nippily laced conversations. I had meant to enroll for classes. Scratch that. I did enroll for classes until Gage pointed out that twins typically come early. Childbirth and finals simply don't mix. Not to mention my morning sickness still rears its ugly head whenever the hell it wants. So that leaves me with Lizbeth Landon to whittle away the hours. I've become her very own pregnant pet project—her uterine ingénue whose body is no more her own than it is Lizbeth's. Mom's daily lectures are often followed by glossy pictorials and quasi-gruesome discussions, such as the fact my baby will be born bloody and wet, covered with thick white goo, which is classified under the scientific name of *cheese*.

My days are filled with all things newborn as my mother prepares me for my own maternal state of mind with the meticulous guidance of a prenatal master. I may not be experiencing the first semester of my sophomore year, but there is a distinct scholastic semblance with all the oral sex oration. My mother has no shame when it comes to deep thoughts on the benefits of kick-starting labor through cunnilingus—which comprises a great portion of the prenatal pep talks that start before I say good morning and end just after I say good night.

Like today, for instance, I learned that the alarming amount of pus that was leaking from my nipples is actually called colostrum, a yummy, fortified liquid that packs a nutritional punch. My mother highly suggests I let Gage feast on this delicious oozing fare. The breakfast of breastfeeding champions is terrific for new fathers' immune systems as well—especially since the baby (*babies*, but she doesn't need to know that little duplicating nugget just yet) isn't here to benefit. The focus of our mother-daughter time together is strictly focused on my vagina and the human contents it is about to pump out in a few short months.

Prenatal coaching might occupy my days, but my nights, well, my nights are consistently set to a pattern you can set a clock to, or better yet, an orgasm. Marshall Dudley is an animal—a highly uninvited one at that. Those tiger-eyes of fire, the body of a sexed-up gorilla hell-bent on conquering its mate, the stamina of every earthen creature combined. Each and every midnight he stalks me through my dreams, although he denies it to a fault, and if that's true, then my subconscious must be stalking him. This is sexual warfare in its prime, our bodies battling it out with stealth determination, Jacob and God wrestling until dawn, the unholy version. This is no friendly battle. This is a flat-out hostility. His body and mine both in enemy territory, his penis versus my vagina. All holy hell breaks loose from midnight till dawn and leaves me breathless, depleted of sound body and mind. But I am a very married woman, and this is carnal treason at its best. I'm done—ready to drive a stake through that Sector's unbeating heart if I have to. This has got to stop once and for all.

My hands flatten over his granite wall of a chest, his chiseled abs cut hard as marble.

"Marshall," I pant into him. "Why in the name of all that is holy are you doing this to me?"

He continues his forceful thrusts as he surges to completion, his body trembling violently over mine, his hot mouth moving over me like lava.

His lips drift near my ear. "I thought that was your favorite position?" he whispers heated and rushed into my ear.

"No, not that. In *general*, why are you here? And why am I unable to resist you? This needs to end, and it needs to end now."

"Skyla." He pulls up enough to examine me. The tender sunlight of this manufactured world offers his comely features a salmon glow. "You mean to tell me, you don't know?"

"Know what?" Here it is, the key I've been looking for. The shut-off valve might literally be just a breath away, and my heart pounds anxious for him to spit it out.

"Hey!" a familiar voice barks. "Get the hell off her!"

Both Marshall and I crane our necks to get a better look at the shadowy figure as he comes into the light. Logan shines like a topaz god in this sodden field of erotic dreams.

"Logan?" I'm slightly confused and more than slightly hoping this isn't going to turn into a full-blown orgy. I haven't climaxed yet, and usually Marshall always knocks it out of the park before leaving me to return to my slumber.

Logan swoops in with a broom appearing in his hand. He swats the junk out of Marshall until he rolls off and dissolves into the light pouring down from an opening in the dismal sky.

"*Skyla.*" Logan gets down next to me and waves his hand over my body until I'm wearing something that loosely resembles a toga, and my giant blooming baby belly is magically restored where it should be. My feet feel slightly stifled, and I glance down to find them snug in a pair of turquoise cowboy boots.

"Cute!" I click my heels together and run my hand over my bloated stomach. "Marshall never includes my belly. I think he likes the maneuverability of the old me. So is this another one of those fucked-up dreams?" I sit up on my elbows as his eyes expand a bit at my expletive. "Sorry. But it's my dreamscape. I think I'm allowed to be as salty as I like. And I hate to break it to you, but if you're looking for a quickie, I'm way too exhausted to please, not to mention I'm feeling rather lucid, so at this point it can't be excused as a dream. Honestly, I don't know how Marshall gets me to do those things. I swear, it's like a spell, only that's not right. More like a mind trick? A dick trick! That's what it is at the end of the day."

"I'm not here to have sex with you." He gently moves the hair from my forehead. "And for the record, this is now *my* dreamscape. Welcome."

I glance around and note the dingy landscape is replaced with a far more familiar territory, a lush hillside, a crystalline unblemished sky. I've been here before with Logan many times. It's relaxing, safe.

"Oh God, I'm so embarrassed." I bury my face in my hands a moment. "I can't believe you just witnessed that."

"Tell me about it. I'll have to wash out my brain with a blowtorch just to scour it out of me."

"I didn't want that. He just comes. No pun intended." I shrink a little. The greedy bastard did come and then left me to quiver just shy of the finish line.

"I heard that."

"Never mind. I'm sure Gage will accommodate as soon as I get back." I wince. "Sorry."

"No, I'd much rather he than Dudley. Don't worry. I'll get to the bottom of this bullshit he's up to. But I actually pulled you in for another reason."

"Is this about the traitors? Those Barricade bitches who think turning on their own people is the only way to save their asses?"

"Skyla," he says with a hint of disappointment. "They have families, little ones. They're frightened. And no offense, but with all the illusions Wes is providing, it doesn't look too promising for us. The world is on the edge of its seat. They want whoever it is that's invading this planet contained in a locked cell—preferably dissected for research purposes. And if they ever say 'take me to your leader,' it will not be Wes, Skyla. It will be you."

"He has framed us well, hasn't he?" I sigh into the grim reality.

He gives a curt nod and helps me up. "There's a man named Ichabod Travers. He's elusive as shit, and I've finally tracked him down. He's responsible for all the wild stunts going on in South America."

"The equator phenomenon." I nod. Drake and Ethan have been filling me in for weeks. Hell, they've been filling everyone in, anyone who will listen for that matter. "How are we getting there?"

"Just a simple, light drive, and then we wait until he shows up."

"Then what?" I was very clear to everyone that the prisoners need to be taken alive. I don't want Nephilim blood on my hands—again. Last time we committed a globetrotting slaughter, it turned into a real can of whoop ass directed at the two of us. Suffice it to say, I really do want them to live.

Logan takes my hands, and the earth moves beneath our feet. The atmosphere changes to something hotter, muggier, the scent of something deep fried hangs so thick in the air you can take a bite of it.

"What kind of name is Ichabod?" I ask as Logan takes me by the hand through the small, winding cobbled streets.

"A name you don't mess with."

"He's that tough, huh?"

Logan leads us into a bar with castanets and a mariachi band lighting up the night with a festival of sounds. "He's tougher."

"How are we taking him down?"

"I'm taking him down." He offers a quick smile. "Dudley has an arsenal of weapons to choose from. I found something that looks like a mini spirit sword but has the net effect of a stun gun. He'll be out long enough for me to toss him in that magic mirror." He pauses a moment to take me in. "You're beautiful."

"Thank you, I think. I don't feel very beautiful these days."

"You should. You glow with the light of a thousand stars." His eyes linger on mine a moment too long before he leads us through a thick crowd, through a dense cloud of cigarette smoke, and the heavy scent of tequila. Voices rise around us at riot levels, laughter mixed with screams merged with carnal groans of delight. He points to a table in the back where a dozen men play poker.

"God, this is all so cliché it might as well be painted on velvet." I struggle to catch my breath from the midnight jaunt we just endured.

"That's him in the red shirt." Ichabod is buff, tall, dark, and handsome in a stunning sort of way. That explains all the cantina girls ogling him and snapping his picture on the sly. "This might be cliché at first sight, but every single person in here is one of our own."

"Oh my God." I stagger forward. "Nephilim?"

"Celestra."

My jaw goes slack. I've never seen such a large group of our kind congregated in one place, let alone Celestra in general.

"How can you be sure?"

"Candace. She told me everything I needed to know about this place." He takes a deep breath. "After my stunt with Dudley a few months ago, I ended up on her back porch so to speak. I asked for directions to the ever-invisible Ichabod, and she spat in my palms until this place showed up in a vision. She's the one who mentioned it."

"He's getting out of his chair." I smack Logan in the arm as we flatten ourselves against the wall—a ridiculous notion for me altogether. "He's leaving!"

"Even better—he's headed to the restroom. Stay here." Logan starts to trek in after Ichabod, and I follow.

Two men stand at the urinal pissing their poor little hearts out, and for one of them, this will be his last night of urinal pissing freedom.

The one to the left staggers as he begins to sing and shout.

"He's wasted." Logan heads over to the redshirt freshman we're about to send to Haunted Speculum U and lifts the spirit sword to his neck as it illuminates a bright electric blue.

This reminds me of a time in our past that I'd just as soon forget with all the heartache and pain it ended up costing the two of us. *Ah*, the old days. Suddenly, I'm serendipitous for those worldwide murderous sprees Logan and I partook in. Only this time we're not sending anyone to paradise. Nope, those one-way tickets will have to wait until—

Before I know it, Logan is in a chokehold, and Ichabod Travers has his knee buried deep in my dearly departed husband's back, shouting something in Spanish.

Dammit. Why did I have to go and get a D in Spanish? *Why?*

"Get off him right now, or I'll stick your head in the toilet and—I will flush!" *Really?* That's the best I've got?

Logan struggles to look up with an expression that suggest the same, but Ichabod laughs, a deep guttural gurgle that lets me know he's undeniably amused.

"First, I kill your boyfriend, then we dance." He hacks the words out as if they were a joke—as if Logan and I were a joke. "Maybe baby fall out of your belly?" He gives a greasy smile, showing off a perfect picket fence smile.

"First, you *kill my boyfriend?* I don't think so." I summons all my Celestra reserves, and before I know it, my Fem-ininity kicks into high gear as well. This sleazy asshole doesn't stand a chance. Nobody but nobody threatens to make my babies fall out of my belly, although, technically, my back would feel tons better.

My foot imprints into his face so hard his entire body blows back into the wall, his head hitting the urinal for bonus points. He staggers on his knees, his face a bloody mess, but I'm not too worried because everyone knows a head wound always looks way worse than it actually is. He swoops forward, almost snatching me by the ankle, and again my mama bear instincts kick in. He could have landed me flat on my ass. He could have jostled the unborn children in my womb, and for once, they're napping and I'd like to keep it that way. I've grown accustomed to the wrestling match they like to play out at least ten hours a day.

Logan tries to storm him with the spirit sword and manages to jab him in the neck.

"Let me get another good one in." I pull my foot back.

"Skyla, no!"

No sooner does my boot meet up with his face than Ichabod goes limp once again, only this time I hear a distinct crack and a thud. It takes a moment for me to remove my foot from...oh my shit—his skull! Ichabod's handsome face is suddenly replaced with a very nasty looking, bloody as all hell, hole.

Logan scoops me into his arms and runs me the heck out of there, dissolving us back to Paragon, into his dreamscape where I'm suddenly stark naked again, only this time it's Logan holding me tight. "Sorry, but I have a strict no blood and brains policy to adhere to." He presses a kiss to the top of my head. "I'm sending you home. Forget about tonight. It was all just a bad dream."

I wake up with a start in my own bed. Logan's arms replaced by that of my husband's—an orgasm the last thing on my mind.

Ichabod Travers is dead.

Looks like I've got blood on my hands after all.

On September thirteenth, the exact day of my one-year anniversary with Gage, I shower and make a gallant, yet impossible, effort to shave my legs. Upon aborting the mission and tugging on my robe, I waddle into Mia's room and do the only thing I can—ask for assistance.

"Sorry," I say, handing her the razor. "Gage is out running an errand, and I can only guess that it has something to do with me."

"No problem!" Mia gets right to work preparing the workspace with a towel, a glass of water, and a can of shaving gel designed specifically for our species. It says so right on the little pink label.

"That's disgusting. Can't you do this someplace else?" Melissa chirps.

I choose to ignore her and wave at Emerson instead. She's been a great little ol' owl and doesn't seem to mind a bit that

Mia refuses to douse her in toxic dyes each month to gift her a touch-up. So for now, her feathers are sort of a salt and pepper color. It's a look I think really works for her.

Mia hums as she pulls the razor along my calves, inspiring Emerson to gawk at the two of us with curiosity.

"I'm having a baby," I mouth to my feathered friend as I point to my belly.

She rolls her eyes, technically her entire head, and takes a few side steps in the opposite direction.

Mia pulls the razor in long slim tracks over my calves and Melissa pretends to retch.

"You know what's really disgusting?" Mia drags the words out as if relishing what comes next. "The fact Marco DeMiro told everyone you swallow. And really, 'Lissa? Describing it to Jackie P. as warm pudding?" She sticks her finger down her throat. "Gag me."

Gag *me*. God, I hope none of that is true, and yet, a very sullen part of me is afraid it might be. Melissa is panning out to be quite the little whore.

A stuffed rabbit bullets by like a missile. "Oh, I *will* gag you—in your *sleep*." Melissa pelts Mia with an entire barrage of stuffed animals. "Believe me, it will be my pleasure. I suppose you'll want to run off and tell your little boyfriend."

"Which one?" Mia muses without looking up.

And really, Melissa? I want to say. Swallowing is something not even I can do without testing out the dependability of my hypersensitive gag reflex. Who knew all those times I told Gage 'I want to drink you down like a tall glass of water' I was essentially teasing him with a vaguely suggestive, utterly disgusting—sorry, not sorry—promise that I couldn't quite keep. At least it's not for the lack of trying. If I had succeeded each and every time, I would have drunk a bucketful by now.

A roll of nausea passes through me at the thought, and I moan.

"*Eww* sick!" Melissa cries. "Get the fuck out if you're going to puke in my room."

"No, I'm fine, I swear. And you should really do something about that mouth of yours. It's not a trashcan, Melissa." I meant with the cursing, but hey, if the warm pudding fits.

"Anyway"—Mia gives my leg a little massage before patting it down with a towel—"I'm seeing Revelyn tonight. I think he's going to ask me to break it off with Gabe, but I don't know. I kind of like having two men warring over me. I'm kind of like you in that respect." She looks up at me with her large puppy dog eyes, and suddenly, I want to cry because I've been such a poor example to her—to both of my sisters.

"You're too young to have two guys warring after you. And, for the love of all that is holy, do not put your mouth on anything that might ejaculate something with the weak promise of a comfort food. Your sister is lying."

"I'm the same age you were when we came to Paragon," she protests. "I'm in the tenth grade. That's when you amassed your male harem, remember?"

"No, God, I was a junior." I was a junior, wasn't I? "And I didn't amass a harem. I met two really nice guys. Logan was my boyfriend, and we broke it off, and then I was with Gage, still am." Something like that. God, it all seems so long ago, and yet, it went by in a blink. The babies jostle, and I land my hand over them as if trying to catch a knee or an elbow in the process.

"And don't forget that math teacher." Melissa pumps her foot though the air, and my mind flits back to poor Ichabod's brain, or more to the point, mush for brains. A chill runs through me at the thought I might have actually given the poor guy an inadvertent lobotomy. I know I did, but a part of me doesn't want to believe it. How could I do that? How could I do that while my unborn children kicked alive inside me? It's atrocious behavior. I'm a terrorist to my own people. It's a terrible, terrible thing I've done.

"*Hello*? Skyla?" Mia waves the razor over my face. "I asked for your opinion. What do you think I should do? Should I leave Gabe for Rev?"

"No, you should leave Gabe *and* Rev. Find someone who won't run around with two other girls behind your back."

"Ha!" Melissa croaks. "Even Skyla knows they're both cheating on you."

"Technically, I'm the cheat." She waggles her bows and hands me back my razor.

"That's nothing to be proud of." I jump off the bed and make my way to the door just as Emerson squawks up a storm. "All right. Come here." I pull her out of her cage, and she leaps to my shoulder. "I'll let you see your brother. Just please don't take a crap in my room."

The windows rattle. The fog presses against the glass with strained fingers as if readying to burst inside. Brielle called the phenomenon a mist storm. Drake suggested it was simply some fucked-up fog. I suppose the truth lies somewhere in the middle. Paragon is prone to its fair share of crazy hazy days, but today, this white coat of armor Paragon has pulled over herself—that has all but made the island disappear—is the most dramatic of them all.

"It's a white out," I whisper to Gage as we stare out the bedroom window. "I went to Bree's place and almost landed on my head. It's disorienting. You don't know which way is which. I swear, I almost ended up at the bowling alley."

"Skyla," he moans directly into my ear, and I melt. Gage has made mindboggling love to me for the last few hours. As soon as he came home, he helped me hoist myself up the stairs and shed my clothes, lashing me with his tongue while my body all but begged for his. To say I've been a little hungry for his touch these last few months is like saying Chloe is a little bit dangerous. Wait—no Chloe references allowed while discussing my voracious sexual appetite for my husband—especially not on this, our very first anniversary.

He pulls back and gives me a stern, slightly stoned with lust, look. "Do not put yourself or the babies in danger," he chastises between kisses. "If it's crappy outside, don't bother going in that direction. I promise, I will meet all of your needs."

He dots the tip of my nose with his tender lips. "Bree would have come to you with a simple text. Stay inside where it's safe, Skyla."

"Wow, that sounds like an order." I lift my shoulder playfully. "You know how I like it when you shout orders."

He moans out a smile, his dimples igniting as he takes a bite from my neck. "I've got an order—fuck me." He does a double take at his phone and picks it up, checking the time. "On second thought, hold off until we get back."

"Get back from where?"

"We might be taking a quick little trip." He winces again as if it's not the greatest idea.

"It's too late for a trip." I press my bare chest against his arm. I know for a fact Gage is defenseless against the superpowers of my newly enhanced bust line. I've tripled in volume, if not quadrupled. My nipples are the size of dinner plates—not necessarily a good thing, but Gage doesn't seem to mind. All the more room to bury those oh-so-happy-to-see-me dimples. So far, this pregnancy has managed to take our sex life to a whole new level with the one tiny detail that actually has only cropped up as of late. I'm officially Gage's number one backdoor girl, a formal title he bestowed upon me last week when he decided there was no other position available to us while my stomach does its best rendition of a beach ball.

Honestly, I cannot get much bigger than this. My skin is stretched so taut it's purple. I've amassed an entire slew of stretch marks that closely resemble enormous blue lightning bolts scattered over my hips and thighs. My stomach looks as if it's cracking apart in the underlayers. My inny has since become an obnoxiously protruding outty, and there's an eerie dark line that runs vertically from the top of my belly to my pubic line. I can officially no longer see my feet, and good thing because last I remember they were soft swollen pillows filled with salty regret. Have I mentioned I'm breaking out like a thirteen-year-old going to her first school dance, and that my bones hurt so bad I wished they'd turn to powder already? My pelvis literally feels as if someone is trying to pry it apart with a crowbar. This entire bodily experience has been just a smidge on the hellish side.

The babies give a few kicks and nudges—and ironically, it suddenly feels like heaven. This sort of psychotic flip-flopping is precisely why I've been so erratic. A bonus to having the babies will be having my sanity back. Brielle swore up and down as soon I pump these puppies out, I'll be right back to my old self, dress size and all. She's even encouraged me to bring something sexy to wear home from the hospital like a miniskirt and a crop top.

"Tonight's the night." He gives a slight shrug. When I don't say anything—because, for one, it's not registering—he gently assists me off the bed. "I'll help you get dressed."

Demetri's face blinks through my mind. "Oh God, the nuptials? Do we have to renew our vows today of all days?"

Gage gives a hearty laugh. "It would make sense."

"You know what I mean," I say, tugging down one of the many quasi-slutty maternity clothes Bree has gifted me over the last few weeks. My wardrobe has become her little pet project. And as a natural recourse to my clothing dilemma, she's developed a whole new baby and me line that ties into the Made in Paragon brand. I must admit, both Gage and I get a kick out of the nightshirt that says *Made in Paragon* with an arrow pointing to my overgrown belly. But so far, that's the only hit. Everything else is a little too tight, too see-through, too bedazzled to be anywhere near a pregnant ogre of my size.

For today's fashion disaster, Gage has selected a white tissue weight dress that hugs my generous, ample hips and accentuates the fact I'll be able to breastfeed the entire Western half of the island by Christmas.

"You can see my bra," I muse as I study the newly formed shelf just beneath my chin.

"I like your bra." He pulls one of my caplets from the closet—not that I have many. Capes and their caplet micro counterparts are the things that villains are made of. Just the fact I'm running low on the furry little shrugs assures me I'm on the right side of the Celestial law.

THE SERPENTINE BUTTERFLY

"Wow! I haven't seen this since homecoming a bazillion years ago, and as fate would have it that night, I forgot it."

He wraps the furry white stole around my shoulders, and with the white dress, I sort of do look like a bride.

"I should dress like a nun for Halloween." I take in my beautiful disfigurement.

"I was thinking more like Little Red Riding Hood, and I could be the big bad wolf."

"Oh?" I curl my fingers around his shirt as he pulls and tugs himself into a suit until he deems himself acceptable. "Why do I sense a little bestiality on board for that horrible haunted night?"

"Because there will be." He dots my lips with a kiss. "You bring out the beast in me," he says it sad, forlorn, as if he really were that mythical creature. "Will you take us there?"

"It depends. I refuse to get married in Demetri's Fem trophy room."

He shakes his head. "It's worse than that, but first, if you don't mind, I promised him we'd bring a guest."

The Transfer on a normal unassuming day is bleak and dreary, but on this day—night, actually, or better yet, eerie combination of both as it stands—the Transfer is alive, festive, adorned with dusty, dirty roses that look as if they were ripped straight out of a casket. Translucent bodies shuffle about in a whirling swirling tornado, all of them yipping about, yammering on and on about *the wedding!* I feel like I'm trapped in some horrible demonic version of *Alice in Wonderland*, where instead of frantic bunnies and Cheshire cats, I'm met with ghosts with serious fashion hang-ups strictly tied to the seventeenth century—large hoop skirts, bonnets and parasols, men with curled mustaches and funny looking suits. Every day is dapper day in the Transfer.

"Lizbeth!" Demetri welcomes my mother with open arms.

It was an odd invitation to begin with, but not altogether shocking. Demetri extending an invite to his baby mama is status quo as far as the demonic oaf goes. But, of course, it wasn't Demetri who actually extended the invitation. It was me. And it went something like this, *"Mom, guess what? I'm getting married again, and this time you can totally come!"*

"Oh, great, honey! Where will the blessed event take place?"

"Why, hell, of course!"

Technically, the Transfer isn't hell per se. That would be Tenebrous—ha! Nephilim humor at its finest. I slay me. Actually, that's not Hades either, just a couple of close seconds and thirds.

"Can you believe this, Skyla?" Mom beams. "I've been working for months helping Demetri get ready for a very special wedding he said he was hosting. If I only knew then it was for my very own daughter!" She lets out a raucous squeal. "Demetri is the very best at surprises. He always knows how to make my most special dreams come true."

I bet he does. I bet she was really surprised—wink, wink—when she suddenly found herself expecting after months of pleading, *kneading* Tad's dried up body parts.

Gage leans into him. "What's with the festivities? I thought you said we'd keep it simple."

"Ah, yes." Demetri sinks his head back, his lips readying the lie. "It seems we've an unexpected guest list. Once rumors began to circulate, you could say things got a bit out of hand." He turns to my mother. "Pardon the décor, my love. I'm sure you could have turned this into a five-star spectacular, but the kids insisted we keep things to a minimum."

"Right," I quip. "Don't you love how he turned his lousy dead roses right back on us?" I jump on my tiptoes to get eye level with Gage. Now that I have this huge belly driving a literal wedge between us, I feel like I have to work harder to get close to him. Everything is a feat now no thanks to Ellis and his procreative advice. I still can't believe that my children's existence will forever be tied to both Ellis and failed anal sex. The thought alone makes me cry a little on the inside. Perhaps those bits of information are best long forgotten. In fact, I'm already thanking Ellis for gifting me—in a roundabout way—two of the most precious treasures on the planet.

"Come now." Demetri leads us to the haunted mansion, the OG one with the crooked doors and windows, the dusty musty halls, the pounding of the endless player piano. I'll have a headache until December, and I can already feel it coming on.

The Transfer transplants glide around us, *through* us, barreling ahead with their horrible warbling laughter. There's nothing more I'm wary of than disembodied spirits with a sense of humor.

Ichabod comes to mind. God, I cannot believe I killed him, *killed* him, as in dead, dead, *dead*. It weighs so heavy on my heart that it hurts to even think about.

We step onto the creaky porch of the mansion proper, and an entire fleet of gossamer waves in our presence.

Gage leans in. "You ready to do this?" He presses a heated kiss to my cheek.

"You two are adorable!" Mom sings, and I turn to find her arm interlinked with Demetri's. Usually I'd frown over this, but considering the circumstances, I'm sure it's partially safety related.

We hit the entrance to the cursed piece of architecture, and Demetri instructs Mom and me to wait until we hear the "Wedding March" before proceeding. The doors swing open to the flickering of malfunctioning dusty chandeliers. Endless rows of candelabras are strewn about with their wax piled knee high over the floor, with their long finger-like drippings. It's so murky inside you can hardly see your hand in front of your face, but every now and again the candles flicker in unison, and an entire thicket of frightened faces stare back at me.

This is such a horror—it's more than a horror, it's a bona fide nightmare—so much so that I'm half-tempted to call off my second wedding to Gage. No offense to the groom, but his father sure knows how to scare the living hell out of me.

"There will be another joining you soon." Demetri winces at me. "Try not to think too deeply on it." He gives a slight bow.

"Thank you for agreeing to do this, Skyla. You've no idea how much this means to Lizbeth and me."

I smirk as he and Gage walk through the opened doors. Gage gives a disparaging look back and nods as if to assure me that everything will be all right. It won't, but that's beside the point.

The fresh scent of apples wafts from inside, and Mom takes in a deep breath, her smile widening with delight.

"Isn't that just heaven?"

Actually, it's hell, but I refuse to travel down that thorny road again.

"It always smells like that," I say. "Most likely to cover the scent of rotting corpses."

"Oh, Skyla, you always have to be so negative." She waves me off with the flick of her wrist. "There are no rotting corpses here. The Transfer is simply one of the many realms belonging to the Countenance—this being the principal locale, of course."

I tick my head back at my mother's sudden Wikipedia-like knowledge on the house of horrors.

"Have you been here before?" I rack my brain, trying to remember when I could have lugged my mother down here on accident, or heaven forbid, on purpose.

"Tons of times. Demetri has given me the tour, and I've tagged along while he took care of business a few times."

Business? She looks deep into the haunted mansion as if this were simply another jaunt to the nether world with her personal Prince of Darkness.

"Are you freaking kidding me?" I don't even know where to begin with this. Demetri has been dragging my mother to the Transfer God knows how many times like some demented tour guide? Does he honestly expect me to believe they were simply here under the guise of party planning? I'm onto that rat bastard. It's clear he's grooming her to be his Mistress of the Dark. Soon, she'll grow her hair long, dye it black, and parade around in slinky dresses—taping her boobs together just to get cleavage because God knows it ain't happening otherwise.

"Boo!" an ultra-cheery female voice sings from behind, and for a happy second, I'm convinced it's Bree.

But it's not. It's the real Mistress of the Dark. The girl without a heart and soul—Chloe.

There she stands in a white ensemble that loosely resembles a cocoon.

"You're not Brielle." Any hope of a smile glides off my face as I examine the strange white webbing she's ensconced herself in. "Shedding your skin?" I muse before turning back around and awaiting my cue. The sooner I'm reunited with Gage the better. The sooner we say I do, the sooner Gage gets his feel-good vibes as a door prize, and the sooner I can bed my human vibrator of a husband. Ha! Gage Oliver is about to turn into a real live human vibrator! God, I really am the luckiest girl alive.

"All I'm shedding are my bachelorette days." She muscles her way to my side. "It's my wedding day, too, Messenger."

"What? I thought you and Wesley already did the white wedding misdeed. Demetri introduced you as Chloe Edinger at his stupid summer shindig!"

"He was stretching the truth." She turns to my mother. "Why, hello, Lizbeth. You look stunning in that color. You should always, always wear fuchsia."

Figures. Demetri is the father of lies. Of course, he was lying that day. And to think poor Laken got worked up over nothing, well, until today. Not that she really cares. Coop is the real prize, and she has him. Wes is nothing but a *boobie* prize, and, well, Chloe deserves him. And fuchsia? Chloe is right up there with Demetri as far as distorting the truth. My mother should never wear fuchsia. The only reason I approved that outfit, once she modeled it as an option, was to A, get this debacle over with—and B, to ensure I can spot her a mile away in this haunted hovel if need be. I was honest in telling her how I felt about that shade of pink working against her hair color, and if Chloe really cared, she would agree.

"Really?" Mom's cheeks flush to match her dress. "Skyla just hates this shade on me. Are you sure?"

Chloe chortles out a laugh about as fake as her existence. "Well, Skyla must be color-blind!"

I snarl at her. "Or maybe *Skyla* doesn't want her mother looking as if she's strayed from the circus? Stick to cool hues," I say to my mother. "They compliment your eyes. Take it from someone who really cares."

Mom rubs her hands over Chloe's belly bump, and to my horror, Chloe actually looks smaller than me. It irks me to no end, partially because I know she's due way sooner than I am. But I get it. I'm getting a twofer. Double the Olivers, double the fun—that has always been my motto. Wait, did I just take a swipe at myself?

"Would you look at this?" Mom coos. "You're beautifully firm. I know it's soon yet, but keep an eye out for your plug. Once it dislodges, you'll notice bucketfuls of cervical mucus. It could be anywhere, your panties, the toilet—I was in the shower when I lost my plug with Mystery. I was pulling out mucus for days!" She and Chloe titter into one another as the music cues up. It sounds like a cross between a warped record and a year-one violinist trying to make the neighbors cringe.

"I'd hate to break up your bonding sesh over vaginal fluids, but I believe that's our cue to trot to the finish line."

"Isn't this exciting, Skyla?" Chloe leans her shoulder to mine as if she's getting chummy with me. "I'm marrying Gage."

Not happening—not even on accident, but secretly, I'm thankful for her heads-up in the event she's plotting a mix-up.

I choose to ignore fake, chummy, soon-to-be-plucking-mucus-from-her-vagina Chloe and start down the long, dark hall lined with its horrific cast of characters. The sound of warbling voices carries up over the music, loud like rushing waters. I lean in, inspecting a few of the faces up close and holy hell! There are real flesh and blood people mixed in with the poltergeist posse! *People* in the Transfer? Shit! What kind of people?

"Where do you hail from?" I ask a younger girl with wide eyes, green as a streetlight, but Chloe pulls me back into formation before the girl can answer as we continue to plod our way through the darkness.

"Where do you hail from?" Chloe scoffs. "Really, Skyla? Is this 1692? Anyway, what I'm really psyched about is the fact we're going to share a wedding date. Isn't that something? Each day our lives become more and more intertwined."

"Same wedding date," I whisper because no coincidence with Chloe is ever a good one. Oh crap. What if we really are about to share the same groom? "Swear to God, Wesley had better be there ready to pooper scoop you back into his life because I refuse to include you as a part of my holy matrimony."

She belts out a laugh that gets drowned out by the ever-increasing furor surrounding us. It's as if we were approaching a very large, exceptionally dangerous beehive. Let's hope we don't get stung to death, although it would serve me right for being stupid enough to agree to this. The only reason I did comply with the circus at hand was to help Gage procure those feel-good vibes that Marshall has. Even though most of my nausea has dissipated and kindly relegated itself to the proper time of day—e.g., the morning—I still can't wait to see how amazing it'll be to bed him with his good vibrations turned up all the way.

"Dear sweet Jesus!" the wail of a frightened woman emanates from somewhere deep in the crowd. Sobbing ensues. "*Please*! Forgive me of my sins!" Violent sobs, downright hysteria takes over the poor woman.

I glance around at the worried looking crowd. The Transfer transplants are oblivious, of course—all having a gay old time, whirling and twirling, and only half-cognizant of what's going on. In other words, they are totally themselves, but the people, those still nicely tucked in their coats of flesh, look petrified to be here.

"Jesus, forgive me! Save me, Jesus! Save me!" More violent sobs and wails.

Dear Lord! Yes, please save us all—that woman specifically.

Mom's eyes bug out as she leans toward Chloe, and the three of us all but cower along hoping to see a few familiar faces coming up soon, but it's so dark you can only see a few feet out at a time. Who knows how long I'll have to walk through hell with Chloe by my side? This place is as deep and wide as a football field.

"Skyla, Chloe," Gage calls out, and I step forward until he comes into focus. "Oh, thank God." I lunge forward and wrap my arms tight around him, my lips magnetize to his, and suddenly, I'm pulled away abruptly.

"Hey!" I'm about to deck my assailant, but it, too, is Gage. "Oh! Sorry," I say, stepping away from his annoyingly good-looking brother who, apparently, I just made out with. Not an ideal way to begin our wedding.

Both Demetri and Wes offer an understanding nod as I take my proper place next to Gage, and Chloe does the same with Wes.

Demetri clears his throat. "Ladies and gentlemen of the underworld and those visiting from the planet proper, welcome!"

A dull cheer erupts around us.

"Who are these people?" I whisper to Gage.

"Videns." He gives a little shrug. "I had no idea. Sorry."

"Not a problem." I'm sure this evening will be laced with interesting surprises. "By the way"—I lean into Demetri—"our wedding guests are very fucking afraid." I'm not amused by his constant usury and trickery, and now real live people are being subjected to his lunacy.

"Don't be silly." Demetri waves me off with his hand. "Everyone is delighted to be here." He clears his throat. "Today we are gathered in the presence of God and man alike to commit into a divine holy union of both my sons and their brides. It is a father's great pleasure to see his children enter into holy matrimony, so you can imagine my sheer delight to be able to not just witness this blessed event but to officiate it as holy council."

I grimace a moment. Demetri is far from holy.

A dark-haired girl springs up next to Chloe and gives a non-smiling wave.

"Emily?" Of course, she's a Viden.

"I'm here to stand up for Bishop," she grunts.

"Oh, nice." Did I just say *nice*?

Mom scoots in close to me. "I'm here for Skyla."

Demetri starts in on some cultish chant that sounds like a hellish version of *hallelujah*, and the rest of the crowd joins in. Just what I've always wanted— a singing demon in the armpit of hell. It's every little girl's dream—more like warped dream.

Gage smiles at me. His fingers hook to mine as he draws me near. The only barrier between us is my belly.

He cocks his head to the side, an amused smile playing on his lips.

"*I love you*," he mouths as Demetri calls the great haunted hall to order.

Chloe stands stoically by Wesley's side, and I can't help but give him the stink eye before Demetri gets underway. If he's so hot and bothered over Laken—like he wants everyone to believe—then why is he making it quasi-official with Bishop? Chloe is a monster. She doesn't deserve a wedding day, a devoted husband, or a child.

Demetri bellows something out over and over again that sounds suspiciously like the words *Magna Carta*.

"Wesley, my son, the one after my heart like no other"— Demetri smiles with those lying eyes, only I'm pretty sure this is the one time he's telling the truth—"do you take Chloe Jessica Bishop to be your lawfully wedded wife—in sickness and in health, in misery and in joy?"

I lean to Gage. "Misery being the operative word."

Wes takes in a mean breath as if marshaling all of his resolve. "I do," he says it solemn as shit, not an ounce of joy in his eyes.

"And, Chloe, do you vow to worship, to fully mind, to adhere to the laws that Wesley puts in place for you?"

The feminist in me hates this, but the fact those are the vows Chloe needs to abide by while married to Wes makes me want to smile—although Wes, like his twisted bride, is evil incarnate. He might look like Gage, and even come across as a pretty nice guy, but he has a one-track mind, and it's world domination. Some people will do anything to get their way. In that respect, Chloe and Wes are perfect for each other.

"I do." Chloe takes up Wesley's hands. "In fact, I want to add that I'm willing to sacrifice my time, my talents, and my expertise to help you in any and every endeavor. From this moment on, we are a team—Team Edinger."

"What is she talking about?" I whisper to Gage. "She has no talents or expertise."

His brows rise as if equally amused.

And Team Edinger? She'll always be Bitch-Face Bishop to me. Good thing nothing is truly legally binding in this special hell. Hey? I bet that's why Wes agreed to this in the first place.

I catch Em wiping the tears from her eyes. She can't be serious.

"And Gage"—Demetri turns his countenance fully to the two of us—"the apple of my eye"—wow, Wes runs around like hot shit on a silver platter, but thanks to Demetri doling out his highest accolades to his little bro, I bet he feels like cold diarrhea on a paper plate right about now—"do you take this lovely vision set before us as your one and only eternal bride?"

"With all my heart." He looks lovingly into my eyes, and all of the wickedness surrounding us, the wicked people themselves, disappear.

Aw, Gage and his expressive eyes know how to dissolve me to water.

"Skyla, do you promise to love and enjoy the company of my most beloved son from this moment until his last dying breath?"

First, he didn't toss in any of that anti-feminist bullshit he flung at Chloe, so for that I'm grateful. But, he did manage to take another swipe at Wes by calling Gage his most beloved son—oh hell, we all know it's true. But that last phrase—asking me to love Gage until *his* last dying breath?

"I will love you, Gage Oliver, in this life and the next. I look forward to spending each and every moment with you, from waking up in your loving arms to falling asleep in them each night, ending the day the same way it began. I vow to love you through each new decade of our lives together, right through to *my* last dying breath."

Chloe scoffs as if I've just spewed a lie. But truer words have never left my lips. I love Gage Oliver, always will, and I want him right by my side until I'm old and gray, my own body in the ground before his ever gets there, so I'll never have to grieve him.

Demetri nods, his features at perfect peace with my response. "Wesley, Chloe, Gage, and Skyla, I now lock you in a binding covenant, a treaty of blood and of the bond of love. You are now, and forever more, husbands and wives."

The crowd gives a deafening cheer filled with warbling screams and chilling cries. Not your traditional whooping round of applause—more like half the guests are afraid this is the part where we skin them alive and line our closets with them as winter coats.

Okay—wait, rewind—that last part Demetri espoused sounded a little kinky. He didn't actually mean Wesley, Chloe, Gage and me, right?

Gage leans in as if reading my mind. "It's just you and me, forever."

My lips twitch, readying for a kiss, and a warm tingling sensation fills my belly. I pull back slightly, and my hand glides over my quickly heating stomach.

"Skyla?" Gage gives my shoulder a firm squeeze with worry. "What's wrong?"

"I don't know. I'm not in any pain. It's just—"

"Oh my God!" Mom screams so loud the hall of horrors quiets down to a demonic whisper. "Did your water break? Are you having contractions? Let's get you off your feet."

"No, it's none of that. I'm fine." My belly begins to swirl as if a washing machine were turned on inside me, and I can feel the babies stretching, and kicking—and slowly, ever so slowly, a blue glow appears from underneath my dress.

"Shit." Gage is not amused with the Las Vegas review going on inside my stomach.

My sky blue tummy brightens, illuminating a brilliant ethereal shade of sapphire, reminiscent of the spirit sword. It's a swirling electric movement of color and light, rotating endlessly in a clockwise pattern. Such a radiant, dazzling, cobalt that the entire structure around us glows the beautiful hue.

Demetri steps in with his shaking hands and places them over the large hump of my belly. "Your child is powerful—I've never seen this kind of energy before." He looks up sharply at me. "I will grant you up to half of my kingdom, Skyla. Just name it, and it will be yours."

Anything? "For Gage to live a very long, long life." I don't even hesitate with that one.

Mom coos as if it was the sweetest of sentiments. Little does she know it's a very real need.

"That's not for me to grant." He looks to Gage as if it were entirely up to him. Obviously, he doesn't understand how my mother in the sky works.

I consider it a moment. Speaking of my mother and her kangaroo court, I do have a very real need.

"Then I know what I want," I say with confidence. "But I'd like to ask for it in private."

Gage

Demetri stares at Skyla as if she's just caught him by surprise. You can catch Demetri by a lot of things—most of them having to do with something nefarious, but surprise is not one of them.

Skyla and I have jumped through his latest hoop in the name of holy matrimony, so I'd say he owes us a little wedding gift in return. I know exactly what my old man owes me—some of those vibratronics that make Skyla sway like a reed whenever Dudley is around.

Chloe pipes up, "Oh, oh, oh! I want something, too! No fair if Skyla gets something and I don't. You don't want to play favorites, do you, *Dad*?"

Chloe is laying it on thick, and as for playing favorites, wasn't she paying attention to the ceremony? I felt like a dick when Demetri spouted off about me. As much as I don't agree with Wesley's politics, I still care for the guy on some level. I believe he's looking for love and acceptance like the rest of us. I believe he's lost his way, but that he can be redeemed. Can't he?

Demetri nods to Lizbeth who's busy cooing into Skyla's dimming belly. For the love of God, I can't have Skyla glowing like a traffic light, albeit a blue one. This had better be a one time only stunt of his.

"Lizbeth, dear—" he strums the words cool and soft as if he's trying to seduce her. He doesn't need to go far if he is. Lizbeth looks a little more smitten with him than usual this evening. "Would you tend to the guests and help them into the main dining hall? The buffet should be up and running, but you may want to supervise. It's been so long since I've hosted such an extravagant soirée."

"Why, it would be my pleasure." She sticks her fingers into her mouth, letting out a sharp whistle that cuts through the noise and effectively herds the masses—both the living and the dead—into the cavernous room next door.

"Wesley, Chloe"—he gives a slight bow—"if you'll excuse us for a moment, we'll join you again shortly."

Chloe steps in a little too close and flicks my collar. "Don't be long, big boy. Wouldn't want you to miss the first dance." She smacks her lips at Skyla. "Welcome to the family, Bitch-Face, and, yes, now that my powers are extrapolating, I heard all of your asinine thoughts. Don't stand so close to me next time."

Demetri leads us farther down the corridor until we hit a door that expands and retracts as if it's struggling to breathe.

"It's like seeing an old friend," Skyla muses as Demetri holds the door open for us. Skyla was held captive here for a while. It's not shocking that she recognizes the breathing hardware. Inside, a wall of candles lights up the cobweb-riddled room, complete with creaky floors and partially downed green velvet curtains.

"You should really get Bishop to clean up the place." Skyla pumps a bleak smile. "Now that she's sworn into a lifetime of remedial chores in the name of all that is marital domestic bliss, redecorating this dump should be priority number one." She glances to me. "Plus, it might keep her off that overgrown rock we live on."

"Is that what you're going to ask for? Put a lid on Chloe and all her comings and goings?" I'm impressed. Most people would have asked for something far less innovative and potentially crime stopping. It is Chloe's fault the entire world has turned its spotlight on Paragon after that stunt she pulled on Logan's birthday. And the fact those lights still hover over the Cove has turned the entire island into somewhat of an unwanted tourist attraction. Scratch that. Circus attraction is the more appropriate term.

"No, actually," Skyla hugs her protruding stomach, which has thankfully dimmed the light show, "I want *this*." She fans her hands out.

"*This*?" Demetri expresses my sentiment exactly. "This room?" His entire face lifts an inch, amused.

"This place."

"The mansion." His head pulls back. "Consider it done. I'd like nothing more than both of my sons to live in the same neighborhood. It is a bit of a fixer as you've pointed out, but I must say the phantasms that haunt the place do prefer it that way. And they will be a bear to evict, but those are mere details." His chin ticks up a notch. "Congratulations to you both on your first home."

"No." Skyla shakes her head, much to my relief. "I want the entire Transfer."

"It's a realm, Skyla." Demetri is further amused by the request. I'm not so much amused as I am baffled—*fucking* baffled to be exact. But that's Skyla. She's full of surprises.

"Then make it my realm." Her voice rises a notch.

"It's doesn't work that way. The Countenance achieved this centuries ago on their own volition." He frowns at the battered décor a moment. "Not that they're bothered to do much with it. The laboratory is a nice perk, though. I suppose that's why you're interested."

Not true. The lab Logan built for Ezrina makes this one look like it belongs in the Stone Age. Besides, Ezrina pilfered the shit out of this place on her last day. A little petty theft from the workplace was both necessary and deserved on her part.

"Okay." Skyla glances at me a moment before staring off at the broken window, her wheels churning a million miles an hour. "How about Tenebrous? I want the Tenebrous Woods."

"*What?*" Now it's me stunned and seeking an explanation. "You hate that place. It reeks of shitty history—countless Celestra died in those tunnels."

"I know." She closes her eyes a moment. "But I want it. I want Tenebrous," she reasserts, this time with a renewed sense of confidence.

Clearly, something is happening that I don't understand. Perhaps it's her way of ensuring it'll never be put to use again. In that case, it makes total sense.

"The Tenebrous Woods." Demetri's smile melts from his face, first time, if ever. Skyla must have really thrown him for a loop. "It's where we conduct the Barricade meetings." He nods to me as if the thought of disrupting those haunted roundtables would throw me into a tailspin.

"We could live without them," I offer.

"Nonsense." He gives a tired blink. "We'll simply host them here. Wesley won't like it. He prefers to keep his home separate from his office. And, of course, you have your own realm—Paragon in Nocturne." Demetri nods as if agreeing. "With the Videns"—he continues—"Wes does like for me to keep things even, a realm for a realm, and now all that he'll have is his home."

"Are you talking about our Wesley?" Skyla balks. "Listen, I know you like to play the role of sugar daddy—I've seen this firsthand with my mother—but, trust me, your little Wes doesn't need to be handfed from a silver spoon. A dominion here, a realm there—you can see how this much coddling could result in spoiling your eldest son—perhaps turning him into a megalomaniac. And the entire world is suffering because of it."

He doesn't look too impressed with her line of thought. "And gifting you Tenebrous will alleviate this?"

"I can't make any promises when it comes to Wesley. But as far as my gift, yes, I would like Tenebrous. And I'd like an all-access pass to bring down whomever I please, and the power to transfer my keys if need be to eligible people."

"Yes." He plucks at his chin. "In the event your friends decide to throw a party."

"Exactly." Skyla closes her eyes a moment as if he hit the nail on the demented head.

What in the hell are they talking about?

"Done." He lifts a finger, and the stale air stirs around us. "You have roaming privileges as of now. I'll file the necessary documents with the Justice Alliance, and it will be yours by daybreak." He glances at her stomach, and his lips curl with approval. "Anything for the mother of my grandchild." He gives a sharp look my way as if he's waiting for us to admit to twins. We won't, so there's that. "And you, Gage?"

I look to Skyla, my mouth opened, my voice already cracking as I struggle to get the words out. There is one other thing that I'd like to tag onto the mad vibratory skills he's about to impart on me, like the completion of that birthday gift from last year he's yet to payout. In a couple of months, I'll have another birthday, and then he'll owe me two lifetimes—not that it were possible. Hell, the first one may prove to be a pipe dream.

"Skyla, why don't you go see how your mother is faring?" Demetri expands his ever-blooming smile. "These vellum sewer rats have been known to border on aggressive when things don't go their way."

"Gee, wonder where they get that?" She hikes up on her tiptoes and gives me a kiss before waddling out of the room.

Demetri sheds a simple smile as soon as the door clicks shut. "I sensed your need for privacy. I take it the vibratronics are a surprise for your beloved?"

"No, she's well aware, and very much looking forward to them. It's just—there is one more thing."

"Speak."

"My birthday last year—you said you'd give me a long life in exchange for a body. I gave you one. Where's my guarantee I'll be pumping air through my lungs well after I'm old and gray?"

"Yes, that was the exchange, wasn't it?" A rustle of unsettled, unearthly voices magnify from the hall before dissipating again. "It looks as if someone is getting a room." He bares his teeth, proud of the earthly euphemism. "But back to the task at hand. Yes, I can gift you what you desire. It is against your destiny, Gage. Both you and I realize that, or I assume you wouldn't have asked. I can give you what was promised. A long life, Skyla, I'm assuming, will remain by your side. You can raise your child—your children together." He eyes me a moment too long as if trying to call my bluff, but I don't give in.

"What's the catch?"

"You'll have to alter paths on the day you were set to separate from the planet."

"Meaning?" My stomach ties up in knots because I don't like the sound of altering my path.

"You must take your rightful place as my heir and run the new dominion. You'll vow to remain loyal to me and carry out the path of righteousness that ushers the Fem and Countenance alliance to fulfillment. You will be the leader of both—Wesley to serve beneath you in accordance to the law. Of course, the Barricade will be forever his, as will the Videns remain your people."

"I'm not following. I run the dominion. That's it?"

"You're further off track than you realize. Not only do you run the kingdom, you will side with the Fems and the Countenance. Therefore—"

"Therefore, I'll be Skyla's enemy."

"Now, now, she could come into full compliance and lay her people at your feet. Once the Sectors bow to our majesty, we can all live in harmony the way it should have been all along."

"You want the Sectors to bow down to you and me? Have you met Marshall Dudley? If the rest of his kind are anything remotely like him, you are in for a shit surprise, my friend. Besides, I can't be Skyla's enemy. She's the love of my life. Ain't happening."

"Then I'm afraid neither is the fulfillment of your wish. Enjoy the remainder of your days, Gage. I've requested and seen your final hours. Time flies, my son, and they will be upon you before you know it." His gaze falls to the floor a moment. "Think things through. There is your expanding family to consider. You have the power in your hands to remain on this planet—heavenly air in your resurrected lungs until well after you should have been old and gray. All you have to do is say yes."

Heavenly air? *Resurrected*? Why do I get the feeling the fine print is what I should be reading?

"I'll be alive?"

"Alive, yes." His brows hike. "We are all eternal beings, Gage. Life after life is promised to all in some capacity."

"No, it's not. Hell equates death."

"You are bound for dominion. Accept this extension of time for the sake of your wife, your children—your kingdom."

Extension of time.

"It is tempting." I would love to be on this planet right alongside Skyla and the kids.

He steps in close, the whites of his eyes glint in the darkness. "That sounds a lot like yes to me." He strides away. "The vibratronics will kick in when you see Skyla. They are exclusive to her and will end upon the birth of my grandchild." Demetri leaves the room, and the door clicks shut behind him.

I stagger to the fireplace, the air in my lungs stills to nothing. "Shit!" I kick a basket full of pinecones clear across the room, and a fire roars to life in the mouth of the charred pit.

I can't be Skyla's enemy.

Can I?

By the time I get back to the party, there's a band playing. They all look relatively alive and human, and yet, I'm not that impressed. The dim chandeliers flicker on and off as the Transfer's residents spin in ghostly circles to the music. I spot Skyla near the buffet with Logan, both of them huddled and whispering feverishly. I pause a moment, watching them like this. I'm sure she's already mentioned her newest acquisition for her people, Tenebrous. I'm almost half-afraid to ask what her plans are with it. Partially because I may not like the answer, and partially because I'm afraid she won't give it—at least not to me anyway. In some respects, Skyla and I are already on opposite sides of the angelic sphere. What could be so bad about adhering to a few different rules as long as our marriage remains intact? I would never do anything to harm her people. If anything, I would drag my feet, slow down Demetri's demented plans to a crawl. Skyla would want me around for the kids, wouldn't she? I know she'd want me to be there for our children. I swallow hard. I'm not looking forward to breaking this bit of news to her—at least not the prospect of me considering the position.

A hard slap falls over my back, and I turn to find Ellis with his glazed over grin, and my sister with her much more perkier, lucid smile.

"Come here, you." I pull her into a deep hug. I wasn't expecting to see any family here outside of Skyla and Lizbeth, so this is a treat.

"Heard you were tying the knot again, and I wouldn't miss it! Mom is going to be so mad!" She giggles because I think we both know she's not going to be that torn up about it other than the fact that I did the deed twice. I'll admit, Skyla might be onto her.

"And I heard there would be a killer spread." Ellis smacks me in the stomach, his eyes glued to the carving station. "If you need me in the next few hours, I'll be in that direction."

"Wait!" Giselle pulls him back just as Skyla and Logan make their way over. Skyla wraps her arms around me and gasps once she feels those good vibrations oozing off me.

"That's right, baby," I whisper with a greedy grin. "And they're all for you."

"Sweet." She closes her eyes a moment. Her pleasure gauge just kicked up a notch. Pleasure *Gage*. I like the sound of that one better.

"Ellis has a very important new job." Giselle nudges him to tell us all about it.

"Oh—right." His eyes grow big as he subtly shakes his head at her.

"Don't be shy! You're going to be famous, remember? Everyone is going to know Ellis Harrison sells the best grass in the West. Isn't that right?"

"Shit," he mumbles, his chest rattling with a dull laugh. "That's right." He scoops her in. "Let's divide and conquer. You hit the surf, and I'll hit the turf."

"Grass?" Logan is about as amused as I am. "Please just deny it. I don't want to have to hear how passion met opportunity."

"Oh, but it did!" Giselle squeals. "His father introduced him to the board and everything. Ellis is going to have the biggest pot farm in all of Washington State!" Her lids hood, her smile is traded for tight lips. "And before any one of you gets all uppity and smug about it, it's all legal, and you can't do squat about it." She nods to Ellis as if to ask if she quoted him correctly.

Shit. "So, when do we get to see this field of green dreams?" I wonder what would happen if I accidentally on purpose lit the place on fire. It might make for one mellow night on Paragon, or at least behind the gates.

"For you guys? Anytime, man. Anytime." He high-fives me before hitting the food lines with G.

"Crap," I mutter. "I think I just saw both of their futures mapped out in front of me in one weed-filled haze, and it's not pretty."

Coop and Laken come up with Liam, Lexy, and Nat—so much for keeping it small.

"We're here strictly for the two of you," Laken is quick to assert. She pulls Skyla into a hug.

"Sorry for the lack of an invite." Skyla doesn't let go of Laken's hands. I'm glad she finally has a friend with a good head on her shoulders. "We hardly got the invite ourselves."

Coop nods at me. "Ezrina and Nev are working overtime on something important, or they would have been here. They asked me to extend their apologies and also their congratulations on making it official once again."

"Thanks." Skyla looks to me with a question in her eyes.

"What's this new project they've got going?" I ask for her.

Coop looks over his shoulder at Wes, who's just a few feet away chatting it up with Morley and Arson. The only real friends he has are twice his age and out for themselves. I won't lie. I do feel bad for the guy.

Coop shakes his head. "Not here. Check in with her, though. You might like what you hear."

I glance to Logan, who looks as if he's ready to bolt right now, and see what's going on. "Will do."

Skyla twitches by my side. "I wonder what's kept Marshall away."

Logan shakes his head. "I don't know, but that is one depressed Sector. He hasn't been his insulting, demeaning self as of late. He's been *nice* to me. Something is definitely up with Dudley."

Skyla winces. She probably feels bad for neglecting the old coot. She's made it a point to keep their friendship alive and well, with Dudley, of course, going the extra mile and inserting his penis into her dreams whenever he can. I don't buy that I-have-no-idea-what's-happening bullshit.

The band starts in on a cover song that the girls all swoon to at once. A scream of delight comes from the player piano where Demetri dips Lizbeth over the precariously decrepit piece of furniture. It looks as if a good time is being had by all. Let's just hope Misty doesn't have a brother or sister brewing before the night is through.

Ellis shows up with a plate full of promise—and that promise is indigestion. "Dude, this band is fucked up! I need to SoundHound the shit out of this." He pulls out his phone and proceeds to do just that.

Lex grabs Logan by the collar and starts swinging her hips, not waiting for the invite herself.

"You know it is a bit freaky"—she grinds into him, and he winces—"but if you're into crap like this, I don't mind if we hold our wedding here."

"Among the dead?" he muses. "I'm one of them, by the way."

Lexy laughs, pulling him in closer, and Skyla raises her shoulder in that direction in an effort to deny it's bothering her. But I know it does. Hell, it bothers me to see him molested that way.

"I'd like to dance with my husband," she coos. Her fingers slowly clasp the side of my face, and her features melt. Her eyes roll to the back of her head. "So sweet."

The party goes on for hours, surrounded by a handful of family and friends. It's nice like this. Skyla melting in my arms, our bodies moving in time, lost in our own universe.

Even a place as dismal as the Transfer can't hold back our love.

Tonight, it only magnifies it.

Skyla and I finally head home where I make love to her like it's the very first time. Her body sings under mine, literally. Skyla is in paradise. So am I. We may never come back.

The very next night, Wes sends a series of spastic texts regarding the fact he can't seem to get into Tenebrous. Figures. Dear old Demetri has neglected to fill him in on the one tiny detail that his favorite playground haunt is forever off limits.

Wes picks me up for our nightly meet-and-greet with the Videns. He went alone last night to the town hall meeting. I wasn't about to leave Skyla on our anniversary, on our second faux wedding night, so I let him go on his own—told him not to break anything or anyone while he was there. He hinted at a special project he's enlisted a few prospective members, something about helping the Barricade in an effort to develop an elixir to hide their markers.

Every news station, every talking head in the country—scratch that—the *world* is focused on these mysterious lights, these mysterious people able to perform super human feats. But as fast as Wes seems to recruit those willing to betray the Nephilim, they disappear just as quickly. I'm the one who gave Skyla and Logan that list. I haven't given them an update, but the new recruits are just as scarce these days. I'm almost afraid to ask. As long as I'm in the dark, Wes and Demetri can't guilt me into laying it all out before them. I don't really need to know what Skyla is up to, but, then, she is my wife, and I want her safe. The world is going to hell in a handbasket, and it's Wes who has lined that handbasket with lead.

"What the fuck?" he rages as he speeds us toward Devil's Peak. "I can't just get locked out of a dominion like that, can I? Do you think I'm losing my powers?" He seems genuinely baffled.

"No. And it's a realm, not a dominion. Have you talked to Demetri about this?"

"No." His eyes narrow in on the road as we take the winding hillside down toward the rocky shore. There isn't a single car in the parking lot up top. Back when I was in school, that lot would have been full of the stoners and moaners and girls in short skirts. And both Logan and I would be warring over Skyla. I give a silent laugh. Can't believe I just had a thought that started with, *back when I was in school*.

"I said no I haven't talked to Demetri, and what's so funny?" He revs the engine, readying to drive through that wall of granite, defy gravity, and end up in a realm that belongs to the Countenance, our brothers in darkness—correction, his.

"Nothing. I was just thinking about how long ago high school felt. You ever wish you could turn back the clock just a bit? Hit pause for a little while?"

Wesley stares off at the jagged stretch of rocks that spike through the whitewash and gives a slight nod. "Wish I could go all the way back to Cider Plains, back to where both Laken and I were alive and desperately in love. She was my best friend. We were inseparable, and now she won't even look at me. She spent hours at the reception last night avoiding me. Coop even congratulated me, but Laken wouldn't blink in my direction. She hated me before, but by marrying Chloe, I've wounded her even deeper."

"That's some ego you've got."

"Shut the hell up." He frowns at the wall he's readying to speed us through. "Imagine a world in which your love for Skyla never ends, and yet, you become her worst enemy. I bet you think Skyla would love you right through it, don't you?" He shakes his head wistfully as if relishing the thought. "She wouldn't. She would despise you—but deep down, she would still wish you were the boy she once knew." He nods while staring vacantly out the window. "She would be with him—that Coop knockoff of a cousin, *uncle* of yours, and then we'd both be up shit creek with nothing but Chloe to show for it."

The wheels to Wesley's SUV spin beneath us as he gives a raucous roar and flies us toward the blue wall of sheer solid rock.

My stomach twists so hard, and I wince with pain, but it has nothing to do with the fact we're flying toward an impossibility and everything to do with the fact Wesley just might be right.

Could Skyla love me just the same if I were her true enemy? What if that were the only way for me to stay in her life? The lives of our children? Just how much pain is Skyla willing to endure just to have me around?

I saw the way Laken was avoiding the hell out of my brother last night. I could never bear it if Skyla treated me with so much contempt.

She wouldn't. She couldn't.

We're in this forever. We're desperately in love.

At least with this version of one another.

Logan

The night sky above Paragon offers the illusion that it's moving at a haunted clip—that it is perilously defying the laws of physics in an effort to bypass this overgrown rock on its way to greener pastures. The night fog swims over the landscape, cloaking Paragon in a robe of heavenly beauty.

Dudley's backyard, if you can call this spacious plane something so meager, offers a certain serenity that ensures it's just the island and me, Paragon and I having an affair of our very own. Every now and again the stars shine through, revealing a sparkling twinkle of light, and I wonder what this night would look like if I could draw back the misty curtains, see the stars in all their glory like the rest of the world. The fog has overtaken my life in so many ways. I felt that fog sinking into my pores, running through my veins as I witnessed Skyla and Gage renewing their wedding vows. It replays like a tape in my mind over and over. They exchanged their *I dos* followed by a kiss. Nothing out of the ordinary, nothing you wouldn't expect to see at a wedding, but, then, it was no ordinary wedding—maybe that's why the entire event has given me nightmares.

A heavy exhaustion settles over me as I attempt to rub the sleep out of my eyes, but I know I should hit the sheets. I still can't believe I witnessed Wes tying the knot with Chloe. I guess you could say that he sold his soul to the devil when he agreed to play the part of his number one henchman, but marrying Chloe? What the hell was that about? Is he honestly concerned with what his child might think about their nuptial standing? Never mind the fact its mother is a killer. I think I was number three on her hit list, but, hell, in all honesty, I don't keep track of Chloe's body count.

The back door glides open, and I groan because Dudley is the last person I want to deal with.

"I'm closing up for the night. Would you prefer to be locked in or out?" He stalks over, hovering with his general discontent.

"Both, I suppose."

"Don't plague me with your impossibilities. I'll leave the choice to you. I've a protective hedge over the mansion proper, so it makes not a difference to me. A spiritual shield puts modern-day home security devices to shame." He turns to go.

"Why weren't you there?" I roll off the bench and sit upright for a moment, trying to get my bearings as my head gives into a quiet rush.

"There?" He sounds less interested than he does mystified.

"No need to play clueless. It's me, Dudley. You can ditch the head games. We're like family." He winces as if I sucker punched him with that one.

"I was there. I felt no need to be seen at the event, so I kept my presence to myself. Will there be anything else you'd like to interrogate me over, or may I retire for the evening?"

"You know, it's not always about you. Sure, you were there, but you weren't there, *there*."

"There, *there*?" he muses. "And they let you into Host with your vast usage of the English vocabulary? Perhaps I shouldn't have been so generous with the letter grades when you were my charge. I'm not sure you deserved that A. And, judging by your lack of linguistics skills, you clearly flew under the pedantic radar when it came to English."

"Are you kidding? I more than deserved that A in your class. I'm practically a math genius. I'm just as good at numbers as you are. It's otherworldly the way I can calculate with the best of them."

"If you're so 'good at numbers,' then why aren't they falling in the bowling alley's favor?"

Sucker punched. I groan at his verbal victory. "Okay, you got me."

I'm about to get up just as the figure of a woman emerges behind him, shuffling along in flip-flops.

"Can anyone crash this party?" Skyla materializes from the shadows with her hair damp and combed back as if she just stepped out of the shower, a flannel gown with a white fuzzy robe draped over her enormous belly. How I love that belly. I can't help but smile. She's so beautiful like this. A part of me thinks this entire pregnancy is moving way too fast, but I'm sure it's not fast enough for Skyla. It's clear from her attire that she's teleported.

I talked to Em about taking a few pictures of Skyla in her new, lovely form, but Lex demanded she take them. Turns out, photography is yet another hobby she's picked up.

"I've been warming the bench for you." I slide over and pat a seat for her.

"Actually"—she gives a nervous glance to Dudley—"I was hoping we could take a little trip."

"Why don't I like the sound of this?" I don't mean to sound negative, but Skyla and I have a history of taking exceedingly bad trips. We're proving to be quite the deadly travel companions.

"A dive bar in South America?" She looks hopeful.

Dudley ticks his head to the side. "A dive bar, Ms. Messenger? In your condition?" He lifts his brows as if expecting the most outlandish reply, and unfortunately, the answer is a little darker than that. "I see you've dressed for the occasion."

"You wouldn't get it." I wrap an arm around Skyla, hoping she'll take the hint and we can take off on our own.

"Try me." Dudley is digging in his heels. Dollars to doughnuts he's coming along for the ride. "Or should I say, explain on the way?"

And there you have it.

Skyla latches on to both my hand and Dudley's, and her belly begins to glow from beneath her dress. It's that same ethereal blue that shone through the other night in the Transfer.

"I think they're girls." She presses her hand, along with mine, over her stomach. "I mean, I don't really know boys like I know girls. And all the miniature pink clothes are to die for." She bites down on her lip while examining the newly illuminated globe that sits inside her.

For a moment, I envision twin girls, blonde hair—hers, deep blue eyes and dimples—his. It still carves a fresh wound over my heart each time I think of how they came to be. But, nevertheless, it doesn't change how happy I am for the two of them.

Skyla takes in a deep breath as if staving off nausea, but it's the way she squeezes my hand that makes it feel more like an apology.

"We're going back." She nods as if centering herself for a moment—redirecting herself to the task at hand. "Back to South America—back in time far enough to before I took off that asshole's face."

Dudley groans as she lowers the boom. I think he has all the details he needs now.

The atmosphere changes, the muggy weather makes my jeans cling unnaturally to my body. Music pours from every orifice of this dive bar, loud and raucous, as if a marching band were on acid. A strange warbling fills the air, and I give a hard blink.

"I think my eyes are having a hard time adjusting." I give Skyla's hand a squeeze as if that were somehow able to fix it.

"Your eyes are perfectly fine, Oliver." Dudley runs his finger through the air and cuts through a stream of violet wavelengths. "Skyla? Explain yourself. You not only lack the knowledge to obtain a Treble Lock—you lack the powers."

She grunts out a tiny laugh. "Never underestimate the power of a woman who wants to undo a rather gruesome error—especially when the Justice Alliance is about to get all over her ass about said indiscretion." She treks on ahead with me by her side.

"Language!" he calls as we head into the liquor-soaked pub.

What's going on? I tap my thumb into her palm, letting her know I need an answer quick. A Treble Lock isn't anything I've heard of before. Not to mention the fact the sole reason I exist at the moment is the Treble I happen to be locked into. The last thing I want is for Skyla to somehow unzip that.

Oh, ye of little faith. She frowns my way before heading upstairs to the parlor where we found Ichabod Travers on that fated night.

A group of men sits at the poker table, and, holy shit—there he is— Ichabod Travers, boisterous and cocky and about to have his nose pushed into his cerebellum.

Dudley points to the far left, and everything in me freezes. Can't breathe—don't need to, but, regardless, not one autonomic response, forced or otherwise, is able to kick in. Huddled in the corner are Skyla and I—the version from so many nights ago. Here, we are in duplicate, watching ourselves as we follow Ichabod to the bathroom where his face will soon meet up with Skyla's turquoise boot.

"*Shit.*" I pull Skyla in, my eyes wild with questions and outright confusion. "What the hell are we doing here?"

Her stony affect melts to a somewhat guilty expression. "I'll be glad to answer all of your questions in just a moment." She slips her hand from my grasp, running after our former selves as Dudley and I follow.

"Tell me how to fix this, now," I bark at him.

"Young Oliver," he says it tired and a bit sorry for me.

Either Skyla has pulled us into a new vat of crap or—well, that about covers it. And, technically, it was me who decided to let her tag along on this little outing the first time, so I only have myself to blame.

Skyla holds her hands out as the Logan and Skyla of the past wrestle with Ichabod. It's pretty damn clear they can't see us.

"Shit," is about the only thing I can seem to say or come up with in general.

Skyla, from the previous light drive, goes ballistic, and just when poor Ichabod is about to meet up with a beautiful blue boot that happens to be adorning the prettiest foot on the planet, Skyla—this one that apparently has powers beyond my comprehension dives over it, strangling the shit out of her own leg as if it were a turquoise snake.

Ichabod drops to the floor from my hearty blow with that miniature spirit sword, like he was supposed to, and the Skyla and Logan of days gone by fizzle out of existence.

A brief wave of confusion filters through me as the memory of the two incidents collides.

"Let's get him up," she pants, tugging at his arm.

Dudley and I scoop him to his limp feet, pulling his arms over our shoulders.

"Where to, Ms. Messenger?" Dudley asks, still pissed yet markedly compliant.

She cuts me a knowing glance. "To the tunnels."

The Tenebrous Woods smell like fresh shit that's sat out in the July sun, frying over the desert landscape.

Skyla and I gag as we materialize in the dark, damp, violet-lit perennial night.

Dudley takes a quick look around before closing his eyes with instant regret.

"No, no, no," he says mostly to himself. Marshall Dudley is not one to panic. Hell, Dudley isn't even one to bat an eye after his "charge" has had his head lopped off in the prime of his life. I should know. So the fact he's having such a visceral reaction—at least as visceral as he can get—gives me pause that this was ever a good idea.

"Follow me." Skyla leads us to the structure in the heart of Tenebrous, the tunnels themselves. She opens up the familiar doorway that leads down a black and white checkered hall, into a mindfuck of a world that only brings back bad memories of being trapped here. In actuality, they weren't terribly bad memories since I had the pleasure of being trapped here with Skyla, but, otherwise, this is a no-fly zone as far as sanity in general goes.

We drop Ichabod off in the first room we see, and Skyla locks it from the outside.

She gives Dudley a sharp look that says *I'm not shitting around.*

"I need the people in the Speculum deposited here tonight. The clock is ticking, and I'm already on the line with the Justice Alliance for being married to Gage. Ridiculous charges..." She averts her gaze.

Dudley gives a quick glance around, sliding his finger over the wainscoting and inspecting it for dust before giving his answer. "I'm afraid this is something I cannot participate in. I'll lose far more than my wings if I mix business with pleasure. What you do with the traitors of your people is strictly up to you. My hands are as dirty as I care for them to be." He holds up his blackened finger. "You'll need a curator. They'll need to eat. See Ezrina about fixing the ventilation system around here. The Counts and Fems are prone to making a pigsty of whatever their wicked talons procure. We, my love, adhere to higher standards." He glares past us at the opened door we just came from.

"Tenebrous very much has a curator," a male voice calls from a short distance.

We turn to find Ingram with his sallow skin, his glowing clipboard—the only modern device in the vicinity.

"You're a Count," Skyla sneers. Actually, he has a diluted genealogy, some Count, some Deorsum, but as Ezrina has mentioned—not enough of either to matter. "You're the Barricade personified. I doubt you'll do what I need."

"I'm a mixed-breed. My bloodlines are of no concern to me anymore. I've been bound to these parts for so long I'm my own faction—faction Tenebrous." He offers a brief toothy grin. "These are my stomping grounds, Skyla. I bode you to consider letting me stay on. I'm familiar with procuring food for the masses and the incidentals beyond that. I know the layout of these woods better than any Count or Fem, living or dead. Of that I can be certain."

"Give the man the job." Marshall ushers both Skyla and me out of the overgrown madhouse.

Ingram secures his clipboard, keeping pace with us as best as he can. "Bring the prisoners to the holding cell just outside to your left. I'll distribute them to their rooms, create a file on each one, and offer you daily reports of their life and times behind these iron walls. What do you say?"

She looks to Dudley once, and again, and he gives the briefest of nods.

Skyla holds a hand out to Ingram. "You've got a deal."

Skyla and I have done the unthinkable.

We've reopened Tenebrous—to imprison our own people.

I spend the next few hours dumping very much alive and protesting bodies into the holding cell down in Tenebrous while Skyla transports us back and forth from Dudley's living room. Now that the Haunted Speculum is empty of its unwilling inhabitants, I'd like to smash and trash the damn thing. Dudley doesn't need a portal to the seventeenth century. He's a Sector for fuck's sake. Besides, why is he so obsessed with those dancing damsels in STD distress anyway? He has Skyla mapped out in his future like an hourglass constellation, or more of a rounded constellation these days, but beautifully so.

Afterward, I make sure to get Skyla home safely, then head over to the bowling alley. It's just after two, and Ellis should be locking up the place. It was his idea that we stay open a few extra hours past midnight on Saturdays, and judging by the cars still lingering in the parking lot, it was a damn good one.

I hop inside, where the music is still pumping through the speakers. It's dim, save for the neon lights snaking through the place. A couple stands at the shoe bar talking to Giselle, and as I make my way toward them, it registers who they are, and my blood runs cold.

"Giselle, go find Ellis," I say as I approach them.

Agent Mosley and Agent Killion expand their chests as they turn their full attention to me.

"Logan Oliver?" Killion lifts her chin in defiance. Her orange painted lips are a little reminiscent of Emma's.

"That would be me."

Mosley takes a step forward, barring me from the exit. "We'd like to ask you a few questions if you don't mind."

10

Sweet Child of Mine

Skyla

Gage and I make our way down rain-soaked Paragon streets, traversing puddle after puddle en route to the Gas Lab. Actually, he's the one traversing with the sophistication and ease of an athlete. Thank God his back is all but healed from the miraculous fall he took last spring. There's just the tiniest trace of a limp in him, and, at that, you have to inspect him with extra careful attention to spot it. I, however, am not traversing. I'm hobbling, hopping and waddling my way through life these long, drawn-out October days.

"What do you think Nevermore's surprise is?" I ask just as a giant blackbird dive-bombs me from the eaves and lands haplessly over my shoulder. A pale version lands gracefully on Gage's shoulder—Holden's main squeeze. It figures. All girls are attracted to Gage, no matter what species.

"Looks like you just got another surprise." Gage gives him a look of fury, and my panties practically melt right off. It's never taken much to get me going when Gage is involved, but now that my hormones have been kicked up about a dozen notches, it's like I've got a fire burning in my vagina that only Gage Oliver and his piping hot penis can put out. Ever since he's been gifted those vibratronic superpowers, I've found myself in a sexual seventh heaven. Gage has literally been my savior with this new gift. I've all but sewn a cape for his penis. All I want to do is lie in bed all day and let Gage have his vibrating way with me. Gage has always had the power to arouse me, but this is unnaturally so. Now if I see him from across the room, I want nothing more than to leap over tables and chairs just to impale myself over his body. I think if all newlyweds, the world over, were gifted with these good vibrations, there wouldn't be a divorce rate, or at least there would be a markedly lower one.

"What is with you? Get *off*. I'm with child." I try to jerk Holden from my shoulder, but he's resistant to my remedial plea. I'm still a bit testy from the hormonal takeover, and I really do feel bad about being such a grade-A jerk all the time. "Okay, what's going on?" I land my fingers over him softly and nod for Gage to join me. I'll simply forward Holden's thoughts to Gage. God, I love my new powers. Who knew a simple thought could accomplish so much? "You'd better have something great to tell me. I'm having a serious craving for some good news."

Justice Alliance says today is the day. Sorry I lost the note from your mom, but it kind of went like this: you know the way, today's the day, hope things go your way—some rhyming shit like that.

"Lovely." I take up Gage's hand and squeeze the crap out of it. I'm terrified of being brought to court. I almost hate the celestial legal system as much as I do hospitals, and thanks to Gage, I'm sort of bound to both. Mom—as in Lizbeth—still thinks there's an off chance she might be able to convince me to have a home birth, but the thought of me naked, spread eagle in the living room, flailing defenseless in a kiddie pool no less, doesn't seem to strengthen her argument regarding it being a much richer experience. I still remember coming home from prom and finding her in the kiddie pool the night she had Mystery while Demetri chanted who knows what in the darkened candlelit room. Of course, he was there. He's the father.

Holden lets out an ear-piercing caw.

"Go on." I land my palm over him again, and Gage does the same.

I need a favor. You think you can ask that Sector friend of yours to officiate for me?

"To *what*?" My irritation with Holden only seems to grow, especially now that I spot Lexy inside the Gas Lab pawing all over Logan.

Officiate—you know, a wedding ceremony. Serena, here, is a bit old-fashioned. She's from another time. She doesn't want me to brush feathers with her until we're legally wed.

I glance to her blonde eminence and give a dry smile. "She does realize she's a bird, doesn't she?"

Yes. Geez, Messenger, rub it in, why don't you? Why don't you remind us we'll never be human again, and that I'll never be able to fill her belly with babies the way Gage did yours.

"Okay, okay, I get it. I'm sorry I was so callous. Yes, of course, I'll talk to Marshall for you. Check back, and I'll let you know what he said."

Thanks. And one more thing, your mother mentioned there was a little surprise she had for you. She said she could hardly wait to give it to you.

I glance to Gage with a look of contempt. "I bet she does."

Holden and his pretty winged friend flap their way back under the eaves as Gage and I make our way inside the Gas Lab. Ever since Ezrina and Nev revamped their menu to include more gourmet fare, the place has been packed. They've even had a write-up about them in a bunch of foodie magazines. Some say they're single-handedly responsible for at least ten percent of the uptick in tourism. The other ninety percent is attributed to Logan and his huge glowing balls—not those balls—the ones Wes and Chloe gifted him at the Cove.

I glare at Lexy as she cozies in the booth next to him. I can't stand her, with her perfectly tanned, perfectly toned body. If I wanted to, I could fit all of her skin and bones into my granny panties and haul her around like a papoose. I frown at her a moment. It's clear I'm just jealous that I've traded my familiar frame for that of a sumo wrestler. Hell, I don't even think I can fit behind a booth.

"You're here." Nevermore pulls me in for a quick embrace. "I'll fetch Rina." He takes a step back and soaks me in. I've pulled a giant winter coat over me the size of a tarp, but I need it in the event the babies decide to rise and shine, literally. My glowing belly seems to be a phenomenon that just sort of happens whenever it feels the need. I'd like to think the kids have no idea what they're doing, but if they have any of Demetri's genes woven through them, they might be well aware of exactly how bright they are. It scares me in a sense. What comes next after glowing? *Flying*? Am I going to have to tie them down with a string on their ankles in the event they decide to float away like a pair of Femtastic helium balloons? I shudder at the thought. That can't happen. My babies will be Celestra like me. Positive thinking, positive thinking. But, regardless, I'll love them deeply, already do.

Logan calls us over, and Gage and I slide across the booth from him and Lex with my belly touching the table just like I predicted.

Lexy looks undeniably cute in her tiny denim jacket, her size negative zero jeans. I can't help but frown at her miniature, delicate frame. Lexy has always had the body of a prepubescent boy.

I growl at her a moment. "And why the hell is she here again?" *Oops*. Did I just say that out loud? Whatever will I do when I lose the excuse of my hormones?

"Nice, Messenger." She forces a smile to come and go. "I happened to be hanging out all by my lonesome when my favorite Celestra wandered in—I'll give you a hint. It isn't you."

"I was just talking to Dudley." Logan motions to him, and Marshall takes a seat next to me. His thigh touches mine just barely, and with Gage still holding my hand, it's as if I'm in a vibratronics sandwich. Dear God, *yes*, please.

"This is the life," I moan. Again? Out freaking loud? These hormones have made me practically insane.

"There's a meeting tonight of the Council of the Superiors." Logan doesn't look amused. "They've put an all-access stop to your invite." His brows tick up a notch.

"Ha!" Lexy barks out a laugh. "How do you like that, Messenger? Your own people put out a restraining order against you."

"Can they do that?" I look to Marshall for clarity. He's like my legal eagle for all things celestial.

"They can, and they did." He scowls a moment at Gage. "I'm afraid the longer you're wed to Jock Strap, the longer you'll be banished from chapter meetings. However, it's no loss. They're powerless against the Barricade."

"Speaking of which." Lexy runs a finger over the rim of Logan's glass, and something about that quasi-sexual motion makes me want to claw her pretty little eyes out. "Wes says he's tired of people dropping out of the Immunity League. He says he's found a way to circumvent this. And all those flashing lights and what-not that have the world in such a tizzy? He's done with that crap, too. This new thing he's launching is going to eat that shit for breakfast."

I glance to Logan briefly. Wes thinks people are dropping out? I want to laugh. Doesn't he realize I have Tenebrous? You would think the missing people math would be easy for a genius like him.

Logan lets out a sigh. "I didn't want to say anything, but I spoke with you know who."

Dudley grunts, "Do we look like a bunch of mind readers to you? We most certainly do not know *who*."

I'm a bit shocked by Marshall's outburst. It's not like him to be so short with people. On second thought, maybe it is.

"Tweedledee and Tweedledum," Logan growls to Marshall sternly, but that children's book reference melts me to my core. Logan will make a wonderful uncle. "Relations of yours, I'm assuming."

"Apparently so," Marshall snipes back, but I don't really get what he means. Usually, Marshall is sharp as a whip with his comebacks.

"The agents," Logan clarifies. "I spoke with the feds. I managed to piss them off with a bunch of vague answers, and they accused me of willfully covering up to government officials. The entire conversation went sideways."

"Shit." Gage slams his hand over the table.

Shit is right. Everything seems to be going sideways as of late.

"*Look*"—I plead with Lexy—"tell us anything you know. Lives depend on this. Any tidbit of information that you might remember can potentially save thousands." The thought that the entire human race might actually be dependent on two ex-West Paragon cheerleaders doesn't bode well for the civilized world in general.

"He said something about the Videns. Hell, I don't know." She looks to Gage. "Ask Emily. She wasn't the valedictorian for nothing. She knows like everything."

Gage swallows hard. His eyes bulge a moment as if something just slipped down the wrong pipe. "I'll talk to Em as soon as I get home. Wes, too."

"Oh no, you don't." Lex gets fidgety. "There's no way in hell I want him to know I'm the one who said anything. He'll throw my ass right out of the Barricade, and then I'll be up the government creek like the rest of you. And until you've got a cave you can hide the masses in, I'm staying on the safe side of the fence."

A cave I can hide the masses in—Tenebrous. I glance to Logan, and I can tell he's thinking the same thing.

Ezrina and Nev come up pulling two seats to the table.

Nev lands a manila folder onto the table and slides it toward me. "I hope you don't mind if we offer you an early birthday gift."

"Me? A birthday gift? I'm in." I pull the envelope over and open it to find a check secured to a packet marked *Gas Lab Earnings Report*. "What's this?" My eyes gravitate to the sum total on the check, and I have to blink twice to make sure I'm not seeing things. "Did you guys win the lottery or something? This is more money than I'll see in two lifetimes." Come to think of it, maybe Ezrina and Nev aren't too keen on math? Perhaps in a dizzying fit of excitement, one of them added one too many zeros to the end of the five. Heck, even fifty dollars would have been too much to gift me. "I can't accept this."

Gage peers over and blows a steady breath from his lips. "Perhaps there's an error."

"Let me see." Logan pulls it toward him. "By chance, the two of you didn't hire Gage as your accountant, did you?"

"Very funny." Gage pulls it back.

"No," Nev chirps without missing a beat. "But perhaps we should consider this. It's tiring keeping up with all the laws and taxes."

"Hired," Ezrina says in her slow, methodical drawl.

"Hear that?" His hand rubs over mine, and I fill with inexplicable pleasure. "I just gained another client. I think I've just become a one-man accounting firm." He gives my hand a firm squeeze, inspiring a throbbing pulse to ride through that tender spot between my thighs. Usually, that's where the fun ends, but for some reason, that tender spot of mine won't stop quaking. In fact, oh dear—

I pant my way through it, and, just when I think I've got it under control, a cry of intense pleasure rips through my lungs.

"Oh God!" I shout, completely out of breath. "Yes!" I blink back to reality, back to face the fact I've just enjoyed an orgasm in front of four of my closest friends, and Lexy Bakova.

All eyes are eerily on me.

"I'm just so excited for you, Gage." I glare at him a moment. He totally knows how powerful his touch is by now. He's been chasing me around the bedroom all week just to watch me have what he's dubbed an "insta-gasm." Suffice it to say, he's pretty proud of his trembling "superpowers."

"*Ooh*, sorry." He raises his hands like a thief.

"Nothing to apologize for." My eyes enlarge with a vague threat. "Now, what's this about?" I try to push the big, fat birthday check back to Nev and Ezrina, but Marshall snags it instead.

His brows twitch at the sight. "It seems you are suddenly a very wealthy woman."

Lex leans over and balks at it. "The government will take like half."

"Is that true?" Nev's mouth falls open. He looks as if he's about to faint.

"Sure is," Gage muses as he checks out the Gas Lab Earnings Report. "Not quite half, but it's a shame to lose any."

Ezrina groans. "These are truly the best of times and the worst of times." She seems pleased with her quasi-literary reference. "It's simply your fair share of the Gas Lab. It's your initial investment, plus profit. We thought the two of you could use it with the expanding family."

Wow. It never ceases to amaze me when Ezrina manages to string together entire sentences. All that time in the Transfer had hardened her to the point of refusing to speak to anyone with the exception of utilizing the fine gift of brevity. I don't blame her. I wouldn't want to talk to a bunch of bossy Counts who kept filling my shop of horrors with corpses either.

"Not if you 1031 exchange it," Logan offers. "If it's a part of your business, then you have the right to identify another property and exchange it for investment purposes. It could even be a home for the two of you." He looks pleased with his non-ubiquitous bit of legal advice.

"Yes." Marshall cinches a wry smile as if he's in on some big joke and is about to deliver the punch line. "In fact, I spied a *For Sale* sign on that choice property next door to your in-laws. It's as if the planets and the stars have aligned for the two of you." He gives an obnoxious smirk. "Shall I phone the realtor?"

"God, no," I hiss so fast Nevermore blesses me.

"We'll, I'm off." Marshall stands and dusts his trousers as if shaking the debris of this conversation off him, sort of like I'd like to do—the housing portion of it at least. "I've a very important meeting with one Lizbeth Landon." He offers a quick wink my way. "She'll be responsible for the festivities taking place at my humble abode in two weeks' time. I assume you'll all be there." He glowers at Logan. "Some of you never seem to leave."

"Wait for me." I get up and offer both Nev and Ezrina a brief hug. "I can never accept this, but the gesture is very kind."

They look mystified by my response.

Nevermore shakes his head. "I'm afraid we won't take no for an answer."

"We'll deal with Gage," Ezrina assures him.

I look to my handsome husband. "I'm off to get this nightmare with my mother over with. Wish me luck!"

He closes his eyes a moment. Gage would love to come with me, only he's not welcome for the most part, and actually, he might hurt my case since he's the sole reason my head is on the chopping block.

"Be careful." He offers a brief kiss.

Logan raises his gaze to mine, speaking to me with simply just one look. It says *don't forget what you've done, Skyla—what we've both done. Don't make this worse.*

Too late, I want to tell him. *We've already made everything a thousand times worse than we could ever imagine.*

Marshall and I step out of the Gas Lab and into the pouring rain.

"Anxious to see your mother, are you?" He extends his elbow, and I hook my arm through it.

"Yes. Just not that mother."

Ahava forms around us, crystalline and clean. The scent of gardenia perfumes the air. Candace Messenger rises from her seat in the middle of the lake and glides over the water to greet us as if it were concrete beneath her feet.

Odd. She seems happy to have me here. If I didn't know better, I'd say downright jovial.

"What's with the new attitude?" I whisper to Marshall. Usually, she's a little slower to warm to the idea of seeing my smiling face. She's not this cheery unless Logan is around. He's not around, is he? I give a quick glance at the expansive clearing, and a figure emerges from the distance, moving forward at an inhuman clip. A wave of elation fills me, and instantly, my belly glows a swirling sea of cobalt.

"Logan?" We just left him at the Gas Lab. He didn't mention coming to Ahava—unless, of course, this isn't the version we left behind. "Oh my God, Logan!" I run over and give a little jump onto his leg. Initially, the thinner me would have hurled myself clear onto his hips and let him spin me as we gave way to a wild embrace, but this new version—clumsier, much, much bigger—can only pull off something akin to dry humping him.

"Skyla." He gives a hard sniff to my neck before pecking a kiss over my cheek. He pulls back and takes me in. "Wow. Motherhood becomes you." He places his hand over the indigo glow emitting from beneath my shirt.

"I miss you like crazy, and yet, we're together nearly all the time." I'm not sure how that statement works. It just does. Logan—the one on Paragon—is in a Treble, a tiny slice of time just after he gets back—so, technically, it's the future version of himself, although he's zapped of any memories that might spoil things in the interim. This version, the completely deceased version, is buying time in paradise until my mother sees fit to gift him the rest of his unfinished life—but that would mean Gage has to go, and, well, it's all one big bloody mess.

"I miss you, too, but I trust I'm doing a good job of getting in your hair." He gives one of my curls a gentle tug. "I couldn't stay out of it if I tried."

There's a fire in his eyes, a passion minus the absolute agony the one on Earth coats his loving gaze with. It's as if this version has made peace with the fact we'll be reunited if and when the time is right—or not.

My stomach knots up because, well, the version on Earth and I are working diligently to make sure that isn't going to happen.

"Does she know why she's here?" he asks my mother who is busy conversing in private with my favorite Sector.

"I was just about to tell her." She nods to Marshall as if she's just filled him in. "Skyla, dear." She swoops over and takes up both of my hands. Hand holding? Funny, the last time I was here, we left off on less than amicable terms.

"That's right." She shakes her head as if that very moment were to blame for what comes next. "That very moment *is* to blame for what comes next." She closes her eyes, and the light dims around me just a touch. My mother has the clearest blue eyes, an exact representation of my own. "The curse you put on me—the only agony I could ever feel would be strictly related to you or your children. The only thing that would truly bring me agony is the untimely death of any of you."

"No." I shake my head. I don't like what she's implying. "I didn't do this. I didn't curse you. I was just making a statement." I rush to Marshall and shake him. "I didn't do this. I didn't mean to kill my baby!"

He shakes his head, but, before he can answer, my mother cuts him off.

"Statement, curse—potato, pota-*toh*." She averts her eyes as if it were irrelevant. "My heart did break when you lost one of those precious beings taking up residence in your womb. But, not to worry, she's with me now in paradise. My heart has fully mended."

"She? I had a girl?" I don't know why this suddenly shocks me. I'm convinced they were all female in my belly. "Where is she? Can I hold her?" My heart drums so fast its echo deafens me.

"Of course." My mother looks amused that I would even ask. "As soon as she came home, I took her under my wing."

My stomach clenches because I'm not sure what the effects of that might be. What happens to a person when Candace Messenger actually raises them? For some reason, Chloe comes to mind.

I turn to Logan. "Have you seen her?"

"Yes." His amber eyes warm at the thought of her. "She's beautiful, and sweet, just like her mother." He brushes his finger over my cheek. His eternal flame burns straight down into the deepest chamber of my heart.

Candace gives a little clap. "Come now, child. Your mother is here!" she says it in a sing-song fashion much like my earthly mother would do.

A little girl skips out from the clearing, four or five years old, and clutches on to my mother's leg, peering out from around the trunk of her thigh to inspect me. Her long hair runs down her back like a silken ebony river. Her eyes burn with a curious intensity, the same hue as the deepest part of the ocean. Her full ruby lips give the hint of a trembling smile, and two deep-welled dimples dig into either one of her cheeks.

THE SERPENTINE BUTTERFLY

Dear God Almighty, I have melted.

Marshall wraps his arm around me as if to steady me. "She truly is beautiful, Ms. Messenger," he whispers.

Beautiful is an understatement, but this can't be my child. Then I see a whisper of myself in her features, same nose, same bowtie lips, the outline of our features are one in the same.

My mother pets the little girl's ebony waves. "I've named her Luzy with Z." It sounds almost identical to Lucy. "It's a very soft Z—*Luzy*. Go ahead, try it."

My mouth falls open. "You can't name her *Luzy*. There is no such thing as a soft Z." I drop to my knees and coax the sweet angel to come to me. My heart tries to pound its way out of my body, demanding to touch her itself.

"Are you sure this is her?" There is no denying that face, those eyes. I've seen them both before. In an irony that only genetics can provide, she is the exact representation of her father as well. Standing before me is a perfect combination of both Gage and me. Here she is, the sleeping serpentine butterfly from Emily's haunted graffiti. Tears blur my vision as my entire body trembles for her touch. "She's a bit older, isn't she?" My fingers beckon, but she's not budging from the safety of my mother's limbs.

"Good grief, Skyla. She's *five*." Candace takes the little girl by the hand and walks her around to the front of her person so I can take her in fully. "I have no patience for infants. You cured me of that. I'll keep her this way until she catches up, and then I'll let her progress in human years. The form ceases to age once it reaches perfection, about thirty-three your time. Though she won't be issued a true body until the last day, you can still touch her—feel her. Go ahead, Luzy. Go to your mother so she can hold you."

The little girl gives a shy smile before plodding over, arms open wide, leaping right at me as if we've rehearsed this on a daily basis.

Time stills. It stops its beating heart as tears stream down my cheeks, watering this child with all of my love, with the very nexus of my grief.

"My God." I sob into her heavenly soft hair that holds the scent of honeysuckle. My cheek warms to her preciously soft skin as my tears continue to rain down over her. I pull back and look into her stunning eyes, so heartbreakingly familiar. "You look just like your daddy."

"A man named Gage is my daddy." Her words come out soft and sweet as the hum of an angel, but there's a stillness about her, a knowing that runs deep. It's anything but childlike.

"Yes." I swallow hard, hitching her hair behind her ear. "That's exactly who your daddy is. Would you like to meet him?" My gaze gets lost in those cobalt spheres of hers. I'll never look at Gage's eyes the same after this.

She nods eagerly. "Very much so. Your Grace, Candace, has told me that he shall come to live with me soon. And I will have him all to myself for many, many years while you live far away."

I take in a quick breath. Who knew her words would be the sharpest blade to my heart?

"No." I pull her in tight, her tiny frame conforming unnaturally to mine. "I want to live with you, too." It comes out a combination of a sob and a whine. It's heartbreaking to think I've done this to my own child. A thought comes to me, and I spring to my feet. My hand secures over her tiny fingers, and I don't plan on letting go.

"I'm taking her back," I warble as I wipe the tears away.

"Skyla." My mother scoffs at my proclamation. "She's perished. It's done. This child will wait for you. Consider her a gift at the end of your life—sort of like a reward. I'll keep her plenty safe, and once her father arrives, the two will be inseparable."

"No." A ripe anguish rips through me, so powerful and painful it might land me in Ahava before too long myself. I drop to my knees once again without thinking. *"Please."* My chest bucks as a fire of grief consumes me. "I beg of you. Let me have my daughter back."

"Rise, child." My mother's voice is heavy and without mercy. "I've had enough of the dramatics. We won't go down that beaten path. She must remain, and you must keep from curses."

A silent sob runs through me as I latch on to her little frame. My face gets buried in her hair as I wash it with my tears—mother's tears, and this separation is a mother's greatest anguish. I couldn't care less if I were making a scene, embarrassing myself or my mother with my "dramatics." I can't bear it. I've done this. I've brought us to this painful place, and the price is simply too damn high.

Marshall pulls me to my feet. Logan takes my daughter's hand and pulls me in as well. It feels safe with him holding her, holding me.

"I'm taking her." I sniff hard and give a curt nod to my mother as if it meant anything. "I've already changed one circumstance on Earth that entailed death, and I plan on doing so again."

My mother's features go slack. That soft, loving gaze from a moment ago is quickly replaced with a hardened gaze as outright anger pours from her being.

"Yes." She takes a step forward. "You did change a circumstance, didn't you?" She isn't amused. "Taking life away, giving it back—do you think you're God, Skyla?" Her lips cinch in that sarcastic manner they seem to do just before she lowers the boom. I didn't grow up with this mother, but I sure as hell know when I'm about to get crushed by her.

"No, not God. I'm powerful, though, powerful enough to have finally figured out that I don't need to adhere to a bunch of silly rules." My heart thumps wildly in protest. "If I have the power to bring my daughter back, then that's what I'm going to do. Any other mother on the planet would do the same." I turn to leave with this precious baby girl's limp hand still in my grip, and an invisible force spins me back around.

"I'm not ready for you to leave, Skyla." My mother's eyes light up like boiling white flames. "Come." She holds out her hand, and my daughter breaks my iron hold and appears by my mother's side in one heartbreaking leap. "She cannot go with you. It's not ordained. As for your dance with Mr. Travers' death, I won't charge you with the grievance since your state of being as the mother of two incubating Fems—half-breeds, as they may be—seem to have induced a psychological haze. Do not, and I repeat do not navigate your way around a corpse that way ever again, Skyla. It's a life for a life, and the life that is called to exit the human plane just might be yours. As for Luzy, there will be no such exchange. She stays. I claim her. She is mine."

There you have it. She claims her. What my mother wants, my mother gets. Her rules. Her way. Her damn universe.

"Not true, Skyla. Although, considering the circumstances, I'll forgive you of the emotional outburst. Luzy stays. Your acceptance of the situation is neither here nor there."

"I see." My gaze falls to the ground, defeated. I won't have her. I never will—at least not during my planetary stay on Earth. "In the least, let me name her. Luzy just doesn't seem to fit." I bite down over my lip, struggling not to crumble.

"Very well." My mother softens, and why wouldn't she? She's getting her way. "I heard that."

I was hoping.

My focus shifts to the black-haired beauty in front of me once again. Names. God, I haven't even thought of names. What was that name Brielle was going to give to Beau if he was a girl? Calliope? Yes, that's right, and Lie was going to be her nickname. No, wait, I can't do that to a child, let alone my own. Another conversation I had with Bree at the Gas Lab bounces through my mind. The ship name! "*Sage.*" A rush of heat pulses through me as I say it for the very first time. I bow to her. "It's my name and your daddy's put together. It's beautiful like you. It's special like you, too—a symbol of how much we love you."

"It rhymes with Gage," she says without any real emotion before nodding. "That's my name. Sage—I like it."

"I'm so glad." I launch forward and pull her into another tight embrace. I don't ever want to let her go.

My arms go limp, and just like that, she's gone.

"I'm not one for long, drawn-out goodbyes." My mother waves her fingers through the air. "She's with your father—who actually allows her to call him Grandpa. Can you believe that? I suggested Your Grace, but Nathan wouldn't hear of it."

My chest rattles with both grief and elation. "That's because he's down-to-earth, mostly. Thank you. I'm glad she's with him." A thought comes to me regarding the Justice Alliance, and I struggle to banish it. If my mother's forgotten all about that good time, then I highly recommend I do, too. I swat the air in front of me as trying to get the stench of the idea to dissipate.

"I've not forgotten. I've simply postponed. I've decided that your visit with your child should remain pure. No faction business allowed."

"Sounds good to me. Besides, I'm sure Sage wouldn't appreciate the idea that her mother is temporarily banished from her overseer duties simply because she's married to her father." And why can't I keep my mouth shut and well enough alone? "Something good has come from our union. Sage's very being should invalidate all of the charges against me."

She lifts her chin as if considering this a moment. "Only a true rebellion that consists of the majority can invalidate the Justice Alliance in this matter, Skyla." She gives the slightest wink, and something enlivens in my heart. My mother just threw me a celestial bone, and I'm running with it. "Besides, you haven't been temporarily banished as the overseer. You've been expelled."

My heart drops. I fought a damn war for that role.

"As for you," she snarls at Marshall, "I've never seen a Sector more aloof, or dare I say, cowardly?"

What the—?

"I beg your pardon, Your Grace, but I am neither." He gives a slight bow. I bet a million bucks that Marshall wishes he could let an expletive or two fly right about now.

"I have given you the answers which you seek, and you have avoided the knowledge for months." She huffs a mocking laugh. "Skyla, it will bode well with you if you would escort your spirit husband to Ezrina's current lair. He's a bit in need of some hand holding." She smacks her lips, her lids lower, unimpressed, as she scowls at Marshall. "Return, both of you."

"No, wait!" I turn back and latch on to Logan as if my life depended on it. "Take care of her," I breathe the words hot into his neck.

"Of course." He pulls back, his sad gaze dragging over every inch of my face. "Skyla?" He tilts his head almost apologetically. "We're still going to happen."

I open my mouth to deny it but don't have the heart to do it to his face.

"Ms. Messenger." Marshall clamps his hand over my shoulder, and we quickly fade to nothing.

I look right into Logan's beautiful eyes and think, *No, we won't. We won't ever happen again.*

Gage and I have a family now. I've already cursed us once. I refuse to do it again.

The laboratory forms around us, white glossy walls, a matching floor that makes you wonder which way is truly up or down. The heavy scent of ginger and spices emits from down the hall as Marshall leads the way, the two of us already walking in stride.

"That was some meeting." My heart is still threatening to give out as a result of it. "My mother is some piece of work."

"Tell me about it." He offers my hand a squeeze.

"I fear the woman." I shudder as I say it.

"The fact you fear anything is amusing," Marshall growls and gives the curve of a smile, and at the same time, looks comely as all hell. It's a talent only a Sector can perfect—this Sector to be exact.

A thought comes to me. "Is that why you were disguised as a clown the first time we informally met? Then again, you donned that ghastly clown face last Halloween? Because my fears amuse you?"

"Precisely. Is this something you'd like me to reprise in the bedroom?"

"Do it and see how far it gets you." We pause a moment. "So, what's this big secret?" I nudge his ribs, but my mind is still back in Ahava, still with Sage—*Sage*—my own precious child. The very child that Gage and I made with love, and, well, some very dicey advice per Ellis, but I'm ready to put that to rest now. My hand rounds over my belly. As far as I'm concerned, these children were meant to be. A sharp pain of grief spikes through my heart as I remember why Sage is in Ahava to begin with. How am I ever going to tell her father that I was the one that put her there?

"There is no big secret." Marshall winces. "Or perhaps it is a big secret, but nevertheless, I've no real interest in it to begin with other than the mere details."

We step into the lab proper to find Ezrina hunched in the corner, chopping something with a machete—something small and delicate. Upon closer inspection, they look like...mushrooms?

"Oh—*oh*!" I'm more than a little disgusted when I realize what they are. "My barf-shrooms. Are they good for anything?"

"Regeneration." She shrugs as if she wasn't so sure herself. Ezrina wipes down her hands while glancing past us. "Heathcliff! It seems the Sector is finally interested to see where the die has landed."

Nevermore strides in with a laugh. "Goodness, no one is blaming you for the scope of time in which it took you to come to terms with this. But, I for one, would have thought the suspense would've kept you up at night."

"The nitwits that have squatted in my home keep me up at night," Marshall snaps. "This is simply a hiccup to an otherwise ordinary day."

"I just found out I have a child." I swat him.

"Correction, you've just met your child." His eyes glow a clear amber and remind me strikingly of Logan's. "Your child is an emerald in an endless sea of sand. She is our child, Skyla. In my heart, your children are my children as well."

My entire person dissolves at his sweet proclamation. "Thank you. That means a lot to me."

Ezrina titters.

My eyes widen. My mouth falls open. I've heard Ezrina do quite a few things, and tittering isn't one of them.

Ezrina nods to Marshall. "Are you ready, fine sir?"

Fine sir? Why does this all seem incredibly strange? Have I landed in another Fem-induced psychosis?

"Give it to me, Ezrina—and give it to me now," Marshall barks.

Again, words I never thought I'd hear.

She tips her head back, and her glasses reflect the florescent lights above like flashing coins. "They are indeed of your lineage."

"What?" I'm terribly confused by this conversation. "I'm pretty sure these belong to Gage." I wrap my arms around my flesh-covered beach ball protectively. "What are we doing here, Marshall?"

He straightens. "It seems I'm looking into a bit of genealogy."

"Whose?"

"Mine."

"Wait...You don't have any. You were created." That conversation we had a few months back comes vaguely floating to the forefront of my mind.

He groans. "It turns out I've done a little creating of my own."

"Oh my God, what? Then it's true!" I'm completely floored. My entire body is numb with shock. "Oh my goodness! Marshall, you're a father?"

"It's nothing new." He glances to Ezrina. "Tell her that it's nothing new. This happened centuries before we ever met."

"True." Ezrina is about as excited as a blank wall.

"Oh right! That whole seventeenth century thing." I make a face without meaning to. "So, it's been confirmed?" I look to Ezrina, and she gives a single, solemn nod. "*Aw!*" I clutch my chest. "Marshall! You have an entire sea of miniature Dudley's running around out there somewhere. I bet you're a great-great-great-great-great-grandfather. Probably more so, but I was growing a bit tired of saying it. We have to find them! I've got to meet them. I bet they're all wildly gorgeous."

"You've met them," Nev flatlines.

"What?" I jump with excitement. "Who? What? Where?"

"Coop, Gage, Logan," Nev says in keeping with the cadence. "Oh, wait." He looks to Ezrina—"Gage isn't one of them, is he?"

She shakes her head.

I suck in such a sharp breath it sounds as if I've just inhaled a scream.

"I can't believe this! Oh, wow! Oh my God!" I howl straight into Marshall's face. "You're like their long-lost dead relative that just walked out of a sarcophagus!" I clutch his shoulders as he openly growls at my analogy. "Coop and Logan are going to flip when they hear this! You're their fantastically long-lost grandpappy!"

"Hush, woman." Marshall glowers over my shoulder at nothing in particular. "Just the thought makes me sound decrepit. They're nothing more than a failed legacy. Something culled from my flesh to replicate me on a cellular level. All the very worst parts, might I add."

"Dear God." I'm so floored I might actually fall flat on my well-padded ass. God knows I've acquired enough adipose tissue to insulate more than just the three living beings that occupy the largest organ of my body—the third being me, and my heart breaks for Sage all over again. "This is amazing. I have to go tell them." I no sooner turn to make a run for it than he reels me back a good foot.

"Now, now, Ms. Messenger, no reason to incite an unwanted family reunion. I'm not about to claim any distant relations wrought from my bastard."

"Marshall!" I gasp at the expletive. "That's a very bad word."

"Believe me, when I think I might be responsible for every Oliver known to man, it's as close to a term of endearment as I can ever get." His head writhes over his shoulders. "I must leave."

"Wait!" I follow him out. "I want to be there with you when you break the big news."

"Of course. But I'm not telling, and neither are you."

"Of course," I parrot. "I won't tell Logan or Cooper."

I'll tell Gage.

Gage

"What?" I gape at my beautiful wife, safe in my arms, the moon dancing over her curls as if skipping a stone.

"You heard me—he's sort of an Oliver baby daddy."

"And Coop?" I can feel my brows hike up in disbelief. I'm not too into *Dudley*, and neither is Logan. This is a shock to say the least.

"It turns out they have a blended lineage."

"Geez." I close my eyes a moment. "Wow, talk about a genetic surprise lurking around the corner." I pull her closer. It's nice like this in bed with Skyla. I'm gone so much of the night that a part of me misses this.

"Actually, there is one last genetic surprise, sort of." She gives a little shrug.

"What?" I twist my neck as if gearing up to take it on the chin.

"I met her." Tears swell in her eyes.

"Met who?" I wipe them away as fast as they fall.

"Our little girl. She's perfect." She buries her face in my chest a moment, and my heart demands to stop at the news. "She has your dark hair and gorgeous eyes. She's not an infant either. My mother can't stand babies, apparently, so she's five."

"Five?" My voice goes up an octave.

"Around that."

"Skyla." My lips twitch as tears of my own come to the party. "Does she have a name?"

"Sage." She shrugs again. "If you hate it, we can change it. My mother named her Luzy, and it didn't fit her, so I gave her our ship name—you know, Skyla and Gage smushed together."

"I love it." I wrap my arms tight around her. Skyla's bulging stomach presses hard against me, and the babies give a swift kick.

We both indulge in a hearty laugh, our joy mixed with so much sorrow.

"Let's think of names before my mother tries to get involved again." She gives a gentle pat to her stomach. "How about Sadie and Angel?"

Ooh. I wince. "How about Max and Mitch?"

Now it's her turn to wince. "You think we're having two boys?"

"Only to off balance the fact you think we're having two girls," I offer playfully.

"I guess we'd better have two of each picked out, and then decide what to do if we're having a boy *and* a girl." The combinations of our newfound joy seem endless.

"We could name them after our parents. That would make things easy, and it would be meaningful."

"Lizbeth and Emma?" Her mouth gapes in disbelief.

"Sorry." A dull laugh rattles from me. "Sage was already taken."

"I'm glad you like it. I think Sage is a perfect name, too." She leans forward and takes a soft bite from my lips. "I guess we can nickname them Izzy and Emmy. At least that way they could have something of their own."

"Izzy and Emmy." I let it swill in my mind a moment. "I like that."

"I think I do, too."

"And the boys—which we are having," I tease.

"Very funny. And by the way, if we did have boys, we'd be in trouble because I really wouldn't know what to do with them."

"Are you kidding? Pop Warner, here we come. Think of all the T-ball games, soccer, the endless football practice in the yard."

"We don't have a yard."

"We will someday." My stomach clenches because I've been holding off on a bit of news that I know won't exactly make her ecstatic. "Speaking of someday, my mom called—turns out, the Walshes have decided that if we want the house, they'd be happy to negotiate a fair price. They've even offered to forgo a realtor, so we won't be out any additional fees."

"Oh?" Her face bleaches white. "How generous of them." She takes a breath and holds it. "So, we come up with a fair number, and that's it?" She hikes up on her elbows, and I can't tell if she's suddenly interested or pissed.

"That would be it."

"Let's see." She tilts her head, her eyes flame with a familiar look—sarcasm—so that's where this train is headed. "We could offer them ten dollars, but then they'd owe us nine."

"All right—you're funny. Forget I ever brought it up."

She shakes her head. Her eyes settle over me. "No, I can't. You wouldn't have brought it up if you weren't at least a little bit interested. Do you want this place?"

"I don't want this place, but I want *a* place, and, well, opportunity sort of came to us. It is behind the gates. We could trick it out and have a kick-ass place with just a little elbow grease."

"Just a little? Try food grease and a match." She falls back onto her pillow and closes her eyes.

"Never mind. It's done. Back to the names." My gut feels as if it were just dealt a blow. I need to get Skyla and me out of this shit box, and, according to what they want for rentals out there, the only place we might be able to afford, emphasis on the *might*, is right back in one of Morley Harrison's slums. An image of our twins with scabies comes to mind, and I quickly banish the thought.

"I'll look at it again," she moans without bothering to open her eyes.

"No. You don't need to do me any favors. I'm okay with it. We'll just have to save up a little longer. We'll rent. Everyone is doing it. We can do it, too."

"Rent?" Her shoulders hike up. "I guess owning would be better."

"We could always fix it up and flip it." A shard of hope cuts through me. I just know the Walsh place is a goldmine waiting to happen. If Skyla isn't into it, I was going to try to convince Logan and Liam to go in on it—someone might as well turn a profit.

"Flip it? So, we wouldn't have to actually live in it?" Her eyes brighten at the prospect.

"We should live in it for at least two years to get the full tax benefit, but then after twenty-four months, we might be able to double our money."

"Really?" she sighs. "Two years, huh?" Something tells me if Skyla and my mother got along better, two years wouldn't feel like such a prison sentence.

"It's entirely up to you, though. I wouldn't dare force you into a thing."

"What do you think a fair price is?" Her cheeks blush a light pink as the color comes back. Skyla looks as if she has fight in her once again.

"Too much." My stomach sours just thinking about it. "But we can always lowball them and see what they say."

"I guess it couldn't hurt." Skyla snuggles up against me, and we lose ourselves in thought for a good long while. "Back to the names...Did you think of anything else for the boys?"

"Actually, I have. How about Nathan and Barron? First one out can have your father's name."

Skyla takes in a huge breath. Her eyes fill with water the color of Paragon skies.

"Gage." She presses her lips to my shoulder. "That's perfect. And what if there's just one boy?"

"That's easy. We'll name him Demetri." I give her ribs a quick tickle, and she bucks with laughter.

"I think we should call him Gage."

A moan rumbles from me. "I was thinking something more like Skyler."

"I don't think so. It would be strange calling my name out over and over, even if it did have a different spin on it. Maybe we should just give Tad the honor?" She gives my side a quick pinch, only I groan instead of laugh.

"Speaking of Tad, who do you think you'll want in the delivery room?"

"You, of course."

"Glad to hear I've got the golden ticket. Anyone else?"

"God—you're not campaigning for your mother, are you?" Her surprise seems genuine, so I take it with a grain of salt.

"Ouch, that was harsh." I take a soft bite from her ear. "Harsh but not unexpected. No, I was wondering if you were planning on having anyone else."

She pulls back to get a better look at me. "Are you talking about Logan?"

"I was thinking about Laken, but since you brought him up—is he invited? I don't mind. In a way, he probably should be." I was thinking about Logan, too. It's just too hard to outright admit it.

Skyla sags in my arms. "I don't think it would be right. I mean, well, I'll be naked in all the places that count—"

I'm assuming he's seen those places, memorized them, but decided to leave that out of the conversation.

"Why are you thinking about having Logan there?" She taps my chest, her gaze unwavering from mine.

My gut wrenches. It's one thing to think about this stuff, and another to admit it out loud.

"I just thought when I'm gone he'll be raising those kids right alongside you. It might be nice to start building that bond with the babies from day one."

A small cry escapes her throat as she wraps her arms around me tight.

"No, no, *no*. You are *not* going anywhere, Gage Oliver. Logan will make a great uncle, but that's as close as he needs to be. You are the father of these children. You are my husband." Her eyes meet with mine, lost in a sea of crimson. "I'm doing my part, Gage. I am moving heaven and Earth to make sure you live as long, if not longer than I do. As far as I'm concerned, my mother's prophecies are full of shit."

A wild cackle of lightning goes off outside, sending a hairline fracture popping through the window. I pull back the curtain. Sure enough, there's a spider web of a crack embedded in the glass.

"Crap." Tad is going to hang me by the balls if I ask him to fix it. I'll have to take care of it myself. "Okay. I'll do my part.

I'll see what I can do." My hand glides over her damp cheek. "I want to be here for you, and I want to be here for our babies. Believe me, there is nothing more important to me than our little family."

My lips find hers, and just as I'm about to dive into her mouth, Skyla pulls back in a burst of excitement.

"I know who I want in the room!" She wiggles with glee. "A couple who really needs to have a messy birthing experience right up in their faces. One of which has landed us in that very delivery room."

"Ellis and Giselle." I give her a high five. "Finally, Harrison and my sister will have a dose of reality hit them."

She holds up two fingers. "Two doses of reality. Two bloodied, screaming beings that will most likely be ripped from the center of my body like aliens."

Skyla has recently added a fear of C-sections to her list of phobias. I can't blame her. Having what amounts to a major surgery while you're awake doesn't sound appealing to me either. Although, shooting a couple of bowling balls from a birth canal doesn't have a much greater appeal. I realize women do this every day, but this is Skyla, *my* woman. And she's tiny, like really small. Hell, I barely fit inside her. I'm just praying the experience doesn't split her in half, or worse, kill her.

Her chest rises and falls with a dull laugh as she rattles my hand with hers.

"I hope it doesn't kill me either, Gage." She slaps her thigh. "And thanks to all those Burger Shack runs, I'm not so tiny anymore." Her head snuggles in the crook between my neck and shoulder. "So, Ellis and Giselle?"

"Ellis and Giselle." I shake my head at the pairing. "Here's hoping they don't have any watermelon babies in their future."

"You mean *near* future."

"No—I'm pretty sure I mean future."

"You don't mean it." She scratches lightly at my chest. "We want everyone to be as happy as we are." Skyla leans up and presses a kiss to my lips. "I love you, Gage Oliver. Now, satisfy my craving for something hot and stiff deep inside me."

"Yes, ma'am."
We are happy.
Aren't we?

The month wears on, and classes at Host U start picking up steam. I've got Kresley in two of my courses, and I've yet to tell Skyla. I don't really see a need to stress her out, and I have a feeling Kresley and her constant pestering might do just that.

Mom called and asked if Skyla and I would come for dinner. The Walshes have taken a look at our bid and dropped off a counter-offer back at my parents' house. Mom also informed me she made the bizarre move of inviting Tad and Lizbeth for dinner as well. Initially, I wanted to rage. Why? I eat dinner with these people on a regular basis. I need a break, but I suppose since the babies will be here soon, I'd better get used to having both sets of parents mingling quite a bit. I'm assuming they'll all insist on being hands-on grandparents, minus Tad. He's pretty much hands-off with his own kids, so I don't expect any special treatment for my own.

We all head over together, separate cars, but a caravan nonetheless. Once we arrive, it's a greet-fest at the door as my parents make sure to welcome the Landons as if they were royalty—as if they've never *met* before.

Since Skyla's siblings weren't invited, what appears to have been an olive branch by my mother was still interpreted as a snub by most of the Landon clan. Mia and Melissa went on and on wondering why "that witch" would exclude them. Both Lizbeth and Skyla asked them not to speak of my mother that way, but that didn't seem to stop them from feeling insulted. I would have reprimanded them myself, but, in truth, I know what it feels like to be snubbed by someone you'd like to at least have acknowledged you. I glance up at the sky in the event Candace decides to play toss the lightning bolt at her least favorite Oliver.

Inside, we find Liam and Michelle, Logan, Lexy, Kresley, and her chesty friend, Grayson. Ellis and G are in the kitchen helping with dinner.

"What's up?" I slap Logan five and pull him in. "Have I got a surprise for you," I whisper, doing a quick sweep of the room for my least favorite Sector. Skyla might have to keep his secret, but I sure as hell don't.

"What is it?" He gets that serious look on his face that usually springs up when we're dealing with faction business.

"Nothing important, trust me. Just something—I don't know, laughable." I shrug it off.

"So, Liam"—Kresley says it loud enough to get the attention of the entire room, or more to the point, me—"tell me all about that racecar of yours. I'd love to see it sometime."

Skyla comes over with Giselle in tow. "I bet she'd like to see it—test out the seat, see if it reclines. She's going to defile the Mustang."

"What?" My ego takes a tiny hit as I scope out whether or not Kresley's hard-hitting tactics with Liam are simply a ploy. Come to think of it, I'll be better off if they're not.

"Sure thing, my little sweetheart," Liam coos, and both Michelle and Lexy grow proverbial horns and tails right before our eyes. He has no clue who he's messing with. I lean into Logan. "Liam is about to have his ass handed to him by Miller."

He shakes his head. "It's probably a good thing. Plus, Lex is getting tired of my hard-to-get antics. I think she might be throwing her hat in the ring as well."

"Exciting!" Skyla sings. "Looks like a bloodbath will ensue. I hope the three of them die a slow, painful, completely non-sexual death at the hand of your brother-slash-uncle."

"Skyla!" Giselle inches back, appalled. "That's completely vile of you."

"You know what's vile?" She steps toward Giselle until her belly bumps into my sister. "The fact a certain Sector I know told me about how you were in his AP Geometry class and then poof!" She snaps her fingers. "You weren't."

Giselle slips her hand over her lips. I must admit, it's adorable as hell the way she's so innocent, and then at the same time, it's scary as hell.

"What's going on?" I gently pull my wife back. Skyla has a temper like never before, and as certain as I am that it's temporary, I'm sort of digging it. I do find the Hell-on-Wheels version of Skyla entertaining to no end—as long as her temper is directed far away from me.

"Giselle dropped out."

My sister's mouth falls open so wide it looks like a silent scream. "You're a little snitch!"

Lexy strolls up and locks her arm over Logan's. "Looks like she's got you all figured out, Messenger."

"Stay out of this, Lex, and get your hands off him." She turns back to Giselle. "If you don't get your butt back in school, Ellis Harrison is going to be your biggest mistake! And don't try to deny he has anything to do with this."

"So, what if he does?" Giselle's eyes narrow with venom. "Ellis is the smartest person I know!"

Shit. Both Logan and I groan in unison.

Giselle plucks Ellis over to the conversation as he strolls into the room with a plate full of appetizers. "Tell them about how the school system in this country has systematically been dumbed-down since the fifties. Tell them that I can earn a better education watching reality TV than sitting in that bureaucratic"— she leans into Ellis—"what's the next part?"

"It's not important." He pats her arm.

"Ellis?" I shake my head. "I thought we talked about this. She stays in school, and if she doesn't, I'm not cool with this." I flail my hand between the two of them.

"Sorry, dude. She does her own thing. Do you run around telling Messenger what to do?"

"I sure as hell don't tell her to stop going to school and sit around all day watching TV."

Skyla winces. "Actually, you sort of did."

My phone goes off. It's a text from Wes. **Why the hell is my Immunity League shriveling to nothing?**

I bury the phone back deep into my pocket because I don't have time for any of his Immunity League bullshit at the moment.

"Skyla"—my voice softens as I plead—"I suggested you take the semester off and relax with your feet up—catch up on our backed-up DVR, because when the 'baby' gets here, that might be a little hard," I say as kind as possible. My heart is pounding right out of my chest, because like a fool, instead of letting it go I had to have my say. To be honest, it's Logan I wanted to offer the explanation to. I would never want him to think I was anything but loving toward Skyla.

She dips her chin, and her eyes narrow in on mine in that I'm-about-to-school-you way, and the irony isn't lost on me one bit.

"And I suggested I try to finish the semester because the *baby* isn't due until after finals. Now, I'll be a whole semester behind, and you'll get to lord the fact you graduated before me for the rest of our lives."

I pause a moment. There's something endearing about the way she insists I'll be on this spinning rock long enough to lord anything over her for long.

"If the baby comes early, you'll thank me for the money we saved on tuition." I turn to Logan. "At this point, her good luck scholarship has run dry, and we're hoofing it from here on out."

"Good luck?" Skyla howls, incensed. "Those were hard won dollars, Gage Oliver."

Logan frowns at me as if I were anything but loving toward Skyla. It seems I can't get anything right tonight.

Michelle and Kresley hit a crescendo in their tug-of-war over Liam down at the other end of the room just as Mom walks in waving a manila envelope, and I couldn't be happier for the distraction.

"Why don't we end the mystery before dinner? I've got a good feeling about this!" she says it loud—alarmingly loud, and everyone stops what they're doing and tries to decode what the hell she's talking about.

"Skyla?" Lizbeth scuttles into the room along with my father and Tad. "Is there something we should know about? Is this one of those gender-reveal parties?" She claps up a storm, and the room fills with a dull buzz over the idea.

"No." She touches her belly protectively. She's wearing a bright blue dress that Brielle somehow procured for her. It's the exact shade of blue that her stomach has warmed to over the last few weeks, and lucky for Skyla because I think the babies just lit up like a Christmas tree. "It's silly, actually." She gives me a look that stings. "Gage and I thought it would be funny if we put an offer on the house next door. Something so low and ridiculous, no one in their right mind would accept it."

Funny? *Silly?* This funny silly stunt has the potential to nail us to those creaky floorboards for the next thirty years—at least mortgage-wise. I'm sure she's just trying to save face with her mom.

"You're really moving?" Lizbeth does her best impression of that sad looking theater mask. Her mouth in a full open frown, a difficult feat that leaves me a little in awe more than it does grieved to be leaving the "Landon Lap of Luxury" as Tad likes to remind me. I've got news for him, an orange shag rug in the family room and an avocado stove do not a luxury make. No one ever said the Bishop's had taste. Lizbeth just sort of inherited the mess.

"I can't believe this." She staggers forward blindly. "I thought I'd be right in the next room when you cried out from the pain of cracked nipples. I bought six tubes of lanolin to surprise you with." Her eyes water on cue—and crap, Skyla is falling right into this lanolin-lubed tub of melancholy. I can't blame her. Skyla and her mom are pretty close even if they don't always see eye-to-eye.

Misty whines, and Beau kicks at Lizbeth's shin, but she's too focused on her newfound grief to pay them any attention.

Tad's head spikes up from his overladen plate brimming with bits of smoked salmon. When he walked in, I heard him ask my dad if he ever tried using it as bait.

"Ha!" Tad crows. "Like you two could ever afford property on this forsaken rock." He turns to Skyla. "Your mother and I had to find a haunted house just to afford a place on this swanky island."

Lizbeth gasps. "Wait a minute…Is there something wrong with this house?" Her hand cinches over her neck at the thought of us finding another home infested with the ghost of a Bishop.

"Oh"—Skyla glances to my mother—"it's the house we showed you—right next door." She lays a heavy emphasis on those last three words.

"Isn't that something?" Mom gloms onto the conversation like the idea of it being directly within stalking distance is suddenly a good thing. "Open the envelope for heaven's sake. I'm dying to know what the Walshes have counter-offered."

"A whole lot we can't afford, I'm sure," Skyla says as I take the envelope from her and slide out the contents.

"Speaking of *afford*…" Tad grouses while cinching up his trousers with his thumbs. It's an annoying habit, and I'm hoping one day he'll pull his pants right over his head and get lost in them. "What are you two planning to put down on the place? A dime and a smile?"

A dime and a smile. I shake my head. Although, that's not far from what we offered. And sadly, these days, all the Landons have to show for themselves are a dime and a smile. Althorpe cut Tad's hours and pay to near nothing. All he does now is scheme with his poor wife on ways to rip-off local businesses. The promise of the big racket looms over the Landon house like a dark cloud. I'm worried about the kind of example they're setting for Mia and Melissa—Beau and Misty. If they're not careful, they might raise a houseful of con artists before they know it.

Skyla tenses beside me. "Pierce Kragger bought me out of the Gas Lab," she sighs into her mother as if to further explain away her new housing pickle.

"Oh?" Tad staggers forward. "What about Ethan? That's his baby. If anyone deserves to be bought out, it's my son."

Amen to that. *Out* being the operative word. I'm not too sure Nev and Ezrina will be quite as financially generous to him, though.

Before Skyla can answer, I spot the word *accepted* in big bold letters across the top of the page wilting in my hand.

"We got the house." The words string from me numbly. What happens next is an odd celebratory shout from everyone at once as the room breaks out into loud raucous cheers.

Mom rallies the troops to the door. "Let's head on over! The Walshes won't mind one bit!"

Lizbeth wags a finger as she follows her out. "Now that it belongs to Gage and Skyla, you might want to wait for an invitation. If what goes on in that bedroom of theirs is any indication of what will take place in that house—expect a new grandchild every year for the next few decades!"

They break out in unified cackles, and, as much as I detest the pretense, deep down I appreciate the camaraderie.

We head over next door as a single mob of overly excited villagers.

"Congratulations, you two." Logan looks from me to Skyla before giving a worrisome glance to the overgrown weeds, the slightly crooked pitch on the roof, the dingy white clapboard panels, splitting and lopsided, and let's not forget the door hanging on its hinges for dear life.

"It's a fixer," I say apologetically to those who seem to have fallen in a what-the-fuck induced trance.

"I'll say." Tad is the first to venture inside. And with Tad as our fearless leader, a slight sense of buyer's remorse sets in before any money, or in our case—roll of dimes, ever changes hands.

It's dark inside the house, right up until a bevy of cell phones turn into flashlights, and suddenly, it looks like a CSI crime scene.

"Skyla!" Lizbeth takes a few brave steps forward, and the house gives an unfortunate creak that sounds a bit threatening. "It's so much more spacious than I remember! There is so much untapped potential here."

Grayson, Kresley's breasty buddy, lets out a titter. "Is she serious? This is a fucking haunted house if I've ever seen one," she whispers a little too loud, and both Misty and Beau begin to wail.

"I'm totally serious." Lizbeth continues to marvel and touch her hand to things that might actually gift her a medical grade bacterium that not even antibiotics can hope to conquer. "I've always loved the idea of molding a place from the ground up and watching as it becomes exactly what I desire." She pats Tad on the back. "I'm a sucker for a good fixer-upper."

I look to Logan and shake my head because she just made it way too easy.

"From the ground up is right," Tad balks. "You'll need to raze this place before you ever get started. And none of that *keep one wall standing* bologna. This is a take-it-to-the-rubble kind of trouble. Boy, I wouldn't want to be your savings account right about now. Talk about your shrinkage."

"We're just planning on doing a little work as we go." It comes out a little gruffer than I wanted, but Tad seems to bring out the douche in me. "We're pretty much moving in just as it is."

A horrific crackle emits from the kitchen as a good portion of the ceiling falls to the floor, creating a mushroom cloud of chalky, most likely asbestos-riddled drywall dust.

Everyone runs like hell out the front door with me protecting Skyla and the babies, using my body as a human shield.

"Shit." I glance back at the house as a plume of white dust blows out of its every orifice. "Are you okay?" I plant a kiss on Skyla's temple.

"Yes, I'm totally fine, I promise."

Logan slaps me on the back. "I'll call that builder I used for White Horse." He looks to Skyla with an apology in his eyes. "Skyla, why don't you Pinterest your heart out and design a house you'll love. I'll do whatever I can to make it happen." Logan would take on the debt of the world to make her happy, so would I, but I happen to be a little more destitute and have no access to my own piece of real estate to take out a double mortgage on if I had to. Logan has always had a leg up on me, and perhaps a bigger heart.

Skyla shifts from foot-to-foot, her face expressing an entire range of scowls and grimaces at the property we're about to acquire—or not. But something in me doesn't want to lose this. Something in me doesn't want Logan to continually be her white knight, riding in and saving the day—especially when I fuck up.

"We can always back out." And I'm a wimp.

"Are you kidding?" Skyla wraps an arm around me as we gawk at the disaster in front of us together. "Fixing up a house is one of life's greatest adventures." Her lips twitch the way they do when she's treading just this side of the truth. "But in the meantime, it looks as if we'll have to stay where we are, at least until this place is livable." A tiny satisfied smile buds on her lips. "I have a feeling I'll have plenty of time to use six tubes of lanolin."

It's clear that Skyla would rather live under Tad's roof than shack up next to my mother in this hard-to-love money pit that just screamed get out with all the drama of a fire-breathing dragon.

Fire-breathing dragon...I tilt my head into the house as if it just gave me an idea.

And it did.

Logan

A wild wind blows through Paragon on this three-dog night, and knowing that I'll be sprawled out alone in bed later makes me think it's time to go out and get a few good dogs. I could use the company. No offense to Lex, but, not only is she not my type—I'm taken. My type happens to be Skyla—simply Skyla. And when I thought I was making love to her last spring, it was the highlight of this Treble thus far. And, now, knowing it was Bishop makes it the lowlight of both this life and the last.

Speak of the devil. Chloe struts over in her sky-high heels, her belly distended, although not quite as far as Skyla's these days.

"Why isn't Skyla here helping with streamers until her fingers bleed?" She examines the pale underbelly of her unblemished hands and scoffs.

"I don't know. Ask Brielle or Lizbeth. I'm not hosting this party."

The bowling alley is in the midst of being festooned with a flurry of pink and blue streamers, balloons, you name it, as Brielle and her army of ex-West Paragon High cheerleaders decorate the night away. Brielle rented out the entire facility to throw Skyla a baby shower.

"Why is it just a surprise for her? I don't get it," Chloe continues to whine. "Shouldn't *I* have been shuttled here under the premise of bad pizza and rounds of free foot fungus?" This visibly agitates Chloe. Her hair is slightly frazzled, her skin moist with perspiration from listening to Bree bark out orders for the past hour.

The shower *is* actually for Chloe, too—which assures me of the fact that Brielle has officially lost her mind. If she still worked for me, I'd fire her on the spot. I need to have a talk with Bree and gently remind her that the girl she still calls a friend removed my cranium from the rest of my body, and although my head was meagerly sewn back on for the sake of posterity, I'm still fucking dead so perhaps we shouldn't entertain Chloe in mixed company anymore—and perhaps never again at the bowling alley.

"Take a seat," I offer. Chloe is with child, and I'm not the monster around here. I nod to the stool at the end of the counter where I'm putting away freshly disinfected shoes. They're all showing wear, and I know I should order new stock, but I want all the extra cash I have chipmunked away to help Skyla and Gage on their desperately needed remodel. It doesn't much matter that they won't take my money. I'll figure out a way to get around that. "Have some water." I pull a cold bottle out of the mini fridge.

Chloe scowls as she snatches it from me. "As soon as that little bitch gets here, I'm going to vomit on her lap and chalk it up to this leech sucking me dry from the inside."

Chloe has nicknamed her future child a *leech*. Charming. But, right now, I'm more concerned with the expletive she's chosen for the love of my life.

"Don't call her a bitch. You're in my house, Chloe. You're lucky you're here at all."

"She is a bitch. Skyla Oliver nee Messenger is a bitch. She's a bitch, bitch, *bitch*. A bitch face. A fat ass bitch. Soon to be the mother of many, many bitches." She takes a long swig and downs half the bottle, gasping for breath when she's through.

"How does it feel to know she's better than you?" I ask. I'm over Chloe's incessant need for attention. If she wants another reprimanding, she's not getting it. The only reason I haven't tossed her out on her rear is the fact she's Bree's guest, and Bree has anted up to the moon to call this place her own from seven till midnight. "Skyla gets Gage," I continue. "You get the knockoff. She lives freely on Paragon. You dwell in the sewer with the faction rats. She has two babies. You have one. She has you beat on every count."

Chloe gives a facial hiccup of a smirk. "I can ask you the same question. How does it feel knowing he's better than you? Gage gets Skyla. You get to jack off. He lives freely on Paragon. You dwell in a Treble with the faction rats. He has two babies. You have none. Gage has you beat on every count."

I shake my head, holding back a laugh. "Damn it all to hell if you didn't get me there."

Sometimes, with Chloe, you just have to call it a draw.

"You ever think how things would have been different? You know, if you ended up with Skyla and I ended up with Gage?" She gives a wistful shake of the head. "I just don't get why the powers that *be*-little us didn't pan things out that way." Chloe is lost in thought over this, and, for a moment, so am I.

"Wish I had an answer." Honest to God.

"I have an answer," Chloe grouses. "That heavenly mother of hers is a rotten old twat. She has twat breath and a twat face, and the next time I see her I'm going to punch her in her twat throat."

The entire bowling alley shakes like a snow globe, and the decorating committee lets out a few shrill screams.

"Just a tiny trembler!" Lizbeth does her best to calm the masses while corralling her little ones.

I lean into Chloe. "I'd be careful if I were you. Although, I'm not entirely sure why I'm so concerned for your safety. You weren't exactly for mine."

"Oh, shut up," she gruffs. "You know I love you. If I ever thought for a minute you wouldn't be back on this God forsaken planet, I would have turned around and stabbed Ellis in the eye to alleviate my pent-up rage. I knew that celestial battle-ax in the sky couldn't stand to shut down the Logan and Skyla Show."

An aftershock rolls through the bowling alley as she says the word *battle-ax*. Chloe's mouth is solely going to be responsible for the big one. As always, destruction first—remorse is optional.

"If you didn't kill me, that wedding Skyla and I had would have taken place with the correct version of myself, and we wouldn't be having this conversation. Brielle wouldn't be lightheaded from blowing up little blue penis balloons—or maybe she would." Now it's me with that faraway look. "Those would be my babies in her belly." I swallow hard, envying this revisionist history and where it could have led. I'm not sure it's true, but for whatever reason, I've boarded Chloe's crazy train.

"So, you think I'm the one who fucked things up, huh?" Chloe is slow to assume responsibility.

"As usual." I pitch the last of the shoes into their cubbyhole—size seven women's, the most popular, and, coincidently, the most dilapidated of the bunch.

"You're mistaken, buddy, because it's my supervising spirit who pissed all over your parade to begin with, not me."

"Ex-supervising spirit."

Speaking of supervising spirits, Dudley stalks into the place, looking as if he's just pissed on his own parade. It's no secret that he's been as much as a hormonal bitch these days as Chloe, minus the biological excuse.

She follows my gaze and gives a dissatisfied grunt at the sight of him.

"What is it?" he gruffs, taking a seat next to Chloe. "Make quick work of it. I've a meeting in a few celestial minutes with the warden."

The room rattles once again.

"Could the two of you hold off your acrid comments about Skyla's mother until you're say—at your own damn place?"

"Language." Dudley scowls. "Ms. Messenger said there was something pressing you wanted to discuss."

Chloe chuckles. "I think it's adorable the way you still call her Ms. Messenger."

"No, you don't." Dudley doesn't miss a beat. "You find it titillating to know that someone is as vehemently opposed to her marriage to Jock Strap as you are." His cheek glides back on one side as if he were considering this. "I'm not entirely opposed. It's her heart's desire to flog him with her body until he's evicted from Paragon proper. Rumor has it there's a place warming in the Transport with his name on it."

The Transport? As in the place where fresh dead souls get their final elevator ride up or down? Crap. As much as Gage and I haven't seen eye-to-eye, there's no way I want to lose him.

"Do you know something? Is this a sure thing?" I want to reach across and shake him until he spills every last detail regarding my nephew's impending demise.

"Rumors will swirl." He gives a casual glance at the door. "Skyla is about to walk in. Summons the circus to scream and shout. I do have a tender spot for Lizbeth and would be remiss if I had to listen to her moan about not being able to pull anything off on one of the most important events for her eldest child."

"What the hell did you just say?" Chloe leers at him as if she's drunk.

I motion to Bree, and, before long, the girls all duck and cover.

Skyla walks in, and the room breaks out into a spontaneous roar of *Surprise!*

"You're early!" Lizbeth scuttles to her daughter with a toddler attached to each hip. "Where's Gage? This is a couple's party!"

"Oh my goodness!" Skyla turns slowly, taking it all in. Her hair is gloriously long and shining like gold floss. Her face radiates a glow as bright as the sun, beautiful as moonlight. She's wearing a dress with thick black lines running down the sides and a tiny curvaceous white cutout in the center, and oddly enough, the dress gives the illusion of a shapely silhouette. She looks amazing, and I can't seem to break my gaze.

"I can't believe this!" She hugs her mother and Bree.

Lizbeth pets her daughter's hair as if she were a cat. "I think it's serendipitous that the shower is right here at the same place we had your birthday party when we first moved to the island. And they were both a surprise! What a coincidence."

"And somehow Chloe managed to crash both parties," Skyla is quick to point out before excusing herself and heading this way. "Here you are." She swats Dudley over the shoulder playfully with the clutch in her hand. "You didn't start without me, did you?"

"*Kinky*," Chloe quips. "You three do this often?" She winks my way. "I'm almost afraid to ask what 'starting without Skyla' might entail. I'm guessing there's no tongue involved. It's all fleshy spirit sword fights and wrestling. How about it,

Oliver? You up for spearing *me* with your spirit sword again for old times' sake?" She gives a heavy wink.

"You're disgusting." Skyla fans Chloe away. "And you're also dismissed. Go find a grenade to play with."

"Testy, are we?" Dudley pats the seat next to him, and Skyla plants herself on it. "Where's the rest of the party? I've places to go—Ahava to be precise. There's a team meeting regarding a newly acquired dimensional plane by yours truly."

Chloe arches a brow.

Crap. I shake my head at Dudley, hoping he'll take the hint.

"Just waiting for"—Skyla glances to the door and flags Coop and Laken over—"never mind. Here they are."

"Whoa, back up." Chloe slaps her hand onto the counter. "Demetri gave you a dimensional plane? That's what you asked for that day, isn't it?" Chloe's eyes shine with fury. It's her best look. Chloe has always been her worst enemy, only she's not bright enough to figure that out.

"None of your business. And why are you still here? Go toss baby bottles around with your bestie." She shoots a look to Bree for inviting Chloe to begin with.

"Not moving."

Dudley shakes his head. "It matters not. I see where this is going." He gives a curt nod to Coop and Laken. "Please proceed, Ms. Messenger. I've no intention on keeping your mother waiting."

Her mouth opens as if curious as to what Marshall might be doing with her mother before she reverts to me. "Logan, Coop"—she smiles sweetly at Cooper and Laken—"I have big news for you that will forever change how you look at yourself in the mirror."

Chloe grunts, "Oh, honey, if you're pitching some acne bullshit Ezrina helped you pound out, I'd work on clearing up your own face before you start hawking it. People won't spend their hard earned money on something that clearly isn't working."

Skyla gags a moment. "Why are you speaking?"

Brielle bops up and slings an arm around Chloe's shoulders. "What's going on?"

"Skyla is trying to be innovative like you." Chloe pulls Brielle into a partial embrace.

Dudley motions for the show to go on.

"As I was saying—" Skyla glances over her shoulder at the door. It's Gage she's looking for. I know this because I half expect him to walk through there as well. I crave his presence almost as much as she does. "It turns out Marshall is a father." She nods to both Coop and me as a few moments of stale silence go by. "Haven't either of you wondered why you look so strikingly similar? Especially to the Sector in question?"

Laken's mouth falls open. "Oh my goodness, really?" she squeals as if this meant something.

"Is that it?" Chloe crows. "Logan and Coop are related to *that*?" She gawks at Dudley as if it was an insult of the highest order, and for once, I happen to agree with Bishop.

"Cool beans." Bree traipses off as if it was no big deal, but Coop and I continue to stare blankly at Skyla.

"Isn't this great?" She nods encouragingly, but we don't take the bait.

"Dudley doesn't have kids." I put it out there in the event no one has bothered to pay attention to the facts.

"Not true." He takes a remorseful breath. "I thought the same, but as it has been recently proven, there was a bastard that lived long ago, thus leaving me the purveyor of the Oliver branch that produced you as well as the Springers that your mother hails from Mr. Flanders."

Coop takes his time reacting, looking Dudley up and down as if trying to figure out how to navigate the rest of this conversation. "Okay." He nods, not saying another single word.

"Okay?" I'm stymied by his sudden acceptance. "This isn't *okay*." I hold my breath a moment, trying to figure out exactly why this isn't acceptable. For one, I'm in love with Skyla, and so is he. Dudley and I don't get along the way Gage and I do, nor will that ever happen. So the fact he carries a torch for my girl creeps me out. "What am I supposed to say?

Glad the boys showed up that day? Thank you for the great genes?"

"You're welcome." Dudley jumps to his feet and bows to Skyla. "I must run. The biggest gift of the evening is from me. It's my undying affection to you and yours." He offers a wink before kissing the back of her hand. "Any words for your mother?"

She shakes her head. "Tell Sage I love her."

He offers a sad smile. "Will do."

Did she mean Gage? It sounded like Sage.

"I'm sorry." She pulls both Coop and me into a huddle. "As soon as I found out, I thought I should let you know." She looks to Laken and shrugs. "Honestly, I was sort of hoping for a little more enthusiasm. Marshall does a lot to help us, and he doesn't have a family—or at least he didn't until now." She gives an accusing glance my way. "I'm serious. You should consider being a little more respectful, and maybe even think about building a relationship with him. He's a great person."

"Wow," Laken muses to Coop. "He's your great-grandfather on some scale. I think that's pretty cool. Do you think there's any Sector magic left in your blood?"

"I don't know about that." Skyla shakes her head. "It's pretty diluted—seventeenth century. But I guess there could be."

Gage walks in, and, before we know it, the baby shower is in full swing with enough people in the bowling alley to qualify as an angry mob. Emma and Barron show up, and I share the news with my brother.

"Is this true?" He looks as stumped as I was.

"It appears." Gage smiles as if he's relishing this on some level, most likely because he's not a part of this family tree in that way.

Emma clutches at her pearls before relaxing into the idea. "We should invite him to dinner as soon as we can. I think a proper welcome to the family is in order."

Lizbeth comes over clapping and squealing. "Did you see that? Nobody even got close to cutting the ribbon to the size of Skyla's belly! She's presenting very forward and bullet-like, which calls for one big baby!" she sings as if this were the best news possible. "I'm betting it's a girl. I have an intuition about these things."

"Gage was of a normal height and weight," Emma insists. "You could fit three of him in that belly of hers." She and Lizbeth chortle at the idea of triplets—little do they know.

After a long evening of blind taste testing mashed sweet potatoes and almost vomiting them from my nose, things wind down as bodies storm the exit. Skyla and Gage sit in a massive pile of prizes, as does Chloe who huddles with her old West groupies.

I take a seat between Skyla and Gage. "Looks like you might have a storage issue on your hands." I run my finger along a set of twin matching white-flocked caskets. Skyla played it off by saying one is for her bedroom, and the other casket is for downstairs. The lids have been removed to avoid the inevitable suffocation. The "casketnets" is something Brielle invented a while ago for Beau Geste, and now she's raking in the green by selling them to every twisted mind that's willing to shell out one hundred and ninety-nine dollars plus shipping on these casket-bassinet combos. Barron sells them to her wholesale.

"I still think White Horse is the perfect home for the two of you. It's yours whenever you wish to claim it. Or, in the least, until the renovations on your own home are done." I throw it out there, hoping at least one of them will come to their senses. In truth, I don't think renovations on their home will ever be complete. There simply isn't that much time left in human history.

"I got this." Gage offers up a handshake that morphs into a hug. "Thanks for the year supply of diapers." He motions to the mountain of boxes standing next to him. I hardly think twelve boxes a year makes. I asked Lizbeth to pick them up for me just so I wouldn't screw up the sizes. Besides, she said it was all that could fit into her van and tried to give back the cash she had left over, but I wouldn't hear of it. I told her to consider it gas money. I know the Landons are hurting, and I do feel bad about that.

Skyla comes up and offers a heartfelt side hug, her belly pressing over my hips. "Thank you for offering us White Horse, but I think I might need my mom's help, at least in the beginning." Her forest-like lashes glance to the ground. I know how she feels about the house.

"I wish you'd take me up on it. I built it just for you."

"Maybe at a later time. Does that sound okay?" She winces, pressing her hands into mine. *The Justice Alliance removed me as the overseer for now. I've officially been banned from any faction meetings, and for sure the Council of the Superiors. How are we doing on dwindling down Wesley's chain gang?*

"Excellent." I nod, trying to give it the appropriate inflection as Gage pats me on the back.

"Lizbeth!" Tad screams at his wife who lies strewn in a twisted position. "Lizbeth!" he bellows, looking to me as if to make sure I heard. "Oh my God!" he says it stale, too contrived to be believable. "She's fallen, and she can't get up!"

Skyla groans as she takes in the sight. "It looks as if they've finally found their racket."

"What does that mean?" I'm almost sorry I asked.

Gage closes his eyes with brief remorse. "It means the books are finally going to show that dramatic loss you've been fearing."

"Do you have good insurance?" Skyla lands her palm over her belly as if protecting her children from the sight.

"It gets the job done. Why?"

"Because someone's just done a job on you."

Forever October

Skyla

Fall is simply a season in most every part of the country, but here on Paragon, it's a way of life. It's as if this entire island were in some time warp, unable to escape the brilliant color of fiery autumn leaves, crisp morning breezes. The thick blanket of fog that lies over Paragon dips in and out of her crevices, filling every last orifice of her being with its love. If fall is our immortal realm, then Halloween night is Paragon's crowning glory.

"It's too tight!" Mia cries as Melissa adjusts her corset in the living room.

"Just what is it that you're supposed to be?" I ask while adjusting my not-so-little red cape. It was my brilliant husband's idea for me to dress as Little Red and for him to play the part of the Big Bad Wolf. And, apparently, Gage is chock-full of brilliant ideas, because as he left for school this morning, he promised our little role play would trickle into the bedroom. My body burns just thinking of it. I blame all these damn Kegels my mother has me doing. Whoever heard of squeezing your vaginal muscles for hours on end? My mother, that's who. It's supposed to be great for me, something about my bladder—but the more squeezing I do, the more I seem to take myself to the sexual brink. I'm insane with all kinds of inappropriate thoughts. The first thing I'm going to do when I see Gage is drag him off to the nearest dark corner. Only he can truly detonate this Kegel bomb brewing inside me.

"A sexy librarian." Mia gasps as Melissa ties her off with her foot planted into her sister's back for maximum inflexibility.

"Oh, right." I cock my head, looking at her costume from a different angle, but no matter how I slice it, she just looks straight-up hooker to me. "That's nice." I give up. Somewhere down the line I failed at my role as big sister, and now Mia and her six-inch hot pink heels are going to have to pay the price.

Melissa leans into the mirror and teases her hair toward the ceiling. "I'm an eighties punk princess."

"You're a punk all right." Mia hands her a pillowcase. "Go on with Beau, and I'll catch up with you."

"Not without me, you don't!" Mom clanks her way over, dressed as a gypsy with her full, multicolored skirt, her large gold hoop earrings, and an arm full of bangles. Her makeup is ten times heavier than she normally wears it, and she looks drop-dead gorgeous. Little Misty is dressed as a tiny cute bumblebee, a costume that my mother actually spent time at the sewing machine to make happen. Since her little slip and fall routine at the bowling alley, she's been relegated to more sitting less shopping.

"Cute," I say, patting Misty on the head. My stomach is so big I can hardly bend in any direction, and I haven't seen my feet since July, so I have no idea if my shoes match. Speaking of shoes, I frown at my mother's walking cast. "So, are you going to file that domestic abuse claim anytime soon?" It turns out Tad had the balls to trip her the night of my shower, causing her to break an ankle, and has since relegated her to a walking cast.

"*Skyla*," she hisses, reprimanding me while covering Misty's ears. "I've already told you he was trying to help move your gifts to the car. Everything was so jingle jangle all over the place that our feet got tangled." She herds Beau Geste the purple dragon and little bumbling Misty together.

"Well, that little jingle jangle tangle is going to set back Logan's insurance a nice plump sum of fifteen *thousand* dollars. I believe once Tad heard that bit of monetary payout news, his words of remorse were *cha-ching!*"

Mom looks disgusted at her husband's moronic scheming, as she should be. "I think Misty's messed her pants. Girls—go ahead and start with Beau, and I'll catch up. Oh, and, Skyla, we'll catch you at Mr. Dudley's place tonight. I've practically been living there for the last two weeks getting everything just right. I think you're really going to love the theme we went with this year. It's to *die* for! Get it? It's Halloween!"

I am *dying* to see it. Marshall has forbidden me to visit for the last two weeks because he wants it to be a genuine surprise. I'm betting it's a heavenly theme—a real Ahava-like getaway. It would be just like him and my mother to try to throw the crowd for a loop by going against the haunted grain.

"I really do get it." I give a brief wave as I head out to Brielle's place out back. She and Drake are giving me a lift since Gage has a class that runs late this evening. He promised he'd go straight to the party in costume. He said if I looked too hot he'd have to take me to the woods and show me exactly what put the *Big* in his Bad Wolf moniker. I made sure to wear easy access panties in the event we feel the need to turn this into a Halloween to remember. Although, I'll probably have to lean up against a tree trunk for support while he fills my "basket" from behind. I'm a little off center these days.

Speaking of my ginormous baby bump, Lexy came by this afternoon in her continuing effort to take a few pictures of my growing belly. It's something Logan talked her into around the time that Gage and I renewed our vows. Today, she actually coerced me into taking them in the nude with just a long piece of fabric snaking across my privates. I'll admit, I'm dying to see them. I already told Lex that I'm going to gift one of those naughty shots to Gage for his birthday.

Bree meets me halfway, decked out in a gorgeous pale blue ball gown that shimmers underneath the moonlight. Her hair is up in a loose bun, and she's wearing a black velvet choker around her neck.

"You are *beyond* gorgeous!" I mean it. Brielle really does clean up nice, and by nice, I mean supermodel. "What are you supposed to be? A fairy princess?"

She lifts her dress just enough to expose a pair of clear plastic pumps. "Cinderella. And Drake is Prince Charming." I glance over, and he waves, all decked out in a white military-style uniform with his hair coiffed back. I'm in complete shock that A, she actually has him in something that might be misconstrued as a suit—nobody tell him—and B, she has Drake in a freaking suit! "At midnight, I'm going to lose a shoe, and Drake is going to lose his shit looking for me in the forest." She gives a hard wink.

Sounds as if there's going to be more than one kinky fairy tale playing out in those woods tonight.

Drake drives us over to Marshall's, and, all the way there, Bree fills me in on how well her line of Paragon Polish—Spellbound is doing. Apparently, Ezrina was meant to be in the beauty biz because stores can't seem to stock the product fast enough. The formula she created not only doesn't chip, but it lays on thick, and gives a professional look that you can only usually find in the salon.

"I'm really proud of you," I say as we arrive, and she helps extract me from the front seat. "You're really carving out a place for yourself in this world, one polished nail at a time."

"Isn't it funny how everything's turned out?" She helps adjust my cape and pulls and tugs until my stomach is fully covered. "Here I am—this multimillionaire mogul, and you're married to Gage."

"Hold the fucking phone. You and Drake are multimillionaires?"

"Well, you know"— she continues—"I don't actually *count* the money. But I feel like a multimillionaire. I mean, I can go to Starbucks anytime I want and load up on lattes. Plus,

I bought like three Louis Vuitton bags last week, and Drake didn't say squat."

"That's insane! If you run out of room to store them, feel free to use my closet. And what's the matter with the fact I'm married to Gage? You made it sound like he's some conciliatory prize. And before I forget, please use him to count your money. He's a great accountant." Pregnancy brain is a very real thing. I've noticed that half the time I walk into a room, I have no clue what I set out to do or how I got there. My worst fear is that the babies have harnessed the power to teleport me without my knowledge.

"Yes to the accounting, for sure." Bree groans as if this is a much-needed relief. "We've got so much cash stashed in our mattress it's actually getting hard to sleep. It keeps sloshing around all over the place, and Drake accidentally wiped his ass with a Benjamin the other night."

"God!" I can't even fathom the thought. "Did you make him wash it like a thousand times?"

"God no—we flushed it!"

My blood boils in an instant rage because here Gage and I are scrimping and saving every single dime. "The next time Drake has a bowel blunder call me over, and I'll dispose of the BM Benny for you." I will gladly glove up in triplicate and disinfect to my heart's content. Honestly, the bank would never know the difference.

"Done." She shrugs it off as if it's bound to happen again. "And what I meant by that Gage comment was that when you first came to Paragon, you really didn't pay him any attention. Remember that time he told you the two of you would marry someday, and you actually got mad?" She laughs as though it were the fondest of memories. Actually, it's far from it. I was Logan's girlfriend at the time, and when I relayed the news to him, he almost passed out.

"I didn't realize Gage had the gift of knowing—at least not while he was relaying the nuptial news." That's back when we believed Gage was simply a Levatio. He was my favorite one. I loved Levatio Gage. Still do.

"How's that gift doing now? Is it stronger? I think between him and Em we can open up the best little psychic shop in Paragon. And, since both Gage and Em are from the island, it would totally qualify as organic."

God. I shake my head. "No and no. For one, mediums are strictly forbidden by the good book, thus ixnay on the psychicnay. And people are generally never considered organic, even though technically they are."

"I'll never understand you, Skyla." She adjusts my cape one last time.

"Ha! And I'll never understand—" I turn to face Marshall's home for the first time in weeks, and a scream gets locked in my throat. My entire body goes numb with shock, weak as water all at once.

Out in the enormous driveway sits a decrepit old Ferris wheel with dead bodies dangling from it. The corpses look eerily familiar, their hair a shock of orange, their faces ghostly white—large painted-on grimaces adorn a majority of the ghastly creatures. Everywhere I look, dozens and dozens of demonic dead clowns.

"So freaking cool!" Bree swats me in the arm. "It's like a zombie clown carnival has taken over!"

An obnoxiously loud band starts from somewhere in the rear of the property, and I frown at how "freaking cool" my favorite Sector's home has become—more like uncool. Clowns are never cool. Marshall knows how I feel about the satanic beasts. Sure, I've *almost* overcome my insane phobia of the nefarious vermin, but must we test my limits on a haunted night such as this?

Bright lights flicker from the backyard where intermittent screams are met with howls of laughter. A giant hand-painted sign reads *This Way to the Cursed Carnival* with a large red arrow leading to the back of the property.

"Oh my God, oh my God, oh my God!" My voice breaks as Bree leads us to the side yard, ushering us past a wall of clown heads impaled on posts, blood dripping from their necks to the ground, their ghastly grimaces still impressed on their very real faces, worms crawling from their eyes. "I'm going to kill Marshall for festooning these haunted fairgrounds with those ghoulish phantasms."

"In English, please." Bree hikes up on her toes. "Oh, look! There's Nat and that new Host football player boyfriend of hers. She is going to make Pierce so freaking jealous."

"No, she's not." Pierce has been dead for years. Heathcliff O'Hare is the happy recipient of Pierce Kragger's body, and poor Nat is still nursing a broken heart thinking he's left her. I'm not sure why, but I suddenly want to right this wrong.

"You're such a cynic." She takes off skipping in that direction, her dress shimmering under the thousands of twinkle lights strung up in orange and purple, giving the landscape a macabre bruised effect.

"Skyla!" I turn to find Chloe headed over as Cruella de Vil, dressed from head-to-toe in a giant Dalmatian print coat. Knowing Chloe, it's a bona fide fur, patched together from real Dalmatian puppies. What else does she have to do with her wicked time down in the Transfer?

I spot Laken and Coop not too far off and waddle my way over. Each step feels as if someone is twisting my hips out of joint and simultaneously pulling my pubic bone apart. It hurts. It burns like a white-hot flame at the base of my body. How have women put up with this for so long? How is the human race even still in existence? I've just barely crested my all-day morning sickness, and by the time I go to bed at night, the twins wake up and decide it's time for their aerobics workout.

"Trick or treat," I say as Laken pulls me in for a hug.

"Looks like Chloe decided to forgo the costume," she whispers into my ear. "Bishop at six o'clock."

I decide to ignore the warning and pull back and take in Laken's costume instead. She's dressed like a flapper in her black beaded gown that ends precariously close to her upper thighs. Coop looks like a dapper gentleman, and it warms my heart because he truly is one.

"Hey, you didn't happen to acknowledge your grandpappy yet, have you?"

Coop opens his mouth to answer, then closes it, giving an icy stare over my shoulder.

Chloe steps in front of me and commands my full attention. "You do realize it's rude to walk away from someone when they're summoning you."

"You invented rude. I suppose that's why you're so familiar with the rules," I quip, rather proud of myself for the spontaneous snark. It's been few and far between these days, as my brain has turned into a gummy piece of taffy. My mother insists the "baby" must be a girl because she's stealing my beauty, and, that may be so, but she, or should I say *they*, are stealing my brain cells faster than I can reproduce them. Do brain cells reproduce? Dear God, I'm almost afraid to Google that one.

"I need you, Messenger. Where's Gage?" Her dark eyes flit around the vicinity, the color of boiled whiskey. "I need to get in touch with him asap."

"Fuck off." I shift my entire person back to Laken and Coop, who look a little amused by my harsh comeback, but, in reality, it's my go-to response when it comes to the Bishop Beast.

Chloe pulls me back by my shoulder, and I take a few unsteady steps to center myself in what's become known as my sumo wrestler's stance.

"Don't you touch me." I stop shy of stabbing her in the chest with my finger. "You're not just messing with me anymore. You're messing with my unborn children. My body is off limits to you. So go back to Wesley and pretend to be Laken because you and I both know that's the only time he'll ever touch you."

"Listen, you little twat"—Chloe's belly bursts forth and grazes over mine—"I am tired, and I am cranky, and as of right now, this body that's hosting me is putting forth a great sacrifice to benefit the beings that your husband represents."

Laken titters to Coop. "It's like watching Mothra and Godzilla go at it."

I shoot her the side-eye. Usually, I would have laughed right along with her, but when your body takes the shape of a

1960s film character that is known for his undesirable girth and lizard skin, it's really not all that funny.

"My husband is on his way over from school, and, when he gets here, he has me and my very important needs to tend to, so you'll just have to take a backseat for now. Oh, wait, that's every day for you, isn't it?"

Chloe touches her hand over her stomach. Her face peaks with color. Her dark eyes flit to mine with a heavy cloying gaze that says both *help* and *die bitch* at the same time. It's a neat trick only Chloe can pull off, I'm sure.

"You're the sole reason for all of the misery in my life."

"Here we go again with that poor little bitch girl routine of yours. I'm so sick of you shoving all your bullshit down my throat, Chloe."

"You took my house, my room, my husband, my life. If that ridiculous mother of yours never blinked you into existence, Gage would have been my husband. How does that fit down your throat, Skyla?" I chew on this for a moment with nary a handy comeback in sight. "Tell him I need to see him. It's of grave concern." She stalks off toward Nat and Em.

"Good riddance," I say, running my hand over my blooming belly just as it lights up like a swirling glowing globe with some serious climate issues. "Crap," I hiss, pulling my red velvet cape over my ginormous baby bump, but it's no use. It's dark enough out to look wildly suspicious. "Please, knock that off in there," I say sweetly.

"Aw," Laken coos. "She's talking to the babies."

"She's reprimanding them, and they're not listening," Coop points out with a smile. "Perhaps a sign of things to come?"

"You're not funny, and neither is this. I'm like an electric current these days. If you stand close enough, I can charge your cell phone."

"What do you think it means?" Laken carefully touches my baby bump, and it illuminates brighter just under her fingers.

"It means Agent Killion and Agent Moser will be able to close their case soon and head back to Washington with their first specimen. Me."

"Now that's not funny, considering they're standing right over there." Laken nods toward the barn, and, sure enough, I spot them dressed in matching silver foil jumpsuits. "I think they're supposed to be aliens, which is an irony in and of itself."

"If they were smart, they would have dressed like angels," I'm quick to point out.

"Or devils." Coop wraps his arms around Laken, still staring off in that general direction. I follow his gaze and find Wesley in their midst.

"Wow, there's a shocker." I want to laugh or cry, but all I can muster is a grunt. "He's all but given them a roadmap to the Nephilim people. I bet he's stumped as hell as to what's become of his little exercise in futility known as the Immunity League. Good thing that rat bastard father of his gifted me Tenebrous, or I wouldn't have known what to do with—" Oh my shit! Someone should really staple my lips shut for good. Good thing I stopped cold turkey before I spilled all the nasty details. I'm not sure how Laken would feel about me reopening the tunnels, even if it were for a worthy cause.

"Tenebrous?" Coop is intrigued with the idea I can tell, but I'm afraid I've opened that can of worms as far as I care to for the evening.

"What do you mean—gifted you Tenebrous?" Laken steps in, ready and willing to block my path in the event I decide to waddle away. "He gifted you the tunnels? Why would he do that? What are you going to do with them?"

Laken is really too smart for her britches. I'd love to pull an *oh, look, shiny!* But she's no Bree or Giselle for that matter.

Logan comes into view with Liam, and I can't quite make out what they're supposed to be outside of their normal selves.

"Oh, look, Logan!" He's much better than anything shiny. Logan has a shine all his own.

Laken turns just enough, and I take the opportunity to wobble right past her. Both my glowing bundles of joy and me hightail it over to the Oliver side of Marshall's immense estate.

"Happy Halloween." I flash my illuminated belly at Logan and Liam a moment before covering it back up under the red velvet cape. The threadbare dress I've donned underneath it is hardly able to contain the brilliant luminosity.

Logan takes me in his arms and buries what feels like a kiss on my neck. "Just humor me," he whispers, hot and sultry, as he single-handedly takes me to the brink of the big O with simply a whisper—damn Kegels.

"Sure," I say, carefully untangling our limbs, lest I tremble to completion right here in his arms under the watchful eye of all of Paragon and the government—not to mention Logan's telepathic capabilities. "What's going on?"

He pulls me in, and we begin to sway to the rhythm of the slow song currently seeping through the cool night air.

Logan settles his amber eyes over mine, and his side lying dimple goes off. "Would you believe I just wanted a chance to hold you in my arms?"

"I'm hardly in your arms." I glance down at the glowing mass between us. "I'm more like hardly within your grasp. What gives, Oliver?"

A hard tap comes over my shoulder, and I turn, fully expecting to see Lexy Bakova in her sex kitten du jour costume, but it's not petite, perky Lexy. It's Grayson, Kresley's breasty BFF. Normally, I wouldn't reduce another girl down to bare boobs, but honest to God, she's a walking mammary gland. I've only seen one other woman so proud to bare her tits—I hate using that word, but Gage says it so often it has sadly morphed into my lexicon—and that other chesty woman would be Demetri's niece, Isis, aka Taddy Dearest's main breasty squeeze.

"Buzz off," I say as I try to maneuver my body closer to Logan's by moving my bump to a more convenient position.

"I'm cutting in." She slips her arm between us like a skin-covered anaconda, and we begin a threesome sort of a move.

"You can't cut in, because I'm not letting you." I look to Logan for help. Surely he's not going to let another woman get between us, literally.

"I think I see someone I need to say hello to." Logan graciously bows out and steps away from both of our grabby hands. "Skyla—perhaps you should join me?"

It takes a lot of focus not to stick my tongue out at her. I don't think I've stuck my tongue out at a single person, well, maybe Gage once or twice, but that was an act of seduction.

I heard that. Logan rattles my hand as he treks deeper into the crowd.

I choose to forgo the fact. "Looks like Lex has some heavy hitting competition."

"That she does." He gives a wistful smile. "But I'm not into either of them. You know that. And I want to keep reminding you, because my soul is buried in that beating heart of yours, and I never want it back." Logan leans in and brushes his thumb over my cheek ever so softly. "I want you to keep it safe inside of you forever."

The babies give a heavy wallop, and it's not until he bucks do I see that his arm is resting on my tummy.

"It looks like someone has an opinion about that," he muses.

"Sorry." I give my belly a pat and lean in toward it. "You're going to love your Uncle Logan. He's harmless, I promise."

He winces as he gives my belly a rub as well. "I hate that I'm harmless." Logan leads me right into Landon Central. Mom and Tad are showing off their bean sprout, Misty, along with Beau to a couple of friends dressed as salt and pepper shakers. It's not until they pull back the mesh that covers their faces do I see that it's Emma and Barron.

"And what are you two supposed to be?" Emma smirks at the sight of Logan and me as if we were a couple. Her eyes ride down to our conjoined hands in judgment. It's as if she's saying *I knew it.* How I'd like to knock her over on her salty side and watch her roll down the embankment. How far do I have to go to prove that I'm madly in love with her son?

"I'm Little Red Riding Hood, and *Gage* is the Big Bad Wolf." My entire body warms with pride. The idea of a couple's costume should speak volumes to Mrs. Salt and Mr. Pepper.

"And I'm an ex-jock." Logan gives his old West T-shirt a tug. "An ex-dead jock to be exact."

"Speaking of dead." Tad starts to ramp it up. Just crap. I don't know why my mother allows him to leave the house. "You're lucky the Mrs. isn't pushing up daisies! Funerals aren't cheap, you know. That lousy fifteen grand your insurance company ponied up would have never covered the funeral expenses."

Barron leans in, his glasses poking through his ridiculous costume. The fact his wife coerced him into dressing like a condiment for the evening begs the question *just how much does Emma love Barron?*

"Actually, fifteen thousand can get you a lot more than you imagine for your money. People tend to believe funeral expenses are unapproachable, but the truth is, we have packages to accommodate even the most frugal of budgets."

Swear to God, there is dead silence in a ten-foot radius. Barron really knows how to kill a conversation, no pun intended.

Mom holds up her walking cast for a moment. "On the bright side, this contraption comes off in the morning!"

"But the emotional damage will linger for years!" Tad is quick to point out. "She's seen three psychologists, and not one of them can figure out what the hell is wrong with her. We have an appointment to see that nut job that let you go a few years back." Tad says it so casually I'm not entirely offended. He's taking about Dr. Booth. I'd better track him down before the night is through and give him a heads-up.

Hey! I just had an interesting thought. If Dr. Booth and Laken's mother marry, Laken will be quasi-related to Rev. And, if Rev and Mia ever get married, we'll all sort of be family. I shake the not-so-interesting thought right back out of my head. Mia may not marry Rev—not now, not ever, not in this universe, or any alternate dimension. *Gah!* Pregnant brain attacks again! I don't want that rebel without a cause anywhere near my kid sister, let alone putting a ring on it. He's all but cheating on her in the open and convinced her to do the same. And are they still having their secret meet-and-greets on the side? I don't even want to know. All I do know is that the dog they share custody of, Bullet, aka D-O-G, keeps reappearing at the house every now and again just to take a giant shit on the carpet. The dog itself is so large and quiet it's mostly just a living ottoman that eats and stains the rug.

"I'm sorry about everything." Logan doesn't waste time in trying to figure out exactly what to apologize for and simply goes for the gold. "I'll talk to my insurance and see if there's anything they can do to help cover any mental health fees you might incur."

"No." My blood turns to lava just thinking of the ways my mother and Tad are trying to fleece poor Logan. "The bowling alley is not a goose that lays golden eggs. It's more like a chipped cup that no one has the heart to throw away, and it's hurting financially just like the rest of us." As silly as it seems, it felt incredibly adult to put myself in that financially pained category. Come to think of it, that sentiment will most likely ring true my entire life.

I reach down and wrap my hand around Logan's fingers. *I totally didn't mean that chipped cup analogy. I just want Tad to feel like the ass that he is. And trust me, our entire cupboard is full of chipped mugs. I was essentially speaking his language.*

"Ha!" Tad balks at the truth as if he knows better. "He's got you fooled. That meathead you married is cooking his books. I know for a fact what he's making because good old Greg left the laptop open last week."

"Tad!" Mom whacks him.

"What? It was at the dining room table. Everybody knows there are no secrets at the dining room table. Zippo!" He wags a finger at Logan. "It's because of those slippery floors of yours that my marriage is in peril."

Dear God.

"My wife can't even hobble up the stairs to the bedroom. It's been an entire month of no nookie for me."

I take in a sharp breath. *Nookie?* Did I hit my head? How is this happening?

Emma groans, and poor Barron looks physically repulsed by the idea. That makes two of us.

"I have a solution." Logan sags, wavering his worn-out smile I've seen one too many times since the end of the Faction War. Come to think of it, dealing with the Faction War was probably easier for him than dealing with Tad. "How about instead of cleaning out the bowling alley, you take my house at White Horse?"

"No!" both Emma and I shriek in unison. Finally, something we can agree on. Or at least I'm pretty sure we agree on.

"Excuse me?" Tad straightens as if suddenly ready to listen.

"It has a ground floor bedroom, and you're welcome to stay there as long as you like. That way the two of you can sleep in the same bedroom and resume your—*nookie*, did you say?"

Shoot. Logan sure is cute when he's turning up the charm.

"I don't know." Mom shakes her head. "My cast is coming off tomorrow, and Skyla is about to have that baby any minute."

"Take her with you. She and Gage can take the entire upstairs. It'll be like their very own place. There's plenty of room for a nursery and even rooms for Misty and Beau. And then when you're a hundred percent better, Skyla and Gage will have a place to call their own—until, of course, their new home is ready."

So that's where this was headed. My lips twist as I contemplate Logan Oliver's brazen sneakiness.

"No thank you," I say it as sweetly as possible. "Gage and I don't mind staying where we are until the house is ready. But I promise, if we do get cabin fever and our house isn't ready, we'll take you up on it."

Logan locks eyes with mine. His sincerity bleeds through to the bone. "Thank you for at least considering it."

A loud pop and a crash emit from somewhere inside, and Mom spasms.

"I'd better go see what that's all about." She gives Tad a firm tug. "Why don't you come in the event I need backup?"

That's one way to keep a muzzle on him.

"*Logan*"—Emma leans in, perturbed—"I will never understand why you bankrupt yourself building a house that you never intend to live in. And now, trying to pawn it off on the Landons?" She gags as if offering it to my family was the ultimate cry of desperation, and in a way, it was. "Is there something wrong with it?"

"No—nothing at all. I just—I'm a little lonely there. I hope you don't mind me at the house now and again."

"You're always welcome," Barron says it in the event Emma won't. She can be iffy. "I enjoy our late-night talks and poker. You still owe me thirty-seven dollars." He winks at his brother.

"There's one sure-fire way to cure your loneliness," Emma says with a strange determined look in her eyes. "We'll just have to find you a good woman."

Kill me.

"No thank you," Logan says it with a fevered undertone as if he didn't want to induce some jealous rage in me. If I can withstand Lexy Bakova throwing herself at him, and Grayson's boob attack, I think I'm good.

"Kresley Fisher was destined to be my daughter-in-law."

"Kresley?" I will cut a bitch.

"Emma!" Barron throws his arms in the air, because for one, he understands what an insult she just gave me.

"Please, I practically raised this boy." She dusts Logan's shoulder as if readying him for his moment in the sun. "Kresley is a beautiful girl both inside and out. As soon as she and Gage arrive, I'll arrange for you to have some private time."

Gee, throw in a condom, why don't you?

"Wait, did you say 'she and Gage arrive'?" I lean in a bit. "As in arrive together?"

"Yes." She blinks as if it were common knowledge. "Gage and Kresley always commute together from their night class."

"*Their* night class?" I'm suddenly simultaneously amused and pissed. When was Gage going to fill me in on this little witch tidbit?

Giselle hops over, looking every bit the cute playboy bunny she's inadvertently dressed as. "Don't you love it?" She wiggles her fluffy little cottontail at her not-so proud parents. "Ellis helped pick it out! He says bunny love is his favorite."

Gross. If Harrison doesn't die by Gage's hand, he just might meet his maker by way of Barron. I've never seen his face this shade of purple.

"And hello to my little dolphin niece or nephew." Giselle rubs her pink satin bottom over my belly, and Emma actually groans.

"Please, Giselle. Do not refer to the baby as a dolphin." She glares at me as if it were all my fault. It is, but that's beside the point. "Skyla, explain to my daughter that, though you will give birth to a mammal, it will not be of the aquatic variety."

Typical Emma ruining everything for me. "There's an off chance I might have a dolphin." I bite down on my lip. There's something in me that demands to make Emma insane. Besides, if there's anyone to blame for Giselle's massive misgivings regarding human reproduction, I'm betting it's Ellis—who, by the way, is responsible for just about every other misgiving Giselle has about the human race.

A tall, rather well-built wolf-looking creature catches my eye from the edge of the woods. He gives a slight nod toward the evergreens before ditching into the darkness and away from the party. It looks as if I'm about to claim my prize for the night, and I'm going to enjoy every last Kegel-loving minute of it.

"Well, I gotta run." I take a step away, and Logan slides over, blocking my path.

"Where to?"

"I just saw Gage by the woods," I whisper. "I think he wants me to ditch the 'rents, if you know what I mean."

"Got it." He dons that sad smile once again as if he knows I'm simply making up an excuse to get busy with my husband in the woods. "Coop and Laken are inside. I think I'll track them down." He starts to take off, and I catch him by the wrist.

I'm not sure what to pinpoint for the deep ache that's settled into my heart at the moment—the wicked night, the sudden rush of serendipity for who we were, who we could be, the fact that a part of me wishes I could turn back time, and even then I wouldn't know what to do with it. Tears come as I wrap my arms around him.

Someway, somehow we will survive this. I say, not entirely sure of what exactly I mean, but with everything in me, I know those were the right words.

I know. He presses a kiss to my cheek just shy of my lips and speeds out of sight.

My feet lead me toward the woods where I spotted Gage a moment ago, but my cheek still burns like a live coal where Logan planted that softer than air kiss. Then it hits me. This will never get easier. Not now, not in a million years. That's just something I need to accept—that we both will. Maybe it's time Logan and I have a hard-hitting conversation. Perhaps we're long overdue on that.

The evergreens engulf me in their black shadowed wings as I follow a thin seam of moonlight down to the stream that runs through Marshall's property. The dark figure of a man leans against the railing, his knee casually up on the lower rung, his hands spread wide as he relaxes his sexy self with that inviting come-hither look in his Big Bad Wolf eye.

"I thought you'd never show." I waddle toward his way, trying to do my best to seduce him. My stomach has dimmed to the faintest blue glow, the babies are clearly napping because they're not trying to pound their way out from the inside, and it feels nice like this, like it's just Gage and I, alone under a bright autumn moon.

"I'm not wearing any underwear." I blow him a kiss. That mask is totally convincing with the full snout, the gaping mouth with a rubber tongue hanging partially to the side. My finger traces over his elongated snout, and I give a nose-wrinkling smile. I turn around and rub my well-padded bottom over his crotch in an effort to get this party started.

"My entire body is sizzling to have you," I mewl like a kitten. "I've been doing those damn Kegels, and it's like a sex grenade is about to go off in my vagina. It's like no matter what I do, I'm about to have an orgasm. The other day my foot was itching, and as I scratched it, the sensation ricocheted deep into that greedy part of me. If I sneeze, I bring myself to the brink. And the Kegels themselves—don't even get me started on the freaking Kegels! I'm supposed to be doing them all the time, and you want to know what it feels like? It feels like I'm masturbating in public. I almost climaxed the other day in the *car*—and I was with my mother! This is really just starting to get out of hand. I need someone to put out this fire once and for all." I try to insert a little grinding action into it, but it's more Weeble Wobble than it is sexy shimmy. "You wouldn't happen to have a hose, would you?" I blow him a kiss over my shoulder. It was much easier to seduce Gage when I could actually reach him. Between the fact my body has turned into one solid chunk, and the not-so tiny detail that his mask makes him all of seven feet tall, we'll be lucky to get the plumbing inserted into the correct fittings. I lift my cape and reach back, placing his hands square on my bare bottom.

Gage pulls away and carefully places my cape back where it came from.

"Knew it." My voice carries over the stream like the wail of a child. "You find me repulsive. You think I'm too massive to make love to. You think my ass has gotten way out of hand. Just admit it."

He reaches under his chin and plucks the mask off, only to reveal it's not Gage looking down at me. It's a dismayed Marshall.

"*Gah!* You touched me!"

"You touched *me*. That hard protrusion was my knee, Ms. Messenger. I thought you had a hard-to-reach itch. And, please note, I replaced your clothing where it belongs. What in heaven's name made you think I was Jock Strap?"

"Oh, I don't know—could it have been the costume?" My voice echoes back to me as irritated as it left.

"And how was I to know that? I simply saw my lovely spirit bride waltz in this evening and decided what better accouterment to don than that of her counterpart?" He gives a slight devilish grin. "Do you like the décor?"

I swat him over the chest. "That's for pretending to be Gage." I swat him again. "And that's for the lousy *décor*."

He gives a crude chuckle. "I may have enjoyed the deception." He measures his forefinger and thumb an inch apart. "And the décor was purely your mother's genius. I did find the clown theme a bit unnerving, considering your phobia of the creatures, but she insisted."

"Ex-phobia, or at least it was before tonight. I'm going to have nightmares for weeks." I lean against the post next to him. I'm at the stage of my pregnancy where standing is simply a spectator sport. "What's with luring me out to pasture?"

"I simply wanted to say hello in private. I had no idea you'd be throwing yourself at me. Did you see the aliens? Oh, what fun we're going to have with them."

"Yes. What a joke. And are they ever going to go away? Or is this lifetime experiment in lurking their new undertaking? I'm not sure what I'm more wary of—their presence or this new body of mine. Did you know that my pubic bone is expanding—on *purpose*?"

"If two tiny beings are planning to fall out, then I assume a lot of things will be expanding on *purpose*."

A shiver runs through me as Emily's horror of a birth echoes in my mind. "I'm sure once I meet the twins I'll be thankful for the experience, but, up until that moment, the day I give birth will be the worst day ever."

"Says every mother in existence."

"How are there people on this planet?"

"I don't know, but I suppose it has something to do with women like you who are willing to put a stranger's hands on their bare bottom. You do realize, I could have been a wanderer."

"Hey, you gotta start somewhere." I press my shoulder to his and give a little laugh. "Speaking of bare bottoms, I need to firmly insist you stop stalking my nightmares. I know that you claim you're not to blame for my pornographic wanderings, but come on—really? Just knock it off already." I press my determined gaze into his wildfire eyes. "I'm starting to moan your name in my bed as much as I do my husband's." He's actually surpassed Gage in that department, but I'm not here to stroke his ego.

"My dear love, are you still vexed with those fantasies?" His cheek glides up one side because it's obvious he doesn't mind at all. "Come." He lands his hand over my forehead and closes his eyes. "Oh dear," he sighs. Marshall's lips tug into the idea of a smile as he continues to scoff out loud. His brows rise and fall with amusement.

"You're watching them all, aren't you?"

"Heaven's no. I don't have that kind of time." He removes his hand and shakes it off as if to cool it. "I'm afraid that's all you, my love."

"Trust me—it most certainly is not me."

"It's you, Skyla," he assures. "Perhaps you're experiencing a light drive into the future?"

"Wishful thinking on your part. Besides, I'm not that talented. Can you at least find the shut-off valve?"

"That I'm afraid I cannot. I've no abilities to wander into your mind and disconnect your insatiable lust for me." His eyes hood over with that cheesy leering grin.

"You're the biggest clown of them all, you know that?" We stand there a few minutes just listening to the howls of laughter, the music emanating from the heart of his big bash. The moon sparkles from above, looking far more like a star than its usual dreamy, creamy self. Speaking of dreamy. "I've been meaning to ask—"

"Anything." Marshall doesn't hesitate in answering.

"Tell me what that haunted chess set means. You mentioned you fashioned it from dream stone straight from Ahava. It's important, isn't it?"

"Did it help during the war?"

"Not particularly— although, I do enjoy seeing the miniature versions of all my favorite and least favorite players." I think on it a moment. "It has something to do with control, doesn't it?" Marshall gifted me that chess set while I was still at West, still in the throes of the Faction War. It's beautiful, the pieces each carved to look like people I know—carved from a gray glassy stone with a similar opacity to jade.

"Indeed it does reek of control. You're so close to surmising its meaning on your own. Shall I proceed?"

"Please." I rub my hands over my burgeoning belly. "My deductive reasoning skills go down with each passing day of this pregnancy."

"Very well. This life—this existence is likened to a sport."

"A game," I flatline. "I'm aware."

"Good. A game, as you suggest, has winners. It has losers—allies, enemies—it has someone who is very much in control." His lips rise with a demented smile. "That would be you, Skyla. The dream stone has properties. You are very much in control of the game, of the players." Marshall leans in and looks deeply into my eyes as if he were hand-feeding his love to my very soul. "You have the control. The game is yours to play. You, my love, will be and very much are the victor. Don't be afraid of the game. Don't be afraid to make your very next move."

My gaze stays trained on his for a very long while. His words ricochet inside me as if they had a life of their own, and they do.

I glance back at the party, at Marshall's palatial estate, and that playful side he seems to bring out in me bubbles right to the surface. It feels like home here, and a thought comes to me. "Hey—you said I was the lady of the manor, right? So, technically, this is my home. I think I should move in a little early."

"With Jock Strap?"

"Exactly. That way we can strategize for this so-called game at an intimate proximity."

"My bed wasn't meant for three."

"Don't be silly. You'll be in the poolhouse."

"I neither have a pool nor a poolhouse."

"Well, start digging. Soon, you'll be my cabana boy." I give a little wink, but Marshall isn't amused at my stab at matrimonial humor.

"Correction—I'll be your husband. Jock Strap can be our cabana boy."

"Oh, and will we get married on the thirteenth as well?" I tease.

"Why would we do that? Everyone knows it's bad luck."

I belt out a laugh that shatters the silence around us effectively as blown glass.

"Why is it always so easy with you?"

"Because we're simpatico. Our lives were designed to dovetail into one another. Don't think for a moment that everything about your life isn't about design, Skyla. If I were you, I'd keep an eye out for the coincidences."

"Coincidences." I tilt my head just so. "Did you glean something new at that meeting you had with my mother?"

"Perhaps." He leans in and dots my forehead with a kiss. "Perhaps it was something I already knew."

"Did you see her?" I nod as her name gets hitched in my throat. "Sage?"

His entire person softens. "I did, my love—and your father, too. I'm proud to say, we have a lovely young lady." He brushes his thumb over my cheek with a warm sweep. "She's just like you." He clears his throat. "I'd best get back to my guests. Agent Moser and Killion asked for a tour of the house. I can't ever imagine what they expect to find."

"I'd hide the whips and chains if I were you. And good Lord, don't show them the mirror!" I shout as Marshall dissipates into a translucent version of himself, gifting his glory to the woods as he becomes one with the evergreens. The Paragon fog slowly seeps into the forest like silent probing fingers, and I'm suddenly all too aware of the fact I'm out in the middle of nowhere all by my lonesome.

The moon shines down on the clearing where Marshall stood just moments before, and a whistling wind explodes through the forest like the cry of the damned. The faraway noise of the party is drowned out, and, for a moment, I turn to look at the stream with the white kiss of the moon riding over its back. There is something golden about solitude—about the need to have a complete moment of silence to rein in your thoughts, and apparently, your orgasms.

A dull howl comes from deep in the woods, and my ears perk in that general direction. I'm not too sure I'll be so eager to lift my cape for the next werewolf I see. I'm lucky that it was just Marshall and not some homicidal, horny-as-hell serial killer.

Another yelp ensues, only this time it's followed by intense hissing of some kind. Crap. I should have known Halloween is no time to go exploring the concept of solitude.

My heart bucks unnaturally as blood pumps through me in wild, spastic spurts.

"*Help*," an anguished female voice carries from my left, and I hesitate before heading in that direction. First, I'm in no condition to "help" anybody, and, second, I've never really been a help to anybody to begin with.

A horrid animalistic cry emits from that same corner of the haunted woods, and my bones turn to glass. One more step and my body will make good on its promise to shatter with fear.

"*I hate my life.*" Each word is drawn out with more agony than the last, but there is something in that tone, something in that sardonic drawl that I've heard more times than I'd like to remember.

"*Chloe?*" I say it just loud enough, maybe too low, but, hell, who am I kidding? Do I really want her to answer?

"Messenger?" It comes out more of a victory than a question. "Please, you have to help me. I can't do this alone." Her voice is breathy.

"Who are you decapitating now?" I stalk my way toward the edge of the stream where her demonic bellows emanate from.

Another hard moan evicts from her.

"Come on." I hold back a laugh. "It can't be that hard for you to chop off a head. What's the matter? Can't hack your way through a couple of vertebrae, Chloe? A little connective tissue getting you down?" A high-pitched squeal echoes near an umbrella oak, and I head over. There she is, sprawled over the ground with her back leaned up against the trunk, her puppy fur coat spread underneath her like a blanket. Chloe has her legs parted, bent at the knees. Her fingers press white into the earth as her face wrinkles with pain.

"The only one who's dying here is *me*." She pitches her head back and lets out a blood-curdling scream.

"Oh God! Are you having the baby? You're having the baby! I'll go get help! My mom is here. I swear, I'll find her and bring her right back." God, my mother is going to *thrive* in this medically bare environment. I'm sure there's no ideal birth next to a kiddie pool other than the backwoods of Marshall's llama farm. Normally, I wouldn't lift a finger to help Chloe, but there happens to be a completely innocent child lodged between her legs at the moment.

"No!" she roars to life. The whites of her eyes flash like flames. "You will *not* leave me, Messenger. It's too late for that. This thing is coming right fucking now! The contractions are right on top of one another." She lets out another harrowing cry as if to prove her point. "I wouldn't wish this on my worst enemy"—she pants while looking right at me—"not even you, Messenger."

"Wow, this must really hurt like hell," I muse mostly to myself. Carefully, I drop to my knees beside her.

"Pull my dress up." She helps with the feat I wasn't about to participate in. "Take off my underwear—please."

It's true. I had imagined myself taking off someone's clothes tonight, yet Chloe's granny panties were not anywhere near the list.

I tug at her dress until it's nesting below her slightly inflated boobs. After witnessing what Grayson had to offer, both Chloe and I are basically still flat chested. To my surprise, Chloe really does have a pair of granny panties on. They're so huge they balloon right over her stomach.

"It looks like you're in on Victoria's grandma's secret."

"Oh, shut up, Messenger. You know they're comfortable."

Okay, so I might have a pair or twelve myself, but only because there is no such thing as a comfy thong. Women who say they're *oh so comfortable* are fucking liars, and trying to look hot in a G-string during your last trimester is just wrong.

"I totally get the granny panties," I say, pulling them off and wincing. There she is, the dark Bermuda Triangle that is Chloe Bishop's flytrap, the place where she's lured Logan to wallow in the mire more than once, and poor Wesley just long enough to get herself knocked up. "Did you ever have sex with Ellis?" I ask, bunching her panties up and tossing them to the side. If I'm going to be staring at her pink parts, I may as well be apprised who's been there before me.

"Who the fuck cares?" she groans so hard, so painfully long that a primal fear resonates in me.

"Oh, that's right. You have. You broke his heart before I ever landed on this overgrown rock." I make a face at the thought of Chloe defiling poor Ellis before I could get here to save him. Her body lurches, and I scoot back, giving her room to shoot this kid out like a missile if need be. "Chloe, I really think I should run and get some help. Childbirth takes a very long time—this might take hours. Trust me, you really would be more comfortable in a hospital bed."

Chloe starts to pant and mumble incoherently for a second before clearing her throat. "I am witty, feel shitty and bright," she bellows it out in song—badly, might I add. "And pity you're not me *tonight*."

"Oh, is that what happens when you go into labor? You break out into show tunes?" Bastardized at that.

"It's coming!" Her legs widen as she bears down.

"Stop!" I shrill into her so loud she actually ceases from pushing and looks up. "I can't deliver your baby in the woods! It's not sanitary! For one, this is where bears shit. And two, it's just not safe. This could kill you!" On second thought. "Next time you feel a contraction, go ahead and push with it."

Chloe lets out an agonizing cry, and her face turns a dark shade of demon as if she's struggling to take the dump of a lifetime.

Chloe lies back in the dappled moonlight. Her girl parts bloom like a rose, expanding into a round bulbous nightmare as if it were one giant zit about to pop all over my existence. Something about this does not feel right. I distinctly remember an entire flurry of doctors and nurses rushing around, collecting pots and pans and surgical equipment while Emily was at this stage of the exploding vaginal game with baby Ember. And all I have handy are my ridiculous wicker basket and a belly that's beginning to glow.

"What is that?" Chloe stops her panting long enough to focus on my talented children.

"Oh, it's a Fem thing. But that's good. It can take your mind off the pain. Just stare at my belly, and hopefully, this entire nightmare will revert, and you'll be back to your nasty self in no time."

"Okay." She nods stupidly into my stomach until her head rolls back, and she grunts a wild series of moans that sound as if I'm hacking her to death all over again. Hell, when I was actually killing Chloe, she didn't make this much noise. "It's here. I have to push!"

Chloe bears down, and a clear, plastic-looking cap begins to swell out of her vagina.

"What the?" I lean in further to get a better look. "It's not a head." My voice warbles.

"Is it a foot?"

"No, it's—it's just weird." God, why didn't I pay better attention when my mother was giving a detailed play-by-play of Misty's birth?

Chloe bears down again, and the plastic-looking membrane pushes farther out.

"It's—a pod." I back away a few inches. "This isn't the part where you confess to being an alien, is it?" Dear God, what if this is the way baby Fems are born? In pods! Only to hatch at a later time! *Shit*. Now I'm going to be forced to have a home birth whether I like it or not. An image of my mother and that fishnet she used to catch any unwanted "guests" from that kiddie pool she crouched in for hours pops up. I will not be taking a surprise crap in a kiddie pool during labor. That's where I put my swollen foot down. Demetri may have gotten me with that whole *your husband is a Fem* thing, but my babies are coming into this world in a sterile, cold, surgical environment filled with strangers, not in the loving comfort of my own living room with my mother and a shit net.

"It's not a pod. I think it's the sac," she grunts hard into her words.

"You're having the sac? I'm pretty sure you're not supposed to have the sac, Chloe. Your baby isn't done cooking. Can't you shove it back inside?"

"NO! Break the stupid bag, and the fluid will gush out, and then you can yank the damn thing out of me!"

"What the hell am I supposed to break the sac with?"

"Chew it open with your teeth! I really don't give a flying fuck! Rip it open with those claws of yours! Hell, you can use your toenails. I really do not care." Her voice cuts through the night, hostile and about as welcome as a broken mirror.

Chloe screams and pushes, and sure enough, more of the sac protrudes like a stubborn water balloon that just won't break.

"*Shit*," I hiss in anger, rubbing my hands raw over my cape in a weak attempt to sanitize them. Chloe bears down again, evicting the sac out farther, and the pressure builds as the fluid bottlenecks at the top. I reach down and touch it, retracting just as quickly. It's wet and slippery and feels slightly like every jellyfish I wish I had never touched. I land my fingers to it again, and it bursts onto me, leaving a gush of warm fluid running over my hands. "Well played, Bishop—well played," I say, holding up my glossy hands a moment.

Chloe screams, loud and viral, drilling her agony well into tomorrow. I reach down between her legs as a warm head emerges. Tiny shoulders pop out, and I slip my fingers around them, pulling the poor innocent baby straight out of its mother.

"Oh my God!" I hold it up to the moonlight. Dark hair, pale skin, and the cutest tiny toosh. "It's a girl!" My heart vibrates right into my skull. "She's not crying. What should I do? Should I spank her?"

Chloe lunges forward and snatches her from me. She swoops her face toward the infant's tiny head, and OH MY GOD! SHE'S EATING HER YOUNG!

Chloe turns her head and spits. "Spank her. I cleared her airways."

I take the baby back as she slips and flops into my hands and give a swift swat to her bottom. The tiny being gives the hearty cry of a lamb before taking in a lungful of air and giving the lusty cry of a newborn—piercing through the night with a battle cry that rivals anything her mother gave just a moment ago.

"Hello, baby girl." I pull her toward me, warming her in my cape, supporting her flaccid neck in the crook of my arm. The top of her head is covered with a dark cap of hair. Her tiny eyes are dark and glossy as she gives a curious glance to her new surroundings. Little tiny dimples go off on either side of her cheeks, and, for a brief second, I see Gage in her beautiful face and wonder if this is what the daughter we lost would have looked like at birth. "What's her name?" I coo sweetly into the baby's tiny face, and her lids flutter.

"I don't have a name." Chloe falls back onto her elbows and sighs. "What about Chloe?"

"No," I flatline. "Try again."

"Fine—then, Bishop."

"Again no." My head ticks back in awe of her poor choices.

"Then Brody. He's my hero, and I think it's a great honor."

"How about no again, and you hold off on the Brody thing until you have a son."

"Okay." She closes her eyes shut with a squeeze. "How about a combination of Brody and Bishop? Bishop."

"How about we chalk this conversation up to delirium, and you think of a name in the morning?"

"I couldn't care less what its name is. Give her to Wes. I'm sure he'll figure it out."

The baby's lips quiver as she starts in on another tiny cry, so sweet and fragile it makes my heart ache. "It's okay, I promise. You made it just fine." I give a little laugh before looking back to Chloe. "I'm impressed you knew to clear her airways. This is probably the only time your sucking face maneuvers benefited anyone." I give a lopsided smile at my stab at humor. Chloe and I have just experienced something monumental, and for a brief window of time, a very very brief window that is quickly closing, this moment we share feels pure and right. "Here. Take your precious baby girl. She really is beautiful." I lean in to hand her the baby, and Chloe waves us both off.

"I've done my part. She has a father."

"Chloe, you can't be that cold. She needs you. She needs you to love her, and more to the point, to *feed* her."

"Get away from me with that thing!" she shrieks in my face, and the baby jumps and startles in my arms. "I said go find her father!" Chloe sobs between words, and as much as I want to see her as a monster, the only thing I feel is sorry for her.

"Have it your way. It's probably just hormones," I say to the tiny being squirming in my arms as I begin the long trek back to the party. I give one last glance back at Chloe as the moon sheds its light over her like a silent silver teardrop. Her head is bent, her chest bucks with grief. Doesn't she know that the one thing that can make it all better is lying here swaddled in my cape? I'm disappointed in Chloe. For as much as she's obsessed over Gage through the years, she gave the impression that she knew what love was, what it could be, and here I have a slice of love in my arms, and she doesn't want a thing to do with it.

The party comes up too quickly, and I tuck the tiny being close to my body, my own belly blaring like a beacon. It's as if the closer Chloe's baby gets to my own children, the more obnoxiously my belly illuminates. Soon, I'll qualify as a bona fide searchlight.

The crowd comes into focus as Emily and Nat hang out with Ethan and Nat's new boy toy. I find Laken and Coop, and I don't dare go in that direction. I spot my mother and Tad, and just as I'm about to take the baby to her—she might as well be a registered safe haven for baby drops-offs—I spot Gage and Wes hanging out with Logan near the fountain full of fake blood and bobbing severed heads, each one with a grisly painted clown smile. My mother really does hate me. So, of course, I head off to Baby Girl's father.

"Trick or treat," I say, handing the sweet princess off to Wes, cape and all.

"What's this?"

"More like who. You'll have to think of a name, all of Chloe's ideas were lousy. But aren't they always?"

Wesley's face turns white as a sheet, so deathly pale that for a moment I think it's a part of his costume, but he isn't wearing one. Wesley is simply flat-out afraid.

"Help me, Skyla. I can't do this. I can't do any of this, and she needs a name."

"You must have a name in your heart you've been thinking of. It's been nine long months, Wesley."

"Laken," he exhales into her with a look of relief as the color comes back into his cheeks.

"No! Absolutely not. You can't name her Laken. You're about as useless as Chloe. Must I do everything?"

Gage wraps his arms around my waist, marveling at the tiny being. "She's amazing."

"Where's Chloe?" Logan asks.

"In the woods. Can you call for an ambulance? And get my mom. She needs to go to her."

His dimple digs in without the hint of a scowl. "Sure thing." He steps away with his phone in hand. Logan really is a prince among men. Not too many people would go out of their way help ensure their killer received proper medical attention after a bodily trauma.

"Any ideas?" Wesley asks, his gaze never leaving the face of that precious little angel.

"I don't know. Some people name their girls after the month they're born in. How about October?"

"You can call her Tobie for short," Gage offers.

"October," Wes sighs with relief. "Hello, Tobie. You're so sweet and beautiful." He sniffs back tears. "I already love you so very much."

"You should probably get her checked out," Gage says it tenderly as if we were talking Wes off a ledge. "Get her warm and fed."

"I will. I have a doctor on standby in the Transfer. I need to get her out of here." His eyes meet with mine as they pool with joyous tears. "Thank you, Skyla. I won't forget this."

He takes off into the crowded midway set up in Marshall's palatial yard and disintegrates to nothing right in thick of it all. Appearing where he stood just a moment ago are a stymied Killion and Moser. Their gaping astonishment quickly transfers from that empty space to my shining star of a belly.

"Great," I whisper. "Now they're never going to leave."

"We may not want them to."

"What?" I look at Gage in his partial costume, the mask of a wolf dangling from his hand.

"I think I've thought of a way to turn Wesley's game around and have it bite him in the ass. I don't think the Nephilim people are in any real danger, at least not those outside of the Barricade."

"I like how you're thinking."

"It's not how I'm thinking. It's what Wesley's done."

The thought of Wes nailing himself inside his own coffin pleases me.

But my heart wrenches for that poor little girl who dropped into the world tonight.

Some kids hit the parent jackpot, and some kids simply don't.

Gage

Dudley's zombie clown-fest continues without a hiccup even after the ambulance arrives and tries to whisk Chloe away—*tries* being the operative word. Chloe throws one of her classic tantrums and threatens to sue anyone who looks at her sideways, so the ambulance takes off empty as Chloe's heart.

"My God, where's the baby?" Lizbeth shrieks. Even with all of the hysterics, the partygoers are far too enthralled in the haunted midway, the bloody cotton candy, and deep-fried fingers-on-a-stick to care.

"In the Transfer with her daddy," Skyla says through clenched teeth. My eyes ride up and down my beautiful wife's attire, and I can hardly wait to sink my big bad teeth into her later tonight. There's just something about Skyla in that dress that gets my engine going. Skyla always seems to get my engine going.

Lizbeth covers her mouth and nods as if realizing the gravity of the situation. "I'd better find Demetri. He's a grandfather now." She fans herself as if overcome with emotion herself. "Is there a way I can escort Chloe there? I'm sure she wants to reunite with the baby as soon as possible."

Skyla gives me a nervous glance.

"I'd better take care of this." She heads off with her mother.

It seems the more Lizbeth becomes entangled with Demetri, the more she delves into the dark chambers of the Nephilim world. Speaking of which, Wesley is a father now. I guess that makes me an uncle. It sickens me to think how Chloe, Wes, and Demetri are going to brainwash my poor little niece. She has a trifecta of wickedness working against her. Skyla and I might be the only light in her life. I'm not sure why I feel a sudden familial duty toward her, but I do. She's something good in this membrane of evil we're embroiled in. I'm hoping she'll take Wesley's mind off the fact his Immunity League has a dropout rate higher than West Paragon High these days. He hasn't added a single person to his trusty dream team, and it's no wonder. Emily's brother and the Videns flash through my mind. Wes says he's not doing anything with them, but Em begs to differ. It makes me wonder if Wesley has found a loophole in that blood covenant. If he's up to no good, I damn well better know about it.

Logan catches my eye as he heads over.

Speaking of dark chambers, I should probably have a talk with him. Let him know the terms of Demetri's deal—become the enemy and live. Me—a fire-breathing dragon for decades to come right here in Skyla's face. I'm sure that will go over well. Or I can simply die and give Skyla and the kids a headstone to visit. I tried walking on the wicked side once before, and it didn't work for me—not too sure it can ever work. From afar, Skyla's belly glows a faint blue hue right through her dress, and my heart wrenches. Those babies, *our* babies, didn't ask to be here, to have Fem DNA infused into their destinies. They didn't ask to have a father who leaves the planet early. They didn't ask for any of it, but they're getting it all, and then some. How could I ever think of leaving them to navigate it all on their own? They'll have Skyla, but, in truth, it feels as if I'm leaving her, too. They'd have Logan—sooner than later. He'd swoop in quickly. He proved that a few months ago.

"You ready to roll?" Logan offers a firm pat to my shoulder. He's wearing his practice jersey from West, and my gut pinches for those golden sentimental days.

"Skyla's wrapping things up with her mom." I take a quick look around, and the party is still hopping. "Hey, there's something I want to run by you when we get a chance."

"We've got a chance right now." He ushers us out to a darkened area of the corral. "What's up?"

"I'm up." I tap my chest and stifle a laugh. "We never did finish that conversation about my last birthday wish."

"The one that cost me a body?" Logan isn't impressed with my tactics, but I think deep down he knows how desperate I was. "It's time to drink the Kool-Aid or quit. I have a decision to make, and I'm not sure how to do it. You've got a pretty good head on your shoulders. I thought maybe you can help me do it."

"I don't have a head. Chloe arranged for that. What are you talking about? What Kool-Aid? What's Demetri up to now?"

"He wants to ante up, and I'm not too sure about where this might lead. Hell, I know I'm not."

"You finally read the fine print." He gives a knowing nod.

"You never get waylaid by bullshit, do you?" I run my hands over my face hard as if trying to wake myself from a bittersweet dream. "What I mean is, you wouldn't have found yourself in this shithole of a deal—with a devil hoping to fill my father's shoes no less."

"No. I would have gotten myself killed and locked in a Treble, only to watch some other dude fuck the woman I love." Logan tries to laugh it off, but it comes out depleted and worn, much like his soul these days.

"I get it." I wipe the sleep from my eyes once again. "I'm being a pussy. I've got the good end of the stick, and believe me, I know it. But it all feels like it's slipping by too quickly. As much as it sucks for you, I don't want to miss out on a life with Skyla and the kids. She loves me. It's real. I don't feel like a replacement or second best. Maybe I should, but I don't. I buy what she's selling, lock, stock, and barrel. And with those kids..." I blow a breath out to the stars and watch as the fog swirls above my head. "Dude, who the hell is going to protect them from Demetri? He's determined to make them his new pet project. I know you'd be here for them, but Demetri will go around you in a hotter-than-hell-fire minute. You won't even know he's pulling the wool over your eyes. He'll have them eating out of his paw." I swallow down the stone forming in my throat.

"You need to be here. I'll be the first to advocate that," he says it soft, careful, as if walking on eggshells. "Honestly, I'll be the second to advocate that because Skyla is the first. She's been championing your cause since the moment the Faction War ended. As soon as she heard your life was in peril, she wanted to stop anything bad from happening to you. She is in love with you. She's loved you from the beginning. You're her everything, and, to be honest, if something did happen to you—things wouldn't be the same with Skyla and me. Her need for you is enormous. You would leave a hole in her heart so big that nobody, certainly not me, could fill it."

My own heart pounds like the surf just listening to him talk that way. Tears come, and I choke up, unable to say a single word.

"So, what's the fine print?" he whispers as if not wanting to alert any unwanted entities.

"If I want to linger on this planet, I go the full Monty. I'm a Fem of the highest order, taking *orders*, giving them. I don't say shit to Skyla."

His chest bucks. "So, that's what this was about. The reason he has you tied to Wesley's hip—you relaying whatever you wish from the enemy lines right into Skyla's ear at bedtime was simply a primer. He knows you're working for Skyla, and he wants to gain your trust. He wanted you to see the inner workings of his twisted mind, that of his son—Wesley—so that there aren't any big surprises."

"Only this time I keep my mouth shut. I'm not allowed to take my work home with me, or my heart shuts down, literally. This time I play by his rules. If I want to stick around—I'm his bitch, Logan. I have to commit. I have to reprogram my mind to work against my own people and pledge over to the dark side."

"Like your brother." His gaze drops to the ground.

Logan is the only brother I'll ever acknowledge in my heart.

"Like Wes."

"Only you'll have Skyla." He tosses up his hands. "You get to kiss her first thing in the morning and last thing at night. You'll have two beautiful kids to raise. Skyla can teach them right from wrong. All you'll have to do is keep your mouth shut."

A piercing howl goes off in the distance, and we ignore it. Logan comes in close, his eyes wild with anger, smoldering with disbelief at how far I've managed to wedge myself beneath Demetri's thumb.

"You really want my opinion?" he seethes as if he's sorry he has to give it. "Do it. Whether or not you're sitting on the throne makes no difference. Demetri and Wes are going to jam their bullshit down everyone's throats for as long as they're both in existence. Is it really going to make a difference if you sit there going along with it? At the end of the day, you don't have to contribute to the demise of the Nephilim people—just oversee it."

A strangled silence closes in on us as if there were nothing left to say.

"What about principles? What about morals and the foundation of things I believe strongly in? What about my alliance to the Nephilim, to Celestra—hell, to Levatio, whom I believed that I was one most of my life?" My voice shakes the sanctuary around us, disrupting the llamas to the point of stirring them through the corral in an uneasy rhythm. "What about staying true to myself and my wife and my kids? At what point do I say, okay, today I sell out?"

"Get over yourself." He starts to walk away before turning around. "It's a fucking job. Do you know how many people on this planet hate their fucking jobs?" Now it's his voice carrying over the expanse. "They hate their coworkers. They hate their boss. Hell, I have an idea—skip the Christmas party!" His eyes bulge with rage. "You have an opportunity to love Skyla until you both walk through that ethereal plane one last time and meet up with me on the other side." His voice softens. "You can shepherd your children, protect them from Demetri. You can have it all, Gage. Sure, it's not always going to smell like roses, but whose life does?" He shakes his head. "Is there really a choice to make here?" He takes a few steps into the darkness before the night begins to digest him. "Sleep on it. I know you'll do the right thing." He takes off for the house, sullen and uninspired to get there any quicker than he needs to. He talked a good game, but he left out one significant detail— himself and the sacrifice I offered to make for him. But Logan is selfless that way. He'll never admit that he needs Skyla, too. According to him—I have the kids. I win.

But I don't think I win, not in the way he's implying. This isn't the forever I had hoped for with Skyla, just a cheap imitation that has me compromising the hell out of my morals.

Logan is right. I need to sleep on it.

Skyla and I head home, and I make love to her like only a Big Bad Wolf can. She hits a record number of climaxes as her *I love yous* pour down into my thirsty soul like rain. Skyla sure makes the thought of leaving hard as hell. I don't think I can. With the babies, I don't see how I can even consider it.

I think I know what I need to do—have another talk with Candace. Let's hope this time I don't end up on the losing end of Devil's Peak.

Early in the morning, just as the sun crests the horizon, I land a soft kiss onto Skyla's forehead and carefully get out of bed. I head down and find Mia rummaging through the fridge, so I give her twenty bucks to make Skyla a pancake breakfast in bed and tell her I'll be back soon. It doesn't dawn on me until I see the taillight of Rev's motorcycle that Mia isn't up early. She's getting in late. Shit. I'll be sure to tell Skyla so she can have a talk with her sister, and I'll be having a conversation with good old Revelyn later. Or more to the point, my fist will. He'll be easy enough to find since he's still interning at the morgue with my dad. The idea of corpses has never creeped me out, but the idea of Rev around a bunch of corpses sends a chill up my spine. I don't care how psychologically grounded his father is, Rev is no mini Dr. Booth. This is one rotten apple that has rolled all the way off the damn farm.

I hop into my truck and head to Dudley's, giving a firm knock on the door until a groggy-eyed girl finally answers. It's not until she winces at me and gargles out my name do I figure out it's Lexy beneath that tumbleweed sitting on her head.

"What are you doing here?" we ask simultaneously.

She gives a superstitious look over her shoulder before letting me in. "Don't tell Logan."

I step in and catch a half-dressed Liam coming down the steps, and right behind him a partially nude Michelle Miller.

"What the?" I'm not even sure I want to know. "Dude." I shake my head at my uncle. "No. Two girls together spells out trouble like nothing else can."

"Speak for yourself." He rolls his head back and winces, trying to fully wake. He looks so much like Logan it makes me uneasy. Are Miller and Lex tag-teaming him for who he is, or who he looks like? At this point, I don't think it matters to anyone involved, least of all Liam's dick. Hope to God it doesn't fall off for his sake.

"I'm here to pick up Dudley."

"Pardon?" Dudley strolls in from the kitchen looking as if he's ready to take off for a business meeting.

"Look at you!" Lexy coos. "You always look so dapper. Do you even sleep?"

"No, dear, I've better things to do with my time than fade from reality." He hasn't taken his stern eyes off me. "What is it? Is it Skyla?"

"Yes." It's technically not a lie. "And I need you to come with me right now to fix it."

We head out, and I wait until I'm parked at Devil's Peak to lay it on the line.

"I need to talk to Candace."

"I'm sure you'll have a memorable time." He kicks open the door with his foot.

"Not without you I won't. I have questions, and she has the answers—and, unfortunately, only you can get me there. But don't do this for me. Do it for Skyla. You know she would want you to."

He pauses, partially out of the truck, and gives a dissatisfied grunt.

"You realize I'm only doing this for my spirit wife."

"That's all I'm asking." *My* wife, I want to correct him, but I don't.

The truck shifts from underneath me. The luminescent morning fog is traded for crystal clarity on a blue-sky day. The lake appears, then Candace, an irritated, hard-lined version of the woman I love.

"Yes?" She looks from me to Dudley, her hair sparkling like champagne. "Is there something I can help you with?"

I'd be lying if I didn't admit to being scared as hell. "I need some guidance, and I know that you're the only one who can truly give it to me."

"Ha!" She gives a quick sarcastic chortle. "Does you wife know of the insult you've just heaped on her? What is it you wish to hear?"

"Your opinion. You see, last year, I traded Logan's dead body for a very long life on Earth—to Demetri. It was my wish for a long life with Skyla, and those were his terms. I foolishly took him up on it."

Her brows rise as if I've just amused her.

"Demetri is willing to gift me a long life if I'm willing to turn a blind eye to the enemy's dealings."

Candace folds her arms over her chest as if considering the ramifications.

"How is this any different than your role today?"

"I'm free to tell Skyla whatever I wish about the Barricade, of anything I glean while haunting the underworld with Demetri and Wes. But should I agree to his proposition, that all ends. I'm to report for duty. My wicked service would be required, and I could tell Skyla nothing of what's about to happen to her—to my people."

She waves me off when I say *my people*. "Do you think your wife confides in you about all of her 'underworld' dealings?"

"Skyla doesn't have any underworld dealings. She's on the righteous side of the fence." I'd add *in case you forgot*, but I like not knowing what it feels like to have my balls struck by lightning.

"Wise," she muses. "And yet, foolish. What about Tenebrous? Has your bride confided in you regarding the infernal state of—"

"Your Grace." Dudley gives a slight bow. "Perhaps it's best we let Skyla deal with her property and who she cares to inform rather than offering it up ourselves like a delicious morsel of revenge?"

"Are you suggesting I'm a gossip?"

"Only if you're suggesting to speak of something that your daughter would loathe you breathe a word of."

Her eyes shine sharp as knives. Her hair illuminates bright as the sun for the briefest of moments. "Duly noted. Gage, you are on your own. Know this—your decision has the power to alter the lives of everyone on the planet."

"Everyone?" I was expecting there to be a rather short list with just two names on it. Logan and Skyla.

"Everyone," she flatlines.

"What's the right decision?" I press her for an answer that I can already feel she's unwilling to give.

Dudley leans in. "Let me give you a clue, Jock Strap—she's still Team Pretty One."

"Don't whisper about me as if I'm not in your presence," she grinds the words out, slow and even, her stern gaze never leaving my face. "And to answer your question, *Jock Strap*"—she says the obscure moniker slow as if trying it on for size—"what has your experience been like with Demetri so far? Has he disclosed to you the innermost darkest plans he's yet to initiate? Has he shown you the same love and care that the Nephilim people have offered? And what about Skyla? Has she confessed anything of Tenebrous? Was she outraged when she was nixed as the overseer of the factions as if the war never happened?"

My lids spring open wide. I can't take in this new reality fast enough.

"Wait—" Fuck. "What's this about secrets and Tenebrous?" Skyla hated the tunnels. She wanted that place closed forever. That's the reason she asked for it in the first place, isn't it?

"Certainly you and Skyla hide nothing from one another. How can you not know this? And your father? " she says it so fast I can tell she's relishing this. There's a touch of malice in her tone that's undeniable. "And, finally, did Demetri truly save you that day you fell from Devil's Peak, or was he the one to push you, and made it look as though it were me all along?"

My blood runs cold.

Shit. "Did he push me only to act as my savior?" My heart thumps so loud it echoes through my eardrums. I think I already know the answer.

A thin-lipped smile curves up her lips. "Isn't it just like your father to throw you in a fire and then douse the flames? How thankful you've been—how perfectly sincere in your acceptance of him. You're worried he'll pull one over on your children—and here you can't even help yourself. What real use will you be if you decide to stay? Who will it benefit in the end, really?"

I may not like Demetri, hell, I push aside the fact he tossed me over the edge quite literally a few months back just to try to rein in the anger I'm feeling toward Candace right now.

"What real use will I be if I stay? Who will it benefit?" I can hardly get the words out as my voice shakes with rage. "I'll be both useful and beneficial to Skyla and my children, that's who. I may not be able to save the Nephilim, but I think both you and I know that wasn't my course in life to begin with. I was made to love my family, and I already know, for certain, that alone is enough."

She lifts her chin, watching me from those long, thick lashes, pissed, still so palpably pissed.

"Now, if you don't mind, I'd like to see my daughter."

She glances to Dudley with a look that says *the audacity*.

Instantly, we're transported to a watering hole, a small lake. I can't quite make out the details. The periphery is lost in fog and soft light, but the focus, the true beauty of this new landscape, are the two little girls swimming in the water, a lanky blonde with a smile the size of her face, and a brunette with eyes the color of the bluest sky and a pair of hesitant dimples dipping in and out of her cheeks.

"Sage, look!" The blonde laughs as she holds up a bright pink starfish.

The dark-haired girl admires it for a moment before her friend tosses it into the water.

Sage. My heart melts and dies all at once. She's so beautiful. Her tiny features undeniably belong to Skyla. Those eyes, that dark hair—it's all me. There we are, a perfect combination of our love in a tangible form. Skyla and I made that tiny perfect being. Skyla and I are perfect. We belong together. Our family belongs together.

"*Sage*," I call out to her with my hands outstretched.

Dudley places his hand over my arms and slowly lowers them. "She can't hear you. This is simply a viewing."

And just like that, the ethereal plane dissipates, and we're sitting in my truck again, the Paragon fog filling the space between us, pecking at us as if asking where we've been.

"Did you get the answers you were seeking?" Dudley asks the question kinder than I would have imagined.

"I think so."

I think I gave them to myself.

Logan

A week into November, Emma and Barron decide to host a welcome-to-the-family dinner for Dudley. They've invited Laken and Coop, and both Laken's and Cooper's families. Liam has called both Michelle and Lexy to court, not sure how he's able to keep them both lassoed in his corral, but their underlying resentment for one another is shining through bright and clear. Ellis is here as Giselle's hard-to-shake appendage, and, of course, Gage and Skyla are here. Skyla shines like a gem, even if she's not convinced of it. Her beauty has only magnified over the last eight months. I didn't think it was possible, and here she's proving me wrong. Nev and Ezrina are present as Dudley's extended family, and it's actually starting out to be a pleasant night.

"So, do you think we can hit a movie later?" Kresley licks the rim of her glass, slow and seductive as she corners me in the living room. Oh, yes, how can I forget? Kresley and Grayson have set down roots by my side. Emma has been trying her best to fan the flames of love, but to no avail. I've proven harder to get than the Ark of the Covenant.

"I don't think so." And just like that, I run out of excuses and lies and other quick-fix remedies I've tried to get girls like Lex and Kresley to back off my dick. I'm not offering any more joy rides to Chloe, or anyone else for that matter. And both Lex and Kresley have made it abundantly clear they would be up for a quick and dirty romp, any way I like it, all night long. Except for the minor detail that Lex has stopped sniffing around ever since she's thrown her ponytail into my brother's ring. Liam, unlike *Logan*, uses and abuses his God-given reproductive equipment quite liberally. A thought comes to me. "I have erectile dysfunction."

Both Kresley's and Grayson's faces drop like stones. You would have thought I had just informed them sex was outlawed, and perpetrators would be executed on sight.

"And crabs." I hold a hand out as if pleading for their understanding. "The latter caused the former. But do you know who doesn't, and has been asking a hell of a lot of questions about the two of you, is my brother Liam." Grayson looks mildly confused, but Kresley is skeptical. "He's especially been asking a lot about you, Kres." I give a secretive nod as if suddenly we're old friends.

"Like what?" She leans in, her eyes never leaving mine as if she's far too interested in the subject matter to abandon the conversation.

"Like, what's your major—are you in grad school—things I have no clue about."

She bites down on her lip as she looks over at him. Both Michelle and Lexy are busy pawing at him, each on one shoulder shooting venomous looks to one another.

"Maybe I'd better head over there and fill him in on the facts." Kres takes off without waiting for a response.

"Me, too!" Grayson jiggles and wiggles behind her. Knowing my brother, he'll simply take both.

Skyla migrates my way while Gage settles into a deep discussion with Barron and Rev about the mortuary.

"I thought she'd never leave you alone. She's such a skank." Skyla cradles her belly from underneath with both hands as if she's literally holding it up. I can't blame her. It does look heavy.

Gage pops over. "Which one is the skank?" He eyes Liam's harem and shakes his head.

"Kresley, *Gage*." Skyla lays his name out hard as if he's done something wrong. "Speaking of Kresley, don't you have something you'd like to confess? I have been waiting and waiting, and yet, you choose to keep suspiciously quiet on the situation."

"What situation?" Gage has that deer-in-the-headlights look going. It's clear Skyla is gearing up to rip him a new one, and he has no clue why. And should I be here for this?

"The you-give-her-a-ride-home-from-your-night-class situation."

Gage opens his mouth, and his head tips back as if it's all coming together.

"Actually, I don't give her a ride home." He winces. "I do, but it's not like that. She lost her dorm and has been staying on Paragon, and it's just a few blocks from the ferry. She asked—my mother begged. What was I supposed to do?" His shoulders hike up clear to his ears. He's in major defense mode, and, as much as I'd like to look away, I can't seem to do it.

"I can't believe you!" Skyla swats him over the chest several times in a row, soft yet erratic. "I don't care that you're giving her rides, Gage. I care about the fact you decided not to tell me. It feels sneaky. I actually feel betrayed."

"Betrayed?"

I'd echo the sentiment, but I'm wise enough to stay out of it.

"Yes. You're letting this other woman get between us. Correction, your mother is coercing you into letting this other woman get between us, and I'm sick and tired of all her bullshit." She drills a finger into his chest. "How long are you going to let her manipulate our relationship like this?"

Oh shit. Skyla is flying off the handle, and maybe she has a right, or maybe it's all hormone induced, but I no longer care to bear witness.

"Excuse me," I say, backing up while frowning at Dudley from across the room because he happens to have a goofy grin on his quasi-related face. I'm sure he'd like nothing more than for Skyla and Gage to have a blowout in front of everyone.

"No, excuse *me*." She stalks off, waddling with her hands spread to her sides for balance.

"Dude, don't worry. She's just—"

Gage cuts me off, "Right. She's right. I should have told her. Even if she wigged out in the beginning, at least I would have known where she stood. It's just I didn't want to stress her out, and I didn't want to say no to my mom. She can throw a mean guilt trip when she has to."

"Don't I know it." Emma has lectured me profusely about how Skyla and I are right for one another and wanted explanation on how I could simply let Gage *steal* her away. It's true. Emma isn't a fan of Gage and Skyla. "What's up with

Liam?" I gesture over where the women of the party have gathered like pigeons, awaiting those magical breadcrumbs to fall out of his Levi's.

"You haven't heard?" Gage leans in, so this has got to be good. "Last week, I caught him with both Lexy and Michelle. Dude, this guy is getting some heavy hitting threesome action." His eyes are wild as if he doesn't approve, and neither do I.

"Shit." I let out a sorrowful sigh. "I'll talk to him." I have before but to no avail. "Threesomes? With Miller and Bakova?" We glance over at the two of them openly scoffing at each other. "They don't look too thrilled with the idea."

"I think it's all in the name of competition. Liam is a hot commodity, and they're doing what they feel they need to in order to snag the prize."

Kresley and her friend, Grayson, squeeze into their midst, and Michelle looks as if she's a moment away from clawing everyone's eyes out.

"The competition just got a little stiffer."

Emma calls us all to the dining room, which is a little more crowded than usual with tables connecting with tables, à la the Landon family get-togethers. Skyla sits by my side, and Dudley flanks her on the other end. Gage simply takes a seat next to me and doesn't flinch.

"I'd like to make a toast," I offer, holding up my glass, bidding the others to do the same. "If you didn't know, Marshall Dudley came to Paragon several years ago to serve as a math teacher at West Paragon High. He saw some of us at this table through algebra, geometry, trig, and calc, but mostly, he saw us through our formative years, and along the way offered some well-needed guidance. For this reason, I say thank you. And for whatever reason, you have always exuded a familial bond toward me. It's nice to know that even through distant relations we are just that, family. So with that, salute and thanks for the killer genes." I give a quick wink.

A round of cheers breaks out as we down our drinks. Dinner gets underway, and Skyla and Dudley begin discussing faction business, or lack thereof. Ellis leans in.

"Any more names we need to discuss?" he whispers it low enough where no one beyond me can pick up on it.

Skyla shakes her head and shrugs. "Let's have a meeting tonight to regroup."

"I think we need to," I agree.

Coop glances up from his rack of lamb as if we've aroused his suspicion.

"What's going on?" Gage nudges me in the ribs. Both Skyla and I exchange glances. It's not exactly a secret we're keeping from him, except at the moment it's obvious that it is.

Skyla reaches under the table and touches my bare arm. *Wow, and I was giving him crap over offering some skank a ride, three blocks in the rain? I feel like an asshole. I think we should come clean. You in?*

"Yes," I whisper. "Great meal." My hand taps over my stomach for show.

"Nice." Gage's eyes glaze over, somewhere between anger and resentment. "But you haven't touched your food. So, what's the story?" He directs the question to Skyla, but all she's able to do is open and close her mouth.

"We'll talk." It sounds cryptic when she says it, and I almost feel sorry for the guy. He spends the rest of dinner moping by my side, half-afraid that Skyla already has a foot out the door.

The rest of the meal ebbs by as Dudley regales us with story after story about our much-hyped highly diluted lineage. It occurs to me that somewhere down the line Marshall's DNA has interbred with Celestra. Why not give him dominion then? Why is Skyla the key to all of these masterful planes? Candace pops through my mind like a bolt of celestially charged lightning, and a picture comes into focus. A chessboard where all of the pieces look oddly familiar—all of our faces carved into bluish gray stone. This is nothing more than a well-orchestrated game. They need her. They need Skyla's special DNA to unlock whatever porthole leads to the next phase of celestial domination. Candace is the one that gifted Skyla this power. Put her in this unique position. I wonder what she gets out of it.

After dinner, Emma has us playing a round of charades until things get pornographic with Liam's coital circle. I want to shake my head at him, but a part of me wants to salute him. I miss sex. I miss sex with Skyla. I miss losing my mind, forgetting my name, what and who I was as my body readied to detonate inside her. I miss burying my face in her wild hair, in her wet heated slick that opened for me like a flower. I miss the smell of every inch of her body and wish I could wear it like perfume. I miss pressing my lips against her soft, very soft tits. The curve of her hip against mine. I miss the way her breathing quickened as she was about to lose her own mind from the way I was loving her.

A hand waves over my face, and I look up to find Emma with her hand on her hip. "Somebody was completely out to lunch. If I didn't know better, I'd say you were lovestruck." She gives an obnoxious wink. "It's your turn. You'll need a partner. Kresley? You up for some fun?"

"You bet!" She hops up and pulls a ticket from Emma's straw hat. It reads *bend over backwards*.

Great. I shoot Skyla a look that says *I'm sorry* before we ever begin, and, as expected, there is enough touching, feeling, squeezing, loving during that horrifically long ten minutes than my body will probably ever see again in my nonexistent life.

After midnight, Skyla calls a meeting of the Retribution League in the butterfly room at White Horse. There, at least she's using it for something. It's an exact replica of the original butterfly room at the Landon house, only about fifteen times the size. It's dim inside, save for the bevy of sapphire-colored butterflies illuminating the darkness. It's stunning, like a sky full of tiny angelic stars.

Skyla requested that I set up a round table and about ten chairs. It's the ten chairs part that has me worried since there are only four official members in the League as far as I know. It was a tight group with a laser focus, and now with more bodies to fill the seats, I'm afraid it'll balloon into a beast sooner than I thought.

"I don't really have a head count," Skyla says as she materializes into the room with Gage by her side. "So it's a give or take ten seats. I thought that might bother you." She pulls me into a quick embrace, her cheek searing over mine for a white-hot minute. *I pray to God Gage doesn't flip.*

I'm not sure if that was meant for me or not, but I nod in agreement. He won't. Gage is an encourager when it comes to Skyla and the Nephilim. I'm sure they'll hug it all out in a creative way later in bed. And I'm guessing with the size of her belly, they need to be very creative. An entire series of obscene images flash through my mind, and I swat them away.

There's a knock at the door, and Dudley shows, along with Ezrina and Nev, Laken and Coop, Ellis sans Giselle—thank God for small mercies—and Brody Bishop.

"Exactly ten!" Skyla marvels. "Everything is so damn hard to do these days with my pregnant brain. Math was never my strong suit."

"What's going on?" Laken asks as everyone finds a seat at the table. "We just saw you a few hours ago. This all feels kind of secret society," she says while wiggling her fingers, her voice dripping with sarcasm. "Are we here to throw baby names into the hat?"

"Nope." Skyla's features lose their softness, and she looks more like her mother than I'm sure she would ever want to. "You had it right the first time. Welcome to the Retribution League."

Gage cuts me a look that says *what the hell*, and I tilt my head toward Skyla. This is her baby. I'm going to let her roll with it.

"The only members thus far are Ellis, Brody, Logan, and me." She lowers her lashes as if confessing something dark and dirty. "I'm sorry I kept this from you, Gage. I don't know why I did, but I thought since I was opening up to you, there were a few others I wanted to let in on this as well." She casts a sweeping glance around the table. "I trust each of you not to say anything. Lives are at risk. I'm not too sure how the Justice Alliance would feel about this either."

"And that would be my cue to leave." Marshall stands and gives a polite bow. "Enjoy the rest of your evening—early morning as it were. I'm afraid I value my proverbial wings far too much than to ever become an accomplice. The Justice Alliance isn't nearly as lenient toward Sectors that go awry. You Nephilim can take up a fine-feathered friend, but we're relegated to less savory creatures, and at that just a few particular parts."

"Like donkey balls?" Ellis leans in, his eyes glazed into tomorrow, bright red, and it's not from a lack of sleep.

"Yes." Dudley has that look that says *I would like to stone you myself.* "Like donkey balls, Sir Harrison. Now, if you'll excuse me, I've research to do regarding the transference of my DNA. Ezrina and I will be conducting a few mundane experiments with you, Mr. Flanders." He turns and gives me the stink eye. "Oliver."

I'm amused by his word choice. "How come he gets to be Mr. Flanders, and I'm simply Oliver?"

"It's better than Jock Strap," Gage cuts in.

"Far more respectful than The Pretty One," Skyla adds.

Dudley's lids lower to the point it looks as if he's sleepwalking. "Perhaps you prefer The Not Chosen One, the Dearly Departed One, The One that Embroils Ms. Messenger in Mortal and Spiritual Danger Time and Time Again."

Crap. The last thing I need is Dudley's vengeance. "I prefer something that involves a bit more brevity." And I can't seem to let him win.

"Very well." His chin dips in an inch. "Dimwit or Ass. Take your pick." He evaporates into the darkness, leaving his fiery eyes as the last to go.

Laken shakes her head. "He's not one to mess with, is he?" She turns to Skyla. "And if he's not impressed with what's about to go down—should we be?"

Ezrina taps her nails, the color of dried blood, over the table. "End this misery."

"Excuse my lady love." Nev gives her hand a quick pat. "It's far past our bedtime, and Ezrina commands at least nine hours of shut-eye. You don't want to meet up with her with anything less." He gives her a sly wink, and her cheeks darken a shade. Flirting under the guise of an insult, huh? If I were Nev, I'd hide the cutlery.

"I'll make it short and sweet." Skyla fans her fingers over the table, exasperated before she ever begins. "A few months back, Gage showed me a list of names that were on Wesley's Immunity League. The fact Wes was teaming up with people from all walks of Nephilim life, all over the globe, made me insane with worry. And, well, I couldn't just stand around while he trained the best of the best to destroy my people." Her belly heats up a brilliant shade of blue, causing her face to glow a sickly hue, and yet, on Skyla, it looks magical, ethereal, and highlights those fairy-like qualities she's always possessed.

"What did you do with the people on the list?" Coop glances around at Brody and me as if he's onto us.

"The people have been missing for months." Gage ticks his head. "Did your Retribution League do this?" His voice spikes with worry, and yet, I'd swear there was anger layered just beneath the surface.

"We did." She faces him fully, her eyes locked onto his. "Gage—I had to. Wesley had them programmed to illicit paranormal activity. They were sending the world into a tailspin. He was infusing them with more power than they rightly deserve."

Gage swallows hard as if he's beyond worried and well into afraid. Why the hell is he acting so strange? I would have bet my donkey balls he was going to be the loudest in the cheering section.

"What happened to the people on the list?" Laken carefully clutches onto Coop's hand as if she needs it.

"They're somewhere safe." Skyla looks from Laken to Gage. "They're in Tenebrous."

"Shit." Gage closes his eyes a moment. "I gotta go." He rises from his seat.

"No." Skyla latches on to him, trying to pull him back down, but he takes a step back. "I have a meeting with the Videns. It can't be missed." Gage squeezes his eyes shut tight. "I don't think I should hear any more of this, Skyla. I'll see you at home. I'm sorry." Gage takes off, leaving a void of silence in his wake.

"What the hell was that about?" Ellis moans. "You two having a spat or some shit?"

Brody sighs. "He said he shouldn't hear any more. You think it's for the same reason as Dudley?"

Coop nods. "Only it's the Justice Alliance he's worried about. Is he a double agent?"

"He has been before," Ezrina points out.

Nev juts his chin out in a bird-like manner. "May I ask who might be running the tunnels? Do you need catering services?"

"We have it covered," I offer. "Ingram's signed on to help. But you can check with him as far as catering."

"Ingram." Ezrina contorts her features. "One minute you think he's on your side, and the next he's ratted you out to the Justice Alliance."

Nev leans in toward her. "I believe he had a bigger bone to pick with the two of us."

"Not to mention he's bound," Skyla adds.

It never occurred to us that Ingram would be trouble. Sloppy. Each time I forget to watch myself, I manage to put Skyla—everyone in this room, in a little more danger. And what about Gage? Is he the mole we really need to watch out for? Ezrina is right. He has been before. As far as I know, he hasn't taken Demetri up on the offer and crossed that line—yet.

"I can't." Laken rises. "You know what I did to shut those tunnels down." Her voice is shaking. "It's like you're spitting in my face." She plucks at Coop, and they head for the door.

"Wait! I promise it's not like that," Skyla pleads. "These are the bad guys."

Laken pauses. "With us running the tunnels, we're starting to feel a lot like the bad guys. I'm sorry, I just need to think about this."

She and Coop disappear down the stairwell.

"Good night, all." Nevermore hops to his feet. "I've an exhausted bride I'd best lay to rest."

"No rest for the wicked." Ezrina gives him that strange wink once again, and they take off with her giggling like a schoolgirl as soon as they clear the threshold. At least romance is alive and well at White Horse, even if it is relegated to the basement.

"That went well." Skyla slumps over her belly.

"Don't feel bad." I rub my hand over her back and feel the tension knotting up her shoulders. "The good news is that there are a hell of a lot less people out there putting the Nephilim in danger."

Brody gives a short-lived laugh. "They're dispensable. Have you noticed the names stopped coming? Lexy says there aren't any more meetings. She said the mass mutiny was bruising Wesley's ego. He's setting up something new, and you can bet your last green dollar that whatever it is, it's ten times worse. Face it, we've run from a lion, only to meet up with a bear."

"We're not giving up." I offer Skyla's shoulder a firm squeeze, and she moans into it as if that was just what she needed. "We'll figure out what he's up to and put that fire out as well."

"And how do we do that?" Ellis carries all the enthusiasm of a dental drilling.

I'm pretty sure that *I don't know* isn't the answer anyone wants to hear, so I'll keep quiet.

"Emily," Skyla says it calm. "I'll ask her to help. Her visions are divine. They're bound to tell me something."

"Whatever it is, I'm sure we'll hear of it soon." In fact, I know we will. We've pricked Wesley's ego, proven that he can be infiltrated, *discovered*, stopped in his tracks. We've emasculated him both physically and spiritually, as Dudley would say, and I'm not too sure one is more efficient than the other. When your ego is the size of the island, either way it has to hurt.

Ellis and Brody take off, and it's just Skyla and I staring one another down.

"You think we did the right thing, reopening Tenebrous?" Her voice is low and raspy as if she were trying to seduce me, but in reality, she's so damned depressed you can see the regret pooling in her eyes.

"Yes. It was the only thing we could do. They were murdering our people—about to cause a mass extinction for all we know. We had no other choice."

"What do you think Wes is going to do next?"

I glance down at that enormous belly of hers, glowing like molten lava.

"Are your powers still growing?"

"As much as the rest of me. Why?"

"I want to see if you have the gift of knowing."

Skyla's mouth falls open as she glances down, her belly sparking like blades sharpening against flint. She clutches her stomach as her eyes set on some faraway place. "Logan," she breathes my name. "I see it."

"What is it?"

"Wesley, no," she whispers as if speaking to him directly. The light in her belly goes out like the flipping of a switch as if she managed to drain it of all its power. Skyla looks up quick, worry rife on her face. "Oh my God, Logan." Her clear eyes round out over mine. "We may have made dozens disappear, but Wesley has done something with thousands."

"What?" I'm not sure I can wrap my head around the idea. "I haven't heard of thousands missing. It doesn't make sense."

"All I know is they went willingly, and now they're gone."

"As in he put them someplace?"

"No—as in dead."

Another week passes, a sluggish holiday that involves ungodly pounds of tryptophan occurred less than twenty-four hours ago, and I'm still stuffed as a turkey. Perhaps everyone else is, too, and that explains the fact the bowling alley has been dying a slow death all afternoon. It probably doesn't help that it's Black Friday. But more importantly, it's November twenty-second, one of my favorite days of the year because it just so happened to usher in the most beautiful girl in the world—about twenty years ago. Lizbeth asked if we could do a double birthday party here for Skyla and Gage tonight, and, of course, I said yes. She mentioned this was their special place, and I just grinned and beared it. Little does she know that this very bowling alley (I'm looking at you, lane number three) is where Skyla and I proposed to each other—first, her to me, and then, me to her.

Speaking of my former wife.

Skyla glides in wearing a stunning dress with a white hourglass cutout in the center and thick black bands on either side. I've memorized Skyla in this outfit from the last time she donned it. I remember its great illusionary powers. It gives the impression that she has a tiny hourglass figure. Ironic, since she does have more of an hourglass figure now than ever before, just not in the same sense.

"Happy birthday, gorgeous. You're looking good. Loving the hourglass. Can I say that?"

Giselle giggles. "You just did!" She's been hanging out all morning with Harrison and me, eating pizza and guzzling down sodas, talking about Ellis's new reefer farm as if it were the Garden of Eden. It's nice to see Ellis is such a good influence on her.

"I don't look gorgeous. I look huge." Skyla steadies herself against the counter as she takes a seat, her belly positioned to the side because it simply can't fit behind the bar anymore.

"You look perfect." I slide a cold water bottle her way.

"I look like a whale." She winces as she struggles to readjust herself.

Giselle's mouth opens with delight, her eyes widen with a dangerous amount of glee, and I shake my head at her. *No, Giselle, I want to say, do not go there.*

"You *do* look like a whale!" Giselle sings.

"No, she doesn't." I squint a nervous grin Skyla's way. Giselle should be out hitting the mall, scoring some deals on new school clothes to wear to West, not juxtaposing her very pregnant sister-in-law with the largest living marine mammal.

"Yes, she does." She nods with enthusiasm toward Skyla. "You do look like a whale. In fact, you look like an *orca*!"

"Shit," I mutter.

"Well"—Skyla's brows peak—"it seems you paid careful attention in science class." She's giving poor G the stink eye, but Giselle is too innocent to put the pieces together. "I think you would make a great marine biologist someday." She tilts her head as if hoping Giselle will take the bait.

"A marine biologist?"

"Yup. You can work right here from Paragon because we're surrounded by the big blue sea. You have keen observation skills, and I think you'd be a very valuable addition to the marine biologist community." Skyla shoots me a sly look before continuing. "They'd probably put you in charge of all the dolphins." She points to her belly because G is convinced that is exactly what Skyla just might birth.

Giselle sucks in a sharp breath, her hands suctioning over her lips. "Oh my God!" She fans herself spastically. "Dolphins are my favorite!"

"I know." Skyla shrugs. "They're everyone's favorite. And how lucky is it that you would be in charge of every single one of them? You'd be the dolphin princess. I bet they'd have T-shirts with your pretty little face on them."

Giselle stumbles back in shock, clearly taken with the idea of becoming the one and only dolphin princess.

"But"—Skyla shakes her head, forlorn—"you'd have to finish high school and then go to college. It would require some patience, and lots of hard work."

"I don't care what it takes." Giselle is hysterical with enthusiasm. "I'm going to go back to school right this minute!

College doesn't frighten me either. I'll go to Host and live in one of those scary dorms that Morley runs. I'm not afraid of anything. I'm going to do this, Skyla. Thank you. Thank you for making my destiny on this planet very, very clear." She gives a stoic nod. "It's not going to be easy, but I'm going to be the best dolphin princess that ever lived!" She takes off toward the breakroom. "Ellis? Ellis, I have great news!"

"Good job?" I'm not sure what to say.

"Thank you." Her demeanor sours.

"You do realize she'll glom on to this life mission. Emma is going to be ecstatic that you've motivated her daughter to get back in school."

"Emma hates me." She gives a dead look to the sweaty bottle in front of her. "And, Gage still won't talk about why he left so abruptly the other night. He says he wants to get on the other side of our birthdays before we go there. I'm beginning to think that Gage hates me, too."

"Who hates you?" Liam pops up from nowhere and slides next to Skyla.

"Never mind how people feel about me." She bumps him with her shoulder. "Rumor has it the ladies are really loving you."

"That they are." He flicks his fingers at me, and I toss him a soda.

"How do you plan on getting them to stop?" I ask, knocking that shit-eating grin off his face.

"Who the hell is going to make me?" His greasy grin glides up once again.

"Me." I deadpan. "Get over yourself. Pick one and stick with her. Love isn't some game. You're messing with hearts."

"I'm messing with bodies." He tips his soda my way. "Love is the furthest thing from anyone's mind. Trust me, the things they say in bed are hardly loving by anyone's standards."

"Threesomes, dude?" I forego the kind warning I was about to offer and go straight to pissed. "You're lucky they're tolerating that shit from you. Knock it off. We get it. You're a sought-after commodity. But you won't be for long."

"He's right," Skyla interjects. "As soon as they figure out that they don't really like taking turns hopping on pop, they'll go rabid, and it won't be pretty. Instead of having half a dozen girlfriends ready and willing to rumble—in a group setting apparently—you'll be all by your lonesome, left to your own devices to alleviate the tension." She casually glances at his hand currently wrapped around an aluminum can.

"Really?" He inches back as if she just slapped him, and in a way she did—she slapped him with his soon-to-be new reality. "Pick one, huh?" He stares off into space with a wistful look on his face.

Dudley walks in—looking for the birthday girl, no doubt.

"Look who's here," I say, leaning in toward Liam. "If there's anyone on this planet who can help you narrow your beautiful choices, it's him."

Liam hops up and heads over without wasting a second. That should buy me about five extra minutes with Skyla.

"Happy birthday, princess." The words trickle from me sad, and strangely victorious. Skyla was and will always be my princess.

Her cheeks take on a dark rose hue. "You already wished me a happy birthday."

"I haven't hugged or kissed you."

"Is that my gift?"

I'm about to say something when a couple walks in, and I clam up.

Shit.

"National security at six o'clock."

Her mouth falls open. "What do you think they want?" she whispers it heavy and thick with worry.

"I don't know, but they're headed this way."

"Skyla Oliver?" Agent Killion grins a wide, toothy smile, and that act alone unnerves me. "May we have a word with you a moment?"

Skyla looks to me with that what-should-I-do look on her face, and I give a slight nod. I'm standing right here, so I don't see the problem.

"Sure." She rubs her belly, and her entire dress lights up a brilliant blue.

Fuck.

"That's an interesting trick." Agent Moser grins like the Cheshire cat.

What the hell is up with all the grinning? Maybe they got their walking papers, and it's time to leave this overgrown rock. Although, thanks to Skyla's belly, they might have just found a reason to stay.

"Oh, it's not a trick." Skyla shakes her head a little too quickly.

Agent Killion tilts into her. "Your dress was white, and now it's blue. You're going to tell me that didn't just happen?"

"Oh, this old thing?" Skyla tries to pluck at the fabric, but it's stretched taut. "This is that stupid dress everyone was talking about on the Internet. Is it blue? Is it white? Some say it's brown." She shrugs. "I saw it and had to have it. Lucky for me, they come in el gigante." She laughs a little too loud.

"Well, this won't take a minute." Agent Killion thumbs through the apps on her phone until it's clear she's recording the conversation. "Agent Moser and I have been residing on the island for months now. We've interviewed a vast demographic of the populace and reviewed endless amounts of documentation, coming up with a single conclusion."

"Congratulations." Skyla goes for a smile, but comes up with a smirk. "Did you find Sesame Street? Because that's always been our best kept secret. Keep it low, would you? The last thing we need is to be overrun by a bunch of three-year-olds looking for the Cookie Monster. Ooh—" She taps the counter in front of me. "Do you have anything fresh baked? It's been an hour since I've eaten."

"They'll be ready in a minute." There's no way I'm leaving her, not even to fetch her a fresh baked cookie. I'll give her the entire jar once this trauma is through.

"No, Mrs. Oliver." Agent Moser loses his smarmy smile. "We discovered that true to what our superiors reported, Paragon Island is a hotbed of paranormal activity."

"Oh my God." She does her best to jump with surprise. "You mean to tell me, you found real live—or should I say dead—ghosts?"

I want to laugh because I happen to be one of those alive-dead phantasms.

Agent Killion looks as if she's beyond perturbed. "Something along those lines."

"Well?" Skyla holds back a laugh. "Who you gonna call?"

Neither Thing One nor Thing Two from the government institution of I-Hate-the-Nephilim is amused.

"They called *us*, Skyla," Moser informs her. "Our research led us to the west end of the island, to one person of interest in particular."

Skyla glances over her shoulder at Dudley, who seems oblivious to the situation, as he carries on a spirited conversation with Liam regarding the perils of a polyamorous relationship. Figures. He's an expert. I bet Dudley is reliving his own threesome glory days. It's no wonder they're related.

"The person of interest is you, Skyla." Killion ironically goes in for the *kill*. "All arrows point to your delicate frame. If you don't mind, we have a list of questions we'd like to go over with you." She pulls out a clipboard without waiting for Skyla to answer.

"Oh, I'm the furthest thing from a ghost." Skyla pats her belly. "In fact, as you can see, I'm brimming with life." The color dissipates in Skyla's cheeks for a moment before shooting back a brilliant shock of pink. "Wait." She gives a little laugh. "You're not trying to tell me that my babies are dead, are you? You mean, I have ghosts in my belly?" Her voice rises, and I give a nervous glance around to see if anyone heard her let the cat out of the bag. Only a handful of people know that Skyla is having twins.

"That's far from what we're saying." Moser leans over the counter, boxing Skyla in with Killion on the other side of her. "Mr. Oliver"—his rectangular features relax as he looks to me—"would you mind giving us a minute?"

"I'm not leaving." There. No head games.

"Very well." Killion doesn't look up from her notes. Something about her orange lips and matching hair manages to turn my stomach. "What deity or life form is it that you stem from, and how have you acquired your alien powers?"

"Alien?" Skyla shakes her head.

"We're using it in the general sense—as in not belonging to the norm," Moser assures. "You have powers, Mrs. Oliver. No point in denying them. We have them well documented. We have witness accounts. We have everything we need but your cooperation."

"Oh, I'll be cooperating"—Skyla's face lights up with color again—"with the *police*. I suggest you leave. In fact, Logan, please call Detective Edinger down here and inform him we have a stalking situation." Her voice pitches unevenly as she grabs on to her stomach and gasps. "Oh God."

"What's wrong?" I jump to the other side of the counter and blast through Moser to get near Skyla. "Is it the babies?"

"Yes." Her face turns a strange shade of blueberry as she bends her head back in obvious pain. "These two—" She points aggressively at them. "You did this! You've sent me into labor!"

"Nice try, Mrs. Oliver." Killion lands a fist on her hip. "We happen to know that you're not due for another few weeks. If you don't mind, we can narrow it down to five questions and schedule a more extensive interview for another time when you're feeling up to it."

Skyla struggles to rise, and I help her to her feet.

"I'm not faking this," she pants, holding her stomach with a look of agony on her face that I'm starting to believe. "The two of you are really fucking pissing me off."

Even I wince whenever she lets an expletive fly. Maybe I'm more like Dudley than I thought.

A loud splat lands over the dusty wood floor as if someone just launched a water balloon, and I glance down to Skyla's feet where a wide puddle has suddenly formed.

"My water just broke!" she shrieks. "Oh God, this is really happening." Tears brim in her eyes without warning.

Moser and Killion take a step in as if to inspect the glossy fluid.

"Get the fuck out!" I bark. "And don't let me catch your faces in here again."

Skyla lets out a hefty moan as they scramble their way to the door.

"Nice work." I give her a high five, and she's slow to reciprocate. "I think I'll nominate you for an Oscar this year. The statue, not the grouch." I glance to the water bottle still full on the counter. "How did you manage to pull that off?"

"I didn't." She swallows hard. "Mother Nature did." She gives a slight nod. "It looks like I'm about to have a baby, or two."

My body numbs with shock. My heart kick-starts back to life as I stand here holding her hand. Skyla is about to become a mother. Things are about to change for the rest of our lives. This is happening.

"Let's get you to the hospital." I help her to the door. "I love you, Skyla Oliver," I whisper, still trying to pull myself from my stunned stupor. "I'd do this for you if I could."

"I know." She pauses, giving my hand a squeeze that mangles me right down to the bone. "You may not be able to do it for me, but you will certainly be doing it with me."

My heart warms at the idea. I was hoping she'd ask. Hell, I know it's strange, but a part of me doesn't want to miss this. One thing is for sure—I'm scared as hell for Skyla.

"I heard that." She removes her fingernails from my palm as she takes a prolonged breath. "Only positive thinking or I'm calling Ghost Busters on your ass, Oliver."

"Duly noted. Have I ever told you that Logan can be used as a gender neutral name?"

We step out into the thick arms of the afternoon fog, and Skyla laughs.

It feels good like this with her, natural, and in the *mother* of all ironies, not one of these moments was meant for me.

I glance to the sky and think of Candace. If none of this was meant for me, she sure chose an interesting moment for Skyla to go into labor and an interesting person for her to be around once it hit.

For once, I'm glad to be the teacher's pet.

Candace has given me a gift, and I'll never forget this. Now to call Gage so he doesn't miss a thing.

A peal of thunder goes off overhead, and the ground gives a slight tremble—a celestial you're welcome if I ever heard one.

12

Babies Breath

Skyla

There are moments in life you anticipate, plan to the very last detail. This moment, this hugely anticipated life event was not supposed to go down like this. In a perfect world, I would have been at home—in bed with Gage. It would be too late to bother my mother, thus avoiding the hurricane of panic that would inevitably ensue. Gage would have calmly grabbed my overnight bag (which I was totally going to pack this weekend). We would drive to the hospital in his truck—oh, wait. Crap.

"Where exactly are you taking me?" I pause in the parking lot of the bowling alley, staring at Logan's white truck as if it were a threat.

"The hospital." His eyes are wide with worry, his knees slightly bent, his hands spread over my belly as if he's on high alert to catch the babies should they decide to fall out. "There's just one on the island. That is the one, right?"

"Oh, that's right. Just the one." Oh God, oh God, oh God! There have only been two nonsensical fears of mine that have managed to plague me well beyond my preteen years, and those were clowns and hospitals. I would say I'm ninety percent over my fear of clowns (It was a hundred until Marshall threw that ridiculous circus-themed party last month, and I managed to take a giant leap back), and then there are hospitals.

A sharp, searing pain stretches over my stomach, tight like a noose strangling my belly. "Oh, wow, this is going to hurt like a son of a bitch." That wily Sector flits through my mind. "Son of bitch! *Marshall*. We need Marshall!"

We turn to find Marshall and Liam already jogging out of the bowling alley. The expression on my face must say it all because they both look well apprised of what's about to happen.

"Skyla." Marshall takes ahold of my arm and—oh my shit.

"Where is it?" I snap, looking into his blood boils for eyes. "I am not amused. Do not fuck with me. This is painful, Marshall. More so than anyone with a penis will ever comprehend. Now get those oh-so-happy vibrations happening, and let the good times roll!"

Liam ticks his head back an inch. "Is that code for I'm really having the babies?"

"No," Logan flatlines. "The code for that was in the puddle she left near the counter. Can you get Ellis on that?"

"Sure thing." He offers me a quick pat to the arm. "Congratulations, little mama. I'll get on the horn and contact Emma and Barron. I'll call your family, too. It's time to get this party started!" He lets out a barking howl before heading back into the bowling alley.

"No, wait!" I squeeze my eyes shut as another contraction comes on, far more vicious than the last. I was about to tell him to stop, to please refrain from alerting the cavalry. The last thing I want is my family, worse, *Emma* breathing down my neck for the next fifteen hours while I try to figure out a way to escape my body.

Marshall and Logan usher me to his truck—and, through a Sector-based miracle, Marshall hoists me into the passenger's seat.

"Where is it?" I moan, not willing to let go of his big, strong hand. "Where are your feel-good vibes?"

"Skyla"—he leans in so close his breath tickles my cheek—"it appears someone has decided that my 'feel-good vibes,' as you say, would be inappropriate in this situation." He gives a quick glance upward.

"Oh my God!" I scream the words until my throat shreds raw. "*Mother!*" My voice shrills into the stubborn iron sky, but not even the clouds bother to part for me.

"I'll be with you," he assures.

"Oh no, you won't! Go to her and plead, plead, *plead*!" I sob out that last word. "And don't come back without your powers." I cup his cheeks and pull him in. "This is a direct order from your leader."

He gives a crooked grin. "You are not my leader, Ms. Messenger."

"Then it's a very heartfelt request from your future wife."

"Now that's something I can work with." He presses a tender kiss to my cheek. "Be strong. I'll be back."

"Spoken like a true terminator of my hope." I sag into the seat as he dissipates. "My mother isn't going to give an inch." Another contraction comes, and I breathe my way through it just the way my earthly mother taught me. Lizbeth Landon would never withhold anything from me, let alone *feel-good vibes* in my most desolate hour. A brief visual of my mother spending countless hours attempting to brainwash me into going "natural," feeling every little morsel of love that nature is willing to gift me comes back to mind, and I quickly eschew the thought of venerating my earthly, slightly sadistic mother.

The pain knifes through me, with its white-hot razor's edge, sawing me in half, burning me to my core with an intense level of agony no human should ever have to endure. It's horrible. Unthinkable. *Completely* sadistic. Pain to end all pain. Chloe was right. I would never wish this on my worst enemy. My breathing hits a crescendo. Thank God Almighty I was halfway paying attention during all those breathing lessons because, holy wow, this feels like a belt of fire just cinched around my swollen belly. Then, as if on cue, my entire abdomen lights up blue like a Christmas tree.

"No, no, no," I moan as Logan dodges through traffic fast enough to get us both killed, well, me and my anxious-to-get-here children. "Maybe you should slow down."

He hangs a hard left. "No need." He slips into a parking stall and expels a toothy grin. "We're here." His gaze drops to my stomach, which is busy bulging like an overgrown sapphire. "Oh shit." His voice spikes. "Can you turn it off?"

"Don't you think I would have done that by now?"

"Okay, okay, we got this." His hands fly to his temples because we so do not *got* this. "I'll call Dr. Booth." He gets on the phone.

"He's a psychiatrist. The human brain and my vagina are on two very different playing fields."

"Yes—hello?" he barks into the phone. "Skyla is in labor. She's—her stomach is glowing like a blue fucking moon. Is there any way to get ahold of a doctor who happens to be one of us?"

Why didn't I think of this? And much, *much* sooner, might I add.

"Great." His face irons out with relief. "We'll wait." He hangs up much to my horror.

"We will not *wait,* Logan! You and I might decide to wait, but these babies are currently trying to squeeze their way out of my uterus. I've got news for you, Oliver. Nobody in there wants to wait."

A quiet smile presses from his lips as if it took great effort on his part. "He said there's a board for this. He's having a doctor summoned as we speak. As soon as he calls, we'll head on in."

A severe flashback of Chloe giving birth in the woods comes to me. I can't usher these babies into the world in the cab of Logan's pickup. This is insanity!

"Call Gage." Just the thought of talking to Gage sends a mild sense of relief through me.

"Gage?" He looks momentarily confused as if he has no idea who this Gage person might be. "*Gage!*" Logan's phone slips from his grip a moment until his fingers swipe the surface. "He's not picking up." He shoots him a text and flashes it to me before he hits *Send.*

"Great." I close my eyes. "The one time I desperately need him, and his phone is who knows where."

A sharp knock emits over my window, and we glance over to find a handsome, dark-haired man whom I wish to God would morph into my husband.

Logan rolls down the window to a grimacing Dr. Booth.

"I was in the area." He winces at me. "I'd ask how you were feeling, but I can see that you're blue."

"Please, no psychiatric humor." Although, it did add a bit of levity to the situation.

"There's a nurse named Allegra on duty. She's a Deorsum. I explained the situation, and she's ready to greet you. In the meantime"—he passes a navy blanket through the window—"I keep this in my car for emergencies. This, I suspect, is one of them."

After a tussle with my seatbelt, both Dr. Booth and Logan help extract me from the truck and to the door of this dreaded medical architectural wonder. The large, *dirty* mind you, glass doors whoosh open, and a blast of ghastly hospital breath overcomes me.

"Why does it always smell like ketchup and rubbing alcohol in these kinds of places?" I retch without meaning to.

Dr. Booth gives a quiet smile. "Because it needs to be regularly disinfected, and the hamburgers are better than you'd think."

Another contraction hits, and I breathe in and out like I'm desperately trying to blow out the last candle on my nonexistent birthday cake. The idea of a smile comes to me as the pain begins to subside.

"I just thought of something," I pant. "I'm going to have these babies on my birthday!"

"Babies?" Dr. Booth chortles a small laugh as he helps me into the elevator.

"Surprise." I give a lame smile. So much for keeping it a secret, although, soon enough, the entire world will know.

"You could have them on Gage's birthday." Logan shrugs. "But that's like ten hours away."

"No thank you. The sooner these babies and their happy feet exit my womb, the better. I can't handle a contraction stronger than that last one."

We exit onto the labor and delivery floor, and Dr. Booth escorts us past the security doors marked for expectant parents and staff only.

"Allegra." Dr. Booth flags down a tall, waif-like nurse with a face that vaguely reminds me of Ellis. I've always suspected he'd make a decent looking girl.

I take the fact that the nurse standing before me is named after a popular medication as a very good sign of pharmaceutical things to come. We follow her through the bowels of the labor and delivery unit, amongst the unmistakable shrieks, the screams, the primal calls for help. The moaning, the groaning, the drumming of robotic machinery—it all has a bit of a human torture chamber effect. The smells, the unholy sights and sounds remind me a little too much of Tenebrous—back when the Counts still held the keys. The unit itself is cold and sterile, with its neutral walls, laminated counters. There's a giant white board in the back with patients' names jotted down like a human grocery list.

Nurse Allegra helps me to a room and hands me a gown to put on—open in the front. Dr. Booth offers a gentle side-hug before leaving, and soon it's just Logan and I—a yellow worn-out gown taking up the distance between us. Tears come, and I begin to silently sob.

"It's okay." He rubs my back. "You're here, safe. We made it." His heated, tender breath strums over my neck. "There's nothing else to do but relax and bring those babies into this world."

The warmth of his cologne envelops me like an old friend, and I linger in that scent that's shared so many memories with us.

"That's not why I'm crying. I can't take off my dress." Okay, that was so why I'm crying, but admitting to it would have only made things worse. And where the hell is Gage?

Logan helps with the task of stripping me down.

"Please don't laugh," I whisper as he plucks off my shoes. My feet are so swollen he actually grunts before taking off the left one.

"I would never laugh at you. I think you're beautiful." He inches up my dress, and his lips twist as it bunches around my belly. "How exactly did you get this on?"

"I had gravity working in my favor." I lift my arms. "Let's see if physics can help me out of this one."

Logan tugs, and tugs, and *tugs* before it finally suctions off my body, allowing the air in the room to cool me.

"Ah, that's better," I coo, opening my eyes to a startled Oliver.

"You're magnificent," he says with his eyes glued to my extended navel.

"*Gah!*" I cry as soon as I spot my granny panties, the size of a hot air balloon. "I'm so embarrassed." Please, God, kill me now.

"Don't be." Logan lovingly places the gown over me, and I pull my arms through it.

He gives a few tugs to my underwear, and I help shimmy them off.

"There. You're ready to party." He helps me climb onto the bed, and the nurse comes in, hooking me up to a myriad of beeping, burping machines. She wraps a Velcro band over my belly like she's strapping me to a bomb, and then, right on cue, a contraction kicks in.

"Look at that climb," she says admirably while pointing to the monitor. "Yes sirree, Bob! This is going to be a big one!"

"I need drugs." I press the words out through panting. My hand clasps onto Logan's so hard I squeeze him to the bone. "Where the hell is Harrison?" My voice hits its pinnacle right along with my contraction.

"Skyla." Logan does that thing with his brows—the one where he so desperately wants to communicate his disappointment with me. "I promise, I'm not disappointed. Ellis can't give you anything."

"That reefer field of his begs to differ!"

A smile tugs at his lips, but he refuses to give it. "I won't let him."

The nurse averts her gaze. "I guess whenever you're ready, I'll contact the anesthesiologist."

What's with the attitude?

The door flies open, and, like a human piñata, in spills every single familiar face I've ever seen. Mom tags me first like it's some playground game both she and Emma were engaged in. Mia and Melissa quickly pull up a chair facing my privates as if they don't want to miss a minute of *The Rocky Horror Vagina Show*. Drake and Bree brought snacks that smell like stewed feet, and Ethan and Em showed up with matching looks of mild boredom. Tad and Barron hold up the rear, hardly able to squeeze into the tiny space. Tad has both Beau and Misty attached to him, a first as far as I know, and Barron is sporting a rather large camera with a lens as long as a baseball bat.

"Whoa." My legs clench at the thought of me having to entertain everyone in here by way of opening wide. "I'm fine. I've got this. And where are Ellis and Giselle?" They're the only ones I truly want to punish with my prenatal peep show.

Emma pats my hand. "In the gift shop, buying some balloons to surprise you with."

It's hard not to roll my eyes at my mother-in-law routinely.

"More importantly"—she leans in a with a stern look that frightens me just a little—"where is my son?"

"That's what I would like to know."

"Did you call him?" Her eyes widen as she spots Logan's fingers interlaced with mine, and she gasps as if she were affronted.

"We can't get ahold of him," Logan offers. "Would the two of you go check out his usual haunts? He needs to be here. His phone is probably dead."

Emma and Barron scuttle out in a flurry of flailing arms and shouting. I think I actually heard Barron curse at his only son and his "idiotic phone." It's clear they want Gage here as much as I do. I'll be the first to say this is ridiculous. Gage, who never missed a single doctor's appointment, would die before he missed the birth of his children. *Gah!* God, what if he's dead? He had better be dead. I'm quick to evict the thought from my mind.

"You're getting another one!" Mom belts it out with the enthusiasm of a World Series umpire. This is the big leagues— her playing the field, and, judging by that look in her eyes, she plans on running a play-by-play.

"Nurse!" I scream with everything in me, as the dough-faced girl appears without incident, ready and waiting for duty. For once, something in my life seems to be on track. "Go ahead and call the anesthesiologist. I'm more than ready to have my entire body, every hair on my head numbed to oblivion." I squint into the blinding pain that's overtaking my body. This one is a far cry from the last few, and those were steadily more significant than the ones prior. "Oh *God*."

"Don't hold your breath!" Mom sounds off like a drill sergeant. "Breathe the damn thing out, Skyla." She pants right along with me, and I ride that thorny wave until I see the needle on the monitor mercifully decline.

Holy mother of God.

"*Okay*." I can hardly catch my breath. "I'll need to see him quick," I pant to the nurse who seems mesmerized by all the bells and whistles attached to me.

"You will not!" My mother gives a dark laugh. "No grandchild of mine will be brought into this world, sleepy and weak from narcotics. We expect a bright-eyed and bushy-tailed bright pink bundle of joy, not an infant with the shakes and a glazed look in its eye."

Holy shit. Is she for real?

"All newborns have a glazed look in their eyes!" I shout so loud my voice rubs raw. "*Bree*!" It's clearly time to call in the reserves.

"I'm so proud of you!" Brielle skips over as if I've done something worthy of her praise. "You two are going to make great parents." Tears glisten in her eyes. Her face is flushed with a genuine sentimentality that has me questioning if she's chemically altered herself. Hey, maybe Bree brought the drugs.

"This isn't Gage," I say sweetly. "We can't find him."

"I know, but Logan is just as good. At this point, they're practically interchangeable."

Logan's brows rise in amusement.

"Would you stop?" I scold. This is no time for Bree and her ditzy ways.

The monitor burps, and Mom gives a hard clap. "This is the big one!"

Oh God! Not the big one!

Tad hustles over and inspects the screen, and just the sight of him annoys the ever-living shit out of me. Too bad it couldn't annoy two babies out of me a little quicker. And why the hell is everyone in this very room? I begin on my breathing, following the rhythm of my mother's—who has managed to embarrass me freshly in front of Logan in ways I never thought possible. Her eyes are enlarged, her mouth puffing in and out like a blowfish. Her arms flap like wings, and dear Lord, am I supposed to do that, too?

Then, in an instant, the pain ratchets up to alarming new heights, sharp, piercing, blazing-hot agony that paralyzes me from any further panting—hell, it just extinguished any desire in me to ever breathe again.

"*Kill me,*" I mouth to Logan. **Kill me right fucking now!** I scream internally.

"Do something," he barks at the nurse who continues to stand by like a wooden soldier, simply studying the graph that stupid machine spits out. How dare she! As soon as Dr. Booth hears about this, her Deorsum ass is fired. I'm canceling her membership to Nephilims United—revoking her powers as soon I can. I'll make sure she gets one hell of a vacation in the tunnels for a good long while, right after I encourage Ingram to make her his boneyard bitch.

"Would you like medication?" She nods to me with a blank stare as if this were a topic we hadn't broached before.

"*Yes.*" My voice comes from me deep, unrecognizable as if a demon had stepped in to answer for me, and nurse Allegra scuttles out the door. "Thank you!" I squeak as my bodily torture tones it down for a moment.

"*Skyla*! You can't have drugs. I won't let you!" Mom spits it out, desperate. "Do that thing, Tad! The one that got me through the thick of it."

"Your wish is my rear's command." He lets one rip so loud and toxic the room clears out, save for Mom and Logan. Hell, I would have run far and fast had I been able.

"Oh my fuck." I sink a little on the mattress. I take it back. My mother is not the embarrassment. It's Tad.

"Make them leave—all of them," I say it weak to Logan.

"Skyla!" Mom sits on the edge of the bed and swiftly pulls back the covers until she's cradling my bare feet in her hands. "If I leave, who's going to do this?" She starts in on what I'm guessing was meant to be a massage, but ends in a tickle-torture routine that promptly initiates the mother of all contractions. I'd kick her into tomorrow, because both Logan and I know how lethal my feet can be—but my body is currently frozen. I'm holding my breath again, and Logan taps my lips lovingly and does the same with his until I'm fully focused on his beautiful whiskey-colored eyes.

"Breathe soft with me, slowly, in and out." **None of that panicked shit.**

I hear that last part, but I don't think it was meant for me.

Mom points to Tad, and he lets another one rip. She gives a soft giggle, momentarily pausing from the foot strangulation she's pursuing. "Oh, I laughed each time he did that." She reminisces with the flick of her wrist. "I would get down on my hands and knees, and he'd get right in front of me. And, at first, I thought a dog was barking, but when my nose told me different, I laughed. Oh, how I laughed. It took the edge off right away."

I give Logan's hand a bone-crunching squeeze. *I will never forgive you if you don't toss them both out on their insane ears right this minute.*

"But then, I got called to work." Tad folds his arms across his chest proudly. "When duty calls, Tad Landon answers. Althorpe relies on *me* to get things done."

Mom lifts a finger to his point while Logan continues to help me breathe my way down this mountain of treachery.

"Good thing Demetri was willing to step in," she continues. "He lit candles and warmed the tub with a kettle. It was all so very cozy." She sniffs at the surroundings. "Not sterile and cold—the smell of antiseptic clinging to your clothes. The first breath this child takes will not be the freshest."

No thanks to Tad.

And really? Antiseptic? She has a bag of gas exploding in her face, and the scent of rubbing alcohol is what sets her off? I would rather *drink* a gallon of rubbing alcohol than have Tad exploding anything from his rear orifice—in my face no less.

"You did it." Logan presses a kiss to my forehead before turning around. "I'm going to have to ask all of you to step outside for a few minutes. She just needs some quiet time. Lizbeth? Would you mind seeing if the cafeteria has a decent cup of coffee?" He drops a twenty onto her lap. "Maybe you and Tad can grab a bite first, get your energy up."

Her mouth opens to protest, but Tad shuttles her toward the door, giddy at the prospect of a free meal. "This hospital is rated in the top one hundred in quality care—that includes the kitchen staff, Lizbeth! I think we're in for a culinary treat."

"Labor is going to take hours—days maybe," I assure my mother.

"I'll be right back!" she wails as they head out.

"Dear God, bolt the door." I check the floor to see if this has turned into a sanitation issue—what with my mother barking at Tad to shit his pants on command.

"Logan," I moan, pulling him in close until his head is over mine. "Help me. Make sure I get the strongest damn drugs on the planet—or just knock me out. In fact, do it now before I have another contraction. No one will have to know. I swear, I won't say a word, and I'll never press charges. Belt me right now"—I point to my chin—"put me out of my misery."

He gives a soft chuckle. "Skyla, I would never hurt you."

"You're hurting me by letting me remain conscious!"

Tears come to his eyes. The room stills around us for a moment. It's just Logan and I—and my body's diabolical need to punish itself for failed anal sex with Gage.

His eyes round out the size of eggs.

"Oh, sorry." I give his hand a tug. "It's true. This is all Ellis's doing. It was a condom issue. He and Giselle should be here to experience every last drop of the bloody baby fun."

THE SERPENTINE BUTTERFLY

Before he can respond, my body starts in on that excruciating pinch once again, and a viral panic goes off in me.

"Remember that time you switched bodies with Ezrina?" Logan combs the hair out of my eyes, and I give a furtive nod because I like where he's going. "Maybe this would be a good time to look into that. Only I think you should switch bodies with Dudley."

"Ha! My mother will never agree to that. It's hopeless, isn't it? I have to do this." The machine chirps, and the needle starts its inevitable climb. "I would give every pint of blood in my body to the Counts to make this stop. Oh, I know!" I sit up as far as I can. "Text Wesley! He'll think of something. You and I both know my mother is relishing the fact she gets to shoot down Marshall. It's me who she's really punishing. She hates me. She's making this ten times worse than it needs to be." My finger fumbles with the buttons on the bedrail, and I spastically hit the diagram of a nurse's hat. "And where the hell is that nurse?"

The contraction sinks me in its icy pit of agony, and I keep my eyes glued to Logan as our lips pant for our lives in tandem. Logan Oliver is my savior. If anything, this bodily torture, this abject misery, has bonded our souls onto one another in ways that sex and marriage and perhaps even love simply couldn't. There is no way that I could even have considered not jumping from the window—which incidentally I noted is hermetically sealed with chicken wire. I'm sure they've had a woman or two "put a crack in it—to get some fresh air." This is hell on Earth—a living sacrifice to bring forth life into this world. Chloe comes to mind, alone in the woods, save for her worst enemy whom she wouldn't have wished this on. And for a tiny moment, the briefest of them all, my heart weeps for her. There wasn't a nurse or the promise of an anesthesiologist in those woods. There wasn't a warm and burgeoning crowd of family ready to offer their love and support—and bodily functions. Chloe literally has no one. And then, just like that, the contraction subsides, and I'm right back to seriously disliking the skank who killed my father and this beautiful man holding my hand.

"You don't have to hate Chloe." Logan gives a sad, lopsided grin. "It's not important. Hate takes too much energy, and Chloe isn't worth it."

"Right. I should pity her." Too bad for Chloe because I only seem capable of pitying people I like. "So, what do you think happened to Gage? He said he was going to get some work done at school, but he was supposed to be back on Paragon an hour ago. He was already late when I walked into the bowling alley." And here I thought that was simply code for running out and getting me a last minute birthday gift or a bouquet of flowers.

Logan shifts uncomfortably. He suspects foul play. I can tell by the way he's trying to shrug it off as if it were no big deal that Gage is missing out on the most important moment of our lives.

My mother comes back and swoops around me as the hours run out on the day.

That demon of a machine ticks like a bomb, and my body decides to cut to the chase and get right to the good part.

"Oh God." My chin dips to my chest as Logan begs me to breathe it out with him. "How could he do this to me? I never want him or his penis around my body again!" My voice warbles into a whine as I dig my head back into the pillow. "All he did was enjoy one short-lived orgasm, and my body has had to pay for it ever since! And now he's not even here doing the hard part with me!" Tears sting as they trail down my face. "He was supposed to be here toughening my nipples." I sob through the pain. "And showing off those damn vibratory skills his demonic father gifted him." My eyes spring wide as a thought comes to me in the height of my delirium. "Demetri!" I shout between hiccupping bouts of panting. "Get him down here!" I nod to Logan who's holding his finger to his lips, still breathing even-keeled.

"Don't you shush me!" I let out a horrific cry, joining the labor and deliver choir a little sooner than expected. As soon as this infernal fire in me dies down, I dive into Logan's jeans and excavate his phone. I put in a spastic text to Demetri that says **GET GAGE AND DRUGS, YOU**

MOTHERFUCKER! And then a group text to Harrison and Giselle. **Get up to my room quick! They're handing out morphine like candy! And DOLPHINS!**

It doesn't even make sense, but with those two, it doesn't really have to.

Within thirty seconds, Ellis and Giselle burst through the doors with pink and blue balloons, along with two giant Mylar monstrosities that read *It's a Boy!* And the other *It's a Girl!*

"Covering your bases?" Logan slaps Ellis five.

Giselle springs to my side. "Where are they?" She pecks her gaze around the room, her eyes glowing with delusional delight.

"Oh, they're coming. You and Ellis should have a seat. Trust me, you don't want to miss a thing."

"Really?" She clutches her chest. "Oh, Skyla, this is the best day ever!" She pulls Ellis toward the peanut gallery set up at the foot of the bed.

"You're not moving, Harrison." It comes out a little gruffer than intended. "I'm having these babies because of *you*, so it's only fair you get to witness their birth. Not only that, but Gage is so not over the fact you're doing his sister."

"Ellis and I love to do things together." Giselle gives a dreamy smile to the stoner in our midst.

"Do you like those special hugs that Ellis gives you?" Ridiculous code for sex in my opinion. Ellis is practically a predator.

"Skyla!" Giselle blushes fifty shades of embarrassed. "I won't talk about those things. Not with my uncle in the room." She mouths *sorry* over to Logan.

"I think what Skyla is trying to say"—Logan glances to me for a second—"is that what you're about to see is what can happen to girls who get those special hugs. It's a very natural part of the human experience, and she's really glad to share it with you." He glares at Ellis a moment. "With both of you."

"Shit," Ellis whimpers, wiping the sweat off his brow. "I might need a barf bag."

The needle spikes again, and my contractions start in wild and mean. It's going to be a hell of a night if these babies don't get here soon.

Long stretches of time pass. The nurse comes back in with my mother, and I have the sudden urge to throat punch both of them.

"Is he coming?" I wail to the nurse.

Mom touches her cool hand to my forehead. "The Olivers are still looking for him."

"Not *him*." Who the hell cares about Gage at this point? As far as I'm concerned, he's no more than a sperm donor who long since fulfilled his part of the bargain. "The doctor!" My voice breaks. "Dr. *Drug*." My mind is so warped and twisted I can't even remember what kind of doctor he is.

Nurse Allegra gives Logan a side-glance. "There's been a slight delay, but I assure you he's on his way."

Shit. "On his way from where? The Mars expedition?"

"The mainland." She smiles as if this were great news. "He's in the middle of a back surgery in Seattle."

"Seattle!" I sob into the word. "It might as well be Mars."

"Oh, hon," Mom coos before looking to the nurse. "What are her stats? Is she dilated? Is she effaced? Her water broke hours ago. My daughter is not going to have a dry birth."

"That's why I'm here." The nurse gloves up, and her hand is quick to disappear beneath my gown. Her roaming fingers enter my body rather unceremoniously and set off a nuclear bomb of a contraction. FUCK! Swear to God, I want to kill her by way of shoving more than my lethal foot in her face. In fact, I've just added slaughtering both her and the anesthesiologist (Just remembered!) onto my to-kill list. Gage is surprisingly at the top with Tad cluttering the bottom for tooting his way into my birthing experience.

Allegra jumps as if she just won the lottery while her hand remains steadfastly embedded in my body. "Ten centimeters and one hundred percent effaced!"

"You can stop fisting me now," I growl through the pain.

Both Mom and the nurse scream with glee, exchanging high fives like they were old college buddies with bets on the game. Only too bad for me because I'm still holding the ball—*balls*—in this one-woman sport.

"No need for the anesthesiologist now." The nurse gives a knowing nod to my mother.

"Thank heavens we evaded that nightmare!" Mom is equally on board with this complete nonsense.

"What?" I wail. "*No*! Don't cancel a thing! I still want it! I want all the drugs he has to offer! I'm a pill popper, too! It doesn't have to be a needle." Because, dear God Almighty, I hate them.

The nurse frowns, still fishing around in my body like she lost an earring in there. "No one's dropped into the canal yet."

"Oh hell." Mom panics. "We'll need to do some nipple stim." She shakes her head while eyeing my chest.

"Oh no, you don't." I cinch the fabric around my chest.

"Normally, I would ask Gage to do it, but since he's up and done a disappearing act, I'll have to step in." Mom peels open my gown, exposing my oversized breasts as if this was totally acceptable—but, then, this is her we're talking about.

"Logan!" I cry as the pain amps up, so hard, so fast I can't breathe.

The next thing I know, fingers are twisting my nipples, and I look down, horrified to see that the hand is rather masculine in nature, rough to the touch, yet gentle considering the circumstances. Logan! Gah! I shake my head, and he retracts.

"One in the hole!" the nurse belts out. If I didn't have a lead weight between my legs, I'd kick her.

"Go ahead and push!" Mom roars like a ravenous bear.

"You can do this." Logan smiles at me sweetly while wiping the hair from my sticky face.

"Come here." I press his forehead to mine, as his panting cools me. "Logan," I whimper, digging my fingers into the back of his neck. Logan has become an extension of my body, my soul in these last few grueling hours.

I bear down, girding myself for the birth of my first child. A life that Gage and I created—*bastard* as he shall be known to me from this day forward—but, still, it's a token of our undying affection robed in flesh and blood. I push so hard I'm shocked I don't have an aneurysm right here on the spot. And nothing. The contraction subsides, and so do the once joyful expressions of both my mother and her first-in-command.

Giselle and Ellis hardly take note as they busily plug into their phones.

"Oh no, you don't!" I shout. "This is a technology-free zone. Put away the cellular and pay attention to the data about to pop out before you!"

"You're going to push again with the next contraction," Mom instructs. "And go!"

Pushing turns out to be something I'm not very good at. Shocking, I know. It takes eight exhausting, demanding as hell grunting desires to expel these beings from my body before my mother lets out a warbling yelp.

"You're crowning!"

A flashback of Emily's birth hits me. I remember my mother shouting those very words as Emily's vagina blew up like a balloon, and a red angry alien tried to fist its way out of it. "Hair! Lots of black hair!"

"Oh God!" I pull Logan in close, with his crimson-laced eyes, the sweat beading around his temples. His body wants this to be over with just as much as mine.

The door swings open, letting in a gush of cold air, and my heart leaps out of my chest because in this one moment all is forgiven, and all I want is my precious husband by my side.

"Ga—shall," I say as I give a half-hearted push. It's not Gage at all, but my favorite trusty Sector. Unlike that flighty Fem I've apparently married—Marshall is ready to report for duty. Holy hell, what was I thinking gifting Gage the keys to my vagina? I bet this is his way of giving me the big FU—leave it to him to defect to the enemy's side in the most dramatic fashion.

"Touch me, Marshall!" I call out, breathless. "Twist my nipples!" I cry in agony. "Anything! I really don't care. I just need your touch." I hold out my free hand to him. There's no way in hell I'm letting go of Logan.

Marshall comes around and clasps his hand to mine. That sad expression in his eyes says it all. I ain't gettin' no satisfaction. Crap. It turns out my mother is a wicked witch after all. It looks as if I've been bamboozled by everyone and everything. The only mother pure and true is this one in front of me with her cell phone pointed squarely at my nether regions.

"Oh God, no filming!" I squeal.

"Your mother says hello." Marshall gives a kind-hearted smile. "She wishes you well and—"

"Stop. If you want to live with all of your parts, do not repeat a word that monster has to say."

The lights dim a moment.

"Skyla!" Mom gives a spirited cry. "Push!"

My body, my entire being works to expel these children.

"There's a head!" Ellis barks in fright. "It has a head! The fucking head is out!" He gets up and staggers toward the window. "*Shit!*"

"That is not a dolphin." Giselle sits pale with shock, and, in a tiny satisfied moment, I realize my work is done in that respect. I have a feeling those special hugs Ellis doles out will be few and far between. "Skyla? There's a bloody baby stuck in your—"

"Suctioning!" the nurse calls out.

Mom plucks off my gown, fully exposing my oversized, sore, and slightly chaffed nipples, my legs spread wide with my pale, enormous belly spiking in the air like a skin-colored weather balloon.

"I got this." Mom dives down between my legs and pulls it right out from under its arms. "It's a boy!" she shouts, and they're the most beautiful words I've ever heard in my life. Carefully, she lands the slippery being over my belly.

Logan presses a quick kiss to my mouth, his hot tears mingling with mine as he lingers with his trembling lips.

"You did it." He offers a partial embrace before touching the baby over its precious, glistening back. The nurse picks up the tiny angel and gives a swift pat until he starts in on a beautiful cry, lethargic and quiet like the trembling of a lamb. She lays him over my chest once again.

"He's beautiful." I warble through tears. He's perfect, with his tiny nose, his ears peaked and slightly pointed like that of his father. His eyes are squinted shut, but even like this, I can see Gage in him. Miniature Gage. I cry and laugh at the same time.

"Look at that! He's got dimples." Logan rubs my arms as I pull the baby up and see them for myself.

Sure enough, there they are, blinking in and out as if to annunciate themselves.

"Oh my God!" My chest trembles as a laugh strums through me. "He's so precious." Logan and I laugh through tears. "Hello, you." I nuzzle in close and touch my nose to his. "I love you. Yes, I do. I love you."

"He is beautiful, indeed, Ms. Messenger." Marshall gives my wrist a light tap, and I pull his hand forward and kiss it.

"*Thank you*," I mouth. I'm so thrilled Marshall arrived just in time to witness my miracle.

Our miracle. He corrects, and I can't help but nod.

The nurse holds a pair of scissors toward Logan. "Would you like to cut the cord?"

"Yes," I tell him. "*Please*, Logan." I'm pleading with him to do this. "It would mean everything to me if you would. You were here for me when I needed you the most. I'd much rather it be you than"—I nod toward the nurse and my mother who are busy wiping down the baby, mumbling about his excellent Apgar scores.

"Okay." Logan takes the scissors and follows the nurse's command. With a wince and a pained smile, he squeezes the blades over the cord, and just like that, it's severed. My hand cradles my sweet son's back. His skin is warm and silky to the touch. There. Logan has done the precious deed, and now my heart will forever walk around the planet outside of my body in the form of this beautiful child. I land a soft kiss to his thick black hair, and my heart melts with an agonizing delight.

The door whooshes open, letting in an iced breeze, and standing over the threshold is a familiar, dark-haired, dimpled newly-minted daddy. His hair is shorter, he's fresh shaven, wearing an inky navy suit, and below his left eye is a bloody gash that is quickly bruising.

Gage has finally bothered to show up.

Gage

"*Skyla*." I rush over. My aching legs move with nothing more than sheer willpower. Skyla's beautiful limbs are spread wide, her pale, naked body exposed for all to see—but my focus, my heart spears at the sight of a tiny baby lying prone on her chest. The room dissipates. It might as well dim because the white-hot spotlight of my attention is on that precious little being.

"Oh God." My voice breaks as I make my way to Skyla. Logan moves, and I take my rightful place by her side.

"Gage!" Lizbeth screams and claps up a storm. Behind her Ellis and Giselle sit in the corner, huddled and murmuring to themselves in a fright-induced frenzy.

"You have a son." Skyla hands me the baby, light as a feather, still naked and raw from her womb. The baby—my son—has a head full of hair—and dimples. A lone tear falls from my face to his, and I wipe it with my thumb. He's soft as silk, and his cry sounds like an idea more than an instigation. I swallow hard, looking to my beautiful wife, her swollen ruby lips. Her damp hair sticks to the sides of her face as if she's just fought a war.

"I'm so proud of you." My heart shatters when I say it because I wasn't here to witness the event myself.

The nurse swoops in. "This will just take a second." She takes him from me for a moment, rubbing him down with a sponge and wrapping him tight in a blanket.

Logan pulls me in and offers a deep, heartfelt hug. "Congratulations, man." He sniffs the words into my neck. "He's truly beautiful."

He sets the scissors down, and I try to evict the image of him cutting the cord—knowing he was the one who was here for Skyla, not me. My mind fails to wrap itself around the impossibility of it all.

"I was detained." It's all my stupid mouth can offer. If I told Skyla my theory on what really happened, I'm not too sure she'd appreciate it.

"Detained?" a voice gruffs across from me.

I glance up to find Dudley with a smug look on his face, and now I feel like twice the ass I did a second ago.

"Yes, detained." I suddenly have the urge to kill him. I want to love my son and my wife, perhaps punch then hug Logan, but I most definitely want to kill Dudley. In all of this madness, how is *he* here? It's as if Candace is sending me a message. Even Dudley is permitted. She's not entirely Team Logan. She still has room for one more. It's just not me.

Skyla's mouth opens to say something before she bucks violently forward, chin to her chest.

"It's a big one!" Lizbeth shouts. "Don't worry, Skyla. This is just the placenta. It's not like your little boy brought along a friend or anything." She gives a hearty laugh while patting Skyla on the foot.

"Don't push yet," the nurse calls just as Dr. Baxter walks into the room. He's a touch too tan with a patina of Oompa Loompa, and his teeth are bleached white as lightning.

"I see you didn't wait to start the party!" His stab at humor is met with his own laughter. He gloves up and evicts the nurse from her seat. "Let's see what we've got here." He plunges his fingers into my wife for all to see, and I recoil, closing my eyes a moment, trying to erase the image from memory. "Beautiful, beautiful. So beautiful," he moans as if he's having a damn good time down there. "The head's dropped. We'll wait out a contraction before we resume pushing."

"What?" Lizbeth bounces off her stool. "Oh my God! Skyla!" She grips her hair and spins in a circle. "This is fucking unbelievable!"

For a brief moment, Skyla, Logan, and I freeze. Lizbeth isn't known to toss around the expletives.

My hand finds Skyla's, but her eyes are glued on Logan as he helps her breathe in rhythm, soothing her with that soulful look in his eyes—holding out a finger as if to alert her to the fact it's going to end soon.

"Gage?" Skyla looks to our conjoined hands, horrified as if I've just put a dead fish in her palm. "You're not working!" She lets out a groan of disbelief. "Where are the feel-good vibes when you need them? Why?" She cries toward the ceiling. I'm assuming that last question was for Candace. And since Dudley isn't lying on top of her, I take it he's not in a vibratory state of mind either. I suppose we both have Skyla's mother to thank for that.

The doctor probes freely again. His hand lodged between her legs is a sight I can never get used to. Shit.

Skyla lets out a wounded cry.

"Give me the epidural now. I'm ready," she pleads, her voice threadbare and worn thin just as her will seems to be. The last time I saw her so depleted, begging for mercy, was at the hands of the Counts after a spontaneous blood drive. Skyla is hurting. She needs me—hell, she *needed* me, and I couldn't do a thing about it. Until now.

"Give her the damn medicine!" My voice cuts across the room, sharp and intrusive, causing Dr. Bastard, the angry nurse, and Lizbeth to pause a moment and glare at me. The baby cries a little louder from the incubator.

"It's too late." The nurse clicks her tongue. "We don't give epidurals once you start pushing."

"I'll stop," Skyla volunteers.

"No, sweetie." Lizbeth tries to coax Skyla back from the ledge. "You're doing so great. Only a little bit more. You're a super mom, Skyla." Tears are running down her cheeks, quick as a river. "I can't believe you held this from me."

"I'm so sorry." Skyla weeps into her words.

"No"—Lizbeth shakes her head with a tear-soaked smile—"this is the best surprise ever."

"*Skyla,*" Logan says it sweetly and glances to the monitor as he begins on an exaggerated long breath.

"Push with this one," the doctor insists, and Skyla bears down, letting a scream curdle from her throat, drowning out the sound of the sweet baby now nestled in Dudley's arms. Okay, I take it back. I no longer want to kill him. When my son needed someone to hold him, he was there, and that's enough for me to forgive a lifetime of indiscretions.

Skyla takes a gulping breath and bears down once again—her face turns pink, then purple. A solid roar comes from her as I see a dark cap of hair bursting through, then quickly a shoulder or two.

"Father?" The doctor looks from me to Logan. "Would you like to do the honors?"

"*Yes*." I carefully reach down and extract the tiny, slippery being from under its arms and land it safely onto Skyla's belly.

Skyla looks up at me and smiles while trying to catch her breath. My entire body fills with joy and light, with a warmth that only true love can bring. All of the anxiety, all of the angst that today had brought has effectively dissolved now that my children are both here safe and sound.

The nurse suctions the baby, and it begins to bleat a velvet cry.

Lizbeth claps up a storm. "Tell us what it is, Gage!"

I gently lift a leg. "It's a boy!" I shout. And there is no greater feeling.

The room erupts in cheers with even Ellis and Giselle blinking back to life.

"Congratulations." Dudley gives a sincere nod my way as he places a tender kiss to the baby in his arms.

"Two baby boys," Skyla pants through a smile, pulling the tiny infant to her own lips. "We did it." She looks to me with sheer exhaustion, sheer delight.

"And it looks like baby number two was born at 12:04!" the nurse belts it out like they were winning lottery numbers. "That means you had two baby boys on two separate days!"

"Are they fraternal? Identical?" Lizbeth is frantic while cooing at the tiny angel in Marshall's arms.

"Fraternal," the doctor volunteers.

Logan leans into Skyla, accidentally dislodging my fingers from hers.

"Good job. I love you." He lands a kiss to her temple before pulling me into a hug. "Glad you made it."

"Thank you for being here." I swallow down my pride. "Thank you all for being here."

The nurse hands me the scissors this time. The baby's cord has been its life link for eight and a half months—leashed to the woman I love. Carefully, I open the blades and clamp down to where she points. It's a little tougher than I thought, but I power through, and within seconds, the precious cord is severed. My heart pinches knowing that they're finally here—out in the world without the shroud of Skyla's womb to protect them. Skyla and I will need to take care of these two angelic beings all on our own. It's horrifically daunting, and at the same time, I'm ecstatic to do it.

"Gage." Skyla shrugs with a smile trembling on her lips. She struggles to pull up the covers while Giselle helps adjust her gown. "We had one on my birthday and one on yours. Happy birthday!" She wipes her tears away—tears of immense joy and perhaps a touch of sorrow that I missed *part one* of the most important acts of our lives.

"I can't think of a better gift—two perfect little boys and a perfect wife."

The nurse wraps him up tight like a burrito and hands him to me. Dudley comes over and tries to do the same with the other baby.

"I can't. I'll drop them." I'm scared shitless. All these months of listening to Lizbeth tell us how fast this moment would come—and now it's impossible to believe it's actually here. I knew twins came early. It was damn foolish of me to even think of leaving Skyla's side this morning. What was supposed to be a half-hour detour from our well-orchestrated day together turned into an emotional scar for both my firstborn and me—not to mention Skyla.

"You'll do fine." Lizbeth takes the baby from Dudley and helps lay him in the crook of my other arm while Giselle incoherently mumbles through tears, snapping away pictures with her phone.

"Dude, I have to tell everyone." Ellis takes off.

Here they are, both safe in my arms—so soft, so light I wonder if this is all a dream.

"My boys." My chest rumbles with pleasure. Tears blur my vision, and I lose it. My boys. I lean over and kiss the baby Lizbeth placed in my arms, then switch to the younger of the two. As my lips connect with his tiny, soft forehead, an image of

Wes rips through my mind. *Then the heart of one you hold dear will turn against you—and everything you think you stand for.*

My pulse quickens, my skin bites with heat, and, for a brief moment, I'm physically ill.

"Here, let me." Lizbeth takes one baby, then the other, and her face literally glows with pride. "Hello, you two! It's Mee-Maw!"

Skyla and I give a slight chuckle. Before we know it, the room explodes with everyone bursting through the door at once. My parents give us a round of congratulatory hugs as everyone takes turns cooing over the tiny princes.

"Two?" Mom gasps as if she's just realized there was an extra baby in the room.

Ellis slaps me on the shoulder. "That was your surprise, dude, not mine. I just told them that Skyla did her part."

"Good job, man." I turn from Ellis and rest a hand on each of my parents' shoulders as if to stabilize them. "Twins. Two sweet baby boys."

The room erupts in elations once again. Every single person is full of joy. Even Skyla's sisters are hugging it out and crying. Then there's Tad.

"Twins?" He looks affronted as if we planned this just to further syphon off his resources. "You were trying too hard!"

We weren't trying at all, but that's beside the point.

Lizbeth shakes it off with a laugh. "That just means he has excellent aim." She offers a sly wink my way.

Did we really just go there?

"Thank you, I think."

"What are their names?" Brielle asks while taking a baby from Lizbeth and sniffing him. "God, I *love* new baby smell! I like want to have ten of these!"

Skyla and I exchange a quick glance. We've volleyed names a few times, but there were too many combinations to settle on.

Skyla sits up in bed. "We'll let you know soon. I think both Gage and I want to spend a moment with them before settling on anything."

Beau Geste demands to climb up Bree's leg, and she hands the baby back to Lizbeth.

Bree comes in close, wielding Beau like a weapon, and he smiles at Skyla. "I picked you a flower with my toes." He hands her a balding dandelion.

"Oh my goodness, thank you!" Skyla's eyes are still tear filled from holding the twins, and yet, she seems genuinely grateful of Beau's gesture.

"My body makes brown playdough," he says it so matter-of-factly I'm afraid for him. I make a note of picking up actual playdough to gift the poor kid.

Brielle nudges him.

"And lemonades." He holds up a chubby finger as if to annunciate this point.

"And lemonade." Bree nods, proud. "Don't let anyone tell you I don't teach you nothin'!"

I bend over and pat him on the head. "Remember, don't drink the lemonade. And I wouldn't mess with the playdough either."

Dudley kisses Skyla good night before shaking his head with disappointment my way. "What's the expression—you had one job?"

"It was out of my control." I subdue a moment of joy to properly growl at him.

He ticks his head to the side as if evaluating this from a spiritual point of view. He glances to the babies, and his face takes on a somber expression.

"I see." He gives a slight nod. "Enjoy your family, Gage. I'm very happy for you both." He takes off, and I'm too stunned to move. Dudley just said my name and was uncharacteristically kind.

One by one the room clears out with everyone offering an outpouring of congratulations and sheer joy at our expanding family.

Giselle comes in. "Happy birthday, big brother. I'm so in love with my new nephews! They're much better than dolphins." She gives a little wink. "You're going to get sick of me because I'm going to be around those precious little angels all the time. Get it? Little angels?"

"I get it." I plant a kiss to the top of my sister's head. "Thank you for being here tonight. Stay away from those special hugs. Do you see what they lead to?"

"Very bad and bloody places." She gives an aggressive nod. "Anyway, think of names quick. I want to know what to call them. Cutie Pie One and Cutie Pie Two are just temporary names for now."

"Got it. I love you, G." I pull her in tight with tears still near the surface.

"Love you, too, big brother."

Ellis gives an exhausted wave as they take off.

Mom rocks the baby nestled in her arms. There's a bright blue wristband on his foot that reads *Baby One*. The one in Lizbeth's arms reads *Baby Two*. I know they're fraternal, but from this vantage point, they look identical, with the same dark caps of hair, same twitching dimples, and bright pink skin.

"We might need to leave those on for a while, like years," I say, running my finger over the tiny blue band. "Look at this," I marvel, circling my hand around the ankle of the newborn in my mother's arms, and I can't stop smiling—can't stop crying like a loon. "They're so little," I moan inwardly at the thought. They're so fragile, so in need of every living detail to maintain their survival. It's at that moment the gravity of what's happened sinks in. Skyla and I are parents. These precious little boys are our charges for the next eighteen years and counting. They'll need us just to survive. My gut cinches at the magnitude of what that means.

Dad places his hand on my shoulder, warm and reassuring. "It's going to be okay, son."

"You always know what to say." I try to sniff back my emotions and fail miserably.

"Not true." His bushy brows peak over his glasses. "I don't know what to properly call my grandchildren."

"The answer to that is on the way." A dull laugh rumbles from me. "Tomorrow for sure."

Mom hands the baby to Skyla, and Lizbeth does the same. My wife is so beautiful with her arms full of love. Skyla has never been more perfect than this moment right here.

"You did good." Mom gives a slight tick of the head as she looks to Skyla. "This more than makes up for the fact you killed Charlie." A muted laugh trembles through her.

Crap.

Skyla just shakes her head, unsure of what to say. She's wiped out. I can see it in her eyes. Not even my mother can get a proper rise out of her.

"Good night." Dad gives her a kiss before escorting Mom out of the room.

"*Sorry*," I mouth.

Tad grunts and moans as Misty claws at his neck. "I think she's trying to kill me." He tries to pluck her off his chest, but Misty is insistent as she laughs up a storm. Her hands clamp violently over his throat as she shakes her velvet black hair back and forth. "See this? She's going for the jugular!"

"It's well past her bedtime. She tends to get a little animalistic if you feed her after midnight," Lizbeth says, hoisting a sleeping Beau over her shoulder. "Let's get these two little monkeys home." She gives each of the boys a tender pat to the head. "Two more precious little monkeys are about to join us tomorrow. I'll get everything ready for you two." She blinks back tears.

Tad gesticulates while trying to avert a medical incident of his own. "That officially makes us a zoo, Lizbeth. Believe you me—it brings tears to my eyes, too." His brows dip into a hard V. "Good night, kids. Try not to procreate while we're gone. You're shooting with a defective weapon, Greg."

"Tad Landon!" Lizbeth hurls his name across the room like an expletive. "Take that back."

"Take what back? Everyone knows you're supposed to have one at a time."

Lizbeth smacks him on the head and keeps doing so until they're well out the door.

"Both of you"—Lizbeth turns to Skyla and me—"take your shirts off and bond with those babies! Skin-to-skin, Skyla!

Just the way I taught you!" The door closes before she can get another word in.

A quiet hush falls over the room. I glance around, and it's just the four of us.

"Where's Logan?" My stomach drops. I hope to God I didn't offend him. In all honesty, I don't remember what I was actually saying or thinking when I walked in. I'm hoping that I kept all the negative comments to myself.

"He left—*Daddy*." Skyla breaks out into a huge grin. "Can you believe this? God, they're so adorable. They're the spitting image of you!"

I lean back and examine them in detail, tiny warbling dimples that dig in and out in their sleep—twitching smiles, those familiar lips, the high cheeks—God, they even have my brows.

A gentle knock erupts over the door, and we turn to find Demetri darkening the entrance.

I'd kick him out, but I know this moment is inevitable.

"I won't stay." He slashes a line through the air with his hand. "I simply wanted to see them with my own eyes." He speeds over, moving quicker than I've ever seen him slither.

Skyla takes in a breath and gives a single nod.

Demetri steps in close until his dark presence hovers above us. I study his face like my life depended on it. I know what I heard when I touched the second baby with my lips. It was that cryptic warning Wesley delivered almost a year ago regarding what would happen if I broke faith with the Steel Barricade. I did break faith with the Barricade. And now the price is suddenly far too high, and there is nothing I can do to stop it. But he's here—Demetri, the master of disaster. I'm his. Perhaps there is still a way.

"Magnificent," he says as if he were admiring expensive art he was about to acquire. "You did well. Both of you. All of my love." He gives his evil villain half-nod and heads out the door.

"Creepy." Skyla shudders, and Baby Two stirs to life. She offers him up, and I take him, cradling this inexplicably light, beautiful being in my arms.

"I'm going to protect you forever," I say it straight into his sleepy eyes. "And your brother and Mommy, too."

A tear glides down Skyla's face, fast as a shooting star.

"Names." I try to clear my throat. "Let's do this. Any ideas?"

"I don't know." She twists those bright pink lips, and I can't help but lean in and steal a kiss. Our little family in such close proximity feels like heaven. "In the meantime, you heard my mother. Shirt off, Oliver."

"You first." I twitch a smile. I help pull her gown back, and she unswaddles the newborn in her arms until his soft pink flesh is lying over hers.

"Heaven," she whispers, closing her eyes.

I hand her the baby in my arms and unbutton my shirt.

"Okay." I pull the baby close to my chest, unwrapping him just enough until his searing skin lands over mine. "You're right. This is heaven. This, right here, is paradise personified." Skyla and I bask in the glory of this beautiful moment for an unmarked stretch of time. "I was thinking that baby number one should be named after your father—Nathan." A smile curves up my lips as Skyla buries her gaze in mine. "And this one, we can call Barron. I know we talked about it, but I'd like your father to have our firstborn's name. And, I know my dad will be pretty excited, like through the roof to have one of our children named after him."

"It's perfect." She laughs through tears. I want to remember her like this forever. Skyla with the baby's glowing pink skin next to hers. I'd swear on my life they just sighed at the same time. It's a beautiful sight, and I never want to forget it.

"Is your dad's full name Nathaniel?" I'm embarrassed I don't know this, and in the back of my mind wonder if Logan does.

"Just Nathan. And I know he'll be excited—through the roof as well."

Another knock comes from the door. This time an illuminated body walks right through it—Candace followed by the Sector twins and Rothello of the Soullennium.

"Well, that was subtle." Skyla holds Nathan a little closer. "You know, on Earth we still go through the trouble of opening the door before walking into a room. I see you brought your posse." She holds up the baby slightly. "I have mine right here." She grins with pride.

"Congratulations!" Candace glides over and plucks Nathan right out of Skyla's arms. "Oh dear, aren't you the most precious little thing!" She reaches down and scoops up Barron as well. "And you are equally splendid!" she sings, her eyes sparkling with happy tears. I would be lying if I didn't say I feel immense relief that she's just as pleased with Barron as she is with Nathan. For a minute, I was afraid this would turn into a Logan-Gage situation. "I'll have you both know I've ordered a jubilee in the ethereal plane in your honor." She pecks a kiss to each child before looking to Skyla. "Sage sends her love."

"Why didn't you bring her?" Skyla struggles to sit up, so I fluff her pillow and raise the bed for her.

"She's with Nathan, love." There's a genuine sadness in her eyes. "We all agreed it would have been too much for you. It's nearly four in the morning, Skyla. You haven't slept. You've had a hard labor. We'll do something soon." She gives a sly wink like maybe we won't.

"I did have a hard labor, didn't I?" She unabashedly glares at her mother. "What the heck was up with that?"

"Should I gift you a free pass out of every rough patch, Skyla?"

"Ha! Do you ever?"

Candace softens. "If I gave you that honor—if either Gage or Sector Marshall alleviated you, then what camaraderie would you have had with the women of the world? Skyla, you are a leader, and a leader cannot sidestep harsh realities. It's your job to be one with the people."

Skyla's cold, blank stare says it all. "And no epidural? Did you have a natural delivery, Mother?"

"Yes—in fact, I did."

"And you wanted the same for me?" Skyla waves her off. "You're worse than Lizbeth. I wish the two of you would go off in the woods with Chloe and have a million natural childbirths one right after the other. But, please, for the love of God, let me make my own decisions—especially when it comes to my body."

Candace lets the words sink in before carefully handing the babies to me.

"Oh, Skyla." She swipes her finger over her daughter's cheek. "You were bought with a price. You are no longer your own." She lowers her gaze. "I apologize for the discomfort you went through. Let me know if there's something I can do to make it up to you."

"I'll have a list to you by morning."

"And I'll have a basket full of muffins sent to the Landon residence," she counters. "Expect me more often. Those little boys each bear a piece of my living soul." Her eyes snap to mine. "A piece of me, and a piece of your father. Can you imagine that?" She strides toward the door. "I love you all. It's hard for you to believe, but it is the truth. Words written in blood like fire over stone." She walks right back through the door, and each of her entourage follows suit.

"Creepy." I give a lopsided grin at my beautiful wife—at my beautiful life. "Nathan and Barron." I test it out on my lips as I lift them each in turn.

"Nathan and Barron." Skyla holds her finger over Barron's hand, and he curls it around her finger. "My heart just exploded into a whole deeper level."

I press a kiss to each of them. "We really do have it all."

"Forever."

Logan

There is a lot to be said about experience, about traveling in someone else's footsteps and gleaning the inroads of forsaken knowledge. That's what last night felt like. I was right there with Skyla every breath of the way, and yet, I wouldn't let myself forget those babies, her life-altering experience, was strictly tied to Gage. It would have been too easy for me to glide in the opposite direction. Me clinging to the woman I love as she's about to give birth to *our* child—children. I had to keep reminding myself this wasn't a dream, some fantasy come to life. This was Gage Oliver's reality—my privilege to attend, nothing more. My heart ached for Skyla and for Gage. What the hell was he thinking? More to the point, where the hell was he? I didn't want to probe. Once the room was bum-rushed with any and everyone we knew, I figured it was their moment to shine, no use in me bringing down the party. I'm sure Gage feels worse than shit for missing the birth of his firstborn. My heart breaks for him all over again.

My phone buzzes and twirls on my nightstand, pulling me further from this hazy fog I've been in for the last few hours. Sleep couldn't find me. Not that I need it.

My fingers fumble for my phone. It's a text from the proud papa himself.

Would you mind coming to the hospital and keeping Skyla company? I need to help Lizbeth get some things together. The boys are coming home later.

I answer right back. **Be right there.**

I'm out of bed and into the shower, dressed, and out the door in record time. My heart pumps wild with a renewed adrenaline. The fresh Paragon morning fog offers its wet kisses as I jump into my truck. I'm feeling more alive than ever, and a part of that is due to the fact Gage asked me to be with Skyla. I'll admit that a majority of last night's lack of sleep had to do with the fact it felt as if a door had slammed in my face. It's stupid and selfish—especially since I love those little boys as much as Gage does. I suppose my greatest fear is to be shut out of their lives. Unneeded. Unwanted. Gage has achieved every dream I've ever had with Skyla, and, it's right for them, especially considering the fact I'm dead. Not only am I dead, but I'm practically dead twice over.

I cast a heavy glance to the sky.

Just what in the hell is Candace Messenger doing with my life anyway? She brought me back, only to let me fall by the sword once more—literally. I know she wants me with Skyla, but I also know she has no clue that it will never happen—and I'm going to be the one that makes sure of it. She might think she's moving me in that direction, but I'll snatch heaven right from under her in order to keep my nephews' brand new family intact.

Skyla was Gage's destiny all along. I'm just some transplant from a different time, handpicked by the high priestess of destruction to rein more horror on Skyla's life. Nope. I'm done playing along—hell, I didn't even realize I was a pawn until last night. Skyla's life is no game. Gage is her forever. I'm simply a bump in the road they had to endure.

I pull up to the hospital and glide into the first spot I see. My eyes ride up seven levels to the floor that houses Skyla and those sweet baby boys. My stomach boils with agony.

Hell, I still wish she were mine.

I take in a sharp breath. That's it. No more moping like a pussy. Skyla belongs to Gage, and I'm damn happy for them. Something settles over me, a calm that I can't quite explain. It's as if finally every single cell in my body has surrendered Skyla to Gage. A sad smile comes and goes. About damn time.

I head on in and bump into Barron as we hop onto the elevator at the same time.

"Congratulations, Grandpa." I pull him into a soft embrace. Barron swims in a cloud of Old Spice, his signature scent, and something about it makes me feel safe—at home.

"Thank you. I was just on my way to the morgue for an early appointment and couldn't resist dropping by." He holds up a fresh bouquet of roses. "Something for the new mother." The apples of his cheeks plump as he squints out a smile.

Barron has always smiled with his whole face, his eyes turning into half moons that are quickly swallowed up in the action.

"Now I feel like an ass." All I have for Skyla is a warm hug. "Gage asked me to swing by—said he needed to help Lizbeth with some stuff back at the house. The twins are coming home later."

"That soon?" His eyes expand with astonishment. "It's a drive-thru delivery these days, I tell you. When Emma delivered both Gage and Giselle, she was here nearly a week." He gives a wistful smile. "It seems like just yesterday, and here I am, a grandfather—of two no less." His voice cracks a bit, and I pat him on the back. The elevator yawns open, and we head straight for Skyla's room at the end of the hall.

I give a gentle knock before peering inside. "All clear?" I whisper.

"Come in!" Skyla sounds cheery, but more so she looks amazing, with color in her cheeks, her hair up in a messy bun, a never-ending grin on her face. Her beauty has magnified a thousand times since I last saw her. Her entire countenance is beaming. Two acrylic bassinets sit at the edge of the bed, each filled with a sleeping bundle of joy. There they are, two dark-haired angels lost in a blissful slumber.

Gage steps out of the bathroom. "Hey." His smile lights up the entire room. "Dad." He lunges for Barron before he slaps me five. "Thanks for coming, man." He looks to his father again. "I was just about to head over to the house to pick up the car seats and some of Skyla's things."

"Don't forget the coming home outfits!" she struggles to whisper. "The cute ones that Bree bought last week."

"I wouldn't dare." He jiggles her knee before reverting to Barron. "I'm really glad you're here, Dad. Skyla and I have made the names official—in fact, just a few minutes ago we filled out the paperwork."

"Well, don't keep us in suspense—what are they?" Barron's face flushes with color. He can hardly stand the excitement. "Out with it."

Gage looks to Skyla and swallows hard. "The older is Nathan Gage Oliver, and the younger is Barron Logan Oliver."

"*Barron?*" My brother stumbles over his own moniker for a moment. "Barron." His forehead creases as he bows his head into his hands for a moment and sobs. "Thank you." He pulls Gage into a hard embrace. "I'm so very humbled by the honor. Thank you both."

I look to Skyla and give a playful wince. "You didn't have to include me. Thank you, princess." I give a tender kiss to the top of her head. "Thanks, man." I pull Gage in and dig my hand into his back, just trying to hold it together. I'm so damn glad they included me. Didn't expect it, but really appreciate it.

"These are for you." Barron hands Skyla the lavender roses, her favorite color. "I have an appointment in a few minutes, but I wanted to drop by and take a gander at my two favorite grandbabies in the world." Tears come to his eyes as he takes them in. "So precious. Emma will be thrilled with the news." He says a quick goodbye and speeds out the door.

"I'd better run, too." Gage gives Skyla a quick kiss.

She wrinkles her nose a moment. "Make sure you're back before they're eighteen," she teases.

"I'll be back long before then. An hour tops, I promise." He looks to me and ticks his head to the door. "You mind?"

I follow him out into the cool hall as an antiseptic breeze envelops us. The sound of a woman moaning comes from the left.

"What's up?" I ask, inspecting the fresh scar under his left eye. He came in battered and bruised last night—still not sure why.

Gage gives a heavy sigh and glances down the hall as if in desperate need for privacy.

"I had a hell of an afternoon yesterday. I won't lie. I miss my powers more than I ever thought I could."

"No harm, no foul. I went through a human phase once myself."

"And a dead phase, a Skyla phase. You always beat me to the phases, don't you? And, apparently, the birth of my first child." He closes his eyes a moment. "What happened yesterday—it was no accident. I went out to cut my fucking hair—put on a suit to surprise my wife for a birthday lunch, and things got botched twelve ways to Sunday."

"Meaning?"

"Meaning, my mother-in-law didn't want me anywhere near the birth of my first son."

"What?" I inch back to get a better look at his face. "Are you kidding?"

"No. It was supernatural. Whatever happened had to do with the fact that baby was being brought into this world. At some point, it was like a leash snapped, and I was finally able to jump into my truck and scramble here. My phone was in the glove compartment. Every turn I took I was derailed. It was a living nightmare." He grips his hair at the temples. "After hours of trying to fight it, I realized there was no way around that bullshit. It was as if I had to endure whatever it was to eventually get to Skyla. I had no clue she was in labor—giving birth, but after a few hours of playing tug-of-war with my time, I figured something big was going down—and, of course, this was my greatest fear." His Adam's apple dips and rises.

"What makes you so sure it was Candace?" I'm not really her biggest proponent. I just so happen to know that there are other celestial fish in the sea. Sharks. All of them.

"Who else would—" he stops short. "Shit." Gage squeezes his eyes shut as if remembering a bad dream. "About a month ago, I met up with Candace. She brought something up that I've been trying not to deal with. She mentioned that she wasn't the one who pushed me off Devil's Peak last spring. She heavily hinted that Demetri might have had a hand in it—that he did."

"It makes sense." I'm not floored by this, but it is shocking. "He was the only one willing to save you. Who doesn't appreciate someone who saves their ass?" And that's how Demetri has managed to get so much mileage out of Gage as of late. "He nearly killed you to get in your good graces." Piece of shit.

"God." Gage wipes his hand over his forehead. "So, how does it make you feel to have your name carried on through my son, even if it is a middle name?" He presses out a sad smile until it bleeds genuine.

"Are you changing the subject?" I frown. "I'm touched—*honored* to have my name in any way associated with your child. But if Demetri stopped you from helping Skyla in her time of need, missing out on Nathan's birth—if he's the one that broke your back, don't you want to find him and pummel him?"

Gage takes one heavy breath after another. His temples break out in a sweat the way he does when he gets excessively stressed, and, at that, it hardly ever happens.

"There's something else going on." He swallows hard as if pushing through some tough emotions. "Last night when I held Barron for the first time, I had a vision—a playback of a scene that I lived not too long ago. It was Wes telling me that if I broke faith with the Barricade, the heart of one I hold dear will turn against me and everything I think I stand for." His eyes knife into mine. "Logan, both you and I know that I broke faith with the Barricade."

I open my mouth to refute Wesley's lunacy, then remember who their DNA is tied to—not to mention the double package that arrived last night.

"*Shit*," I whisper without meaning to. "You think it's—" I struggle to say what comes next.

"I don't know." His fingers rake through his hair with marked aggression. "I"—he chokes on his words—"I love those boys so damn much I can't bear that I might have fucked things up for them before they ever had a chance in this world." Gage fights the tears as his cheek twitches and pulls. "Just—no matter what happens to me—keep an extra eye out on my boys."

"Hey." I pull him in by the shoulders. "It was a long night. This entire experience is a little mind-bending. You're just stressed. Nothing is going to happen to you. Understand? Skyla and I both are fighting"—I dig my fingers into his rocked-out deltoids—"we are fighting hard to make sure your feet stand on solid ground for the next eight decades. We are gunning for a very long life for you, my friend, so don't go throwing in the towel just yet."

Gage blinks hard as if coming to. "You're right. But I'm more worried about my boys." He backs up, still trying to get his bearings. "I don't know—it just threw me. That might have been what he wanted." His dimples invert. Gage is tired, upset, and overwhelmed with all of his blessings at once. "Demetri is just trying to get under my skin. And as for missing the birth, my money is still on Candace."

I'd hate to say it, but I'm betting he's right.

"Talk to Skyla and me. Don't leave us out of the loop. And for God's sake, and the sake of those two boys, don't go doing anything you might deem heroic."

"Got it." He gives a light sock to my arm. "You're pretty good at pep talks, you know that?"

"Yeah, well, you don't look so convincing. You're sleep deprived. Drive carefully, and be back soon. You have a small crowd in there that needs you."

"Will do." He pulls me in quick and hard. "Thanks for everything, man."

I wait until he's on the elevator before ducking back into the room where Skyla radiates her beauty bright as the sun.

"Hey, beautiful."

"Please. I'm far from beautiful." Skyla makes a face as she struggles to sit up in bed. "Don't look at me. I look like a witch."

"You look like an angel."

"You're just being literal."

A dull laugh rumbles through me. "I'm not here to spar with you." I glance at the twins, who seem to be sleeping soundly. "It looks like my two new favorite nephews are good sleepers."

"I wish. They fell asleep the second you and Barron walked in as if on cue." She looks down at her chest where two wet spots sit just above her nipples. "Let's just say they went to bed hungry. I'm afraid I might not be destined to be a heroic boob slinger like my mother."

"You'll get the hang of it." I fluff the pillow behind her.

A nurse breezes in and strides right over to Skyla. "Everything going well, Mrs. Oliver?" She peers at each of the babies, only partially interested in Skyla's response. "I'm here to give you a tiny massage." She pulls Skyla's covers down and adjusts the gown over her swollen belly.

"Oh God, yes." Skyla scoots up a little in the bed. "My shoulders have really been—"

The nurse dive-bombs Skyla's stomach and starts pounding away as if she were kneading dough.

"Holy shit!" Skyla smacks her over the back, but she refuses to relent.

"Now, *now*, Mrs. Oliver. I need to make sure everything is falling into place."

Skyla lets out a blood-curdling scream just as I pluck the psychotic woman off her. In truth, I thought she was falling when she dove into Skyla's stomach.

"All done." Nurse Ratchet smiles at Skyla as if she actually did her a favor and leaves.

"Dear God." Skyla reaches for my hand and gives it a squeeze. "Thank you for helping me. Sorry you had to witness that little bit of medical misery."

"I'm sorry you had to live through the medical misery. Are you okay?"

"I'm fine. It's their job to make sure I scream and bleed." She tosses up a hand as if she's resigned to this new brand of torture. "Thankfully, the boys slept through it."

The boys. I can't help but smile. I love the sound of those words. There are now two miniature versions of Gage ready to run around this planet—literally. It couldn't please me more. I glance over at their matching caps of thick, black hair, and it warms me to imagine them as full-grown men, the exact representation of their father.

"Why don't you get some shut-eye? I'll hold down the fort," I offer.

"What if they get hungry?" Her face fills with worry for her tiny brood, and it makes me smile to see her this way. I always knew that Skyla would make a great mother.

"I've got nipples, too, you know," I tease. "I've got to

use them sometime."

Her lids lower with mild disgust at my stab at humor. "It won't be very productive."

"No, but it'll be entertaining as hell. Get some sleep. I'm getting cranky just watching you try to keep your lids open."

She settles into her pillow and turns slightly to face me fully.

"I want to talk about things," she says it quiet. "The things we've done. The haunted places we've dared to go again."

The tunnels.

I give a slight nod. "We're in control this time, Skyla. We're protecting our people the best we can. The Faction Council couldn't argue with that."

"The Faction Council means nothing," she spits it out so fast I try to catch the words as they fly by. "It's simply a means of control. The fact I was the overseer made me nothing more than my mother's favorite puppet. I was her pet, to be put in my place. Well, no more. This is a new day, a new way. Hopefully, we'll create something that actually benefits our people. This was never about the Nephilim. This was about dominion from the beginning. We're rewriting all the rules—you and me, Logan." She bows her head and closes her eyes a moment. Skyla is pensive, sad, her shoulders heavy with the best interest of the Nephilim—of her new sons. "The war was God's," she whispers. "You and I are vessels of the house of the Master." Her entire body sags into a sigh. "Logan." Her fingers extend toward mine. "Did Gage say anything to you that I should know about?"

And now I know her hand in mine is more than simply a friendly gesture. It's a listening device.

"I need to know the truth," she whispers.

I pull my hand free, and that says it all.

"He would lay down his life for these little boys." She bites down on a painful smile. "I think he should fight twice as hard to keep it."

I offer all I can think to say. "He's a smart boy." Most of

the time.

My gaze drifts to those sleeping little angels. Gage charged me with shepherding his boys, Barron in particular.

Skyla reaches out and takes me by the hand again. "With the twins here, Demetri officially has dominion." It's as if she can feel the window of Gage's life closing on her.

"What are you thinking?" I put up an iron shield over my innermost thoughts—not an easy feat. Gage, on the other hand, is an expert at it.

Thick glassy shards glitter in her eyes as she fights the tears. "I'm afraid maybe he's done with him."

Maybe he's done with him.

I was thinking the very same thing.

13

The Sickle Rises

Skyla

In the still of a perfectly tranquil and gray Paragon afternoon, Gage drives the babies and me home in my mother's minivan with her in the passenger's seat and me nestled between two plastic bins that house the most precious beings in the world, my sons. Demetri was the one who purchased the car seats for us—one for each of our cars, but I suspect he knew of the twins all along. Gage and I looked up the car seats online and were shocked to see they were not only by far the most expensive, but that they were practically approved by NASA to take part in a space mission if need be. I almost wanted to laugh. We all know I could be hauling these boys around in a wicker basket and not a hair on their heads would be harmed. I'm sure Demetri has an entire infantry of Fems watching, protecting, monitoring his grandchildren, or more to the point, his dominion insurance. In that respect, I feel a sense of relief. For so long, I felt hunted as a Celestra. At least my children won't have to go through that—at least not by the enemy. They already have all of wickedness on their side. Not really something I'm proud of, but it takes a burden off my heart, heavy as this wicked world.

We pull up to the Landon house, and Mom begins clapping up a storm and singing, "Happy homecoming to you!" to the tune of "Happy Birthday."

"Check it out." Gage points to a huge blue banner above the door that reads *Welcome Home, Nathan and Barron!*

Mia and Melissa race down to the minivan with all the enthusiasm of trying to escape a poltergeist.

"They're here! They're here!" Mia cries as her giant pit bull-mastiff mix lumbers on her heels. "Down, D-O-G!"

Melissa swats at him as he tries to jump into the van and see what all the excitement is. "God, he's going to eat them!"

"He's not going to eat them," I whisper, secretly hoping I didn't just make up that entire Fem secret security theory just so I could feel better about a very dark and dismal future. On second thought, I'd better be vigilant in the event my own lackadaisical behavior is what ultimately harms my boys.

Both Gage and Mom grab a car seat and carefully tread toward the house.

"Wait here, Skyla. I'll be right back to help you," Gage instructs just as Brielle and Drake appear from the back of the property.

"You're home!" Bree screams, practically knocking me over with a diving hug. "It feels like you were gone forever!"

"Nope, just one day. In fact, it's still Gage's birthday. Hey! Would you mind picking up a little cake for him? Double chocolate if you can?" I scoot out of the car and try to navigate my own way up to the house.

"Not a problem. Chloe and Pierce have this Dobash that's to die for. It's chocolate chiffon filled with a chocolate pudding. I'll order a couple of sheets."

"Bree." I pause halfway up the porch. "A tiny eight-inch round is plenty, trust me. We're not that big on dessert." Which is a total bald-faced lie, but since I woke up just as big and round as I did yesterday, I'm pretty sure dessert should be low on my nutritional priority list. Besides, I have absolutely zero willpower, and I'd eat every single sheet of double chocolate goodness Brielle can get her hands on. Plus, Nev and Ezrina made it? I would so be dust.

"You can't stop me from spoiling the birthday boy!"

Oh hell, what's another ten pounds?

By the time we get into the house, she's already on the horn with Ezrina and Nev.

"I'll go pick them up, and be back in a sec. *Drake!*" she belts so loud I brace myself for the trembling cry of the boys, but nary a whimper is heard. So far they've been very good. If they keep this up, this mothering thing will be a breeze.

Emily and Nat are hanging out in the family room when I finally arrive and plop myself onto the couch.

"I think that's all the stairs I can manage for now." I smile at Gage as he arranges the car seats in front of the sofa.

"Skyla!" He twists into me, worried that I might have risked life and limb just to get here, and judging by how my body feels, I might have.

"I'm fine." Only a tiny lie. This fishnet underwear the nurse helped stuff me into, in lieu of real panties, has about three maxi pads lining it that I'm sure are all soaked by now. The walk from the car felt more like a hike up the Matterhorn.

The babies squirm in their sleep, still tucked safely in their seats by the sofa.

"What do you want to do with them?" Gage wraps an arm around my shoulders as if trying to cheer me up for no reason. Come to think of it, I do feel like I'm about to cry. Everything has changed, our worlds forever altered. I feel strange. I can't quite put my finger on how or why, and to make matters worse, a horrible fear shakes me right down to my bones. Damn hormones.

Nat belts out an explosive laugh. "They're not socks, Gage. You can't put them away. Get a couple of bassinets and bring them down here, or hand one to Skyla and she can start nursing. My sister has six kids, going on seven. She says the first five are a breeze."

Nice. I don't even know what to say to that.

Mom clucks her tongue. "I've got two bassinets in the living room. I'll wheel them right over. Gage, you make sure Skyla has plenty to drink. We need to keep her hydrated, and her nipples in tip-top condition!"

A curtain of newspaper comes down at the dining room table, revealing a bedraggled-looking Tad. "If you're going to be nippling all over the place, maybe you should take this cantaloupe roadshow upstairs? Isn't this what I built you a soundproof room for? Feel free to nipple all you want behind closed doors. But as far as the rest of us are concerned, this is a nipple-free zone."

"Em rolls her eyes. "She can cover up or not. We all have tits. And it's not like we didn't already see yours, Skyla."

I'm perplexed by Em on many levels—one, she just said *tits* in the family room and took the general discomfort up a notch, and two, when did she see the ones that belong to me?

"It was during cheer, Messenger," she grouses. "I wasn't spying on you. I'm not a freak," Em manages to say the words without an ounce of affect, and it only begs to differ.

"No one said you were a freak, Em. Besides, I saw every last bit and piece of you when you had Ember, so we'll call it even."

Nat sighs, "You didn't see every last bit and piece of what I have to offer." Her gaze drifts out the window. "But, since Pierce wants nothing to do with me, I suppose I won't be having kids anytime soon."

"What happened with that football player from Host?" Gage asks, setting down a glass of water for me.

God, I can't even deal with the fact she's still hung up on that long-dead Kragger. It must be really hard to see Nev running around in his body and not to have gotten the memo. I think it's time someone delivers that little bit of news, and it should probably be me. An idea goes off in my brain, bright as a haunted light bulb, and I make a mental note for later.

"Derek the linebacker?" Nat scoffs. "He's dead to me."

I hate to burst her bubble, but so is Pierce.

Gage takes off to help Mom as they wheel in two small rectangular cribs from the other room.

"Here, let me help," Mia says, unbuckling Nathan from his car seat and carefully handing him to me. He squirms and grunts, his face turning a bright orange in the adorable process. "Babies should be held, not shoved into boxes." She picks up Barron and takes a seat beside me.

I plant a kiss on Nathan's soft as velvet forehead and pause a moment to take in his sweet baby scent. He smells like a fresh L.A. springtime, like a sea breeze off a warm beach—off

Rockaway. He blinks up at me with those serious eyes, and, swear to God, he's gazing right at me.

"We have company!" Mom's voice hits a soprano, and Nathan's poor body bucks as he beats his fists in the air.

Mia places Barron in my other arm. "I think he wants his mom. He smells like a Landon."

"Hey," Melissa snaps. "You're a Landon!"

"Yeah, but my body still smells like a Messenger."

"You said it, not me," I whisper, and Mia gives a full wicked grin.

Marshall appears with a bouquet of white roses, and both Em and Nat swoon in a chorus of "*Hello, Mr. Dudley!*"

When Marshall first came to the island, he gave the entire female population a lady-boner. And then, in return, he boned half the female population. He was our very own resident playboy until I put the kibosh on that good time. Actually, he volunteered to stop sleeping around in my vagina's honor. I'll admit, it pleases me on some level that he's no longer casting his penile net far and wide, catching skanks of every variety. Marshall is an equal opportunity "penilizer." I give a dry chuckle at my own ridiculousness.

"Ms. Messenger?" Marshall leans in. "You look a bit sleep deprived. Perhaps I should go."

"Oh, sorry, no. I just zoned out. I've been up all night, and I couldn't sleep if I wanted to. I'm too nervous to take my eyes off these boys."

"Speaking of shut-eye." Mom looks to Tad, who has managed to nod off at the table, sitting upright while his head bounces back and forth like a bobblehead. "Tad Landon, are you sleeping?"

"Nope" He startles to life. "Just checking my eyelids for leaks."

"Very funny." She takes off to the kitchen. Em and Nat leave the room while discussing something in a fury of whispers, and my sisters bolt upstairs.

"What's up, Dudley?" Gage takes Nathan from me and sits by my side. "You come to get a better look at your new adversaries?"

If I weren't holding Barron, I would smack Gage—playfully, of course. Marshall would never consider my children anything but his own.

"Not at all." Marshall is affronted by the idea. Ha! *Told you*, I want to say, but in reality, I didn't say a thing to begin with. "In fact, I consider them quite the opposite." He leans over and touches his fingers to the dark plume of feather soft hair on Barron's head. "These special boys are my relation."

Gage frowns. "I think you're forgetting they're mine, not Logan's. You and I are not related."

"No, but they are related to my bride, and that is all that matters. I'll arrange for a sanctification ceremony with the Sectors right away."

"You'll do no such thing," a deep voice comes from over my shoulder, and I turn to find Demetri grinning like an evil kook. "These children require a *Fem* sanctification, a ritual sacrifice and a chalice of suffering. This, my friend, will be done the *right* way and not half-cocked by a bunch of mediocre celestial bodies who are no more useful than a dictionary used as a doorstop."

Crap. I look to Gage. The last thing I need—*anybody* needs is a showdown between good and evil in the Landon family room.

"Demetri! You're here!" Mom bursts into her operatic octave once again. "And you brought flowers, too! Gerber daisies, Skyla's favorite."

Marshall holds up his pristine white roses for me and nods, pleased by his selection.

"The flower of the gods." Marshall kisses a bloom before handing my mother the bouquet.

"You boys are too much!" Mom takes off with an armful of flora and fauna as Nathan begins to stir in Gage's arms.

"I'd better feed them."

Both Marshall and Demetri head for the door.

"Wait!" I call to Marshall, but unfortunately, they both pause. "I need to see my mother," I whisper, giving Demetri the stink eye for listening in.

"I'm sure I can arrange it." Marshall motions to the baby in my arms. "Let me know when you have a free minute."

"Oh, I plan on taking them with me."

"Absolutely not." Demetri snaps before straightening and forcing that manufactured smile back to his face. "It's against rules and regulations. They're far too young for intercellular disbursement. It's simply not recommended at this stage of life."

Funny, they disbursed just fine in utero.

Marshall frowns. "Translation—your mother draws the line at newborns. She's banished them from the lake. It's a binding even she can't undo. I'm sure Jock Strap is capable of minding them for a moment."

Gage shakes his head. "I'm going with you."

Marshall steps back into the room and caresses Nathan's little cheek with his finger, but Demetri lingers in the doorway like a phantom.

"What is it you might be needing to see Candace for?" Demetri directs the question to Gage just as my mother appears with two glasses of fresh squeezed lemonade. She hands one to Demetri and the other to my spirit spouse.

"Nothing in particular." Gage cuts his father, aka the sperm donor, a hard look. "I just so happen to like supporting my wife. She has a tough time with her mother."

"Just like you do with your father," I say it sweetly in a show of solidarity with my husband.

Mom's jaw drops as if she's just heard the juiciest piece of gossip. "I didn't know that you and Barron didn't get along." Her eyes widen as she drinks Gage in. The Olivers are a pretty perfect family—sans me, of course. So I can see how something like this might be shocking.

"We get along fine," Gage flatlines, and my mother is left to do that patriarchal math.

"Oh, I see."

"I don't see." Demetri smiles. "It's simply not true. Lizbeth"—he turns to my mother—"I'll be throwing a christening ceremony next week for the boys at my home. I'll need you to make quick provisions."

"Of course! I'll get right on it!" Mom hops to his will like an obedient puppy. "Oh, wait." She chews her fingernail a moment. The enthusiasm on her face sinks like a stone. "The boys are far too young to be going out in a week—especially around an entire group of people."

What's this? Lizbeth Landon shutting down one of Demetri's demented soirees? Delicious!

I glance back at Marshall to make sure he didn't miss my mother's daring display of bravery, and he offers a wink.

"I'll take whatever suggestion you offer, my lady." Demetri gives a little bow, and Mom loses it in a fit of schoolgirl-like giggles. My stomach churns just watching the display. I glance over at Tad who's busy jiggling a finger in his ear.

"About a month," she concludes. "That gives the boys time to build up their immunity, and it gives me some time to create the best christening party known to all mankind." She clasps her hands together midair as if catching a fly.

Gage and I sniff at each other. Mankind implies *humans,* and we all know there won't be a single full-blooded one of those in the vicinity.

Marshall takes a breath and expands his chest wide as the sea. "I'll see to it that a proper consecration takes place. We Sectors have our own rituals."

"You can save them," Demetri quips with a greasy grin. "We Fems have a ritual that cannot be tampered with."

I growl at Demetri. I don't mean to growl, but it must be the Celestra in me reacting to the Fem in him. Just the thought of Demetri performing a ritual around my sweet baby boys sounds perfectly perverted.

Gage nods as if he's read my thoughts. "I think Skyla and I are just shooting for your average dedication. No consecrating or rituals necessary." He looks to my mother. "A simple cake will be enough. No need to go overboard. No champagne, no hors d'oeuvres. If we need to, we can order a pizza."

Her mouth gapes as if she's just been shut down herself. Go, Gage! It's about time we took back our lives. After that wedding vow renewal fiasco, in which half our guests were crying out to the Messiah himself for mercy, I think putting our foot down should be routine from here on out.

"Duly noted." My mother shrugs to Demetri.

"Ms. Messenger." Marshall gives a slight bow. "Mr. Oliver, you both did exceptionally well. Young Nate and Barron will enjoy a bright future, I'm sure"—he frowns at Demetri—"gene pool considering."

Demetri mumbles something about visiting again soon, and both he and Marshall take off, but I'm too busy noticing a horrid, rock-hard feeling in my breasts to say a proper goodbye. They've gone from cow-like udders to concrete bowling balls in the span of one hour.

"Mommy," I whimper, clutching at the granite spheres attached to my chest.

"What is it?" She zips in front of me with the finesse of a poltergeist.

"My boobs just turned into boulders—solid, hard, and explosively large. Oh God." I give a little cry. "This can't be good."

"Oh, silly, that's normal. It's time to nurse. Come, come." She flicks her fingers at me. "Take that top off. These boys are hungry, and it's mealtime."

Gage gives my hand a soft squeeze. "Shouldn't we go upstairs?"

For the first time ever, Gage Oliver actually looks frightened. Ironic since not even the most disfigured wicked Fem could shake him, but the thought of me whipping out my newly lead-lined boobs in the middle of the family room rocks him to his very core.

"I can't. Just the thought of climbing those stairs right now makes my lower half cringe and my upper half want to scream. Sorry, but I need to do this here."

Mom helps lift off my tent of a T-shirt, and I vaguely see Tad speeding out of the room with his hands in front of him like Wile E. Coyote.

"We've got to get that house of theirs fixed up quick!" Tad shouts as he ascends the stairs. "There are enough exposed teats in this home. We don't need another set!"

"Who's exposing their teats?" Mom rolls her eyes as she shouts back.

"You, me, the boys—who, by the way, are the only people allowed to bare their nipples. No other teats allowed! You hear me, Lizbeth? This is a breach of Landon code of nipple conduct. All female genitalia shall henceforth be banished under layers of brassiere wear and conservative dress. It's the new law." His voice vanishes with the rest of him.

"Oh, he's just teasing." Mom gives a little wink as she helps push poor Barron's face onto my freshly scolded nipple. "We need to get a good latch." She plunges two fingers down onto my boob. "Goodness, you're hard as sheetrock. You'll have to sit here a good hour at least. Here—" She beckons Gage to give her Nathan. "Normally, I'd suggest just one at a time. Of course, it'll take twice as long, but who are we kidding? You're going to live to be doing exactly this, right here, for the next four to six years!" Her voice shrills like a siren.

"Four to six *years*? I don't think so." I wince as Nathan latches on as well, and soon, I can feel their urgent little suckling mouths pulling on me in tandem.

"I think it's working!" I marvel at the two tiny dark heads doing their best to gain sustenance. "They're really nursing. This feels so strange."

"It feels wonderful is what it feels," Mom corrects as she plunges a finger near each of the boys' lips as if inspecting for leaks. "How did it go last night when I left? Were they big eaters?"

"I don't know. The nurses gave them a bottle, so I could try to get some shut-eye."

"*Skyla!*" Mom shouts and disrupts the homeostasis we just took five minutes to engineer. "You do not let a single bottle near these babies' mouths. Do you hear me, young lady? You need to train these boys to take only from you. Once you start giving them options, they'll choose the easy way out. It's our nature. Sometimes, the right decision is a hard decision—

painful even at times." Her eyes enlarge as she nods. It's as if she's speaking between the painful lines. "I'd better go check up on Tad. Whistle if you need me!"

I'm almost afraid to look at Gage, afraid he'll be green and squeamish watching his wife utilize his fun bags for something far more functional—like udders.

"You're beautiful." He strokes my hair lovingly. The softness in his eyes makes me blush.

"Oh, come on"— I jostle into him with my shoulder— "say what you really mean like *I wish you had another one so I could join in on the fun.*"

"All right, I get it. You're a mind reader." He presses a kiss to my ear. "But I'm okay with just the two. The boys will have to share with their pops."

It's nice like this, just the four of us together—alone at last.

The front door bursts open, and Bree waltzes in singing "Happy Birthday" while carrying a sheet cake over her head. Drake straggles behind carrying his own sheet cake sized box—and holy crap, there's an entire procession with Emily and Ethan holding up the rear. They set the oversized pastries down onto the table, all the while keeping their rubbernecks craned in my direction. Drake and Ethan plop down onto the couch near the window, their faces contorting into a dozen different looks of horror.

This is probably the part where I should cover up, or scream, but my body is in too much discomfort to care if an entire football team were watching.

"Cool." Em picks up Ember and shoves her under her shirt to do the same. "Did it get painful yet?"

"What? No. It's fine." My boys are easy, apparently, and I'm feeling perfectly smug about it.

"It'll get painful," Em assures. "*Really* painful."

"All right. She heard," Gage grumbles as he fumbles for something to cover me with, but comes up empty. He puts his arm protectively around us as a shield, his hand caressing the side of my neck. **You got this. Heck, we *got this.***

Bree snaps a couple of birthday hats onto her head like horns and watches with a look of longing. Brielle has never really had the full mothering experience with Beau. My own mother sort of took over in that department. Come to think of it, my mother had Ember for almost a year—some people even mistook Em for the tagalong babysitter on occasion.

The boys grunt and squirm, and every now and again give my nipples a good tug. Their warm bodies are snuggled up together, their limbs tucked in a ball, their backs rounded like turtles. I soak in their tiny perfect noses, their tiny adorable dimples blinking on and off like Christmas lights as they continue to drink down deep. They are so precious, so completely beautiful. Tears come to my eyes, and I'm unable to stop them from falling.

Gage and I have got this.

With Nathan and Barron in our lives—we have got it all.

Hours bleed by. Weeks pass in a blur. Gage and I haven't slept since November. My body aches constantly. The sound of a baby crying sets off a grenade of acid in the pit of my stomach. And the nursing, the incessant feedings—my cracked and raw nipples can't take another knife-piercing minute of it all.

Mom comes at me with Barron, and my fingers tremble as I take him. He latches on and—

"*Shit*," I cry.

"You'll have to watch your language," she reprimands lightly.

"I know, but it feels like needles are being jabbed into my nipples." I let out a quiet groan. "They're cracking and so raw it wouldn't surprise me if they fell right off." Bleeding is probably next, but I can't even think about that.

Gage has gone to the bowling alley to help Logan repair a lane. I wish to God I could have gone in his place, and he could be the one here nursing the boys. Two healthy little angels really are a blessing, but they're wearing me out in ways I didn't think possible. I remember when bathing was so easy and necessary, and now, like the rest of my hygiene, seems rather optional.

"You know, Gage has it so easy." I sit up in bed. Gage and I have both bassinets in the bedroom, making the already tiny room impossibly small. It's like playing a game of *Tetris* just walking to the bathroom.

"Don't they all," Mom quips, taking a seat at the foot of the mattress while cradling Nathan. "But we're the lucky ones. You get to hold these precious little beings and let them suckle off your bosom for hours while doing absolutely nothing but staring lovingly down at these perfect little creatures. Oh, how I wish your father could be here." She nuzzles her nose into Nathan's neck. "I'm sure what's-her-face has already told him that you've named a child after him."

I glance out the newly repaired bedroom window in the event Candace What's-Her-Face Messenger decides to lash out at my poor earthly mother for the quasi name-calling and break it again. Demetri sprung for the repair, and, even though it inspires a frown from me, I'm more than grateful. Wow—grateful to my father's killer. I shake my head, disgusted in myself.

"We thought Mia might be a boy," she goes on. "We already had you, so all of our pink dreams were fulfilled, but, I guess, it wasn't meant to be. If only your father knew you had *two* boys!" Her voice becomes strangely distant, and my head fills with a quiet rush as I nestle into the pillow. I clutch my arms tight around the tiny, warm bundle as I feel myself slipping away, slipping straight out of my body, out of my room.

"What's happening?" I whisper as my mother's laughter warbles like a dream.

Ahava forms around me. Candace Messenger is at the helm of this divinely inspired nightmare, and here she is—in the flesh. It's just like looking into a mirror if that mirror hadn't given birth a few weeks ago. Personally, I'm still sporting maternity wear, but I'd swear on a stack of Bibles it's because I'm too tired and busy with the boys to dig out my old wardrobe. Not to mention, I might be a tiny bit afraid to pull out my old jeans. It's like someone replaced my entire wardrobe with a bunch of miniature Barbie clothes. When was I ever that tiny? And will I ever be again? Tough questions with potentially scary answers.

"What in the—?" I gasp as I note my empty arms. "Where's Barron? Mother!" I gape at my lookalike relation. "I am nursing a baby! As in my body just can't up and disappear!" Oh my dear God, the inmates really are running the asylum.

Her eyes widen and retract. "You are most definitely not here in body, Skyla. I have ways, you know."

"Dear God, your ways are putting both my child and my left nipple in peril! By the way, my left nipple might not survive this latest debacle."

"Be still, child. Your mother is in the room. She thinks you're sleeping. She's already steadied the baby, and he's sucking away blissfully. I trust Lizbeth's supervision, and so should you. After all, I chose her to supervise my own child."

My mouth opens to say something, but I just can't.

"You're soulless, Skyla. It's a cheap party trick in my neck of the woods, and before your pretty little head goes there, I've wrapped you with a hedge of protection. So you need not fear a possession." She touches her finger to my nose, and I gag.

"Under no circumstance can I ever be possessed. Are we clear on that?" I'm not so sure what Candace Messenger understands anymore. Knocking me unconscious while I'm nursing an infant—her own grandchild no less—takes soul-knapping to a whole new level.

"We are most certainly clear." Her lids lower in annoyance. "Sector Dudley apprised me of the fact you were anxious to see me."

"Yes, I was—three weeks ago. Gage wanted to come along for the ride." I glance around and note his absence. "I can see the request was met."

"He'll get his." It comes off as a threat as her expression sours.

"Your disdain for my Fem of a husband astounds me, Mother."

"Your disdain for your own destiny astounds me, Skyla."

"What's that supposed to mean?"

"It means why are you fighting his unstoppable death? It's his destiny to go the way of the world, Skyla. You're to be with Logan—your true love—the one you've wanted from the beginning."

Her words sting like a fresh slap to the face. "I love Gage. Logan and I had our moment." Each word rips like a blade through my vocal cords. "Logan and I are in agreement that we both want Gage to stay. Gage and I have a family now. Besides, Demetri has achieved dominion through him. He's—"

"He's done with him," she says it so matter-of-factly the words breeze by me as if they were insignificant. But they aren't. They're perfectly tragic, and it makes me want to howl in this crystalline paradise that my mother calls home.

"Do you love me?" The words tumble out from me, numb.

"Of course. Why in heavens would I go through the backbreaking work of producing an heir to deliver a people who otherwise had no hope? The Nephilim need you, Skyla. I need you. You were designed for a higher purpose. A purpose of light, not darkness."

"But?" I can feel it dangling between us a like a viper.

Her gaze falls to the ground. "But, two dominions are to be born of you. And since you've accomplished the first, it's time to accomplish the second."

This strange world stills around me. Ahava itself seems to hold its breath at the audacious thought.

"Is that all I am to you? Some cheap breeding machine?" A wild rage strums through me, fueled with all the bullshit the celestial sphere has put me and those that I love through over the last few years. "I'm not putting up with it anymore. Yes, I love Logan, but Gage and I are together, and

I'm begging you to keep it that way. Lock this in. Make it last. You and I both know you have the power to make this happen."

Her features harden as she drills her lucent-colored eyes into mine. "Let's talk shop, shall we? What have you done regarding the factions?"

"Not a damn thing since your kangaroo court kicked me off the hot seat. I've been evicted, remember? You nullified the war and declared the last few years of my life a joke. Not to mention, spit on the graves of the ones that paid the ultimate price during that ten stage battle."

"Skyla." Her demeanor shifts as she closes her eyes and shudders. "As the overseer of the factions, your authority could never be stripped. Yes, you have been removed from the chair, but the power still lies in you. In other words, you are their leader. Lead the people, for God's sake!" A nest of lightning forms over her head, crackling and barking, flickering on and off as if a child were at the helm of the switch.

"What are you saying?"

Her eyes remain on mine as if we're having a showdown.

"Oh my God," I whisper as I piece it all together. "You're defying them." A dull smile twitches on my lips as the gravity of what's just happened comes over me. "You want me to do the same."

"Not true. You've already done it. I'm simply suggesting you take it to a grander scale."

"The Retribution League."

"Yes. That." She folds her arms across her chest, her hair flying around like a golden electrical current. "Skyla, while you've been holed up in your bed, nursing your pups, listening to Lizbeth preach from her *Mother Earth Handbook*, your people have been placed in grave danger. There are no more hours left to save them. There are only minutes." She glances back at the lake, and coming into view are her three backup singers—the Marshall twins and good old Rothello who got the ball rolling on the war to begin with. "The Decision Council has come to present you with a gift in honor of the precious princes you've ushered into the world. I'm aglow with pride these days. Sage is beaming at the thought of being a big sister."

My body (soul as it were) warms at the mention of her.

Candace nods to me. "We will grant you one good deed—of no monetary value—to be done at once to the person of your choosing."

"That's my gift?" It's so odd, but, then, look where I am. "Okay. I choose my daughter, Sage. And my good deed is to land her in a body and make her my legal child on the planet so I can put my family back together again." Well done, if I don't say so myself.

She closes her eyes a moment too long, letting me know it's a no-go.

"A living person. Is there someone in your circle of friends you'd like to bless with a kind gesture? A surprise bouquet of Mylar balloons perhaps?"

I study this version of myself a moment. "Do you say silly things to mock me, or just to get my juices flowing?"

"Both." She's quick with the answer. In truth, that's what I like about my mother. If anything, she's a straight shooter.

"Very well, I choose Gage—I generously gift him a very long life. He's to step into eternity only after me."

She shakes her head. "Try again. We cannot alter length of years."

Figures. "Okay"—I say it measured because I can already feel a no coming on for my next request—"I choose Chloe Bishop, the one in the Transfer. I want you to tighten her leash and freeze her morphing capabilities." I raise a hand. "Before you say no, at least freeze her ability to morph into Laken and me. She slept with Logan under false pretenses. That alone should be enough to call her to court." Although, no punishment ever seems enough for Chloe.

"Yes." She taps her chin.

"Yes?" I jump with glee that I'm finally getting somewhere. Had I known my mother would go for it, I would have gone for the gold and banished Chloe's soul from existence.

"Yes—no." Her brows rise as if to annunciate her confusing answer. "Chloe is residing in Ezrina's flesh. Ezrina worked very hard to harness those powers. Who am I to stagnate her spiritual synapses?"

"Who are you?" I'm not even going there. "Her leash is tight enough. And Logan is a dead man. The Justice Alliance isn't the least bit interested in the dead. Come, come—I've places to be. Pick someone."

Crap. Who to help...Who to help...

Nat and her forever broken heart come to mind. I know we're not close. In fact, some might call her an enemy of sorts, but we were in cheer, and I did kill her best friend *and* boyfriend, so I suppose I owe her a solid.

"Natalie Coleman," I say flatly. "I'd like her summoned at once, as well as the souls of Pierce Kragger and Kate Winston."

"Waking the dead, are we? What jurisdiction do you think you have around here?" Her eye twitches, as does her lower lip, alerting me to one of her schemes.

"That's right. We're waking the dead. They are my people, and I have waited too long to right this wrong."

My mother takes a step back, and a brilliant glow envelops her. "There you are, my girl. I've been waiting for you to come into your own."

She waves her hands, and out of thin air appear Nat, Kate, and Pierce.

"Oh, wow," I marvel. They all look so, well—*alive*.

"Crap!" Nat runs over to me and cowers for a minute, her rust-colored curls bouncing like springs. "What the?" She gives a hard look to Kate, and for a brief second, I wonder if they even liked each other. "Katie?" She turns to gawk at the Kragger being. "Pierce, what's going on?"

Pierce steps up. He's well-built and fit, just like Nev, but there's something different about this version of the O.G. Kragger. His demeanor is softer than I remember. He's far more humble in spirit. If he were half this decent on Earth, Nat would have had a whole lot more competition.

"Natalie"—he says her name sweetly, the look of love still alive in his eyes—"I'm the Pierce you once knew, but I've long since passed. It's not me in my body anymore." He shakes his head as she runs into his arms. "Babe, if that was me, you know we'd be together." He peppers her face with kisses.

Tears come to my eyes, and Kate comes over and wraps her arms around me. Her hair is the palest color of butter, and her eyes glow bright as the sky. Kate always was, and still is beautiful.

"Greatest good deed ever." She squeezes me, tight. "Thanks for thinking of my bestie."

"No biggie." I try to shrug it off, but the urge to blubber keeps getting stronger. Again, damn hormones. "Sorry again about killing you," I whisper. I've already had a chance to meet up with Kate in the celestial sense. "I still feel awful."

"It was my time." Her eyes cut to my mother. "But there is one more task left for me to do down there."

My mother and Kate enter into a standoff—their faces wash of all expression, their gazes locked like a vise.

"What is it? Do you want me to start a foundation or something?" My mind goes wild a mile a minute. I could start up the Accidental Slope Beheading Fund, but I'm not too sure who exactly would benefit.

Both Kate and my mother shake their heads in disapproval at me at the thought they heard.

Nat and Pierce pull away and join us after their alone time. They each have an arm wrapped around one another, and it looks easy as if they never spent a moment apart.

"So, what's the news with my sister and brother?" Pierce asks it kind, not at all smeared with Kragger-tude.

"Your sister is an owl, safe in the Landon house. She's one of our favorite pets. And your brother is a raven. He has a girlfriend who happens to be in the same plumbed predicament. They're quite cute together."

Nat's mouth drops open at the revelation.

"Good for him." Pierce shrugs at the idea. "But you need to do something about Emerson. She's not a caged-up kind of girl. I don't need to assess the situation to know she's miserable. Isn't there anything you can do for her?"

"I don't know. Chloe killed her ages ago, and then Marshall resurrected her in the form of an owl to help me glean some information. She's been trapped ever since. I don't think there's much I can do. She can't survive in the wild. My sister's been feeding her table scraps. Her cravings for mice have long since dissipated."

"Keep her, then. But give her something to do. Put her in charge of something. She's never been good with alone time. Like all Kraggers, she tends to crawl into her head a bit too much."

"I'll see what I can do." Talk about your far-reaching good deed. But I do like Emerson. And I hate that Chloe killed her. I will find something for her. Hey? Maybe now that her palette is more refined, I can convince her to dine on Chloe's eyeballs. I recall Nev gobbling a few of those delicacies down in his prime.

Nat and Kate spend a few minutes chitchatting, lost in hugs and tears, and, before we know it, my mother calls time.

"The two of you back to Earth!"

"Wait!" I cry as my body begins to tremble, my soul loosening from this world to the next. "Let Gage live, once and for all! Please!" I shout those words with all of my hope, all of my love, all of my anger and fury rolled into one desperate plea.

"Skyla, my love." She bends over and picks up a small ebony-colored rock from the edge of the lake. "His destiny is written in stone." She tosses it to me, and it feels cold and hard, dangerous, in my hand. "Etched over the top is the amount of time he has left. You must wet the stone to read it. This is my gift to you, Skyla. I'll be down soon to see my precious boys. Please, slather some lanolin over those cracked sores you're feeding my grandchildren with. Celestra blood is not their choice of beverage."

I open my palm, revealing a smooth black stone. I rub my thumb over and flip it, but it's blank on both sides to the untrained eye.

The stone warms in my hand, igniting a pure shade of cobalt, identical to my husband's eyes, and I drop it back at her feet. I don't want it. I never want to see it again.

I startle back to life, back in my body with Barron gumming me into regular intervals of wild pain.

"Lanolin," I cry out, and Mom blinks to life herself.

"Good call! I think it's time. I have some in my room. I'll be right back."

I glance down at my empty palm. No stone—and I'm relieved. There is no way in hell I'm interested in seeing what that stone says. The only thing I'm interested in is reversing its curse.

If it's one thing I learned tonight, it's the fact my mother, the womb donor, is more than okay in sponsoring my rebellion.

In fact, you might even say she's leading it in a roundabout way.

The Retribution League will expand, usurping the Faction Council's power, and Gage will live.

I'll see to both of those things.

Now—how to go about rallying the masses—and how to go about saving a life? I have no idea what either of those entails...

But something tells me I'm about to find out via my mother, the not-so subtle leader.

The baby's mouth falls away from me, and we both give a sigh of contentment. I'm exhausted, delirious even. It wouldn't surprise me one bit if I hallucinated that entire scenario with my mother. My body needs a solid eight—make that eighteen—hours of sleep just to recoup from the trauma of childbirth three weeks back. I couldn't care less if it's the middle of the afternoon. The inside of my eyelids is calling, and I'm not about to deny my body its due.

I place Barron down into the bassinet, happily squirming in his sleep just as Nathan lets out a lusty cry.

A hard bite of acid explodes in my stomach as a surge of adrenaline courses through my veins.

A tiny whimper escapes me.

I didn't really think I was going to get any sleep, did I?

Gage

"What did the stone say?" My entire body goes rigid, waiting for Skyla to answer. She's just relayed the bizarre details of her visit to Ahava to both Logan and me. Logan swung by the house this evening and came up to the room to pay a visit to his new nephews. I'll be the first to admit, it feels strange with him sitting on the bed that I make love to Skyla on—not that we've been hitting the sheets for the last few weeks. Her body isn't healed quite yet. But the exhausted moments we've shared since the twins came home seem far more intimate than anything we've experienced before. For about an hour each night, Skyla and I lie over the bed, shirtless, with the boys' bare skin over ours. Of course, Skyla is doing something far more productive in feeding them at the time, but while she has one, I'm bonding with the other, and it's been magic every single night, every single day with our children finally here with us.

"It said nothing as far as I'm concerned." She leans back onto the pillow, cradling Nathan while Logan holds Barron. "I gave it back. Besides, she mentioned it needed to be wet to read. It was dry as a bone, and I plan on keeping it that way—safe in Ahava." Her lips twitch. "There's hope for us yet. We don't need my mother—as evidenced by her rebel-at-the-speed-of-light speech. She's useless. I'm in charge. Get used to it." She gives a sad wink. "The fact she gave me the green light on the Retribution League shows she's all about bending the rules. Death may be eyeing your expiration date, but she's just proved that nothing, and I mean nothing, is written in stone." She winces because my expiration date is quite literally carved into a rock somewhere.

"That's okay, Skyla." I reach over and take her hand in mine. "I've got a few strings I can pull. I wouldn't worry too much about me. Wes is full steam ahead in phase two of his make-the-Nephilim-look-like-psychotic-sadists."

"Meaning?" Logan plants a gentle kiss to the top of Barron's head. It warms my heart to see Logan so loving with him. Thanks to my reckless act, I'll forever be fearing for

Barron's destiny. If I knew that breaking faith with the Barricade would cost me my son, I would be driving that crazy train right alongside my brother. A tight knot builds in my stomach because I'm afraid it might still be an option—hell, with Demetri, I'm sure that was the intent all along.

"Meaning, the Videns are freaked out," I continue. "A third of their youth is missing."

"The youth is missing? Track down their phones. Shut down their Wi-Fi. You'll find them." Logan shifts Barron to one arm and holds him like a football.

"These are consenting adults—eighteen to thirty—ninety percent males. Em says they were recruited to work as a part of some underground army."

Skyla's mouth falls open. "He sidestepped the Immunity League, so soon?"

I shake my head. "I'm thinking this underground army had a completely different purpose. The Immunity League was built from the best and the brightest. This Viden harvest was indiscriminate. Come as you are, ready to serve, no questions asked. And they came by the droves. And now, every single one of them is unaccounted for."

"Shit." Logan glances to Skyla a moment as if they had already discussed this awful scenario. "Anyone file a missing persons report?"

"Not to my knowledge. The Videns asked for answers, and I told them I'd shake down Wes myself."

"And when are you going to do that?" Skyla sighs hard because we all know that Wesley and straight answers are strangers to one another.

"Tonight. I have a meeting with the Videns after that, and I'd sure as hell had better have something to tell them. Once the authorities get involved, we'll all be eating a shit sandwich."

Logan nods in agreement. "About how many people would you guestimate are missing? Fifty? A hundred?"

"Try two thousand, worldwide."

"Oh my God." Skyla closes her eyes like she might be sick. "Gage, the Videns are my people, too. They're an affiliate faction, and they need to be treated as such. If Wesley is hurting our brothers and sisters, he needs to be stomped out like a flame."

"He's bulletproof. Demetri made sure of that." And so am I until I'm not. It's a funny thing to be on top with your father one minute, then sail so far down to the bottom you can't even see the surface anymore. A thought I've been stifling struggles to break free. "There's something you should know about Demetri."

"He turns into a pumpkin at midnight?" Skyla yawns as she says it. She's exhausted. It might as well be midnight. Hell, every hour of every day feels like one long, drawn-out midnight.

"That would be too easy. More like a child killer after midnight—attempted child killer, and I'm the child in question."

"Excuse me?" Skyla shelters Nathan's ears with her hand as she says it. She doesn't want the filth of my biological father to trickle down into his precious mind. I already wish it didn't trickle down into their DNA.

"That day I almost bit the big one off Devil's Peak—it wasn't Candace who pushed me." A grievous smile comes and goes on my lips. I don't like to share dicey things her mother has done to me. I know deep down Skyla desires the love and acceptance of her birth mother. In a strange, twisted way, I think I want that from Demetri—for him to accept me as I am, his enemy.

"Are you saying Demetri pushed you?" Her eyes widen, each their own pale blue globe.

"I'm saying he might have liked the attention he received when he saved me." I place air quotes around the word *saved*.

Barron starts to fuss, and Logan hands him over to me. "He needs his daddy."

"He can rest assured I'd never push him off a cliff just to make him grateful to me. I fell for Demetri's bull once, but never again."

"Never say never," Skyla whispers the words almost catatonic.

"What's that supposed to mean?"

"It means Demetri is a master manipulator. Be careful."

"Watch your every step," Logan adds. "Wes and Demetri are out for blood—and I think we all know they have a pretty tight track record of getting what they want."

"Except Laken," Skyla points out. "She's the one who thankfully got away."

"Laken." My wheels start turning. "Out of seven billion people on this planet and counting, Laken Stewart—*Flanders*, is the only person who might have a shot of stopping my brother." I try to digest this for a minute. "I think I know what I have to do." I get up and drop a kiss over each of the boys' foreheads, handing Barron to Skyla. "Don't wait up for me." I plant a kiss onto Skyla's lips. "This is going to be a late one."

Logan says good night, and we walk out together into the dismal Paragon night.

"Do what you can to get to the bottom of this mass disappearance, and fast." Logan gives my back a tap as he heads to his truck. "If you don't, we'll have to find a way to bind that Fem brother of yours. Demetri won't have it, so we'll have to strip him of his balls as well. You know how easy that will be." His eyes narrow with a threat before he loosens and slaps me on the back. "We can do it—and we will."

I give a quick nod in lieu of words as I head toward the street to wait for my ride to the underworld, Wes.

There are two things I know to be true: Wesley can't be bound, and Demetri's invisible henchmen aren't letting anyone near his balls, with the exception of my mother-in-law.

Logan is wrong—simply talking to air, pumping me up with useless words.

We can't do it. And we won't.

I, on the other hand, might be able to defuse two bombs that I just so happen to be related to.

THE SERPENTINE BUTTERFLY

There has never been an impotent feeling in my life like that of being human, or more accurately, devoid of my Fem capabilities. In hindsight, there isn't a very good reason to have asked Candace to remove my powers, considering my DNA remained intact, spiraling like a nefarious stairway to wickedness. I text Wes once again to pick me up, which he's been doing diligently, but I haven't paid too many visits since he had Tobie and I had the boys. We've both had a few more pressing things—people on our minds. He's not usually late, and I'm starting to freeze my ass off just standing at the bottom of the Landon's driveway.

Nevermore shows up unexpectedly in the sensible sedan he and Ezrina purchased. He kills the engine and comes around dressed in a suit, his face a charmingly handsome version of Pierce Kragger.

"What's up?" I slap him five, a concept he's been working on. His arm swings at me like he's going to throw a punch, and for a second, I'm sure he is. Nev latches on and our bodies vibrate violently until the landscape changes around us, and we're standing in the Transfer.

"I'm your new pickup." He gives a cheery grin as he holds a hand out at the dismal surroundings. "Wesley gifted me the privilege to come and go as I please."

"Do I want to know why?" I glance around for my brother, but he's nowhere to be found, just a bunch of Transfer poltergeists swirling and whirling their way through this hellish oblivion.

"Perhaps not." He ushers me toward my brother's overgrown home. "But you're about to find out."

We head inside, no need to knock since the front door sits wide open.

Wesley is in the living room, his arms filled with a tiny pink bundle, a bottle in his hand as he feeds his precious baby girl. Instantly, I'm warmed by this. I wish that I wasn't. I came ready to rip his balls right off his body, but seeing him as a father, holding his child, makes me feel desperately happy and sad for him all rolled into one.

"I'm pissed at you." I walk over and touch my finger to my tiny niece, her pink bow lips still wrapped around the clear nipple. She's beautiful. And a part of me is relieved that I see Wesley's face in hers and not Chloe's.

"No rough language around my daughter. She's pristine—perfect, and I plan to keep her that way."

"Then you'll have to give her to Skyla and me to raise because pristine perfection is the last thing she'll find down here."

He lifts a brow before calling over his shoulder, "Ezrina."

"What's she doing here?" I look to Nev who's currently mesmerized by the watery globe in the center of the room.

"My how the world has changed in two hundred years," he muses without answering me.

Ezrina comes and takes the baby from Wes. "There, there, sweet love," she coos.

"What's going on?"

Ezrina nods to Wes and makes a face. "Can't speak now. I have a beauty to bathe." She whisks off down the hall. "Come, Heathcliff!" And Nev is quick to follow.

Wes tosses the tiny white towel off his shoulder and onto his dusty velour sofa. "I asked Ezrina to help. I couldn't quite ask my mother since she's dead." He motions for me to take a seat. "Take a load off."

"No thanks," I say, and he stands to join me. "Where's Chloe?" Not that I'm interested in her whereabouts, but it might explain what Ezrina is doing here.

"Upstairs counting Cheerios. You'd think she was administering round-the-clock care the way she bitches and gripes. She hasn't seen her daughter twice, and she's acting as if she's losing her mind. Kresley offered to help, but I know how off-putting that would be to Laken."

"Off-putting?" I grip his shoulder and make him look at me with those familiar features I've grown to hate when looking in the mirror. "Do you want to know what's off-putting to

Laken? You messing with the rest of the planet. She finds that very fucking off-putting. And sadly, I still believe she's the only one who can stop you from committing one of the biggest catastrophes to our people." I twist his shirt in my hand and pull him in close. "Where the hell are the Videns? You and I have a deal. You're to report to me any bullshit you're about to pull. Do I need to drag Demetri's ass down here to clarify?"

"No need," a deep voice booms from the foyer as Demetri makes his way over with the clapping of his thousand dollar Italian shoes. "Wesley, is it true? You've denied your brother knowledge regarding his people?"

Wes tips his head back, his nostrils flaring with a silent rage. "They'll be back."

My heart thumps wildly. Adrenaline spikes within me. If Wes isn't keeping his end of the bargain, it must void out the covenant.

"What are the consequences?" I look to Demetri. "He broke the covenant. It's null and void. I want that curse lifted from my children." Barron, to be exact, but I'm simply going off a feeling, off the fact I had one lone vision the moment he was born. I could be wrong. Hell, I pray I am.

"I'm sorry, son." Demetri looks down a moment, somber, utterly sincere, and it frightens me. "You broke faith with the Barricade, Gage. There is no one who can help you." Those psychotic smiling eyes of his begin to glow.

"All right." I rake my fingers through my hair, razoring my nails over my skin. "Shit. What do I have to do? Sit on the throne? Drink your blood? I'll drink a fucking gallon. You need me to claim dominion? What?" I shout that last word so loud, the baby begins on a high-pitched wail from down the hall.

"Mind your manners!" Ezrina howls back.

"Shit." I pinch my eyes shut. "Tell me." There's desperation in my voice, so raw and visceral it makes me squeamish just hearing it. "I love my wife, my life, my brand new baby boys. But, God Almighty, I don't want them cursed. I do not want them turning from all I believe in."

Wes smirks. "Because you think what you believe is right. Your boys might think otherwise."

I pick him up by the shirt and slam him to the wall. "Because he won't have a choice!"

"I get it," he whispers, raising his arms in surrender. "I would feel just as destroyed if Tobie turned her beliefs from mine—or, more to the point, if he took hold of her brain and heart and made her do it." He glares a moment at our father, and it feels like a brief show of solidarity. A real come-on-Dad moment between two brothers.

"What if I let the curse fall on me?" I pant, wiping down my brow. Wesley has that fucking fire turned up to hell, and the entire room feels like a sauna. Tobie might choose to live with Skyla and me simply for the air conditioning.

"Gage, Gage, Gage." Demetri walks a clean circle around me. "What kind of curse would that be? Of what consequence? You would feel vindicated, proud to have done something noble for your child. There is no punishment in that."

"Trust me, I'm plenty punished. Not to mention that I lose my wife." It's one thing to listen in on Wesley's schemes, to play along and pay attention, but it's a whole other thing to cross my heart over to the dark side.

Wes shakes his head. "There's no reason Skyla wouldn't let you be your own person, let you carry out a sentence to spare her child. You wouldn't lose Skyla."

"I'd lose Skyla for the same reason you lost Laken."

"Bullshit." His eyes bulge, his jowls vibrate with rage as he grits the word through his teeth. "You're married. She knows you've got a hard-on to please her and her people. Everyone would know you're a fake. You think you're going to team up with me and then go home and sleep with the enemy? How is that going to work? And, if it did, what difference would it make in our children's lives when they decide they want to be just like Daddy when they grow up? You'll lure them both to my side without meaning to. You don't win at this Gage—and that my friend, my *brother*—is the point."

My head pounds, blood courses through my veins, steady as a hammer. He's right. I don't win.

I blow out a mean breath and turn to Demetri. "Lay it out for me. What is the worst-case scenario? What rot and filth will enter my life once I spare my child?"

"Just one?" Demetri toys with a demonic smile.

"Fine. Children."

"You lose Skyla. You lose the boys. You lose your life." He bleeds a black smile. "It's as simple as that."

I swallow hard. Worst case is pretty damn bad.

"And what do I gain?" A loss that magnificent in Demetri's twisted mind is easily replaceable—I can feel it in my bones.

"You gain my kingdom, the throne—you are the king."

And there you have it—the gains, the losses, all the same in value to him. I look to Wes. "You'll give the Videns an explanation alongside me tonight as to why they lost so many damn men." I clear my throat, trying to get my bearings before shifting to Demetri. "When does this need to happen?"

"The binding covenant is instantaneous upon ritual rites. And your era on the throne begins when Your Grace"—he lifts a finger presumably to Candace—"decides it is your time. I'll give you until the christening to decide."

I look the bastard who brought me into the world dead in the eyes. "Is this what you've wanted from the beginning?"

His hand rises to my face, his thumb caressing my cheek. "Yes, my son. It is."

Logan

Shit. I continue chewing on my burger, trying to swallow it down while staring at Gage. I should have known something was very fucking wrong when he summoned me to Dudley's at this late hour—invited Dudley in on this burger-laden meeting no less.

"So he's not done with you after all." I toss my food back into the bag. "Why are we eating?" I suck down my water. "This is shit news."

"Because I need to eat." He takes an aggressive bite before choking it down. "Skyla wanted me to pick up a burger for her on the way home. It's been weeks since she's had one. I want to give her whatever she wants." His voice breaks. "A happy wife, a happy life." He shoots me a glassy-eyed stare. "You might want to remember that."

"Gage." I lean my head onto my hand like I might vomit.

"What is the alternative here?" Dudley says it so tenderhearted you'd think he was speaking to Skyla.

"I die anyway, and one of my boys turns his heart against all Skyla and I stand for—in other words, to the dark side. He sits on that throne of Demetri's and rules the demonic roost." Gage's mouth contorts as if he's holding back tears, and he is.

"Is that so?" Dudley leans back, folds his arms across his chest as if he's contemplating this. "I'm afraid you've missed the point here."

"Tell me it's good news." Gage crumbles his wrapper in a wad and tosses it against the wall.

"It is, but you won't see it that way. What you have here is Demetri trying to demonstrate his mercy. His dominion needs a leader. Ideally, one of your sons, considering their pedigree, but since you have found that weak spot in his heart, he has decided to gift you the option to take over the throne yourself. Which is a wise move on his part, considering how violently protective a parent can be toward a child. He knows you would serve with all your heart to shield your children from his wickedness. In essence, he has you where he wants you, and, if you love those little boys nestled in your wife's bosom, you will do what pleases him best."

"Or else one of the boys picks up the baton." I sink in my seat. I love those boys as if they were my own. "If Gage doesn't sit on the throne, if he chooses to live out the rest of his days in peace, what will happen? Does a bomb go off in the child's mind, suddenly programming him to eschew what's right? I think this reeks of brainwashing, a technique the Counts have spent centuries perfecting. Look at that fiasco that took place at Ephemeral? Why didn't anyone take them to court for that?"

"The Justice Alliance isn't too concerned with what Demetri does. He's kept to a different code of ethics. He knows the laws and all of its loopholes. He swims in the loopholes for the fun of it." He looks to Gage. "I'm sorry, young Oliver. It seems you've been caught in a loophole the size of a throne."

"Don't apologize to me." Gage's voice shakes with anger, his eyes set on Dudley, rife with fury. "Figure out a way to get my children and me out of this mess. You"—he digs his finger in the air at Dudley—"are my only hope, my friend. I don't have a celestial leg to stand on, and we all know what happened the last time I went begging my mother-in-law for assistance."

Something in me lurches. A sick feeling weighs me down because I'm the one Candace loves, and yet, I haven't gone to bat for Gage.

"Run from this." Dudley steadies his cutthroat gaze over my nephew's. "There is a third solution. Find it."

"Why don't you get going?" I slide the bag toward Gage. "Get this to Skyla. Kiss your boys. Don't overthink this."

I know for a fact she's preparing a speech to give at the Council of the Superiors. Gage and Skyla each have the weight of their own unique worlds on their shoulders.

"All right." He scoops his food up and heads for the door. "I know what I have to do. It just kills me to do it."

"Do yourself and everyone else a favor"—Dudley calls after him—"do nothing."

"Story of my life." He lets the door click softly behind him.

Dudley shifts his sharp glare to me. "Why the eviction?"

"Because we have places to go."

Ahava winks and sparkles in pale tonal blues as if it were the only color that mattered, the only one we needed.

"You might want to segue into the topic at hand," Dudley suggests in a whisper as the perfect representation of Skyla looks up from her glass throne in the middle of the lake. Her eyes, her face, her entire being lights up with a shower of sparks emitting from her the moment she sees us.

"Logan!" she says it high and clear, sounding so much like Skyla I want to cry. How could this version of my beautiful wife, ex-wife, ever want to remove Gage from the planet?

"Segue how?" I hiss to the Sector by my side.

"Talk shop," he whispers sideways from his lips like a B-list ventriloquist. "You know, how the Treble is going—how the twins are doing."

Candace frowns and bats him away before pulling me into a long, vibratory embrace. She holds the scent of a summer afternoon and clean sheets, a scent I wish I could bottle and keep for myself. Candace is so beautiful. It sometimes hurts to look at her.

I wince as we pull away, hoping she won't catch on to the ego boost I'm trying to invoke.

"The twins are doing great," I say.

"Of course, they are." Her eyes widen as if I just affronted her. "I've given them the very best mother. Skyla's neuron matrix is carefully designed to make sure her mothering skills, her need to protect her young, is seven times stronger than that of your average human. It's a vicious thing to come between Skyla and those boys. Make no mistake—she will be the victor."

I glance to Dudley. Not sure if this is what he meant by segue, but it feels right.

"You know who else loves those boys fiercely?"

"You," she says without missing a beat, a slight look of irritation in her eyes because she knows where I'm headed with this. "Did you come to see the stone?" There's a touch of giddiness in her voice, and now I'm the one who's irritated.

"No."

She smacks her lips. "I didn't think so, but, nevertheless, some people do like to be apprised. We receive inquires by the dozens."

"We're not inquiring. Gage wants to stay. He broke faith with the Barricade, and now the heart of the one he loves will turn against him. He had a vision when Barron was born. He's afraid it might be him." There, no shitting around, just straight to the point.

"Barron," she whispers, looking grieved in the process.

"So you know?"

"I know everything, Logan. I even know what you're about to ask next." She doesn't look up from the ground. "Gage Oliver has a destiny. His children each have their own destinies as predicated long ago. The thing is, Demetri has become quite powerful and generous, I might add." She looks up abruptly. "Adding to his realm—giving out options to those who least deserve it." She clucks her tongue and waves me off. "I know what you want—Gage with Skyla until they're old and gray—you, of course, getting to play the part of martyr."

"Not true. I'm dead."

She glances around. Her eyes enlarge as if this surprised her. "Yes, you are—for the time being. How is the situation with the Steel Barricade?"

"Dire. They've eaten the Videns for breakfast."

"And my daughter? Has she begun her so-called retribution?"

I glance to Dudley before answering. She can't be serious. "She's a tad busy," I say. "And what exactly is she to do for retribution?"

"She'll think of something." Her eyes burrow into mine, sharp as knives. "Or perhaps you will."

"Me? My destiny is wrapped up in here somewhere, isn't it?"

"Somewhere," she echoes, her features growing cold.

"Help, Gage," I plead. "Help him live for those boys. I'll sit on the throne of filth and lies, do whatever it is you want me to. I'll switch allegiances. I've already done it once for Skyla. It would be an honor to do it again."

"You're not a Fem." She softens again. "You're my special angel." Her finger curls under my chin, soft as velvet. "You and Skyla together will be—"

"Miserable without Gage," I finish for her. "So will those boys. Candace"—I fall to my knees, and Dudley groans and looks away—"I beg of you with all that I am. For your precious daughter's sake, for those boys, for my sake, help Gage out of this mess, and for the love of all that is holy, protect those children from ever choosing wickedness."

Her mouth falls open. She takes a small breath of surprise, her eyes searching me as if I've betrayed her in some way. Candace walks to the edge of the lake, her thumb tucked to her lip as if deep in thought before returning.

"The boys have free will—and are bound with the potential curse should Gage refuse Demetri's offer. Just the one—of course." She lifts a finger when making the point. "Gage is being gifted a unique opportunity. Demetri is willing to forgo the original agreement, which is to take the heart of the one Gage loves and turn it against him. He does have all legal authority to do so—but, in this case, he's offered the position to his own son—that being Gage." She shrugs. "If Gage decides to take the curse upon himself, wickedness will reign in him. That is not the Gage you know—you will not be miserable because he is gone—you will be miserable because he is still in your midst. Prior to any of this taking place, death will come and free Skyla from her covenant with him. It's the one mercy I'll allow. Be gone."

Ahava dissipates, and Dudley and I find ourselves back in his cavernous home, staring at one another with nothing productive to say.

"He's screwed, isn't he?" I ask, still trying to wrap my head around the conversation.

"It would seem."

I spend the night at White Horse, at the home I once hoped I would share with Skyla, and now more than anything I hope I won't. It's funny how you can hope, dream, beg God for something with all your heart, and then once the details shift, it becomes the worst outcome in the world. Well, maybe not the worst, definitely not the best.

Sleep finds me, throws a cloak of darkness over my head, and kidnaps me into its murky oasis. I fumble from one strange dream to the next before Devil's Peak forms around me. A familiar blonde with those deep ringlets running down her back catches my eye as she speaks to another girl.

"Skyla?" I call out to her, and both she and Laken jog over.

"Logan." Her arms collapse around me, tight. It feels real, and it's only then I note the icy air against my skin, the sharp bite of fog choking up my lungs. "We're so glad you're here."

"What's going on?"

"I don't know. I thought this was your dreamscape." She shakes her head.

Laken glances around, unsettled. I can feel the fear rattling her bones like castanets. "It's Wesley. He's done this before. Not since Coop, but he has."

"What do you think he's called us for?" Skyla's voice trembles as she takes in the dark edges of the parking lot, the borders of the lawn that dive down the cliff not quite drawn out. Wes is playing fast and loose with details. It's amateur hour compared to what I can do. "And why Devil's Peak?"

"I know why." Laken hooks her arm through Skyla's. "He's about to summons us the hard way." Laken isn't a fan of cliff diving in an effort to see her ex. I'm not either.

The ground trembles. A dull moan emanates from around us, and suddenly, we're thrust into a bad sci-fi movie. Devil's Peak vibrates as a stampede of some sort heads this way. The ground bounces and shakes as if Wesley himself is trying to make a point. The three of us struggle to balance ourselves, holding our arms out, holding each other, so we don't fall over.

"Wes?" Laken cries out, but her voice is drowned out by a steady, horrific moan coming from the woods just past the lot. She shakes her head. Her face grows pale as the eye of the moon. "No—please," she pants, the panic in her rising. "They're coming. He's done it again!"

"He's done what?" I shout over the thunderous groans. "Who's coming?"

Laken looks to the forest and screams, "*Run!*"

Skyla and I follow her gaze. Out of the woods, stabbing through the darkness, is an entire army of pale, twisted limbs, shredded clothes, blood everywhere. Hundreds, if not thousands, of men and women stagger from the shadowed evergreens. Their bruised eyes and their chalky skin give away the fact they are no longer among the living.

They tumble out onto the parking lot, spreading over the lawn like a disease. Their limbs move at an exaggeratingly quickened pace, not your traditional zombie trot.

Laken takes both Skyla and me by the hand and runs us off Devil's Peak via the sharp knives of the rocks below.

We'll never touch them.

We never do.

Laken hits the ground running once we hit the Transfer and races straight into Wesley's nightmare of an abode.

Skyla and I skid in after her to find Wes sitting in a chair, rocking his baby girl in his arms, innocent and pure like some Norman Rockwell painting.

"Ezrina!" he says as loud as possible without shouting.

As if on cue both, Ezrina and Nev appear looking a bit haggard.

"Ezrina? Nev?" Skyla is shocked as hell to see them here, as am I.

"He needs a woman's touch." She waves us off. "It's a temporary situation."

"And she looks like Chloe," Wes is quick to point out. "I'm hoping that might help her bond when Chloe feels the need."

Figures. Chloe needs a body double as a mother.

Laken leans in to get a better look at the baby, and her eyes fill with tears. "She's beautiful."

"Thank you," Wes says, hushed and heartfelt, never taking his gaze off Laken. His obsession with her is about as sick as Chloe's with Gage, although Wes and Laken actually had something once. They could still have something if he hadn't thrown her into Coop's arms so long ago.

"So, Chloe's really not stepping up, huh?" Skyla touches the baby's cheek, and the tiny tot begins to fuss as if she still hasn't figured out the fine art of the scream. With Chloe as her mother, she will more than master the fine art of screaming.

"Oh!" Skyla touches her hand to her chest as dark pools of liquid grow over her breasts. "My milk just let down at the sight of her. My body seems programmed to respond these days." She gives a slight shrug. "Sorry."

"Don't apologize." Wes hands her a towel, which she drapes around her shoulders. "It shows you're attentive to your children's needs—a loving mother." He offers a forlorn look to Laken. "You will be, too, one day."

Skyla tips her head in sympathy. "And you're a good father, Wes. You're just a lousy leader. Who were those

Spectators? Where did you get the bodies?" She sucks in a deep breath. "The Videns!"

"You're smart, too." He motions to the bar. "Can I get anyone a drink?"

Laken lets out a moan. "We're not here for your hospitality, Wes. Why pull us into this nightmare? Are those Spectators real? Is that your next move?"

He pauses from putting the cap back onto the bourbon. "Because I can. Yes. And why not?"

"Shit." I walk over to that enormous globe bobbing in a barrel and give it a spin. It's heavy, mostly onyx, I think. "You can't have the world."

"No." He takes a quick drink, and his jaw sets from the burn. "That's my brother's territory, along with everything else."

"You sound bitter." Laken goes over, her voice wavering as if trying to steady itself. "You don't need to be." She's sweetening her tone, too much saccharin. Wes is a smart boy. He already knows it's an act.

"I'm sorry." He puts down his drink and steps toward her. "I don't mean to be." He offers her a sad smile, pained, the very present look of agony stamped over his pompous features. "Gage believes you are the only one in the world who can stop me, Laken." He gives a slight nod as if it were a reality. "Do you believe this to be true?" The room stills. "Soon, Laken"—he threads his fingers through her hair, and she stiffens—"very soon, I'll have my kingdom in place. The Steel Barricade is already reveling in its victory. The Spectators are simply a show of force I'll use if I have to."

"Is that what you're doing?" Skyla heads over and bats his hand from Laken's hair. "Don't touch her."

Wes gives a depleted smile. "Yes. I was simply sharing what's to come if things get—complicated."

"Does Gage know?"

He nods. "He's been briefed. I'm sure he'll spill the details come morning. He's probably letting you enjoy your beauty sleep. Such a gentleman." He shakes his head before taking another sip. "You know all of my moves, Skyla. How fair is that? It's not, but I still have the upper hand. That counts for something, right? It's a testament to my fortitude, my greatness."

Skyla wraps her arms around Laken as if she were her child but doesn't say a word because she knows he's right.

"Enjoy your victory while you have it," Skyla says it calm, cold as her mother. "It won't be yours for long."

The moaning picks up right outside the walls, and I look to Skyla and Laken, shaking my head, beckoning them not to move. Within seconds, the room is inundated with the putrid stink, the rotting flesh of the Spectators', their arms swinging through the air with a primal savagery. A deteriorating arm swings my way, slamming me against the wall with supernatural strength. The decrepit creature presses his nasty face into mine. His dead eyes, laughing the way I've only ever seen Demetri's do. He plunges his mouth to my neck, locking down over my throat with his teeth, and pulls back, ripping my flesh with a searing pain that spreads like a flame through my body. A scream begs to rip from me, but I'm staring at my vocal cords, my larynx dripping from his mouth.

Wes steps forward and touches Laken gently on the cheek. "Good night, my queen. Sleep tight."

I sit up with a start, panting into darkness—back at White Horse—back in the safety of my home—neck intact and all.

My hand slaps the nightstand for my phone as I send a group text to Skyla and Laken. **Everyone okay?**

Laken responds first. **I'm fine. Sorry he dragged you into it.**

Then Skyla. **I'm fine. There's only one solution to this madness. Wesley and Demetri must die.**

Laken: **They're not able to—at least not Demetri. And I'm sure Wes is untouchable.**

She's right. I hit *Send*.

Skyla: **Then they'll have to be bound, immobilized, or destroyed.**

Most likely all three, and in that order. The sooner, the better.

I beg sleep to take me one more time, but she never comes. Instead, my mind reels on how to bind, immobilize, and destroy a Fem.

Deep down, I wonder if that Fem will be Gage.

14

Avenging Angels

Skyla

There are many seasons in life, and, for Gage and me, this is both a season of mind-bending exhaustion and insurmountable joy. This microcosm of our existence is much more precious than any hard-won victory. It is a selfish endeavor, the salvation of our spirits found through the eyes of two cherished, blessed souls. Gage and I have soared to our own private nirvana. We've found a harmonious solitude among the chaos that only this sweet hour of life can bring. Nathan and Barron, their cries, their every coo have become our heart song, our lover's anthem, something wild and beautiful born to us as the tangible representation of our union.

I slog downstairs with sleep still locked in my eyes. The bassinets were empty when I finally managed to rouse myself, and I find my mother at the table holding one of my precious dark-haired angels, and Gage the other. I never knew my heart could expand so much, that the tendrils of my affection could grow and coil around such tiny precious beings and wrap them in the invisible matrix of my undying love. My heart has jumped outside of my body and split in two. I never knew that love could grow deeper than the sea or higher than the stars, but these two perfect creations have tapped into a part of my soul that I didn't even know existed.

Drake, too, is in the family room catching up on his favorite show, *Naked and Betrayed*, or *Naked and Lost on a Group Date*, or *Renovating Naked*, *The Naked Cupcake Cook-*

Off. He seems drawn to shows that feature ass crack as their most important attribute.

"You were really out." Mom lifts the baby over her shoulder and gently pats his back in an attempt to burp him. I'm secretly terrified my mother will try to breastfeed the twins while I'm not looking. Gage has forbidden me to let her anywhere near her baby-happy boobs, as if she would stoop to that level of crazy. But I can't help to note that her blouse is neatly buttoned up. In fact, she's suspiciously dressed to the nines.

"Yeah, I was pretty dead." I give a depleted smile to Wes—*gah*! I mean Gage! I blink back in horror. "Good morning, *Gage*." Crap. I cannot ever make that mistake, not even with my sleep-deprived brain. "Where are you off to?" I ask my mother just as Tad walks into the room, sporting a wrinkled suit, his lime green tie slightly askew.

"We're off to see the wizard!" he squawks, and I wonder for a brief moment if I'm trapped in another one of Wesley's nightmares where Ezrina is his scullery maid and Logan's neck is being chomped on by zombies. "And the wizard's name is Mr. Pete Daugherty."

"Who's that?" I take up the baby's warm body in my hands and turn his precious face toward mine. "I know who *this* is," I coo into my son's tiny, sleepy face. "Mister Barron, that's who!" Barron wrinkles his nose, and those adorable dimples go off in either side of his cheeks. Both boys have the most beautiful olive skin—or I should say Oliver skin, their dark hair is thicker and glossier with each passing day, and those eyes, those navy baby blues only seem to brighten up as the weeks go by. I'm in love. My heart swells just touching his cotton soft cheek to mine.

"It's our attorney." Mom shrugs as if to apologize. "Logan insisted we get the payout we deserve."

"You've got to be kidding me. Logan is family." I walk over to where Tad is doing his morning monkey-like workout while downing an entire pack of uncooked hot dogs. "And what the heck are you up to?"

"You can't look well when you walk into those kinds of places." He swallows down the food in his mouth with a heroic gulp. "You need to come in smelling like you need some help."

"You're going to need to be dewormed." I'd snatch the nitrogen stick from his hand but don't dare expose Barron to it.

"Skyla is right. Logan is family," Mom says it stern. "This doesn't feel right."

"What?" Tad chokes it out with a hot dog mashed between his teeth. "She's married to the other Oliver in the event you hadn't notice—Demetri's kid, remember?"

My blood runs cold at the mention of it. Something about that solid truth coming from Tad and his hot dog riddled mouth makes it a filthy finality. If Tad has accepted this horrible reality—it's pretty much official.

"Logan is an Oliver." Mom charges at him while snapping up her purse. "That clearly makes him family. We love the Olivers!"

Tad grunts at the thought. "That's not what you suggested a week ago when you said that *battle-ax*—and I'm quoting here—threatened to call child services if you tried to tuck one of Greg's kids under your shirt one more time."

She slaps a hand over her mouth. "Let's get you out of here before you get us banished from these children's lives forever." She tugs him to the door. "Emily has Misty and Beau. Rest when the babies sleep, Skyla!"

I look into Barron's bright eyes, blue as his father's, and press a kiss to his ruby red lips.

"Please sleep for Mommy today," I whimper as he offers a quick wink. I jolt a little at the sight but quickly chalk it up to gas. I'd much rather he have gas than any Femtastic capabilities at this early stage of the game. I suppose, in a way, his Femtastic capabilities are inevitable. But that's why I'm here—to ground my boys in all things celestially right.

Emily and Ethan stroll in from the backyard sans one child.

"Where's Beau?" I ask in the event he was left to his own devices. God knows if he toddles into the woods, we may not see him for weeks.

Em scowls as she hoists both Misty and Ember in her arms. "We pawned him off on his parents."

"Yeah." Ethan laughs as he plucks a box of Twinkies from the cupboard. The Great Hostess Scare last summer had them stockpiling the confections, and, now that they're back on the shelves, Ethan and Drake pop them like they were vitamins. "We had to formally introduce them. The way Drake was grunting under the covers was like he never heard of the kid before."

Gage and I exchange glances.

"Dude." Drake pauses the television, and a bare ass is frozen over the screen, seventy-two inches wide. Drake and his newfound fortune have technologically benefited our parents somewhat, although, apparently, not enough to leave poor Logan alone. "I'm right here."

Ethan bucks as if shocked to hell. "Then who's that fucking your wife?"

Drake shoots down to the mobile home, and Gage and I scoot to the porch, too afraid to run through the muck below with the babies in tow. When they said kids really slow you down, they weren't kidding.

Mia speeds out of Bree and Drake's love shack with little Beau in hand. Her hair is doing its best impression of a haystack, and her shirt is on inside out with the tag licking the front of her face like a giant white tongue.

"What the?" A glimpse of a man, clad in leather, dissolves into the forest behind the property. "Oh my God!" I shout with venom. "Take him." I hand Barron to Gage and bolt barefoot down to my sister. "This is *stat rape!*" I shout into the woods as the fog braids itself through the trees. "You will not get away with this, Revelyn Booth!" I shake my fist in the air.

"Would you"—Mia bats my hand down—"knock that off! You're embarrassing me!"

I shuttle Beau to his father. Clearly, Bree is nowhere to be found. The two lovebirds shacking up in the trailer were none other than my sister and the man far too old to bed her.

"You have lost your ever-loving mind! What the hell are you *thinking*?" I give her shoulder a bone-clenching squeeze as

I glare into my sister's wild eyes. The idea of that womanizer taking advantage of my little sister makes me insane. "What if you get knocked up? Do you see those boys up there?" I point toward Gage with an armful of babies. "In the event you didn't notice, twins run in the family, and you might even have triplets!" *Like me*, I want to say, but decide to leave Sage out of this.

Mia's eyes widen in horror. "I'm not having a baby—or ten or twelve. I'm not like you and Mom." She gives a childlike wail. "I don't even want a kid!"

"Why are you with him, anyway? He's too old for you!"

Mia takes in the crowd amassing around us—Drake, Ethan, Em, and the girls, Gage above with Melissa, who's just joined him, each of them holding a twin.

"Gee, thanks for embarrassing me, *Skyla*!" The words smother from her thick with tears. "Is this what your first time was like, too?" She gives me a hard shove, and I fumble in the mud to keep from falling. "Did you have your entire family outside the door just waiting to embarrass you?" Tears spout from her like a fountain, but her anger overrides her need to sob.

"Your first time?" I whisper, so sad for my sister in so many ways.

"What? Did you think I was a *slut*?" she screams in my face. "Because that would be your other sister in the event you were wondering. Rumor has it Gabe is back to making nightly visits! Did you know there's a secret attic in our room that leads to the roof?"

Oh my shit! Who the hell designed this stupid house! I've checked that labyrinth of an attic for another closeted space, especially above my sisters' bedroom and came up empty. Dear God, this house grows secret spaces as efficiently as a tumor. It would figure that the Bishop's old abode is up to no good.

Mia barges past me, sobbing, pushing her fists deep into her eyes.

I turn back and watch as she bypasses Melissa's heavy scowl on her way inside.

"Way to go, Messenger." Em hands me Misty, and I take her.

"I didn't know." I glance at all the startled faces around me. "Um—I guess I overreacted." In truth, I don't know what the right reaction should have been. I'm certainly not penning Rev's dick a thank you letter—more like a restraining order. And I will most certainly be telling his father. Maybe he can keep his son's penis in check—or, in the least, away from my underage sister.

I care deeply about Mia, and, now that I'm a parent myself, I just want to protect her and keep her safe. It's incredible to think that merely weeks ago the boys were tucked safe inside me, my maternal instinct yet to fully blossom, but, now, not only could I never envision a life without them, I'm willing to snap into a deranged lunatic to protect them.

"What was your first time like?" Em asks casually as Ethan and Drake scuttle up to the house to watch the rest of their nudist marathon.

"My first time? Nice," I say it quiet as a vision of Logan thrusting above me comes to mind, that heavy look in his eyes, his lips curling up at the tips, satisfied to finally bury himself deep inside me. I shake it out of my head, replacing the image with Gage and his dark, furrowed brows gliding over me—the ridge of his neck bent back in ecstasy. The first time with *Gage* feels far more appropriate to think about, considering my matrimonial status.

Misty giggles in my arms and claps for no reason. Dear God, did she see that completely inappropriate reel that just cycled through my mind?

"How about you?" I volley the slightly awkward virginity ball into Emily's vaginal court.

"It was Dudley. You know, it was when everyone was doing him. He was practically a graduation requirement."

I cringe. Remembering Marshall's Studley Dudley days is not something I try to do often.

"How was it?" I regret the words before they leave my lips.

"Did you ever see all the shit I drew for him? I painted? That man has an art gallery dedicated to your future lovemaking. You'll find out for yourself, Messenger, and when you do, the entire island will hear you scream with pleasure."

Not what my tired brain wanted to hear at all. A part of me is still hopeful this entire morning is one of Wesley's twisted nightmares. If it's not, it should be.

"You have any pressing diagrams you need to share with me?" I've tried every other path to try to save both Gage and the Nephilim people. Maybe the future me can send a very clear message through Em. Not that it works that way.

"Nope. Not a doodle." She heads inside with Ember.

"Boo," I say as I give a weak smile to Misty. "I'd do anything for a hint of what's to come."

Misty grabs ahold of my ears and laughs as if I'm the funniest thing she's ever seen. Her fingers grip my neck as she twists and points to Gage.

A dark fog creeps over the stairwell, crawling up the porch like a body, slowly, ever so methodically, circling his ankles. Gage looks to me, his blue eyes traded for piercing glowing rubies. Horns sprout in a burst from the top of his head, thick and black, at least three feet high, curved like half moons like that of a ram. His skin is traded for serpentine scales, the color of rust and soot, and, in an instant, he grows in size and girth, exploding into a demonic creature with black webbed wings, a horrific snout, a tongue of silver fire.

Omen—the dragon from Host—Gage has morphed into an exact replica of that nefarious mascot, and my heart thuds audibly at the terrifying sight. A horrible sound thunders from him as he rises on his hind legs and lets out a roar that expels a fire fifty feet into the sky. He flaps his wings with great might and speed, propelling himself into the dismal Paragon sky. Gage—the hideous creature he's become, soars into the stratosphere with a baby locked in his talons—Barron.

My heart stills, my breathing ceases, as Paragon transforms back to its weary self as if nothing ever happened. Gage waves to me with one of the baby's hands, and I give a weak wave back.

"Oh, Misty, that must never happen." I stagger back toward the house. "Not to Gage," I whisper. "Not to Barron."

I wipe the hideous vision from my mind. It's Demetri who needs to pay for putting us all in this position. For a moment, I picture his smug self in the middle of the Landon living room while I plunge a butcher knife into his skull again and again, Ezrina style, in an effort to alleviate my pent-up rage.

Misty startles and begins on a piercing wail.

"Sorry." I pull her in and rock her, trying to both comfort her and shield my thoughts as I think up horrific new ways to kill her father.

In the late afternoon, while Gage is at the morgue and the boys are enjoying a rare moment of content silence, Mom and I sit at the kitchen table pouring over far too many details for a simple christening.

"I've ordered fifty thousand ice blue twinkle lights." She wiggles her fingers, dazzled by the extremely luminous idea. "The theme is going to be a winter wonderland. Demetri has all those birch trees lining the property, and we're going to paint their trunks white and wrap them in lights. Everything will be elegant and blue. It's going to be simply enchanting!"

Everything will be blue like the Counts, like apparently the Fems—but more to the point, like baby boys, as in the two that the night is in honor of. I need to focus on those two tiny little details and try not to get worked up over the deeper meaning of the hue that my mother chose to run with.

"There's nothing as magical as baby blue twinkle lights. Tad will agree!" she belts it out as she yelps to him from across the table. "Remember the Althorpe Christmas party last year?" She beams, but Tad is still hiding behind his journalistic wall of parchment. Both Tad and his newspapers are quickly becoming archaeological relics.
"It was as if we were lost in a fairy tale!"

Althorpe? A fairy tale? I bet it was—an old school Brothers Grimm with real live monsters and unhappy, downright gruesome, endings.

"Are you sleeping?" Mom whacks him on the arm.

"Nope." He startles as if coming to after a bad dream. "I gave up sleep right after we moved to this haunted island. You ever think we should have stayed back in L.A. with all the glitz and glamour?"

What glitz and glamour is he talking about? We survived off Ramen noodles and tap water as soon as he claimed my mother as his bride. Our rental home faced a parking garage.

"Are you kidding? And miss out on these lovely grandchildren? And *Gage*?" Mom's voice pitches unnaturally.

Smooth, Mom—real smooth.

"Anyway, we're discussing the christening. I'm not sparing any expense." She frowns at Tad a moment. "And by me, I mean Demetri."

And together, they just became one—I've suspected an unholy union all along.

Tad tosses down his paper as if acquiescing. "Will there be caviar?"

God, he asked it so smug, with such expectation. Dare I say, our multiple jaunts to Demetri's home have ruined everyone's expectations of a real family get-together? Oh, how I yearn for my mother's questionable cooking. Not only did we keep the calorie count to nil by not actually ingesting the malodorous fare, but we didn't have to stare at Demetri's ugly mug while trying to digest our dinner.

"Of course." My mother fans herself as if the thought of not having buckets full of beluga on demand makes her nauseous. "Beluga. Only the best for our grandchildren." Ha! I so called it.

I try hard not to roll my eyes since neither the boys nor I will be sucking down glibbery fish eggs.

"As long as Edinger is footing the bill"—Tad slaps his round belly—"bring on the pricey eats!" Tad is really packing on the pounds ever since Emily has claimed the kitchen as her domain. "Hey, how about you order up some barbeque for the big day, too? Something Cajun?" And there you go. Emily has added a variety of meals to the menu and has become a master griller as well. It's pretty clear she's expanded Tad's culinary horizons for the tastier.

"*Tad*"—Mom lounges in his name as if affronted by his suggestion—"this is an *elegant* affair."

"Well, you can't stop me from coming!" He lets out an atrocious belch that rattles the windows and sets poor little Nathan astir in his bassinet.

I wish we could stop Tad from a lot of things. Putting a plug in all of his disgusting bodily functions is at the top of the list.

"Speaking of the guest list, add two more." He straggles over and taps the table as if it were an order. "Althorpe asked me to entertain those VIPs that have been working their tails off around the island. Said they wanted to soak in some island culture."

My antenna goes up. There's no way I want Killjoy and Moldy at my children's christening. And working their tails off? Ha! On second thought, for all I know they might actually have tails. "Sorry, but it's a family affair."

Mom gives a curt nod as if agreeing.

Tad lets loose an assortment of bodily functions. "On second thought, ixnay on the BBQ. I'm about to blow like a volcano from both ends!"

"Nice," I whisper, looking up to see Mia ushering Laken into the room. I hop up and give my good friend a strong embrace, hoping to somehow shield her from my stepfather and his offensive odors. "Everything okay?"

"Yeah." Her eyes squint into me in that fake I'm-totally-fine way, and I can tell it's the furthest thing from the truth. "I just needed to ask you a favor." She says hello to Mom and Tad before heading to the boys and cooing over their tiny bodies. "Skyla, they're just so perfect." Barron's dimples press in, and she covers her mouth as if holding back tears. "Dear God, that dark hair, those eyes, these gorgeous faces—Skyla, they're doppelgangers of their father." Her joy diminishes as soon as she says it. I know she's thinking of Gage's nefarious brother.

"Are you busy?" She winces. "I mean, I know you're *always* busy nowadays, but do you think there's any possibility I could drag you away for a tiny bit? Maybe a half an hour?"

"I don't know...Gage is at the morgue with his dad, crunching numbers—"

"I'll do it!" Mom volunteers. "Go on, get out. You haven't left this house since you came back from the hospital. You need some fresh air. And what better way to get it than with a girlfriend?"

"I object." Tad holds up a hand like he's under oath. "Once you open this can of escapist worms, there won't be any stopping her. She'll be gone at all hours of the day *and* night getting some 'fresh air,' and you and I will be saddled with two more diaper dwellers. I'm not tripping over one more casket in the night! You hear me, Lizbeth?"

"Ignore him." Mom attempts to shoo me away. "This is a perfect time, since you just fed them, and, when you get back, I'll pull out the breast pump, and we'll start building a reserve!" She claps as if it were the best news ever. "I have one for each breast, so it cuts the time in half. And I know what you're thinking—no damn bottles! But I assure you the nipple system I have is as close to Mother Nature as it gets. It's that fantastic pouch setup I once used. The one you strap to your body." I clearly and regretfully remember. She duct taped that thing to her chest in order to feed Beau. It was the artificial third nipple she flashed at us for years. How can I ever forget? "And guess what? Great news! Gage can breastfeed, too!"

Crap. I offer the idea of a smile. "That's going to be something." I lean in and kiss Nathan and Barron each on their delicate, buttery cheeks. My heart wrenches at the thought of leaving them here all alone with Mom and Tad. Gage might divorce me if he hears of it. "Promise you will watch them like a hawk!"

"Like a mama bear!" Mom one-ups me in the animal kingdom.

"Keep your phone near you," I scold. "And turn it up all the way!" I shout as I snatch up my purse and scoot reluctantly to the door.

"Have a good time! Nothing will happen to the boys, Skyla, I promise!"

"Famous last words," I whisper as Laken and I head outside.

As soon as we cross the threshold, my heart begins to race.

"Where are we going?" My mind spins, trying to wrap my head around the fact I'm actually going to leave without my two favorite appendages. And also, I'm secretly calculating how many Burger Shack fries I can buy for Laken and me with a twenty-dollar bill.

Laken's lids lower as she gives a mean shiver, and there isn't a single gust of wind. Wherever we're going, it already has her spooked.

"We're going back to the Transfer to see Wes."

"Oh, is that all? Couldn't you call him to come and see you?" I'm desperate to run back into the house and hold my babies. This entire outing feels tantamount to child abandonment. Everything in me screams *don't fucking do it!*

She shakes her head, her caramel curls stiff and bountiful as my own this morning.

"I need you to protect me."

"*Please.* Wesley would never hurt you. You're golden in that regard." True as God.

"Not from Wes." She takes my hand and leads me to the car idling in the driveway. "From me."

Laken drives to Devil's Peak with the radio turned up all the way, the speakers crackling from the weight of a familiar, yet warbling Christmas carol. God, I love this time of year.

The parking lot is full, and bodies brim all over the grassy areas that lead to the lookout. Billows of fog unfurl like batting over the ocean, but they haven't quite touched down onto Paragon's shoreline yet. Not sure how Laken thinks we'll unassumingly toss our bodies over the side of the cliff anytime soon.

She turns down the thick music that's ricocheting off the ceiling, vibrating the windows with its melodic twang.

"I didn't know riding with the bass all the way up was your style, Flanders." I give a little wink at the mention of her new last name, and Laken's features wring out any trace of joy. "I get it, though. That was your way of saying don't ask me any questions."

Laken's cheeks darken with color. "You guessed it."

"So, can I ask you *any* questions?"

"No." She kills the engine. "What are we going to do? I'm desperate to see him."

"Is calling him on the phone out?"

She gives a solemn nod.

I hope that doesn't mean Laken doesn't want Coop to find out. Already I don't like where this is headed.

"Switch seats with me."

I get behind the wheel and drive us slowly down the twisted road that leads to the base of Devil's Peak. That wall of granite lies ahead as I rev the engine. The fog rolls in, flipping cartwheels over Paragon's rocky crags like a herd of happy ghostlike children. Its fingers curl at the edge of Laken's hood as if readying to swallow the car.

A crowd of teenagers bucks with laughter at the top of the cliff while doing a lousy job of hiding their beer bottles.

"They'll see us, Skyla." Laken's breathing grows erratic just watching that mountain before us shining like steel.

"They won't. We'll be too fast for them to see."

My foot hits the floorboard, and we fly across the graveled expanse straight into the barrier that penetrates us into the next plane with a pleasant hum. The car vibrates and shakes. The world around us transforms from the gloomy landscape of Paragon to the dark armpit of the Transfer. The car lands over the cracked soil with a thump, mowing down a dozen or so of the literal deadbeats that populate this place.

"Sorry!" I say, getting out and following Laken to Wesley's tall, dark, and scary hideaway. My heart is in literal agony at the thought of him trying to raise a little girl in this hellhole, all alone with no potential friends, no humans, no Nephilim—no good ones anyway.

Several of the Transfer transplants get in my face with rage and warble out a few unintelligible words. A man with a unibrow pounds his chest like a gorilla.

Laken and I head inside, leaving the people of this underworld to pause at the edge of the walkway leading to Wesley's monstrosity of a home. It's as if they know not to step on his turf, not to enter these unhallowed walls. I would be lying if it didn't make me feel important to know that Laken and I could simply waltz in, uninvited, and be total bitches to Wesley himself. I don't think Wes would ever revoke our invites.

"You're here." Wes looks perplexed. Little Tobie lies nestled in his arms while Bishop sits with her feet up on the rococo-inspired coffee table, the wood sculpted like the waves of the sea with a plate of glass in the center. The entire piece is gilded from top to bottom, as fake and useless as Chloe's heart. She pauses from filing her nails to glance at us over her shoulder.

"Congrats on the brats, Skyla. I hope they both had big heads."

Typical Chloe, always ready with a dig.

"Hello, little one." I touch my finger to Tobie's chubby little hand, and she grips it tight with her finger. Her lips curl into a wide grin as she looks right at me, blowing bubbles and cooing happily. She's the exact representation of Gage—or Wesley for that matter, in miniature female form. "God, her whole face lights up when she smiles. She's beautiful, Wes." So much for being a bitch to my worst enemy. Only a baby can have the power to defuse me.

"We need to talk, Wes." Laken ticks her head toward the hall. "Do you think Chloe can take the baby for a second?"

"Oh, I will!" I volunteer, scooping her cute chubby self into my arms. Tobie is heavier than the boys by far, but, then, she's older by a month, so it's to be expected. She starts kicking and fussing, her head twisting toward my chest as if she knows I'm carrying a delicious concealed weapon—two of them to be exact. "Where's her bottle?"

"I just ran out of formula." Wesley's dimples ignite as he gazes lovingly at his little miss. "Ezrina will be back soon."

"You ran out?" I squawk, incredulous, doing my best impression of my mother. "You don't *run out* of formula! You need to build up a stockpile! Buy two or twelve of those cans at a time just to ensure she'll get what she needs, day or night." I press her tiny body to mine, momentarily forgetting who she came from. A part of me doesn't seem to care. Tobie is as innocent as her big blue eyes suggest. I'm not about to pile the sins of her parents onto her tiny little shoulders. God knows that would do her in.

"You're right. I need to be better prepared." Wes strokes her tiny cheek with his finger. The look of love in his eyes makes my heart melt—but only because he looks strikingly like Gage at the moment. Wes may be a lot of rotten things, but he's shaping up to be a wonderful father. "It won't happen again."

He turns to Laken, and they begin their little powwow, only I'm catching every third word because Tobie is rooting like crazy, trying to get my chest to turn into a flesh-covered bottle. Just listening to her cry and fuss makes my rock-hard boobs perk to attention. And now both of our bodies are aching for relief.

Laken says something, bemoaning the idea of being disloyal to Coop.

What? I rock my way over, trying my hardest to listen in, but Tobie starts in on a wild fuss, inspiring Laken and Wes to step further away. Crap. How exactly am I supposed to be protecting Laken from herself when she keeps sashaying in the opposite direction? For all I know, Laken is signing up to be sex slave in exchange for world peace. God forbid she enters into some kind of a coital covenant.

"Bishop, take your daughter a minute, would you? I need to be a part of this." I shuffle over to Chloe, and she gets up and passes me right by as if I wasn't holding the most precious baby girl in the world.

"*Huh*—I did my part," she huffs. "No one said anything about holding her. Besides, she doesn't want to be held. Lock her in her room and shut the damn door. That'll teach her."

"God, Bishop, I don't know why I expected anything more from you."

Tobie's face begins to change colors as her frustration rolls to a boil. I shoot a quick text to Ezrina and ask her how far away she is. Couldn't she concoct something in the lab for goodness' sake? This is a serious situation. A child is starving. I scan the area for a pacifier just as Ezrina pings back.

At Cost Club. Line is terrible. Another hour at least.

An *hour*? Little Tobie starts in on an all-out assault on my boob as if she, too, were vexed by this.

Oh, screw it. I pull up my blouse and undo what Gage refers to as the "secret hatch" on my bra. It takes three tries before Tobie latches on and begins sucking away as if her cute chubby little thighs depend on it—which they probably do. I gasp as she finally goes at it—that feeling of a needle embedding straight into my nipple hasn't quite gone away yet. At least they've stopped cracking and bleeding. One gift at a time, I suppose.

I look down at this hungry child feasting at my bosom, this *hungry* child who is not my own, and I'm shocked to hell at how quickly I've become my mother.

"Well, well," Chloe muses, popping up from behind and inspecting the breasty malfeasance. "Like mother, like daughter."

"Hopefully, they'll never say the same about you and Tobie." I scoot over to where Laken and Wes are in deliberations and keep my back to them in the event Wesley decides to go ninja on me.

"I want to know, Wes." Laken is speaking in an exceedingly kind tone. Hey? I thought we were coming in as wicked bitches, and here I am playing nursemaid while Laken is trying to sweet talk him. No wonder our enemy is prospering. We're making provisions. "Is it true if I give myself to you wholly that you'll come to your senses?"

Give herself wholly? In what way? In *that* way? Why? I hold my breath, scooting in ever so carefully, afraid to hold back their momentum.

"What are we talking?" Wes grunts. "A night? A week? A year?" He sounds just as frustrated, and it's a tone I've never heard him evoke with her. Wesley Edinger worships the ground Laken walks on. Hell, he longs to kiss her feet, kiss any single part of her. But thank God, Laken is a bright girl and chose to side with Celestra and *Coop*.

"You tell me. A lifetime? Do you want me to live out the rest of my natural days in the Transfer? I wasn't fed the specifics." Laken's tone just took a turn for the pissed. Pissed is good, Laken—very, very good.

"What?" I squawk. Again, is this another twisted nightmare? Wesley's once-upon-a-midnight-stomp in this hellhole seems to have spawned an entire slew of real-life horrors.

Laken holds up a hand to me. "Answer me right now, Wes."

"Laken." His fingers tremble as they touch her arms— as if he were only moments away from ravaging her. "What you're asking—does Cooper know?"

"I just wanted to be clear if this is an option." She skirts the question and answers with something far more outrageous. "If I gave you my life—my body, to do as you please—would you cease all of this wickedness? And what kind of insurance would you give me—a covenant drawn up by Skyla's mother? I'm sure it would be airtight. No more evil poured out on the Nephilim," she scoffs. "Would you really call off your army of the dead *and* the government? Would you put things back the way they were and forget about power, and money, and every vile thing that's churning in your stomach?"

What in the hell has gotten into her?

Chloe glances at me with eyes the size of saucers. "So wait." She saunters on over. "You think he's actually going to give all of this up?" She fans around the room as if it were a prize. "Give up his rightful place as ruler of the Fems and the Steel Barricade just so he could fuck you nightly? Oh, honey." She honks out a laugh. "You're hot, but you are not *that* hot. Get a grip, and lose the ego. Wes isn't giving anything up for you, or he would have done it a long time ago."

Laken's face piques with color as if Chloe had just slapped her, and basically, she did.

Of course, I could have told Laken all of that—minus the insults. Laken *is* that hot. Wes is just too stupid to deserve his next breath.

Wesley takes a moment, centering himself to the idea. "Is this something you would seriously consider?"

Poor Coop. I'd better do something fast.

"No way, no how," I say, looking over my shoulder at the two of them. "Chloe is right." And I hate myself for both admitting it and saying it out loud. "Wes is going to lie to you. Or worse, attempt to have his way with you and then get right back to dismantling the world. Don't kill your brand new marriage over nothing, Laken. You're not being a martyr. You're just fooling yourself if you think you are. If he wanted to leave the coven that lives in his father's armpit, he would have done it when you gave him the option the first time all those years ago. He *chose* this living hell over you. He's a killer, a destroyer, a beast with no morals. No matter how good you are in bed, this boy isn't changing his wicked ways."

"Skyla?" Wes creeps over, filled with suspicion. "What is it that you're doing?"

Crap. I try to pull my nipple out of Tobie's tiny mouth, but she's hanging on with a death grip, and it stretches unnaturally long as if it were taffy.

"Skyla?" Laken calls. "You can turn around. I got my point across."

"Oh, that's okay. You two continue hashing things out. I'll just keep rocking sweet little Tobie. She really seems to like it."

Wes pops his head over my shoulder. "Shit, Skyla."

"I'm sorry!" I give a half-hearted shriek and trot away a few feet. "She was *crying*!" I turn around, and Laken slaps her hand over her mouth. "And I sprung a leak, and, well—I don't think it'll actually kill her."

Wes comes over and brushes Tobie's dark hair back. A loving look of affection warms his face as he stares down at both his daughter and my left boob. I decide to overlook the fact he just accidentally grazed my nipple with his hand.

"This is what I wanted for her. A mother—a bond like this." He shakes his head, disappointed in his useless nipples, I'm sure.

"Anyway." I plunge a finger next to her tiny pink mouth and break the suction. Tobie rears her head and gasps as if she's coming up for air. Her mouth is still rooting for more, so I do the sensible thing and switch sides. "My boobs were turning into rock-hard boulders, so it's sort of a win-win situation." I cover up as much as I can. I hate that the tally of people who have seen my boobs in the last month has climbed to double digits. "Laken, it's very admirable of you to throw yourself on the sword." Or, in this case, the penis. "Wes, tell her you're too big of a megalomaniac to consider such a ridiculous option so we can get on our way."

"I don't know." He takes up Laken's hands in his own. "This is Laken—the love of my life. What good is all the power in the world when you don't have love?"

I suck in a quick breath. Wesley has picked a lousy time to come to his senses. Coop will kill him, and so will I, if he ever touches Laken in that way.

"Power is everything!" I gasp, trying to manufacture reasons why Wes needs to stay firmly on the dark side. "When it comes to wickedness, you're the man! Not even Demetri can do it better. If you switch teams, who am I going to go up against? I need a worthy opponent." God! What am I saying?

Laken's selfish plot just might work. Sure, it will help the Nephilim, but where will that leave poor Coop?

"Laken"—I plead with her—"you have a husband—who by the way is an Adonis, a Greek god amongst mere mortals—a marble statue come to life—Mount Olympus yearns to have its favorite son back. And, Wes, you seem pretty happy here in this multi-level home with a wicked view of the badlands. You're an evil *genius*. Not even Ezrina is good enough to crack your codes."

A throat clears from behind, and I cringe as Ezrina appears.

"Skyla!" Her eyes widen as she spies Tobie latched to my boob. "Give." She flicks her fingers, and I'm slow to surrender the little suckling. "I'll have you know, I can crack codes with the best of them," she snarls as she leaves the room with my new little boob buddy. If anyone ever told me that Ezrina and I would be caring for Chloe's offspring more than she does, I would have never believed it. On second thought, maybe I would.

Wes caresses the side of Laken's cheek. "The thought of being with you, sharing our lives once again—a *bed*. It makes me genuinely happy. But knowing that you may not want me, that it's simply *work* for you, a sacrifice, makes me feel like it wouldn't be worth it for either of us."

She shakes her head. "But what if I were devoted?" She narrows her gaze on his as if she were testing him. "What if I bear your children? What if I love Tobie as if she were my own?"

Obviously, I've already beaten her to the punch.

When Laken made it clear to Wes, a few months back, that she was determined to shut down the tunnels, he suggested they date, that they share one last kiss before he opened the gates of hell in her honor. But it wasn't really in her honor. Wes was about to do it anyway. It's no wonder Laken feels as if her body is the portal to freedom for millions. He's convinced her of just that. And Laken is just sweet enough to feel tremendous guilt for at least not trying to save the masses. Thankfully, Wes is being honest and letting her know it wouldn't work. Wow, here it is—the day that I'm actually thankful to Wesley Edinger for something.

"Well, we'd better get going!" I snatch Laken by the arm and drag her to the car. "I get it." I close my eyes for a moment as the Transfer transplants cage us in from all sides. "You think this is productive in a major way, but trust me, it's not. Wes used you for that kiss last year. Your vagina isn't the solution you're hoping it'll be."

"You don't know that." Her face pinches with grief.

"Stop it!" I'm one ounce shy of slapping her back to reality myself. "I'm not impressed with this sacrifice you're willing to dish up, and you shouldn't be either."

She gets in my face. "I don't give a shit if you're *impressed.*" Her jaw sets in a snarl. "You know who's impressed? The captives *I* freed." She beats her chest. "What Wesley showed us last night was just his opening number. He's going to raze this Earth and its people. You think the death toll is high enough? Be prepared to watch it climb. And the future? It's going to be a living hell for everybody. Sometimes, a person has to sacrifice themselves for the greater good of the people."

"You don't give up a marriage to quell the devil!"

"Sometimes, you do!" she shouts back, tears streaming from her eyes.

She turns to leave, and I reel her in with all of my Celestra strength and hold her trembling body until she stills beneath me.

"I don't want to fight with you," I whisper, her chest heaving against my own. "This is not an option. Wesley made his decision years ago."

"I just thought"—she hiccups through tears—"he's had a chance to see what the power is like—how empty it is. I thought I could circumvent what's to come. Skyla, the Spectators are frightening. A world filled with monsters is going to change everything."

I grip her by the shoulders and shake her. "The world has always been filled with monsters. Wesley is one of them."

She nods, sniffing back her emotions. "I just wanted to be sure I did everything I could. Coop and I both agreed I should come after discussing what Gage told Wes. Coop knew it was the only way to keep me sane."

My stomach lurches. "What did Gage tell Wes?"

"You know, that I was the only person who could ever stop him." She waves her wrist. "God, I would never have even entertained coming down here if it weren't for him. Of course, Coop and I knew it was bullshit. That's why I was giving Wes such a hard time. Besides, as heroic as I sounded a moment ago, I'd never go through with it. In truth, I'd make a lousy sacrificial lamb."

My heart stops. I want to smack Gage into tomorrow for ever getting this ridiculous ball rolling. And leave it to Wes to bring it up and guilt Laken with it. Although, suspiciously, he wasn't jumping at the chance. I'll bet anything he already has another plan cooked up to snatch her away from Coop.

"Cooper and I discussed it—he said I should come so that I would forever know that I didn't have to carry an ounce of guilt with me for the rest of our lives. He assured me Wes would either lie or deny me. He was right. The funny thing is, I didn't for a minute think Wes would say yes." She shakes her head as if waking from a dream. "I really don't know why I'm in tears." She blinks back a smile. "I swore on all that is holy to Coop that I was just here to clarify—even if Wes agreed to it, I had you here to drag me back to safety."

"'Kay." I'm slow to nod—still pissed at Gage for sponsoring this insanity. "I get it. You can sleep at night knowing you did all you could. Sorry Gage had anything to do with this. I'll make sure he apologizes to Coop for putting you in this position." She shakes her head as if that won't be necessary. "You needed to know you did everything you could. And you did." I push a kiss to the top of her head as she bucks beneath me.

"I hate myself for coming here, Skyla. I don't know why I let Gage fill me with self-doubt," she says it so sweetly I can tell it wasn't meant to send a barb through my heart, but it does. Darn Gage.

"Don't hate yourself." *Hate Gage*, I want to say. "It was noble—and stupid, but mostly noble," I tease.

She gives a little laugh, wiping down her face. Her mascara washes her cheeks with soot.

"How about we head to the Burger Shack? My treat."

"Sounds good."

We evict the ghostly bodies from every orifice of Laken's car and get out of Wesley's private hell.

Although, I might have to give Gage a tiny piece of Hades as soon as I get home.

"What the heck were you thinking?" The evening is wearing thin as my patience with him. I've just fed my own children with my bosom, and now I'm finally getting dressed for the Council of the Superiors meeting.

"I'm sorry." Gage actually manages to look agonized over this. "I knew I put my foot in my mouth the second it slipped out. It was stupid. Coop asked how things were going with Wes and—I swear, it's like this lack of sleep has turned a filter off in my brain. Forgive me."

I cringe a moment. I so get it. "Come here." My arms slip around his neck. "Of course, I forgive you. My own brain isn't exactly up to par these past few weeks itself—which is sort of scary, considering where I'm headed. Come with." I dot a kiss to his lips, and he relaxes a bit. We're almost at the one-month mark of no sex, and I'm starting in on some serious withdrawals. "It'll be fun." I bite down over my lip. "You can hang out in the back." I run my hand down his jeans as the twins lie side-by-side in Barron's bassinet. I hate separating them at night. I think they'd sleep better if they were together, but my mother threatened me with life and limb, so apart they shall be.

"Trust me, you'll get further without me. People see me as the enemy." He lands a kiss to the nape of my neck, and I melt into him with a moan.

"Speaking of the enemy...I'd hate to see you make any."

"I'll talk to Coop—and Laken. And I'll never repeat anything idiotic Wes and I exchange," he moans, closing his sleep-deprived eyes. "All I want to do is kiss you, Skyla."

My stomach boils just thinking of Wes and Gage having heart-to-hearts. It's downright frightening to think he's that close to pure evil.

A steady breath plumes from me. "Okay. And I want that kiss tonight." My lids land heavy when I say it. I take his hand and guide it between my thighs. "I want it right here, Mr. Oliver." My body shakes because I don't want to wait that long.

He inches back as if readying to call my bluff. "You ready for that?"

"I'm always ready for that." I rub my thigh over his blooming crotch. "In fact, I'm ready for whatever you want to give me."

A dark laugh rumbles from him. "Then that's what you're going to get."

"Be gentle with me, though. I'm like a virgin again." It's true. I needed a few stitches when all was said and done, and I'm convinced Dr. B tightened my chastity belt a notch.

"Like a virgin." That devilish grin breaks out over his face. "It's going be an interesting night."

"You'll use a condom," I charge him with the duty. "And I'll use my mouth." I take a bite from his ear. Even though we've had oral options since the twins were born, we haven't exactly exercised them. Truth be told, we've been a little more preoccupied with sleep and scavenging to get it.

"My body misses your mouth." He runs a kiss from my ear to the hollow of my neck.

"We need to stop, or I'll never want to leave. Come with me," I plead once again.

He shakes his head just barely. "I'll stay behind and map out all the things I'm going to do to you later." He rubs my shoulders, and I moan into him.

"Can't wait to see what you come up with when I get back. I have two bottles in the fridge." My mother hooked me up to electronica like a cow and expressed two full bottles in an hour's time. She was more than impressed with my ability to produce enough human dairy to feed the boys twice over. And, after seeing those two white glowing bottles, so was I. "Don't wait up." I nuzzle my face in his neck a moment. "I'll kiss you in all the right places and rouse you from your sleep myself."

"I'll hold you to it."

Gage and I each snatch up a twin as he walks me downstairs, where we find Logan already waiting, talking to Bree and Em while Drake and Ethan gorge in their visual au natural fun-fest. Their eyes are literally set agog at the television.

Beau Geste pops up from the other side of the couch with an ear-to-ear grin on his face. "I see butts!"

"That you do." I make a face at Gage. Our children will not *see butts* if I can help it. I dot Nathan's forehead with a kiss as if to prove a point.

Gage nods as if agreeing with me just as a bevy of beautiful blondes exposes their toddler-tight derrières.

"It's like freaking Christmas," Ethan chokes out the words.

"Speaking of the fat man's big day," Drake barks over to Mom and Tad. "Pay attention to the list this time, Pops. You gave us pillows and socks and shit last year. It's like you forgot the true meaning of Christmas—*stuff*."

"I'll get her back soon." Logan offers Gage a quick pat to the shoulder, whispering something into his ear, and Gage shakes his head in response. My curiosity is piqued, but my nerves are overriding my need to snoop. I hand the baby to Mom and press my lips to his soft as a peach forehead.

We start to head out, and Mom waves with Barron's tiny hand. "Goodbye, Logan and Mommy!"

"Have fun on your *date*," Tad yelps, upset that I'm once again stepping foot off the property without my two tiny twin engines that never seem to shut down and sleep.

"It's not a date," I whisper under my breath. Because really? What's the point?

Gage and I kiss goodbye at the door, and I coo into Nathan's precious face before dotting his nose with my lips. It's swoon-worthy seeing Gage hold his tiny doppelganger in his big strong arms. There is nothing hotter on this planet than Gage Oliver as a father.

Soon enough, it's just Logan and I standing outside of the Landon house with the fog sealing our bodies like a membrane. Something stirs inside me like a memory, like a premonition. Logan interlaces our fingers as we head to the Mustang. It feels safe like this with him, and yet, hollow without Gage.

We can never lose Gage.

Logan pulls my hand to his lips as he helps me into the passenger's seat. "I agree."

The Council of the Superiors is held on the outskirts of Ahava just east of my mother's sparkling domain. A portal is open to those in attendance, so it's the one time I don't need to beg Marshall for a ride—although, my favorite Sector is present in support of me, as are Brody and Ellis. Of course, there is Logan, but he's like my other half in this operation. The Retribution League is just as much his baby as it is mine.

Logan wraps an arm around my shoulder. "Dr. Booth to your left," he offers the heads-up. "Do your thing."

"Dr. Booth!" I wave him over. "You look great—ten years younger at least." It's a genuine compliment. He's lean and mean and dressed pretty decent, too.

"It's all thanks to my fiancée. She's taken to me like a pet project, I suppose. Which is fair since I came to her as a fixer-upper." He pats his trim belly.

"Speaking of fixer-uppers." I realize I should segue into faction business, but Rev's obnoxious face bounces through my mind. "Revelyn has made quite a presence in my family as of late." God, what else can I say? Just about everything that wants to fly from my mouth is perfectly perverse.

"That's wonderful!" His eyes light up with a touch of pride, and my stomach wrenches. "It's been so long since he's had any good influences in his life." He rubs his wooly brow with a finger. "I've always thought I did him a disservice by letting him navigate through life on the coattails of his whims. I should have put my foot down a few times with little Rev-Rev.

He's landed himself in quite a few rough patches over the years."

"Is that so?" I bet accosting underage girls wasn't one of them. "Is he here?" I scan the area for the man who thought wise to deflower my sister in her own backyard.

"No. Heavens no. He's got some hot date. He's quite the ladies' man."

"Oh, I'm aware." I seethe a moment at the idea that Mia was just one in a long string of girls he took the penis plunge with that day. "Anyway, I'm addressing the factions today. I'm proposing a break in tradition, and I'd really appreciate your support."

He twists his lips, unsure of what I'm saying. "Skyla, the factions are born and bred on tradition. I'm afraid I can't support a youthful whim without examining it in detail. These things take time. I'm sure you understand."

My mouth falls open, and the urge to beg him to side with me rises up like vomit in the back of my throat. "Revelyn slept with my sister, and now she's not a virgin. Did I mention she just turned sixteen?" Dr. Booth's eyes bulge the size of soccer balls. "I'm afraid I can't support his youthful whims either, and, unfortunately, I have examined this in far too much detail. I'd like to forgive him, but these things take time—and perhaps a police officer or two." His mouth falls open at the legal implications Little Rev-Rev seems to have ensnared himself in. "I'm sure you understand." I take a full step in. "I really need your support, Dr. B. You have the respect of the elders. If you have my back, I've already won half the battle."

Nicholas Haver slams the gavel down and calls the room to order from inside the cave-like dwelling. Bodies rush past us in an effort to get a seat, and both Dr. Booth and I do the same. I'm more than familiar with this end of Ahava, the lilac scent, the beautiful waterfalls that dress the outer opening of the cave-like sparkling curtains. Inside, the walls pulsate a strange shade of crimson. It's markedly warmer in here, no thanks to the tornado of fire that towers toward the rear of the structure. But, tragically, what I remember most about this beautiful cave is the fact that Logan Oliver lost his life here. I'll never forget that horrible day—the final day of the Faction War. Logan died in an effort to help me win that damn battle and become the overseer of these very people, and, here I am, at the big meet-and-greet, as a lowly observer—an unwanted one at that. There are at least three hundred people here tonight. Usually, there aren't this many representatives, but, as of late, every faction is shaken at the thought of what the Steel Barricade might do next. I take that back. The Counts have dwindled to nothing at these shindigs. Thanks to Wesley, they're all doing the Steel Barricade Shuffle.

"Rest assured, you have my full support." Dr. Booth looks past me, stern, like a father readying to administer a beat down. "I'd appreciate some time to speak with my son once we get back. If you so wish to involve the authorities, I completely understand."

I don't—for now, but I give a curt nod. No use in taking the incarceration card off the table just yet.

Nicholas starts in on his usual spiel—weather, local news, ridiculous antidotes to regale the foreign nations, then the hard hitting stuff—Nephilim misconduct around the globe, his shared expression of worry over what the Barricade might be capable of.

A woman stands up near the back. "I've heard there are serums they've administered to their members in an effort to shield their Nephilim DNA! What's being done about this?"

A man with a dark beard that neatly outlines his jaw as if creating an exterior mouth ready to swallow him whole stands up. "All this UFO shit is terrifying my kids—not to mention putting a target on our backs!"

Then a flurry of verbal attacks hit hard as hail. *We've heard the tunnels have reopened! And this time they're not just taking Celestra! What about the rumors that the government already has us in its sights? Are we able to survive this as a people?*

Their horrified faces, the terror in the hearts breaks me.

"Enough." I hop onto my chair and look around the monolithic entombment. Nicholas pounds his useless gavel, but I choose to ignore it. "I realize I am no longer your overseer, but I also realize that the protection the faction leaders promise is virtually nonexistent."

A few brave souls dare to audibly agree.

"And I also realize that the old way of doing things is obsolete. The Barricade has fine-tuned itself, and I propose we do the same." The cheers roughly double—the majority still not sold. "I'm aware that the Barricade has enlisted a small army of its best and brightest to terrorize the citizens of this world in an effort to make us look like monsters ready to devour the human race." The room slips to a hypnotic silence. "And, I'm aware of the fact the Barricade has enlisted a vast number of our Viden brothers and sisters to do something far more sinister." A rumble breaks out into the crowd. "If you think the world is afraid of us now—when the Barricades' next phase of intimidation begins, the world and the Nephilim people will never be the same." A few gasps circle the room. "I am breaking with tradition." I look to Dr. Booth when I say it. "I am fighting this wickedness among us with my bare hands, my mind, my very soul. I will not let evil prosper. Is anyone with me?" A dull round of cheers breaks out—still not enough for an outright rebellion. My mother's words come back to me—*only a true rebellion that consists of the majority can invalidate the Justice Alliance.*

An exceptionally tall man stands up across the aisle. We're the same height, and I'm standing on the seat of a chair. If all the Nephilim were his size, they wouldn't need to scour for a DNA imprint. The world would have long since learned our secret.

"What is this next phase of intimidation?" he gruffs.

The crowd shouts along with him, asking for the truth.

I take a full breath and look to Logan for help. Even the mention of the resurrected dead sends a shiver up my spine.

"The next phase of intimidation will be the final phase—it will be all the Barricade needs to land us where they want us." I swallow hard because there is no good way to stop this. What am I without solutions? Just another helpless face in the crowd. "Spectators."

A quiet hush fills the cavernous space. Faces bleach white. A few bend over with their head between their knees.

Nicholas claps his gavel. "Skyla, I bid you to take a seat. These are serious matters that call for serious resolutions."

"I have a resolution." It might be a lie at the moment, but I'm hoping what comes out of my mouth next is something we can run with. "The tunnels are open. It's true." Loving it so far, despite the adverse reaction from the crowd. "It's me who has opened them." More gasps, a little bit of honesty never hurt. "I've imprisoned members of a special unit of the Barricade known as the Immunity League. Members of this league were deliberately causing disturbances for our people—making it look as if we posed a threat—assuring the world that we were one." People are rapt at attention. Who knew the truth could actually work in my favor? "I have a place, a holding tank not in an earthly realm, ready to accept as many Spectators as we can capture. We'll need hunters. I'll accept as many volunteers as you'll give me. We also need spies. This is a call to any and everyone with family, friends, coworkers in the Barricade. I am one of them, but their leader, Wesley, only feeds me what he wants me to know." I look around at the crowd, my eyes scorching over theirs. "My husband tells me everything." If it's one thing I need everyone to understand, it's that Gage would never turn on us. There isn't a deceptive bone in that boy's— *man's* body. "We need all eyes and ears on board to pick up even the faintest whispers of a wicked plan. We'll need all the information funneled down from faction districts straight to Paragon where I'll set up a centralized communication force, along with a Nephilim Bureau of Intelligence. This is not a war—this is a preservation of our people. These are not times to lean on old unreliable practices. This is a time to band together and forge a future devoid of the danger that our brothers in the Barricade force upon us." The crowd breaks out into a wild cheer, and my heart soars. "The Earth is our home, and we will not be disrespected in our own house!" A roar breaks out as the room erupts in agreement. "This meeting is adjourned. All interested parties please see Dr. Booth who will record your information in our database. It is your responsibility to inform your constituents. There is no time to waste. We have remapped, regrouped, and restructured. Tonight, we stand as one faction, and our name is Retribution. Yesterday, we were caught in evil's snare, unable to fight off its stronghold, but today, we stand united together—and tomorrow, we are set for victory!"

All of Ahava seems to ignite with a thunderous applause. Dr. Booth gives me a big thumbs-up as Logan helps me down from the chair.

"Thank you." My breath sweeps over his face with victory. "And, as your newly reinstated leader, I revoke your status as a traitor. You, my love, are going to lead right by my side."

"Thank *you*. This is going to work." Logan pulls me into a congratulatory embrace.

"It has to."

Gage

There have been seasons in my life that I've been exhausted to the point of feeling drugged, feeling run over by a truck or falling-from-a-cliff-tired, but never have I experienced a fatigue quite like I have since the twins have arrived. How in the hell society has ever evolved to include more people stumps me—on second thought, a fresh crop of unassuming parents is truly what keeps the planet spinning. Nature relies on our ignorance, our inability to believe our elders, our friends when they warn us of the dangers of having children. Not that Skyla and I set out to defy anybody's logic and have kids—it just happened. And, now, seeing how in love we are with them, it sways the needle from mistake to the best surprise destiny has had in store for us since the day we met.

With Skyla at the faction meeting, it's my first night on daddy duty. Lizbeth felt sorry for me at one point in the evening—about five minutes after Skyla left—and asked, correction, *demanded* to keep the twins in her room for the night. An entire night. I fell asleep before my head hit the pillow. Every muscle in my body drinks down sleep, thirsty and savage.

A sharp cry comes from somewhere in the room, and I sit up, slightly nauseous from the sudden movement, and squint at the light emanating from the closet.

"Who's there?"

"It's just me," Skyla whispers, her voice wailing in disappointment.

"Are you okay? Did you fall?"

"No, I ate an entire bovine thanks to that stupid Burger Shack, and now I have to live with the bloated consequences." She steps into the room, taking off her top. Her bare legs glide forward, providing me with enough evidence that she's not wearing any bottoms. "I wanted to surprise you and put on my old West uniform, and I couldn't even get it past my knees. That means my legs are fat, Gage!" she shouts it in my face like it's all my fault. "You know that old saying, 'you are what you eat'? I've literally morphed into a cow."

A dull laugh pumps through me. "Come here, beautiful." I pull her over me. Her cool limbs touch mine, and my hard-on springs to life. I hope she's open to offering some serious alleviation because I am in desperate need. "You look perfect to me. And if it's any consolation, I like you better naked." I give her thigh a gentle pat. "I was hoping you'd wake me by sitting on my face."

"You have a dirty mind, and a dirty mouth." She sits high up on my bare chest as if readying to take me up on the suggestion. Just feeling her there, her wetness kissing my flesh makes me harder than I've ever been in my life. "Were the boys good?"

"They were great. Your mother insisted on taking care of them until morning. They're in her room." I trace along her thigh with my finger. "That means we get the night off."

"Her room, huh? If I hear them cry, my boobs won't know the difference. I'll probably spring a leak."

I lean back onto the pillow and pull her knees to my ears in one aggressive move. "Make it rain if you have to. I just want one delicious taste of what I've been missing." I pull her close and bow a quick kiss into her wet silk and watch as her eyes close with pleasure. My mouth lands over her sweet spot, shaking with hunger, and every muscle in my body tenses as it silently begs for me to fall into her. Skyla is home—always has been, always will be. A deep guttural moan evicts from my throat as I suck down, lick, French kiss the most delicate part of her body. My mouth devours her tender folds. My tongue runs a line up that new scar she earned while gifting us our boys, and I peck a kiss over it as a thank you. She's still as honey sweet as I remember. I work her over with my tongue, quickening my pace until she's panting above me, hard and urgent, as if she might have a cardiac episode if this doesn't happen for her soon. My teeth graze over that one magical tender spot, and she loses it in record time. Her body shakes out over me, begging to get off the ride, but my hands are buried in her hips, and I refuse to let go until I drink down the very last drop.

"You're an animal," she pants through a smile as she falls onto her back.

I take off my boxers and land over her on my elbows. The moon kisses her beautiful face, and my stomach pinches with a bite of pain. It all feels as if it's ending way too soon. Skyla and I have just started our family and already I'm forced to tear us in half, make choices I will never be ready to make. That bionic shield that protects my thoughts from her ability to read them erects itself as if on cue. I don't think I'll let down my guard again any time soon. The christening will be here before I know it, and I'll have to give my answer to Demetri, risk one of my children falling prey to his twisted mind—or surrender—save them, save Skyla's heart from getting wrenched out of her body while it's still beating. Regardless of my decision, I have to die. That doesn't change. I should have known that asking Demetri for the one thing I craved—to live alongside Skyla for as long as she's on this spinning blue rock—would only be granted so long as the end suited his needs. My first covenant with the Barricade was simply his way of getting my feet wet for things to come. He knew I wouldn't last—that I couldn't. Breaking faith was inevitable in that sense. Demetri has played me brilliantly, and now I am staring down the barrel of a celestially loaded gun. Ironically, this piece of shit news doesn't hasten my death by a single second. In that alone I find comfort. A part of me wants to believe that Skyla and I could raise Nathan and Barron to do the right thing, make the right choices, but how can I ever risk it? If Demetri took them for himself, I could never forgive myself, not on Earth, not in heaven. No. If any one of us is bound to become an enemy to the Nephilim people, it's going to be me, not one of my boys—never them.

I pull a condom from the nightstand, and Skyla sheds a mile-wide smile.

"How did your meeting go?" I ask as I tear open the package with my teeth.

She laughs. "Is that what our passion has been replaced with? Updates on diaper duty and faction meetings in the middle of lovemaking?"

"Sorry." I wince.

"I love it." She runs her fingers through my hair. "And I especially love that you and I are on this crazy train together."

"You know what else we're going to do together?" I roll on the condom and navigate my way to the entry of her body. "Are you ready for me?"

She lets out a tiny grunt, biting down on her lip nervously as if suggesting she's not.

"As ready as I'll ever be." Skyla braces herself against my arms, wincing in anticipation of the pain. My heart aches for her. Her body has been subjected to poking, prodding, and unimaginable agony for close to a year, and now, even this act of love will bring her more of the same. It seems vindictive the way the female body was designed, unfair. I'm betting Candace had a hand in that.

"I love you, Skyla Oliver." I land a kiss over her mouth, evicting all thoughts of her mother out of my mind. "I'm so proud to be your husband. You astound me with what you can do with both your body and your mind." I push in carefully, and she takes a quick breath. "Guide me," I whisper.

Skyla carefully navigates me inside her, achingly slow. We're both on pins and needles until I'm in deep, filling her without another inch to move.

"You okay?" My lids hang heavy, drugged with the ecstasy of being deep inside her once again.

"I'm okay," she pants into my ear. "We did it. We're Skyla and Gage again."

"Plus two." My mouth falls over hers.

The babies begin in on a faint wail just as I begin to thrust, but it's too late. I can't stop. I couldn't if they were right here in the room with us. I need Skyla. I need to have this moment with my wife. It's been far too long, and far too much has happened in both of our lives. I'm craving her in the worst way.

The babies quiet down, and Skyla's body relaxes beneath me once gain. I thrust into her with ease and care, my zenith coming all too quickly as I grab onto her with a monstrous grip. I come for weeks, in gallons, lost in the pulsating heartbeat of our love.

A dark laugh echoes through my chest as I kiss her just under the ear. "Looks like you weren't the only one feeling like a virgin. That was short and sweet. Sorry."

I lie over her, and a gush of warmth covers my chest as her milk lets down.

"Oh, geez." She slaps the mattress, getting up on her elbows. "It looks like I'm the one that owes you an apology. I'm a mess."

I lean in and lick her chest as if I'm about to lap it up. "You're a convenient mess. I was getting thirsty."

"Stop!"

We share a quiet laugh as I roll over and pull her to me. "We should probably shower."

"And then pass out."

"How was the meeting? You never did say."

"They're *in*, Gage." She locks eyes with mine, her chest squirting at me intermittently, and that impenetrable brick wall goes up around my thoughts without trying. "We've got them on our side. It's happening. The Barricade will never prosper." She sniffs. "I'll die before I let it."

Skyla folds into my arms, and we lie there, each lost in our own thoughts.

Skyla would rather die than let the enemy prosper. And I feel the same. The irony is I'll die, and then I'll become her enemy.

I'll make a lousy enemy.

Perhaps that makes me the very best one.

A week trickles by as the christening inches ever so close. My feet sludge into the future like a dying man walking to the electric chair.

Wesley does his nightly pick up and delivers me to the Transfer. It's been our routine before he takes me to the dark side of Paragon—Paragon in Nocturne, but I can't bring myself to call it that—that's where we traditionally meet with the Videns.

Chloe sits at the edge of her seat once we enter his haunted abode. Wes has told me that she spends the entire day primping for my nightly visits, ignoring any pressing needs baby Tobie might have. Ezrina has been a saint in taking care of that child—and she's also been a spy. Wesley is well aware of both.

"So, what have you decided?" Chloe offers me a cauldron with a bubbling brew, and I decline—probably some underworld version of a roofie.

"I haven't." I look to Wes as he takes a seat by the fire. He wants to know if I'm in. If I've decided to remain on Earth after my demise and spend the rest of Skyla's life tormenting her. "If I do this, how will it work?" I need the fine print. That's one lesson I don't need to learn twice.

"He didn't tell you?"

I'd like to think that Wes and I have developed a friendship over the past few months. Lately, especially since we've become fathers, we've been shooting from the hip with one another. The walls that have been up from the moment we met have finally crumbled to dust, and I can say with certainty that I have a brother in him—a twisted brother, but nevertheless.

"I don't know shit."

"You know the rules," Chloe points out. I'd ask her to leave, but she's like a gnat, so there's no point.

"Okay." Wes leans over his knees as if assembling his thoughts for a moment. "If that is the direction you decide to go in, you'll partake in a covenant ritual, which will bind you to this agreement. Then, you simply wait out your time—once you're deceased, he'll take charge over you. There's the issuing of a new body—a rarity, with the exception of a few. The marriage supper of the lamb is the big renewal for everyone else, so you'll be ahead of the curve in that respect. After your death, you'll be brought back and expected to perform."

"How does anyone think my heart will change course the second I step back on this planet? I love Skyla. I love our people."

"Nobody believes that you'll transform like some robot who's been freshly programmed—but the stipulation was that the heart of the one you hold dear will turn against you and what you believe. Since you're taking the brunt of the curse on yourself, you'll be the one whose heart is turned and all that you once believed. You'll question your old beliefs. Doubt will set in. And that, my friend, will be the downfall—or in your case—the pathway to the *light*." He raises a glass filled with a dark amber liquid before knocking it back in one quick swig.

"So, it's like a spell of some kind?"

"Absolutely not." Wesley's eyes enlarge at the audacity of my question. "Shit like that is strictly forbidden." He plunks down his glass like the sounding of a gavel. "This is a swaying of your heart. Now—here's the kicker—if you're strong enough, you can fight it, but it's like swimming against the current. Eventually, you'll wear out and give in. You'll feel relief once you go with the tide."

I look from Wes to Chloe and wonder if that's what happened to them.

"Skyla will be safe," I say, still trying to process this madness. "Logan will protect her—but I still want a relationship with her—with the boys."

"You'll get it. Just don't hold your breath, because things are going to change. I'm suspecting she'll have a hard time accepting some of the decisions you make." He looks to the floor, shaking his head. "She might even offer to be yours again just to make you change your mind. She'll convince herself you're strong enough to fight this—that she could help you do just that."

Something about hearing Wesley's thoughts about my wife—about my life with Skyla, makes me shake with anger so I change the subject.

"I heard about what happened with Laken." I take in a breath because I'm at the root of the blame. "Quite frankly, I'm shocked she did it." It's true. My heart broke for both her and Coop—especially when I know that it was my big mouth that started her in that direction.

Chloe chirps a laugh. "Desperation breeds all sorts of misdeeds. I can't wait to see how Skyla is going to handle this. I suppose she'll be offering to sleep with both you and Wes just to keep your head in the Celestra game. Little lucky slut." She takes a swig of her drink, and a plume of smoke trails her goblet.

"Chloe, would you leave?" I ask as calm and kind as possible. "You're really starting to piss me off." So much for being kind. "I've got a life and a wife who I love, and, if you haven't noticed, I'm in a shit situation. I'm trying to evaluate this from all angles, and I need to make a clearheaded decision."

"Really?" She looks less than amused. "What does Little Miss Priss make of all this?"

"She doesn't know. I'm asking you as a friend not to tell her." Shit. Can I really blame my lack of sleep on that little verbal blunder? I probably can.

"Oh, wow!" Her mouth falls open. "Skyla is going to freak! I fucking love this."

"You know what I'd fucking love? Some privacy."

"You won't get the privacy, but I promise not to tell."

"Don't get too excited, Chloe. I'm telling Skyla myself as soon as I make a decision."

"Oh, dear, dear, *sweet*, Gage." A ripe look of pity crosses her face. "You and I both know you're too nice of a guy to think there's a decision to be made."

I swallow down the lump building in my throat. Chloe is right.

There never was a decision to be made.

This is bound to happen.

Skyla officially has a new enemy—and it's me.

Logan

Three days until the christening means that Gage has three days to swallow that shit sandwich Demetri is shoving down his throat.

"This is happening," he says matter-of-factly as we sit in the back of the bowling alley while a group of middle school teenagers scream a riot with each strike and spare.

"I'm sorry to hear it. But, if Wes is right, you *can* fight this. You can still be a valuable ally for Skyla and the Nephilim people. You'll have a new body—indestructible. No one said you need to leave Skyla. You can have it all. You can beat them at their own game."

"She won't be my wife." He takes a dejected swig of his drink. "According to Wes, I'll give into the darkness, and she'll eventually grow to hate me."

"Not true. Skyla can never hate you. In fact, I've thought about it. You don't need a marriage covenant to be with her. Remain as her husband—keep your family intact. The human world doesn't need to know the dirty details."

"That I'll be clinically dead?"

"You'll be *alive*. Gage, you're one of the few who will ricochet right past the most painful part of existence. You can have Skyla in your heart, your home, and your bed."

"I don't think it'd go down like that." He touches his fist to his chin. "It is a nice thought to hold on to."

"Think about it. You'll outsmart Demetri. Beat him at his own game. Your sons remain pure, and *you* keep your life, the former and future, forever together with the woman you love by your side."

"And what about you?"

"And I run this ridiculous bowling alley into the ground." True as God—that, right there, just might be my purpose in life.

"You know that's not how this works. I die, and you come back. Your Treble has an expiration date, my friend."

"I'll forgo the trip back to Earth. I'll live it up in

paradise knowing you'll both be with me soon enough. In other words, I'll be happy knowing your family survived Demetri and all his wicked schemes."

"I don't know. Worst-case scenario is that I lose my fucking mind and start to hurt you, to hurt Skyla, and the people I love. Wes said it would be hard to fight for long. I know I can fight. I know I can persevere, but a part of me is already tired of all this bullshit. The easy route would be to head into paradise myself. But I could never rest knowing that one of my children will be lost. Face it, Logan. I am done. I made a covenant with wickedness—broke it, and now I'm going to lose everything. It was a part of the plan from the beginning. Don't you see? It's too ironclad for this to have been some massive misstep. This has destiny written all over it." His voice breaks. "I never thought I was evil. Never thought I had a bad thought about the Nephilim in my heart, and now everything I thought I knew is about to be chucked out the window." Tears pool in his eyes. "Would you do me a favor?"

"Anything."

"Set me straight. Don't give up on me. Have Ezrina, Candace, anyone help release my children and me from that damn curse, and I'll go easy into that good night. Believe me, it would be a privilege to die knowing I wasn't going to bring Skyla any more pain."

"You're not a bad guy. You're not going to set this world on fire in any wicked way. It's not like you'll be out of your mind. You'll still be you." A thought comes to me. "This might actually turn out to be a blessing in disguise."

"Let's hope so, man. Let's hope so."

Skyla calls a meeting of the Retribution League, just captains—about fifty people including Brody, Ellis, Laken, Coop, and me. The rankings that Dr. Booth designed for this new system are genius.

"We need as many volunteers for tonight's effort as

possible." Her voice hums through the hollow walls of the Havers' old barn. "We're storming the gates of the Transfer and making a show of force. I have a feeling Wes has the Spectators locked in holding tanks under the lab. It's where they were kept before. Brody and Cooper will escort them to Tenebrous. If we can round up as many as possible, that will dwindle the number he can terrorize the planet with."

Brody gives a slow blink. "He can have a new batch whipped up by sunrise."

"Then let him," Skyla snaps. "The important thing to do is demonstrate that we are innumerous, and we are not taking his crap lying down. We'll only have hours, maybe minutes to do what we need before Wes has the place on lockdown."

"What about Demetri? He can do it far quicker than that." Laken makes a good point.

"He's a Fem—not a drop of Nephilim in him. He can no more interfere in a rebellion than Marshall can."

"Sounds good." Brody mock salutes her.

The mobilization of troops is staggering. Within hours, Skyla manages to bring forth a nation's worth of people ready and willing to serve.

Skyla and I meet up with Ellis, Brody, Laken, and Coop at the base of Devil's Peak.

Ellis clears his throat, looking shockingly lucid. "How are we going to get everyone into that shithole?"

"We won't—I will." For months, Dudley has been priming me with new skills, teaching me how to forcefully appear and disappear, how to take people, *things*, with me and now I know why. Dudley was grooming me for just this very moment.

"You three, get to the Transfer. I'll send the masses in groups."

It takes almost an hour for me to complete the mission. By the time I dive through stone, and vibrate my way into that dark and lonely plane one last time, the Transfer is teeming with people in the underbelly of the woods just south of Wesley's haunt.

The group remains silent, staunch, while waiting for

Skyla's signal.

Skyla climbs onto the highest hill and crosses her arms over her head as if launching a race.

In an instant, the group enlivens, shouting and screaming its way over the hillside, down through the desolate village, and bleeding into Wesley's home without warning.

He swims out amidst the crowd and jumps onto the pedestal that sits outside his porch.

Skyla made sure Ezrina would be here tonight caring for Tobie. She wanted to ensure she was safe and unafraid in the attic until the melee subsides. No one is to touch that child per Skyla's orders.

"What the hell is going on?" Wesley's voice carries over the sea of people.

Coop leans in toward me. "You know, sometimes, I feel sorry for the guy. Tonight's not one of those nights."

Laken wraps her arms tight around Coop in a show of solidarity. I know they've had a rough patch. I pray it's the last one that Wesley—and, apparently, Gage brings into their lives. My stomach sours at the thought of Gage causing any unrest, and I pray it's not a sign of things to come.

Skyla makes her way to Wes. "This is the face of the Nephilim people. This is the face of your enemy. Make no mistake. We are here for blood. And it's our own we came to save."

The crowd goes wild with cheers, and per Skyla's order, they ravage the place—pillage the already barren landscape. An entire crowd runs into the labyrinth of Ezrina's old lab with Brody leading the way to the Spectators.

"Shit." Wes gets down, his face white with shock. "You think this is funny?" he pants into the crowd as people scatter like ants.

"We think this is serious," I say, standing shoulder to shoulder with Skyla.

He huffs a dry laugh. "So this is what I'll have to look forward to when my brother is no longer with you." He looks from me to Skyla. "Your own preview, I assume."

Skyla shakes her head vehemently. "This is no preview.

This is not a test. This is an actual emergency."

A horrid moan emits from behind as the Spectators emerge from their captivity.

"If you'll excuse me, I have the dead to deal with." Skyla takes off to banish as many of the shits that volunteered to give their lives for the wrong cause.

Wesley takes in the scene, the look of fear, the look of defeat spreading over his features, clear as the morbid handwriting on the wall. We've finally done it, managed to stump him, to prove that we—that *she*—is a worthy opponent.

It takes three hours before Wesley is able to wrangle enough binding spirits to shoo us the hell away. One by one we disappear, satisfied knowing we knocked out half of the Spectators in one swift move.

"That was a blow to his campaign." Skyla slaps me five as we appear in front of White Horse together. I don't dare point it out, but the binding spirit's job is to place everyone where they belong—at home. Laken and Coop disappeared together; Ellis and Giselle—and Skyla is right here with me.

"You did it." I offer a platonic embrace.

"We did it." The smile quickly slides from her face. "Wish Gage could have come. He would have loved it."

"I know."

It's sucked not having Gage as a part of our plan, to see the lowlights, the highlights of what we've accomplished. It's as if Demetri's ultimate strategy has already been set into motion.

"Skyla"—her name falls from my lips like a star—"I think—I know that after tonight, the Nephilim trust you again. I also think they're ready to accept Gage as your husband."

"I hope so." She wraps her arm around my waist, tight. "I can't move another inch without him."

Skyla and I fall onto the cool, dew-laden lawn, ripe with exhaustion, making snow angels in the grass, laughing like children at the monstrous feat we've just accomplished. The penetrating fog is a welcome relief to our aching bodies.

Skyla stares up at the sky, panting, relishing her victory.

But my mind wanders to how far Skyla might have to

move without Gage. It might be far more than an inch. And it breaks my heart to think about it.

15

The Greatest Sacrifice

Skyla

Rain falls over Paragon, hard and weighted, like bodies tumbling from the sky. Then, in a show of defiance, it clears up before evening, the air warmed and sweetened, perfumed with lilacs as if Ahava has blown its breath over the island. But this weather phenomenon is as far from the perfection of paradise as one could get. This is the handiwork of the devil himself, Demetri. It's the night of the boys' christening. My mother's party planning tour de force will be exemplified for all to see—family and friends only, Gage and I insisted on keeping it small, *simple*. It's the day before Christmas Eve, and the entire island is in a festive holiday mood.

Bree and Drake hitch a ride over to Demetri's estate with us. Mom has all but gifted her minivan to Gage and me. In the meantime, she and Tad have been sharing his Althorpe issued Corolla.

"This is going to be the shit!" Drake leans in as he inspects the rotating searchlights that greet us at the gate.

Multicolored searchlights? At least a dozen of them? I sink in my seat. An infantry of searchlights does not *simple* make. What the heck is my mother thinking?

"Shit," I whisper as Gage offers a look of dismay. We've made a conscious effort to keep our expletives in check. There won't be time to train ourselves how to speak like dignified adults in a year when the boys will be free to mimic us, so we've decided to cull the cussing asap. "I told her to keep it small—intimate. I even gave her a guest list."

"Skyla," Gage rumbles it low, laden with the kind of concern that thinly veils my name as a question.

I follow his gaze to the side of the property where the fog kisses the fence line and see for myself what has him so gun-shy to speak up.

"Oh God." I bury my face in my hands a moment. The Transfer transplants parade freely about in their old school fashion choices, full bell skirts, twirling, whirling, and weird for all to see. "You do realize that State of the Union Crypt Keepers will be here this evening. That beckon of light is practically an invitation. It looks like Demetri and my mother will be serving up steaks with a side of paranormal tonight—so much for a peaceful evening. Kill Me and Poser Moser have been dying to finish grilling me."

"Speaking of grilling." Drake opens the side door while Gage is still crawling up the driveway and hops out. "I'm down for that all-you-can-eat lobster bar." He plucks Bree out of the van, and they shut the door, capsulizing us inside with the boys.

"We can make a run for it," I offer.

"We can't. We happen to be the parents of the guests of honor." He winces before pointing over to a young man in a tuxedo. "Besides, he's got valet. This is going to be a great night." His features sag when he says it as if it's the last thing he believes. "Who's in for the lobster bar?"

We get out and each grab a diaper bag—the expensive leather kind with the brand name stamped all over it a thousand times. Gage loathes these ritzy overgrown purses, but mostly because they make him feel like a forty-year-old housewife proud of the fact she can afford a luxury bag on her husband's dwindling salary. Gage and I hoist a car seat a piece—and with the boys snug safe inside, they weigh as much as the Mustang.

What I thought being a mother would be like, and the harsh reality of it, are two entirely worlds apart. Although, the joy is insurmountable, more than I could have ever imagined, so is the fatigue. Gage and I have found pleasure in the littlest of details, the boys silky skin over ours, the powerful force of love we feel when gazing deep into their eyes. The simple way their fingers curl over ours makes our spirits soar. We waited two patient weeks for their excess belly buttons to fall off, only to seal the tiny prunes in their baby books. I'm sure they'll forever be disgusted in our need to preserve all things, but, they are precious, and we don't want to lose a single memory. Last week, the boys urinated in tandem once we took their diapers off to change them. Gage and I laughed, but it was mesmerizing on some level. Our own marble fountains come to life. Michelangelo couldn't have carved a greater perfection. These boys have now become our life force. There was no us before them.

Once we unload in Demetri's vacant living room, we each strap on our BabyBjörns and place Nathan and Barron in their shearling slots, only to remove them once again, ditch the suede baby holsters, and bundle them up in snowsuits so they can be passed about freely to family and friends in Demetri's expansive, quasi-haunted backyard. Even though the boys are just hardly a month old—on one hand it feels as if they've been in our lives forever in a blissful I-can't-believe-we-ever-existed-without- them kind of way—and, on the other hand, I wonder how four weeks zipped by without my permission.

"Hey, little guy," I coo into Barron's sweet face as he struggles to steady his glassy cobalt eyes on me. Barron and Nathan are carbon copies of their daddy through and through. His tiny lips purse as he purrs and stretches to life. I drop a kiss to his smooth forehead, and his body squirms with delight. The boys slept all the way here, and, if I had my way, they'd continue to sleep right through the party.

"You ready to do this?" Gage picks up my hand and offers a firm squeeze.

"As ready and exhausted as I'll ever be," I whisper as we make our way to the back where voices carry with laughter and buzzing conversation. It feels more like a New Year's Eve party where everyone is getting happily loaded, and where Gage and I simply don't belong. All we want to do is go home and collapse on our mattress. "Are you getting the feeling this was a damn bad idea?"

"Language."

THE SERPENTINE BUTTERFLY

I turn to find Marshall twitching his fingers at the baby, and I make my first hand off of the evening as he takes Barron from me like a doting uncle.

"Come, Jock Strap. Give up the little goat. I'm taking them both," he insists.

Gage scowls a moment before handing over Nathan.

Marshall heads outside like an Olympic victor holding up my precious babes for all to see, and the crowd breaks out into a raucous cheer.

Gage pulls me back a moment.

"There's something I want to say"—his brows crease in that tortured handsome way that only Gage Oliver seems able to pull off—"I've wanted to say it all day, but I couldn't find the words." He presses out a painful smile. This lack of sleep has taken its toll on our sanity, and even our affection is marred by fatigue's wicked clawing for attention. "I love you." He pinches my chin between his fingers. "You are the love of my life. I worship you and our little family." His eyes bear into mine as if he were carving the words right onto my heart. "Know this— there isn't anything I wouldn't do to ensure your safety or the boys'. There isn't any sacrifice too big to make sure the three of you have the best life—the one you deserve. I would die to keep you and the boys safe, and I would sacrifice my sanity, my very soul to make that happen." His words swirl from his lips like musical notes, like a love song I've been aching to hear. I was thirsty for that reassurance. Gage—his DNA to be exact—has made me twitchy as of late. After that vision I had in the yard, the sight of him morphing into the dragon with Barron in his talons, my mind has been buzzing with the psychotic "what-ifs" ever since. But these words, these truths, quell that silly side of me that ever thought there might be a shard of a possibility to the nefarious scene. It was right after I had that big blowout with Mia. My hormones were rampant. Of course, I was seeing dragons. I was out of my mind with worry for my sister.

"I needed to hear that," I whisper. "I needed to hear that no matter what, you are for the light." I touch my hand to his sexy stubble and pull him in. "The dark came and tried to steal you away, but we won. You are my hero—my beating heart that walks outside my body. I love you forever, Gage Oliver." I lean in and land my lips over his, soft as a wish. Only Gage can kiss me as if writing a poem over my mouth. His tongue mingles with mine, hot and alive, and it feels just as exhilarating as that first stolen kiss we shared so long ago.

The door opens to the rear of the house, and voices tremble in. Mom bumps into us holding an empty silver tray with the glossy tracks of something that once occupied its dimensions.

"Would you look at the two of you?" she cackles so high I'd swear she's inebriated. Considering there are no more pump and dumps in her future, I don't see why not. When she first explained to me that if I happened to imbibe I'd have to sit under my electric udders for an hour only to flush all my mommy milk down the toilet—for the next two days, I decided that not a sip of anything stronger than sparkling cider was worth it. "Don't go making baby number three just yet! You want to let the sheets cool." She gives a hard wink. The light catches on the shiny red gloss ringing her lips. Mom looks pretty, despite the blinking Christmas tree on her sweater and the miniature stockings she managed to turn into earrings—one reads *Nathan*, the other *Barron* in gold glitter. She made them this morning with an unsurpassed sense of pride, and it warmed my heart to see her do it.

Gage and I make our way outside where Demetri's spacious estate is blanketed in a sea of baby blue twinkle lights just as Mom had promised. There's a buffet spread that runs the entire length of the swimming pool surrounded by throngs of friends and family, not to mention netherworld creatures stirring in frenetic circles.

"Is there another definition of simple that I'm not aware of?" I whisper.

Down by the woods, the bitch squad holds a quasi-reunion, and Nat offers up a friendly wave. I reciprocate just as Laken and Coop pop over.

"How are your eyelids holding up?" Laken gives me a power hug. She's been my rock as far as letting me vent freely about my lack of sleep and newfound crusty boobs, which finally healed no thanks to sheep in general and their greasy manes. Lanolin will forever be a cure-all for all my dry, cracked skin, crusty, bleeding boob needs.

"Are my eyelids supposed to be up?" I tease. "I thought I was dreaming."

Coop gives a quick embrace. "Wes is here." His expression sours as he glances to Gage.

Gage winces as he takes them in. "I'm so sorry, guys. If I'd have known that what I said would have set into motion what it did, I would have kept my mouth shut."

Laken pulls her gorgeous hubby in tight. "Believe me, it's been a relief."

"I encouraged her," Coop confesses. "I knew Laken wouldn't be able to sleep at night knowing she might have had the power to stop this. I also know Wes is too much of a power-hungry SOB to have left his unholy throne."

My gut wrenches because I know for a fact that unholy throne happens to have Gage Oliver's name on it. Thankfully, that's one seat he'll never take.

"Coop." I reach over and offer him a firm embrace. "But what would you have done if Wes lied just to take Laken?"

He glances over in the nefarious Fem's direction. "He can't lie to her any more than I can."

Laken pulls him in. "Coop and I were both certain he wouldn't do it. And, in truth, I do have peace in my heart knowing there's nothing I could have done to stop this."

"I know it sounds twisted, but I thought it was commendable." Coop pulls his wife in tight. "Laken would sacrifice herself in any manner to make sure the Nephilim didn't have to suffer at the hands of that madman—in theory." He hikes his brows at his bride, and she kisses him on the lips.

Coop and Laken are solid. I love that. I love how it flies in the face of Wes and all of his wicked intentions. The good guys really do win. I should know. Gage and I are proof of that ourselves.

"A sacrifice like that wouldn't have been worth it." I pull Gage in as if to prove a point. "Wickedness only knows how to lie. Even if he agreed to end all this madness, it would be a fabrication. Making a covenant with evil is a mistake every single time. You think you're doing something noble, then *bam*! They have you by the balls, ten times worse than before."

Gage tenses beneath my arm. I know he's taken a liking to Wes. Heck, I've taken a liking to Wes, and that bastard once sucked me dry in the tunnels himself. I do wish he would change, but not for Laken's sake, for his own.

"I'm so glad you were there for me." Laken takes up my warm hand in her gloves. "I just had to know. And when the shit hits the fan, I'll feel less responsible for it."

"You won't be responsible for it at all." I smile at her handsome counterpart. "Besides, I have never seen a better looking couple than the two of you. As soon as graduation hits, you two should seriously consider procreation. That is, unless you take an unexpected detour like we did."

"Be careful." Gage winces. "And enjoy the hell out of a good night's sleep."

"We do have a bit of news." Coop gives Laken a sly wink as if they were conspiring this entire time.

"Laken! How could you not tell me? Oh my God! How far along are you?" I can't spit the questions out quick enough.

"No, not that." She glances around in the event a stray ear glommed on to our miscommunication. It wouldn't be the first time.

"I've taken a paid position at West Paragon High." Coop leans in with a self-deprecating grin. "I'm the new assistant coach. Come next spring, when I get my degree from Host, I'll be bumped to head coach if I want. They're filling the position with temps in the meantime."

"Son of a bitch." Gage pulls him into a man hug.

"And I want to know if you're willing to help out. There's another paid position. It'll be tricky with school, but not impossible. You in?"

"Hell fucking yeah, I'm in." They engage in a knuckle bump, secret handshake combo, and Laken and I are just as giddy for them. Gage's entire life revolved around football until last year when he hurt his back.

"This will be just as good as getting on the field myself."

Gage beams. "And at West? Can you believe that, Skyla? It's like I'm going home."

"Say hi to Cerberus for me," I tease.

"Here's the party." Logan gives Gage and me a hug at the same time. "Just spent some time with my two favorite nephews."

"I guess I've been booted from the top of the totem pole." Gage ruffs up Logan's hair.

Logan is quick to shrug him off and slick it back down to perfection. "You're more of a brother to me anyhow. Speaking of brothers." He glances over my shoulder, and we turn to find Liam with Michelle Miller snug in his arms. "It looks like he made his choice."

"Or was it made *for* him?" I nod over at Lexy with her arms draped over Brody Bishop's shoulders. It's no secret that his on-again, off-again relationship with Brooke is off-again. I've seen her sniffing around Marshall. I scan the vicinity, and there she is, trying to latch on to him like a tick, ready to get fat off his Sector eminence. *Dream on, sweetheart*, I want to say. In truth, I feel pretty bad for caring at all.

Marshall spots me and points in my direction, breaking up his little powwow with Brielle's big sister. She smirks as he makes haste in this direction.

"Modern girls just won't take no for an answer," he muses, giving a swift tug to his tweed jacket as if to annunciate his frustration.

Coop gives a dull laugh. "She's on the rebound. Coming on strong is par for the course. Speaking of rebounds, any luck with that elixir Ezrina whipped up?"

"What elixir?" I don't like being out of the loop when it comes to Ezrina's lotions and potions.

"Your magic mushrooms," Laken interjects. "When you vomited in the Transfer—"

"Oh, that's right. It had the power to harvest an entire crop of insta-shroom." I cringe at the memory. "Please don't tell me they hold some psychedelic side effects. I'd hate to think I had the power to sponsor crazy."

"Nope." Coop grins. "Something better. You have the

power to sponsor life. Turns out, Ezrina thinks the regenerating power she's harvested from them is enough to bring back the Spectators."

"Thank God." Gage leans his head back, allowing the moon to kiss the ridges of his neck. "The Videns will be relieved to hear that. It's been a shit ride for the families of the 'volunteers.'"

I shudder. "See? I bet Wes promised them one thing, then did another. No offense, but your father and brother are masters of bait-and-switch."

Gage extinguishes a breath as if he's been holding it all night. Logan slaps an arm over his nephew's—scratch that—*brother's* shoulder as if to comfort him.

"Your dad—Barron is looking for you," Logan says to Gage as they politely excuse themselves from our circle.

"I'll be there in a second!" I call after them.

"Ms. Messenger—" Marshall clasps my hand and begins ushering me toward the edge of the party. I give Laken and Coop a slight wave as I'm so rudely carted off.

"Do you mind? I have guests to mingle with."

"Yes. About those guests." His eyes shine red like cranberries as he glares into the woods. "You have an unexpected visitor."

I crane my neck trying to get a glimpse of whatever it is he sees, but all I can make out is a tall, lanky couple—

"Oh, it's just them. Killion and Moser. They make my stomach turn almost as much as Chloe does. And clearly the good-for-nothing feathered Kragger isn't here because she's gracing us with her awful presence."

"Young Holden is nesting in my rafters with his pale-plumed betrothed."

"Oh! I've been meaning to ask—"

"It's already done." Marshall marches us on without skipping a beat.

"You mean—"

"Yes, I've done the deed." He looks positively perturbed. "Joined together in holy feathered matrimony a bird and his chick."

"Ha! That's pretty funny actually." Only Marshall isn't laughing.

"You wouldn't think it so humorous if they were cooing away in your rafters. Have you heard what a bird in heat sounds like? Now that's an awful presence."

"I don't think heat is something birds typically experience."

"Believe you me, these birds give heat a new meaning. I expect a baby batch of Kraggers come spring."

"That sounds dangerous to the entire species."

"It will be." Marshall shoots a crinkled eye into the woods as if trying to make something out. "But those Althorpe postulants weren't the guests I was—"

"Here you are!" Mom hooks me with her claw, and, before I know it, I'm front and center with the Olivers as Barron holds his namesake and Emma cuddles with Nathan.

Mom squeals as she wraps her arms around Tad. "Who would have thought a year ago we'd all be standing here today?"

"Not me—that's for dog dang sure." Tad deadpans. "I told you we should have splurged and bought them a box of Willie Warmers last Christmas."

Mom swats him like the annoying fly he is.

"But no—" Tad weaves his finger through the air. "You thought it would be *crass*." He says *crass* with air quotes. "You know what's *crass*, Lizbeth? Stepping on a dirty diaper in the middle of the night! Do you really know what number two feels like squishing between your toes?"

"That was a one-time deal. I did not plant them all over the bedroom like a minefield just to watch your blood pressure spike like you accused me." She gives an incredulous huff. "If I were trying to kill you, I'd think of far more clever ways."

Shit.

Emma and Barron exchange uncomfortable glances. And suddenly, I want to snatch the boys from their arms and make a run for it.

Talks of plotting your spouse's homicide is something the Olivers simply cannot relate to—although, I couldn't blame

Barron for a fantasy or two.

"Skyla!" Emma chirps as if she heard me, and I jump.

Tad gesticulates wildly as if he can't get his words out fast enough. "And you can bet your bottom tootin' dollar that they'll each be getting a box of baby stoppers in their stockings tomorrow night!"

Emma chooses to ignore him while rocking Nathan. "Speaking of gifts—I have an early Christmas present for you, Skyla. It's in my purse. Would you mind reaching in?"

Gage gives a smug look my way that reads *told you she loves you*.

Emma angles her purse toward me, and I pull out a small box the size of a paperback wrapped in black and white print with a bright red bow on top. I can't help but think it looks so cosmopolitan and chic, and, for a second, I'm bursting with pride until I realize it's simply wrapped in one of Barron's discarded newspapers. An entire row of happy yearbook-like pictures spans up and down the girth of it with birthdates and death dates below their photos. Gah! It's the freaking obituaries! Emma Oliver wrapped my Christmas gift in the obituaries! *Figures*.

"Presents!" Giselle pops up on cue, all giggles and smiles, with Ellis hanging on by her fingertips. "Did Santa come early? If he did, it's because I begged and begged!" She gives a few quick hops. Giselle is so stunningly beautiful with her dark hair and deep-welled dimples. Even though Emerson Kragger wasn't related to Gage, her features really did resemble his. I can't help but think of Sage, what she would have looked like at that age. Stunning. She would have been stunning.

"The gift is for Skyla." Emma gives a tight-lipped smile. "And it's not from Santa. It's actually from me, just a little something."

I pull the paper off carefully, and just before I'm about to fling it to the side, I stop cold. Staring me in the eyes is a familiar, dearly departed soul I may have accidentally sent to paradise before her time, Kate Winston.

I glance up at Emma and meet up with her sharp stare. There's something cold, calculating in her eyes as if this were no error, no accidental wrapping mishap that I'm contending with. There is a very real reason that Kate is in my hands doing her obituary best to pull a guilt trip on me—well, not Kate, Emma. Maybe this is Emma's way of saying *you will never be good enough for my son because you are a homicidal murderer*. Or better yet, I'll never be a good enough mother because I'll forever run the risk of lopping off one of my poor children's heads. Who knows what twisted thoughts are running through her mind?

"Oh, the suspense." Marshall connects those poppy red eyes with mine and gives a single nod before glancing down at poor Kate. And for whatever it's worth, I feel vindicated knowing that this discretion of Emma's didn't get past Marshall. Gage, on the other hand, coaxes me to open the box, completely oblivious to his mother's morbid slight.

I unearth the box and hold my breath. It's blue, Tiffany blue, which under normal circumstances would excite me, but given the delivery, it has sort of knocked the sheen off that pricey shade of turquoise. I pull off the lid and am met with the glare of two tiny silver spoons, their handles curled up at the ends.

"They're engraved." She beckons me to inspect this myself.

I shoot Gage a smug look myself that says *see? It wasn't for me after all. It was for the boys*. The wrapping was for me—makes total sense.

"That's so thoughtful," I say. Thoughtful in a cryptic-reminder-of-my-darkest-hour sort of way. Kate's life was cut short because of my ill attention. I gasp in horror. "God, is that what you're trying to say? Is this some passive-aggressive attempt to let me know I'm going to accidentally kill my children because of my ill attention?"

"*Skyla!*" Tad and Gage shout in unison. Good God, if those two are joining forces on anything, the world must be coming to an end.

"It's just hormones." Mom flicks a wrist at Emma, trying to defuse my odd outburst. "It takes months for the human brain to come back from Babyville." Or apparently years.

I frown at my mother for the vagina-based defense.

Tad grunts, "Every day I hear the exact same excuses." He gives an exaggerated shake of the head to Emma as if to sympathize. "*Ignore her*"—he does his best impression of my mother—"*she's got bloody, crusty boobies!*" His hands dance in front of his chest as if to add to the mimicry.

"I apologize, Emma." I choke on my words. "But I think I need some air." I push the gift toward Gage and head to the rear of the yard.

"I'll come with you!" Giselle catches up. Her dark beauty shines against the pale glow of twinkle lights the color of a tropical sky. "Where do we go to get the best fresh air?"

"Probably deep in the woods." So the government can haul me away before I go psycho batshit on your mother again.

"*Dude.*" Ellis appears like a ghost on my other side. "You just need something to mellow you out—you know—take you down a notch so you can roll with the Oliver punches."

"I know what you're rolling, Ellis, and no thank you." I'd hate to think how long it would take to express those laughing gases Ellis infuses himself with daily out of my not-so-fun bags—or "bloody, crusty boobies" as Tad lovingly refers to them. Ellis doesn't even bother to hide his pot addiction anymore. You can smell it on him. His new cologne, Eau de Reefer. I bet all the gifts Emma has for Ellis this Christmas will be wrapped in the obituaries, too. I'm also willing to bet she'd love for him to star in one of those morbid ads himself—right along with me.

We hit the first layer of pines and hear the distinct moan of a girl followed by giggles. The fog dances around our feet, swirling, pulling us forward with its elongated fingers. Paragon is flirting, casting her spell as she lures us deeper into the woods.

"I should be getting back to the party," a female voice chortles unconvincingly. God, it sort of sounds like Mia... "But only after you put that nightstick of yours in my—"

"Oh my God!" I stalk over to the shadowed figures, ready to rip Revelyn Booth's nightstick right off his body and beat him senseless with it. Only it's not Rev and Mia—it's Drake and Brielle.

"Oh!" I try to turn away, but I'm afraid I've exposed my corneas to Drake's flesh-covered nightstick, and my lids burn as I squeeze them tight.

Shit! Shit! Shit!

"Geez, people!" Brielle bops over, still buttoning her blouse, a bare nipple ogling at the three of us. "Where do you have to go to get some privacy around here?"

"Mars." I glare at Drake a moment, holding back the suggestion he sign up for an upcoming mission. He is a father—of two. Not to mention the fact my mother, keeper of the destinies, seems to have gifted him with the Midas touch.

"*Shh!*" Drake puts his finger to his lips. "I've been hearing weird shit out here all night." He gives a mean stare into the fog, and I half expect a hand to reach out and snatch him.

"I know—it's totally freaking me out." Brielle shivers. "It's like the woods have eyes, and something sinister is watching us."

I take a quick breath. "It's those idiots who keep trying to question me. I've had this foreboding feeling all night like they're coming at me with a big giant net. We'd better get back to the party. I don't want them cornering any of us. If they come near you, remember, you know nothing about nothing." An easy task for the majority present.

"What's nothing?" Giselle whispers as a billow of haze spreads from her lips.

"About faction business—about angels," I whisper, touching my finger to my mouth. I've learned that with Giselle you need to be very upfront with nary an analogy between you and her ears. She needs to be told point-blank which way is up, and then she's good to go—mostly.

"They're coming!" Brielle clamps her hand over her mouth as two elongated shadows, forty feet in length at least, head in this direction.

"We're not angels!" Giselle shrieks as if she's being filleted with the sharpest blade.

Holy, *holy*. I close my eyes.

"Just follow me," I hiss, leading us to the left, but Killion and Moser make the turn right alongside us. "*Shit.*"

This is it. I can see it now—the five of us thrown into government-issued cages while they strip search us looking for alien markings, or battery packs. Worse yet, they'll probe our every orifice! Darn Wes. His hunger for world domination is going to cause my vagina to be surveyed by yet another stranger. And what about *Gage*? He'll have to raise the twins without me. Chloe will probably claw her way to the surface just to try to fill my bedroom slippers.

"Mrs. Oliver?" Moser sets his rectangular jaw in our direction. "Just the woman we wanted to see. Would you and your friends mind stepping over here so we can chat for a moment?"

Oh my God. This is it. They'll buy Ellis with a dime bag, Giselle with *oh, look, shiny!* And Drake with a handshake. I suppose that makes Bree the wild card. Perfect. All of humanity rests on Brielle's ability to remain calm and focused. We are so very fucked.

"Skyla?" Gage's voice booms over the vicinity, his tenor vibrating through the branches. "Time for cake!"

"Time for cake!" I jump, buzzing past them. "You're welcome to join us if you like!" *Not.* But no thanks to Tad and his ridiculous faux position at Althorpe, they're a part of the party package.

I bolt from the woods with Giselle and Bree in tow. Drake stayed behind, mumbling something about "that moaning shit." God, I had better see Mia, or I am going to freak.

Mom presents the twins with an enormous white confection, the piping on the borders outlined in baby blue in keeping with the theme.

"It's gorgeous," I say as Gage and I admire her ability to order a sheet cake with the best of them.

"It's time for the dedication." Gage takes hold of my hands, his eyes burrowing deep into mine. There's a distinct aura of mourning in his gaze, and it throws me for a moment before the pieces fall into place.

"I get it," I whisper, with tears just below the surface. Gage is overcome with emotion just thinking about how quickly everything is moving in our children's lives. "I can't believe an entire month has gone by either. And I know that in a blink we'll both be standing at their high school graduation, then college, then they'll have weddings of their own." My lips tremble as I hold back the dam that begs to burst. Mom is right. My hormones are still raging like a tempest, still trying to navigate their way through the body morphing that's currently taking place. I'm still not able to fit into my jeans or my old emotions, but every day I'm one step closer.

"It's true." He can hardly whisper the words.

"But the one thing that keeps me centered is knowing you'll be there, right alongside me for all of those milestones. I couldn't do this without you, Gage. I wouldn't want to."

Mom gathers everyone around while Gage and I each hold a happy cooing child—me with Nathan and he with Barron.

Marshall says a simple prayer, blessing each of the boys in turn. His voice strums through the night like a poem.

"That was beautiful," I whisper.

"I'm not done." He places a hand on Nathan's, then Barron's forehead. "May the living God bless you both. May He ignite a path of righteousness before you, cast a pall upon your enemies, and may you never want or suffer so long as you both shall fear Him."

A round of applause breaks out. A few of the Transfer transplants start in on an odd looking jig, the girls' opulent dresses shake like rag dolls.

"I, too, would like to add a blessing!" Demetri's voice rings out like a demented gong, putting an immediate damper on the joy in my heart. A blessing from Demetri is pretty much tantamount to a curse. "Barron and Nathan"— he begins with that twisted never-ending grin of his—"two boys after my own heart. You've already captured it."

"That's because it's so tiny," I whisper to Gage, and he chuckles.

Demetri lays his fleshy mitts over each of the boys just like Marshall did. Only now it doesn't feel so holy and right. It feels downright creepy. The warm fuzzies are quickly replaced with the need to swat him away and call social services.

"May you find your true path in life. May the destinies you were designed for prevail and lead you to life everlasting, with power and majesty and glory at your feet. May the world acknowledge you as the royalty you are. May you be delivered from all of your troubles, from those who seek to destroy you. Blessings upon you both in this realm, and the next."

A shiver runs up my spine. The fog swirls and dances, flossing over us with a brilliant blue patina.

The crowd cheers, the voices of thousands thunder like the hooves of an army riding in to capture us. In a way, it feels as if we've already been taken prisoner—Gage, the twins, and me. Somehow, deep down inside, I feel as if there is no real escape from Demetri and his realm.

Gage and I slice into the cake while Melissa and Emily help plate it up and funnel it to the crowd.

"Where's Mia?" I ask my far more snarkier, hopefully far more virginal, younger sister.

"On her knees with Gabe, where do you think?" she snipes.

"*Gabe*? You mean Rev, right?" Not that I have a preference, but reputations are built in quantity not quality of lovers.

"Nope. She's going for it. She bought glow-in-the-dark condoms and everything." Melissa sticks a fork down her throat and gags before jabbing into a slice of cake and handing it off to the nearest person aching to quell their sweet tooth.

"Crap," I whimper, turning to Gage. "We need to find Mia," I plead as the twins bob contentedly in our arms. Nathan holds that fresh baby bottom scent I've grown to love, and I bury my nose in his hair a moment.

Gage glances toward the woods. His dark brows hood over his glowing eyes, and my sweet spot quivers for him. This is one time I totally approve of my hormones' behavior.

"Let's take a walk." He nods for me to follow him into

the crowd.

We scan the vicinity in hopes of spotting Mia, or her male suitors, but there's no sign of any of them. Most people have taken seats at the rows and rows of tables Mom has dotting the length and breadth of Demetri's palatial estate. I realize she was just following the demented Fem's orders when going along with this over-bloated guest list, and to Demetri, this most likely meets the criteria of an intimate gathering.

"I see her." Gage leads the way into the woods I came out of not too long ago. Dear God—the *moaning* woods. I have a feeling the moaning mystery has come to an end.

"Is she having s-e-x?" I cover poor Nathan's ear when I say it.

"Not unless she does it standing—and fully dressed. She's laughing at something."

"Hopefully at Gabe Armistead's ridiculously tiny member." A boy's ego can never recover from something like that. They fear that sizable rejection just as much as girls do showing up to school without any pants on. They're both very high up as far as reoccurring nightmares are concerned.

Then I spot her, her fingers entwined in that Armistead head of his, her knee tucked between his legs, riding up and down his body like a carnal promise.

"Mia!" I bark as she comes into view. "Step away from that asshole right this minute!"

Gage touches his shoulder to mine. "I'll give you a pass on that one."

"Thank you." I cringe. I just pray Nathan's or Barron's first word is not *asshole* because, while humorous on some level, they would be housebound until they worked that out of their system. This parenting thing is a lot harder than it looks.

"Skyla?" Mia looks mildly confused. She's wearing a long velvet cape, which she stole from my Halloween costume, but it does look strikingly sexy. I'll have to "borrow" it back sometime.

Two figures step out of the dark and into a patch of moonlight.

A breath hitches in my throat when I see who they are.

Mia wasn't touching Gabe. She was hugging her father.

"Daddy!" I stride over at a quickened clip and wrap my free arm around his waist, sobbing at the sight of him.

"Skyla, my darling little girl." He kisses me on the forehead. "How I've missed you." He touches his finger to Nathan's cheek.

"This is your namesake." I carefully hand him Nathan, and Gage does the same with Barron.

"Barron and Nathan." My mother steps beside him, her face illuminating unnaturally as if she swallowed a flashlight.

"Candace," Gage acknowledges her before I do.

"You've come to terms with the night?" She flits her eyes over his before pulling me into an embrace.

"If by 'come to terms,' you mean christened the boys, then yes." It's a real struggle not to roll my eyes around her sometimes. Although, there is a Marshall-esque charm about her that warms me.

"Marvelous." She glances to Mia who takes her place by my side. "You, my dear, are the spitting image of your big sister." Her lips expand with pride. "Who is, of course, a spitting image of me. It was my pleasure." She gives a solemn nod as if Mia had thanked her.

"How is Sage?" I look to my father. He's so youthful looking tonight. The silver hair he usually wears by his temples isn't present in this dim light. I miss him. I miss the scar beneath his right eye, the thickness of his skin, his full bottom lip—those eyes like sea glass. My father is a beautiful man both inside and out.

"Sage is wonderful." My father beams at the mention of her. "I would have brought her along, but you know how your mother is." He rolls his eyes, and I laugh.

Mia ribs me. "Who's Sage?"

"Um"—I look to Gage, and he gives a combo of a shrug and nod as if to say he's fine with letting her know—"the daughter I lost." My voice breaks. "But she's with Dad. She's the treat that waits for me at the end of my life." A tear slips down my face, leaving a glacial trail, and I shiver.

"I'm sorry." Mia wraps her arm around me. "I want you

to keep me in the know about things like this. I want to be a part of your life, Skyla, but I can't be if you don't let me in. I'm the same age you were when we moved to Paragon, and I used to think you were so mature." She gives a soft laugh. "I'm ready to be friends now—and sisters forever, of course." She tightens her embrace. "I want to hear all about Sage when you're ready to talk about her."

"Thank you." I give her a kiss. "I appreciate that, friend."

"Oh!" She jumps as she spots something behind my shoulder. "I gotta go." She lunges at our father and kisses him on both cheeks. "Don't be such a stranger!" She turns and waves at my mother. "Catch you later! Thanks for the face!" She laughs as she runs full steam into the woods. "Rev!"

Rev? Should I be relieved that it's not Gabe she's hunting down with her glow-in-the-dark prophylactics? God, I pray Dr. Booth knocked him into tomorrow, and that his dick shrivels at the sight of her.

I glance back to my father, ready to dish about any and everything, and he's scowling, downright glaring at Gage.

"I'd like a moment alone with your husband, Skyla."

"What?"

Candace takes Barron from Gage and hands him to me while scooping up Nathan for herself. "We'll scoot along." She snatches me by the arm. "I've things to discuss with you, young lady." Her tone is scolding, and now I'm starting to think both Gage and I are in hot water.

We move away from the woods and into the clearing that borders the big bash.

"What was that about?" I ask, struggling to pick up on anything they might be saying.

"Oh, you know, it's probably one of those manly heart-to-hearts. Now that Gage is in charge of Nathan's grandchildren, your father probably wants to outline what's expected of him."

"Doesn't sound like Dad, but then again, he's never had grandchildren before." I rock Barron, and the hair on his head wafts like dark feathers.

"Put his cap on, Skyla. For goodness' sake." She adjusts both boys' snowsuits until all that's visible is their tiny faces, those piercing blue eyes that threaten to keep their father's cobalt coloring—and I sincerely hope they do—those dimples that go off every now and again indiscriminately. "You lose most of your body heat through your head. These poor boys will have pneumonia before New Years if you keep this up. Whose brilliant idea was it to have a night affair in the middle of winter? Don't answer that. I already know it was your ditz of a stepmother."

"No name calling." Although, I may agree on a few points.

"Please, she has a child harvested from Demetri. She's a dolt through and through."

"And I'm married to his son. What does that make me?"

She grunts, waving off my idiocy with her hand. "You not only married him, you bore him dominion." Her brows rise as if I've one-upped my doltish stepmother.

"They are children, not a place."

"Same difference where their lineage is concerned." Her brows furrow as she looks to the two of them. "Do you remember that curse you bestowed upon me?"

"On accident," I clarify. "How can I forget? It's the reason my daughter is in paradise denied her rightful life on Earth." Actually, I don't fully believe that. I believe that somehow I played into her destiny-wielding hands, and that Sage was meant to live in paradise from the get-go. If I choose to place the blame of her death on my shoulders, I won't be able to breathe. "What about it?"

Her hand falls to my cheek as her touch enlivens me with a joy unspeakable. Those vibratory powers Marshall has—the same ones that Gage acquired for the term of my pregnancy—my mother trumps them all. They say there is nothing like a mother's touch, and, in my case, it is most definitely true.

"The curse is about to be lifted." Her face wrinkles with grief. "But, now that it will be gone, an echo of its biting sting will resonate with you for the rest of your life." She nods as if I must accept this.

"Yes," I whisper. "Sage is gone, and that pain will never leave me." It's true. It won't.

Her eyes narrow with sorrow once again as if I haven't understood at all.

"The time has come for a benediction." She smiles sweetly at Barron before looking to me. "Skyla Messenger, born under the fifth seal, I charge you with the task of supervising these human-angelic beings to the best of your abilities. May you meet their needs, and surpass their desires in all that they long for in keeping with the Holy Order." Her eyes narrow in on mine. "May you take what is rightfully yours without hesitation within the angelic realm and protect your people in any manner that you see fit regardless of heavenly jurisdiction and bylaws." She gives a curt nod as though this shouldn't be spoken of again. "And lastly, may you topple the wicked one you are legally bound to in holy matrimony. In due time, may you put an end to his splendor and cast his throne down to the ground."

My stomach cinches at her caustic words. Gage is far from wicked. I'd start a war of words with her, but she's holding my child, and I don't feel like jumping in a celestial fire at the moment. But her words bite around the edges of my sanity, threatening to take down my sleep-deprived mind. What throne? Should I be bothered by the fact Gage is leading the Videns? Everyone knows Wes is really running the wicked show. Perhaps she has them confused.

"It seems I've left your gift in Ahava. Why don't Nathan and I retrieve it? We'll be back soon enough. Tend to your guests, Skyla. Come, Nathan, let us check on young Sage a moment," she calls to my father, and we offer our temporary goodbyes.

The kiss he lands on my cheek feels like heaven personified. He leans into my ear and whispers, "Tell Logan we need to speak as soon as I get back. It's urgent. Don't say a word to anyone else." He pulls away, the worry in his eyes quickly replaced with joy as if he were putting on a show on some level. "And thank you from the bottom of my heart for gifting me the honor of being a part of your lives again." He kisses his namesake. "These boys are destined for great things." He lands an equally saccharin kiss to Barron before he and my mother scoot into the woods. The blue fog finds them and wraps them like a cloak. A shower of sparks goes off around them as my parents dissipate in a show of glory. My mother never was one for subtlety.

"I love you both!" I shout and mean it. "Don't be long!"

Gage and I huddle together as they dissipate from the woods—from the earthly realm altogether.

A breath gets lodged in my throat as a couple stands just beyond where my father and mother dissolved into thin air, a tall, lanky man with a lantern jaw and his redheaded accomplice.

"Shit!" I hiss. Gage and I pivot on our heels and dive into the crowd, threading our way into the thick of things. "They saw everything."

"It was dark," he tries to reassure.

Demetri heads over with Wes, and I wish I had the power to make them disappear.

"You look great, Skyla." Wesley offers a partial embrace.

"Where's Tobie?" I spot useless Bishop cackling away with Michelle and Lexy, no baby in sight.

"With Ezrina." He rubs my arm a moment. "You really do look good. The boys are amazing." He gives them each a loving glance. "Where's Logan?" He looks to Gage.

Odd. Logan seems to be the man of the hour. I'm dying to know what my father wants to tell him—and now Wes?

"Right here." Logan pops up, the warm scent of his cologne washes over me like an old friend.

Demetri nods. "If you boys have a moment, I'd love to show you something in the trophy room."

I shudder just thinking of the demented rows and rows of taxidermy Fems on display. There's no way in hell I want anything to do with this.

Marshall comes up, and I hand him Barron and take Nathan from Gage. "Marshall and I will cruise the crowds.

Don't be long. I think it's almost time to call it a night." My rock-hard boobs agree.

Gage lifts my chin gently and meets me with a steady gaze. There's a sadness in his eyes, a distinct look of pain that I haven't seen since those West Paragon days. "I love you," he whispers. "Everything I do is for you, Skyla. Not heaven or hell, not the most wretched evil could keep me from loving and protecting you and our boys." He lands a molten hot kiss onto my lips, and for a moment, the party, the small crowd around us dissipates to nothing. There is something pure about this kiss, this intimate moment Gage and I share. He's telling me something far deeper than words could ever express. It's an *I love you* mixed with something unidentifiable—an apology?

He pulls back, blinking hard, as he and Logan rush after Demetri.

A swell of relief settles over me. It's done. Gage and I are finally on the path to taking control of all that was pulling us apart—all that was threatening to destroy the factions.

The tunnels are open—with better intentions. The new mushroom-inspired serum Ezrina is working on just might be the saving grace my people need to shelter our markers and regenerate the Spectators. I'm ready and willing to stomp out any new scheme Wesley dreams up like a flame. The Retribution League will continue to net as many Spectators and as many traitors as possible. Wesley is no longer two steps ahead of us—we are neck-and-neck. And finally, yes finally, I am in charge of my people. It feels good. It feels like home.

I sigh as Gage disappears out of sight. "I already miss him." I love him that much, and more.

"Parting is such sweet sorrow," Marshall quips. "I find the drama almost charming. Where is Jock Strap off to? Is it time for a potty break?" His left cheek twitches in my husband's direction a moment before his eyes widen, and he takes a quick breath.

"Stop." Nathan begins to fuss, and I shift him from one arm to the other. "Gage and I are deeply in love." I smile into Nathan's perfect features. "Not to mention, it's a special night for us."

Marshall gives a vacant stare to the woods. His jaw ticks as if he were pissed. "Indeed it is. You might even say it's sacred." His nostrils flare as he takes in some invisible scene far away. "Find your mother and Emma. The twins should go inside for a while. You and I are going on a little adventure."

Gage

My feet trudge forth, involuntarily, weighted as if carrying me to my death chamber. Death would have been easier. If only a simple departure is what would break Skyla's heart. But this is no earthly departure, no temporary parting—this is a stake driven right through the heart of who we are. This is my greatest sacrifice, my most intimate betrayal all rolled into one.

Logan takes up my hand, and I look at him as we follow Demetri and Wes like diligent soldiers. I can't recall a single memory of the two of us holding hands, not even as boys. Instead of pulling away, I lean in, assuring him of my decision, of my false bravado. I give his fingers a squeeze—saying thank you—saying please fucking help me because I'd rather die a thousand deaths than do what I'm about to, what I need to.

We bypass the party, snake our way through a thicket of bushes, and end up in a clearing deep in the woods, a stone of sacrifice lying flat and round the size of a dining room table, and here I am offering myself up to Demetri for the feast.

Wes pulls a duffel bag from the bushes and extricates a goblet dipped in gold. I recognize it, the exact one we used to seal the covenant between us that day I joined the Barricade. Ironic since breaking faith with that shit parade is what's brought us here to drink from it again.

Logan leans in. "You want to walk, just say the word."

I pull him in quick, his nose just a hair from mine. "You listen to me, and listen good. My hands are fucking tied. If for any reason I thought I could walk the hell away and not have my children placed in that madman's clutches, I would have never begun the journey." I swallow hard, struggling with the sudden rage that's overtaken me. "I am not doing this for pleasure. This is pain all the way around." Tears blur my vision as I let him go. "Sorry. I know you meant to help."

"I know your heart," Logan whispers as Demetri and Wes busy themselves with the details of the wicked undertaking. "I also know that when Skyla asks why, when she rages against your decision—and make no mistake, she will—I will go to bat for you. I spoke with Candace." His jaw twitches with anger. "There is no other way. It's you or your sons, end of discussion. You're making the only decision that works. If it were me, I would do the same."

I let his words soak in a moment before agreeing with a nod. "It's the right decision," I say as if convincing myself.

"This covenant kicks in after your death, Gage." Logan cocks his head. "That means the longer you're alive, the longer this madness is put off."

I look off into the woods, trying to go along with Logan's brand of logic and come up empty. "Demetri doesn't need me on the throne to prosper."

"He wants you. You're the prize. He's not going to do anything to stop your death from happening, but others can, and I'll make sure they will."

"Death will come." A slight smile ticks on my lips, anemic and weak. "But I will never be Skyla's enemy. It might be in my blood, but it's not in my heart. Any actions I might take to the contrary are the work of that devil." I glance to Demetri. "Looks like I'll be the boy on a string that he's always wanted me to be."

"You're stronger than he is," Logan says it with so much conviction it's hard to deny him, almost as hard as it is to convince myself of those very words. I don't feel strong. I don't feel like a hero. I feel weak—with all the markings of a coward. How will my boys, how will Skyla ever view me as the hero I so desperately want to be in their lives? I'm not so sure Skyla will ever see anything heroic about this. But I'm here for her as much as I am for my sons. And even if she never believes me, I'm here for our people, too. If I am strong, if I can overcome Demetri's black heart—I might just stop his madness.

"Come," Demetri calls us over just a few steps away from my old life and a few closer to the demon I was destined to be.

Wes nods. "You okay, man?"

It's strange that over the months I've known him he's starting to feel like family, like the brother he was promised to be, and even now, his concern feels genuine. It was because of him that I joined the Barricade in the first place—to keep an eye on him, to be Skyla's eyes. What could it hurt? I would never do a thing to harm the Nephilim—until my ego landed me right where Demetri hoped—and then I broke off my love affair with darkness, only to land at the bottom of Devil's Peak. Now I would pay the price. My soul. Perhaps that's all a bit dramatic, but, knowing that Demetri's influence over my future has the capacity to bring me to my knees, that the conviction I once held high and strong will one day be reduced to cinder and become the very thing I loathe, makes my stomach churn.

"One question." I look to Demetri. He's not my father. He's a DNA factory and nothing more. I feel like a frightened kid at the dentist office asking *one question*, just before he sinks the drill over my rotting tooth, no Novocain. "Are the consequences everlasting?" Consequences. I refuse to call it a curse, even though it is. Consequences eventually end. Curses take you down with them to the miry depths of eternity.

Demetri looks to me, his eyes always laughing, always one-step ahead, in on the greatest secret. "You are an eternal soul, my son. Eternity is far too long to contain anything but love."

His words go off in my gut, first with an acidic bite, then the quiet spread of relief as it fills my body. I can read between the thorny lines. This is temporary. All of the hate, the wickedness he's determined to fill me with will eventually evaporate to nothing—his efforts as futile in the distant future as they are now.

"There will be no manipulation of your morals, no pulling of your heart strings as if you were a boy on a string." His eyes sharpen over mine. My heart gives a hard thump. He heard. "You will wield your might, and you will drink your power—willingly. The shadow of doubt will flee, and you will have opened your eyes to what is just and who is in the wrong and who is in the light."

I don't move—don't show a single emotion. Demetri just spoke in one big circle—saying everything and nothing at the same time. Somewhere in that murky pit the truth is circulating. I heard it, though. I will wield my might, and I will drink my power—willingly—because love wins. That's all I need to know for now. My heart races at the thought of this horrible nightmare one day coming to an end. When I finally do confess this disaster to Skyla, it will be the first thing I say.

"And my boys—am I guaranteed their safety?"

"Your boys—*our* boys"—he pauses to lap it up—"will not be under the duress of the covenant, Gage. Should they join forces with the Barricade one day, it will be of their own volition. There is no need for me to sway their hand."

I look to Logan, satisfied with Demetri's answer. Nathan and Barron are safe. Their hearts are their own. They won't side with wickedness, no matter how hard Demetri hopes this to be the case—not with Skyla as their mother, not with Logan looking after them. I'm not so sure I can trust myself to be included in the equation just yet.

"It's time." Demetri pulls something that resembles a wine bottle from a slender velvet pouch, the dark glass reflects the midnight moon as it slowly glows an eerie shade of blue—Celestra blue.

He pours a sanguine liquid into the goblet Wesley steadies in his hand.

"Logan will imbibe," Demetri says, filling the cup to the rim. "The covenant requires two witnesses bearing representation to the Barricade and the reformation upon us." He hikes the bottle up a moment. "Celestra issued. 'Tis precious. My reserves are the lowest they've ever been." He holds the chalice among the four of us. "This is the claret of your own beloved—Skyla's cherished blood."

Shit.

He lets the idea sink in.

Logan shakes his head. "No way. I'm out."

"This blood will act as a signet for our new journey"—Demetri is undeterred by Logan's protest—"it's the same blood that fueled our covenant to the Barricade." He takes the time to frown at Logan. "Procured during the time of her captivity, her blood is stored only for rituals concerning Gage. These are sacred fluids, for a sacred covenant, her blood sealing the protection of your children, Gage Oliver Edinger. Do you accept?"

"Like I have a choice." I glance to Logan. "If you want to take off, go ahead."

Wes clasps his hand on Logan's shoulder. "I'd say the same if we didn't need you. Gage needs you, too."

Logan shifts like he's about to turn over this stone table, kick the goblet from Demetri's hand, and spill Skyla's blood to the ground.

"All right," Logan seethes at both Demetri and Wes. "Let's hurry up and get this over with."

Demetri begins in on a long, terrifying chant that hums and drones into the night, scrolling out before us like the years of my life. A thick carpet of clouds dispenses over the moon, expanding over the stars as a nest of lightning circles overhead, purple and white, a dazzling show of power and might. His voice rises above the thunder, above the sizzle of electricity threatening to take us down. Demetri steps up onto the stone, and the three of us follow him as he raises the chalice, full of my precious wife's blood, to God himself.

"May the Lord of Glory find favor upon my son, Gage Edinger, who is willing to war against the enemy in the name of the Steel Barricade, in the name of the glorious Fems, upon the dissolution of his soul from the flesh that is mortal. At that time, the King of Glory will see fit to issue him a new body, a new incorruptible flesh built to last for all eternity. Though, in his old flesh, he broke faith with the Barricade and brought upon himself the terrible affliction—the heart of one he holds dear to turn against him and everything he thinks he stands for—in the beauty of his sacrifice to spare his own children from what he believes to be a grievous error, he has agreed to take the covenant upon his own heart, turning against what he thinks he stands for—turning against his old self and toward the warmth of the truth. All of this shall come to pass in the hour of his death, upon which his kingdom will thrive—and his heart will flourish for his true destiny, his people." Demetri locks those dead eyes of his onto mine. "Though there will be a struggle between the powers, I assure you, son—you will be the victor."

Logan shoots me a quick look as if he picked up on something I didn't. And he could have. My head is thick with self-hatred. Half of what Demetri said sailed right by me.

"From this moment on—your God-gifted abilities have been restored. You are a Fem through and through. Power and glory and honor are yours." Demetri raises the goblet higher, and the crown of lightning above spins faster, illuminates brighter. A stray tendril drifts down to touch the golden chalice as if it were the finger of God. "May this living sacrifice be found holy and righteous in your sight, precious Master!"

A bolt of lightning curls around the cup like a cat and ignites Demetri like an x-ray before crackling back to the sky.

"Let us partake of the blood of Celestra." Demetri takes a sip and passes the chalice to Wes. He does the same and hands it carefully to Logan.

Logan glares at the liquid until all of his anger melts away and replaces itself with sorrow. He takes a sip, wipes down his lips hard with the back of his arm, and hands it off to me.

I can't help but pause as I lose myself in the somber liquid. It might as well be a dark, watery grave. So much blood—all of it Skyla's. I stare down at the inky black water as it dances in this dim light, expecting to see some hint of my own reflection, of my own betrayal—instead, I see two little boys, growing fast, morphing into young men right before my eyes. I see one of them lured to the darkness, his interest piqued, his beliefs swaying, his heart drifting further from the light. Lastly, I see the wicked glance he gives his mother.

I don't need to see any more. I knock back the cup and drink down every last drop, swallowing down all possibility of those boys ever turning against their mother.

The work of Skyla's marrow bubbles with the acids in my stomach. I thrust the goblet over the stone with a marked aggression, and the night explodes into a shower of shooting stars, of lightning that spears to the ground, stabbing the granite, through Demetri's body, through mine.

I step to the middle of the stone of sacrifice and lift my arms to the heavens as the electrical currents rain down from the sky, rain over my limbs, jolt me, electrify me, and walk me to the brink of this new era that awaits me.

I lean my head back and whisper, "Skyla, I did it for you—for us—for our boys. Forgive me."

I know one thing.

I can never truly forgive myself.

Logan

The groaning of the pines—I try to focus on the way the evergreens whip their branches against the night, the pepper of rain beginning to fall, anything but the fact the boy I grew up with, the one I proudly call brother has lightning coursing through his veins, his hands raised to heaven, begging a quiet forgiveness I'm not sure he will ever receive. My heart weeps for him—weeps for Skyla. I never knew it would be this unbearable. If only I could rewind time, take us back to that fateful day Skyla Laurel Messenger set foot inside the bowling alley, both of our tongues wagging at the sight of her, I would make sure everything was done differently. I could reason with Gage, with Skyla, with the punk kid that I was at the time. I could. But a part of me knows not one of us would listen. Somehow, we would still end up at this juncture of our lives, right here on this stone of sacrifice, with the power of the living God raining down his terror over us. If only—if only we could go back to the start. Although this rings reminiscent of the night he gave his life to the Barricade, this is one covenant Gage can never break—he wouldn't want to in an effort to shield his children. Demetri found a way to lure Gage right into the bear trap he set out for him the moment he was conceived. But Demetri is no victor. I'll make sure of that.

A primal scream comes from beyond the thicket as hundreds of bodies erect from the ground. A cry of terror rises from them, followed by a howl of delight as Demetri encourages the crowd to give into wild cheers, cries of ecstasy, of inhuman pleasure, at the sight of Gage Oliver Edinger ringed in a bolt of lightning. It is a vision. That I cannot contest.

I recognize a few of the jackals jumping and pumping their fists at my nephew. My lungs seize up. Every one of these bastards was placed in the tunnels by Skyla, Ellis, Brody, and me. And shit. Demetri just hit the *Reset* button.

"A celebration of the ages is unfolding." His voice is calm, yet unmistakably loud as a megaphone. "Let us feast the night away. I hereby proclaim your freedom by the power vested in me. The hour of the Dragon is upon us. The age of the Serpent has arrived."

I jump over to the wicked demon and shake him like a rattle. "What the fuck? You said the curse wouldn't kick in until after his death, not one second sooner." Saliva pulls across my face as I struggle to spit the words out.

Demetri glances down at my fists cuffed to his shirt. "Hands off."

A jolt of pain sprays through me, and I drop him.

"The hour tarries." He glares at me a moment before broadening his ever-present grin. "Welcome to the feast of the covenant. If you find the celebration offensive, I suggest you leave the premises." He jumps off the stone and strides toward his estate, and the wicked crowd follows along. The lightning ceases and lands Gage face-first onto the granite below.

Wes turns him over and helps him sit up. "You okay, man?"

"I'm good." Gage gets up, staggers for a minute before righting himself.

"You did good." Wes pulls him, whispering something into his ear before grafting his discontent over me. "I'll see you at the party." He takes off after his father and the rowdy crowd. Tenebrous is empty. It seems there is a growing list of the things Skyla will be pissed about this evening.

"What'd he say?" I'm only half-curious.

"He said 'welcome to the light.'" Gage and I stare one another down, stuck on the stone as if our feet were rooted into it.

A shrill cry comes from the woods. "Let *go*! Don't you ever do that again if you plan on keeping your balls!"

My stomach tightens because I recognize that voice.

Skyla blooms from the darkness like a rose illuminated from the inside. Despite all the insanity, her presence, her beauty, is a balm from this madness.

"Shit." Gage's face bleaches white as if he were sucker-punched.

In a moment, she's side-by-side on the stone with us, her fierce anger directed at Gage.

"How long were you standing there?" I really didn't need to ask. Her fury is an answer all to itself.

Her hand flies over his cheek, connecting with a crisp, angry slap, the sound just as lusty as the thunder still grumbling overhead.

"I'm sorry." His own hand rises to meet the sting. "Let me tell you everything."

"Shut up!" she seethes as if she were about to knock his teeth out to make sure he never uttered another word. "You don't get to talk to me."

I try to pull her gently back. "There are things you don't know." My voice is deliberately hushed, deliberately pleading.

Her face pinches with grief as she nails me with her piercing stare. "That's because you bastards get off on that."

"Come, love." Dudley appears at the base of the stone, his arms firmly crossed over his chest as if he's just as pissed as she is. He's trying to win her over by siding with her. Covenant. That's been Dudley's game all along.

"Let me guess"—I scowl over at him—"you made sure she watched the show front and center," I spit it out, trying to control the urge to destroy him for the damage he's caused. "You betrayed Gage."

A hint of a smile curves on his face. "I have no allegiance to Jock Strap. My allegiance is to my spirit wife, and that dolt has made her life more difficult than it ever needs to be."

I glance back to where Skyla and Gage stare one another down—Skyla with fierce indignation, and Gage with remorse and sorrow.

I look back to Dudley. "You were there when we were discussing it. You approved it."

"I listened to his idiotic plan, and I told him to *run*."

"I'm going to run," Skyla says the words to Gage, slow and melodic, the wild anger still alive in her eyes. "With our boys, very far away from you."

"*Skyla!*" Gage shouts her name as if she had already bolted, the cords in his neck popping thick with frustration. "Let's go home. There's too much to tell you here. I'll start from the beginning. I swear—"

"I swear sounds like a vow, like a *covenant*," she grits the words through her teeth. Her entire body shakes with anger. "You're good at those, aren't you? What happened to no more secrets? That—all truth, all the time bullshit?"

He reaches for her hand, and she knocks his feet out from under him in one blind-siding move. Skyla proceeds to level him with a series of wild kicks—one swift blow after the other, and Gage grunts and takes it. He's already beaten on the inside.

"Stop," I plead, pulling her away, my arms tightening around her waist like a belt. Her elbow comes at me, knocking me in the chest like a gravity hammer. If I were in working condition, she would have stopped my beating heart.

Gage jumps to his feet and attempts to bind her flailing arms, only to have her coldcock him square in the nose.

"You don't touch me! You don't *look* at me!" she shouts over his squinted eyes. "You piece of shit!" She gives him a hard shove until he stumbles from the stone back to the ground, right off the pedestal of her heart. He'll never get back on, get anywhere near her playing field if she has anything to do with it.

"Skyla." I bind her wrists and pull her in as a wild wind pushes the fog back through the woods as if punishing it for leaving in the first place. This entire damn island is haunted. We should all run. I touch my mouth to her ear. "Once you know the truth, you will understand why he had to do this."

Her body writhes and flexes, her gaze pushes from mine as if what was once magnetic is now uncomfortably polarizing—and now it were impossible to connect with me on such an intimate level.

"You never gave me a chance." She hawks back and spits a long wet one right into my eye. "I don't want an explanation after the fact, Logan. I'm done with this bullshit!" She hops down from the stone and turns to her husband. "You think I'm good enough to lead our people—*my* people—and yet I'm not good enough to let in on your schemes, your wicked, wicked dreams?" You can see the lava-hot anger rising around her. "You never believed in me." She scowls into my eyes. "Neither of you."

Dudley links his arm through hers, and they head back to the party.

"Shit." Gage pinches at his eyes. "Every time I try to make things right, I manage to fuck them up twice as bad."

"She'll come around." I'm not entirely convinced of this, but it felt right to say. I drape an arm over his shoulder as we begin the slow amble from the woods. "She sure kicked our asses."

"Sure as fuck did." His dimples dip in, no smile. It's his art. I've only seen Gage pull off that feat.

"Come on." I weave us through the pines, out into the clearing that leads to what's panning out to be Demetri's holiday rager. "Let's apologize to her. We'll get her to listen. In the least, you can tell her you love her—that you did it for the boys."

A scream comes from the pool where a mass of humanity has congregated, and we spot Skyla holding something blue in each arm.

Killion and Moser look frazzled with their outstretched arms. They're both shouting at the crowd as if trying to break up a fight.

"What's that glowing in Skyla's arms?" I try to make heads or tails out of it and come up blank.

"The boys." Gage sprints over.

"Shit." By nature I'm a problem solver. By nature I am frustrated as hell when I can't fix something, make something right—and looking at the bizarre sight, the inflamed excitement budding in those agents posturing by her side, whispering into her ear—I can only try to fix this for her, no matter what the cost is to me.

Dudley nods at me from the poolside as if answering the burning question of what the fuck to do.

Then it hits me—his lightning move. This is the very reason he's been priming me, making me an expert at one very distinct, unique Celestra talent he was hell-bent on extrapolating from me.

My arms rise, eye-level the way he taught me, my anger burns for justice—my passion burns for Skyla, always the perfect combination. A rush of electricity pours from my limbs, shooting a line of ragged lightning that stops shy of those precious bundles. To the naked eye it would be my tour de force causing the strange discoloration. The energy of my own hand will have to satisfy as the answer, or I would have tried in vain.

I stop the show and jog over just as they're trying to pry the babies from Skyla's death grip. Her feet sway, and she shifts her weight as if she's about to go around them and dunk the game winning slam.

"You will never take my children!" she cries.

Her mother, Emma, and an entire crowd of friends and family balloon around her in support.

"Mrs. Oliver!" Killion shouts over the melee. "We need a pediatrician to inspect the children. We'll summons a specialist come morning, but they'll need to be detained in the interim."

"Did you like the show?" I pant, forcing a smile to pin itself on my face. I hold my hand out and light up the Transfer transplants on the other side of the pool a bright electric blue, the color of those butterflies Skyla and I once nestled under. It's for her I'm doing this, for my very precious nephews. I'm giving it all up just like Gage. I'm all in.

Moser flashes his badge at me as he and Killion turn their full attention in my direction.

"You're doing this?" Killion's mouth drops as if she thought she had us pegged, and I threw her for a loop.

"It's me you're after," I pant. "I'm not of this world. And there are more of me." There. Sound like a threat and they'll treat you like one—anything to get the focus off my nephews.

"Mr. Oliver, I'm afraid we're going to have to take you and ask a few questions." Killion looks to her accomplice. That strange orange hair of hers glows green under the lights, and it makes me wonder. "Get command to send reinforcements. We'll need them stat." She pulls out a set of silver bracelets and has me turn around, binding my wrists with the cuffs, and I don't fight her.

Gage hands one of the boys to Emma—Skyla hands the other to Lizbeth, instructing them to take them inside.

"I'm one, too." Gage steps in, the color of his eyes brightens as if someone illuminated him from the inside. They pulsate in concert as if he were flicking on and off like a light switch. Gage has become his own warning signal, his own doom for the second time tonight. It's clear Gage's powers have been reinstated, and for his sake, it happened at the very worst time. He should've let me handle this.

"Turn around." Moser cuffs him as they quickly shuttle us out of the crowd.

"No!" Skyla's voice rises over the chaos, her panic just as viral as her anger. "You don't get to do this!" she rails at the two of us as we're led out to the clearing. She lands her body in front of Killion, creating a barricade as if she were blocking a pass. "I will *not* let you do this." She's still hopped up on rage. Her sanity fled an hour ago when Dudley dragged her to the field.

Moser growls at her, his lips drip with saliva as if he were rabid. "Out of the way, or we'll have you arrested as well."

"Never mind," Killion seethes, irate as she snatches Skyla by the wrist. "You're coming with me. The evidence on you is rich. You were our only suspect. These two are an unexpected bonus."

"No." She takes a step back, her hand pressed to her chest. "My babies need me. I'm not going anywhere."

"Yes, well"—a greasy smile floats on Killion's lips—"we would never dream of separating you from the babies. We have a vested interest in them, too."

Skyla turns toward the woods and bolts.

Killion and Moser shove Gage and me toward the forest.

"You stay here with them." Moser pushes me to Gage as he cuffs us together.

"The hell I am." Killion cuffs my leg to a lifted root, struggling to get it to lock for a moment. "Stay put, gentlemen. If you run, we can't make any promises regarding what will happen to your little lady friend."

The two of them take off, shouting for Skyla—for *Mrs. Oliver*.

Gage and I look at one another and share a depleted grin.

I summons my Celestra strength and pop my leg free from the root, snapping the metal like a candy cane.

Gage closes his eyes as he pulls his cuffs apart like chewing gum. I break loose from my own stronghold with one solid snap.

"Fucking morons," I say as we head into the woods.

"Skyla!" Gage calls out as we split up. Gage and I never objected to the idea of going with them. We weren't enthused, but we weren't about to fight it. But they can't take Skyla. They simply can't have her.

"Skyla!" My voice comes back to me as an echo. The woods behind Edinger's estate are wide and vast. This is a search that can span days. "*Skyla!*" Her name cuts through my lungs with the power of a jet engine.

A horrific scream comes from the left where a thicket of birch trees intertwines with the evergreens.

A horrific moan, inhuman in nature, shakes the forest floor.

"What the—" before I can get the question out, I spot a man's leg lying prone as if he were passed out.

Skyla must have kicked the shit out of him. She's getting good at it, too, because he's not moving.

"Hey? You okay?" I give his shoe a slight kick, and it glides over a few inches. I bend over to rattle him, and his leg rolls over unnaturally. My heart jumps up into my throat. My head pounds with adrenaline. "Moser?" I pull out my cell phone and shine the light over him, blood at the knee—no fucking knee. I give his leg another kick, and it goes flying solo into the trunk of a pine. "Shit." I glance around. The screaming of a woman shrills into the night.

"Skyla!" I roar it out over the expanse.

Gage comes upon me and retches at the sight.

A series of screams go off, wild, nonstop, and we run

trying to find the source.

"Logan!" Skyla wails, her voice layered against the ceaseless howls.

Gage and I hurdle through the twisted roots that snake throughout the backwoods, and I shine a light onto a tangle of flesh.

A creature looks up, wild eyes, dead as a December sky, its flesh partially decayed, blood rinsed over what's left of its face.

"*Skyla.*" Gage tries to pull her from the carnage, but she's clamped on to a set of arms. Killion holds on to Skyla with a death grip, her nails tearing into Skyla's flesh, leaving deep crimson welts at the wrists.

"Help me!" Killion pleads to the three of us, her hip embedded in the creature's mouth.

"I'm not letting go!" Skyla wails, trying to pry her loose.

Gage gives a swift power kick to the moaning beast, but he only pisses it off. Its jaw unhinges, slicing up Killion's back until it has her vertebrae between its teeth like a bony tail.

Killion's mouth opens wider, no scream—her eyes avert to heaven never to move again.

The beast lets out the animalistic roar of a cat on fire and lunges on top of Skyla.

Gage and I throw our bodies over it. My fingers dig into its eyes, culling out its brain before it devours the woman I love. Gage plucks out its heart and tosses it across the forest like he was gunning for a touchdown.

The beast writhes and bucks in waves of spastic fervor as it bounces to its feet.

A swift wind moves before us.

The creature smacks into the trunk of an evergreen with an arrow piercing through its skull, nailing it to the tree. I glance back to find Dudley gearing up for another shot.

And sure enough, an arrow lands swift in my leg, effectively pinning me to the ground. One hits Gage right through the foot.

"That was for Skyla," he growls at the bloody mess around us as if it were our doing. "Clean this place up. These woods will be crawling with authorities in minutes." He helps Skyla to her feet and wipes the splatter of blood from the edge of her lips. "Come, love. Your children need you. Let's get you home."

Gage and I watch as their silhouettes shrink in the distance.

"Spectators," Gage growls as he plucks the arrow from his foot.

"Demetri opened the tunnels tonight." I yank the razor sharp stick from my leg and grunt through the pain. "We are in for a shit ride, my friend."

"As always." Gage helps steady me just as Coop and Brody show up.

"Welcome to the cleanup committee," Gage muses as we stare at the monster lying limp against the tree—at the limbs strewn around the forest as if poor Killion stepped on a landmine. "Let's get this shit done."

"Let's," I say, landing a hand on Gage's back. I offer the idea of a smile that says *my brother—we are in a fine mess. How did we ever get here?*

Nobody ever said it would be easy.

Nobody ever does.

Coop and Brody insist on disposing the bodies, so Gage and I head back toward the estate.

Skyla stands at the base of the fountain as the party swirls around her. Emma and Lizbeth are both there, each with a baby nestled in their arms. Barron waves us over. The distressed look on his face lets us know he's aware there is trouble.

"Shit. What should I do?" Gage moves with apprehension as we speed in that direction.

"Do what you always do—love her." I offer a pat to my nephew who has his work cut out for him if he wants anything with his wife ever again.

"Well, here's the man of the hour!" Lizbeth reels Gage in. "Skyla was just about to leave. Something has her very upset." She leans in toward us. "Not to worry—it's those darn hormones rearing their ugly heads again." She gives a hard wink to her son-in-law, and I cringe because I know for a fact Skyla heard.

Skyla tips her back with an incredulous growl working from her throat. "I can assure you my ripe anger has nothing to do with hormones."

Dudley comes our way. Candace and Nathan close in on our circle, back from paradise just in time to experience the hell Skyla is about to dole out.

"I'm glad everyone is here," she pants through her visceral emotions. "The more witnesses, the better."

Shit. A part of me wants to whisk her away, to remove her from this madness before any more of Demetri's disease can eat away at her life. No matter what she believes, she does not want to have it out with Gage in public.

Skyla huffs in my direction as if she heard me.

"Gage Oliver." A whisper of baby blue fog plumes from her lips.

Gage steps in close to her. "I know it was dangerous—"

"You don't know dangerous. You *are* dangerous." Skyla's words are effective as a slap, stilling both Emma and Barron in their tracks. Even Lizbeth's eyes round out with surprise. Candace looks to me with a smile tugging at her lips, and for a moment, I contemplate begging Nathan to drag her out of here. This isn't going to end well, and Candace is only fuel for the fire.

Skyla sets her face to the wind, her steely eyes on the man she loves. "We've been through a lot, you and I. You might even say we've grown up together." There is no sweetness in her tone. She's gearing up to gut Gage right here in front of friends and family, and knowing my nephew, he believes he deserves it. "You knew me when I was weak—when I was a little girl, when I behaved like one—foolish and irrational. But no more. I'm putting my childish ways behind me. I'm going to tear a hole in any dominion you or your father procures. I will not tolerate the exploitation, abuse, or injury of my sons or my people. The days of my confusion, of my weakness—of needing the slightest bit of rescue are over. I am here now, in all of my fullness, and you shall witness my momentum. You will know my power, and you will have to deal with me. This new war between the Fems and all of creation, between the Steel Barricade and its malevolence—it starts here—it starts with you."

A stunted silence clamps down over us, and even little Barron seems to turn and look up at his mother.

Candace starts in on a slow clap, eating away the false tranquility with her vigorous approval. "Bravo"—she cheers her daughter on—"*bravissimo*! Dear child, I could not find more pleasure or pride in you at the moment." Candace beams as she steps in close to her daughter. "I've a gift for you and the boys. It seems you left this at my home, and I'd relish you to have it." A stone appears in her hand as she holds it up for Skyla to see—smooth, dark onyx no bigger than her palm. My stomach clenches. I know for a fact it's the same stone Skyla mentioned that sealed Gage's fate in something as arbitrary as a number.

A single tear rolls down Skyla's cheek, falling to the rock, and the stone glows a haunting shade of butterfly blue.

"There," Skyla whispers, taking it from her mother's hand, holding the stone out for Gage to see. "You come to this number"—her voice hitches as silent tears rain down—"and then you are no more."

"Yes," Gage says it with a marked finality, a bead of acceptance, the undertone of resentment. But his eyes—they're still fixed on that stone.

My heart turns to granite. Gage has minutes, hours, days, weeks, months, or very few years—I'm pretty certain it's not decades. My body begs to peer over and see which way the numerals fall, but my feet have screwed themselves to the ground.

The rain starts in, and both Emma and Lizbeth run inside with the boys. Barron is slow to leave, glaring at me as if he somehow knew what this ominous truth meant. Dudley gives a solemn nod before heading toward the woods. The goodbyes that Candace and Nathan offer fall on deaf ears. But Skyla and Gage are still locked in a death stare that might end in more limbs being strewn around the property—namely that of my nephew's.

Nathan pulls me into a partial embrace before he takes off. "We have a lot to talk about—Skyla, strategy, the government boots that are about to land on Paragon. It won't be easy, Logan. Skyla needs you more than ever."

Candace tugs him away. "She doesn't need anyone. She is most certainly her mother's daughter." Her voice lingers in the air as they dissipate in the night.

Gage and Skyla remain locked in their misery, her anger, his grief. This is a moment I shouldn't be privy to—one I should swiftly walk away from but can't. I can't leave these people I desperately love, alone, each in their hour of need.

The rain hammers over us with its needle-like wrath before letting up just enough for us to catch our next breath. Paragon is weeping, flooding the planes with her outrageous grief.

Gage takes a step toward her, his angst written in those demanding dark brows. He tries to take up Skyla's hands, but she coolly pulls them back.

"This is not where we end." His voice is strong, yet wavering through the storm. I can tell he's a moment from losing it.

"This is where we begin—as adversaries." Skyla nods into her words, her jaw set in defiance as the rain slicks her hair to her back. "This is the nexus of our unraveling. No matter what Demetri has convinced you of—all arrows will forever point to this night as the moment we became what perhaps you knew we would be all along—enemies."

Gage closes his eyes as she eviscerates him with the most damning words of all. He looks to me with hurt, with anger locked in his stare before striding past the two of us toward Demetri's palatial estate.

I catch Marshall dissipating into the woods now that his dirty deed for the day is done. "Figures—Dudley was the one to lead you to this misery."

"Dudley?" She shoves me in the chest, incredulous, as the rain picks up pace again. "Marshall is the only one willing to tell me the *truth*!"

"When it's convenient for him." A ripe anger boils in me toward the slimy Sector.

"Maybe I should just fast forward and marry Marshall, and I wouldn't be party to *this* misery!" she rages in my face as the rain pummels us with its fury.

"That's one shit parade I'm not sticking around for."

"The hell you're not!" Her hands pummel against my chest once again. "I blame *you* for getting me into this mess to begin with. *You're* the one who withheld things from me! *You're* the one who tried protecting me with your fucking lies! *You're* the one who promised to love me forever!"

"And I will!" I roar back. "I sacrificed *us* to keep you safe!" The wind mixes with the driving rain, and it's all we can do to stand upright, to keep from dropping to the ground and staying there.

"Then love me like you mean it!" She crushes her body to mine. "You can't leave me. You can never leave. I demand you be here when I draw my last breath." She lets out a pained cry into my chest, rattling my bones with her agony. "It was always supposed to be you and me." I'm not sure if she's espousing some hard truth from Candace or slashing at Gage with the sword of what we once had, but this isn't the time to claim her. She and Gage will fix this. Once she sees there was no other way—that she will have Gage right here on this planet for the rest of her life, things will change. It will be the balm that heals the wound from this blow. A small eternity stretches by as the rain lightens its fury.

Skyla pulls back and sets her shoulders to the house, to where her boys sit waiting.

I want to tell her that I'm here for her, that Gage is not the monster she thinks he is.

"He is exactly the monster we dreaded." Skyla doesn't take her gaze from those haunted windows lit up peach in the night.

She heard me. We're not touching flesh, and she heard.

Skyla's powers have manifested in a whole new level.

"That's right, Logan. I'm stronger, leaner, meaner than ever before." Her dead gaze remains staunch at the home her husband, her lover, her seeming enemy just entombed himself in. "Make no mistake about it, Logan. He is the enemy."

My heart wrenches just hearing her say those words—knowing what I know—knowing what she doesn't.

Those precious baby boys run through my mind—her marriage to a man we both deeply care about takes center stage in my heart. "What do you want to do?"

"Forget about Wesley and the Counts. I'm taking down Gage."

"I thought we were a team?"

She cuts her gaze to mine, a fresh fire brewing in her eyes.

"Not anymore."

Skyla heads toward the house, and I watch her long, confident strides, the weight of her grief resting on her shoulders, heavy as the world.

Destiny is reshaping all that was, redefining battle lines, molding new enemies out of old companions. Destiny is having its way with us. We are ragdolls in a tempest, lost in its dominating sway. We are helpless in our cry for power, losing control of all that we thought we knew, all that we were. Here we are askew, Gage donning the cloak of the enemy, Skyla carving herself out to be the exact replica of a woman she once despised—her mother, and me with my lifeless body, my unbeating heart still pining for the girl I love, still aching for the boy I call a brother. We had come so far and gone absolutely nowhere. There has to be a way to turn this around, to say *screw you* to the powers that be, and right this ship. There has to be a way—there has to be an answer.

"Hey!" a sharp voice calls from behind, and I turn to find a familiar effigy staring back at me—my own.

"What do you want?" I lack the enthusiasm I once might have had upon seeing another version of myself.

He comes over and lands an arm over my shoulders, leading me toward the woods, toward the glimmer of a porthole shining and warbling in the night like a wrinkle in the fabric of the island.

"I have the answers you seek."

"Are you from the future?" I squint at this seemingly older, wiser version of myself.

He sheds a quiet laugh. That long line Skyla embedded into my face dips in for a moment. "That I am."

"Good." I slap my hand over his back. "Because you, my friend, are not leaving until you tell me exactly what I need to know."

A grimace comes and goes on this version of myself. "Not happening."

"It's happening. And make it rosy, sweetheart."

A dark laugh rattles through him as we enter the opening in time. My bones flex and quiver, my head pounds with a heartbeat of its own as we step into a cavernous room with a sky for its ceiling, floors made of glass, the stars at our feet—the moon down below is but a whisper above a spinning blue marble—it's so far down it seems improbable that life could exist there at all.

"Where the hell are we?"

"Look up."

My eyes are slow to rise as I take in the dry and arid space. A golden throne holds a *meaner*, leaner version of the boy I grew up with, the boy I call brother. Gage sits on his magnificent throne with angels carved into each of the breathtaking armrests. Precious stones of every color and shape adorn the periphery.

Gage is fierce, his eyes set with a determination I have never seen before. His head bows back as he lets out a ferocious roar, and a dagger of fire plumes from his mouth, robing the room in a scalding heat.

"There you have it," this future version of me says. "Gage Oliver will set the world on fire and not in any good way."

My stomach boils at the sight. This will not happen. I refuse to believe it. But the horror that stands before me contests that wishful thinking.

"What can I do to stop it?"

"You can't." He sets his gaze on Gage and glowers. "I can."

"Skyla isn't looking for a teammate."

"Neither am I."

Gage twists and writhes until his skin is exchanged for scales, his head elongating, morphing until he becomes the serpent of his father's dreams. Skyla insisted that Gage was a monster, and I was quick to defend him.

I take a step toward the throne as the dragon elevates from his seat, his webbed wings propelling him to the night sky.

This cannot be. Both Skyla and I will fight to stop it. This thing, this monster, Gage himself would never want anything to do with this horrific destiny.

The dragon ceases all movement, focusing those midnight glowing eyes on mine. He lets out a ferocious roar that rivals the last, and a tornado of flames rain down, baptizing me with fire—my flesh, my bones, my very existence reduced to ashes, my temporal being returning to dust.

Our sky has fallen, the harvest of our people—of our very souls had come, and we are not saved.

We might have been doomed from the start, but we are not going along for the ride.

I groan as my conscience begins to fade.

I need to fight for Skyla, for our people—for Gage.

The room envelops in a fit of flames as if that were the final straw. My bones and my flesh reconstitute themselves as I flex my way through the porthole and fall face-first onto sopping wet Paragon soil.

My lids struggle to open. My mind claws to stay awake.

It's over now.

And yet the horrible undoing of Gage Oliver has just begun.

Wesley

"Some party," I say to Demetri as we wave Skyla and the boys off, fuming as she may be. "Gage left for Dudley's place—odd, don't you think?"

Demetri chuckles at the idea. "It's a temporary separation, I'm guessing, but, then again, I have what I want. There's no need for any further poisoning of his mind by the likes of her." He leads us back to the rear of the property, nodding a polite good night to the last of the party stragglers.

"I'm taking off." I take a breath toward the woods, knowing full well I'll be striding into the Paragon evergreens and coming out the other side in Cider Plains. I'm an expert at "light driving" as Chloe calls it. I've got a standing date, and I don't plan on breaking it, ever.

"Come, let me see you off." The rain sizzles around us, but neither Demetri nor I are affected by its precipitation. It's a perk of being a Fem—you can have just about anything, but the things you really crave—the woman you love, your rightful claim to the throne. But I don't feel too singled out in that capacity. It's the same for Demetri with Lizbeth, with the Fems as a whole, wishing they had what the Sectors seemed to achieve so easily. It will be the same with Gage once he loses Skyla—he, however, will achieve the throne, and I can't say I'm happy for him. It should be me. He doesn't want, nor deserve, that kind of power, those kinds of accolades.

I don't bother looking to Demetri upon having the thought. He already knows how I feel, and I'm well aware of his harsh opinion on the matter. This is where we agree to disagree.

We come upon a body lying in the field. Logan Oliver lies prostrate, with his hair wild, his clothes singed and smoking.

"What should we do?" I roll him over with my foot, and he remains dead as a doornail, not that he wasn't to begin with.

"Leave him be. I'll summons his keeper. I've a few words to share with Sector Dudley as it were."

"All right, Pops." I eye the woods where the tendrils of fog curl like fingers attempting to lure me in. "This is where we part ways. I'll catch you on the flip side. Good work with Gage."

"Your brother's journey is far from over."

"I'm sure you have it all mapped out." I lack the enthusiasm to cheer him on, but I do care about Gage, and I'm damn glad he's slowly coming to his senses.

A siren wails in the distance, the blades of a helicopter roar to life overhead.

"What's this?" I glance to my father without moving.

"It seems those inspectors found themselves in the mouth of a hungry Viden." He scowls at me a moment before nodding to the chopper rotating above us. "They've come to look for their own."

"Good." I glance around at the silent woods as if they were guilty of the death of those people as much as the Spectators were. "I want them here. I want the government's long nose in everything. Our people are covered. It's time to clue the rest of the world in on the fact there are strangers living among us—aliens, devils, angels, take your fucking pick. I want them all gone." I take a step toward the forest, and Demetri pulls me back.

"Be careful what you wish for, son. Fools rush in where angels fear to tread." He sheds a black smile. "I didn't inspire the phrase for nothing."

I take back my elbow with an aggressive yank. "Careful who you call fool, old man. I still qualify as an angel—so, what does that make you?"

I stride into the woods, demanding that all traces of my temper, any trace of anger I might have for the man who bore me melt away as I walk right through Paragon and back onto sweet Kansas soil.

The night air is electric, glowing in lavenders and neon blue just beyond the old barn. The lake shines bright like a nickel caught in the sun, and there she is, Laken Stewart swinging her feet off the dock before jumping up and running over, so very glad to see me.

"There you are!" She wraps her loving arms around my

neck, and I take a moment to bury my face in her hair, taking in her familiar scent, the feel of her soft body against mine. "For a minute, I thought you stood me up."

"Never." I pepper her face with kisses like I used to do when we were together—like I've done each night since I've revisited this precious time in our lives, and my desperation grows like a plague. I scoop her up and carry her under the willow that sits near the water. "How was your day?" I land us on the ground with Laken square over my lap, my hard-on blooming, begging for a bite of something it will never get to taste, at least not yet, not in this carnation.

"Empty without you." Her finger outlines my features as she lays the sweetest gaze upon me. We were special, holy, and right—Laken and I.

"I wish you would always feel that way," I whisper.

"I will. There's nothing anyone can ever do to change that." She seems so convinced of it I almost want to cry. "The lake is so pretty, and it's warm!" She bounces with a youthful enthusiasm. "Should we go for a swim?"

"Not tonight." In a week's time, I'll drown in that lake right along with her brother. Demetri has already set the wheels of my misfortune into play. Laken and I will meet up again at Ephemeral, and the rest details the end of us. Only this moment, this night is the purest, the sweetest memory of who we once were. That's why I chose it. That's why I love to relive it. I tried going back to Ephemeral, setting myself straight so that when Laken arrived, I'd be better prepared, but there's a binding spirit around any version of myself in that horrific past. I'm impenetrable, a deadly force that cannot be reckoned with.

"Then what do you think we should do?" Her eyes enliven with lust for me as her hands run up my shirt. "You are so strong, you know that?"

I wish I were strong enough to tell her who I really was, and how desperately I wish I could turn back time, make her understand right from the beginning that the Counts are our people, that she only ever belongs with me. But, in truth, it was her wedding to Coop that sponsored my first trip here. I couldn't sleep knowing he was defiling the woman who was destined to be my wife, the love of my life. So I came back, and we've had an amazing night ever since.

"We should do this." I lean in and steal a kiss. "And this." I take a bite out of her lower lip and pull it out slowly. Laken tastes like fresh, sweet strawberries, always has, and it's a pleasure to revisit this. "And this." I bow a kiss to her neck and graze gently against her with my teeth until she purrs beneath me.

"I think we should switch up the roster a bit." Her fingers fumble for the button on my jeans, and I'm caught off guard for a moment.

"Whoa." I catch her hand before she hits pay dirt. Laken is growing more aggressive, more sexual than ever as if my repeat visits are whetting her appetite for the things her body craves. "We'll get there someday." I'm not sure if I just looked into her denim eyes and spilled my very first lie. I'm hoping I didn't. Getting to that magical place with Laken is still a dream of mine. "But, for now, I'll take all of the kisses you're willing to gift me."

She giggles up a storm as she topples over me, and we land on the grass, her hair spilling around us like a love story of the ages written in strands of gold.

Laken's lips find mine, her tongue enters my mouth, willing and demanding as she takes me, makes me her own, and I melt into her. This, right here, is how it should be, how I hope it will be once again.

There is nothing so pure as Laken and me rolling around in a Kansas plain with the moon bleaching us white as snow.

Laken and I are right. We are meant for one another—in the least in Cider Plains, in the least on this magical night that I replay on a beautiful loop.

She reaches down for my jeans once again, and this time I don't stop her.

I can't.

I couldn't deny her if I tried.

Chloe

Wesley's castle of castration is empty and hollow. The sounds of my clicking heels and the unruly child in my arms are the only things keeping me company on this dark, dank evening. Skyla's private baby prom bored me to tears. And those good-for-nothing feds lived up to being zombie bait just like Wes predicted. He also predicted a stronger swarm of replacement G-men who will finally turn the Nephilim world on its pretty pink wings. That's what they get for bowing down to Messenger once again. You would think once they witnessed how useless she was the first time, it would be her they'd toss out to the Spectators at feeding time.

The baby seizes and lets out a sharp cry as if she were witness to a holy terror. Well, I have news for her. She's the only holy terror around here. I plunk the screaming brat down into the casketnet Bree gifted me and sit on the sofa, kicking off my heels, glaring at the fire until that enormous hole in the wall burns with the flames of a thousand suns. I like it hot and bright, two things that the Transfer will never truly be.

"I'd knock, but I really don't care!" a girl's voice shouts from behind, and I startle a moment to find an unwanted familiar face I saw just under an hour ago.

"What the hell do you want, Messenger?" I shove a dusty throw pillow behind my shoulders. My back has been killing me all fucking day. Ezrina's old body is nothing but a crap heap.

"There, there." She goes straight for the screaming little demon. "What's the matter, cute stuff?" She picks up the tiny menace and manages to bring her wheezing to a minimum. "Did you just figure out who your mommy is?" Skyla rocks her on one hip, and I'd swear that little thing just cooed at her.

"I was just about to close the lid on that casket." True story. But it only makes the little witch ten times more agitated. Wesley said he'd pluck my fingernails out if I ever did it again. A little peace around here might be worth a fingernail or ten.

"It's not supposed to have a lid." Skyla lands her hand

against the baby's head as if protecting her from me. As if.

"I had it reinstalled."

"God, I can't believe Wesley lets you near this precious angel."

"He's a moron. We both know that."

Skyla hiccups with delight at the tiny nervous being flapping in her arms. "Did you see that? She just smiled." Skyla doesn't take her eyes off the little mutt. "She's nothing like you after all." The baby claws at Skyla's neck, her mouth pecking at her sweater as if she might actually get lucky, and knowing the nitwit holding her, she just might.

"When did you last feed this poor thing? Where is Ezrina?"

"Don't know, don't care to both of those questions."

Skyla swoops in by my feet and takes a seat. She wastes no time lifting her blouse and getting my own daughter to suck on her tit. Tobie goes at it, greedy, in a frenzy as if she's never eaten before. I've been telling Ezrina for weeks that she's got some freaky food addiction. That child is never happy unless she has a nipple in her mouth. Good thing Messenger is here pulling her tits-for-humanity stunt because she wasn't getting ahold of mine.

"What is it with the titty toddler time? Is that supposed to be some kind of FU to me? Because I'm truly confused by this." I flick her free boob with my foot, and she bats me away with her elbow.

"Your daughter is hungry, Chloe. My God, she's starved. I just fed the boys, so I don't have much to give at the moment." She leans back, making herself at home. Her eyelids flutter as if she actually might be enjoying this on some bizarre sexual level.

"Is that what you came for? Are you making your wet nurse rounds for the night? Why aren't you home fucking your husband?" Skyla obviously doesn't know a good thing when it lands on her mattress since she's often drifting from Gage Oliver's side. "That man is a coital playground I would have bound to the bedroom every dirty loving minute."

"Leave Gage alone. It's bad enough you had Logan."

"Are you kidding? He was no thrilling, all drilling."

"Well, thank God you have Wesley. I'm sure he's attentive to all the dirty details."

The thought of Wesley ever taking Gage Oliver's place makes me scowl. Everything about him annoys me. "Does Gage leave the toilet seat up?"

"No, he's a perfect gentleman."

"Wes leaves the toilet set up."

"That's because all he cares about is himself. He's a megalomaniac. You have to lie down for the master, *and* you have to lower the toilet seat. That's his way of exhorting power over you."

"Speaking of power—heard your people kicked you to the curb once they discovered you were useless."

"Not true. I've been reinstated. There's a rebellion against the Justice Alliance ruling, and I'm spearheading it."

"My, my—someone is smugly proud. Too bad you're going to fuck this up like you do everything else. The tunnels are open. Those blue death tubes of Ezrina's are percolating once again—and Celestra are the new Counts. Way to lead a revolution—morph into your enemy. Who are you strategizing with these days anyway? Demetri?" I scoff at her ignorance. "For once, would you take some solid advice from me? Go home and bed that husband of yours before I figure out a way to do it myself."

She narrows her gaze a moment. "Did you miss the show tonight, Chloe, or are you playing dumb?" Skyla is the queen of playing dumb, so it's hard not to laugh.

"Miss the show?" I stall for a moment. "Last I saw you, Dudley was yanking you into the woods for a quickie."

"Mmm." She shakes her head and moves Wesley's river rat to her other rack. "I saw Gage—he made a covenant with the dark. He'll be your king soon enough—fighting against my people, against Celestra." She blinks back tears. Skyla has always been an idealistic do-gooder who, for fuck's sake, could never actually do any good. If I weren't so bored by her, I'd laugh in her face.

I yawn for effect, but I'm surprised at how heavy my

eyelids feel regardless. "I'd say sorry to hear it, but I don't much care. Was there a blowout? If so, I'll catch the next light drive over." I offer her a wink. "Care to join me?"

"No," she says it stern, with enough force to affirm the trip will be worth my effort.

"So it's safe to assume things will end for you and Gage." Something wrenches deep inside me, and I can't figure out why. I should relish the fact Skyla and Gage will part ways once and for all. God knows they're nothing but a nightmare together. Am I secretly rooting for them? Or am I afraid that without Skyla in the picture, Gage still wouldn't pick me? Oh, who am I kidding? Gage Oliver will pine for Skyla until he's blue in the face and then throughout time immemorial. He's as ridiculously idealistic as she is. I think they both need a dose of reality and heartache—a few dozen broken bones wouldn't hurt either.

"Things will end for Gage and me," she says the words stunted, like a question, as if testing out the theory for the first time on her lips. "His days are numbered." Her eyes flit to mine. "It's written in stone."

"In stone?" God, I have a babbling Messenger here to entertain me and keep the river rat quiet. I should be both amused and grateful, and I'm neither.

"Yes. Just a few more—days, months, you get the picture."

"Do you know how long?" My throat constricts as if waiting for the noose to cinch.

"Yes," she says it almost catatonic. "The prophecy was a gift from my mother." She glances toward the ceiling as if making known which one.

"Oh, come on—snap out of it, Messenger. It won't be long before you have another mustache to ride. Got to love your intergalactic mama. She knows exactly what to gift you for every occasion—*Logan*. That woman has one serious ladyboner for that boy." My finger falls into my mouth involuntarily, and I pull it out slowly. "I sort of have a ladyboner for the fair-haired Oliver myself. He's no slacker in bed, honey. That boy has a tongue, and he knows how to use it." My thighs quiver on cue.

"Oh?" She holds back her amusement. "And what was all that BS about no thrilling, all drilling?"

"Lies, I tell you, all lies." We share a short-lived laugh.

Wait...why in the hell is Skyla bonding with me over bedding her dead ex-husband of all things? I smell a rat, and it isn't just Wesley's spawn.

"Why are you really here?"

"I have a proposition for you." Her eyes steady over mine as if she were pinning me down. Messenger is setting the net, asking me to venture toward the hole in the ground that she just laid her golden hair over, but I'll outsmart her yet.

"Concerning Terrible Tobie?" My foot touches the baby's tiny toes, and her pint-sized leg recoils, repositioning herself to nuzzle better at Messenger's teat. Traitor.

"Concerning Gage." Skyla's eyes enliven with something I've yet to see before with the mention of his name. Is that anger, resentment, and rage all rolled into one delicious confection?

Skyla leans in and dips her hot mouth into my ear, whispering away in a heated fervor. I take in her words, the heft—weighing the meaning of them with great interest.

She pulls back, awaiting my response.

"Oh dear, *Skyla*"—a dark laugh tremors through me as I stare wild into the fire—"this really does change everything."

"Don't get too excited. You know what they say—the enemy of my enemy is still my enemy."

I cut her a dark glance and scowl. "That's not what they say."

"All the rules are mine now, Chloe—and that's what I say."

A scuttle of footsteps comes from the entry as Messenger and I stand to find the OG hag headed this way.

"Explain!" Ezrina's eyes round out, bloodshot and angry, like only hers can. Her finger points hard toward the door. Whatever twisted her granny panties in a knot is outside these haunted castle walls.

"Watch the baby." Skyla drops a kiss to the tiny troll's

head and hands her off to Ezrina. "Come, Chloe." She walks stoically toward the exit, shoulders back, chin up, her tone even-keeled. I hardly recognize this poised, pissing-fire version of the shell of a person I've come to know. I almost admire her. A laugh tries to bubble its way to the surface, but I stifle it.

I follow Messenger to the door like a trained dog. I'm so fucking amused, this time I do laugh, and the sound of my own voice gets trapped in my throat when I see it.

The sky. It's—gone. Every physicist's nightmare brews outside this vessel, this realm that caters to wickedness. Something or someone has ripped the Countenance a new one, and no more is the dismal sky—the arid space replaced with lapping circles of stars and sprays of pastel colors as if we were somehow pulled into a psychedelic nightmare.

"You did this?" The words trip from my tongue.

"Damn straight." The dark brewing clouds bubble with a volcanic furor, angry, swelling, then bursting with a sense of demonic pride. She waves at something in the distance, and a pair of majestic ebony steeds trots up, swift as lightning, each one dark as a starless night.

"Doing a little redecorating?"

"More like a hell of a lot of rearranging."

My heart thumps in my chest with a jolt of excitement at what this might mean.

Her brows narrow as she glares at something on the dark horizon. "Get on, Chloe."

We climb onto the oily stallions and ride swiftly toward a wall of pulsating liquid, red and gold—the scalding oppression emanates with the heat of a thousand branding irons. It's as if time itself were suddenly tangible, and we had harnessed the power to dive right into the beating heart, the nexus of what makes us who we are today. Time has always been honest in chronicling our scars, our hapless victories, our hard-won wounds—and now we own it, the past, the future, the imperfect present.

The ground pulsates with the might of our angry hooves as we head straight out of this obsidian hell, straight toward the eye of this boiling foreign sun, its girth and width weighted with the truth.

The Transfer twists in a kaleidoscope of color, churning in its own agony at the misshapen beast it had become. Messenger is alerting her foes, her adversaries, sounding the celestial ram's horn—she is blowing loud and hard. She has singlehandedly knifed the very realm the Countenance have worked so hard to procure, to preserve, to revel in for as far back as the Nephilim themselves.

She is twisting her enemy by the balls, saying *look at me. Look into my eyes. You will know me. By my might and my strength, you will know my name.*

I almost want to laugh. And I would if I weren't so terribly fucking glad she's finally doing it.

It's quite a romantic pairing, Skyla and I.

We ride ever closer to the flames as they rise, higher and higher, to the hole where the sky once stood—to our destiny.

The world will never see us coming.

There are kingdoms, realms, dominions to dismantle, eradicate, consume.

It's time to burn them all to cinders.

And we will.

A Note from the Author

Thank you for reading **The Serpentine Butterfly (Celestra Forever After 3)**. If you enjoyed this book, please consider leaving a review at your point of purchase. Even a sentence or two is appreciated.

*Look for **Crown of Ashes (Celestra Forever After 4)** coming soon!

Acknowledgements

A HUGE thank you to those of you who are on this Celestra roller coaster right along with me. Thank you for being so patient in waiting for *The Serpentine Butterfly* to finally release its wings. I hope it was all you wished it would be! Your love and support for the Celestra books amazes me each and every day. I'm so blessed to do what I love, and I'm even more so blessed to know that you are on this journey with me.

A special thank you to Lisa Markson for being one of the early betas who viewed this beast and gave valuable input! Big beastly kisses for not balking at its girth!

To the fabulous Kaila Eileen Turingan-Ramos, I am so thankful that you take the time to pour over each word and make sure it is in its place. I am so very grateful for your sacrifice of time. You are a true angel! I can never thank you enough!

Thank you to Kathryn Jacoby who combed through this monolithic text to make sure all of my rambling thoughts spun out a cohesive Paragon tale. You are wonder woman in every capacity.

And to Paige Maroney Smith, I am truly indebted to you for taking this slippery serpent of a book and putting it under your microscope to make sure it shined like a jewel. You are the real jewel! Thank you for sharing your sparkle.

And last, but never least, thank you to Him who sits on the throne. Worthy is the Lamb! Glory and honor and power are yours. I owe you everything.

About The Author

Addison Moore is a *New York Times*, *USA Today*, and *Wall Street Journal* bestselling author who writes contemporary and paranormal romance. Her work has been featured in *Cosmopolitan* Magazine. Previously she worked as a therapist on a locked psychiatric unit for nearly a decade. She resides on the West Coast with her husband, four wonderful children, and two dogs where she eats too much chocolate and stays up way too late. When she's not writing, she's reading.

Subscribe to Addison's mailing list for sneak peeks and updates on all upcoming releases at:

http://addisonmoorewrites.blogspot.com

And, Follow her on:
Facebook: Addison Moore Author
Twitter: @AddisonMoore
Instagram: @authorAddisonMoore
Goodreads www.goodreads.com Author Addison Moore

Manufactured by Amazon.ca
Bolton, ON